"Is it bad that I don't feel anything?"

I turned back to look at the casket, troubled by her question but trying to find a way to deflect it.

"I'd say that it's entirely human. You wouldn't necessarily have known a single soul on that ship. On the *Salmacis*, many of us travelled alone, with no contact with the other passengers. We didn't begin to know each other until we founded the settlement."

"And now?"

"We've become a community. A family, five thousand strong. We have our differences, as in any family: sometimes very serious differences. But there's a unity that binds us. A mutual understanding; a sense of our own fragility. Call it love. We have to look after each other if any one of us is to survive. We're vulnerable without the affection and support of our fellow citizens. Together, provided each plays their part, we're strong enough to wait out the wolves. We've been doing it for thirty years now, through thick and thin."

"I think you must be a good man, Miguel de Ruyter, to have left your family and come out here for me."

"Then you think wrongly."

"You risked your life, left your loved ones, for one passenger you didn't even know."

I was glad she could not see the tightness in my face. "I had a job to do."

Praise for
Alastair Reynolds

"Comparisons to *Dune* abound.... At a time when large-scale SF is flourishing, *Absolution Gap* is as good as it gets, and should solidify Alastair Reynolds's reputation as one of the best hard SF writers in the field."   —*SF Site*

"A book of great fascination, rich description, and memorable action."
                                                        —*Locus* on *Absolution Gap*

"Reynolds writes a lean and muscular prose where the intense action scenes are leavened with the kind of bright, shining, mind-boggling science talk that characterizes the best of post-modern space opera."
                                        —*Science-Fiction Weekly* on *Absolution Gap*

"Alastair Reynolds continues his rise to the top of...SF....Revelation, Redemption, Absolution...Reynolds provides them all."
                                                        —*Guardian* on *Absolution Gap*

"Fulfills all the staggering promise of [Reynolds's] earlier books, and then some....A landmark in hard SF space opera."
                                —*Publishers Weekly* (starred review) on *Absolution Gap*

"An entertaining science fiction tale....The story line contains several brilliantly developed concepts...an intriguing look at religion, war, societies, and economics in outer space."
                                        —Midwest Book Review on *Absolution Gap*

"Clearly one of the year's major science fiction novels....The book Reynolds's readers have been waiting for."   —*Locus* on *Redemption Ark*

"[A] tour de force....Ravishingly inventive."
                                                —*Publishers Weekly* on *Revelation Space*

"An adroit and fast-paced blend of space opera and police procedural, original and exciting, teeming with cool stfnal concepts. A real page turner. The prefect...is sort of a space cop, Sipowicz in a space suit, or maybe Dirty Harry with a whiphound."   —George R. R. Martin on *Aurora Rising*

"[Reynolds is] one of the most gifted hard SF writers working today."
—*Publishers Weekly* (starred review) on *Beyond the Aquila Rift*

"[Reynolds is] a mastersinger of the space opera."
—*The Times* on *Blue Remembered Earth*

"A swashbuckling thriller—*Pirates of the Caribbean* meets *Firefly*—that nevertheless combines the author's trademark hard SF with effective, coming-of-age characterization."
—*Guardian* on *Revenger*

"*Revenger* is classic Reynolds—that is to say, top-of-the-line science fiction, where characters are matched beautifully with ideas and have to find their place in a complex future. More!"
—Greg Bear

"A leading light of the New Space Opera movement in science fiction."
—*Los Angeles Review of Books*

"A fascinating hybrid of space opera, police procedural, and character study."
—*Publishers Weekly* on *Aurora Rising*

"One of the giants of the new British space opera."
—*io9*

"It's grand, involving, and full of light and wonder. *Poseidon's Wake* is one of the best sci-fi novels of the year."
—*SciFiNow*

"Reynolds blends AIs, mysterious aliens, intelligent elephants, and philosophical ruminations on our place in the universe in a well-paced, complex story replete with intrigue, invention, and an optimism uncommon in contemporary SF."
—*Guardian* on *Poseidon's Wake*

"Few SF writers merge rousing adventure with advanced futuristic technology as skillfully as Alastair Reynolds."
—*Toronto Star* on *On the Steel Breeze*

"Reynolds is a master of the slow buildup leading to apocalyptic action, and *On the Steel Breeze* is no exception."
—National Space Society

"His writing mixes spartan style, provocative ideas, and flashes of dark humor. . . . Reynolds excels at weaving different threads together."
—*Los Angeles Review of Books* on *Slow Bullets*

"Alastair Reynolds is a name to watch. . . . Shades of Banks and Gibson with gigatons of originality."
—*Guardian* on *Revelation Space*

"If you like hard SF...with fast-paced action and hard-boiled characters... you're in for a great ride." —*SF Site* on *Redemption Ark*

"Reynolds has a galaxy-sized imagination allied to a real storytelling ability." —Bernard Cornwell on *Blue Remembered Earth*

"Heir to writers like Isaac Asimov and Arthur C. Clarke, Reynolds keeps up the tradition of forward thinking....An immensely thrilling, mind-bending piece of work." —*The A.V. Club* on *House of Suns*

"Reynolds takes quests for vengeance and redemption and places them on a galactic stage." —*Locus* on *Redemption Ark*

INHIBITOR PHASE

By Alastair Reynolds

THE INHIBITOR TRILOGY

Revelation Space
Redemption Ark
Absolution Gap

REVELATION SPACE UNIVERSE NOVELS

Chasm City
Inhibitor Phase

Century Rain
Pushing Ice
House of Suns
Terminal World

THE PREFECT DREYFUS EMERGENCIES

Aurora Rising (formerly *The Prefect*)
Elysium Fire

THE REVENGER SERIES

Revenger
Shadow Captain
Bone Silence

SHORT STORY COLLECTIONS

Diamond Dogs, Turquoise Days
Galactic North

INHIBITOR PHASE

ALASTAIR REYNOLDS

orbitbooks.net

Copyright © 2021 by Alastair Reynolds
Excerpt from *Terminal World* copyright © 2011 by Alastair Reynolds

Cover design by Lauren Panepinto
Cover images by Shutterstock
Cover copyright © 2021 by Hachette Book Group, Inc.
Author photograph by Barbara Bella

Orbit
Hachette Book Group
1290 Avenue of the Americas
New York, NY 10104
orbitbooks.net

First Orbit Edition: October 2021
Originally published in Great Britain by Gollancz in August 2021

Orbit is an imprint of Hachette Book Group.
The Orbit name and logo are trademarks of
Little, Brown Book Group Limited.

The publisher is not responsible for websites (or their content) that are not owned by the publisher.

The Hachette Speakers Bureau provides a wide range of authors for speaking events. To find out more, go to www.hachettespeakersbureau.com or call (866) 376-6591.

Library of Congress Control Number: 2021941941

ISBNs: 9780316462761 (trade paperback), 9780316462778 (ebook)

Printed in the United States of America

LSC-C

Printing 1, 2021

To my wife, for being there.

PREFACE

Dear Reader,

This is a novel set in the Revelation Space universe. While it shares some connective tissue with some of the other books and stories in that sequence, it's my hope that it can be read independently. In addition, while there are callbacks to events and characters from earlier in the history, I've tried to avoid significant spoilers for the other titles. If you want to dive into the book cold, please do so and skip the rest of this introduction.

If you'd like a little more orientation, but not too much, then here is the essential setup:

About five hundred years from now, humanity has spread into interstellar space and settled many nearby solar systems. There have been good times and bad: golden ages, factional wars, a devastating plague. While exploring the ruins of a vanished alien civilisation, humans manage to trigger a long-dormant threat from the dawn of time. Remorseless cube-shaped replicating machines—Inhibitors—emerge from the darkness and begin culling humanity. Over the next two hundred years, humans and their allies (including hive-mind "Conjoiners" and genetically engineered "hyperpigs") band together, squabble, and generally go to ever more extreme ends to find a weapon against the Inhibitors (also known as "wolves").

These measures all fail to one degree or another.

By the late years of the twenty-eighth century all that's left of humanity is a few isolated pockets of survivors, hunkering down with ever more limited resources, and still no real idea how to fight back against the wolves.

This is where *Inhibitor Phase* begins.

Again, if that's enough for you, please dive in. If you'd appreciate some more detailed notes on the chronology, terminology and key figures in the history, then please turn to the back of the book—but be aware that these notes do indeed contain mild spoilers both for *Inhibitor Phase* and the other titles.

That's why they're at the back.

AR

Part One

SUN HOLLOW

CHAPTER ONE

Victorine was painting a wall. I looked down at her as she added a touch of detail to the mural's darkening edge. Cubes swarmed in from space, each rendered in two efficient strokes of midnight blue and black. They stood out against the ruddier background of the dust disk, gathering into sinuous straggly formations, loops, and chains, before coagulating into larger and more ominous forms—dark, dense masses prickling with lightning like an armada of thunderheads. Victorine had done none of that: it was all the work of other schoolchildren, some long grown or long gone.

But she was adding to it, layering paint over paint. From out of the thunderheads burst a pack of creatures: twisted, straining, mad-eyed forms of muscle and claw, fur and tooth.

"I know they're not really wolves," she said, anticipating any remark I might have been about to make. "I know that's just what we call them. But they might as well be wolves."

"You've never seen wolves."

"I don't need to."

"They're a reminder of what drove us here," I said quietly. "That's why they're on the mural. But you're painting them as if they're about to pounce out of the sky. Is that how you feel?"

Victorine set her brush down on the lip of the metal box she cradled in her other arm. The materials inside it were improvised: chemical pigments and stabilising emulsions that had once served some other purpose in the great plan of settlement. There were colours denied to her, because the right ingredients had never been found, or could not be spared for something as frivolous as a school mural. Her brushes were crude sticks tipped with coarse eruptions of stiff animal hair from the cattle stocks we kept for food and clothing. The paintbox was itself the front compartment of a life-support pack, long-since dismantled and repurposed for its vital treasures. That Victorine could make any sort of mark on the wall was something of a miracle. In fact, her wolves were alive with a desperate energy and purpose.

"What do you think I ought to feel?" she asked, in answer to my query.

A deep, resonant thud shook the ground. It shook everything. We looked up: up from the wall, up from the school, up to the ceiling of rock far above us. A second thud came again, and a rain of dirt and dust loosened itself from the ceiling. The ceiling's lights flickered and died. A third thud came, harder than before. Heavier stones and boulders began to detach. Screams sounded across the cavern.

Victorine was calm, though.

"They're here," she said, taking a step back from her work. "They're here and they want to break in." Her tone became quietly accusatory. "It means you failed, Miguel. It means you failed and everything here is going to end."

She dipped her brush into its little jar of cleaning solvent and stirred it methodically.

The thudding became the low throb of the wake-up alarm. The stir of Victorine's brush was the high, cyclical tone of air-circulation pumps purring to life. The sting of the debris against my eyes was the discomfort of forcing them wide, after weeks of sleep.

I was awake.

Awake and inside the torpor box.

For a moment, lying weightless, it was enough to know that I had survived the crossing; that the ship and its components had held together long enough to bring me to the interception point. Given the state of our equipment and defences, that alone was something to thank. The torpor boxes were good enough to keep us in hibernation for a few weeks, but they were nowhere near as reliable as the long-duration reefersleep caskets that we had once taken for granted. Every trip involving a period of torpor carried a risk of death or permanent disability. I had rolled the dice once and survived: I would be rolling it at least one more time before my return to Sun Hollow.

I waited a minute, gathering my strength, and set about removing the box's monitors and catheters. When that slow, painful business was done, I took another few moments and examined myself with the detached, methodical eye of a physician. The box's blue light laid me out unsparingly. Blemishes, scars, poor muscle tone, white hairs: all old news. A few fresh pressure sores, some bruising, bleeding here and there. The usual numbness and tremor in my fingers. Nothing, though, that was going to kill me in the next few hours.

The memories of the last few days before my departure were still fresh. The detection, the confirmation, the decision to interdict. My

4

volunteering for the operation. The arguments against and for; the tears and the strained farewells that followed. Saying goodbye to Nicola and Victorine. The launch boost, blasting away from the false-bottomed crater over Sun Hollow's shuttle pen. The strain on my bones as the shuttle accelerated, gaining speed while it still had the cover of the circumstellar dust disk. Ten gees, four point seven hours. I had been unconscious for most of that, mercifully, and had only endured it because of a suite of aggressive life-support measures, taking the load off my heart and lungs. My spine still ached from the twin abuses of compression under acceleration and now the slow, painful unloading under weightlessness.

Hard on a young man; murderous on a relic like me.

Why had I volunteered for this? I had to dig deeper into my memories for that. Hitting them was like finding a loose tooth jangling against a nerve: an instant, savage hit of raw agony.

Ah, yes. *That* was why.

Political atonement.

I was making amends for a mistake, a blemish on my office, after a badly managed coup against me failed. After a contentious trial and a botched execution.

Rurik Taine, writhing on the floor, not quite dead.

My fault, all of it. Nothing that was enough to unseat me from office—nothing criminal, just a series of bad judgements—but enough to undermine the trust vested in me, the trust I had fought so hard to earn since the founding of Sun Hollow.

I swallowed back any self-pity. Doing this had been my choice, not something forced on me. Allies and doubters alike had tried to argue me out of it. But I had known that the only path to redemption lay in the acceptance of my duty.

Now I had a task to finish.

Once I was free of revival grogginess, I extracted myself from the box and floated through to the control cabin with its pilots' positions and faintly glowing instrumentation. Although the ship could easily accommodate a larger crew, I was alone aboard it. I settled into the middle seat and brought the readouts to normal illumination while keeping the windows shuttered. Satisfied that the ship was in good health—the engineers had done well to keep it spaceworthy—I turned to communications, hoping for an update on the status of the incomer. It would have suited me very well to learn that it was a false alarm, a data mirage, or that the crew had come to some change of heart, reversing for interstellar space and leaving us in peace.

No such respite: it was still there, still coming in on a direct course for Michaelmas and Sun Hollow.

I refined my position, using cold-gas thrusters to minimise the likelihood of being seen. Thirty million kilometres still separated my ship from the incomer, but that was a scratch against the size of the system. Our relative speed was a little under four thousand kilometres per second: two hours until we were on each other.

I moved back to the missile bay, opened a pressure hatch, and peered in to inspect the weapon, making sure no harm had come to it during launch.

There was only one missile: a thick, round-ended cylinder two metres long, fixed into a deployable launch cradle. The arming panel was a flattened area of the casing, set with black controls. At my touch, a matrix of red lights glimmered from the casing. They went through a start-up cycle then held steady, indicating readiness. With the hatch sealed, I depressurised the missile bay, then opened the outer door and lowered the cradle until it was projecting beyond the hull.

I returned to the command deck. Missile inspection, arming and launch-readiness had taken less than ten minutes.

I loaded the tactical input from the shuttle's main console into the missile, giving it an up-to-date model for the incomer's position and speed. I double-checked communications, just in case word had come in to break the attack.

None had arrived.

So I waited until our relative distance had narrowed to a mere two million kilometres, then let the missile loose. The cradle's restraints opened and the weapon streaked away without fanfare, boosting to close up the distance. I watched for a response from the incomer, some sudden evasive swerve, but there was no change in its approach. Nothing about that surprised me: if the incomer had been capable of detecting the missile, the same capability should have given away my position long ago.

According to the console, the missile was maintaining its lock on the incomer. It would slip like a dagger between the drive beams and auto-destruct a microsecond before impact. From a distance, the matter-antimatter blast would be indistinguishable from a Conjoiner drive malfunction: the self-same malfunction that was bound to follow an instant later, when the ship broke apart.

With the deed all but done, I permitted my thoughts to turn to the sleepers on that ship. I still had no idea how many there were, or where and when they had commenced their journey. We would never know. But

I liked to think that they had gone to their hibernation berths with no fear in their hearts; no intimation of the terror that must have detected them, and then chased them across the stars, forcing them to this desperate, final bolthole.

Some day we would find a way to mourn them. It was not that we were murderers by nature, or that we had anything against the crew and passengers of that ship. Doubtless they were just looking for somewhere to shelter from the wolves: a quiet, out-of-the-way sanctuary; an unobvious hiding place. It was why we had selected Michaelmas—why we had selected this whole system—and presumably they had been guided by the same logic.

But we had already done it. We had dug ourselves into the crust of Michaelmas and we had years of survival to prove that we were good at lying low. We had never given ourselves away, and we had no intention of doing so. Which was why this bright, clumsy visitor could not be tolerated. Even if they did not know of our presence, even if they never became aware of it, they might still be leading wolves right to our door.

So they had to die, and in a manner that looked like accidental destruction.

The console flashed red, synchronised with a piercing warning tone. To my consternation the missile had developed a steering anomaly. There was nothing I could do but observe, reading the faint telemetry trace: a low-bandwidth crackle designed to blend in with the radio-frequency noise coming out of Michael. The cold-gas thruster had jammed at one of its extreme deflections, making the missile begin to veer.

I cursed our luck. The steering fault was a known factor with the improvised missiles—we were asking them to perform far outside their design envelope—but we had done all that we could to mitigate the problem.

"Correct yourself," I whispered.

The missile was waggling hard. At any moment, the gee forces might be sufficient to jolt the thruster out of its jammed position. There was still a chance...

But the console flashed again. A different readout now, a different warning tone.

Interception null.
Interception null.
Interception null.

The mathematics could not be argued with. The missile's contortions had pushed it too far off course. Unless the incomer obliged by changing its own course, there was no longer any means by which the missile could achieve a kill.

"Abort and self-protect," I told the missile. My words were reserved for the console alone, which contained just enough artificial intelligence to understand natural language. All that was transmitted to the missile was a burst of prearranged binary code.

The missile would attempt to use whatever was left of its fuel to put itself into a safekeeping orbit, allowing it to be recovered at some point in the future. As difficult as that exercise might prove, it was better than losing a warhead.

I now knew what must be done. I had always known it might be necessary, but I had pushed it to the back of my mind while there was hope that our first line of defence might be sufficient.

Now that the missile had failed, though, I had to fall back on our only other means of stopping the lighthugger. It was not as surgical and, if anything, was even more costly to Sun Hollow...and, crucially, I would not have the satisfaction of knowing that it had succeeded.

But there was no alternative.

"Protocol two," I told the shuttle. "Zero abort."

Validation?

"Cydonia," I said, using the codeword I had prearranged.

The shuttle accepted my instructions. Its own cold-gas jets began to pop, lining it up ever more precisely with the incomer. It would be trying to follow the same intended trajectory as the missile, slipping between the drive beams. Hard for a missile; harder still for a bulky shuttle. But at least it no longer mattered if a little of the incomer's drive radiation seeped through the hull.

I had no munitions, so the destructive power of my shuttle lay solely in its mass and speed. It would be sufficient.

I was calmer than I had expected. There was no room now for doubt or failure of nerve. I had assigned all necessary control to the shuttle and removed any possibility of rescinding that authority. I could wrestle with the controls, beg for my life, but no failure of my nerve would make a difference.

I was going to die.

In doing so I would condemn however many innocents were on that ship. But I would save the five thousand of us who lived in Sun Hollow, including the woman I loved and the daughter she had allowed into my world. I visualised Nicola and Victorine alone at our table, Nicola starting to break the news, Victorine absorbing it, holding her composure for brave seconds, before the truth undid her. I was not her father, and would never know a daughter's love, but I believed that she had become fond of me.

8

I steeled myself and watched the impact clock tick down to zero. There was a white burst, and for a foolish moment I thought it was the impact itself. But that whiteness continued. It pushed itself through the cabin walls, through the shutters, before dying away.

The shuttle jolted hard.

The clock ticked past zero, and continued counting.

So I was not dead. But *something* had happened. Through half-blinded eyes I saw that the shuttle's systems had all blanked out. There had only been one jolt, but my gut told me that the whole ship was yawing, out of control.

I gasped, stunned by my own continued existence. Shocked, confused, and more than a little aggrieved that whatever redemption I had hoped for in the moment of my death was no longer for the taking.

Slowly my eyes recovered from the white pulse, and slowly the shuttle began to recover its own faculties. The console's indications came back on. There was some damage, but not nearly enough to be consistent with any sort of collision. The outer hull had taken the brunt of something, but it was not an impact.

Then came a rain of blows: a soft succession of fist-falls and claw-taps against the hull. It came and went.

I began to understand.

I had not needed to hit the incomer after all. In the last few seconds before the collision, the strain on its engines had finally taken its toll. The white flash had been the disintegration of the drives, which knocked my shuttle senseless, but had not destroyed it. I had sailed through the expanding debris cloud of the former ship.

The shuttle was confused. It had been given a task, but now the object of that task no longer existed.

Null solution for protocol two.

Null solution for protocol two.

Null solution for protocol two.

Revoke zero abort condition?

"Yes," I stammered out, still half breathless from the cold slap of my own survival. "Yes—revoke zero abort condition. Confirm revocation."

Zero abort condition now revoked. Awaiting orders.

Orders. The idea seemed ludicrous. How was I supposed to come up with orders, now? A few moments earlier I had scrubbed my mind of anything except the total acceptance of my own imminent end. Now I was expected to fumble around for the severed thread of my own life, find a purpose, and keep going.

"I...don't know," I said. "Just...stabilise yourself. Maintain course and...assess what the hell just happened. And...call the missile back, if it's got enough fuel to meet us."

Thirty minutes passed while I carried on drifting past the point of the explosion. Then a chime came from the console. It was a soft tone, polite as a cough in a theatre.

The shuttle had detected something. It was not an update from the missile, nor a communication from Sun Hollow or any of the Disciple observation satellites. But it was an electromagnetic signal: a repeating radio pulse, with an interval very close to exactly one second. I let the shuttle gather enough of these pulses to subject them to a close-grained analysis, looking for embedded content. There was nothing: just a smooth rise and fall, followed by silence, then another rise and fall.

As we drifted, the shuttle was able to triangulate the pulse. It was moving away from the point where the incomer had blown up, but on a velocity vector much closer to my own, differing by only a few hundred kilometres per second. If it had been co-moving with the debris field, it ought to have been tens of millions of kilometres away from me by now, but it was not even two million astern of me.

Something had survived the blast, or been ejected just before it happened. Something that was now putting out exactly the kind of signature that Sun Hollow had spent thirty years doing its best not to broadcast: a clear, repeating and unambiguous indicator of functioning human technology. The wolves might or might not have been drawn to the explosion, but a systematic distress signal would be more than they could be ignore.

Unless that signal fell silent. Very quickly.

The missile returned, sidling in from the darkness then latching itself back onto the cradle.

I brought it back into the weapons bay, then began to recharge its fuel tank from the shuttle's own supplies. It was time-consuming, but the only option. While the tank was reloading, I used a delicate but well-rehearsed procedure to extract the antimatter warhead from the front of the missile. The magnetic pen—and its associated arming and detonation system— was a fist-sized chunk of sterile metal, clean and gleaming as an artificial heart. It was much too valuable to waste against a target I fully expected to be easily susceptible to a pure kinetic energy strike.

With that done, and the revised target loaded into the missile, I sent it back on its way.

And waited.

My plan was straightforward enough: I had already commenced a course alteration that would eventually bring me back to Sun Hollow.

This far off the elliptic plane, I did not have nearly so much dust screening as when I had started out. My thrust bursts had to be done sparingly, at pseudo-random intervals, disguised as far as possible to blend in with Michael's own variability.

After the missile had done its work, my course would bring me close enough to the impact point to inspect the field for any clues as to the nature of the transmitting source. I pushed aside thoughts of what that debris might point to.

The missile was thirty minutes from its interception when the voice came through.

It was a woman, speaking Canasian: the language most of us used in Sun Hollow.

"Help me. Someone has to be able to hear this. Please...help me."

The console confirmed that the voice was originating from the same position as the distress pulse. It was a faint signal, but just as problematic.

"Stop talking," I implored, as if she could hear me. "You're going to die, don't complicate things."

The voice carried on. "I don't know where I am, or when. But something's happened, and I'm on my own. I think the ship...I think something happened to the ship, something bad. If you can hear me, and you're close by, I need you to help me. I'm cold...getting colder. Please come."

Some spectral quality attended the voice: thin and otherworldly, as if it were not being made by a human larynx.

"Are you wolf?" I whispered to the emptiness of the cabin. "Are you a trap, designed to bait me into replying?"

"I'm so cold. I don't think this is how it's meant to be. I can't move... can't feel anything below my neck. I'm not even sure if I'm really speaking. I can hear myself...but I don't sound quite right. I sound like a ghost of myself."

"Because you're dead," I said.

I told the console to open a reciprocal channel back on the same frequency.

"Stop talking," I said again, but this time for her benefit. "Stop talking and find a way to turn off that distress beacon."

Twelve seconds of silence. Then an answer:

"Who are you? Can you help me?"

"Who I am doesn't matter. You're making a lot of noise, and it has to stop." I was making noise now as well, but at least the shuttle was tight-beaming my response in her direction only, minimising the chances of it being scattered or intercepted. "If you can't..." But there was no "if" about it. I was going to kill her whatever happened. "Just turn off that distress beacon. You must still be in reefersleep, but you've been raised to a minimum consciousness level. You should still be able to address the casket's command tree. Find a way to stop it pulsing, and stop broadcasting your voice."

The silence again: the lag caused by the distance between us. It stretched so long that I thought she might have taken my warning to heart.

Then she said: "I'm frightened. I don't remember what happened. There was the ship, and then this. I don't even—"

"Stop."

"—remember who I am."

"Listen to me very carefully. This isn't a safe place. I have a duty to protect my people, and you're endangering them."

"Where am I?"

"Drifting, a long way from where you ever wanted to be. Now turn off that beacon."

"I'm so cold."

Twenty seconds later the beacon stopped. Either it had silenced itself, or she had found a way into the command tree. I permitted myself a sigh of partial relief. How much harm had been done, it was impossible to say. But I was glad not to have that repeating tone coming from the console, and glad also not to have to expend our missile.

"I think it's stopped now."

"Good," I said beneath my breath. "Now—"

"Please help me."

I calculated a new course, called off the missile; and told it to put itself on a safekeeping orbit again. We were due to pass through the same neck of space, but at vastly different times and speeds: there was no hope of re-intercepting it this time. But even without its warhead the missile was worth preserving.

It would take three weeks to reach her position. I crawled back into the torpor box, fixed the catheters and monitors back in place, and set the box to revive me when the shuttle was two hours out from contact with the drifting object.

Her casket was floating free, long since separated from any other part of the debris field. It was tumbling slowly, presenting all its aspects to me. It was a round-cornered rectangular box, with a gristle of tubes and cables sprouting from one end of it. A reefersleep unit, but not of a kind that was immediately familiar to me. From the damage at one end of the casket—the end opposite the passenger's head—I saw that it must

12

have been ripped away from some cradle or chassis, perhaps supplying some function that the casket alone could not provide for itself. How long could it have kept her alive, without the sustenance flowing through those severed roots? I thought she would be doing well to last a few days, never mind the weeks that it had taken me to reach her.

I crept closer. I used the shuttle's passive sensors alone, relying on ambient illumination. Never far from my mind was the possibility that this could still be a wolf trap of sorts; a clever imitation designed to bait me in. But the nearer I got, the less I thought that was likely. It was all too real, too convincing. There were scorch marks on the capsule, dents and gashes, a mass of scarred bubbling where some of its sheathing must have registered tremendous heat. A rectangular window lay at the intact end, roughly where the passenger's face would have been. There were grilled bars over the window, protecting the glass beneath. The casket's design looked robust, old-fashioned.

The capsule continued tumbling. Floating beneath the window—was there something?

A serene sleeping face, balmed by Michael's ruddy light, just for an instant.

I brought the shuttle to within a few metres of the casket. Metres or kilometres: if it was a bomb, I was already far too close. I opened the weapons bay then lowered the cradle, using the pincers to grasp at the casket and try and stop its tumbling. It was clumsy work but after twenty minutes of fumbling the casket, losing it, chasing after it, I finally had it tamed sufficiently to bring back into the ship. It was good that there was no missile: there would have been no room in the bay otherwise. Luckily the two objects were not too dissimilar in size and shape.

I sealed the bay, repressurised it, and opened the inner door. The casket had come to rest with the window nearest to me, facing back into the ship. The sudden transition to atmosphere had laid a frosting across the glass beneath the grilled bars, hiding whatever I thought I might have seen beneath.

I had come prepared, a pair of headphones already settled over my ears. I attached a magnetic limpet to the casket's outer casing, then angled a microphone before my lips.

"Can you hear me?" I asked, tentatively. "My name is Miguel de Ruyter, the same man who spoke to you three weeks ago. I've brought you inside my ship. I've fixed a radio transmitter onto the outside of your casket, using the same frequency we spoke on originally. Make some response if any of this is getting through to you."

There was no answer from the casket, but nor was I expecting one. I was going through the motions, mostly resigned to the passenger already being dead, which was another way of saying that she was beyond any possibility of safe revival. Death came in many shades. Everyone was dead at the deepest point of reefersleep: no thoughts, no cellular processes. But they could still be brought back to life—if the casket operated as it was meant to. If one of several things went wrong, though, then a wave of damage could sweep through those cells, rupturing them from inside, tearing apart the connections between them. In the brain, those connections encoded everything that was most dear to us about ourselves. A warm corpse, with a grey mush of scrambled neural pathways, was no better than a cold one.

On other worlds, in better times, there had always been hope. In Sun Hollow, even extracting a tooth or setting a broken bone came with challenges. Remaking a damaged mind was a little beyond our capabilities.

"Rest," I said, as if it mattered. "You're safe now, and I'm taking you back to our world."

I left the magnetic limpet in place, the radio channel open.

I went forward and began readying the shuttle for the rest of my journey home. A few thrust bursts, a course correction or two, some food in my stomach, and I could crawl back into the torpor box again. Someone else could worry about what to do with the macabre trophy I had brought back home.

"Talk to me."

Her voice was coming out of the console, relayed through the magnetic limpet. I dashed back to the weapons bay, grabbed a glove, and used it to swab away as much of the frost as I could from the grilled window.

"I'm here," I said, speaking through the microphone. "Are you...all right? Do you remember anything of the last three weeks?"

"Where am I?"

Her voice still sounded distant and not quite real. There was something too pure, too crystalline about it, like the notes that came off a wine glass when it was stroked by a wet finger.

"In a ship. I rescued you."

"Rescued me?"

I peered closer, trying to get a better glimpse of the face beneath the window. But there was still too much fog on the inside of the glass. She hovered beneath like a dark-eyed moon peeking in and out of threads of cirrus.

"Something happened. You were on a ship—a much bigger ship than this one. There was an accident...your ship blew up as it was coming into our system."

14

"An accident?"

"An engine failure. It seems you were blown free. I picked up a signal from your casket. Yours, but no one else's."

"There were others," she said distantly, as if half a memory had just presented itself. "You have to search for them. I can't be the only one."

"I don't think there was anyone else. Even if there were...I'm afraid we don't have the means to look for them. You had a transmitter; no one else did."

"I want to get out of this thing. I feel numb."

"I don't have the means to help you until we're back in Sun Hollow. Once we're there, you'll be well taken care of."

"What is Sun Hollow?"

I moved around to the other end of the reefersleep casket, where most of the damage lay and where numerous pipes and cables had been severed cleanly away.

"A place of safety. A small settlement, on a world called Michaelmas, orbiting a star called Michael."

"I don't know those names."

"There's no reason that you should." With insulating gloves on, I examined the severed connections, trying to identity familiar technologies and functions. "May I ask...do you remember anything about yourself?"

"There was the ship. They were putting us aboard it. Then they came to put us to sleep, and said that when we woke up we'd be somewhere else. My name's..." But she trailed off, unable to supply the answer she must have expected to come without effort. "I don't...I can't remember."

"It'll come back," I said, fingering two thick lines that had alloy cores, suggesting that they were power umbilicals. "If I said 'wolf' to you... would that mean anything at all?"

"We had wolves in the hills above Zawinul's Landing. They'd come on one of the first ships. I'd listen to them when the moons were high."

"These are different wolves. But it's good that you remember something of home. Zawinul's Landing." I said the words slowly, ruminatively. "That's a place on Haven, I think—one of the first Demarchist settlements. Do you remember when you left there?"

"Not exactly. What did you say your name was?"

I examined one of the other cables. It had a slippery, eel-like texture and seemed to want to coil itself around my fingers.

"Miguel de Ruyter."

"Are you a pilot?"

"No." I smiled at the idea. "An administrator."

"An important one?"

I moved away from the casket in the weapons bay and tugged open a general service hatch in the wall of the shuttle. Behind the bee-striped panel was a mess of power lines and sensor cabling. Like everything else on the shuttle, it showed clear signs of being repaired and adapted several times.

"Reasonably high up the food chain."

"Then why did they send you?"

"I sent myself."

I had brought a tool and repair kit with me to the weapons bay. I opened it and sifted through the items I would need to make some kind of improvised connection between the ship and the casket. I decided it would be feasible, if inelegant.

"Are they really all dead, Miguel de Ruyter?"

"I think so."

"Is it bad that I don't feel anything?"

I turned back to look at the casket, troubled by her question but trying to find a way to deflect it.

"I'd say that it's entirely human. You wouldn't necessarily have known a single soul on that ship. On the *Salmacis*, many of us travelled alone, with no contact with the other passengers. We didn't begin to know each other until we founded the settlement."

"And now?"

"We've become a community. A family, five thousand strong. We have our differences, as in any family: sometimes very serious differences. But there's a unity that binds us. A mutual understanding; a sense of our own fragility. Call it love. We have to look after each other if any one of us is to survive. We're vulnerable without the affection and support of our fellow citizens. Together, provided each plays their part, we're strong enough to wait out the wolves. We've been doing it for thirty years now, through thick and thin."

"I think you must be a good man, Miguel de Ruyter, to have left your family and come out here for me."

"Then you think wrongly."

"You risked your life, left your loved ones, for one passenger you didn't even know."

I was glad she could not see the tightness in my face. "I had a job to do."

CHAPTER TWO

Another six weeks brought me home.

By the time I emerged from torpor, a few hours out from Michaelmas, the shuttle was already on its final deceleration burn. There was no point signalling my arrival: I would have been tracked by the Disciples all the way in, their updates alerting Sun Hollow to my imminent return. Even without the Disciples, the sensors on Michaelmas would have picked up the profile of my ship and determined that I was nothing to do with the wolves. If I had been deemed to be some other kind of threat—a thing of human origin, taking too close an interest in Michaelmas—then I would already have been shot out of the sky by our defensive railguns.

The fact that I was alive at all, meant that I had been tracked and identified as a friendly asset.

When the gee-load had dropped enough to permit mobility, I went back and checked that my passenger was still secure and that she remained at the same level of reefersleep as when I had gone under. The frosting beneath the window had cleared a little since I last saw her and her face loomed more discernibly. She looked bloodless: as pale as a white paper mask. Her dark-rimmed eyes were closed, her lips sealed, her demeanour one of serene repose. I thought of a painting I had once seen: a drowned woman floating in water.

I went back to nurse the shuttle down.

Michaelmas was a dense rock, larger than Mars but smaller than Earth. Other than this short interlude of human habitation, it was doomed to be lifeless. It had no atmosphere, seas, or icecaps. At no point in its extremely short life had any volatile materials ever rained down onto its crust. Nor would they: Michael's bad-tempered flaring episodes had banished all the life-giving compounds from the inner planetary system, never to return. Thus, Michaelmas suited us very well as a hiding place. The constant, continuing bombardment by rocky impactors meant that its surface was a scribble of overlapping craters, providing natural conceal-ment for our surface emplacements, launch silos and access shafts. Each

17

impactor transferred some of its kinetic energy into the crust, warming it almost imperceptibly. Over time, that thermal background served as a camouflage for our own heat-generating activities. The crust rang like a bell, too, meaning that it would be very hard to detect human presence by remote seismography, scanning the surface with lasers or radar. Our own seismophones had to work hard to separate noise from signal, with that ever-droning undertone. Beyond Michaelmas, the dust disk in which it swam provided additional cover, and when Michael grumbled out a flare, we tried to use it to conceal a launch, thrust boost or signals burst.

None of it was infallible; none of it was easy. We had come to Michaelmas not to found a colony, but to hide for as long as it took. Whether that was thirty years, or a hundred and thirty, was beyond the bounds of discussion. It was simply an axiom of Sun Hollow that we waited as long as necessary, always with the understanding that this place of refuge was temporary. Each day that we added to our tally was an achievement; each year a triumph. The forward planners in Sanctum were tasked with looking into our long-term survival needs, but for most of the citizenry that kind of thinking was actively discouraged. Concentrate only on the day ahead, and all the days after that will follow.

Every few years threw us a crisis. Sometimes they were political, like the Rurik Taine affair. Sometimes they were linked to a resource shortage, a systems failure, a chain of accidents. Sometimes, as with the passenger, it was an emergency related to something picked up by the Disciples. We had come through this latest one, and been spared our ultimate fear. Although a human incomer posed a serious threat to Sun Hollow, it was within our means to neutralise. One day, the Disciples would see a more wolfish kind of shadow at the cave mouth. But not today, and perhaps not this year. We had come through again, and I had played a small part in that success.

The shuttle fell tail first, dropping to the surface. It was always an act of nerve, waiting for the crater floor to slide aside at the last moment, allowing the shuttle to sink into the underground silo.

Sun Hollow allowed me in. The engines throttled down. The shuttle rocked slightly on its landing legs, then settled into stillness. There was never any air in the silo unless repairs needed to be done, but a pressurised connecting bridge pushed out from one of the walls, and before long a figure sauntered along the transparent tube to meet me at the lock.

Morgan Valois, plump in sheepskins, dangling a breather box.

"You're lucky man, de Ruyter."

"I am?"

Valois opened the breather box and took out a small bottle. He unstoppered it and held it out. A heavy odour wafted up my nostrils, settling into the space between my eyes. Already sensing brain cells beginning to wither, I took a polite swig for friendship's sake. I had no idea what was in the bottle, nor how Valois had come by it, but that concoction only came out on exceptionally rare occasions. "You get to read your own obituaries. I think you came out of them looking tolerably well."

"I'm not dead."

"We know that now. In fact we've known for about three weeks, once you popped back onto our tracking network. But the obituaries were already written and duplicated: too late to do anything about it now." His eyes narrowed to a hard, penetrating curiosity. "Why in Michael's name didn't you signal back to us?"

"I didn't believe it was necessary. The Disciples should never have lost sight of me."

"They did. You know the system's not flawless. If the Disciples occasionally lose track of one of our ships, that's actually a *good* thing. It means our stealthing measures aren't entirely pointless." He waved a flustered hand near his brow. "Besides that. We've had…glitches…with the Disciples, while you were away."

"Glitches?"

"Never mind. All will soon be mended. Which is better than I dare speculate about the state of your marriage."

"What about it?"

"You've put them through hell."

"Oh, dear God. Are you saying they thought I was dead, all those weeks?"

Valois took back the sacred bottle and returned it to its place of sanctuary. Any trace of bonhomie was gone from his face. "Nicola protected Victorine to the best of her abilities. Of course, she clung to the hope that you were alive, but near the end even she was starting to lose faith." He shook his head, his tone turning censorious. "You didn't have to inflict this on us, Miguel: if something happened out there, something that delayed your return, it would have been acceptable to signal us."

I stared at him. "What do you mean, *if* something happened out there? You know exactly what happened."

"We inferred. We saw the ship blow up. Either your missile had hit it, or you'd gone to protocol two. When there was a silence, we had to assume the latter."

"But the distress signal."

"The what?"

"Is this a game, Morgan? A test to see how well I cope with post-revival disorientation?"

19

"I assure you it's no game at all."

"There was a distress signal. Something contacted the ship. I investigated and found a drifting casket."

"A casket," he repeated carefully, as if taking notes in an interrogation, seeing how carefully I kept to one version of events.

"That signal was broadcasting all across the system. I had to silence it, by any means. There's no way Sun Hollow didn't pick it up, let alone the Disciples."

"We didn't pick up any sort of distress signal."

"Then it must have been...unidirectional." I frowned through a headache: more than could be explained by the tiny sip I'd taken from his bottle. "I don't know how it knew where to find me, but that's the only explanation. We can argue about this later: if you think I'm making this up, or delusional, I have all the evidence you need in the weapons bay. I found the drifter and I brought her aboard."

"Her."

"A passenger from the ship. Which, incidentally, I didn't need to destroy. It blew up on its own, just as I was about to ram it."

He lifted an eyebrow: the merest trace of admiration. "You were that close, in the end?"

"The missile veered off. No chance to return and refuel. So I put myself in the firing line." I lowered my voice. "I was ready for it, Morgan. You'd be surprised how ready I was. How good it felt, to know that I was about to make that sacrifice."

The admiration turned as quickly to pity.

"Until something robbed you of that chance for noble self-sacrifice."

"Unless you were there, you can't know what it was like."

He nodded slowly. "All right, I believe that much of it. I saw it in your face when you left: that need for expiation. Are you serious about this casket? You really brought something back with you?"

"More than just a thing. A survivor. I've spoken to her. She's not some radiation-blasted corpse in a box: her casket warmed her enough for communication. She was on a ship from Haven."

"One survivor, out of how many?"

"She doesn't remember enough to be able to say. I'm hoping she'll remember a little more when we bring her out of reefersleep."

"And this...fortunate soul? She's in hibernation now?"

"Her casket was damaged, but I plumbed it back into shuttle power for the trip home. She went back under."

Valois nodded. "Good. Then she won't feel a thing when we kill her."

*

20

I knocked on my own door: it only seemed polite. A long interval followed, and although it was evening, and out of school hours, I wondered if Nicola and Victorine had made themselves unavailable, delaying the point when they had to see me again. I could not blame them for that. I had been anxious to see them, and at the same time desperate to postpone our reunion because of the difficult feelings we were all going to have to face.

I was nearly ready to turn away from my own home, to go back to Sanctum on some pretence of business, when Nicola let me in. We held each other in the hallway, but there was a tentativeness to the embrace. When I kissed Nicola, she did not pull back, but neither did she rush to reciprocate.

"I am glad that you are back," she said quietly, as if there were a risk of Victorine overhearing from one of the adjoining rooms. "More glad than I may be capable of showing right now. But you put us through something terrible."

I closed the door behind me and shrugged off the breather box and sheepskins I had worn on my way home through the caverns. "Morgan says that you never lost hope that I was alive."

Nicola kept her voice low. There was a strain in it. "Not losing hope is not the same thing as knowing you're alive, Miguel. When we saw that explosion, what else were we expected to think?"

"I thought about signalling. But there's always a risk in any sort of communication."

"You do not need to tell me these things."

"No," I said softly. "You need to understand. That ship wasn't destroyed by my missile. Something else caused it. An engine failure, most likely. But I had to consider the other possibility: that there were wolves nearby. Maybe they hadn't seen me until that point. But it would only have taken one stray photon to give me away. From that discovery, they'd have found the Disciples, and then they'd have found Sun Hollow."

"Don't over-dramatise."

"I'm not. If wolves had come, I wouldn't be talking to you now." I searched her face, hoping the cruelty of my words had served its purpose. "It wasn't carelessness or thoughtlessness that stopped me signalling, Nicola. It was love. I'd have died out there rather than give the wolves a lead on our location."

Some rumination played behind her eyes. "Morgan says you nearly sacrificed yourself."

"The missile had failed. It was the only remaining way of stopping that ship."

I sensed something change in her: not forgiveness, not yet, but a step in the direction of forgiveness. It was the intention on which I pinned the first faint hope of reconciliation.

"How close did it come?"

"I'd made my peace."

"And then?"

"A burst of light. I was spared my sacrifice."

"What were you thinking of, in your last moments?"

"Of you here, alone, without me. I hoped you'd think well of what I'd done."

"It is not me that needs to understand it. I protected Victorine from the word of your death for as long as I could, but I could never shield her completely."

I nodded my agreement. "It wouldn't have been fair."

"When at last the news reached her—which we all thought was the truth—she was shocked and saddened. But as the days passed, and she had contact with her friends, she saw that in the eyes of many you had become a hero. Miguel de Ruyter: the man who gave himself to save Sun Hollow. I think, for that little while, she would have preferred to have been your daughter, not mine. But do you see what happened when you turned out not to be dead after all? You put her through another kind of grief. That figure that she had built up in her imagination died too."

"I can't help what happened," I said. "I can't help that I didn't die out there, or that I'm not the heroic martyr I never set out to be. All I know is that there was a threat, and now it's neutralised. And for a week, or a month, or however long it takes, some of us can sleep easily again." I stepped away from her, offering my palms. "That's all I have. I had a duty to Sun Hollow; I discharged that duty."

"Did you feel you had something to atone for?"

I started to lie, then decided Nicola deserved only the truth. "You were the one who said I had a guilty conscience. I'd have denied it, but part of me knew you were right."

"And now...has that burden lifted?"

"I think it has."

"I hope so, for all our sakes." Her voice became stern, but beneath it was a thread of familial warmth. "You will not go away again, Miguel. Promise me that, and make the same promise to Victorine. Can you do that?"

"I will do my best."

"Not good enough. I want a promise, here and now." She took my hands in hers. "As sacred as a marriage vow. You must not leave us. You will not leave Sun Hollow until the day we all leave. Is that understood and agreed?"

I nodded solemnly. "It is. My bones ache. I'd forgotten how hard it can be, and it was just a few weeks in space. Someone else will go next time. That's my promise."

"Good." Her fingers tightened. "You mean it."

"I do."

"Your hand is shaking. How is the numbness?"

"It'll get better after a few days."

At last there was the easing in her that I had been hoping for. "You will say all these things to Victorine, as well. She is waiting in the kitchen. When Morgan said that you were on your way...I prepared a meal. I was allowed an extra mutton ration, on account of your return. Will you eat with us?"

My eyes began to sting: tears of gratitude and relief, to be welcomed back into the love of a family.

"Nothing would make me happier."

It could never be a normal meal, but it was far better than no reception at all. I made the same promise to Victorine that I had given to Nicola, and when she came back at me with a hundred extra conditions, I accepted them without complaint. That settled—to her satisfaction, at least—she began to probe me for the details of what had happened since my departure. Most of it I could answer straightforwardly, but I was still in no hurry to dwell on the topic of sacrificing myself. Instead, I glided around it, mentioning that the missile had gone wrong and that shortly afterwards the ship had blown up on its own.

"Morgan told Mother that you found someone out there."

"I did," I answered. "A woman, the only survivor of the incomer."

"No one else seems to know."

"They don't, for the time being. Once we have a better idea of the incomer's condition, I'll make a public announcement."

Victorine picked spinach from between her front teeth. "What's her name?"

"We don't know. We spoke to each other out there, but she was still frozen and her memory hadn't begun to come back properly."

"Will it?"

"I very much hope so. There may be things she knows that can help us—even the simplest skill. Even if she doesn't remember everything, and hasn't anything unique to offer us, she'll still be treated kindly, made welcome in our community."

Victorine ate on in silence for a few mouthfuls. "Does she know you went out there to kill her?"

"Not her personally," Nicola put in on my behalf.

"Does it matter?" Victorine asked, lifting her face to both of us. "Her or one of the thousands of other people on that ship. Just because you didn't know any of them by name, it doesn't change the fact that the plan was to kill them all."

"The ship had to be stopped—" Nicola began.

"No, it's all right," I said, cutting her off gently. "Victorine deserves to hear the unvarnished truth. I did mean to kill the passenger: there's no getting away from it. I meant to kill her and however many other thousands of people she travelled with. It doesn't matter if there were fifty thousand of them, and five thousand of us. It's not a moral calculus. They had to die, no matter how many of them were, no matter how virtuous they were, so that our survival wasn't put in jeopardy."

"That makes us monsters," Victorine said.

"It does," I agreed, undercutting her ire. "It also makes us alive, and able to keep being alive. This is the key, Victorine: we've done it. We've proven to ourselves that we have the means to survive in Sun Hollow, and to keep surviving. Every death, every injury, every hard lesson along the path that's brought us here: all of that would have counted for nothing if we'd permitted them to blunder into our system and draw the wolves with them. It's not nice, what we have to do. But until we know that we aren't the only surviving pocket of humanity, every decision we take has to be conducted in that cold light. It's not about *us*: it's about the thread that we carry—a link between the humanity of the past, and the humanity of the future. If we break that thread; if we fail in our duty of self-preservation, we extinguish that future. Every hope, every dream: gone. It will be nothing but darkness, until the end of time."

"Did you come up with those words, or did someone in Sanctum do it for you?"

"You'll understand in time," I said.

"I don't want to understand."

Afterwards, when Victorine had collected her paintbox and gone to her room, and Nicola and I were cleaning up in the kitchen, she touched my wrist and said: "She will get over it, Miguel. It's not that she blames you for coming back from the dead. Deep down, she is very glad. But for a few days you became something else in her imagination, a figment no man could ever live up to, and now she has to deal with the reality again."

"Thank you for speaking in my defence."

"I did not agree with your silence—you should never have put us

24

through that. Even though Morgan said that you were right to expect that we should have worked things out for ourselves. But I believe in what you did, and what you set out to do. Those who think you had something to atone for? They are wrong, and so are you if still think that way." She pulled me in. The wholehearted embrace I had been waiting for since my return. "You are better than your detractors. You are a good man, Miguel de Ruyter, and I am proud that I am your wife."

In the morning I joined Morgan Valois and Alma Chung in Sanctum's infirmary. Like all our facilities it was a rambling complex of makeshift, modular rooms and buildings tucked into a network of caves and caverns, hundreds of metres beneath the surface. Every part of it had been scavenged and repurposed from the hulk of the *Salmacis*.

"I'm confused, Alma," my deputy administrator was saying as I made my entrance. "I could have sworn we spoke yesterday, but I must have slipped at least a day or two."

"We did," Chung answered tersely.

"Then...why is Miguel here? He was encouraged to stay home and recuperate for at least twenty-six to fifty-two hours."

"A suggestion he clearly decided was best ignored." Chung—my head of planetary security—gave an unconcerned shrug: she had no time for these frivolities. "I don't blame him in the slightest, given how quickly his prize is likely to emerge. He wants to see what he's brought back to us."

The three of us were looking into a glass-partitioned annex where the passenger and her casket had been brought after my landing. The sterile, airtight recovery room contained a bed and the usual medical monitoring equipment—not that much—but for the time being the passenger was still in the casket. The reefersleep unit had been wheeled in on a trolley, the sort we used for missile handling, and was now connected to a much more sophisticated battery of support systems. Two technicians, wearing masks and anti-contamination garments, were fussing around the connections, checking vital signs and taking notes on their bulky portable screens.

"Do we recognise the technology?" I asked.

"Older and more sophisticated than anything we brought here," Valois said. "But not so old that our earlier experience doesn't give us something to go on. Pre-plague, most likely—which doesn't mean we aren't taking all available safeguards."

"If you find something in Sun Hollow capable of being touched by the plague, let me know. We're deep in the Dark Ages, Morgan. No matter how far back things might have seemed to slip when she went under, we'll be a step less developed than anything she's prepared for. Have they got any further with that corrupted memory core?"

"Different varieties of scrambled data, but all pointing in the same direction: a passenger manifest for someone embarking at Haven, in '613. An adult female. Her name is Brianna Bettancourt."

"We have a ship record as well," Chung said. "Lighthugger *Silence in Heaven*. Bulk passenger, five point five megatonne displacement, commissioned '329, Demarchist orbital manufactory, Fand, Lacaille 9352. Engines and associated propulsion sub-systems leased from the Conjoiners under the technology sharing protocols of the Europa Accords."

"Good to have a name," I acknowledged. But I was still trying to push away the fact of what that ship had been: an ark full of sleepers, on their way to some better world, some better future. "How long until we bring her out?"

"They've begun perfusion," Valois said. "Say, thirteen to twenty-six hours, before she's conscious and warm and safe to be moved to that bed. Even then she'll likely be weak, confused and amnesiac: don't expect to be playing chess with her any time soon."

"Other than her memory, which was starting to come back, she sounded sharp."

"That was then," Valois cautioned. "We've tried opening that neural channel, and we'll keep trying as her brain comes back to life, but so far we haven't found a way in."

"It was some emergency function of the casket. If the casket no longer detects that it's at risk of failure, it won't invoke that neural interface."

"If that little trick was done with implants," Chung said, "she'll have to have them scooped out and incinerated before she takes a step out of that room."

I shook my head. "Be real, Alma. Even if she was a carrier, she'd be no threat to us."

"Point of principle, dear boy, just like your decision not to signal back to us," Valois answered loftily. "Still, we've scanned the box as well as we can. There doesn't seem to be anything artificial inside her, nor any nasty surprises in the casket itself. We'll conduct a complete set of tests once she's out, but my best guess is that she's come to us without augmentation, innocent as the snow."

"Innocence," Chung scoffed. "That'll be a first for us. If you get a glimpse, tell me what it looks like."

A faint shudder came up through the floor. Beyond the glass, the technicians halted in their examinations. Valois, Chung and I lifted our eyes to the breach light up in the corner of the wall, waiting for the red flash and siren that would mean some part of Sun Hollow was losing air, venting out to the surface. None of us had breather boxes around our necks. Inside Sanctum, which could be pressure sealed in a few seconds, there was no need. Any impactor big enough to puncture Sanctum was not going to leave much in the way of survivors, nor any great need for government.

The light stayed dim, and no siren came.

"Perhaps she'll want to climb back into the casket, when she finds out what sort of world she's woken up to," Valois said.

"She'll be grateful to be alive at all," Chung said, with a fierce lack of sympathy. Then, with a frowning squint. "She *did* know about the wolves, didn't she, Miguel?"

"I don't think she did."

"Then what did her captain tell her they were running from?"

"Nothing. I don't think she had the first idea what had happened to that ship at any point since it left Haven."

Chung was silent for a few seconds. I could almost feel the mesh of mental gears; the whirring simulations going on in her brain. "Something's been niggling me, Miguel, ever since you said you had a passenger. How the hell did she survive?"

I nodded into the glassed enclosure. "I'd say just barely. You've seen the damage to that casket."

"Your closing speeds were on the order of seven thousand kilometres per second," Chung stated.

"They were heading in, and I was heading out to intercept them, on a closely opposed vector. Two fists closing. Of course we had a high relative velocity."

"Yet from the shuttle's navigation log, we know that it was within your capabilities to rendezvous with the casket. The differential motion was much lower than your closing velocities."

"You're quibbling about how a survivor came to us?"

"I'm saying there's more to her story than simply being the one lucky soul who was thrown clear by that blast. There's something else."

"I thought there might be."

"The shuttle log confirms your account of the distress signal."

"I'm glad you didn't think I was making it up."

"But we didn't pick it up, and neither did the other ships or Disciples."

"So it was aimed at me, and not them."

"To aim it at you," Valois said, picking up on Chung's point, "she'd have needed to know where you were. But your account says that she didn't seem to know who you were or where you'd come from."

27

"Maybe something in the casket was able to lock onto me automatically, without the passenger ever being aware of it."

Chung looked at me as if there were blood coming from my nostrils. "Something in that casket? Is that the best you can come up with?"

"It's not an interrogation, Alma," I stressed. "And when we do start asking questions of the passenger, we won't be interrogating her, either. We'll be treating her as what she is: the sole survivor of something harrowing. An honoured guest, to be shown kindness and understanding."

A functionary bustled up behind us. "Pardon me, sirs. I'm afraid your presences are requested in the Red Room."

"What is it?" Chung snapped back.

"Something odd with the seismophones, picked up in the last few minutes. You'd best come."

CHAPTER THREE

The atmosphere in the Red Room was one of puzzlement, rather than outright alarm. The alert level was still amber: the same condition it had been since the demise of the *Silence in Heaven*. It had been red before, and would go down to yellow and then green if there were no further repercussions from the incomer.

Chung's analysts were crowded around the main table. Its display had been enlarged to focus on Michaelmas alone, with the two hemispheres of our planet placed side by side. Both faces were dotted with luminous, prism-shaped markers showing the positions of various sensors and defence assets, with a Neolithic huddle of them gathered around Sun Hollow. Other than that asymmetry, the two faces looked much alike: densely cratered, like a pair of coins that had been left in some corrosive medium, until no part of their surfaces remained unpitted.

"Fill me in," I said, as we joined the analysts.

"Something coming through here, sirs," said one of Chung's senior people, called Cantor. "Quite close to the estimated impact point of that last event, about ninety kilometres due east of us. We have no eyes in that area, but we do have several seismophones."

"Show us," Chung said.

Cantor drew our gazes to one of the screens suspended above the table at eye-level. A wavering green trace ran from one side of the screen to the other, pulsing up and down in a semi-regular pattern, almost like the electrocardiogram of a very slow pulse.

"We're not seismologists," Valois said.

"Something is triggering the seismophones," Cantor said. "And not the normal after-shock pattern we'd expect to see following an impactor. Those shocks fall off in amplitude very quickly. This is...not falling away."

"Convert that trace to an acoustic signal and play it over the speakers," Chung said.

We waited while Cantor made the necessary arrangements. The

29

technicians stopped in their work as the sounds played across the general address system. There was a muffled thump, a crackly silence, another muffled thump. What we were hearing were not sounds conducted through air, but vibrations being sent through Michaelmas's crust.

The pattern continued. *Thump*, silence, *thump*. There was a rhythm to it that none of us could ignore.

"It sounds like footsteps," Valois said, voicing the thought the rest of us shared. "Is this signal coming through all the seismophones in that sector?"

"Yes, but at varying strength," Cantor said. "That's why we don't think it's a fault in the phones themselves, or the cabling linking them back to Sun Hollow. There's a hint..." But Cantor silenced themself, directing a glance at Chung in expectation of permission or refusal to continue with this line of speculation.

"Go on," Chung said.

"The signal might be moving. It's growing in amplitude in one receiver, falling away in the others—but still much too slowly to be anything to do with that impactor."

"If it is moving, would you put a figure on the speed?" I asked.

Cantor looked at Chung again, drew breath. "My best guess? About two kilometres per hour. Quite slow, for a walking pace. But maybe not so slow over the sort of terrain on the surface, given that whoever's walking has to be wearing a vacuum suit."

"And if it's moving," I pushed. "You can estimate a vector?"

"Only very crudely."

"But you have estimated one."

"It could be travelling in the direction of Sun Hollow. If that's the case, we'll have a much better idea within the next twenty-six hours." Cantor gestured at the table. "These other phones should start registering the vibration, and we have eyes on the sector that the signal's heading into. The coverage is sparse, but it might give us something."

"Ninety kilometres," I said. "If someone is headed our way, whoever they might be, they'll be knocking on our doors in about forty-five hours. I wonder what they're hoping to find?"

Sensing that the moment could be delayed no longer I walked up the short flight of stairs that brought me onto the stage, in full view of the gathered citizens. Two functionaries followed me, shorn of their sheep-skins and wearing ceremonial attire only a little less ornamented than my own.

As the crowd noted my presence, there was a palpable shift in the atmosphere. Sweat prickled under my armpits. The air was not as cool as it had been in Sanctum, gently warmed and humidified by the five thousand bodies now pressed into the forum.

Murmuring and fidgeting stopped. There was one last cough, then silence.

I looked out, my gaze sweeping the ranks, trying to take everyone in. The first six rows were set with chairs, but after that it was standing room only, and even with my elevated position I could only see a little way into that press of tired, worry-worn faces. I had asked all of Sun Hollow to come here, with the exception of anyone hospitalised or on essential duty elsewhere. Five thousand was too many to recognise individually, but among the faces in plain view there were indeed hundreds that I did know by name, and with their names was a web of familial, occupational and political relationships.

There was Mina Lofgrind, whose father, Marcus, had died in the opening up of the twentieth cavern. Mina worked in the spinach beds, breaking her back to feed us. There was Nate Masnek, who had lost most of his hand in an accident in the papermill only a few weeks earlier. He was making a good recovery considering the injury but would need different employment once he was strong again. There were Etienne and Mokhtar, tireless scholars of closed-cycle life-support: never a day passed when they were not fixing something or trying to make something work a little more efficiently. No children, of course—or, at least, no children younger than Victorine.

I found Nicola and her daughter quite easily, seated just back from the first row. They were being pressed with questions by the gossip-fiends on either side: fishing for advance news about the announcement. By Nicola's brittle, exasperated look, I thought she'd had more than enough of being probed.

Of the people I recognised, how many were entirely on my side? It had been hard enough to say even before the Rurik Taine affair. Sun Hollow as a whole had not been in support of his attempted mutiny, but there had been many nuances of opinion besides simple disapproval. Some thought I had been too lenient in the past, allowing the dissenters to plot and organise, and that I ought to be held to partial account. Some thought I had been too lenient in the manner of his execution, and that nothing short of hanging, drawing and quartering was suitable for the man who had endangered us all.

Within Rurik Taine's family, I had no doubt where lay the sympathies. Rurik's wife Orva was seated next to his brother (and her brother-in-law) Soren. I tried to look past them, without snagging either's gaze, but it was

31

futile. Some part of my brain wanted me to lock eyes with Orva, as if that were a necessary step in my rehabilitation.

What do you want of me, I wondered: blood?

There had been no desire on my part to have Rurik executed. But the nature of his crime prohibited any other form of punishment. It was there in the tightly framed legislation we had both helped draft, in the earliest days of Sun Hollow. If we were going to survive, if we were going to stay hidden from the wolves, that entailed a simple, binding premise: no one could ever leave the system.

I made sure of that by destroying the *Salmacis*. Once we had stripped the ship of the last of its useful materials, what remained of the hulk had been put on automatic pilot and allowed to crash itself into Michael: timed, of course, to coincide with an episode of flaring, so that the twin detonations of its Conjoiner drives would look like spurts of background radiation. That sacrificial act was well known and commemorated: it was there in the mural that Victorine and her fellow pupils (and those before them) had been painting on the school wall. The principle of the act was understood: since the temptation to leave might prove irresistible, especially after a few decades of hardship—and if the wolves failed to come, year after year, lulling us into the treacherous idea that they might have gone away—then the best way of avoiding catastrophe was to remove the means itself. We had deliberately left ourselves with only the capability to travel within the system, and then only for emergency purposes.

But about five years ago a rumour had taken hold.

Like all the most daring lies, it was insidious and difficult to refute. The story was that the destruction of the *Salmacis* had been faked, and that the ship was still operable: kept somewhere close to Sun Hollow as an escape option for the governing elite, if and when the wolves came or some other catastrophe hit us. Most of the five thousand would be left behind, though, since the ship could only take a lucky few.

Rurik had shrugged off this lie when it first began circulating. Then he had begun to view it with a sort of guarded scepticism: not believing it, but not exactly dismissing it either. Finally, he had begun to nurture it for his own political ends. We had fallen into some mild rivalry over differing ideas for contingency planning—birth control, food rationing and so on—and Rurik had begun to agitate for a change in leadership. At the time I do not believe he put any real credence in the lie. It was just useful leverage, helping him stoke up some public dissent and gather a body of supporters. But over time I think he came very close to believing it, internalising it as fact, even though Rurik himself had been part of the executive operation to scupper the ship.

He and his brigade of rebels had got no further than the shuttle pen, but in attempting to leave Sun Hollow—without direct orders from Sanctum to do so—he had incurred the sternest penalty in our statutes.

I could do nothing to pardon him, but I had done all in my power to spare the lives of his co-conspirators. Including Orva Taine, who had undoubtedly been aware of her husband's plans. At the very least, she should be behind bars in Sanctum's modest detention block. But nothing good would have come of that—she was well liked and a good worker—and so I had used every executive power at my disposal to isolate her from the consequences of Rurik's crimes.

"You are either very wise," Morgan Valois had confided to me, as I laid out my plans for protecting the co-conspirators, "or extraordinarily gullible. I think we may need the benefit of another thirty or forty years to know which it is."

"If we get those extra years," I said quietly, for fear of being overheard, "I'll take whatever verdict's offered."

Valois was watching me now, from just off-stage. His downcast, reproving look confirmed that he thought little good would come of this announcement. He disagreed with me going public about the incomer before we had a better idea of what she represented, or how the seismic disturbances fitted into that picture. But rumours were already in circulation, and I knew all too well the damage they could do if left unchecked.

"Friends," I began, smiling out to the assembly, trying to strike an immediate note of reassurance. "I have news, and for the most part it is welcome. Some while ago, as you are all aware, I set out from Sun Hollow to intercept a ship that was in danger of exposing our existence to the wolves. Even if that ship had never attempted any contact with our community, it was behaving in a way that caused us concern. It had to be destroyed, even though that meant the likely deaths of many innocent souls." I injected the appropriate solemnity into my voice. "It was necessary, but that does not mean I took any pleasure in executing their destruction. And there was, of course, great risk in our own intervention. But it was a risk that we have considered many times; one that we have decided must be borne for the sake of Sun Hollow and the five thousand lives I address today. So it was: the incomer was successfully intercepted and destroyed."

I paused, watching their faces to see if anyone challenged my glossing over exactly how the incomer had been destroyed—how it seemed to have happened despite, rather than because of, my interventions. If they had doubts, they were well hidden.

"That is the less welcome news," I continued. "Lives were taken, and we mourn them. But out of that tragedy we have been granted a gift of life."

A ripple of surprise and interest passed through the assembly. Interest, curiosity, scepticism and resentment, in equal measure.

"A single passenger survived the destruction," I said. "A woman, we believe, and probably from Haven. It's likely that we know her name, but we'll wait until she can confirm it for us. What we can say is that she seems well, given all the tests we can run. She's sleeping for the time being, coming slowly out of hibernation, but we don't think it will be too many more hours before she is conscious and able to communicate." I smiled tightly. "Then we will begin the difficult business of explaining to her what has happened. It will be a shock, I think, and she will need help with that readjustment. She may not like us, at first. But in time, with all the patience and understanding we can offer, I think she will come to accept her situation and perhaps be thankful to be alive. And we, in turn, will be thankful to have her among us."

"Another mouth to feed," called Silus Maurus, one of my more embold-ened and vocal critics. He sat in the front row, squashed into his seat like a toad, arms folded belligerently.

"Yes," I said enthusiastically. "Another mouth to feed. Another pair of lungs to add to the demand on our life-support. Another soul needing shelter and warmth. Shall I tell you what else she brings? Possibility. A mind full of new ideas. New stories, new lessons. New songs. New jokes. She only has to know one new thing to turn Sun Hollow upside down. It might be the tiniest, least important fact as far as she's concerned. It might be about the wolves, or engineering, or medicine. It might be a new way to cook spinach or mutton. It might be a better way to take out an infected tooth, or a new way of stitching sheepskin."

"And it might be nothing at all," Maurus said, smirking to one side.

"That's possible," I admitted, "though unlikely. But I'll tell you this. You don't learn the worth of a human being with a few questions. It takes a lifetime to understand the value of a life. And that's what we'll give her, unreservedly and without conditions. A new life among us, in Sun Hollow." Before any other critics could chip in, I added: "She'll find employment, something that suits her talents. Everyone contributes, and so shall she. But from the moment she opens her eyes, we treat her as one of us. If she has something to offer, something new, she'll give it in due course. But we won't demand it of her, and we won't treat her with anything other than gratitude and kindness."

"What about these noises we hear about?" called out Nate Masnek, rising slightly from his seat and rubbing his good hand against the bandaged remains of the other.

I tried not to bristle. Masnek had been fair to me in the past and his question was well meant. It was not his fault reports of the seismic disturbances had already leaked out of Sanctum.

"Impactor activity has been quite high lately," I said, which was close enough to the truth to assuage my conscience. "As ever, we monitor all seismic activity and respond accordingly. At the moment, there's no cause for any concern."

I became aware of Morgan Valois, shuffling to my side. "Thank you for that extremely helping briefing, Administrator," he said, in the strained tones of one who believed that some sort of embarrassing public debacle had only just been averted. "Since you have much business to attend to— and everyone is already gathered—I think I might seize the opportunity of continuing with some daily administrative announcements?" Pointedly, he did not wait for my assent. "Firstly, I'm pleased to report that the spur into chamber four has now been cleared for use after last month's subsidence..."

Questions were still being shouted from the audience, even as Valois tried to turn the topic over to such matters as seasonal spinach output, mandatory water rationing and the imposition of revised schooling rotas.

I was exceedingly glad to turn my back on the gathering and leave the stage.

Most of a day passed before our guest was ready to be removed from reefersleep. Legitimate Sanctum business (Valois had been right about that) took up the last hours before I returned home, quietly apprehensive about the sort of reception I was likely to get from Victorine. Nicola must have spoken to her, though, or her harder feelings had thawed, or my words at the assembly had worked some effect, because there was little of the antipathy I had felt the previous evening. I wished that adults were as capable as children of moving beyond some impasse, letting go of whatever had been intractable only hours or days ago. I envied them that ability to discard their past selves as if they were old, tattered, useless skins.

"Has she come out of the box yet?" Victorine asked, while we were setting out a board and counters for a game we often played after meals.

"No. Perhaps tomorrow, if all goes well. Nothing needs to be rushed. She's taken decades and decades to reach us, so a few more hours won't make any difference to her."

"Do you think she ever saw the wolves?"

"It's doubtful. We think she left her planet in the years before the

35

wolves came. Much of what we take for granted will be new to her, and very likely difficult to accept."

"Didn't you speak to her, out in space? You didn't say anything about that in the assembly."

"I did speak to her, but I'm not sure how much of it sank in. That's why I didn't mention it. If your mother and I woke you in the night, when you had been deeply asleep, and whispered secrets to you, do you think you'd remember them all in the morning?"

"It would depend on the secrets."

"You cannot fault her logic," Nicola said, smiling at the two of us as she fumbled handmade dice out of a bag. "Still, we will all do our best to help the passenger adjust, won't we? It will be good for us to have a new face in Sun Hollow."

"Do you think she'll be cross that everyone else on her ship died?" Victorine asked, with an unaffected naturalness.

"She'll be sad, I think, when the truth hits home," I answered, laying out the counters in their starting positions. "But she might not have known those people as well as we all know each other in Sun Hollow."

"She still won't be able to talk to any of them about where she came from."

"No," I acknowledged, meeting her eyes. "And that may be difficult for her, until she adjusts to her new life."

"It would change things," Nicola said quietly, "if it turned out that she was not the only survivor."

I nodded once, but did not allow myself to be drawn in. I should have known it would be impossible to prevent news of the seismophone trace finding its way beyond Sanctum, especially as I had decided against placing it under a secrecy order.

We played three rounds of the game, Victorine trouncing Nicola and me, and then tiredness won out and we all made preparations for bed.

"There was a rumour," Nicola said quietly, when it was just the two of us and the last of the tea. "Of something coming in from the east."

"You're exactly right. It's a rumour."

"Nate Masnek asked about sounds, and I heard something about footsteps."

"Which is as good a case as any for dismissing it completely. No one would land ninety kilometres away and walk across the surface."

"Perhaps they don't know we're here."

"In which case, it's an astonishing coincidence they landed as *near* to us as ninety kilometres. Either way makes no sense. A deliberate visitor would land closer if they'd detected our presence. Maybe not right above us, but not tens of hours of travel away. A random stranger would have landed anywhere on Michaelmas but this exact sector." I forced a reassuring smile, trying to ease her fears even if my own were unassailable. "The truth is more mundane: those seismophones aren't as reliable as we'd wish, and the cables connecting them back to Sun Hollow are susceptible to damage. There might not be any weather out there, but there's no shortage of violent geology to make up for it. The temperature variations play havoc, the crust strains and contracts, and it only takes one cable rubbing against a rock to send false signals back to us."

"These recent weeks have been strange. First Rurik Taine, then the incomer. Then you coming back to us, when we thought you were dead. And you bring back a gift for the community, if an odd one. No one knows what to make of these things, Miguel. They start to feel like portents." She smiled hastily to reassure me that she was not yet ready to embrace full-blown superstition. "Too many shadows. We are all surviving on the edge of our wits. This isn't how people are meant to live." She nodded to the bedroom where her daughter was easing into dreams that I hoped were as pleasant and carefree as her life would permit. "You would tell me, regardless of your Sanctum secrets, if you knew things were about to get worse?"

"I would tell you."

"Good. Now sleep, and sleep well, because I have never known you look more tired than these last days. And tomorrow, if all is well, your passenger will speak again."

Late in the morning of the following day I left my office and went down to the infirmary, summoned by a call from the duty physician, Doctor Kyrgiou. Valois must have received the same call, for we nearly bumped into each other in the rock-walled tunnels that connected the two parts of Sanctum.

"Alma not joining us?" I asked.

"Headaches of her own, dear boy, without concerning herself with your pet survivor."

I raised an eyebrow, unaccustomed to such a tone from the normally unflappable Valois. I supposed the strain of recent events was getting to all of us, cracking us open along our lines of weakness. "A few odd noises on the seismophones?"

"No—although I'd say they're hardly helping, under the circumstances." Although there was no danger whatsoever of our conversation being overheard, he nonetheless dropped his voice. "Peter and Saul have dropped out."

I understood his meaning, but hoped that I might have misheard. Peter and Saul were two of our Disciple watchkeeping satellites: our system-wide early warning network. "Dropped out as in...gone silent?"

"They were late with their status pulses. Those pulses aren't sent on a fixed schedule, but there's a window in which we'd expect to see them. That window came and went. We waited for Michael to spike a bit, and sent a query." Seeing my developing concern, he added: "Low-energy, ultra-low bandwidth: the usual protocols, and aimed preferentially at Peter and Saul."

I walked on a few paces. "And?"

"Nothing's come back. Those queries aren't negotiable: if the Disciple receives such a transmission, it's obliged to acknowledge receipt, regardless of Michael's activity or any other security concerns."

"A serious fault could put a Disciple into self-repair and recovery mode. That's happened before after an impactor strike: something small enough to damage the satellite, but not destroy it outright. Sometimes they come back up on their own, sometimes we have to go out there and repair them."

"Two at the same time?"

"Well, that still leaves ten units: ample overlap of coverage. Provided they all keep working properly." I patted him on the shoulder and wished someone were around to extend me the same courtesy. "We'll get around this, Morgan. It looks bad because of everything else going on, but any one of these anomalies is something we've faced before."

"Something is wrong here, Miguel—really, badly wrong." We had arrived at the infirmary in time for Valois to nod through the glass partition into the enclosure where the passenger was being kept. "Something to do with Brianna Bettancourt, if I'm not mistaken."

Doctor Kyrgiou and her fellow physicians were preparing to take her out of the casket. It had already been opened: the entire upper section removed in one piece like a coffin lid and placed to one side. Now the gowned and masked physicians were delving into the interior with gloves and tools. The tall, slightly stoop-shouldered Kyrgiou stood to one side, holding a portable screen while one of her colleagues swept a scanner along the length of the casket.

It was hard to see what was going on. Other than the physicians, there were trolleys stacked with monitor devices, life-support machines (not yet operating, but ready if they were needed) and upright stands loaded with various bags of tinted medical solutions.

I pressed the intercom button set into the partition. "Good morning, Doctor Kyrgiou. Thank you for calling me. May I ask how close she is to revival?"

38

The tall figure looked up from her portable screen, her voice emerging from a grille above the window.

"She'd already be awake if it wasn't for our own anaesthetics, Administrator. Just as she was showing signs of surfacing, we held her under while we double-checked her bloods and ran a few last-minute tests."

While she was still cold, the physicians had drilled into the casket and nipped away a tiny tissue sample; enough to run some basic checks and confirm (to the best of our capabilities) that the passenger was human rather than some devious wolf construct. The sample also enabled them to test for the major transmissible diseases, based on those known to us. They went on to draw blood, extract marrow and spinal fluid, and probably run a dozen other tests too complicated to explain to me. Kyrgiou tipped her screen in my direction as the scan went on, showing a smoky scroll of familiar-looking body parts. Pelvis, ribs, shoulders and skull. I was no surgeon but nothing stood out as being artificial, even at the highest scanning resolution. Her brain was uncorrupted by machine parts, and there was no sign of trauma from her ordeal.

Kyrgiou swept the scanner back along the passenger's torso.

"Stop," I called out. "I saw something. Back up a bit: around the ribcage."

"What did you see?" Kyrgiou asked.

"I don't know. Something solid, somewhere in her chest. A sort of dense mass, like a machine, an implant. About the size of a fist. Like an artificial heart."

"There's nothing, Miguel." She played the scanner back and forth over the area of interest. "Bone, muscle, lungs, heart. Normal tissue, normal organs. Nothing mechanical."

"I swear I saw something."

"The scanner records itself. I'll rerun the capture. Back thirty seconds?"

"That should be enough."

Kyrgiou spooled back and let the recording run forward. I watched intently, until we reached the point where Kyrgiou jerked back to the ribcage upon my request.

"There's nothing there," she said, watching me guardedly, daring me to contradict her assessment. But I could not. I had seen the playback as well, and nothing out of the ordinary had shown.

"I'm viewing it through this window," I said. "There must have been a reflection, a trick of the light."

The masked figure nodded doubtfully, perhaps not fully convinced that I was over the strains of my mission. "The bloodwork and associated tests will need several hours. But provided we maintain our usual hygienic measures, there's no reason not to bring her to consciousness as soon as you're ready to greet her."

"I am ready."

"Good. Shall we say—thirty minutes?"

As she spoke, a gap opened up between the physicians and I caught my first glimpse of the passenger without the grilled window of her casket between us. A small, pale, vulnerable form lay in the casket. She was no longer armoured in metal, invulnerable to heat or cold or vacuum. She was a human being, fragile and easily broken, just like the rest of us.

"Treat her carefully," I said.

Cantor had already prepared the main table with a highly magnified view of the surrounding two hundred kilometres. At that resolution, the projected area of Sun Hollow was about the size of a fat thumbprint: a cluster of twenty caverns buried between two hundred and six hundred metres beneath the surface. A dozen or so radial lines pushed out to between five and twenty kilometres from the settlement: hard-fought tunnels leading to reactor cores, shuttle pens and surface locks. After that, there were no underground digs, just remote monitoring stations, railgun emplacements, and the spidering threads of cables linking remote sensors and weapons to Sanctum.

Cantor had positioned green prisms to denote the seismophones within that two-hundred-kilometre radius, including the three that had picked up the repeating signal. Now there was a luminous dotted trace extending from that cluster, wandering around crater walls and deep fissures, but generally heading in the direction of Sanctum. I estimated it was between forty-five and fifty kilometres long. The trace had already passed close to several other seismophones—the coverage improved the nearer one got to Sun Hollow—and it was now on the threshold of two blue prisms. These were eyes as well as ears, and we had fewer of them.

"So it's not a fault," I said quietly.

"If you find that stating the obvious helps your analytic faculties, please don't hold back," Chung answered in the same low register.

Valois directed his question at Cantor. "Do we have visual contact?"

"If there's anything to be seen, we have our best chance in the next few minutes. Michael's most of the way up, which means low contrast but high illumination: not ideal but much better than darkness. These two eyes are set back behind a ridge, so we can't see anything just yet. But if our seismophone readings are correct, whatever's making the disturbance ought to be emerging very shortly."

"Are those eyes armed?" I asked.

"Negative: passive defence only." But Cantor jabbed a finger towards another pair of close-set prisms just beyond the twenty-kilometre marker of our furthest surface lock. "These have teeth, though, and they should be able to bear onto a slow-moving surface target."

We had two classes of railgun: heavy ordnance aimed at the sky, and smaller units that were our last line of defence in case anything made it all the way to the surface. That final stockade was mostly psychological, but I would sooner have torn out my fingernails than dispense with it. Human beings could be comforted against the night by a drawn curtain or a head buried under bed sheets. It seemed to me that we needed all the comfort we could get.

"Something…" Cantor began.

Two of the suspended screens had been assigned visual feeds from the eyes covering the ridge. Both views looked quite similar, since the two eyes were only a kilometre from each other. The ridge was a ragged, not-quite-horizontal line dividing the views into two halves. Above the ridge was the blackness of space: even though it was "day" on Michaelmas, there was no atmosphere to scatter Michael's illumination across the sky, and Michael himself was behind the eyes. Whatever dust was in Michael-mas's orbital path was far too faint to be seen against the glare from the terrain in the lower half of each view. And that terrain was nearly feature-less; distances, elevations and relative sizes difficult to judge. Michael was not a bright star but even a red dwarf's light was sufficient to blast away shadows and contrast, leaving the ground like a flat ochre smear daubed across a wall, curtailed abruptly by the ridge line.

I could pick out slight differences in parallax caused by the eyes' dif-fering vantage points. And now Cantor had mentioned it, I was starting to see something rising above the ridge line on one of the two views. It was a white prominence, like a pale planet pushing above the horizon. The planet became a white hemisphere. Then, very slightly to the right of it, a second one. Now the other eye was picking up the same projecting forms.

We watched in silence. The hemispheres kept rising. They were heads: or more properly, helmets. They had black slots across their fronts. Beneath them came shoulders, torsos, arms and legs. Two white-clad fig-ures, walking side by side. Not one set of footsteps, then, but two. Though the figures were walking in lockstep, each planting a foot at the same time, lifting, planting, lifting.

They crested the ridge and began to descend. They looked like two pale paper cut-outs sliding down a vertical surface, but that was only the extreme foreshortening of the eyes, coupled with the absence of atmospheric blurring and the lack of any reference points to help with perspective.

I was struck by how slowly they seemed to be walking. Cantor's earlier estimate of two kilometres per hour could not have been far off the mark. Over a day, that was enough to account for the forty-five or fifty kilo-metres of that sinuous trace. A suit could easily keep someone alive for that length of time—much longer, if required—and with augmentation, and volition systems, a suit could walk on auto-pilot even if its occupant were injured or sleeping. But there still seemed to me to be something unnatural, something reminiscent of troubled dreams, in that slow, syn-chronised gait.

My neck hairs prickled.

"Will we get a closer look, as they come nearer?"

"Maybe," Cantor said. "Depends on the path they take, coming down off the ridge."

"I want anything you can give me. Markings, names—anything on those suits that might tie them to the *Silence in Heaven*. I presume you'd have told me if there'd been any attempt at contact?"

"Radio silent the whole time we've been hearing those footsteps. If they're communicating between themselves, it's on some short-range channel we can't intercept." Cantor looked doubtful. "Should Sanctum send someone out to meet them, sir? They're about twenty kilometres beyond our outer lock, but if we sent out a party now, using a cart to get to the end of the shaft, they should be able to meet them about halfway."

"No. Not yet," I demurred. "Wait until we have a clearer view, or until we're confident that they're heading for the lock. Then we'll decide how to respond."

"I don't see anything that looks like a weapon," Valois said.

Doctor Kyrgiou helped me into the sterile garb. "Keep the mask and goggles on at all times. No physical contact until we're sure about that bloodwork. A conversation is fine, but don't stress her unnecessarily. If she doesn't remember too much about her predicament, no need to bring it all back to her in one go."

"I'll go gently. But there are questions we need to ask."

"I'll be watching duplicate feeds on the monitors on this side of the glass: I'll know if her anxiety levels start rising."

I let myself into the partitioned area through a double-door airlock, then walked to the passenger's bedside and sat down in the chair that had been provided on her left, opposite the monitoring equipment. Kyrgiou had told me that our guest ought to be surfacing from the anaesthesia, but for the moment she showed no awareness of my presence. I studied her properly for the first time, finally seeing a human woman rather than a disembodied face in a box.

She looked younger than me, but then so did everyone. She was white: literally the colour of snow. There was no pigmentation anywhere on her skin, except for the black smears around her eyes, presently lidded. She looked hairless: her skull a smooth white dome. Her lips had the tint of smoke.

Her fingernails, where they rested on the bed sheets, were a pearly grey.

I waited, watching her breathing. When I detected the tiniest motion of her head, a quiver in her eyelids as if she was on the verge of opening them, I said: "Welcome back, Brianna."

Her nostrils flared as she drew in a slow breath. Her eyes stayed closed but her lips moved.

"Where am I?"

Her words were faint but perfectly comprehensible. It was the first time I had heard her actual voice, as opposed to a synthetic emulation. It was deeper and throatier than I had expected.

"A place called Sun Hollow. That might mean something to you. My name is Miguel. I found you in space, after an accident, I promised I'd bring you back to my world."

She answered after a few moments.

"What happened to me?"

"You were on a ship that ran into trouble. I found you drifting in a hibernation casket, and we spoke to each other. Then I brought you aboard my own ship and carried you back to safety."

"Where is...Sun Hollow?"

"Under the crust of a world called Michaelmas, orbiting a star called AU Microscopii, which we call Michael."

She opened her eyes to narrow slits. "I remember. There was a red light. A whorl of dust. I was...cold. And you found me."

"I'm glad that you remember. It's a very good sign that you'll remember all the other things as well."

She angled her head to look at me. Within their black margins they were the colour of iron. She was as monochrome as an old photograph.

"The other things?"

"What happened to your ship before it got to us. We think you may have been born on Haven, and probably lived close to a place called Zawinul's Landing. From the records we've recovered, it seems likely that you left Haven around one hundred and eighty years ago. We also think your name may have been Brianna Bettancourt. Does that name seem familiar?"

"Say it to me again."

"Brianna Bettancourt," I replied.

She lifted the arm with the line in it and looked at the bandaged-over catheter, her expression neutral. I wondered what she made of our medicine; whether it inspired horror or reassurance.

"Am I all right?"

"Yes…" I said, tentatively, not wanting to pre-empt the physicians. Then, with more confidence: "Yes—you're doing very well. You can breathe for yourself, move your own limbs, speak and understand us, and you're beginning to remember fragments of your past. I've helped a lot of people come out of hibernation, and I know when the omens are good."

"Omens." A faint smile played across those pallid lips. They were closer to the colour of static, the colour of storm-clouds. "Am I an omen?"

"A guest," I affirmed. "A patient, for now, until you're well enough to leave the infirmary, and then a welcome newcomer." I leaned forward slightly. "Brianna…if that's your name. I must ask you one or two difficult questions. I'd sooner wait, but I'm afraid we don't have that luxury."

The edges of her lips curled, buckling the skin around her mouth. It was as if she were tasting some delicious memory, or anticipating some coming delight.

"What are your questions?"

"Can you remember how you came to be separated from your ship? There was an explosion, and then I picked up your signal. I assumed you'd been thrown free, but it's difficult for us to understand how that could have happened. Is it possible you'd already left the *Silence in Heaven*?"

Instead of frown lines, two perfect dimples appeared in her brow. It was as if they were being depressed into some yielding, resilient surface by two invisible fingers.

"Why would I leave the ship?"

"I don't know. But we wonder if your ship may have sent out a scouting party, long before it reached the edge of our planetary system. Maybe more than one such party, more than one smaller vessel?"

The dimples popped out of her brow, leaving it as unmarred as a sheet of virgin ice.

"Have you found someone else?"

"I…don't know." I smiled—or perhaps grimaced—through my mask, feeling as if Brianna and I were engaged in some sort of parlour game for which only one of us had been handed the rules. "There are indications that another ship may have landed on our planet, or come near enough to set down an exploratory team. Two people, two other survivors."

"Are they here?"

"Not yet. It would help us very much if you could shed any light on them. What they might want, what they might expect...what they might already know of us. Then we can be sure that they're friends, and welcome them accordingly."

"Why wouldn't they be friends?"

"I hope that they will be."

An urgency seemed to grip her. "There was a light: a very bright light. Everything before that is...washed out, faint." Her eyes widened, beseeching me. "Did you see the light, Miguel?"

"I did." I pushed myself up from the chair, unaccountably drained by our short conversation. "It was a terrible thing."

"Were there people in that light, besides the two you just told me about?"

"In that light?"

"Killed by it, I mean."

I nodded slowly. "There's a good chance of it. But out of it, you came to us."

"I hope I won't disappoint," she said.

"Enhance it," Alma Chung ordered, arms folded across her chest as Cantor brought up another video sample of the two approaching figures. The White Walkers, some of the analysts were starting to call them, borrowing the nomenclature from some half-forgotten mythos that had somehow found its way to Sun Hollow.

"This is the best we'll have until the next set of eyes," Cantor said. "I've applied every reliable filter in our arsenal, and then a few I shouldn't have."

"It'll do," I mouthed.

The visitors—as Chung, Cantor, Valois and I were still calling them—had come down off the ridge by a moderately meandering trail and then cut a course that took them to the south of the two eyes, skirting the nearest by two and a half kilometres. Unfortunately, the eyes were designed to scan large areas of sky and terrain, rather than magnify a tiny portion of either.

But now at least we had a side-on view of the suits as they skirted around the southernmost eye. Cantor had isolated about fifteen seconds of video and put it on a loop, so that the figures kept walking past the same bit of terrain. Michael's elevation had decreased since the suits had first come over the ridge, and now the ground shadows were longer, offering slightly

45

more contrast and a chance to pick out details on the suits: markings and tools that might offer a clue as to their intentions.

Even in the enhanced zoom, though, the suits looked smooth and nearly featureless. There were no articulation points between the body parts, just a smoothly flexing white integument. The boots and gloves were seamless extensions of the legs and arms. The helmets swelled up from the necks and upper torsos, with no trace of a pressure collar. The only details, when the suits were face-on, were the narrow, slot-like visors, wrapping around the helmets from ear to ear. Viewed from the side, as we were doing, the suits had hump-like backpacks but again these were formed from an integral extension of the main suit and offered no clue as to what else they might contain besides life-support systems.

The loop kept playing. I stared at it, willing some detail to spring out that I had missed the last time.

"Suits like that would be very handy to have," Valois mused. "The next time we have to ask some poor volunteer to go out onto the surface during a flaring episode, it would be good to get something back with a life expectancy exceeding a few hours. Do you think they'll let us have those suits, if we ask nicely?"

"If they're friendly, and abide by the terms of our community, there'll be no reason for them not to share the technology."

"In exchange for what?" Chung asked. "Sheepskins and spinach?"

"Stop the playback," I said suddenly.

Cantor obliged. I ask for the video to be reversed by a few seconds, then frozen.

"Kyrgiou said you've been seeing phantoms," Valois commented.

"Not this time. Take a close look at the horizon line behind the leading figure." The suits were walking side by side, but because of the eye's viewing angle, the one on the right appeared to be ahead of the one on the left. "Just for a second, it cuts behind the visor. Cantor: advance the playback, but at much less than normal speed."

Cantor let the video move forward, but at a twentieth of its usual rate. The suits oozed to the right, their bipedal gait now all but imperceptible. It was like the movement of clouds: no human quality to it at all.

"Trust Miguel to see something on the horizon line, not the two things the rest of us are looking at," Valois went on.

"It's not the horizon line: it's what happens to it. Look closely as it passes behind the curve of that visor. We can still see it."

"And?" Chung asked.

"Shouldn't there be a head in the way?"

CHAPTER FOUR

The two railguns at the twenty-kilometre margin each contained nine kinetic energy slugs, their normal operational load. The magazines contained ten rounds, but since the rounds were manufactured in batches, and the loading process required partial disassembly and reassembly of the gun, it was always considered necessary to fire one test shot, to verify that the rounds had been machined within tolerance, and that the guns had been put back together correctly.

Fortunately, there had been no false alarms since these guns were reloaded—a difficult, dangerous, time-consuming job in its own right—and so there was only one empty slot in each magazine.

The guns' normal muzzle velocity was one hundred kilometres per second, far in excess of Michaelmas's escape velocity. That was a consequence of their original use defending ships against high-speed collisions: they needed quick reaction times and extreme penetrating power, to shatter micro-meteorites into harmless ions. That made them good as anti-ship defences (not that they had ever been tested in that capacity) but not so effective against over-the-horizon targets like our two suits. To function in that mode, the guns' muzzle velocities needed to be dropped by a factor of ten, preventing the slugs from flying off into interplanetary space, going into orbit around Michaelmas, or hurling themselves halfway around the world before coming back to ground.

With the muzzle velocity damped, it was possible to aim a slug at a point only tens of kilometres away: out of the line of sight, but only just over the horizon. But the downside was that the penetrating force was also much reduced: kinetic energy fell off with the square of velocity, so a tenfold reduction in muzzle velocity meant a hundredfold drop in stopping power.

Still: what could stop a ship should also be able to stop a suit, even if it was a hundredth of its usual effectiveness. But with just eighteen slugs, and no means of reloading the guns in anything less than a day, we had to consider each shot very carefully.

I still wanted some explanation for the suits that allowed us to avoid destroying them. I was even hopeful that Brianna Bettancourt might dredge something up in our next meeting. But until such clarification was forthcoming, or an overture came from the suits themselves, or whoever had sent them, we had to proceed on the assumption of hostile intent. It was agreed that the first two shots (sent in quick succession, but not simultaneously) would be lobbed to fall short of the suits by about a kilometre: presenting no danger to the suits but providing a clear demonstration of our capabilities. Two shots arriving in the same spot meant that we could demonstrate the repeatability of our aiming. If that deterrent failed, the next two lobs would fall closer still. If those failed, the next pair of shots would be intended to land exactly on the suits.

The suits had passed out of reach of the first set of eyes, but Cantor and the other analysts still had their seismophone readings. The signals were faint, but just strong enough to enable triangulation to within an error margin about twenty metres across. That was too imprecise to guarantee a kill, but good enough for the purposes of our warning shots. I assigned all necessary authority to Chung, and was not even back at the infirmary when the lights wavered. That was the railguns sucking power from our already-strained generators.

The passenger had sensed it too. She was awake and alert.

"I didn't think you'd come back quite so quickly, Miguel. Is everything all right?"

I put on a smile under my mask. "Why wouldn't it be all right?"

"There was a power dip just now. I wondered if there was a problem with your settlement."

I eased into the seat next to her.

"You'll have to get used to a lot more than the occasional flicker. Sometimes we have to go onto emergency power for days at a time. We use flywheels, deep underground. They used to be part of the manoeuvring system of the *Salmacis*, but now they help us ride out power interruptions. They can't run indefinitely, though. Sometimes it gets dark and cold in these caverns."

"Perhaps I'd be better off going back into the casket?"

"No—never that. But it's probably going to be a harder life than anything you experienced on Haven. We have very basic medicine; we get by on a restricted diet, though it meets our nutritional needs, and when we get a bad year we have to go onto double rationing, as if our normal conditions weren't enough of a challenge. We haven't allowed children to be born in Sun Hollow in twelve years."

"Then you're not going to live very long."

"We have a little while left."

"Do you have children, Miguel? I can't remember if I asked you before."

"I don't have my own children, no. But my wife has a daughter from her previous marriage. Her name is Victorine. She's as dear to me as if she were my own."

"And your wife?"

"Nicola." I tensed; this was supposed to be about our guest, not my own background. "Brianna, do you remember what I asked you the last time we spoke? About two people who might have been part of your expedition?"

She constructed the frown again, forming those even, symmetrical dimples in her brow. "I tried to remember, but it's still hard to bring things into focus. Maybe if you told me a little more about what you know?"

I reached for the package I had brought into the room. It was a flat, book-sized box with tattered edges. I set it onto her bed, dutifully avoiding any sort of contact and opened the box. I took out a folding board with perforated holes and a bag of coloured pegs.

She looked at me with over-embellished delight, as if I had tipped a bounty of treasure onto the sheet.

"You brought a game! Do you like games? I like games."

"I had someone go to my house and fetch it. I thought it might help to unblock some mental pathways if you have something else to focus on." I jammed two sets of coloured pegs into their starting positions, then explained the extremely rudimentary rules.

"I see it, Miguel. It's not too complicated. I think we can play right now."

"Perhaps a warm-up game?"

"If you say so."

I let her go first, and went easy on her during the opening moves. It was a simple game, but that did not mean that there were not layers of complexity buried within it; traps and subtleties waiting to spring out like vipers. While we took turns, I edged the conversation around to some of the things that had been troubling me—troubling all of us, in fact—since her rescue.

"I asked you about what had happened before the explosion. You didn't remember, but maybe it would help if I explained our difficulty."

"Please, ask whatever you wish."

"Our ships were travelling towards each other with a combined closing speed of thousands of kilometres per second: more than two per cent of the speed of light."

"That doesn't seem terribly fast."

"It isn't—not for interstellar ships like the *Silence in Heaven*. But it's very fast for anything moving through a solar system. After the explosion, your casket should have kept moving with about the same relative speed as the original ship, give or take a margin of error. But it didn't: it ended up on a velocity vector much closer to that of my own ship. Granted, I still needed time to match my speed and position with yours—but it was feasible to do it."

"Lucky for me."

"Lucky for you indeed." The peg game carried on. My opponent had made some predictably poor moves in the opening rounds, but now she was making up for it, putting me under pressure. A quick learner, I thought to myself—or just possibly someone who had not needed to learn the game at all. "There's another odd factor, Brianna. Somehow, you were able to send a distress signal to my ship. But it wasn't picked up by any other of our receivers."

"Perhaps they're not working as well as you'd wish."

"Or perhaps you managed to locate my ship and aim a very narrow communications beam at it."

She broke off from pondering her next move—any one of the available options was likely to put her at an advantage over me. A look of slow puzzlement came upon her face.

"You seem...not quite to trust me."

"I *want* to trust you," I said. "That's normal when you risk your life to save someone—and I risked all of ours by not shooting you out of the sky when I had a chance. But you're not making it easy." I paused. "That power dip you registered? It was two of our guns, firing kinetic energy slugs over the horizon."

"To what purpose?"

"To send a message to a pair of suits that are walking towards us, across the surface of Michaelmas." I watched her reaction as carefully as I could, hoping for some fracture in that flawless armour. "Two empty suits, as near as we can judge. It can't be a coincidence that you've all arrived on Michaelmas at the same time. Those suits must have come from the *Silence in Heaven*, just like you, and like you they must know more about us than we'd like to think. You knew about my ship. These suits know about the location of Sun Hollow."

"And the message you meant to deliver?"

"Stop. Come no closer until you've declared your intentions."

"You think that will persuade them?"

I reflected on my answer.

"More that I worry about what those suits are going to contain in the future."

We played on for a few more moves, with my chances of drawing against her, let alone defeating her, diminishing to distant theoretical possibilities.

"How would that work, exactly? Do you think someone's going to get inside those suits, and then go somewhere?"

"I don't know. I'm currently trying very hard not to rule anything out."

"Right answer."

"I'm sorry?"

"I mean that right now you can't help wondering if I've got something to do with the suits, so you're very wisely leaving your options open."

"I can't help but draw a connection," I said, regarding her with faint unease. "Do you have other friends out there who sent you to us who need to get you back?"

"I think if I had friends, I'd remember them."

We entered the endgame. Although I could have drawn it out for a few more moves, it would only have delayed the inevitable.

I made my last move, a deliberate sacrifice.

"You let me win," she protested.

"No, I just spared us both a drawn-out bloodbath. I could never win from the position you put me in."

"I think you give in too easily. Perhaps that was always your central weakness." She uttered these words as if they were a normal continuation of our conversation, rather than some blindsiding swerve. "Each of you had your faults, but that was yours."

"Each of us?"

She grabbed my fingers before I could withdraw my hand from the board. Although I was wearing surgical gloves, her nails bit through the fabric, digging into my skin. There was a sharp pressure, then she relaxed her grip.

I snatched back my hand, as startled and dumbfounded by that as I had been by her words.

"What the hell are you?"

"I was wondering how long it would take you to ask." She smiled, watching as I rubbed the wounded hand, feeling where she had punctured both the glove and the flesh beneath it. "You needn't worry: that was a formality. No harm will come of it."

"What are you?" I asked again. "Who sent you?"

She laughed once. "I sent me."

She spread the fingers of her hand, the ones that had just punctured my glove. One by one the nails were turning black, not along a gradient from top to bottom but as if each were a screen, filling with interstellar darkness.

I got out of the room, still rubbing my hand. Kyrgiou was standing next to an orderly, leafing through some patient notes, seemingly unaware of anything that had happened with the passenger.

"Are you all right, Administrator?"

I sealed the door behind me. "Get security here, and don't let anyone into that area. She moves from that bed, tries anything at all, they put a boser pulse through her neck."

"You've changed your tune."

I tore off the glove, showing Kyrgiou my palm. "She just did something to me. Jabbed her nails into my skin, and then her nails turned black. I don't think she put a toxin into me, unless it's really slow-acting, but I ought to be feeling the effects by now. And why would she use a slow-acting toxin?" My voice was racing, and so was my heart, but I put both of these effects down to nervous excitement, rather than anything swimming in my blood. "We missed something. Those nails of hers must be artificial."

"What did they do to you?"

"I don't know. Perhaps you should quarantine me. If she's brought an infectious agent into Sun Hollow..."

"We didn't miss anything, Administrator." But Kyrgiou had already pressed the emergency summons button, calling assistance down from Sanctum. Alma Chung arrived first, carrying a small boser pistol, and behind her came three more heavily equipped and armoured Sanctum security personnel, with excimer rifles, stun-truncheons and axes. Just behind them, puffing, was a ruddy-cheeked Morgan Valois.

"What the hell, old man?"

The passenger was still in bed, idly moving the pegs in and out of the pegboard, whispering something to herself.

"Situation," Alma Chung demanded.

"We've been...set up, in some way," I floundered, still trying to assemble the facts into something that made passing sense. "She's not what she seems." I showed them both my palm. "I think I've been sampled. Her nails are some kind of analysis system. Micro-laboratories. Nanotechnology."

"What the hell?" Valois echoed, as if stuck in a loop. "We scanned her. Didn't we, Doctor Kyrgiou?"

"There was nothing. No implants, no prosthetic augmentation, neither mechanical nor biological."

"I saw something," I insisted. "Inside her."

"Your mirage again," Kyrgiou said.

I waved my palm. "If she can do this, then what else can she do? She hid one thing; she can hide another. Maybe I just got a glimpse of something, before she gained control."

"We played back the recording," Kyrgiou reminded me.

"Then she was able to retroactively alter it," I said, shivering a little at the idea. "She dropped her guard for an instant, made an error, corrected it."

Chung's guards were pressing against the glass, checking the readiness of their weapons.

"Orders?" Chung asked.

"Go in. Surround her, but don't touch her. Make it plain that she's only one mistake away from being shot dead. And watch out for those nails."

When she was satisfied that the passenger was under armed restraint, and unlikely to do any further harm, Chung joined Valois and me in the Red Room, gathered around the glowing map of the status table, with its radial markings, surface contours and illuminated marker prisms. Cantor and the other analysts were working hard to keep the table updated, their voices low but urgent, like surgical assistants during a difficult operation.

"You'd better get that seen to," Valois was saying.

"Later," I answered, shaking away the tingle in my palm where I could still feel the puncture wounds. "Whatever she did to me, it's done. Did the over-the-horizon shots work?"

"They struck," Valois said carefully. "Two warning shots, two closer strikes, and the two that were meant to stop them dead. The seismometers took a little time to clear after all those impacts. The suits are still coming."

"For certain?"

"Both suits, same gait. No sign of damage from the seismic traces. It's as if they walked right through the bombardment and nothing touched them."

I nodded and tried to find something to cling to. "Then our positional estimates were off. We still have six slugs in each railgun, don't we? Once they come over the horizon, they can aim more accurately, and we can dial them up to full power."

"I hope so," Valois said.

Chung narrowed her eyes. "Why would you only hope so?"

"Because I can't help feeling our passenger knows our capabilities almost as well as we do." Valois shot me a weary look. "Next time you find a waif and stray out among the stars, old man, perhaps leave it there? I don't know who or what you've brought into our nest, but she's not welcome."

"If I'd known..."

"The oldest litany in the book." But his demeanour shifted to one of sympathy. "I'd have done the same, for what it's worth. We're hiding from monsters, not trying to become them."

"But she might be one," Chung said, reflecting for a moment before continuing. "What's our assessment? Could she be the thing we feared all along: a wolf construct, a biological infiltration measure?"

"She's something else," I said with certainty.

"You know this, Administrator, or you feel it?"

"Just before she grabbed me, she spoke to me in a way that made it feel personal. As if her interest lay in me, rather than Sun Hollow. That's not how a wolf construct would operate. They regard us as vermin, not individuals."

"Perhaps they're evolving new strategies?" Valois said.

"There's a thing inside that biological body: the object I saw in her ribcage. There was easily room in it for a magnetic pen and a few grains of antimatter. It wouldn't even need to be a powerful bomb to destroy all of Sun Hollow—a mini-nuke would be more than sufficient. So why not let it off the moment she arrived?"

Valois scratched under his nose. "Intelligence gathering?"

"Unless she's using a wolf communication channel we don't know about, no signals can escape beyond Michaelmas," Chung replied. "You know this, Morgan." Her subtext: do not waste my time voicing untestable hypotheses.

I caught Cantor's eye. "Time until line-of-sight acquisition?"

"About thirty minutes, Administrator, depending on the exact path the suits follow. Do you want to issue another warning, or engage on sight?"

"We have six slugs left in each gun: twelve in total. That should be more than enough but I don't want a single slug wasted. Decapitating those suits may not be enough to stop them, so reserve fire until at least half the suit is over the horizon. Understood?"

"Understood, Administrator."

Chung said: "I'd like to begin moving a security detachment to the far end of the twenty-kilometre tunnel in case those suits try and force their way in. If we move now, there's time to set up a defensive position with the heavy Breitenbachs. The team can also lay demolition charges to collapse the tunnel if the suits make it through the lock."

I had vetoed Cantor's earlier suggestion of meeting the suits halfway but now there was no doubt in my mind as to their hostile nature. Short of the railguns, the portable Breitenbach cannons were our heaviest anti-personnel weapons. They had never been used.

I had always thought that if we did have cause to use them, the fight was already lost.

"Provided they have time to fall back to safety," I said.

Chung had taken the initiative of having her team already assigned and prepared, waiting for the order to begin moving down the tunnel. A couple of electric carts would get them to the far lock in just under twenty minutes, leaving a small margin of error before we expected visual contact with the suits.

I left Chung to coordinate that part of our response while Valois and I returned to the infirmary. Not much had changed since I was last there. Chung's security detachment were in the revival area, forming a cordon around the bed, their pistols and rifles aimed at the passenger. She was sitting up, musing over the pegboard game, apparently oblivious to the armed presence.

"Has she done or said anything?" I asked Kyrgiou.

"No, it's as if she's in a bubble." She reached for a surgical kit she had been keeping open until I arrived. "I will look at that hand of yours, whether you like it or not."

"Later."

"Administrator...is it possible that this is a bit of an overreaction?" Ignoring me, she inspected my palm and dabbed the wounds with a strong-smelling salve.

"Of course it's not an overreaction. You saw what happened with her nails."

"We've examined the recordings we took during her extraction from the casket. The nails were black."

"How about you examine your memories, instead?" I snatched my hand back. "She can alter our recording systems. That points to a cybernetic capability: something like a Conjoiner. You'll say that we didn't see implants in her skull. I think all that points to is an extremely developed ability to manipulate our scanning devices, altering their data to show us what she wants us to see. I think she can do that in real-time and alter retrospective records almost as quickly."

"I didn't think we were at war with the Conjoiners," Kyrgiou said, reclaiming my hand and persisting in her examination.

"A bit hard to be at war with a group who aren't around any more," Valois said, not disputing her point. "And there wouldn't be any cause for this even if they were back again. So we had a few fallings-out, a few wars. But we're all on the same side against the wolves. Everything else is just ideological nit-picking."

"I'm not saying she is one," I said testily. "I'm saying she has similar capabilities, and we need to be ready for them. Damn it, Kyrgiou: that stings!"

"Capabilities aside, what is it she wants?" Valois continued mildly, indifferent to my suffering.

"I think I need to know." I sighed, letting Kyrgiou get on with her work. "I'm going in there again. Give me something in a syringe, something that will act quickly."

"To kill her?"

"No, just knock her out fast. But whatever dose you think you've calibrated, double it."

I went in with the syringe in my hand. It was loaded with a watery blue fluid whose identity and potency I knew better than to question. I gestured for the armed guards to move back from the bed slightly, allowing me to move closer to the passenger. She smiled as I approached, setting down the pegboard as if it were many hours since we had spoken, and my return a welcome development.

"How long?" she asked brightly.

"How long until what?"

"Until your railguns achieve line-of-sight acquisition? I think it must be in the region of twelve to thirteen minutes by now." She shook her head. "I wouldn't bother. You'd be better off keeping those slugs for another day, and for use against a target you actually have a chance of slowing. Notice I said slowing, not stopping. Good to be realistic."

I was fast. Perhaps she had seen the syringe, perhaps she had not. But I had it tight against her neck before she could flinch. Kyrgiou had given me one of the thicker, blunter needles, so I could press it in without immediately puncturing the skin. "No more games."

"Not even chequers? I liked that game. I like most games."

With my other hand I slapped the pegboard to the floor. "Don't test my patience, Brianna. Should I call you that, or should I accept it was never your name, just an identity you stole for the purposes of this infiltration?"

"Oh, please," she said, rolling those dark eyes. "No crocodile tears, Miguel de Ruyter. You were on the verge of killing thousands of people: every single sleeper on that ship. So I took one name, just to grease my way into your trust. That's not even a crime. She was already dead."

"My missile didn't kill that ship. I didn't kill it. And I'm increasingly doubtful that a sudden engine failure had anything to do with it either."

"Mm." She frowned, making a deliberately exaggerated display of incomprehension. "But then…what *did* destroy it?"

"There's another ship in this system. One we haven't seen."

"Right answer!" she declared excitedly.

"It's probably the same ship that dropped those suits into Michaelmas. Probably the same one that put you within reach of my shuttle." In case she had forgotten it was there, I increased pressure on the syringe. "You arrived independently of the incomer, didn't you? Your ship used the noise and fury of the *Silence in Heaven* as cover. If that was even the real name of the incomer."

"I was coming anyway," she said. "That other ship happened to arrive at the same time. Very bad form. I won't deny that they were slightly useful in providing a limited distraction. But the direct threat that they posed to you—to Sun Hollow—was far more than I could allow to pass."

"You admit it, then. You murdered those people."

"There's no moral distinction between us, Miguel. You were prepared to murder those people. I just happen to be the one who actually did it. History doesn't care about thwarted intentions, only what we *mean* to do. Would we say that the Butcher of Tharsis was a good man, if only he hadn't followed through on his war crimes?"

I ignored her question. "When we spoke before, you seemed to have an interest in me."

"Did I?"

"Any one of us could have volunteered for that operation. Even if I mean something to you, you couldn't have known who would be in that shuttle."

"No. But I wasn't going to take the chance of letting *any* of you die," she said. "Not when I knew that there were unlikely to be more than a few thousand of you in these caverns. Besides, you settled the matter for me ahead of time: Cydonia."

Now it was my turn to frown, and it was genuine. "What?"

"The verification password for your suicide protocol. I read your on-board telemetry. Your shielding measures are nowhere near as foolproof as you think."

"Cydonia was a random codeword. It doesn't mean anything."

"Oh, it means infinitely more than you realise, dear Miguel de Ruyter."

"Who are you, and what do you want?"

"I'm..." The name seemed to stall on her lips. Even with the syringe pressed against her, she swivelled her eyes around the room, moving her head minutely as her gaze scanned. "Let's see. It's on the tip of my tongue. Ceiling? No, that's not it. Floor? Wall? Not quite." Then her attention locked onto the partition, the transparent screen beyond which Kyrgiou and Valois were still watching. "Ah, yes. Of course. How could I have forgotten?" She smiled with a fierce, avaricious delight. "Glass. My name is Glass. And I've come for you, Miguel. You're the only thing I want from Sun Hollow."

"Then you've made a mistake."

"How so?"

"You're alone and unarmed. Maybe there's something inside you that can hurt us, but if it's a bomb you'll be taking yourself with it. Your suits are about to be destroyed."

"Certain of that?"

"Totally."

"I wouldn't be. Let me help you with that syringe." Her hand was on mine before I could react. She had moved so quickly it was as if she had jumped between frames. I made to maintain pressure on her neck, expecting my hand to be forced away. But I had misunderstood her intention. She closed her fingers around the syringe's plunger and injected herself.

"Good. You've saved me the trouble."

"Was it meant to kill me?"

"You'll find out in a few seconds." I eased back from the bed, content to let the drug take its toll. Whether the dose knocked her unconscious immediately, or took a few seconds, I was in no doubt as to the outcome. But as she regarded me, her composure unruffled, my skin began to tingle.

"I'm analysing it. Interesting blend of chemicals. They break down into harmless metabolic products very readily."

I made an executive decision. I snatched the boser pistol from the hand of the nearest guard, checked that it was set to maximum yield, and levelled the fat muzzle in the direction of her head. My hand shook slightly, as it always did. But at such close range there was little danger of missing.

"I'll do it, Glass. I'll blow your head off."

"Will you manage that as well as you handled the execution of Rurik Taine?" She nodded earnestly. "Yes, I've read the political reports. I found my way into your sealed archives very easily. Really, though, it wasn't your fault. Your hands were tied when it came to his sentencing: it was a capital offence, to attempt to organise a coup within Sun Hollow. The best you could do was arrange some leniency for his allies, that political amnesty for his family. As always, you were trying to be a good man in a difficult office. It was his insistence that his execution be a public affair; his request that you be the one to carry out the sentence."

"Stop."

She carried on. "You could have refused that request, of course—deputised it to another functionary. There was nothing in your legislation that said you *had* to bow to his craven, attention-seeking demands. But you felt you had to rise to the occasion. He'd been your friend, once; a valued ally in those difficult early days. So you agreed to put a boser pulse through his skull. Which might have gone well, had he not also refused to wear a hood, so that you had no choice but to look into his face." Her lips creased in false sympathy. "Oh dear, that didn't help, did it?"

My finger tightened on the trigger. "Shut up."

"Your hands shake. Peripheral nerve damage, from the years you spent working with pneumatic drills on the excavation teams, opening up new living space. Even as you led these people, you were one of them, always ready to get dirt under your nails. But that civic-mindedness failed you when you most needed it. Rurik's face, the pressure of the moment, all those eyes on you. Your hand shook when you shot him. Your pulse went wide: ripped the side of his face off, but didn't kill him. Valois had to do that. You were too busy crumpling up into a ball, unable to process what had happened. Everything collapsed in on you at that moment. The mistake you'd never recover from. The mistake you had to atone for, by offering *your* life, to protect your people."

I squeezed the trigger. The boser pistol clicked in my hand, flashed an error status.

Glass said: "There's nothing I can't reach, nothing I can't control. I've already pushed my influence into every part of Sun Hollow. Do you know the disappointing part? It wasn't even difficult. Your defences are like... paper walls."

I lowered the pistol, certain it was useless. Certain that every other powered weapon was equally compromised.

"That's very good, Glass," I said, reaching for one of the axes. I raised it, making ready to swing down.

"I wouldn't," she said calmly. "Not if you want Nicola and Victorine to live. Not if you want any of your friends to live."

The lights faded, leaving us in a darkness far deeper than the power dips that attended the activation of the railguns. With that darkness came a jarring silence—the background sibilance of air-circulation suddenly absent. A second passed, then the lights and life-support sounds returned, but the light was somehow sickly, the sounds maliciously off-key.

"I can do that," Glass said. "I can do it throughout Sun Hollow. Kill me, and you'll never get your systems restarted again in time. You'll freeze and suffocate. Put the axe down, before you do something stupid."

"The stupid thing was rescuing you."

"Perhaps," she allowed. "But out of it, some good may come." She sighed, modulating her tone to one of companionable reassurance. "I only want you, Miguel. I've no interest in hurting any part of Sun Hollow. Quite the contrary: I very much hope this little pocket of humanity makes it through the night. There aren't many others."

"You'd know?"

"Yes, I'd know. I've been to places, seen places. And so shall you. We're going to go on a journey, you and I. To a place called Charybdis. But just the two of us. No one else. We shall have each other all to ourselves."

"Why?"

"Because we have wolves to kill." She smiled at my bafflement. "Now, shall I tell you what's going to happen? Nothing you do is going to stop those suits. They'll make their way here, and you and I shall leave in them. Before they arrive, though, you have a little time. Use it wisely. Make your fond farewells."

"What happens if I resist?"

"The more trouble you make for me, the more likelihood that lives will be lost. Now, I don't want that to happen. But I do want you, and if there is a cost to be paid..." She looked at me sharply. "What are you waiting for? Use the time left to you. You won't get it again."

CHAPTER FIVE

While Chung and I waited in the Red Room for the railguns to start, Valois went back to my home to bring Nicola and Victorine to Sanctum.

"The heads have emerged over the horizon line," Cantor reported. "In about thirty seconds we should have a clear view of the upper half of both suits."

"Open fire at your discretion," Chung said. "But single shots only, unless I say otherwise." Then to me: "My units are in position, Breitenbachs ready and demolition fuses laid along the last hundred metres of the tunnel. Be a nuisance having to dig it out again, but if that's what it takes...are we convinced that the power drop was orchestrated by Glass? I still think it might be worth rushing her with axes; seeing how much of this is a bluff."

I shook my head, resigned to our powerlessness. "None of it's a bluff. She deactivated my weapon, interfered with power and life-support throughout an entire section of Sanctum, and she's been accessing data records—all from that bed. I think if we could see what's inside that skull, instead of what she wants us to see, it would freeze us cold. And I believe every one of her threats."

"What does she want with you?"

"I don't know. Some nonsense about killing wolves. Listen, Alma. I'm prepared to believe her threats; that doesn't necessarily mean I think she's sane."

"Powering up both railguns," Cantor called.

The lights dimmed: the usual drain on our resources. Around the Red Room's walls power dials fluctuated, then climbed back to normal levels.

"Slugs away," Cantor said.

At one hundred kilometres per second, the impact was nearly instantaneous. Screens, relaying remote feeds from surveillance eyes, registered an immense white flash lifting off the ridge. In the airless environment, the flash dispersed very rapidly.

"Confirm the kill," I said, as if every analyst gathered in the Red Room was not already focused on that task.

"Negative kill," Cantor said. "Both suits..." Cantor stumbled over their words, as if not quite believing them. "Both suits intact, still proceeding."

"Impossible," Chung said, as if a firm refutation was all that was needed.

"Did the guns misfire, or did something neutralise the slugs?" I asked.

"Negative misfire. Targeting solutions validated," Cantor said.

"Fire two more slugs," Chung ordered.

The power dipped; the guns discharged. Another white flash.

We waited.

"Negative kill. Suits intact."

"She's got a countermeasure...something," Chung said, a crack of desperation opening in her voice.

"Or she has control of the guns," I replied. "I can believe it, given what else I've seen her do."

Chung leaned into the table. "Advance teams, move into outer lock and report visual acquisition."

"Order countermanded," I called out. "Fall back to the pressure door at the eighteen-kilometre marker. And get there fast!"

"Four slugs remaining in each railgun," Cantor said. "Shall we fire two more?"

I nodded. "Try it."

We waited again, Chung confirming that her teams were in the process of retreating two kilometres back down the tunnel, to the point where they would be protected in the event of an immediate decompression.

"Negative kill. And..." Cantor was staring down at a pattern of numbers on the edge of the table "...guns are retargeting. Both railguns, slewing."

"Lock them out," I snapped.

"Overrides not accepted. Guns are acting autonomously."

I shook my head. "I wish they were."

"Continuing to slew," Cantor said. "Passing one hundred and eighty degrees."

"The safeties will prevent them aiming directly at any part of Sun Hollow," Chung said, with a fracturing confidence.

"Two hundred and seventy degrees," Cantor intoned. "Aiming points are converging on the outer lock."

I looked to the lights. They were growing dimmer.

"Where are your teams, Alma?"

"I don't know. On their way."

The room shook: dust shaking off the ceiling, prisms toppling over on the table. Twenty kilometres away, a pair of fists had just struck the crust of Michaelmas. The monitors covering the surface went blind in the same instant.

"Weapons cycling for two more shots," Cantor said.

I bellowed: "Glass! Stop! Whatever point you need to make, you've made it."

"You think she can hear you in here?" Chung asked.

"I think she can hear me anywhere." I lowered my voice, realising that I had never needed to raise it in the first place. "Glass. You've got me. You can blast your way into us, I believe it now. And if you run out of slugs, I don't doubt that you can override every airlock in Sun Hollow. Our safety interlocks won't stop you. You can probably blow all our air if you want to. But you don't have to. It's done." I raised my hands in a gesture of surrender. "It's *done*. You have me." Then, to Chung: "Word on your teams?"

"Nothing yet."

"Glass! Let them live. I'll come to you. Whatever you want."

Cantor said: "We've lost all telemetry from the end of the tunnel. No idea of pressurisation, lock status...if there even is a tunnel any more."

"Close all intermediate locks. If the air's venting out into vacuum, we won't know it for a minute or so."

"Miguel," said Valois, returning to the Red Room with Nicola and Victorine right behind him, all three of them looking just as confused and frightened as the rest of us. "What the hell is she doing to us?"

I moved over to them, clamping my hands around Valois's shoulders. "I need a moment alone with my wife and Victorine, if that's all right."

Nicola wrenched me away from Valois. "No. Whatever you are about to say, no."

Some part of our predicament must have been communicated to her in the journey to Sanctum. "I have no choice. *We* have no choice. Glass wants me." I had never looked into another person's eyes as fiercely and deeply as I looked into hers. "I have to go with her. If I don't—if we keep resisting—she'll keep damaging Sun Hollow until she gets what she wants anyway. And that will hurt you far more than losing me."

"We can kill her." Nicola's voice was a monotone, the shock of my declaration hitting her like a bereavement. "There must be a way to kill her."

"There might be," I said. "But not without terrible risk to ourselves, and still with no way of eliminating whatever part of herself got into our systems. Kill the body, the soul of Glass remains. I wish it weren't so simple."

Victorine had grasped enough of what was under discussion to ask: "How long does she want you to go away for?"

I had two choices then: the consoling lie, or the blunt truth. As cruel

63

as it might have seemed, I was doing Victorine a longer-term kindness by speaking honestly.

"Forever."

"You do not know that!" Nicola interjected.

"Glass must have a ship of her own," I answered. "An interstellar ship. It's out there somewhere. She mentioned a place called Charybdis, presumably a planet. But it's not one any of us have ever heard of. That means it must be some way out beyond any of the settled systems, which means I'll be gone a very, very long time. How long, I couldn't say. But our lives are short now." I pulled Victorine to my chest, tears stinging my eyes. "I'm sorry. I'm so, so sorry. I wanted to see you grow up. I wanted to see you become the great person I know you will be. And, Nicola..." I turned to her mother. "You've shared these years with me and let me know something of a daughter's love. I'll carry my gratitude for that wherever I go. You are both more than I ever deserved."

All objection was gone from Nicola's voice now. She knew I had made my mind up. All that was left was heartbreak.

"She should not have done this to us."

"No," I agreed, forcing a wry smile through my own tears. "She shouldn't. And I don't agree with any part of it. But here, today, I matter less than Sun Hollow." I stooped down until my face was level with Victorine's. I dipped a hand under her chin, forcing her watering eyes to meet my own. "This is the worst thing that's ever happened to you. But you are strong, and good, and it will not destroy you. I'll carry your love for me wherever I go, and you'll keep mine with you in Sun Hollow. And you'll live, and grow, and love. And you will make your mother proud, and I will always be proud of you both."

"Kill her for me," Nicola said.

"And for me," Victorine said.

"When the chance comes. Which it will."

Nicola breathed heavily. She kissed me, then stood back. "You are a good man, Miguel. We shall remember you. But you must remember us, as well. Wherever you go, whatever happens, hold this in your heart: you are a good man, and you are loved."

Orders were issued not to obstruct us. We walked unimpeded from the infirmary, out beyond Sanctum, past my empty home, out to an electric cart waiting to carry us down the long tunnel. By then we had word that Chung's team had made it to the relative sanctuary of the eighteen-kilometre pressure door, and since they were instructed not to defend the tunnel, nor delay the suits, we passed them as they returned to Sanctum, shaken by their narrow survival—they had been much closer to the impact points when the railguns turned on us—but otherwise uninjured.

Beyond the pressure lock, the last two kilometres of the tunnel had been blasted open to the sky, ruptured by a combination of the railgun strikes and the premature detonation of the demolition fuses. The suits had a clear path down a deepening furrow until they arrived at the other side of the pressure lock.

Glass told me to instruct Sanctum to close the sixteen-kilometre door behind us, sealing us in a two-kilometre tube of air. We got off the cart and walked to the door. Through a thick pane of glass I saw the suits waiting like pale ghosts on the other side.

It was a door, not a lock. There was air on this side of it, vacuum on the other. Either we had to go through the door, or the suits had to come to our side. Either way would result in the decompressive venting of all the air bottled into those two kilometres.

"How do we do this?" I asked. "Presuming you have a plan."

"Don't try and hold the air inside your lungs."

I looked at her sceptically. "Because you don't want me to die?"

"Because I don't want to have to go to the trouble of growing you new lungs. Although given the work I will have to do with you anyway, perhaps I'll treat you to some new ones after all."

"Nice of you not to suggest we brought vacuum equipment with us. I suppose that thing inside you is a life-support device?"

Glass tilted her head, mulling on her answer. "I suppose it is. But I won't be depending on it to get me across a few seconds of vacuum. The suits will close around us: try and stumble into yours, if you wish, or just wait for the suit to come to you."

I had been through enough decompression exercises to heed Glass's warning not to retain the air in my lungs. She moved her hand to the manual release on the door, and I took one deep breath to flood as much oxygen into my blood as I could. Then I breathed out and Glass opened the door.

I remember no part of what happened next. I suppose we were blown out of the lock by the force of the escaping air. At some point I came around to a foggy awareness that I was warm, and breathing, and being made to walk like a sleeping soldier propped up by his marching colleagues.

We were above ground, trudging across terrain that had already been gouged and scarred by the railgun strikes. Me in one suit, Glass in the one to my left, walking in lockstep. I tried to resist that motion, to lag behind her, but the suit's movement was far stronger than my own muscles.

65

"Don't resist it. In time, I'll allow you almost complete command of the suit and its functions. But not today. Not while your nerves are still a little raw."

"Did you hear the promise I made to Nicola and Victorine?"

"About killing me? Yes."

"You don't think I have it in me."

"I think you need to be realistic about your chances."

"I've seen your capabilities, Glass. I've seen how easily you outdid us—how easily you could have killed us all. I've also seen how quickly you can move. Mentally and physically, you might be the most dangerous entity I've ever encountered. But you're not invulnerable. You were frightened of that axe, just for a second. Nothing you could have done about it. You couldn't *metabolise* it. And you make mistakes. I saw that thing inside you."

"How can you be sure I didn't want you to see it?"

"Because the other thing you're not so good at is lying. I think you're so good at being nearly perfect that you haven't had much practice at being human."

"You've read me so well. How do you propose to kill me?"

I shrugged inside the suit. "I'll have to find a bigger axe, won't I?"

Glass halted, and so did I. She lifted a hand, beckoning something down from the sky.

A ship enlarged above us: a cruciform blackness blotting out the stars. A vaguely conical hull with a slight swelling near the rear. Sharp nose, and two engine outriggers.

"This is *Scythe*. Moray class, with augmentations. Fast, dark, and extremely agile. It's going to be your home for some time to come, so get used to it."

"If wolves followed you here, that time might not be long."

"They never saw me. *Scythe* knows how to keep to the shadows; to keep upwind of them. Inhibitor swarms are ruthless and powerful, but slow to adapt to changing parameters. That's our only hope: adapt fast and find something that catches them off-guard."

"You have weapons in that thing?"

"Yes, very potent weapons. But only enough to slow them down. What I have is maximum stealth. They can't see my engines, can't see my hull. Darkdrives, cryo-arithmetics, chameleoflage, nonvelope light-path manipulation—plus six or seven other things you'd need neural augmentation to understand." Glass stretched out her hand, magicking open a glowing rectangle in the blackness above. A ramp tongued down until its lower end made contact with the ground. We stepped aboard and the ramp retracted back into *Scythe*, delivering us into an airlock.

I felt movement, a heaviness in my belly. We were already lifting away from Michaelmas.

I had no sense of air flooding into the chamber, nor any indication of it within the suit. But at a certain point my helmet clicked and peeled itself back. Glass's helmet did likewise. Then the rest of our suits opened so we were able to step out of them, wearing only what we'd had on in Sanctum. The empty suits shuffled back against the airlock wall, then were absorbed to about half their depth.

"How many people are here?"

"Just me. And now you."

I considered the time Glass had been away from *Scythe*. "This whole ship runs itself? It must be half a kilometre long."

"Not far off. And yes, it does mostly run itself. We can communicate neurally, me and the ship, but only in relatively close proximity. Other than that...well, it's quite clever, for a ship."

"I hope it's got a good brig."

"Oh, I won't be locking you away. What sort of manners would those be? No, this ship is yours now. You may explore as you wish. If there's a part of it that I don't wish you to access, *Scythe* will rebuff you, gently at first and then with escalating force."

"Those are the rules?"

"Those are the rules."

"Good. Here are mine. Despite what you've said, and the warnings you've given, I am going to find a way to kill you."

"Good. I like a man with a goal."

"I'll keep looking for opportunities. One will arise, if I'm patient enough."

"*Scythe* will kill you."

"But at least you won't have the satisfaction of witnessing it. And if I find a way to kill you, stay alive, and turn this ship around, I'll take it. There won't be a moment when I'm not thinking of that. Just so *you* understand."

"I'm...relieved. If the man I sought hadn't made such a promise, I'd start to worry that he wasn't going to be much use to me." She reached out, took my chin, and angled my face so that our eyes locked. Her fingers were vicelike, the nails digging in sharply. "It's no lie, is it? I can see the hate in your eyes. So much hate."

"What did you expect?"

"Hate helps. Hate is useful." She made a flicking gesture, batting aside the dark business that floated between us. "That said...may we at least pretend to move onto a more civil plane of discussion? Come forward. I'd like you to see the control room."

We went forward, or up, depending on my shifting perspectives. *Scythe* had parked over Michaelmas in a belly-down configuration, as far as I could judge from that starless hovering form, and then pushed away from the surface at the same orientation. But now the thrust was coming from the rear of the ship, along its longitudinal axis, and the local gravity had shifted through ninety degrees. Floors and walls had swapped function without fuss, corridors constricting or bulging, doors sealing and opening in accordance with the changing geometry.

The control room was a spherical chamber, dominated by two monstrous acceleration chairs, the sort that came equipped with an arsenal of life-support devices so a person could endure days or even weeks of constant operation. Both chairs were mounted on bulky gimbals and pistons that allowed for rapid orientation shifts, compensating for any breakneck manoeuvres that *Scythe* might be required to make. A certain number of controls and displays were built into the chairs' armrests and head supports, while the rest were farmed out to the spherical walls, grouped into functional stations to which either of the chairs could be guided. There were screens, fold-down control panels and a narrow ribbon of wraparound windows.

The view through the windows—looking down at the face of Michaelmas as it fell away beneath us—looked convincing, but it was almost certainly false, relayed through tens of metres of hull cladding. If Glass had gone to as much trouble to make her ship invisible as she claimed, windows were the last thing it needed.

"Take a seat," she said.

I eased into the leftmost chair. It turned out to be far more comfortable than any of the acceleration couches on our shuttles. Pressure supports adjusted silently, conforming to my body shape. I ranged my hands across the built-in controls, trusting that anything dangerous would have been locked-out at the system level. Diagrams and menus sprang into life across the screens fixed to the chair, and those on the walls within my field of view, all annotated in Canasian.

Almost as soon as I had taken note of that, they morphed into Russish. Not some random variant of Russish, either, but the era-dialect with which I was most comfortable.

"How did it do that?"

Glass was busying herself in her own seat. She made much less use of the tactile controls, her hands forming stiff, dancer-like gestural shapes but not actually contacting any of the surfaces. "It reads visual saccades:

involuntary eye movements. It maps the way your attentional focus skips across certain symbols and dwells on others. From that, it uses a predictive model to determine that Russish is your preferred tongue. Did it do well?"

She would have seen through a lie instantly. "Yes. But hardly anyone in Sun Hollow uses Russish. I'd almost forgotten it was easier for me than Canasian."

"You might have forgotten. Your brain didn't. Old wiring is slow to learn new tricks." She made another flicking gesture and I heard a series of rapid thuds from somewhere aft of us. Through the arc of the windows I caught movement: several dozen small objects erupting away from us, showing up as dark specks against the face of Michaelmas. They drifted on natural trajectories for a few seconds, growing smaller, then accelerated on widely varying courses, darting to all quarters of the horizon like a shoal of fish spooked by the arrival of a predator.

"What are they?"

"The first of my parting gifts. Consider them an upgrade to your current defence arrangements. Which were—shall we say—a little lacking? These will supplant your existing networks of seismophones and railguns. You'll have better eyes, ears and teeth. The packages will conceal themselves and tap into your surface cables, repairing them with self-replicating sheathing. They'll digest and reprocess your existing sensors and guns for raw material."

"You said nothing on this ship was good enough to stop wolves."

"It isn't, and these upgrades won't stop them either. But they'll serve Sun Hollow well in other respects: more reliable, more sensitive, more accurate. If another ship blunders into your system, or—perish the thought—another interloper such as I—then you'll be far better prepared."

I could imagine no reason why Glass would overstate the benefits of the packages, nor go to the trouble of dispensing them if they did not offer a significant improvement on our existing arrangements.

"I need to contact Sun Hollow, tell them what's happening."

"There's no need. There'll be a little bit of me in Sanctum from now on, coordinating your security."

"Coordinating, or overriding?"

"So little gratitude," she said chidingly. "But don't worry. They'll get used to me very quickly. And in time, they'll realise that I'm actually on their side. I want Sun Hollow to survive. You're not alone: there are other pockets of life out there, other doughty little bands of survivors, huddled down against the night. But at any point one or more of those groups could fail, or be found by the wolves. So each must be considered irreplaceable."

"You have a strange way of showing charity."

"Charity. Interesting choice of word. Did you think about Faith and Hope at the same time? But it's not that, Miguel. It's species-level insurance. My gifts don't end with these packages, either. While *Scythe* was on its way to fetch me, I had it send out drones to meet your Disciples. It helped me to blind you, a little, but I assure you that was only temporary. One by one the Disciples have been injected with self-replication packages similar to those I've sent to the surface. When the Disciples return to life, they'll be much improved. Again, it's nothing that will stop the wolves. But if you have early warning of their approach, you'll have more time to shut down your noisier processes and sit tight."

"You know a lot about wolves. Or seem to."

"I've made it my life's work. Someone had to." She gestured at the window, where the horizon of my world was already tightening, closing towards a circle. "Say goodbye to Michaelmas, Miguel: it'll be a faint, fading pebble the next time you see it."

I looked at my home for a few seconds, until the thought of Nicola and Victorine still down there, never knowing what would become of me, me never knowing what would become of them, our lives strung together by a lengthening bond of grief, became too much for me to bear, and in shame and despair I averted my eyes.

Glass was wrong. There would not be a next time.

CHAPTER SIX

In another part of the ship a table had been laid for dinner. Plump-backed chairs faced each other, with plates, cutlery, glasses, bottles and jugs set between them. Candle flames wavered in *Scythe*'s air-circulation currents.

"If you want me to eat, just give me some food I can take back to my quarters."

"No, I insist. And when I say 'insist'..." Glass indicated the chair facing the window. "Take that one. They say it's polite to let guests have the view."

Rather than argue with her—sensing how futile it was likely to be—I took my seat. Glass took up the opposing one, with the windows ranged behind her back. There was no sign of Michaelmas now, only the ruddy smear of the dust disk, pricked by a few of the brighter stars. There must have been some trick of contrast going on because even the candlelight should have washed out my view of those stars.

Glass poured wine for me without asking.

"Let's begin anew, Miguel. Let's put all that bad business behind us. I've taken you from your family, and that's not a thing I expect you to thank me for. But I guarantee in time you'll see matters in a different light. Until then, we are obliged to share this ship. Share this ship, share in my quest, and—in so far as your survival is predicated on my own—look out for each other." She dropped her voice confidingly. "We're heading for dangerous waters. Sea monsters and peril. But at the end of it will be a prize worth all our travails."

"Charybdis?"

"You were paying attention after all. Now shall we agree to a truce, of sorts? My ship is your ship." She raised her own glass and encouraged me to raise mine. "A toast. But not to me, or even to us: it's far too soon for that. You despise me and I understand your feelings. But to your friends, and mine, and our mutual struggle against the wolves. The night is cold, the forest full of terrors, but there is a glimmer of light on the horizon."

"To my friends," I allowed.

71

"And to mine."

"And pray they never meet," I continued. "Because whatever you are, and whoever or whatever sent you, I want no part of it."

"My friends aren't the same as me."

Glass sipped from her wine, and I sipped from mine, and as much as I wished it to be otherwise, it was heady and delicious.

Nor did I care that the wine might contain anything, or that it would very likely cloud my judgement. I was on Glass's ship now, entirely at the mercy of whatever she wanted to put into my body or take out of it. If I allowed myself to draw a breath of air, I might as well drink her wine.

"What can I possibly offer that you can't already do for yourself?" I asked her. "Or have this ship do for you?"

"You'll have proven your worth by the time we get to Charybdis."

"Which is where, exactly? I didn't think I'd ever heard of a planet called Charybdis. So I checked Sun Hollow's libraries: no mention of any such place."

"Then you'll have to trust that it exists. But I'll help with part of your confusion. The reason the name doesn't show up is that it's one I gave to the place, not anything official."

"Then where is it?"

"In a system within easy reach of this ship."

"But still decades of flight away."

Glass gave a hopeless shrug, as if we were both caught up in a situation that had nothing to do with her interventions. "Space is deep. What can you do?"

White spheres floated into the room. They were some kind of servitor, each about the size of a human head. Multi-jointed arms came out of each sphere, holding the steaming plates containing our first course. The plates contained a selection of dumplings, glistening with drizzled sauces. The spheres set the dishes down, then departed.

If the wine had been superlative, the dumplings required a vocabulary I no longer possessed. It might have been the contrast with the diet in Sun Hollow, but I could not remember anything more delicious, or anything better suited to the fading preferences of my palette. I was a blind man rediscovering colour.

"To your taste?"

"Don't expect gratitude." I paused, swallowed another morsel of dumpling. "But you were right about your ship. It cooks very well."

I made to set down my knife, then hesitated with it still between my fingers. It was heavy, made of some cold solid alloy. It was not as long or as sharp as I might have wished, but it could still do some useful damage if I were quick enough.

Glass pushed aside her plate. "You're thinking about stabbing me. You're debating with yourself whether or not you could spring across the table speedily enough to reach me. There's another part of you wondering if the knife will melt in your hand the instant you try to do some harm with it, or even if it will turn itself against you."

She must have expected me to put down the knife in befuddlement, astonished that she had read my intentions so unerringly. She must also have thought I would ask how such a feat of mind-reading were possible.

Instead, I lunged across the table with all the force I could muster, the knife before me, scattering plates and glassware, only thinking of whether it was better to go for the eye, the throat, or the chest. I was ready to hack and stab at her until she died. I was ready to test her promise all the way.

Glass did not seem to move. There was simply a discontinuity; she was in a different position, blocking me with her right arm and seizing my knife hand with her left. I stopped as if I had impacted an iron framework, an armature welded into the shape of a woman.

Glass did something to my wrist, barely a pinch, and the knife tumbled away. Then she held me in that posture, suspended over the wreckage of the table, our faces only a hand's width apart.

"I don't blame you for trying," she said, as calmly as if we were still continuing our conversation. "It would have been all too easy for me to bluff." She reached out and retrieved the knife, then slid it back over to my side of the table, through a tide-pool of spilled wine. Then she relaxed her hold on me, giving me a gentle shove back in the direction of my seat. "Try again, just so you're absolutely clear. Go for it with all your will. This time I won't make any sort of countermove. *Scythe* will intervene instead." She dipped her hands into her lap, beneath the table. "No, please try. It will be...instructive."

I thought about it for a second then pushed the knife further away. My hand contained a little hot star of pain where she had pinched my nerves together.

"There wouldn't be much point."

"You're learning."

Glass looked to the door. The spheres came in again and quickly tidied up the mess I had made. The throb in my wrist was starting to die down.

"See the larger picture," she continued, lifting her goblet again. "Make that adjustment, no matter how hard it seems. Come with me and find something that will make a difference against the wolves. Show, if you will, the ultimate love for those close to you."

The spheres brought in the main course. I had no wish to continue playing the subservient guest to my domineering host. But that was only my pride having its say: my appetite was perfectly willing to debase itself.

"Back in Sanctum," I said, lifting my knife by way of emphasis, rather than with the intention of stabbing. "You said something that puzzled me."

"Did I?"

"You were making a point about the ethics of intention. To serve as an example, you dredged up the Butcher of Tharsis."

Glass cocked her head. "I suppose I did."

"Why him? You had all of history to play with; any number of despots and madmen. Why did you settle on the Butcher of Tharsis, out of all the possibilities?"

She met my question with one of her own. "Did they teach you much about him?"

"Enough that I remember that his name was Nevil Clavain." I ate on for a few mouthfuls. "A military figure, something to do with Mars. A long, long way back. Five or six hundred years, I suppose."

"He was involved in the first war against the Conjoiners," Glass said, leaning in with a sort of scholarly eagerness, as if she had just learned something and was itching to parade her knowledge. "He tried to crush them, tried to stop them from happening. He earned that name because of the excessive brutality and cruelty of his methods."

"He'd probably have said he was just doing his job as a soldier."

"I'm inclined to take the same view," Glass said, surprising me. "Different times. We mustn't be too censorious. But a man like that—a man prepared to go to extremes, in the interests of a military end? He'd be quite useful to have around now, wouldn't you say?"

My quarters were several times more comfortable and well equipped than any chambers I had known in Sun Hollow. They consisted of several linked rooms. There was a bedroom, a small lounge, a toilet, a bathroom with a weightless shower and washing basin—which even ran to a selection of soaps, oils, unguents, and grooming accessories—as well as a wardrobe and exercise nook. The water in the bathroom ran so hot that I nearly scalded myself. For my entertainment, there was a small library of printed books, mostly classics, and all of them conveniently in their early Russish or late Russian or English editions. There was a digital library, with a searchable database accessed by a fold-out keyboard suspiciously similar to the ones we used in Sun Hollow. One of the lounge walls was configured to act as a false window, showing the view beyond *Scythe*'s hull, but it could as easily show ocean breakers or a mountaintop sunset or a million other supposedly soothing scenes. The facilities met all my needs and more: it was almost a shame that I would be making so little use of them.

Glass assured me that I was not a prisoner, and as soon as I had explored the room, washed and dressed (there were fresh garments in the wardrobe, and they fitted me perfectly) I tried leaving my quarters.

Nothing prevented me.

I walked in every direction for as far as I could, until I was certain that I had explored every possibility at least twice. I found the hibernaculum, with two waiting reefersleep caskets; I found a sort of games room or weapons-testing range, and near to it another room full of weapons stored behind walls of opaque glass, so that all I could make out were murky silhouettes.

In another part I came upon a corridor that ended in a partition inset with a small window, with a bright space beyond it. I peered through the window and saw what, at first, I imagined to be a kind of engine room, filled with a mass of beguiling, mirror-surfaced machinery. Spherical robots were toiling in and around the machinery, slipping between blade-like vanes and corkscrewing helices that made me think of some immense turbine, stilled for now, but capable of whirling into lethal motion. It could not be an engine room, though, or at least nothing resembling a conventional engine. I had seen little enough of *Scythe* from outside, as it hovered over Michaelmas. But that glimpse had been enough to identify the basic cruciform outline of a ship built according to Conjoiner prin-ciples, with a pointed hull and two outriggers upon which were mounted Conjoiner engines. Glass had mentioned that they were darkdrives, but my instincts told me that this was a variation on the basic technology, rather than something entirely new.

The partition had no hinges or visible seals in it, but that did not preclude it becoming a door upon the right command. Yet despite my curiosity as to the room's contents, I felt an instinctive disinclination to go beyond the partition. A prickling intuition told me that something was going on in that space that was neither safe nor wise, and I wondered what it said about the sanity of my host.

That was the only visible part of the ship to which I was denied imme-diate access, and yet it could be no accident that I had been allowed to get exactly as close as the window but no nearer. If Glass did not want me to see what was happening in that chamber, she could easily have denied me access to this whole area of the ship, or just made the partition opaque. She had done neither of those things, and I did not for a moment imagine it was through simple oversight or neglect. Glass was content—willing, even—for me to see the thing that the robots were working on, and that fact alone told me that it figured in my future.

Or at least the future that she thought she had planned for me.

I touched the glass, felt an astral coldness, then backed off and resumed my explorations. I went as far as I could, along straight corridors and curved passages, through junctions and nodes, and at every point I tried to visualise myself as a small moving dot within the form of *Scythe*, attempting to build a mental map. But the ship's layout was disorientating, the task hopeless. I had been denied no apparent point of entry, except for that partition itself. And except for what I saw through the glass, I had come across nothing that looked delicate or dangerous enough to be a promising candidate for sabotage. I did not want to die, but if I had found a means of crippling the ship, forcing Glass to return to Sun Hollow, even if that did no more than buy me time until she once again bettered us, I would gladly have taken it.

Perhaps it was something in the wine or the food, or it might be the accumulation of recent days, but eventually fatigue got the better of me. I gave up exploring, accepting that Glass was in complete control of my surroundings, and returned to my bedroom. It was easily found, as if the ship had detected my intentions and opened up a helpful short-cut within itself. A fog of tiredness sent me under the sheets, but not before I sat at the fold-down keyboard and attempted one query, typing in a word and seeing what *Scythe* had to say to me.

The word was Cydonia.

A moment later the system responded, an image appearing of the rust-red face of a small, airless planet, before zooming in on a part of that planet where a random conjunction of geological events had produced something eerily similar to a human face, staring back at me with blank eye sockets that reminded me of nothing other than Glass herself.

Superimposed over that image, in green Russish text:

Cydonia: region of Mars, First System.
See also: Knights of Cydonia.
See also: Conjoiner-Coalition War.
See also: Nevil Clavain.

I slept badly.

I had been ripped from my home, torn from the two people I most loved in the universe. I had been severed from the community I had helped build; the five thousand faces that might be all that was left of humanity. In place of family life and the consoling obligations of work and duty—the almost comforting grind of daily worries and pressures—I had been granted the company of a ghoul-faced psychological torment-ress and a dark, dangerous ship I neither understood nor trusted.

It was not what she had done to me that I found most troubling: not the sundering from my people; not the flight from Sun Hollow; not the confinement aboard Scythe.

It was the little cracks she was opening up in my self: fine as the flaws in tooth enamel. And just as surely with the promise of agony to come.

"Good morning, Miguel." Glass was sitting at the table, finishing off a glass of squeezed fruit. "I trust everything was to your satisfaction?"

"If it wasn't, would it make any difference?"

"Ah." She nodded peremptorily, confirming some inner suspicion. "I see that we're going to continue in that vein. I'd rather hoped that a good night's rest would have put you in a more agreeable mood."

"You mean, a more subservient one."

"I'd rather think in terms of cooperation. Still...how about a little diversion, over breakfast? Sit down, please."

As I took my chair I said: "Nevil Clavain was a Knight of Cydonia."

"Was he now?"

"But, of course, you'll know that I know that. There's no way in hell you'd let me access Scythe's data systems without keeping a record of my queries."

"And what did you make of your little detour into early history?"

"You tell me."

"He was an interesting figure," Glass mused. "First a staunch enemy of the Conjoiners; one of the highest-ranking figures in the Coalition for Neural Purity. But something happened to turn him. We know that he was captured and held prisoner by Galiana, the enemy's leader. But he eventually returned to his own side and appeared to still believe in the cause. Something must have changed in him, though; some little seed of doubt planted during that period of capture."

"I read a little further. He didn't defect without provocation."

"No?" Glass asked, as if she did not already have the facts laid out like a schematic.

"There was a peace mission. Clavain went down to Mars to talk the Conjoiners into accepting some kind of treaty. At that point he was still fully aligned with his own cause. But elements in his own side were work-ing to sabotage the peace initiative. Clavain was deemed expendable in that effort. They set him up to die, making it look as if the Conjoiners were to blame. History tells us that he survived, though. And the fact of that betrayal was obviously sufficient to shift his loyalty to Galiana."

Glass widened the black pools of her eyes. "The betrayal must have stung."

"I suppose that it did."

"The architect of that betrayal must have been very glad when Clavain took his leave from human affairs."

"Do you think so?" Without waiting for her answer, I added, "Here's another question, Glass. You dropped that reference into our conversation for a reason. Like a depth charge, trying to sound something out. But I'm afraid it didn't have the effect you desired."

"I'm sure that it didn't. Of course, it's a little telling you felt the need to query *Scythe*..."

"Because I'm still trying to figure you out, and if you throw me a bone, I'll follow it. Even if it leads to a dead-end from history."

"Well, I think all we were talking about was the usefulness of the military mind. I picked a...bad example, is all. I'm sorry if it touched anything raw."

"It didn't..." But I shook my head, exasperated by Glass and even more frustrated by my own reaction to her; how easily I felt played. "But you're wrong, anyway."

"How so?"

"A man like that isn't any use to anyone, now or then. We're fighting monsters. We don't have to become monsters ourselves."

"Let us hope, then, that we haven't already done so." She passed me the other glass of squeezed fruit, and then whipped a cloth away from the thing in the middle of the table. It was the pegboard game we had played in the infirmary, set up for the start of play. Not the game itself, unless Glass had spirited it along with her, but an indistinguishably precise replica. "And to prove that I am not the monster you may think, I'm prepared to offer you back your family."

I shook my head, refusing to accept any part of that statement.

"If you want to mess with my head, Glass, do it some other way. I'm resigned. You wouldn't have gone to all that trouble only to throw me back."

"Ah, but my word is my bond. And I'm perfectly sincere in this. I told you I like games. We'll play three rounds. If you win two of those rounds, I'll turn this ship around and take us back to Sun Hollow. You can go home, live happy ever after." She made a tiny doubtful pucker of her lips. "Well, apart from the wolves, of course. But if I win two rounds, we continue to my next port of call."

Some foolish part of me played along. "Is that Charybdis?"

"No, there's some small business I have to attend to first, in another system. You needn't be woken for any part of that. But of course, you can avoid all that by taking me on."

I shook my head, refusing to be drawn in. "I don't believe for a second that you'll honour your promise if I win."

Glass sighed. "You have a choice here. We'll either play the game or we won't. If we don't, we'll go straight to the hibernaculum. If you do play, there's an outside possibility that you'll see Nicola and Victorine again. And I'll make it a fairer contest: I can handicap myself, de-allocating neural resources."

With a fatal guarded interest, I asked: "By how much?"

Glass looked pleased. "I'll start with a figure; a percentage handicap. I'll make my opening offer generous, but I'll be reducing that handicap by one per cent for every second that passes. The sooner you jump in, the better your advantage—but you'll need to be quick about it. Wait too long, and I'll be playing with almost no handicap at all."

"I know this is meaningless," I said, sighing as well. "But if there's even a tiny chance that you can be beaten, and that you'll honour your promise, I'm compelled to try."

Glass nodded emphatically. "Right answer."

"Start your damned reverse auction."

"I shall. Fifteen per cent..."

"Accept," I said, I jumping in before she had a chance to say another word.

Glass favoured me with a tight-lipped, approving nod. "That was... much quicker than I expected. My opening bid wasn't too low for you?"

"Of course it was too low. What difference is a fifteen per cent handicap likely to make? But it was the best offer I was going to get. It's vastly in your favour, but it's still better than no advantage at all."

"You aren't the first I've played this auction game with," Glass confided. "You'd be surprised how many don't see things as clearly as you did. Others hesitate."

"Perhaps they don't trust you enough to take the game seriously."

"But you did?"

"No, but a poor chance in a weighted game is better than no chance at all. Shall we get this over with?"

Glass let me have the first game. Or perhaps I won it by legitimate means: she was playing well, but so was I. The difference between this time and the game in the infirmary was that I gave no quarter from the outset. In the infirmary I had been playing to keep her amused, not taking it seriously until she began to better me, by which point it was far too late to turn the tide. Now I went in hard, straining to think as many moves ahead as possible, and drawing on the memories of a thousand games won and lost against Nicola and Victorine. It was not about the fates of individual pegs, but the disposition of pieces as a whole.

But the second game went to Glass. I held her off for as long as I could, and at one point thought I had her cornered, but it proved a false dawn. She responded cleverly and soon had me pinned down. I managed to drag out the inevitable for a few more moves, but the game was all but decided. She had bettered me, and yet I could not deny that the game had felt fairly won. I had played against machines, and knew the feeling of losing to an algorithm. Glass was not like that. I only ever felt that I was playing against a person: one who was both ruthless and extremely quick to learn and adapt

Defeated, I leaned back in my chair.

"You knew you'd beat me, even with half your brain switched off."

"But I haven't beaten you—not just yet. We're even: both a game up. The third is the decider."

"I've nothing left to play."

"You've also nothing left to lose. We've each learned from each other. Either of us could make an error. Either of us could stumble on a surprising move."

I sighed, shook my head, but set up the pegs on my side of the board while Glass did hers. Glass permitted me to make the starting move. I accepted, and embarked on a counter-intuitive opening, one that opened up an initial weakness in my flank. It looked like a bid to end the game quickly, but I had lulled Nicola into a similar false security, and it had not gone well for her. I doubted there was much hope of Glass falling into the same trap, but it seemed to offer marginally better odds than a continuation of my earlier style of play.

It worked, for a little while. Glass was thrown...she could dig into the bag of moves she had learned from me, and find that none of them were applicable to this new configuration. She had to improvise, and in doing so she opened up a subtle vulnerability of her own, one that it took my own experience to recognise and exploit. I retaliated, treating her as callously as she had treated me, and I began to methodically shatter her defences.

But as we each depleted our opponents' pieces, so the game fell into a more familiar pattern, and Glass was again able to draw on her developing library of moves and sequences of moves. There came a point where all my instincts told me I was beaten, but I strove not to show it, playing with all the intensity and concentration I had brought to the game from the outset.

Glass won. I had bloodied her, but not enough, and the tournament was hers.

"That was instructive," she said, packing away the pegboard.

"To see how gullible I was, to ever think you would let me win?"

"On the contrary: to see how determined you were, until the last. I've a small confession to make."

"You cheated?"

"No, I kept to my promise. But I had *Scythe* run a non-invasive scan of your neural workflow during all three games. I wanted to see how seriously you were taking it. The answer pleases me. You gave your all, right until the end. No one could have played more valiantly, more determinedly."

"This proves something?"

"It proves that I was right about you. You'll fight until the bitter end. Until your last breath. No matter how the odds seem to be stacked against you."

"I was ready to give in."

"But you didn't, which is the important thing. I'll be frank: after that first game we just played, there was very little likelihood of you winning. But the probability wasn't zero."

"Would you have honoured your promise?"

"I like to think so."

I wondered if that was the first truly sincere thing that had come from her lips since our acquaintance.

"But you can't be sure."

"Under the circumstances, I'd have honoured the pledge...and then looked at other means of persuasion. It wouldn't have pleased me to lose you, especially now I know how tenaciously you'll fight." Glass rose from the table, leaving the pegboard where it stood. "Come. There's nothing to prevent us going directly to the hibernaculum. It will be easier for you, once you're on the other side of reefersleep."

Glass extended a hand across the table, beckoning me to my feet. I got up and moved along the table until we were both at the same end of it. I cowed my head, faking submission, ready to be led to my fate. I doubted very much that she was convinced by it, especially if *Scythe* was still looking into my skull, reading brain activity. My intentions would have been obvious to the dimmest machine. Still, it was all I had.

I lunged, planting my left hand around her throat and punching her beneath the ribs with my right. Glass crashed back against the wall behind her. I redoubled the pressure on her throat and pushed hard into her abdomen. Glass got her right arm up, balled her fist and punched me across the face. She followed through with her elbow, jabbing into

81

my throat. Something crunched somewhere in my larynx or windpipe. I drew a breath and nothing came. Glass wrenched my hand away from her throat, raised a knee and kicked me in the groin. I went tumbling back into the table, hitting its edge with a spine-jarring crack. I tried to snatch another breath and still nothing came.

Glass laughed. It was a deep, broken, wet-throated laugh, like a tumble of rocks in a bucket. She got a foot up and kept me pressed against the table, bent backwards so that it would only take a little more pressure to snap my spine.

"You know..." She paused, rubbing at her neck. "You know, I'd have been ever so slightly disappointed if you *hadn't* tried that."

I made a wheezing sound. A straw's worth of air must have reached my lungs.

"I'll keep trying."

"But not here, not today. Today, you sleep."

Glass yanked me up as six or seven of her white globes came into the room. They bustled around me, pinning me with their multi-jointed manipulators. I wrestled against them, but I had no strength left in my limbs.

Glass gave no audible command to the spheres, but they knew what to do with me. Scooping me up like a doll, no part of me able to touch any surface, they conveyed me to the hibernaculum. We got there easily, as if the labyrinthine puzzle of the ship had straightened itself out overnight. The two caskets waited for their occupants, side by side and set at forty-five degrees to the floor. They were chrome-green cocoons, fluted with radiator fins, control pedestals next to each. Instead of the lidded casket that had brought Glass to Sun Hollow, these units peeled open along their mid-sections, with interlocking hinged petals waiting to close over again and form an impervious seal.

I might as well have been a drowsy baby being lowered into a crib, for all the resistance I was able to muster. The idea of fighting was still there, it was just that my body had already surrendered. The spheres busied around me with surprising tenderness, while Glass stood by and watched, hands on hips.

I managed to croak: "You said you had business in some other system. Where?"

"You don't need to worry your little head about that."

"I still want to know. If I matter to you, give me that much."

Glass looked at me with a distant species of pity. "Oh, very well. We'll be making a short stopover in the Yellowstone system, around Epsilon Eridami. I've made arrangements to collect some items of importance."

"Items?"

"Gideon stones."

"I'm afraid that means nothing to me."

"I'd be concerned if it did."

"What are Gideon stones, Glass?"

She leaned in a little, as if she were about to whisper a lullaby. "They're going to help us murder some wolves. Quite a lot of wolves, if all goes well."

"I saw something through a window. All blades and helices."

"Ah. You saw that, did you?"

"You know what I saw." I wheezed against the effort of speaking. "You've controlled that happens to me since I came aboard this ship. What is that thing?"

"Oh, you do like to spoil a surprise."

"I suppose I do."

She sighed as if I had taken the fun out of a parlour game. "It's something else that will help us. Not so much a weapon as something that will make a weapon. But for it to work the way it needs to, we must have the Gideon stones." Glass touched a finger to the black cupid's bow of her upper lip. "But I'll take care of that, little man. Rest now. I can't have you worrying. You can stay asleep while I take care of the stones. I want you rested: you'll need all the strength of mind and body you can get, for when you meet them."

"Them?"

"The Pattern Jugglers," Glass said, as if that was the fullest answer that I could reasonably expect.

Part Two

REVELATOR

CHAPTER SEVEN

Six sleeping bodies fell towards Mars.

Their re-entry capsule had detached from its mother vessel just beyond the boundary of the interdiction volume. Nineteen decoys of similar size and mass had also been deployed, hoping to confuse and overwhelm our orbital defence systems and allow the occupied Defection Capsule to slip through the screen and make it down to the surface.

It was a familiar strategy. We were ready for it.

In the nine months since the war's outbreak, we had engaged with countless similar efforts, originating from all over the system. It would have been simpler to shoot at the mother vessels before they reached the interdiction boundary, but we had foolishly agreed to some military treaties that made such actions problematic. Often, the incoming ships contained human shields: civilian hostages who were not fully turned to the Conjoiner ideology. It was not good for our cause to be seen to be killing too many civilians, so we were obliged to track these ships, but not to fire on them unless they made a clear bid for the surface. Any re-entry capsules were considered fair game, but only once they had crossed the interdiction boundary—which was just wide enough to include the orbit of Deimos, the outermost of the two tiny Martian moons.

The orbital tracking systems and gun platforms had to operate smoothly to target these Defection Capsules, and lately they had been getting a lot of practice. Our interception efficiency was now at ninety-six per cent, meaning that fewer than one in twenty attempts to reach the surface succeeded. The enemy knew that as well. It was why they had begun to make increasing use of decoys. In response, we deployed more guns and improved our discrimination algorithms.

Against such measures, this new capsule stood little chance.

As it fell into their sphere, the tracking systems had shone lasers onto each of the twenty possible targets. The lasers' photons had been reflected off the hulls and reacquired. By measuring phase shifts between the transmitted and reflected light, tiny vibrations in the interiors of the capsules could be detected. A particular pattern of signals was only coming from one of the capsules. Fourier analysis showed that this pattern was consistent with six human heartbeats. The guns were assigned and prioritised accordingly, concentrating their attention on that one capsule while neglecting none of the other nineteen. It was a given that at some point the Conjoiners would find a way of confusing the heartbeat detectors.

The guns fired, spitting out high-velocity railgun shells. There was no immediate kill. The capsules swerved and veered in a way that made course prediction difficult. We had beam weapons—more powerful versions of the detection lasers—but these were cumbersome to deploy, slow to energise, and not as quick to achieve a kill as a single well-aimed shell. Ultimately, force of numbers was still on our side. With multiple guns spaced around Mars at different inclinations and elevations, a number of different course predictions could be fed into the targeting systems at the same time.

Sooner or later—nineteen times out of twenty—one gun was going to make the correct shot.

One after the other, most of the nineteen decoys were taken care of. One shell each was all it took in most cases. Three probable decoys got through to the upper atmosphere, but subsequent tracking showed that none of them made any attempt to slow down before cratering into the surface at multiple kilometres per second.

That left the twentieth; the one with the heartbeats.

Luck was on its side, for a while. There were three distinct intervals, each lasting several seconds, when one or more guns had ample opportunity to shoot down the capsule. The guns swung and their magnetic barrels cycled to firing readiness.

But the guns did not discharge. Treaty-compliance systems had activated, putting the guns into temporary safing conditions. Areas of the Martian surface remained under Demarchist jurisdiction, even if they had been all but abandoned, and the guns were forbidden from firing if their projected lines of fire transgressed any of those sensitive areas.

That still left one gun that had a clear shot at the capsule.

The gun was in the lowest orbit of any of the weapons, and its position meant that it had to fire up and away from Mars, not down at it. Even if the shell missed the target, or sailed right through, it would just become another piece of fast-moving deep space debris on its way out of the solar system.

Since there were no treaty entanglements, the gun was free to operate. It cycled up to firing readiness, a shell already chambered and dialled to its maximum impact yield. The gun was extremely confident of doing the job it asked of itself. It had fifteen whole milliseconds in which to fire.

Inside the Defection Capsule, the hearts of the sleepers each gave off a single beat.

The gun detected a fault.

It was a malfunction alert, an error diagnostic that had floated up through its decision-action modules without any prior warning. Puzzled, the gun put itself into a temporary safing mode while it conducted a thorough top-down systems review.

The safing mode was scheduled for three milliseconds; undesirably long but sufficient (the gun felt) to resolve the problem and continue with the firing sequence.

The gun needed to know exactly where it was pointed. This was not normally a problem, since the gun maintained a history of itself and was in constant dialogue with the other weapons platforms and tracking systems, enabling a continuous process of error-correction. Until that alert, the gun had never had any cause to doubt its faculties.

Yet now one of its three extremely precise helium-superfluid gyroscopes was giving a discrepant reading. As far as the gun was concerned, the two majority readings were the ones to be trusted, especially as they were self-consistent with its assumed orientation, as well as the verifying signals it had received as part of the last error-correction pulse.

But still. There was a small but finite chance that the minority reading was correct, and too much was at stake for the gun to be able to dismiss that possibility. It would not be the one to break the treaty conditions.

The gun needed more time to get to the bottom of this. It extended its safing mode by another three milliseconds while it ran more detailed functional checks on the gyroscopes. It was now more than six milliseconds into its firing window.

There was still time.

The functional checks were inconclusive. There might have been a hint of a developing failure mode in the suspect gyroscope twenty-two seconds earlier, but the statistics were far too poor to rely on. The gun dithered. using up more of its available firing window. Nothing in its history had prepared it for this. Less than three milliseconds now remained. In two milliseconds, the next error-correction update was due to arrive from the rest of the network. Could it wait that long?

The gun thought ahead, simulating the time it would need to analyse that update and make a decision concerning the gyroscope discrepancy.

The time was insufficient. The gun could arrive at a decision, but there would not be enough of the window remaining to launch the shell. The gun reanalysed its simulation, seeking a way to streamline the process. If it emptied some arrays, and made reasonable guesses about the likely contents of others, and was prepared to proceed on the basis of an incomplete but reasonably robust analysis of the error-correction pulse…

But no.

It could not be done. Not under any circumstances. All pathways that involved a firing solution within the window involved at least as much of a gamble as simply firing now, without waiting for the update.

The gun could not act. It held itself in safing mode, and the window closed.

The six sleepers remained silent. There had not been time for any one of their hearts to beat again. By the time one of them did, the capsule had passed out of range of the interdiction's guns, already feeling the first thin, cold kiss of Martian atmosphere. Beneath it lay the desolate, time-blasted uplands of the Tharsis Bulge.

The opening of the casket's petals jolted me into consciousness. Glass and her robots had put me into it, but now I seemed to be expected to get out on my own. It was tempting to do nothing except wallow in my slowly returning sense of self. Getting out of the casket at all felt like a form of treasonous cooperation.

But at the same time, I did not want to die. The ship sounded quiet. I raised an arm, allowed it to float in front of my face. *Scythe* was weightless, which could only mean that it was not under any form of acceleration.

I eased myself out of the casket, floating free. I rubbed my limbs, inspecting the damage. Whatever shunts, plugs and monitoring devices it might have applied to me before I went under had detached painlessly, leaving only a few sore spots. There was no hint of tremor in my hands, and when I touched my fingertips the old numbness had vanished. The casket must have rebuilt my peripheral nervous system while I was under.

I pushed myself sideways, along to the adjoining casket. It was also open.

"Glass!" I called out, as much to test my vocal cords as to summon my host. My voice was raw and dry, but more than ample to reach beyond the hibernaculum. "Glass, where are you?"

No reply.

I moved around the hibernaculum, drifting from one point to the next. It was easy, since I was never out of reach of a hand- or foot-hold. The air was cool, and I was glad to find a cabinet that held a couple of extra layers I could wrap around myself. Another contained various medical and nutritional dispensers. I used them without hesitation: if Glass was going to poison me, this was an absurdly long-winded way to go about it.

Deciding that nothing was going to be gained by waiting in the hibernaculum, I set off to investigate. Provided the ship allowed me into the areas I had already seen, I fully expected to find Glass up and active, wearing an attitude of detached indifference to my feelings.

But Glass was in none of the places I knew.

The ship made no effort to obstruct or confuse me. For once corridors led where I expected them to lead, doors were where they were meant to be, and all I found was empty rooms.

Finally one of the spheres appeared. It seemed to be on its way somewhere, limbs retracted into its body. I followed it all the way back to the belly airlock chamber, where I had first come aboard. There was still no sign of Glass, but one of the suits remained, partially submerged into the wall.

Where the other had been was a hollow, suit-shaped concavity.

"*Scythe*," I said. "If you can hear me, and understand me, can you confirm that Glass has left the ship?"

No answer.

I went to the airlock, hoping there might be a clue as to when it had last been activated. But as with much of the ship, the readouts and controls were subjugated to neural or gestural channels to which only Glass had access.

I had already searched the control room but I went back there anyway. I had been looking for Glass before: now I wanted to know what might be outside.

Nothing had caught my eye before and there was a reason for that. The windows were a ribbon of blackness. *Scythe* was not near a planet or a star, or in orbit around anything. But if we were in interstellar space, where were the stars? Even if we were mid-crossing, one or two of the brighter stars should have been visible, even allowing for relativistic effects.

Glass had given me authority to learn the control system. Did that set of permissions still apply? I put it to the test, easing into the same acceleration chair I had used before. Sensing me, the readouts in my locus of the control room shifted to Russish. This time I concentrated. None of the configurations were familiar, but neither were any so alien that I could not make some hesitant sense of them. Some related to the direct control of the ship, its engines, precision-manoeuvring systems and navigational functions. Even some hints that I might have limited access to defensive and offensive measures.

Ten minutes later I had learned nothing of the ship's status or position, but I had found a way to reduce the glow from the controls, as well as increasing the transmitted light through the false windows.

It made almost no difference.

If there were so few photons reaching *Scythe*'s sensors, then there was only so much it could do to amplify them for my benefit. There were hints of fixed structure out there: little twinkling emanations coming from roughly the same handful of places—but nothing my eyes or brain could make sense of. If *Scythe* had landed inside one of the caverns on Sun Hollow, without the benefit of artificial lights, the view would have been barely distinguishable from what I was seeing. But the one thing I could be sure of was that we were not inside a planet—be it Charybdis or any other stopping point, or even any sort of moon or asteroid. By now even a weak gravitational field would have revealed itself.

I returned to the airlock. One suit was still present and one still absent. I floated up to the one suit that was still there, facing the tinted band of its visor. There were no controls or seams on the outside; no clue as to how I was meant to get into the thing.

"Open," I commanded.

The suit did not obey. Then I remembered Glass telling me in the tunnel that all I needed to do was shuffle into my suit, or just allow it to come to me—submitting to the suit's programmed desire to shield me from vacuum. It was obvious in hindsight that the suit would be programmed to respond to a postural/proximity trigger. I only had to avert myself from the suit, while maintaining the same body orientation, and drift slowly towards contact with it. The suit gave some wet slurping sounds as it opened up along hidden bonds, and then extended parts of itself to wrap around and guide me in. I pushed aside any inclination to panic: if the suit was clever enough to detect my intention to wear it, then it surely knew better than to suffocate me.

The suit came to life. Around the visor's field of view appeared the same pattern of symbols and readouts I had come to recognise during our exodus from Sun Hollow. The only difference was the suit's annotation had shifted to Russish.

I was still ignorant about many of the suit's functions. But I knew the colour green when I saw it: where dials and needles were displayed, they were all comfortably into that end of the spectrum. The suit was powered up and stocked with all that it needed, and had presumably taken care of any repairs or maintenance needed after Sun Hollow. I had a feeling it could keep me alive for a very long time.

I tried moving my arms. The suit complied with my request, alleviating much of the effort but leaving just enough resistive feedback to remind me I was suited, and at the mercy of its protection. Next, I tried propelling myself away from the recessed berth in the wall. The suit came unglued, then drifted. I put out my arms and legs and checked myself against the opposite wall. Then I turned around until I had the airlock in sight. It was one thing to get the suit working—I had already been allowed a degree of autonomy during our walk. But Glass would never have wanted me to be able to use one of the locks without her consent, in case I did something inconvenient like killing myself.

I used a combination of drifting and handholds to bring myself to the lock. But it would not open for me. I tried pressing my hand against the panel around the door, hoping to work some hidden control, but nothing obliged.

I needed some assistance.

"Can you understand me?"

"Yes," the suit answered, speaking with a fast, buzzy intonation, like a recording that had been speeded up.

"I need to leave *Scythe*. Open the airlock for me."

"Unit Beta cannot parse this request."

"There is a door ahead of me. I need you to make it open."

"Unit Beta cannot parse this request."

"Wait," I said, mentally backtracking. "Where is Unit Alpha?"

"Unit Alpha is extravehicular."

"Is Unit Alpha coming back?"

"Unit Beta cannot parse this request."

I could feel my breathing quicken. I hoped that the suit would be a little more helpful when I asked to be allowed out of it.

"Tell me...how far away is Unit Alpha?"

The suit seemed to think this over. I wondered if it was stupid, or damaged, or labouring under such a restrictive set of command protocols that it could answer almost no request.

"Unit Alpha is one point two three kilometres from Unit Beta."

"Is Unit Alpha on the move?"

"Unit Beta cannot..."

"Never mind," I interrupted. "Can Unit Beta open a communications channel to Unit Alpha?"

"An event-log channel remains open."

"I want to speak to Glass. To the occupant of Unit Alpha. Can you make that happen?"

"Unit Beta cannot..."

"Never mind. Can Unit Beta follow Unit Alpha?"

"Unit..."

"And never mind that, either. Take me to Unit Alpha."

There was a pause.

"Verify directive."

"Yes!" I exclaimed, before the dim-witted suit lost the thin thread of comprehension it had finally established. "Verified!"

"Directive accepted. Unit Beta will assume autonomous control until directive is satisfied. Autonomous control may be overridden at any point. Prepare for vehicle egress and transition to hard vacuum."

What had been impossible for me was simplicity for the suit, now that it had a purpose. The lock opened automatically and the suit drifted me into it. The lock cycled. The exchange was rapid and it could only have been thirty seconds before the outer door opened and the suit accelerated me out of *Scythe*, into whatever volume of space surrounded the ship.

I looked around. I had some lateral view through the visor, but if I averted my direction of gaze sufficiently the symbols around the visor shuffled obligingly and the visible field extended back another ten or fifteen degrees, to the limit of my peripheral vision. If I carried on trying that, the suit created another visual band above the main one, displaying a rear-looking view and allowing my eyes to rest. Apart from the glowing belly lock, which was already sealing up after me, I could see nothing of *Scythe* against the blackness of its surroundings.

I felt a faint, rising acceleration. The suit was gaining speed via its micro-thrusters. Glass had never used them, so I guessed they were only powerful enough to function in a weightless vacuum.

It was unnerving: like closing my eyes and running headlong into a darkened room, not knowing how far away the walls were. The airlock had closed completely, robbing me of a reference point. Within a few seconds I had lost any sense of our speed or direction.

"Slow down."

"Do you wish to amend the current directive?"

"No. I don't want to crash into anything."

The suit pondered my answer. "Collision mitigation measures are in force. Do you wish to review the collision mitigation measures?"

"No, I...yes. Yes! Show me the measures."

A list of items scrolled onto the upper left part of my visor. As soon as I saw it I realised how much was going on without my direct awareness; the suit not troubling me with what it considered to be matters of minor housekeeping. It was scanning the space around us with radar and laser-ranging systems of proven reliability. It was using image amplification to detect visual obstacles. It was running gravitational-proximal spacetime gradient measurements, capable of detecting any large, dense nearby object. It was sniffing for neutrinos, muons, and a dozen other particle types. It was even ingesting the not-quite-perfectly-hard vacuum and running mass spectroscopy on trace atoms and ions...and it was following the course-log transmitted by Glass's suit when it made exactly the same journey.

Now that I knew what the suit was up to—and satisfied that a collision was not my biggest concern—I persuaded the suit to show me a visual representation of its active and passive sensory modes. A lilac-tinted tracery settled over my field of view, annotated with rapidly changing digits showing relative distance and velocity. Rough-surfaced walls surrounded the whole space, which I now understood to be hundreds of metres across. It was a cavern, after all: deeper than it was wide and with sheer, circular ends, like a cylinder. Most of this three-dimensional contour-map was assembled from radar and laser returns, but there were also several pale glowing smudges that must have corresponded to the faint lights I had seen from inside *Scythe*.

Only now did I understand that these smudges were caused by light leaking into the cavern from outside.

The suit conveyed me towards the cavern's wall, heading towards a depression or rent in the wall's surface. Again, it seemed that we were going too fast, but the suit had matters under control. From somewhere in my chest thrusters began to burn, quickly reducing our speed. As the wall approached, so the overlay became sharper, and with a jolt of shifting perceptions I realised that what I had taken to be natural formations were nothing of the kind.

The walls were of artificial construction, yet lacking any regularity or organisation. There were interlocking panels, projecting modules, criss-crossing pipes and conduits, handling arms, clawlike docking cradles, all of it huge in scale while at the same time appearing haphazard and piecemeal, as if a succession of owners had each their own ideas about repair and alteration. The chamber also bore the imprint of the Melding Plague, which is why I had been so easily convinced that the enclosure was natural. The plague's fibrous, branching strands had erupted across nearly every surface, softening and corrupting where it touched. It was like the cloisters of some abandoned cathedral, wreathed in pale worming vines and slowly succumbing to ruin and time.

The presence of the plague stirred the usual fears, hardly blunted after thirty years in Sun Hollow. But the corruptive process appeared to have been arrested here: the plague must have gained a hold then faltered, leaving the chamber's original form still recognisable, and with no projection into the main volume. There might still be traces of active spore, but if I wished to pursue Glass, I would have to put such concerns aside. My quarry had come this way and must have known what her suit was capable of dealing with.

The gap in the wall was just wide enough for me to pass through. The suit swivelled, reorientating me. The gap was a rupture, or what remained of a doorway, allowing entry into what I first took to be a corridor, running in the same direction as the chamber's longest axis. It was very wide to be a corridor, though, and despite the plague's predations it was still possible to make out the linear tracks which threaded along its length, spaced around the walls at intervals of ninety degrees. Buckled and interrupted as they were, I recognised their function: guidance rails for a vehicle; a train or perhaps an elevator.

"Minimum hazard threshold exceeded. Verify continuation of current directive?"

"Verify," I answered, but not without some disquiet.

Still weightless, the suit drifted along this railed shaft. In the confined space, it was content to move at only a little more than walking pace, veering now and then to avoid some jagged protrusion or crimpage that blocked a clear path. There was no danger of anything still moving along these ruined rails, but only the rational part of my brain understood that. I still kept glancing behind, using the rear-angle display. If I was not doing so at regular intervals, my neck prickled.

By now I had narrowed down my ideas about our location to three possibilities. The first was a cylindrical space inside some small, rocky body: say, an asteroid a few kilometres across. That was how some habitats were arranged, with the rock providing radiation shielding and impact protection. The second was a minor variation on that—a thin-walled artificial world in the form of a cylinder, but which for some reason was no longer spinning to generate artificial gravity.

The third possibility, and the one I instinctively knew to be the correct solution, was that I was inside a starship. A lighthugger as large as *Silence in Heaven* or our own *Salmacis*. Such vessels were easily big enough to contain ten or twenty docking or cargo bays the size of this chamber.

It fitted with what little I knew. Glass had spoken of business needing to be conducted before our next port of call—perhaps a rendezvous of some kind. I had never been meant to be awake for any part of that affair, but that assumed that Glass's plan went smoothly.

"How far away is Unit Alpha?"

"Unit Alpha is zero point two four three kilometres from Unit Beta."

Less than a quarter of a kilometre. If there had been air, I could have called out to her.

The shaft forked: a junction where the elevator was able to switch tracks. The suit took the less damaged of the two options, picking up speed again even as the shaft deflected, obstructing my direct view ahead.

"Slow," I whispered, and the suit obeyed, dropping me back down to a walking-pace drift. A faint glow projected around the curve in the shaft, becoming brighter as we approached. I wondered for a moment if it was some outside light leaking in, but as the brightness increased, so I realised that its green-yellow hue owed nothing to Epsilon Eridani or any of its worlds. No stars or planets had that sickly pallor.

A voice crackled into my helmet.

"Speak to me, stranger."

It was not Glass. The voice was deep, slow, and masculine. It seemed to come from everywhere at once. If the voice of God had announced itself into my skull, I do not think it would have been too different.

"Who are you?"

"I think I asked first."

It was not just the voice. There was something behind it: a sort of chorus of other voices, repeating a refrain. I tried to pick out the words, but their meaning was just out of reach. I was hearing one of the older languages, predating the modern forms of Norte, Canasian or Russish. There was still only vacuum around us, so the voice and its chorus must have been finding a way into the suit via its own communications channels. I saw no reason not to answer it truthfully.

"I am Miguel de Ruyter."

My answer seemed to amuse the voice. "De Ruyter. Interesting etymology. The rider, or perhaps even The Knight. Into the haunted castle you ride. What business brings you to me, Miguel de Ruyter?"

"I wish I knew." But guessing that this answer might not satisfy my nameless host, I added: "I'm here under duress, and I don't even know for certain where here is."

"Yet you presume upon an invitation to continue. Are you a captain, de Ruyter? I've met all the captains. I think I was a captain once..."

I spread my arms and legs and made faint, slipping contact with the sides of the walls. The suit had been drifting, so it only took a little effort to bring myself to a halt.

"I'm not a captain. But I have come from a ship and the person who operates it is missing. Her name is Glass and my suit is telling me she's somewhere inside this ship."

"Is Glass your friend?"

"No," I answered carefully. "I think it would be safe to say she's anything but a friend."

The voice deliberated. There would have been a silence if it had not been for that underlying chorus, still continuing. Now my brain picked out the meaning from the words. English, pre-Transenlightenment. Words I understood, with effort.

Tell me who's that writing? John the Revelator.

Tell me who's that writing? John the Revelator.

John the Revelator wrote the book of the seven seals.

The voice said: "You have answered well, de Ruyter. Pray continue. In fact, I insist upon it. While you're on your way, though, tell me what it is Glass wants with you."

As I listened to the voice, I used my fingers and toes to propel myself at a slow drift, hardly faster than a walking pace.

"I know only what she's told me. I've been enlisted to help her find something."

"Something?"

"She's been vague about what it is and where we'll find it. But supposedly it's something we could use against the wolves."

"A weapon."

"I believe so."

"I've seen a lot of weapons that were meant to stop the wolves. Carried some inside me, for a while. Exordium devices, hypometric weapons. None of them made a difference."

"I don't know about those things. I don't even know if I believe anything that Glass has told me. But if I thought there was even a tiny chance of her being right, I'd fight to the last drop of blood."

"I like your spirit."

"I hope it's more than spirit."

"There was a man inside me once. An old soldier. He wouldn't have stopped looking either. He'd have fought to the last drop, as well. But it didn't help him in the end."

"What happened?"

"He gave his life so that another might live. Is that a sacrifice you think you could make?"

"I know it for a fact."

"Not many can say that. Very few indeed can say it and make me believe them. But with you, there's no pride or boastfulness about it. It's just a matter of fact: you've been tested, and you were ready. But I'm guessing the universe played a little trick on you."

"I lived. But it wasn't the universe."

"Glass? Well, that wouldn't surprise me. She has a habit of twisting the fates of others. I'll come clean: we *do* have a little history, Glass and I. Not a long one, but enough to understand each other."

"Have you killed her?"

"Would you like that?"

"I might, in the long run. But she's not much use to me dead. I've come to the conclusion that I need her to operate her ship, or to at least give me control of it. Then I get to turn around and go home to the family she ripped me away from. If either of them are still alive." I paused. "Has Glass done something to you as well?"

"Yes. The worst thing of all. She made me live again."

"I'm not sure I understand."

"You will, in a moment. Come nearer, Sir Knight."

Tell me who's that writing? John the Revelator.
Tell me who's that writing? John the Revelator.
John the Revelator wrote the book of the seven seals.

A rupture in the wall of the shaft was the source of the yellow-green light. I slipped through this ragged, puckered opening, into a room filled with the living dead.

It was a spherical chamber about a hundredth the volume of the docking bay. Jumbled around the walls of this chamber was a haphazard mosaic of reefersleep caskets. They were set at odd angles and alignments, and no two caskets were even approximately the same design. There were at least fifty of them, perhaps a hundred, and all were old. They were pressed back into the walls' fabric like stones wedged into soft cement, half interred. Each was wreathed in the same branching, fibrous structures that I had seen in the docking bay. Some of the caskets were closed, with no easy clue as to who or what might be inside them. Some were open and empty, their lids hinged wide as crocodile jaws. Others were open but still occupied. Bodies rested inside, in various states of corruption or decay. The yellow-green light emanated from the flesh of these bodies, from the caskets in which they lay, from the vinelike growths enshrouding them.

They were dead, all of the bodies that were exposed to vacuum. But some were still moving. Their heads shifted at my approach. Their mouths were working, jaws opening and closing in time to the words of the chorus...

Tell me who's that writing? John the Revelator.
Tell me who's that writing? John the Revelator.
John the Revelator wrote the book of the seven seals.

The horror of this chorus-of-the-dead nearly overcame me. The only thing that moored my sanity, anchoring me to the moment, was the presence of Glass. I had come for Glass. Glass was still alive. Everything else was madness, but if I could hold onto that...

Tell me who's that writing? John the Revelator.

Her suit was being pinned down on a plinth formed from another casket, set on top of a second. About a dozen bodies were ranged around this plinth, each with at least a hand pressed against Glass, holding her in place. They were singing, opening their jaws to vacuum. The bodies used their other limbs to lock themselves together and, in turn, to apply leverage against the other caskets to hold her in place.

Glass writhed under their pressure. She thrashed her limbs a little but even the augmentation of her suit was insufficient to overcome that deadening laying on of hands.

"Can you hear me?" I asked.

"De Ruyter," she said, suddenly and breathlessly. "Get out of here. Go back to *Scythe* and tell it to initiate—"

"Now, now, Glass," said the voice. "Is that how you mean to reward me, after all I've done? By having your clever little ship gut me from inside?"

"Who are you?" I asked, fighting every natural instinct to turn and flee this place of horror. "What is your connection to Glass?"

"Tell him," the voice said. "Tell him everything."

"You'll kill me whatever I do or say."

"Just answer him," I said.

Glass fought the hands, but with dwindling conviction. I wondered how long she had been here; how weakened she had become. Then some acceptance must have come over her. I heard the faintest of sighs before she began.

"I needed a ship."

"You had one."

"I needed a second ship."

"You have one," I said.

"Let me...explain."

I looked around at the ghoulish spectacle. I would have been frozen with shock and revulsion except for the tiny suspicion that my host had marked me as an ally, or at least an enemy of Glass.

"Go ahead," I said. "Now's as good a time as ever."

"I'd been looking for you for a long time. First I went to Ararat, but you weren't there. But you left a lead—a hint as to where I'd find you. Michaelmas, except that world had no name until you landed on it, and I couldn't go to Michaelmas directly. The work ahead of me was too great. I needed allies; individuals who could attack one part of the problem while I worked on another."

"This is not starting to make sense."

"Give her time," the voice said, teasingly. "It's the truth, isn't it, Glass? However outlandish."

John the Revelator wrote the book of the seven seals.

100

Her helmet nodded. The hands permitted her that much movement. "We agreed to travel separately: me to AU Microscopii, my allies to Epsilon Eridani. For which they needed a ship of their own. Fortunately, they had one, though it was a little damaged."

"This is the ship they came in?" I asked. "We're in the Epsilon Eridani system?"

The voice laughed.

"I *am* the ship. But she lies. I wasn't damaged. I was dead."

"Who are you?"

"I've had many names. Before I died, I chose a last one for myself. Now they sing my praises."

"Then your name is...John." I hesitated, wondering how close I might be to giving lethal offence. "You are...were...some kind of construct? A gamma-level, or above, tasked to run this ship?"

"Not a construct. A man, just like you."

"There was a man, a captain," Glass said. "He had been old and strange long before the plague ever touched him. Gradually he seeped into the structure of the ship; became inseparable from it. When I had *Scythe* inject the remains of this ship with plague-resistant replicator packages, it wasn't the plague that fought back. It was the ship, fighting my attempts to bring it back to life. It was John the Revelator."

"They warned you I'd be trouble."

"You think I was ready to abandon my plans at the say-so of a barely sentient pig?"

"A better pig than you'll ever know."

Glass scoffed. I wondered, given her circumstances, if that was the wisest course of action.

"I went in with heavier measures, forced the ship into accepting my treatment. I won. I turned the ship to my will, made it capable of one or two final interstellar hops, and sent my associates to Yellowstone."

"You tortured me back to life."

"I gave you another chance to redeem yourself."

"Please," I said, raising a hand. "Whatever grievances there are between you...I'm not a part of them. But I do need Glass. Please let her go."

"I could take her apart piece by piece before your eyes. Perhaps you think she is strong. Would you like to see how very much stronger I am? Would you like to see the things I could do to her?"

"I want her alive. She turned my colony against itself, paralysed our defences and threatened us with decompression. Thanks to Glass there's very little chance that I'll ever see my wife again, or her daughter."

"Their names, Miguel de Ruyter?"

I swallowed on my answer. "Nicola and Victorine."

"Good names. Did you love them?"

"With all my heart."

"I believe you. We are both old men, and we have a sense of these things. But I wonder even more why you do not want her dead."

"Glass can go to hell, but only Glass knows how to work her ship."

"I could kill her, and then work my way into her ship. I don't think it would be too hard for me to unravel its secrets. There's not much I don't know about ships. It helps... being one."

"Even if you could do that—"

"He couldn't," Glass interrupted. "*Scythe* would destroy him from the inside the moment he tried to breach its defences. He is not stronger, he just caught me at an inopportune moment, my defences not at optimum readiness."

"Put that on your gravestone, Glass."

"There's something else," I said, admitting it to myself as I said it. "Now that I've been dragged here against my will, I at least want the satisfaction of knowing there was a point to it. I want to meet these associates, the ones you carried with you. What was their business in Yellowstone? Our last reports said the wolves had left only ruins, in orbit and down on the surface. I'd also like to know more about Charybdis, and what it has to do with killing wolves. If that means keeping Glass alive a little longer, so be it."

"She doesn't know what became of her two associates."

"Do you?"

"They left. They went off in a smaller ship I carried inside me to this system."

"When?"

"I don't remember. I've stopped keeping track of time. You would have, too. Maybe it was ten years ago. Maybe it was ten weeks."

I directed my next question at Glass. "What happened to the planned rendezvous? How long have we been here, before I woke up?"

"I don't know what happened, only that they're not here." Glass paused. "*Scythe* docked three weeks ago. My associates were supposed to have reached Yellowstone in a smaller vehicle, completed their operation in Chasm City and made it back here to the lighthugger ahead of us. They should have been done years ago: they had ample time—decades to spare. The plan was that they'd seal up and go into reefersleep until I arrived. When I couldn't find them, I went looking for my inertial clock."

"Your what?"

"A device I left aboard, in case I needed to reconstruct its movements. My suit homed in on it. It led me...here."

"Is she telling the truth, John?"

The ship gave a dry laugh.

"For once."

"These two associates...do you hate them as much as you hate Glass?"

"No," he said, after a moment's reflection. "I could never hate them."

"But it sounds as if they were co-conspirators in whatever Glass did to you."

"They never realised how far she was prepared to go in forcing my resurrection. If they turned a blind eye, allowed themselves to be persuaded against their better judgement...there have been worse crimes. I should know; I committed some of them."

"Do you know where they are?"

"They never came back to me after they left. The last indication I had from them put them in the vicinity of Yellowstone, but I can't even say whether they made it into the atmosphere, let alone to Chasm City."

"What was their business there?"

"Ask Glass."

"Please, let her come back with me. You don't have to forgive her for what she's done. Just let me be the one who eventually punishes her."

"Forgive me, Sir Knight, but you don't seem to be in much of a position to be punishing anyone. From what you've said, you're her prisoner."

"I'll make her pay. Not here, not now, but eventually." I stopped myself, worried that I might be making an awful error in appealing to his better nature. "The ones who never came back—were they friends of yours?"

"Close acquaintances, certainly. We'd been through a lot together."

"Then I'll make you a pledge. Give me Glass, and we'll find out what happened to your friends."

"Are you serious about this promise?"

"I am."

"We have something in common, Sir Knight. Both of us were dragged here against our will. Both of us would like to think there was some point to our being here. Go, and let Glass take you onwards in her ship. I won't be so ungracious a host as to prevent your leaving."

"Thank you."

"Fare well, de Ruyter. If we never meet again, and I rather think we won't, I'm not sorry our paths crossed today. Oh, and Glass?"

Her answer came warily. "Yes?"

"Two things. One is that the ends very rarely justify the means. You've made yourself into an instrument for serving one good end. But along the way, you've done many evil things. Reflect on those deeds."

Her voice contained a steely indifference. "And the other thing?"

"I wouldn't want you to leave without your little toy."

One of the zombie passengers jerked upright in their casket, spasming out a stiff-jointed limb, the fingers opening to fling away a dark, grenade-sized object.

Glass caught it and pressed it tight to her chest.

CHAPTER EIGHT

We travelled back to *Scythe*, retracing the path my suit had taken through the corpse of the starship, then back across the void of the docking bay to the waiting shadow of her ship.

"What was that thing?"

Glass was still holding John the Revelator's parting gift.

"My inertial clock."

"I hope it was worth the trouble. Did he really hold you there for three weeks?"

"It was nothing," Glass dismissed. "My suit could have kept me alive for years if necessary. And he was powerless to hurt me. Nothing in the universe can hurt me, unless I choose to allow it. Kill me, yes, but not hurt me. And I'd have got out eventually, once my suit had diagnosed his weaknesses and formulated countermeasures for those zombies."

"What were they?"

"The last few passengers that he couldn't save around Hela, the little ice-moon around 107 Piscium where I first found him, plus a few bodies still left lying around. He pushed his tendrils into them, made their corpses dance like puppets."

"I'm sure your suit would have found a countermeasure sooner or later. Otherwise it would have been very, very stupid to allow yourself to be trapped like that, especially after you went in alone."

"It was not your concern."

"Still, it became my concern, didn't it?"

After a silence, Glass said: "Your intervention may have accelerated the inevitable. In that regard it was ... not unwelcome."

"At least you had the sense to set some wake-up condition in my casket. It would have been very bad for both of us if I'd stayed asleep. I'd be stuck in *Scythe*, and you'd be stuck in that room."

"Until my suit got me out."

"Of course," I said, humouring her. "Until your suit got you out, which was only ever a matter of time. Answer me truthfully, though. Are your associates really late for the party?"

"There is no party." We sailed on across the void for a few more seconds, until Glass added: "They should have returned. They had an in-system vehicle, with anti-wolf augmentations. A small ship that came all the way from Hela, in the belly of John the Revelator. Not as capable as *Scythe*, but adequate for the purposes of their mission. It should have let them get to Yellowstone, and then into the cover of the atmosphere."

"Something went wrong, then. They're dead."

"Or delayed. I'll have a better idea when I read out the inertial clock, if he didn't scramble it."

At some command from Glass, *Scythe* opened its airlock, ready to admit us back inside. I had the strangest reaction to that door. I welcomed it and wanted to be within its shelter. I despised what she had done to me and saw her ship as a silent partner in that crime. But being inside the sanctuary of *Scythe* was infinitely preferable to being outside it, in the plague-ridden bowels of John the Revelator.

We cycled through the lock and stepped out of our suits. I was hardly fresh, after the couple of hours I had spent in mine. If her story was true, Glass had been inside hers for the better part of three weeks. She stretched like a cat and arched her neck back, taking her first deep breath of ship-borne air. A musty tang of sweat, fear and forced confinement reached me. For a second, I nearly pitied her. There was still something human beneath that white armour.

"We take the ship to Yellowstone," I said.

"Right answer."

"And I'll cooperate in any attempt to find your associates. For the purposes of that operation alone, I won't attempt to harm you or sabotage you or the ship in any way. I'll give it my all and offer any insight I think may be advantageous."

"Presumably this is a temporary detente."

"Until we know what happened. But my cooperation comes with terms."

"Oh. Terms." She put on a look of intrigued amusement, as if I were a child who had come out with a big-sounding word. "And what would they be?"

"Some candour, to begin with. Before I went into reefersleep, I think you did something to me."

"Did something?"

"I had the strangest dreams."

She creased her lips in false sympathy. "Strange dreams come with the territory. All those poor little synapses shutting down, then lighting up again as you come out of the cold..."

"These were...coherent. Something about a war on Mars."

Glass nodded sagely. "Well, then we're getting somewhere. You want candour, de Ruyter? I'll give you candour. But you won't thank me for it."

John the Revelator let us leave. A huge circular door opened in the end of the docking chamber, pivoting on a single massive hinge, and *Scythe* slipped out into empty space. From the vantage point of the control room, where I sat in the seat to the left of Glass, I had my first view of both the system into which we had arrived, and the ship where Glass's rendezvous had failed. The latter was as large as any lighthugger, but I saw only disconnected elements of its whole, glimpses that I was forced to assemble in my imagination, much as if I were a traveller catching hints of some forbidding, mist-wreathed castle atop a craggy pinnacle. The ship was as dark as the space around it and gave off no illumination of its own. Nor did *Scythe* throw any light against it as we departed: Glass was very careful in that regard. All that served to define the broken pieces of the starship's form was the light from Epsilon Eridani, and since we were at twenty AU—four hundred light-minutes away—the star offered only a dim, emberlike illumination, picking out certain details in faint, dusky reds and browns, and throwing only a deeper funereal pall over the rest of it. All lighthuggers had a dagger-like form, the better to carve their way through the resistance of interstellar space. But this ship was a dagger that had been rusted and mangled nearly to uselessness. The hull had been ripped away in vast areas, revealing a sort of anatomy lesson on the internal structure of starships. The front part, the stabbing point of the blade, was nearly intact. But halfway to the hilt the ship withered in on itself, as if an iron-gloved fist had closed around the blade and shattered most of it away. The elements that formed the hilt—the outriggers for the Conjoiner drive—were ragged, woodwormed, see-through in places. Stars glimmered through a gristle of ship-sized bones, tendons and nerves. But the outriggers had done their work, I saw. The engines were still in place, even if they showed great and possibly crippling levels of damage.

"Would the wolves know that this ship is here?" I asked.

"By now, almost certainly. But it came in quietly after crossing space from Hela and from any sort of distance it looks like any other drifting, lifeless wreck. It's of no concern to them now. It poses no threat, and there's nothing left of our technology that they have the slightest interest in."

"Is John the Revelator a man stuck inside that ship, or the ship itself?"

"Do you think it matters?"

"Whichever it is, I think it matters that you made him live against his will."

"I needed a ship," Glass answered. Then, nearly under her breath, "John the Revelator suited my purposes. The universe owed him no mercy, Miguel—no clemency or kindness. If I started accounting the bad deeds of his life to you now, we'd be here until the wolves are dust. But that doesn't mean I set out to be intentionally cruel. If there had been another way, or another chance...I might have done things differently."

The console chimed: it had completed its retrieval of the embedded data in the inertial clock. Numbers and curves sprung onto the displays.

Glass stared at them in icy silence.

"Well?" I prompted.

"This isn't right. They've taken too long."

"We already knew that."

"To get here in the first place," she said, irritated. "The clock says they've taken much longer to reach this system than I expected."

"So much for expectations."

"Something happened to delay them," she said, muttering to herself.

"How bad is it?"

Glass breathed in heavily. "I zeroed the inertial clock when I left them on Hela in '750, on my way to you. By then I'd set the repair processes in motion, so I didn't need to oversee them until completion. I knew the condition of the lighthugger, what needed to be done to make it space-worthy. John the Revelator resisted me initially, but I knew that he would see the ultimate righteousness of my cause and accept his place in my plans. Together with his passengers they should have been under way in a year, two years...but the clock is flat for another twenty years!"

"What does that mean?"

Half annoyed by my question, half keen to show off the cleverness of her gadget, Glass directed my attention to a line which started at a low value and moved to the right, staying horizontal for twenty tick marks.

"The clock records local acceleration: that's all it can measure while being inside the lighthugger. After I left them, it holds at a steady quarter of a gee. That's them sitting in the local gravity field of Hela, not going anywhere. It spikes here, after twenty years: that must be the launch event, when the lighthugger boosted itself back into space. Then it drops to zero for a few weeks—engine check-out and final repairs, in weightless-ness—before it then ramps up to one gee, for the interstellar hop between 107 Piscium and Epsilon Eridani."

"So they took twenty years to fix up the ship, instead of a year or two.

That...doesn't seem unreasonable to me. Plans rarely go to schedule."

"Based on your vast expertise of ship repairs?"

"I haven't repaired a ship," I admitted. "But I did dismantle one. It took us five years to strip the *Salmacis* down for useful supplies, after we landed on Michaelmas. We'd expected it to take a year, eighteen months at the longest. Plans do that."

Glass brooded, not quite able to dismiss my point. "They still took too long, even allowing for those twenty years. Look at this." She jabbed her finger at the diagonally rising line of the one-gee profile. "The clock is in the same inertial frame as the ship, so it should record one gravity all the way up to the mid-point. But something happens after a couple of months."

"The acceleration doesn't hold. It drops down to about half a gee, then never recovers. Engine trouble, presumably. Either the C-drives couldn't keep operating at the desired output, the shielding was worn out, or the rest of the ship couldn't tolerate the stresses. So they throttled back: reduced the acceleration to a rate that was sustainable." I shrugged. "Half a gee will still get you to relativistic speed, it'll just take longer to get there. But that's not really a problem if you're crossing tens of light-years; you'd only be adding a year or two onto a trip that was already going to take decades."

"But they never get above seventy-five per cent of the speed of light." Glass's finger hovered over a part of the trace that was flat and zero, until the line dipped into negative acceleration. "They cruise most of the way, engines at idle, until the slowdown. A crossing that should have taken twenty years takes thirty!"

"So, allowing for the delay before departure...that puts them about thirty years behind schedule."

Glass thought to herself.

"They should still have had time. Our differing trajectories allowed for a significant margin of delay. Even with the delay, the lighthugger's still been sitting in this system for twenty-eight years: enough time for them to take the in-system ship to Yellowstone and back many times over. Something else must have gone wrong."

"Can you see how long ago they left?"

"No. Only the movements of the main ship. Their departure wouldn't have created a big enough event to register on the clock."

"So they could have left twenty-eight years ago, or twenty-eight days. You have no idea which, and John the Revelator can't be trusted to be any help either. This plan is going really well, isn't it?"

Glass seethed. "The plan is still viable. If they didn't manage to return to the rendezvous point, that doesn't preclude them—or someone else—still being in possession of the items I need. Can you tolerate three gees, or do I need to put you back into reefersleep?"

"Whatever you can tolerate, I can tolerate."

Glass smiled at my naivety. Even as her plans came apart, it was good to see that she could still take some pleasure in my shortcomings. "It's tragic; you aren't even close to understanding how wrong you are."

Glass could move around unassisted in three gees, but it was too exhausting for me. After watching my groaning, stumbling efforts—as if she was running a book on how long it would take me to break a bone—she had the ship produce a wiry, insubstantial-looking exoskeletal frame which could be worn over or under my clothing. It was surprisingly effective, and clever enough to be able to apply its support without inducing pressure points that would soon turn to sores. It even had a padded rest for my skull, cupping under my jaw and the back of my head to alleviate the load on my spine and neck muscles. I took a few minutes to adjust to the frame, and then stopped noticing it was there. The frame was already learning my gait and gestures, anticipating my movements like a dance partner.

Scythe's acceleration was still arduous. My blood weighed three times as much as normal, so my heart had more work to do. But with the frame easing the load on my bones, muscles and ligaments, and with no risk of injuring myself—the frame wouldn't allow me to trip or otherwise come to harm—I could at least move around and take care of personal hygiene without undue difficulty.

Glass insisted that we continue to take our meals in the dining room, with food cooked and served by the on-board robots. Once I had adjusted to the heavy feeling of the cutlery in my hands, the way the wine jumped from the bottle to the glass, and the way the slimmest goblet felt like a tankard, it was surprisingly normal.

Surprisingly normal, and almost—almost—convivial.

"A confession," Glass said, putting a piece of bread on my plate. "The support unit is only temporary. Over time, it will reduce its augmentation level."

"If you want to see me suffer, there are quicker ways to go about it."

"You won't suffer. You'll need the unit less and less, because you'll be getting stronger. While you were under I had the casket undertake some nanotherapeutic repairs. They're still playing out—hard to move cells around when they're frozen—but as the days pass you'll start to feel the effects. Those old bones of yours are no use to me. I'm rebuilding them, stripping away the years. Nothing magical: just a suite of rejuvenation methods that we wouldn't have batted an eyelid at three centuries ago. It'll ache a little, while they make themselves strong again, but that will be a good sort of pain."

"There are machines inside me now?"

"There you are, being a worrier again. Let me put your mind at ease. The odds of any plague spore touching you are tiny, and I wouldn't even take that chance, unless my medichines were already impervious." She lifted her goblet, unaugmented, not even a trace of a tremble in her hands. "Which they are."

"What are you trying to turn me into?"

"Not turn you into something. Turn you back into what you used to be."

"I was never anything."

"And yet this man, who was never anything, somehow ended up running a community of five thousand people, and holding them together through thick and thin, for thirty years?"

"Someone had to do it."

"Once upon a time," Glass said, eyeing me through the red filter of her wine. "You were a soldier."

"I think I'd remember."

"No. Not after you took steps to blockade and scramble your own memories." Glass laced her fingers, looking at me with a seriousness of expression that was all the more unnerving because I felt it to be sincere. "You were one of two brothers, both destined for military service. Your brother was an important man, born a long time ago. His name was Nevil Clavain and he was a soldier also. More than a soldier: a high-ranking military asset during the first Conjoiner war. He was on the side of the Coalition for Neural Purity, an organisation opposed to the Conjoiner experiments on Mars. But something happened to Nevil Clavain. He was captured by the Conjoiners, and later released. Unharmed, and untouched. The experience drove a wedge into his loyalty to the Coalition. Later, he defected wholesale to the other side. Thereafter he was closely aligned with the Conjoiners, without ever fully committing to their ethos. The perpetual outsider, doomed to never feel entirely at home."

"No," I said angrily. "I've nothing to do with that man; that monster."

And then I thought: but I have been having a strange dream of Mars, of a war from the wrong end of history.

Glass said mildly: "Let me continue."

"Please do," I said, with a sudden defeated sense. "I might as well hear it to the bitter end."

"Clavain's life spans centuries. In his later years, he became involved in the early effort against the wolves. There was factional struggle within the Conjoiners: differences of opinion over strategy. Squabbles over forbidden weapons and dangerous experiments. At some point, Clavain lost his life. That was unfortunate, because I believe him to have had strategic and tactical insights that could help us, including one very important piece of information."

"And you think I have it?"

"Actually, I'm as sure as I can be that you don't."

I raised my glass and drank to the futility of her mission. "Then I'm sorry you've wasted all these years."

"Nothing's been wasted." Glass stopped while the robots bustled in with food, all of it predictably appetising. She watched as they set out the meal, smiling slightly, and no doubt sparing part of that smile for my discomfort. "Because of the manner and location of Clavain's death, there's a chance that the mission-critical information is still retrievable: Charybdis. I tried to retrieve it myself, and failed. But the odds would be better if someone with a blood connection to Nevil tried."

"Even if some part of this were true...I'm no use to you. I'm not the man you think you've found."

"On the contrary, Warren, you are exactly the man."

"Who is Warren?"

"You are," Glass said. "That's your real name. Warren Clavain. You were one of the elite strategists in the Coalition for Neural Purity. A thinker and a warrior in the same cold package. You had a name for yourselves, you and your little gang of super-soldiers: suitably self-aggrandising."

A nervousness stirred in me as I asked: "Which was?"

"The Knights of Cydonia." Glass made an encouraging gesture towards the meal, even as the last certain part of myself collapsed into immense, sucking hollowness. "Tuck in, Sir Knight. We've work ahead of us."

When I returned to my room aboard *Scythe*, I found something new in there. It was resting on the bedside table, secured against sudden shifts in local gravity by a friction pad. It was an ornament of sorts, and heavy as a bludgeon when I lifted it in my hand. A thick wooden base sprouted an upright metal rod which, in turn, formed the support for a chunk of rough, semi-translucent material.

I fingered the material. It was a crudely finished rectangle, about twenty centimetres from side to side, a little wider than it was tall. It was buckled along two gentle curves: side to side and top to bottom, as if what the rod supported was only a section cut from a larger, approximately spherical form. The material was about half as thick as my little finger and ragged around the edges. The surface was pitted and scoured to the point where I could make out an impression of shapes and colours through it, but nothing sharp. Notably, there was a small hole in the middle of the material. It went all the way through it, and radiated a fine network of cracks.

I rolled the ornament in my hands, certain of two things: that it meant something to me—that I had seen it before, in some context—and that nothing about its appearance here was accidental. Glass had left it deliberately, in the sure knowledge that I would find it troubling.

The ornament drew something from my lips, unbidden.

"Faith," I whispered. "And Hope."

Then finally:

"And Charity."

In a fit of rage and denial I slammed the ornament down against the table. But no part of it broke.

Part Three

SWINEHOUSE

CHAPTER NINE

I fell into Mars on the back of a rock.

There were two other soldiers next to me. Each was squeezed onto a single-person dropship that was not much larger than the surface-suits we had on underneath. The chrysalis-shaped dropships were attached to the rock at the head end only, with their tapering tails projecting into space. They were black on black, sheltering on the rear face of the rock as its leading side approached Mars. There was a fourth dropship beside the ones we wore, empty for now.

I looked around, wriggling against the tight binding of my acceleration restraints. The sun was in my eyes, dimmed to a tolerable brightness by my visor's filters. Even in the full blaze of it, though, our dropships were chunks of featureless black, nearly devoid of detail or defined form.

A spray of status graphics framed my visor as systems woke up or rebooted from the long sleep. I reviewed them with a quick, thorough eye. All was well with my body, suit and dropship. The status update from our mission planners showed that the second phase of the operation had been executed without incident. A Defection Capsule had come in ahead of the rock's trajectory, and instead of shooting it down we had allowed that one to slip through, quite deliberately, by arranging our own orbital guns to fail in their interception.

Heartbeat analysis of the Defection Capsule indicated six recruits. They were already down on Mars; had been so for just under a week. Our thermal scans showed that the capsule had survived its re-entry and touchdown and appeared to be keeping its occupants alive. But there had been no movement from them; no attempt to leave, and no attempt by any other Conjoiner forces to reach them from the mother nest.

They would come, though. I was perfectly sure of that. Galiana would find that capsule far too tempting a prize to ignore.

My suit established a short-range comms web with the two occupied dropships. From their biomedical feeds I saw that the other two soldiers were also emerging from hibernation.

117

I sipped on a drinking tube, wetting my lips and throat, then tried to speak.

"Hope? Charity?"

Their answers came back a moment later: groggy but clear.

"I'm here, Faith," Hope said.

"Me too," Charity said.

"Good. Welcome back." I omitted to add: *to a mission that will likely kill us all*. No reminder was needed. The exact probabilities of our individual deaths might not be known to any of us, but none of us were under any illusions. This was an extremely high-risk endeavour, with no possibility of cover or reinforcements if anything went wrong. "You'll have the same status update as me, even if you haven't yet digested it. I'll summarise: a DC lander's gone in, six up. Dust-down eight hundred klicks north of our projected LZ. Been sitting there for six days. Spiders haven't made a move on it."

"Think they've sniffed a trap?" Hope asked.

"No. Why should they? It's a legitimate defection bid that only just made it through our screens. It doesn't become a trap until we touch it. Until then, it's all that it seems—and they *will* move on it eventually. The only reason they haven't gone in already is instinctive caution and an under-standing that they don't need to rush. But we'll give them an incentive."

"Do we have a reference for our rendezvous point?" Charity asked.

"Most favoured location is a Muskie camp two hundred klicks south of the capsule. One of us is likely to arrive several hours ahead of the others. Whoever it is, secure the hideout and begin systems inventory, after sweeping for spider traps."

"As if we'd forget," Hope said.

"You'll be battered and bruised from the impact, and strung-out and sleep-deprived from seventy-two hours hard marching. Nothing in the simulations will feel as bad as the real thing."

Hope laughed. "Well, that's encouraging."

"Look on the bright side," I answered. "Between then and now, all you have to do is survive riding down to the planet on the back of an explod-ing asteroid."

"I'm ready," Charity said.

She sounded as if she meant it, too. I admired her for that. She was a prime asset to the Coalition: brave, single-minded, resourceful, selfless in her adherence to the anti-Conjoiner cause. No one knew what went on in the heads of spiders better than this gifted young woman from Pyschosurgical Ops. It was to her credit that she had been so willing to volunteer for the operation.

Or, to put it more bluntly, not to de-volunteer herself once her suitability had been identified.

I almost wished I knew her actual name.

Glass disengaged the darkdrive, then slipped into the cover of the procession of corpses still orbiting Yellowstone.

Ten thousand habitats, thousands of larger ships, tens of thousands of smaller ones, had been turned into a garland of ashes. There were about three thousand more or less recognisable habitats, but even so they were blasted, airless and tumbling out of control. The rest was rubble: the rubble of miniature worlds, lighthugger hulls, in-system vehicles, people.

Glass was attentive. Traces kept appearing on her displays: spikes and waveforms and gabbling eruptions of binary code.

I shifted in my acceleration couch, trying to find a position where my bones ached a little less.

"What are we looking for?"

"Something with a pulse," she answered in a low voice, as if there was a risk of being overheard. "Ideally, something with a pulse that talks back."

"I thought we'd passed the point of being cryptic with each other."

Glass gave a small shrug. "There are things here that aren't totally dead. Bits of ship that still have some residual functionality left in them. Habitats with housekeeping devices that are still running on minimal power, even though the rest of the habitat is a shell. Space traffic beacons, still putting out transponder codes."

"And this helps us...how, exactly?"

"Some of these things are still sending out localisation pulses, just as if it's business as usual. Range-finding sweeps, requests for identification, approach authorisation and so on. It's like the last few flashes of electricity in a dying brain. Machine senility. But it's still activity of a kind."

"You think one of these signals may be from the ship that was meant to meet us inside John the Revelator?"

"Not necessarily. But if they were here at all, they may have been picked up on a tracking system, and their movements logged. If I can find a tracking device and interrogate its memory, I'll be able to tell when they arrived." She paused, biting her lower lip. "But so far these systems aren't responding in kind."

"You're talking back to them? After all the trouble we've gone to not to be noticed, isn't that a little risky?"

"My, you really *are* a worrier, aren't you?" Her look veered between admiration and the faint, developing disappointment of the remorseful buyer. "How a man like you ever got anything done in wartime..."

119

"I'm not a soldier."

"Your very name says otherwise. When you were small, your brother—when he and you used to play games in the sand dunes near your home—your brother called you War for short. It's mentioned in one of the military biographic files: a puff piece about both of you being promoted to Sky Marshall. Isn't that sweet? He saw what you were to become!"

"You're insane."

She considered. "Well, it's possible, if by 'sane' we mean operating in the functionally predictable attractor volume of mental phase space. I'm definitely not that." Glass gave a kitten-like shudder, as if the idea of being normal was almost viscerally repulsive. "But what I'm also not is reckless, dear War. Those comms we were discussing are all minimal energy, extreme tight-beam. Since I'm mimicking the same signals protocols, any back-scatter will just look like accidental leakage from the same conversation that's been going on here for decades. The trouble is, nothing is showing signs of..." Glass slowed, narrowing the black pools of her eyes at one of the readouts.

"You were about to say?"

"Until now, nothing's answered my requests for an internal data inventory. Probably means most of these transmitters are useless to us, incapable of logging an event history. But *this one* is more promising. It's faint, but its output pulses aren't nearly so garbled as the others, and the way it's responded is in keeping with my return pulse."

"It's sent you the record of movements?"

"No...it may need some further persuasion. But at least it seems to understand the nature of my enquiry. I won't risk further comms until we're right on top of it, though. We have to work our way further along the orbital stream."

Our course was a forced orbit: using thrust to maintain a fixed altitude above Yellowstone, while moving faster than the blasted remnants which still circled the planet at the same elevation. Glass fired the engines in sparing bursts, never for too long, and when she had the opportunity she used any large, relatively solid-looking mass as a cover for our course changes.

After twenty nervous minutes, *Scythe* chimed with an alert: a warning that the concentration of masses ahead of us was denser than anything we had been picking through so far. Glass slowed our approach, reducing our relative speed to no more than a kilometre per second compared with the average motion of the orbital flow.

"I don't know how big the largest structures were," Glass said, in a rare admission of ignorance. "But several of them seem to be moving in a

120

fixed formation, rather than following independent orbits. I don't know why. We'll have to push into that concentration, one way or the other. The beacon I'm looking for seems to be embedded in the same group of ruins."

"We could look for another beacon."

"We have already searched quite thoroughly. This is the only promising candidate."

We drifted between the black icebergs of gored and disembowelled habitats, the spaces between them slowly narrowing. From a range of ten kilometres the structures remained distant, abstract forms, with only traces of their former shapes. Here was a ruptured cylinder, blown wide at one end like a stoppered cannon. Here was the arc of a space wheel, severed along its rim. Here was a half-shattered globe, its guts long since spilled. I thought of the millions who might have called these worlds home, the lives that had been spent within their warm, comfortable cores.

Scythe put out another alert: a different tone this time.

"What is it?"

Glass studied a readout, bit her lower lip in concentration, wore the glazed look that told me she was in intense dialogue with her ship, then undid her seat restraint. "Wait here. I'll be back in a moment."

"Not the ideal time for a toilet break, Glass. Couldn't you try holding it in?"

"If you knew the things I am holding in, you'd be a little more circumspect with your attempts at humour."

When she returned a minute or two later she had an object clutched between her hands. It was a blunt-ended cylinder, about the size of a small oxygen tank. The two bevelled ends were thick metal plugs, flickering with lights. In between was a glass-walled container giving off a pale violet glow.

Something floated in the centre of that glow: a black dot.

"Know thy enemy. You'll have seen their actions from afar, I imagine. But it's quite a different thing to hold extinction between your hands."

Glass passed the cylinder to me as if it were haunted or cursed and I the gift's hapless, doomed beneficiary.

"Of course we saw their actions," I said quietly.

"Before or after you left human civilisation?"

"A little of both."

Though the cylinder was weightless, I still felt the mass of its armoured sides and powerful containment mechanisms. I had understood without asking that the black dot was an Inhibitor machine: a piece of wolf, or in some sense a wolf entire. Magnified, I would have seen a cube of perfect blackness. More accurately: I would have seen either a square or a hexagon, depending on the viewing angle, since the three-dimensional nature of Inhibitor cubes was impossible to perceive. Those surfaces and edges were as slippery to light as an event horizon.

"What happened on the *Salmacis*, to make you choose AU Microscopii as your destination? That can't ever have been the intended destination when the ship set out."

"It wasn't," I said guardedly. "When we left, the rumours of war were already about. But it was confined to a relatively small number of worlds and systems, and many believed it would burn out soon enough: that some revenant alien machines could never defeat the civilisation that had already survived the Melding Plague and numerous wars of its own. So some of us thought there was hope; that all we had to do was regroup and fight back, and we could do that from one of the worlds where there was already a human presence."

"And yet, the plan was abandoned."

"Mid-voyage, the captain and crew thawed a quarter of the passenger complement and raised the others to baseline consciousness. We were polled, like good Demarchists. By then, the *Salmacis* had been running into a blizzard of emergency signals, an ever-rising chorus of alarm and panic. Other ships, other worlds. The only commonality was that sooner or later all those signals got snuffed out. The wolves were emerging everywhere we looked, around every settled star. In many cases it was perfectly clear that they had been with us all along, undetected, dormant, waiting for their moment of activation. All thoughts of a safe haven in the known systems were thrown out. We had to plot a new course to some world where humans had never trodden, and where the wolves would be least likely to look. There were many suggestions, but most of them were deemed unworkable for one reason or other.

"I...advocated for Michael. There was resistance, at first. Who wants to spend the rest of their life sheltering inside an airless, radiation-blasted lump of rock orbiting inside a rubble cloud? But one by one the objections fell away. We could reach the system without straying too close to any of the wolf hotspots, and the circumstellar cloud and radiation environment would provide perfect cover, especially early on, as we worked to dismantle the ship."

"Good then, that you were so persuasive. That your one voice triumphed where others did not."

"If we'd gone somewhere else, then perhaps we'd have made that work as well."

"But you do not know."

"I know that no part of Sun Hollow came easily, and that there were plenty who wanted my neck on the block for ever advocating it."

"And yet, by then, you had become the de facto leader." Glass looked at me with the sort of cold admiration one reserved for a well-tempered blade. "Just one voice out of all those passengers, yet the one that prevailed."

"Someone had to. The crew relinquished authority to a civilian settlement board. If there was a command vacuum then I suppose I helped fill it. But it wasn't just me making those decisions like some kind of autocrat. There was Morgan Valois too, and... Rurik Taine."

"The man you later shot, or attempted to shoot."

"Whatever we were driven to, Glass, it was only ever because of the wolves." I regarded the object between my hands with renewed fascination and horror. No venomous snake or spider could have filled me with more dread. "I saw those transmissions when they came in. There was nothing distant or abstract about the way people were dying. Extinction isn't some bureaucratic erasure. It's screaming, suffocation, desperation and terror. It's pain and sorrow and the certain promise of more to come. I saw it and swore we'd never be touched by any part of that in Sun Hollow." I swallowed, my throat suddenly dry. "I kept my promise, right to the end."

"A promise that drove you to the brink of mass murder. Oh, poor brother War."

"Enough," I said angrily. "You weren't there, down in those caverns. You have no right to judge me."

"Oh, I have every right. Shouldn't the executed be allowed an opinion on her executioner?"

"I said I'd kill you, Glass—I haven't yet." I shuddered, trying to push her questions and madness out of my skull. *A piece of rough-edged glass, bored through the middle.* "This... wolf," I said, focusing on the immediate practicality of the thing I held between my hands, "how did it get in here, and can you really be sure it's dead?"

Glass sighed: I could not be sure whether it was one of modest relief, or quiet disappointment that I had not allowed her to keep picking at the scabs of my past. "*Scythe* detected it. It fell against the hull and was immediately recognised for what it is. Recognised and quarantined, then brought inside for examination. To your second point: it isn't dead. If it were, we would not see it. When they die, the cubes collapse and you're left with a tiny remnant of dust. The fact that the cube is still present, and that it triggered the ship's countermeasures, proves that it's still alive. But more than likely in a dormant or weakened state, and therefore of no immediate risk to us. May I?" Gingerly Glass took the containment device

123

back from me and made some adjustment to the controls in the end. "Watch. I'll reduce the containment strength."

"Are you mad?"

"I said reduce it, not turn it off." Glass's fingers played the controls as if they were the buttons of an accordion. The Inhibitor machine swelled: no longer a dot, now, but a black speck about the size of a skin flake. Still I could see no structure to it, no hint of depth. Glass allowed it to grow a little further. A grain of rice, then a sultana, then a small, blank-faced gaming die.

"Enough," I whispered.

The containment device quivered in her grip. Red lights pulsed on the ends.

"Oh, but there's some life in you, isn't there?" Glass let the cube increase further still in size. Now a fat die, now a child's play block. The violet radiance stammered. The red lights were all lit continuously: the device straining to hold back the cube's desire to expand. "You were sleeping, until you hit me, weren't you? Sleeping and nearly forgetting the thing you are. The thing you are meant to be. But now it's all coming back to you." She lofted the device until the cube was level with her eyes. "Such determination. Such an evil, earnest need to do your duty. Such...self-lessness." She snapped her fingers, and a white flash pulsed out of the device's sides. I blinked, an after-image floating before me. As my vision cleared, I saw that the cylinder was empty, the violet field dimming. Glass opened a little port in the base and out squirted a grey haze of fine ash. She pinched some of it onto her fingers, then held them up to my nose. "Smell it. That's what extinction smells like."

"Fireworks?"

"I've never smelled fireworks. But they say everyone has a different idea about that smell. It races up the olfactory nerve and finds something in each of us. Some memory or connection to death."

"I take it the dust is safe."

"Inert matter. When they collapse—when an external force over-rides their field-generating capability—they're careful not to leave anything useful behind; anything an inferior species might be able to reverse-engineer and turn against them. So yes, safe."

"That really wasn't necessary, Glass."

"On the contrary: it was more than necessary. You've seen the worst of what they can do, via those transmissions. The screams and the sorrow. I've drunk my share of that as well. And you know the slower, more agonising sort of terror that lies in the act of hiding—hiding for years or decades, never daring to make a single mistake. That terror that seeps into every thought, every dream. The terror that underlines every pleasure, the terror that negates hope, the terror that stains every joy with the knowledge that it may all soon end, and horribly. But this is the counterpoint: the truth that we must also carry within us. The understanding that for all they have done to us, for all they have brought us to the whimpering edge of annihilation, they're not invulnerable. That we can kill them, and we shall."

Glass's words resonated within me for a second or two before I answered.

"Perhaps we can kill them. But only when they're kind enough to arrive in ones or twos, and be half-asleep when they do."

"There'll be other means. There *are* other means." Glass set aside the containment device, its purpose—to rattle me, or inspire me, or both—evidently served. "Now at least we know that the wolves are still here, albeit in some state of dormancy. *Scythe* can rebuff them in small numbers, and without drawing too much attention to itself. But we would be advised not to run into any large aggregations."

"And if we do?"

"We should be well to have found ourselves a wolf-killer." Glass was silent for a moment. "Which, with your assistance, we shall."

The habitats crowded nearer. The distances between them narrowed to mere hundreds of metres. It turned dark in those canyon-like spaces, and I had a strong urge to turn back. But Glass was still following the trace from the beacon and she would not be deterred.

"Do you see?" Glass said suddenly.

"See what?"

"Black filaments, black structures connecting these drifting hulks. That's why they're following the same orbit. They're tethered." She ruminated for a moment. "I don't think it's wolf material. If they meant to engulf and assimilate these ruins, they'd have done so in a very short while. There's no need to, not with so much raw matter elsewhere in the system, there for the taking."

"So what is it?"

"Something indigenous, which has broken out of control. An opportunistic regrowth of plague strains, perhaps, erupting from private vivaria or the hidden niches where it was never entirely eliminated. Or something spawned deliberately, some self-replicating biological or cybernetic process now enjoying unfettered growth, far beyond the whims of its creators."

"Wouldn't the wolves have come back to stop it?"

"I doubt that it concerned them enough to go to such trouble. These are maggots."

"Maggots?"

"The wolves have taken apart civilisations before. Many of them must have produced unregulated end-stage growth patterns not unlike these forms. It's a marker for morbidity: a highly integrated society going through its terminal spasms." She waited a moment, then brought up some synthetic image of the intricate, netlike structures binding the drifting ruins. Blue lines, radiating and intersecting. "What does that remind you of?"

"Cobwebs. And where there are cobwebs..."

"Then we shan't delay. The beacon is just ahead, loosely adhered to the outer wall of the nearest habitat. Go to the suiting room. By the time we begin station-keeping you will be ready to leave."

"Can't you send out some of your robots instead?"

"The servitors can't move around very efficiently in vacuum, whereas the suits can. And if I am going to commit a suit, I might as well give it an autonomous capability."

"So glad I get to be an autonomous capability," I said.

The crossing to the beacon was no test for the suit: just a quick jaunt across a couple of hundred metres of open space. The robots had delivered a self-burrowing probe to the airlock in time for my departure, and now it spooled out behind me, trailing a hair-thin line back to *Scythe*. The main part of the probe was a squat, dual-handled cylinder with a battery of gripping, cutting and drilling devices set into its end. Glass had assured me that it would know what to do.

The space I drifted through was the canyon-like gap between two habitats that had come near to each other, but hadn't quite fused. The two surfaces were pitted and scarred, ready to close in like a pair of vast rotten molars. Their surfaces stretched away in all directions, leaving only narrow slots above and below. The blackened and scabbed walls gave off no light of their own, but Yellowstone was below, fully illuminated by Epsilon Eridani. Some of that reflected radiance found its way into the crevice between the habitats, bouncing around and casting a sepia tinge on the ship, my suit, the walls of the habitats, and the cobwebbing that stretched between the walls.

Glass had loaded a navigation trace into the suit, homing in on the beacon, but it still took me a minute to recognise my target. The beacon was a dodecahedron, about four metres across, with panels made of some lustrous substance. It was partially enclosed by cobwebbing, binding it to the wall, but not so thoroughly that it was impossible to reach.

The cobwebbing thickened as I neared. The suit wanted to charge on through, but I slowed it and switched to a fully manual approach. Eventually I had to tuck in my arms and legs to squeeze through the narrowest passages. As I made contact with the beacon, I was able to stretch out again and plant my feet on a ledge-like protuberance of the wall, then rest a hand on one of the dodecahedron's panels.

We knew the beacon to be functional, so it was no surprise to see the occasional pulse of light flicker beneath the panel. It was the only continuing process I had seen anywhere around Yellowstone; the only indication that our civilisation had been capable of more than mute ruins. Before continuing, I looked back through the tangle of cobwebs, reassuring myself that *Scythe* was still there. Glass had said nothing since my departure, not even sending a signal through the line, but I imagined she was studying my progress.

I positioned the cutting face of the probe on the nearest and least-obstructed panel. At the last instant before contact the probe jerked from my grip, fastening itself on. With my palm against another part of the beacon I felt a constant grinding vibration. This went on steadily for a minute or two, then abated. Faint tremors and bumps came from the beacon, but by now I guessed that the probe had dug its fangs beneath the outer armour and was working through the softer tissue of logic arrays and memory registers.

The flickering lights responded in kind: the beacon registering its distress. I watched the lights warily, willing this to be over and done with. So long as it was just those lights, we were not in too much trouble. They were surely too faint for any trace of them to make its way out of the canyon.

The beacon jolted hard, nearly knocking me off my perch. The probe must have broken through some inner membrane...or ruptured some pressure vessel or energy cell. Everything stopped. The beacon was still, the probe pausing in its efforts.

"Glass..." I began to say, invoking her name without contacting her.

I saw the probe twitch as it resumed its work, sending a kink back through the data line—

—and the beacon screamed. Every other one of its panels was flashing a brilliant, blinding pink. It was putting out a clangorous emergency tone across a wide spread of radio frequencies, detected by my suit and amplified into my helmet. I had no doubt that the signal was strong enough to reach halfway around Yellowstone, and probably far beyond it.

I moved to the probe and tried to detach it. It was rooted in place, impossible to budge. It was still drilling.

"Glass!" I shouted, content to use the suit-to-ship channel now that we were already making so much electromagnetic noise. "You've triggered something! Make it stop!"

"No—not yet. The data is beginning to flow back to *Scythe*."

"The wolves will hear this!"

"The signal has already done its damage: nothing would be gained by stopping now. We will just have to trust that the wolves interpret the signal as a natural consequence of the processes going on among these ruins. Besides, I am exploring a number of promising override pathways..."

"Explore faster!"

The beacon silenced. The pink panels stopped flashing. It had happened so suddenly that it was nearly as shocking as when it had begun.

The probe remained in place. I imagined that it had pushed a fatal load of venom into its prey and was now sucking it dry from within. I watched it for a few more seconds, wondering if I had any further part to play in the operation. If I went back directly, *Scythe* ought to be able to reel in the probe without my assistance.

The beacon moved again, shifting languidly in its nest of cobwebs. But it was not the beacon that had initiated that motion: it was the cobwebs themselves, stirring. I froze for a moment, surveying the scene around me. What had been stillness was starting to creep and ooze. The sepia light exaggerated the encroachment of a thousand shadows, as the cobwebs tightened and unravelled and slid over themselves according to some huge, slow, coordinated plan.

I pushed myself off the ledge, into free space. The probe could take its chances: I wanted to get away from the area where the cobwebs were at their densest. They were already wrapping around the beacon more thoroughly than before, cocooning it in a tightening weave of slithering threads. Glass had set up the suit to home in on the beacon, but she had left it to me to plot my own way back to *Scythe*. I could still make out the black absence of the ship, just barely. Like a message that had been scribbled over several times it was becoming harder to keep my attention on it, as the cobwebs criss-crossed the space before me. They were moving now, as well as the ones near the beacon, and with steadily more vigour. Some were as thick as tree trunks, flexing or uncoiling with the quiet, hungry purposefulness of pythons.

"Glass," I said, fear overcoming my inclination to keep silent. "We've started something. You'd better move *Scythe* well away from this area."

"I'm not finished. Stay with the probe, in case it detaches."

"To hell with the probe. I'm already on my way back. But I'd like the ship to be in one piece when I arrive."

"This was your one test. The one thing I asked you to do—"

"You mean, the thing you demanded I do—"

"Get back," Glass hissed.

Something snagged my ankle, jerking me to a halt before the suit had gathered any useful speed. A black tendril had hooked me, forming a loop in itself, and tightening. I thrashed and kicked, loosening myself at what felt like the last possible moment before the loop closed off any possibility of escape. Perhaps the suit would have had some countermeasure in reserve, but it was nothing I was prepared to stake my life on. I gunned the jets, breathing hard. The line still stretched all the way back to *Scythe*, a fine thread catching the last golden blush of Yellowstone before the face below us was swallowed by night. The ship was clearer in my view now, less than two hundred metres away, but the cobwebs were exploring it, brushing against its hull. Glass must have known, but still she was delaying departure, anxious to drink the last drop of data from her prize. If there had been something in my suit capable of cutting that line, I would have done so without hesitation.

The line went slack, and then tautened again.

"The probe is returning," Glass said. "Grab it and ride it home. It will be quicker than coming in on suit power."

I steered close to the line and looked back just in time to see the drilling head speeding towards me, hauled in by the accelerating winch. I only had one chance to seize it, and the velocity difference was already four or five metres per second. The jolt might have torn my arms out of my sockets, if they were not protected by the suit. I held on, my breath rasping in my throat, and then a secondary concern presented itself. Glass was winching me in so fast I was in danger of smashing into the rear wall of the airlock. At the last instant I released the winch, and the suit instigated its own anti-collision procedure before I could begin to command the thrusters. I slowed hard, but remained conscious, and then drifted almost peaceably into the lock. By the time the door began to close, we were already moving.

But not so quickly as Glass must have desired. The cobwebs had furled around *Scythe*, and now they were consolidating their embrace.

CHAPTER TEN

As we slipped free, I think even Glass understood that she had cut matters too fine for comfort.

"I hope that was worth it."

"So do I, because I'd hate to rely on you twice. Fortunately, it won't be necessary to look for any other beacons. I have what I needed from this one. A ship entered the ruins six years ago. Its point of origin isn't determined, but there's no reason to think it didn't come from the lighthugger."

"How can you be sure it wasn't some other ship, and nothing to do with your allies?"

"Because there aren't any other ships. This is the only logged movement in or out of the wider system in fifty-three years. No one has come near enough to be picked up by the beacon."

"Before you pin all your hopes on that one entry..."

"It's them. The pattern fits. They make a direct approach to Yellowstone, then are lost in the atmosphere. Two weeks later the beacon picks up a vessel of the same general profile leaving Yellowstone. But they never continue back to John the Revelator."

"Something still got to them, then. Perhaps they ran into those cobwebs, or some more of those wolf cubes latched onto them—more than they could defend against."

"I don't think so."

I decided that I much preferred Glass when she was certain of things. If I was going to be forced into cooperation with a merciless killing angel, I wanted her to be entirely free of doubt. Doubt was for the rest of us.

"Does the beacon have anything to say?"

My question must not have seemed entirely imbecilic to her, because she answered in a surprisingly civil manner. "It doesn't keep a detailed fix on their movements. It's impossible for a single beacon to sweep all of the ruins at the same time with Yellowstone sitting in the middle. But there's nothing about the way they left the atmosphere that makes me think they had difficulties with their ship. They seem to be moving towards a small body in one of the outer orbits, just before the trace goes cold. They don't reappear. I think they must be still waiting in orbit, but well enough concealed that there's no way to pick up a locator trace."

"I know you want them to be alive. But six years is a long time to sit around for no good reason."

"They must have determined that it was too dangerous to make the agreed rendezvous. Perhaps wolf activity was heightened until recently, or they were aware of some other threat." Glass squeezed her fist, seizing an idea and crushing it until its juices flowed. "They're waiting for us. They knew we'd follow their trail as best we could, but they can't advertise their location. They have to rely on us finding them, using the beacon records."

"All right...supposing we run with this. After six years, can we narrow down their location?"

"It should not tax us. Even if there are a number of candidates, *Scythe* can search them quite efficiently with its remotes, looking for stray emissions or thermal noise. They can't reach out to us across any sort of distance, but if we can get very close they may announce their presence."

"This is going to be like playing hide-and-seek in a darkened room."

"Except the hunter and hunted both have sharpened daggers, and each has reason to be nervous." With that reassurance, Glass flashed a fierce grin. "I have the search volume: it's a little further around the orbit, but *Scythe* can narrow down the candidate list as we travel. The game's afoot, dear War; no reason not to start playing!"

It took us three hours to skulk our way further around Yellowstone, using the ruins for cover where it was prudent to do so. Now and then we saw drifting clusters of habitats or parts of habitats tethered together by something similar to the cobwebs, indicating that the growth had taken root in multiple sites. I was relieved when Glass showed no inclination to curiosity. There was enough to keep our nerves on edge without indulging in dangerous sightseeing. *Scythe* was detecting and neutralising wolf cubes every few minutes as they rained against our hull. These were either lone cells or micro-aggregations of less than a dozen, and in such small numbers were not a serious threat. In all cases the cubes were destroyed before they showed any tendency to begin the assimilation of local matter, confirming that they were in the same state of dormancy as the first. But the threat of the wolves lay in coordinated action, and it would only take one cube to wake up sufficiently to send an alert back to a larger concentration, in the ruins or nearby. This was not speculation: it was a pattern that had been documented time and again as the wolves picked our civilisation apart.

Between them, Glass and *Scythe* had narrowed down the possible hiding places to three bodies, all following a similar orbit. When we were a thousand kilometres out from each candidate, *Scythe* launched a drone.

One object was a ruptured cylinder, blasted open at both ends, so we could see right through it without any special sensors. The interior had been landscaped—shaped with lakes, rivers, waterfalls, little hills and hamlets linked by meandering roads better suited to mules and carts than high-speed travel. Only a grey death-mask of this one-time Eden remained. The habitat must have depressurised quickly, its waters boiling into vacuum and its trees torn from their roots. A few petrified trunks were still floating in the core. A ship could have parked within the gutted shell, but unless it had disguised itself in the remains of the hamlets, or dug its way into the thin skin between the inner and outer walls, the drone should have found it.

The second candidate offered a little more cover: it was a sphere that had only been punctured at one point, meaning that most of the interior was still well concealed. But the drone found almost nothing inside besides some broken lights and the lacy remnants of withered vegetation.

Only the third candidate really offered a plausible place to hide a functioning spacecraft. Rather than a fabricated structure like the first two, this was a lump of rock that had been tunnelled into and made liveable. Being a boulder, it had withstood collisions and impacts that would have shattered a wheel or cylinder. That was not to say it had come through the attack unscathed, or that it would have been easy for anyone to keep living inside it. Something like an energy beam had punched a dozen clean holes right through the boulder, and the entry and exit wounds were wide enough for a small ship. *Scythe* wheeled around this rock, sniffing for emissions. Nothing struck, but when the drone went in and out of one of the tunnels, it picked up a slight but statistically significant excess of neutrinos. The boulder was also a little warmer than some of the surrounding bodies, although not so much that it called attention to itself.

Glass summoned the drone back.

"We'll go inside. They'll know we're here, so the next move is theirs."

"I'd raise an objection," I said sourly. "But you'd only say I was worrying."

"You mustn't let Glass get under your skin," Glass said, commenting on herself as if she were absent.

She took us in through the only hole large enough to accept a ship the size of *Scythe*. This was not one of the energy-beam punctures; the walls on either side of us had been smoothly bored, and as we went deeper they widened into a reception cavern. Here and there were the ghost traces of structures that might have been bracketed out from the walls, but which had now been removed.

"This used to be a docking bay," I said, before Glass had a chance to voice her own opinion. "It's not something that formed by accident. There were berthing cradles here—servicing racks and airlock ports. But it's all been cleaned out a long time ago, leaving just the witness marks. Perhaps a really long time ago—even before the wolves."

Glass said nothing. I had come to realise that this was her silent, brooding acknowledgement that I had made a statement that was neither incorrect nor easily refutable.

"It would have made a good place to dock," I went on. "But there aren't any ships. We can search the other holes, I suppose. But it could be that your probe was just picking up residual radiation from something that happened in the past."

"There's a ship near us."

"You *want* there to be a ship near us. That doesn't mean..."

Something was happening in the back wall of the chamber. A section of what had seemed to be a seamless surface was receding into the wall, leaving a clean-bored shaft behind it. The shape of the section was curious but too deliberate to be accidental: an ellipsoidal middle with two lobelike extensions on either side, each tipped with a smaller ellipse of their own.

Without a word, Glass advanced her ship.

"It could be a trap."

"It's not a trap. It's a lock." She glanced at me. "I mean in the old-fashioned sense, rather than a thing to keep in air. It's a lock and we're the key."

I understood. *Scythe* had exactly the right cross-section to fit into that peculiar slot that had opened up in the wall. The central ellipse was for the hull; the lobes and smaller ellipses for the Conjoiner drives. Through the false view of the control room windows, I watched as the sides of the bore slipped past us. There was ample clearance to begin with, but *Scythe* widened near its mid-section and by the time half the ship was into the lock, the proximity alarms were informing us that we were only centimetres away from a collision.

Terrain! Terrain!

Glass silenced the alarms and pushed on blithely. She barely blinked when the ship ground against the walls.

"If we jam inside this thing, we're in trouble."

"We shan't jam. This lock has been purpose-designed for *Scythe*." Disapproval clouded her face. "It's an unnecessary flourish, but not out of keeping. It reassures me. To have engineered this lock, they must have had time and resources and the means to move matter around without attracting the wolves."

Scythe crunched to a halt, jerking us forward in our seats.

We had arrived at the end of the shaft, and there was no way through.

Glass touched the cold-gas thrusters and began to back us up.

"What are you doing?"

"Reversing a little, then I will deploy cutting devices. Something must have malfunctioned in the lock: the wall ahead of us is sticking at this point. If the cutters don't work, I will use limited-yield energy beams or shaped-charge munitions, but they may require a retreat to the first chamber."

"You're not thinking this through."

Glass looked at me sharply. "Oh, and you are?"

"You said we're the key. What's the first thing you do to a key, after you've pushed it into a lock? Or have you forgotten how keys actually work?" I nodded forward. "Take us back in as far as we'll go, then use those jets to apply a rotational torque. Keys turn."

Glass brooded on my answer then appeared to find some grain of sense in it. She took us back into the limit of the wall, kissing it more cautiously this time.

"Which way? Clockwise or anticlockwise?"

I shrugged. "Whichever works."

Glass applied the jets. At first it got us nowhere. We were already tight against all the surfaces so *Scythe* barely twitched before it stopped moving. Clockwise hadn't worked. Glass tried an anticlockwise torque and that got us no further.

"So much for your one idea."

"You give in too easily. Locks get sticky, and if this one is only meant to work for *Scythe*, you can be sure it won't have been operated for a long time. Waggle us around harder."

"*Scythe* doesn't *waggle*..."

"Today it does."

Glass offered a wordless grunt, then set about doing what I had suggested, applying the jets first one way then the other with increasing force, *Scythe* clunking back and forth against the limits of the walls until, with a lurch, we continued rotating, the lock's barrel finally loosening. It was a clockwise turn that did it in the end, and we must have gone around more than one hundred and eighty degrees before some secondary mechanism activated, causing the obstructing surface ahead of us to drop away. *Scythe* now had a clear path forward again. Glass advanced us, passing out of the opposite counterpart to the lock entrance, into a sealed space about as large as the first chamber, but considerably further into the rock.

Scythe exited the lock and floated in airless stillness and dark.

"You have your uses," Glass said.

After about a minute, lights came on. Around the walls of the chamber, twenty or so beams had activated, pinning us in a cat's cradle of light. The beams were visible in the trace gases of the manoeuvring jets. They slid around the hull, examining it. Then they became still again and a small door opened in the wall.

A much smaller in-system vehicle was docked next to ours, fixed to the wall by a berthing clamp. It was dark red, with a scale-like patterning to its armour.

"Do you recognise it?"

Glass nodded once. "That's the shuttle they brought with them from Hela, carried here in the hold of John the Revelator. It's small enough to traverse the lock, like a universal key."

"It doesn't look damaged."

"Are you an expert on that design?"

"No...but I don't need to be. Is it damaged?"

After a few seconds Glass said: "It appears superficially intact."

"Thank you."

"I admitted no error."

"No, but I'm learning to take my victories where I can."

We watched the door for several minutes, wondering if someone or something (up to and including a weapon) was going to come out of it. When it became plain that nothing of that sort was going to happen, Glass and I arrived at the unavoidable conclusion that we were meant to let ourselves in.

"I'll go," I ventured. "Then you can do the same excellent job of protecting me as you did when I went to the beacon."

"Did you come to any harm?"

"No—"

"Then you've nothing to complain about. I almost *am* tempted to send you ahead, you know, just in case there are any traps we still have to pass. But we'll go in together. The sooner we're all acquainted, the sooner we'll gain the Gideon stones."

I nodded slowly, as if this was all reasonable. She had mentioned these stones already but I was still none the wiser about their nature or function.

"Do we go in armed?"

She looked shocked. "Where are your manners, War? That would be rude. And futile. We're not here to negotiate. They'll be relieved to see us, and fully cooperative."

"It's been a warm welcome so far. And please stop calling me War."

Glass put *Scythe* into safekeeping mode and we went to the suiting bay. We carried no extra weapons or equipment with us, although I was certain that the suits had built-in self-defence capabilities. But as long as we were not flaunting weapons, I supposed we hewed to some tenuous definition of good manners.

The chamber was weightless, so we drifted over the door using suit thrusters. Beyond the door was an airlock of unremarkable design, equipped with a full set of manual controls. It was spacious enough to take both of us. Glass sealed the outer door and allowed air to flood in. She looked back at *Scythe* through the door's small viewing port, her ship still pincered between those beams.

"Misgivings?" I asked gently. "The faint feeling that something isn't quite right, but you can't put your finger on it? If they have these stones you need, and since their ship is intact, why didn't they find a way to get them to the lighthugger, or at least send a message? How hard can that have been? And what, by the way, are the stones?"

The airlock provided an atmosphere determined to be both breathable and absent of any harmful additives, so in the interests of further good manners we stepped out of the suits and left them to wait by the lock. It was colder than I might have wished, wearing my shipboard clothes, but I could tolerate it for the sake of diplomacy. I rubbed my hands hard, urging blood to circulate into my fingertips. Glass seemed untroubled.

Still weightless, we half drifted and half propelled ourselves down a connecting corridor lit by pale yellow strips. The corridor soon came to an abrupt end, with a smooth sheer wall blocking us. I reached out to touch the wall, wanting to get some sense of its solidity. There had to be a means of getting through it: it was absurd to allow us all this way and then deny any further progress.

Glass slapped my hand away before my fingers contacted the wall.

"It's moving, you fool."

"What?"

"We're only seeing a small part of a much larger moving surface, like the side of a wheel."

I stared at the wall, seeing it anew. Though it had seemed flawless before, I now realised that this was only a consequence of its motion. Now and then, a scratch or scuff passed across the width of the corridor very rapidly.

I glanced back to my fingers, glad that they were still attached to me. It would not have taken much—a crack or seam in the surface—to rip them from my knuckles.

"I don't understand why they'd block us this way."

"They aren't," Glass said. "Sooner or later there'll be a gap, a recess, in the wall. This is the transition between the main body of the rock and some part of it made to spin, for centrifugal gravity. When the gap comes around, we have to step into it."

We did not have long to wait. The gap was an interruption in the rim, a recess big enough to take at least two suited forms. It came and went in two or three seconds, then returned around again about a minute later. Glass and I looked at each other then nodded, ready for the next opportunity. There could be no hesitation: if we mistimed our entries, we'd be crushed between the moving and stationary parts of the structure.

The transition was bruising, but my bones remained unbroken. Glass had made it look easy: she was already standing, legs spread for balance, one hand against the fixed wall of the moving structure.

I got up on my feet, readjusting to the presence of gravity.

"It feels heavy."

"Not even close to a gee." Glass strode over to a circular hole in the floor, planting her feet to either side of it and peering into a yellow-lit void. "There's a ladder going down. Your weight will increase as you descend. Go ahead of me."

"Why?"

"Because if you fall off, I don't want you dragging me down with you."

"Your kind concern is noted."

I made an awkward approach to the ladder, wishing there was a handhold on the floor to help as I levered my legs into the shaft and searched for a rung. Eventually I got going and set about a steady descent, rung by rung. Glass was right. The load was steadily increasing as we moved further and further from the centrifuge's axis of rotation. But my muscles were readjusting to the imposition of gravity as well, and the two kept pace.

"Nice of your friends to come all the way to the front door and greet us."

"There's no need. We've come this far; we'd hardly turn back at the last step. Can you see a bottom to the shaft?"

I glanced down into a yellow haze of receding perspectives. "Not yet. Are you going to tell me about these Gideon stones before we meet our host, or would that give you one less reason to feel superior over me? I'd hate to deprive you of one of the few small pleasures in your life."

I went down a few more rungs, grunting with the effort, my palms turning sweaty. The ache in my bones was reasserting itself jealously, as if I had neglected to give it enough attention. Glass followed a short distance above me, moving with an easy, catlike rhythm that only made my own efforts seem more laboured.

"They're devices. Alien technology."

"Something we can use against the wolves?"

"Indirectly."

"I don't like 'indirectly.'"

"You won't like any part of it." Glass continued her silent descent for a few more moments. "They're a defensive system, and a useful one. The creatures that made them put the stones to one use; we shall put them to another."

I was starting to see something below me. Feeling more confident now that there was less distance to fall, even as the gravity increased, I quickened my descent. A floor or platform was coming up. I jumped down the last few rungs, feeling a reckless confidence in my newly strengthened bones. With my feet on solid ground—actually a gridded floor—I stepped back to allow Glass to finish her climb. When she was still above my head she skipped off the rungs entirely and slid down with her palms and feet skimming the ladder's side. The floor clattered under her as she landed.

"You missed your chance," she said. "You could have impaled me as I was coming down."

I dabbed my forehead in mock absent-mindedness.

"I *knew* there was something I'd forgotten. An impaling spike! You know, I wouldn't go around putting ideas in my head. I might start noting them down for future use."

The ladder had brought us to a room no larger than an airlock. There was no sign of the ladder continuing beneath us, so I supposed we had reached the maximum radius of the centrifuge. I estimated that we were experiencing about half a gravity. "They can't operate this wheel all the time," Glass said. "No matter how well engineered it all is, there'll be a heat burden. I left them with some cryo-arithmetic engines, but they can't be used continually."

"They broke down."

Neither of us had spoken. A door had opened in the side of the room and a person of medium height was standing there, wearing a dark hood and gown. They had their arms by their side but the sleeves were so long that it was impossible to say whether they carried a weapon or were empty-handed. The hood projected forward, shadowing the whole of their face.

"Lady Arek?" Glass asked, doubtfully.

"This man with you—" The voice was deeper and raspier than Glass's. "I take it he's the one you went all that way for?"

"He's the one."

"Clavain?"

"No. The brother, as I expected."

"Not what I expected." The hood lingered on me. I heard a sniffing sound. "Smells musty. Smells like old meat. Smells rotten."

"He's old, but I've commenced rejuvenation measures. You should have smelled him before I began."

"You sure it's really him?"

"The gene markers don't lie. Nor do the micro-surgical traces. He's grown himself a new arm, and a new eye—maybe several times over. Swamped his own memories with blockades, so thick he doesn't even remember his real identity. Been living as a kindly old man of the people, under the name Miguel de Ruyter."

"Couldn't let the past go completely?"

"No. A billion names he could have chosen, and he still went for one with a connection to Mars." Glass looked at me with a little sadness. "But it's not who else he fools that matters. No one else cares. No one else remembers. He could have called himself Clavain and the world wouldn't have noticed. But *he* needed to forget who he was."

"Is he coming back?"

"Slowly. I used reefersleep to flood him with mnemonovores. The blockades create distinctive association structures. The mnemonovores target them preferentially, leaving authentic memories intact, and help reconsolidate pathways that have been left to wither. It's not perfect, but..." There was an awkward lull. The hooded figure was still at the threshold and had made no overtures of welcome. "May we come inside, Lady Arek?"

"I'm not Lady Arek." The figure lifted its arms, the sleeves falling back to reveal stubby, trotter-like hands with only two fingers and a thumb. It swept back the hood, disclosing a scarred, snouted face. I flinched in the first moment of recognition, realising that we had been speaking to a hyperpig. "My name is Snowdrop. Lady Arek's head of security. I'll decide whether you take another step inside."

I studied the map of scars that criss-crossed Snowdrop's face. One had gone right through an eye socket, but somehow spared the eye. Some teeth were missing; others yellowed with age. Wisps of white hair straggled back from a low, angled brow. Her pointed, upraised ears were scarred, swollen, and ragged with long-healed voids. They were also punctured by numerous metal rings and studs, and where her skin showed, it was a patchwork of ink, mark over mark.

"If you had any doubts about our identity, you should have acted sooner," I said.

"Got that wrong for a start." Snowdrop shot Glass a quizzical look. "Are you sure he's Clavain? Thought he was supposed to be some kind of tactical mastermind."

"You had to wait until we were out of our suits, and nearly defenceless," Glass said. "There's some barrier across that door, a last line of security. Whatever it is, I can't sense it."

"Then how do you know it's there?"

"Because I don't think you or Lady Arek would be stupid enough not to have something."

Snowdrop gave a half-impressed cock of her head. "There's a thread of filament, moving up and down the length of the doorway too quickly for your eye to detect. The mechanism is hydraulic, driven by shielded pumps. If you'd taken a step across the threshold, half of you wouldn't have made it." She lifted her snout. "Tell me how you found us here."

"We followed breadcrumbs," Glass said. "John the Revelator, then the Rust Belt, then a beacon which had logged your ship movements six years ago."

"And how was John the Revelator's state of mind?"

Glass gave an indifferent shrug. "All that you could expect of a barely human consciousness haunting the bowels of a plague-ravaged wreck from another century. All that you'd expect from a man born when people used chemistry to get off planets. All that you'd expect from a man whose life consists solely of grand crimes and tiny inadequate twitches of reflex atonement. All you'd expect of an eight-hundred-year-old monster. Not that any of that's a surprise. The man was more than mad before he became half-fused with his ship."

"And the rest," I said.

"The rest?" Snowdrop asked me, lifting an eyebrow over that scar-bisected eye.

"I had to rescue Glass. In return for releasing her, I promised John the Revelator that I'd find out what had happened to you. Whoever you are, he seemed fonder of you than he was of Glass."

"From what I was told, he'd be fonder of most things in the universe than he is of Glass." Snowdrop stepped back from the door. "You can come through now. I've disabled the cutter." She called back over her shoulder: "They're clean."

"We passed some test?" Glass asked.

"Old Stinky seems to be speaking some kind of truth. If you'd come up from below—or worse, if you were being run by wolves—you'd never know who John the Revelator did or didn't like."

I took a breath and stepped across the threshold, pausing on the other side to make sure all of me had made it across. Then I turned around to offer a chivalrous hand to Glass. She wrinkled her nose and traversed the door without my assistance.

I lowered my hand.

Two thick-necked, over-muscled men appeared behind Snowdrop, wearing plated and buckled body armour and carrying boser pistols. The men were bearded, one with long hair and the other shaven all the way to the scalp, which was a map of scars and dents, like a planet after a heavy bombardment.

"Stand down," Snowdrop murmured. "These are the incomers."

"Do you know these people?" I asked Glass.

"I don't know any of them, including her. They must be...associates...Lady Arek has collected since her arrival."

"You make us sound like trinkets," Snowdrop countered. "Not exactly how I see it. Or Lady Arek, for that matter."

"Is Lady Arek one of the associates you sent from Hela?" I asked. "The ally you met?"

Snowdrop cocked her jaw in amusement. "Is that how Glass tells it? That it's an equal partnership? Or did she go even further and make out she's somehow running things and Lady Arek's going along with whatever she's told?"

"Lady Arek and I arrived at a basis for cooperation," Glass stated.

"Well, that's one way of putting it," Snowdrop said. "Another would be that she turned you into a weeping little puddle, and it was all you could do to beg for your life and be given a tiny part of her plan to be getting on with, like a doggie thrown a bone." Snowdrop eyed me. "Sorry, Stinky, if this is all news to you. I bet you think Glass is scary. But that's only 'cause you haven't met Lady Arek."

"She's well, I take it?" Glass asked.

"Six years in this place will test anyone's will. But it's a lot better than where we came from, and she knows it."

"And her escort, the pig?"

"Oh, Pinky? He's mostly fine. I see to that."

Glass had told me next to nothing about her associates. But now at least I had some names, or partial names, and the knowledge that one was a hyperpig, like Snowdrop. Also that Lady Arek was in no way acting under Glass's direction, and that their alliance might be built on shakier foundations than I had been led to think.

141

Who were they, beyond these names? I had no idea.

"Gentlemen," Snowdrop said to the two guards. "Would you mind going ahead and warning the Overlook we're on our way up?"

"You sure about that?" asked the balder of the two men, scratching at his temple. "They haven't been searched, scanned, decontaminated..."

"It's them, Omori. And if it isn't—if the wolves are good enough to impersonate living, breathing bodies—we're already in far too much trouble to do anything about it."

"I like that attitude," said the long-haired man. "Very pragmatic."

"We see things similarly, Cater. But don't worry—the only thing likely to overwhelm me is Stinky's old-man smell."

"That bad?"

"Friend, be glad you're not a pig."

The guards went on ahead. Just before they went out of sight they shot Snowdrop a questioning glance, but she waved aside their concerns, shaking her head at their over-protectiveness.

"You're taking a risk, all the same," I said.

"We haven't had visitors in six years," Snowdrop answered, taking us along a connecting hallway where the gravity remained constant. "It makes them twitchy, dealing with new faces. But you're who you say you are."

She had an awkward waddling gait, as if her hip joints were fused.

"If Pinky and Lady Arek are Glass's two associates," I said, "and if no other ship has come and gone from this system, then you must have already been here when Pinky and Lady Arek arrived from John the Revelator. How the hell is that possible?"

"Well, I won't say it was a picnic, Stinky. Anyone you see here is, by definition, a survivor, and most of us came through it with a few scars. Inside and out."

"I don't disbelieve it. But we saw only ruins as we came in. No trace of life anywhere."

"If there was a visible trace, the wolves would've found it. So the trick is to not be visible. Easier said." She patted one of the walls as we passed along it. "Several of us were holed up in this place. It's well shielded, so you can run basic life-support and a few other systems without putting out too much excess heat and noise. Which isn't to say any part of it was easy. It was a cold, dark hell most of the time. Just one step above being dead."

"And the others?" Glass asked.

"There are pockets of survivors down in Chasm City. Or what's left of it. Wolves cratered it pretty good when they hit Yellowstone: blew out all the domes and pancaked most of the bigger buildings. Not much left that you'd recognise. But life clings on in dark corners and hideaways. Survivors. Feral gangs. Crimelords. None of it pretty. And none of it capable of lasting much longer. Breathable air, water, food—all running low. People turning sick and hungry. Any idea what people will do to each other, when they turn sick and hungry?"

"The place I came from had its hardships," I said.

"I bet it did, Stinky. I bet you sometimes went as long as a day between hot meals."

"You don't know me, Snowdrop," I said warningly.

"And you don't know any of us," she replied.

Glass said nothing. I wondered what she was thinking, and how warm and friendly was the reunion she was anticipating with her associates.

CHAPTER ELEVEN

The Overlook was a large room with a stepped floor, numerous seats and tables, and a set of vast angled windows stretched across one wall. Beyond the windows was a grey gloom, hard to resolve in any detail, but with faint suggestions of depth and slow, grinding movement.

A woman stood with her back to us, facing the window. She was tall and imperious in her stance. She had her hands laced behind her back, her legs spaced, her shoulders squared.

"Something illicit used to take place here, is our best guess," were the first words to come out of her mouth. "That's why the shielding is so effective. The people who constructed this environment wanted whatever happened within to remain a secret. Whether those activities constituted a consensual sport, or a form of coercive entertainment, is lost to us now. It was all far too long ago. But we should be grateful for their thoroughness. Their security measures have protected us long after the wolves rooted out every other human hiding place in these ruins." Her voice was slow, measured and extremely deep. Even when she fell silent, the lingering force of her words seemed to deny permission to speak. I wanted to say something, but I was dry-throated, my intentions stalling between thought and deed.

She carried on, still not turning around: "I am Lady Arek. You may call me that. I have had other names, some longer, some shorter, but this one satisfies me for now. My mother was a soldier, my father a revolutionary. I was conceived within the influence of the Hades matrix and carried to term in the artificial womb of a half-sane Conjoiner whose name means 'damage' in a tongue now long forgotten. I carry within me traces of all my antecedents, including those who passed forever into the Hades matrix. I am therefore both a scientist and a scholar. I have lived a hundred human lives and felt the death agonies of a thousand civilisations lost to the Inhibitors. I have seen worlds burn and suns shrivel. I have walked on bones and breathed the dust of the dead. I have wept. Some think me insane, others that I might be a goddess. I am neither of those

144

things, but I am most certainly not to be underestimated." She began to turn. "You will not wrong me, will you? Or disappoint me? I would caution against it."

The shorter, squatter figure who had been standing next to the woman, also with his back to us, said: "So you know, this is her light, easy-going side."

Lady Arek had turned to us. I saw a human woman, with nothing about her to suggest any obvious genetic or prosthetic augmentation. Yet authority blasted off her like a cold, shrieking wind, finding every loose chink in my soul. I had never been in the presence of another person with such a commanding will.

I could not guess her biological age, but I sensed that she had taken no steps to make herself appear youthful. There were lines around her mouth and eyes; a hollowness under her chin. Her hair was black turning to grey, and she wore it combed back from her forehead, without ostentation, and secured by a plain clasp that I had seen when she faced the window. Her deep-set eyes were pale and piercing, though, and all the more striking for the plainness of her features. The manner of her was judicial: as if any ornamentation or vanity would have been not only out of place, but disrespectful to her station. Only her coat offset the impression of severity. It was long-hemmed, high-collared, and marked in blue, red and white with a cross-shaped motif, imprinted diagonally across her back. Beneath it she wore a dark tunic, trousers and boots.

I wanted to speak for myself. But Lady Arek's gaze exerted a squeezing pressure on my windpipe. It took an immense effort to overcome that paralysing influence.

"I was under the impression Glass wanted me for something."

Lady Arek looked at Glass without answering me. "Are you certain of his identity?"

"As I told Snowdrop, the markers confirm it."

Lady Arek's companion was another hyperpig. He had turned around as well, regarding me doubtfully. From halfway across the room he wrinkled his already well-wrinkled snout and wafted a hand in front of it. "He stinks."

"Old-man stink, love," Snowdrop said. She was with us, but standing back with a certain deference to the commanding figure in the multicoloured coat.

"I know old-man stink, Snow. But he doesn't smell like Clavain did."

"He's not the same man," Glass clarified.

"I'm not even sure he's the same species." Pinky came closer. He was short, broad, pugnacious, and very obviously an old pig. There were scars

145

as well as wrinkles, vying for space with each other. His left ear was little more than a fleshy nub, as if most of it had been ripped away. He had a sour smell to him, something lingering on his breath. I had not said a word to him, but I already felt as it I had crossed some line of invisible etiquette, failing to satisfy his expectations in the matter of some arcane, punctilious formality. "Don't look like the old man, either. Looks like something the old man would have chewed up and spat out." His pink-tinged eyes narrowed. "What's your game, exactly? Why'd you let Glass think you're someone you're not?"

"There's no game," Glass said. "He is the sibling. No great familial resemblance should be expected, either. They were of different ages, before centuries of interplanetary and interstellar war took them on different trajectories, through vastly different subjective time intervals." I watched her, thinking how odd and pleasing it was to see Glass on the defensive, being forced to explain herself. "He is Warren Clavain. His older memories are reconsolidating. He is coming back to the truth of what he is, in all its glorious ugliness."

"We shall verify," Lady Arek declared, nodding slightly. "I do not doubt your essential account, Hourglass. You will have conducted the necessary biometric audits: you are nothing if not thorough. But there will be no harm in verification, using our independent genetic samples."

"They will establish consanguinity."

"They will have to, because no other outcome is tolerable."

Pinky sidled even closer. He was measuring me up as if I were some dusty artefact left over at the end of an auction, something no one wanted. "Not sure what I want to believe less. That he's an impostor who's hoodwinked us all. Or that he really is the old man's brother."

Lady Arek looked down at her companion. "Why would you not want to credit the latter?"

"Because if those blood checks of yours prove reliable, we're really fucked."

Lady Arek looked a little disconcerted by this outburst. "How so, Pinky?"

"Look at the evidence. He might be cut from the same cloth as the old man. But the way he's standing there, shivering in his boots, letting Glass push him around like a sack of old meat...can't even find the balls to speak for himself?" He dismissed me. "He's nothing."

"He is all we have," Lady Arek said.

"I am...Miguel de Ruyter," I said, forcing out each word like a hard, jagged stone. "That's what I know. All I know. I didn't ask for this, and I don't know the man you seem to think was my brother." But, needled by the pig's assessment of me, I plumped my chest out and jutted my chin

146

forward. "But that's your problem, not mine. My business begins and ends with Glass."

"Ooh, tough guy," Pinky said. "And the nature of that business?"

"Killing her," I said.

Glass made a dismissive sniffing sound. Pinky turned away, sneering his disregard. Snowdrop was silent. The guards, Cater and Omori, brooded. Only Lady Arek said: "And what if she is too valuable to be allowed to die, Clavain?"

I frowned. The eyes were as sharp and cold as ever, but some of their effect was attenuating through exposure. I thought of the men who developed an increased tolerance for snake venom, through being bitten repeatedly.

"You called her Hourglass just now. That wasn't a slip."

"The name reflects her nature," Lady Arek answered crisply. "Like me, she is a Demi-Conjoiner."

"A what?"

"You know of Conjoiners, if only from second-hand intelligence. Demi-Conjoiners have all the usual gifts of their kind, but few of the restraints. We are none of us alike. Some of us came about by design, some by happenstance."

"And what of Glass?"

"They found her, grievously injured, left for dead by her own supposed allies during a compromised military operation. With grace and kindness—and not a little self-interest—the Conjoiners took her into their compound and rebuilt her broken mind using experimental techniques. Since she was essentially a new person at that point, with only the thinnest threads still binding her to the past, they gave her a new name. It was not uncommon among Conjoiners to adopt forms relating to timepieces, or components thereof. Clepsydra. Remontoire. Hourglass. That is her true name. But she prefers the shortened form, imagining it distances her from her origin and nature."

I looked at Glass. "Is this true? After everything, you're a Conjoiner?"

"I am no more a Conjoiner than Lady Arek is," Glass replied. "Their methods touched us. I was useful to them, once. But that doesn't make me one of them."

"You travel alone," I acknowledged. "Unusual for a Conjoiner, from what I've gathered. They can't handle isolation from their brothers and sisters. It's worse than any sensory deprivation we can imagine."

"Speak for yourself," Lady Arek said. "But you are correct about Hourglass: she is different, as am I. Better to think of her as an engineered instrument, a military tool. She was designed to act independently of the

147

mother nest, without the neural support framework of other Conjoiners. A sociopath, by their standards. But useful, in certain situations. They needed an assassin: an agent of death. She became the very personification. Her name: Death's timekeeper. Her ship: Death's implement. *The hourglass in her hand, her scythe by her side, the Mistress Death leads them on.* Even her face: skull-pale, a mask that both conceals and illuminates her nature. She is a work of art as much as a weapon."

"And you?" I asked, feeling an unexpected bristling protectiveness towards my captor, the very woman I had sworn to kill. I hated Glass, but I hated hearing her belittled even more. "You're better, are you?"

"I contain multitudes," Lady Arek said. "Hourglass is defined by her Conjoinerhood. For me, it is merely a facet." But she dipped her face, some tiny increment of severity dropping away from it. "Hourglass has been effective, in the long run. You are testament to that. And we still have need of her. You will not hurt her, Clavain, nor attempt to. You are useful to me as well, but not irreplaceable."

"Well," I said, forcing a smile. "Now that we've got the warm civilities out of the way..."

Lady Arek met my remark with indifference. "Have you immediate needs, after your journey?"

"I don't even know what you want with me, or what Glass has already done. She mentioned stones. Gideon stones, whatever the hell they are."

"She hasn't told you?"

"I told him as little as he needed," Glass said. "There was no point dwelling on the significance of the stones until I had confirmation that they were in our possession." Some boldness returned to her. "Are they, Lady Arek? You've had six years. Tell me you haven't been sitting around doing nothing all that time."

Pinky dipped a stubby finger into what remained of his ear. "This is where it gets complicated, boys and girls."

Snowdrop moved nearer to his side. She reached for his hand, touching it for an instant.

"Have you, or haven't you, secured the stones?" Glass persisted.

"Secured is an elastic concept," Lady Arek returned. "The stones have been extracted from the wreck at the bottom of the chasm. Nine in all: sufficient for our needs."

"What wreck?" I asked.

"Someone please enlighten him," Lady Arek said, touching a hand to her brow as if she might swoon from exasperation.

Glass angled the white mask of her face to mine. Her black eyes swam in pools of deeper blackness. *The Mistress Death.* Something was

148

battling within her. She enjoyed enlightening me about anything. But she did not enjoy being given orders by the effortlessly superior Lady Arek.

"An alien vehicle lodged itself at the base of the chasm millions of years ago. For years, before the wolves came, it was an open secret among some of the factions within the city. They even extracted the occupant of this vehicle, and coerced it into...well, that's another story. But the technology remained buried under hard-packed rubble and the enormous pressure and toxicity of the chasm's base. Hard to reach, harder to extract. No one managed it in all the living years of the city." She cocked her head at the other woman. "But Lady Arek arrived with the tools and the expertise. She was meant to obtain armouring devices, the so-called Gideon stones, for the purposes of our larger mission."

"Did she?" I asked.

"Yes, did she?" Glass echoed.

"I said nine have been extracted. That is not to say that nine are in our immediate possession." Lady Arek regarded my captor, the Demi-Conjoiner about whom I now knew a tiny bit more. "We have one. You shall be shown it."

"One?" Glass queried.

"I believe my diction was clear enough."

Glass nodded, accepting this news as a teacher might accept a poor excuse for late homework. For the first time I had a sense of the balance shifting between these two antagonistic allies, Glass seeing her chance to press a temporary advantage. "And the other eight? You're going to tell me where they are?"

"In Chasm City, or the ruins thereof."

Glass made an impatient snapping gesture with her fingers. "Give me the location. *Scythe* is atmosphere-capable and still has a full weapons load."

"If it were that easy, Hourglass, if it were a question of mere brutality, do you not imagine we would have already secured the remaining eight?" Lady Arek breathed in through her nostrils. "There is a difficulty."

"What kind?" I asked.

"Me," said Pinky, spreading his arms magnanimously. "I'm the sticking point. I'm the reason she doesn't have the other eight stones. And you want to know why?" He did not wait for an answer. "It's because she likes me too much. Somewhere beneath that scary born-in-a-neutron-star space-goddess exterior there is actually a beating human heart."

"I won't send him to die," Lady Arek said. "Not for eight stones. Not for any stones."

"Damned right no one sends him to die," Snowdrop said, and closed her hand around his again.

Snowdrop was charged with showing us to our rooms. Even Glass accepted the wisdom of this arrangement, since it was far too much fuss to keep coming and going from *Scythe* without good reason. Besides, there were many rooms, and (as I discovered) they were surprisingly well appointed.

"We didn't furnish them," Snowdrop said, keen to make this point as we were led through tunnels. "This rock is much as we found it, except for the extra security arrangements we put in around the lock. Lady Arek mentioned that this place might have been illicit." The hood was pushed all the way back now, allowing her hair to spill down onto her gown and shoulders in loose, colourless strands. "I think she's right. It was a gaming arena, built around a central core where various contests could be held."

"The grey space beyond the windows in Overlook?" I asked.

"Yes, and I'll show you a little more of it after you've settled in. We'll eat later, and then you'll probably want to rest. Tomorrow, I'll give you the tour."

"I'd like that."

She looked at me doubtfully. "Really? It's a miserable, fog-filled rock floating in space. Provided I could take Pinky with me, there are about a million places I'd sooner be than here."

"You forget that for the last few decades I've seen almost nothing but the caves of Sun Hollow. A change of scenery...any scenery...it reminds us of what we've lost, and what we've still to lose, if we're not careful." I stroked my fingers against the rough-hewn wall, thinking of the fingers that had gone before my own. "This place only existed because there was a society beyond it, a civilisation of people and other worlds. The mere fact of it is something marvellous."

Snowdrop made an equivocal noise. "It's been useful to us, that I won't deny. But what they got up to in here wasn't very nice."

"I suppose you have some idea of what it was for?"

"There are some giveaways. The inner core, the arena, is very well shielded in addition to the precautions built into the rock as a whole. We think various sports took place there, and the rooms were for the spectators and bidders. It seems likely that some of the wealthy came with champions of their own: sponsored talent. Highly augmented warriors, with a high degree of cybernetic enhancement. Pampered prize fighters—willing participants, to an extent."

Glass said: "But not all of them?"

"From the evidence we've gleaned, it seems that, on occasion, having a willing participant wasn't enough to keep the spectators engaged. So they spiced things up by bringing in an outsider."

I asked: "An unwilling participant?"

"We can only speculate. What is clear is that the shielding in that arena would have been very hard for a distress signal to penetrate, even one sent by a Demarchist, Conjoiner, Ultra or Skyjack. No neural alerts would have got through it. And the challenges that were deployed against these champions...again, what we've seen of them point to a deliberate attempt to design weapons and traps that are inimical to those with a high degree of cybernetic augmentation. Neural weapons. Nanotechnic weapons. Things that would have made the Melding Plague look like an itch. We think they captured these poor souls, then let them loose in the core while laying bets on how long they'd last."

I shook my head. "Just when I think I've imagined everything people can do to each other."

"Wait until you hear about the Swinehouse," Snowdrop said.

I thought back to the conversation in the Overlook. "Is that something to do with Pinky?"

"In a manner of speaking."

"I don't think he really took to me."

"See it from his side. He was with the old man when he died. The old man trusted him with everything, including being the hand that wielded the blade that killed him. He looked up to him when the old man was alive, and tried to walk in his shoes when he was gone. Hard, for a hyper-pig. And now you show up in the old man's place."

I did not know whether to agree or disagree. "If it's any consolation, I'm not trying to measure up to any man Pinky may have known. I don't even claim to be that man's brother! Glass and Lady Arek can say what they like. I know my past."

"You know what you think you know," Snowdrop cautioned. We had arrived somewhere: a pair of adjoining rooms. Glass in one, me in the other. "We still need to run those genetic verifications. They kept back tissue samples from the old man. Probably Rose will be coming down shortly."

"You're not even sure if she's coming down or not?" Glass asked, plainly resentful that her word alone was not being trusted with regards to my identity.

"You'll see," Snowdrop said.

It might have been two hundred years since the room last hosted a paying spectator. Nothing about the furnishings, though, suggested any comparable passage of time. Everything was clean, and neither scuffed, faded nor stained. The floors and walls were fleeced in grey and ruby, all other surfaces mirrored (and probably reconfigurable, if I had the means to control them) and the bed was enormous. So were armchairs, settees, cabinets and writing desks. They were decorated with inlaid designs showing various exemplars of athletic prowess, martial combat, bloody dismemberment and death. A bathroom as large as my entire office in Sun Hollow, tiled in shades of scarlet and bone and with vein-and-artery drainage runnels worked into the floor. Power, light and warmth. And all of these amenities to satisfy the tastes of men and women who (I was ready to believe) gladly collaborated in murder for sport. The only grace was that they were all almost certainly dead, and had probably perished in the same orbital firestorms that had turned ten thousand habitats to ash. I hoped their fun and games had been worth it.

If the room allowed me to sleep and wash, it was enough. The rest of it I could ignore. I was clean enough, despite Pinky's protestations, and far too confused and anxious for sleep to be an option. But I was hungry, and curious, and wondering when either might be sated.

There was a knock at the door, followed immediately by the door's opening. A human woman came into the room, pushing a trolley. I sat down on the bed, watching her as she propelled the trolley softly and silently across the grey fleece.

"Are you Rose?"

"No. Why would you think I was?"

"Glass said that Rose was probably coming down to see me."

"That's not what she said, no and no. Yes. She would have said Probably Rose is coming to see you."

"Then you are...Probably Rose." I nodded, as if all this made instant sense. "Of course. How silly of me to have called you by completely the wrong name."

She was middle-aged, by my reckoning, with a narrow chin, pointed nose and a lick of black hair combed across her brow. In place of her left eye there was a pattern of star-shaped stitches, drawing her skin drum-tight over an underlying emptiness. She wore an austere grey outfit of tunic and trousers, with her hands gloved. She wheeled the trolley to my side and whisked away a green covering, revealing racks of medical equipment and drugs, nothing of which I had seen before but nothing of which looked entirely alien and unfamiliar.

"Roll up your sleeve."

"Why?"

"So we can tell who you are, yes."

152

"I know who I am," I said patiently, as Probably Rose prepared a syringe, her hands shaking more than I might have expected. "Nothing you can do or say will change it."

She lifted the syringe up to her eye, the needle wavering perilously close.

"They don't care."

"I'm sorry?"

"I'm saying, yes, they don't care what you think you are, so long as, yes, they know, yes and verily, that you are what they think you are, yes and yes." Still holding the syringe, she used her other hand to slap the side of her head palm first, not violently, but in the form of some mild personal chastisement. "Yes and verily! Yes, yes! Your sleeve."

I rolled up my sleeve.

"Why wouldn't they care?"

"Because, yes, you're useful to them regardless of what you think you are. Yes and verily!" Curiously, her hand became steadier as she advanced the needle towards my arm. She drew a small quantity of blood, efficiently and nearly painlessly, and then injected the syringe's contents into some kind of analysis device on the trolley. Machinery hummed and whirred, a centrifugal separator making the trolley wobble and the other items on it clink together. "But you will remember, yes. You're the one, yes. Yes, yes and yes." A string of lights was appearing on the analysis device, illuminating it from left to right. "See it, yes? Genetic correlation. Clavain left samples on Ararat. Close familial cross-match. Definitely you."

"I'm not..."

Probably Rose took a tissue scraping from inside my mouth "Almost redundant. High statistical significance from the blood alone. But blood can be swapped, so need to be sure, yes and yes." Her hands were again shaking as she dipped the sample into another analysis receptacle, but they had been steady enough when she was extracting the tissue. "From this, just this alone, yes, high likelihood you were born on Earth, Northern Europe, natural conception and parental gene mixing, early-mid twenty-second. Which would make you...yes, seven hundred years old, calendrical, yes and verily."

I laughed aloud at the absurdity of what she had just said. "I would know if I were seven hundred years old, Rose."

"Probably Rose. Not Rose. Always Probably Rose."

"All right," I said, accepting her preference. "Probably Rose it is. What... happened to you, Probably Rose? How did you come here? Were you a doctor before?"

"Not a doctor. Not a doctor." She was preparing another instrument now, resembling a magnifying glass. She indicated for me to extend my arm and swept the glass along it, frowning intently as images and data streams played across the semi-transparent glass. "Glass said you'd had it changed, yes."

"Glass can say what she wants."

"See those bone growths? Markers for osseo-integration. You lost the arm, then had a mechanical graft." She nodded to herself. "Fits. Wartime prosthetics, Martian theatre, first Conjoiner war."

"You just took blood from that arm."

"You had it regrown. Later methods. Maybe more than once. Multiple basal nucleation sites." She swung the hoop onto my face. "Mixmaster genetic watermarking. Same with the eye. Lost it, replaced it, regrown it—several times over. Good match. Hard to tell."

"Glass has sold you a story. Now you're just seeing what you want to see."

"Run the same tests on yourself if you like. Yes, and yes. And verily. Nothing to hide. But you'll come to the same conclusion." She put away the scanner. "Still need medicine, whoever you are. Do your bones ache?"

"It'd be quicker if I told you which parts of me don't ache."

"Glass's accelerated rejuvenation, yes. Tearing apart bones, musculature, nervous tissue, rebuilding. Hard on you. These will help." She was preparing a concoction from the coloured vials on one of the racks, pouring a little of each into a small beaker. "And mnemonovores mean headaches. Ripping and reassembling synaptic connections. Like digging up the pavements of a city, putting in new drains and cables. Will get better, with time. But for now, drink."

Since I had nothing to lose, I took the beaker she had filled and sipped at it cautiously then with steady enthusiasm, and then swigged it with reckless abandon.

"I'll bet the medical systems on Glass's ship were at least as good as anything you have here."

"Yes, and verily."

"So why didn't Glass bother to give me something like this, just to take the edge off?"

"Glass doesn't care what you feel. How you feel. Just that you live."

I finished the beaker, tilting the empty receptacle in the direction of Probably Rose. "But you did, seemingly. To you, in that case. Unless you've just talked me into drinking a beaker full of poison." I watched her as she took the beaker from my fingers and placed it into an autoclave. "Did you know Glass before now?"

"No. Not crossed paths. Only knew what Lady Arek and Pinky said."

"Then you're another of the people who were already here, in this rock?"

"No. Not here, yes and verily." She cuffed herself again. Something was not quite right in her head, I supposed. Some neurological gears kept sticking, or going out of mesh. It explained the strangeness of her speech patterns, the shakiness of her hands, perhaps even the twitching self-admonishment, a kind of tic that reset herself. "Down in Chasm City. In the Swinehouse, yes."

"What was the Swinehouse?" I asked gently.

"Bad. Very bad, yes, and verily. Bad, bad. Yes!" She cuffed herself twice, and I felt bad that I had made her revisit something painful. "But I got out, yes. I got out. Probably Rose got out."

"What happened there?"

"Not what happened." She slapped herself hard this time, three times in rapid succession "What *is* happening. What happens. What still goes on. Her Swineness! Yes. Yes! Yes!"

I reached out to grab her wrist before she hit herself again.

"I'm sorry, Probably Rose."

Slowly I let go of her, and she rubbed her wrist where I had seized it too firmly, even as I meant to be kind.

She looked into me with that single wondering eye. "Are you a bad man, Warren Clavain?"

She had called me by that name and I had no desire to acknowledge it. But if Glass had driven a crack into my certainty, initiating a process of self-examination and reidentification, being in the presence of this other damaged soul had blasted that crack into a deep, widening fissure. It wasn't that I believed the evidence presented by the machines on the trolley. But I did believe Probably Rose.

"I don't know," I answered, trembling in sympathy. "And it frightens me what I'll find when I do."

CHAPTER TWELVE

We were called back to the Overlook for dinner. A long table had appeared since I was last there, with its major axis pointed at the slanted observation windows. There was still not much to see through them except suggestions of some formidably jagged terrain, crags and prominences and ravines wrapped all the way around the inner core, but which was still mostly wreathed in mist and darkness.

Lady Arek stood at the table's head, with her back to the window. Everyone else present was already seated: a dozen or so on either side. It was the first time we had seen most of them. Pinky and Snowdrop were nearest to Lady Arek, but seated opposite each other. Two facing chairs were left unoccupied, then came Cater, Omori, and Probably Rose, and then a weary-looking ensemble of pigs and humans, all of whom carried at least a scar or two.

"Be seated, please," Lady Arek said, making a formal, stiff-armed gesture in the direction of the empty chairs. "I imagine you will want to eat, but even if you don't, I have something you will want to see."

We took our places with a certain awkwardness, Glass eyeing me, me eyeing Glass, neither of us sure of our roles. Lady Arek poured some wine into our glasses. "They left us with the evidence of some extremely questionable activities taking place here," she commented. "They also left the contents of several well-stocked cellars, mostly untouched. Should our ethics forbid us from partaking, do you think?"

I lifted the glass and sniffed the bouquet. "My instinct would be to say...to hell with ethics."

"Then we are of one mind, Warren." Lady Arek sat down and scraped her chair forward. "I must apologise for a certain reticence upon our first meeting. I had my doubts about your nature, and by extension I had doubts about Glass's judgement. I wondered if you could really be the man we sought. You seemed, on the face of it...somewhat unpromising material."

"But he is who Glass says he is," Probably Rose said, looking around at the rest of the table. "I've run the tests, all the tests. Yes and verily. This man was born in an insular territory of Northern Europe, Western Palearctic Sector, Earth, called—"

"My guarantee should have been sufficient," Glass interrupted.

"My dear Hourglass..." Lady Arek extended her hand in a show of charitableness. "You are right, as I should have always known you would be. Your methods may be unconventional, even reckless, but you have always shown attention to detail."

Glass shifted in her seat. It was hard to tell whether she considered herself criticised or praised. "Say what you will about my methods. But I wouldn't have sat around for six years doing nothing."

"Matters are complicated," Lady Arek said.

"Nothing's complicated when you're willing to use the necessary force. Unless you lack the nerve."

"Oh, the nerve isn't lacking," Pinky said. He took a quick glug from whatever it was that he was drinking: some clear spirit, rather than wine. "If force was the answer..."

"Then why aren't we in possession of all nine stones?" Glass demanded.

I took a cautious sip of wine and set down my glass. "Lady Arek, Glass? This isn't helping. It's not helping me and I rather doubt it's helping any of your friends. Who, incidentally, I have yet to be introduced to."

"You expecting it to be a long acquaintance, Stink?" Pinky asked.

I met his gaze and answered as reasonably as I could. "The truth is I have no idea. But I thought a little civility wouldn't go amiss, until we've all agreed on the next step—whatever that is."

Lady Arek sighed. "You are right, Warren: I've been a less than perfect host. And you have every right to know your new allies. As does Hourglass." She extended a hand and began naming the figures who took up the other places. "Bruno, Yilin, Chersini, Maude..." Until the names washed over me and I could only nod, trusting that it would not be too long before I committed them to memory.

"From what I've gathered," I said, "some of you were on this rock before Lady Arek arrived, and some of you have come up from Yellowstone. But the navigational beacon we found showed no ship movements other than the coming and going of Lady Arek's shuttle. Those of you who arrived here from Chasm City must have arrived at the same time, on that last flight six years ago."

"That's correct," said the one called Chersini, a male pig who held a long-bladed knife in a leather-gloved hand, scratching the tip against the table as he scraped an outline around his other hand. "We came up with the stone, those of us who made it out. Lady Arek and Pinky saved us.

157

Isn't one of us that won't carry that gratitude to our graves. Unless you were there, you won't know how bad it was."

Pinky said quietly: "Lady Arek wanted to take the shuttle back down, to scoop up another load of survivors. I overruled her. Twenty was all we managed. Three didn't make it through the first week, even with Probably Rose doing her best."

"You were correct to overrule me," Lady Arek said. "Even now, I shudder to think how close I came to making that error. We had been lucky to make the movements we did without alerting the wolves. Another flight in and out of that atmosphere would almost certainly have breached their triggering thresholds." Her fierce eyes latched onto me, and again I felt their intimidating scrutiny. "Then all you would have for dinner company would be ghosts, Sky Marshall."

"First a new name, then a title. I suppose I'm going up in the world."

"Count your blessings," Lady Arek said. Then she reached forward and lifted the domed metal lid off the plate that was set before her. "Behold, the Gideon stone."

In the middle of the plate was a lumpy, random-looking thing that appeared to be a half-fused nugget of ruby and chromium. It was larger than a fist, smaller than a human skull. It gave off a soft scarlet glow, underlighting Lady Arek's face.

Lady Arek picked it up in her fingertips. She passed it to me, dropping it into my grip. I closed my fingers around it. The Gideon stone was cosmically cold, heavy and dense, as if I had just palmed a lump of frozen spacetime, folded and curdled in on itself to the quivering point of singularity.

"It's active," Lady Arek said. "It has its own energy source, its own activation protocols. We can control the stone to some degree, interfacing native human technology, integrating it into our defence systems. But the stone will always have a will of its own, its own moods and temperaments. Squeeze it tighter."

"Why?" I asked.

"Just do it, Stink," said Pinky.

I redoubled my grip, humouring my hosts. I was expecting something to happen and when the stone glowed brighter, its scarlet light bleeding out between my fingers, I wisely avoided dropping it. Then I felt a sort of cold, eruptive ooze emerging from the stone, as if I had cracked it and now its soft, liquid contents were spilling out.

The stone was intact; I had not crushed it. But something was definitely emanating from it. A pearly film was gloving my hand, creeping up towards my wrist. I felt nothing: no cold prickle or itch of contact. It was

158

as if the film adhered close to the contours of my hand without making direct contact. A scale-like tessellation showed itself in the pearly film: hexagonal platelets jostling against each other.

"Chersini," said Lady Arek. "Bring the vice."

Chersini scraped back his chair, reached for something beneath it and came round to my back. Before I could move Cater and Omori had me pinned down, unable to move or lift my arm where it rested against the table, my hand now lost within a faceted mitten of that spreading film.

"Harm him," Glass said, "and I'll send a direct neural command to *Scythe* to flood this entire complex with broad-spectrum nerve gas."

"That would have the slight drawback of also killing you," Lady Arek said.

Glass looked unconcerned. "I'd accelerate my mental clock rate enough to enjoy my last few seconds."

"He shan't be harmed." Lady Arek nodded at Chersini. "We need him to unlock the riddle of Charybdis. But a demonstration of the stone's ability will make my point more readily than words ever could. Do it."

I writhed, but Cater and Omori had me immobilised. Rationally, I did not think it likely that Lady Arek would have any interest in seeing me injured. But I would have defied anyone to cling to rationality as they watched their hand being inserted between the two flat planes of a mechanical vice: the heavy item Chersini had kept beneath his chair.

Chersini tightened the vice by means of a handle. It went around twice, then met the resistance of my hand.

"As tight as you can," Lady Arek said.

Grunting with the effort, Chersini completed another turn of the handle. I had no doubt of the strength he was exerting: I could see it in the muscles and tendons of his forearm, bulging through the fabric of his sleeve.

But I felt nothing. The vice should have crushed my bones, but all I felt was a cold tingling. The pearly membrane that had come out of the Gideon stone was licking around the two jaws of the vice, enclosing them.

"Harder," Lady Arek demanded.

Chersini growled back: "Any harder and I'll shatter the vice."

"I think," Glass said, "that we may consider your point demonstrated, Lady Arek."

"I concur," I said.

Chersini eased back the jaws of the vice until it could be released from my hand. The membrane clung to it, then relinquished its interest. It settled down around my hand again, but with the extreme edge of it still inching up my forearm.

"Armouring skein," Lady Arek said. "A defensive technology known to the Grubs and carried by the member of their civilisation who ended up crashed beneath Chasm City. We have no sense of how it works. We cannot even determine the consistency of that field, whether it's a form of mass-energy or some clever, self-organising origami of spacetime at the Planck granularity. All we know is that we can make it work for us. Release your grip on the stone."

I did, watching as the membrane slithered back down my hand, losing its faceted texture and puddling eagerly back into the stone. The scarlet glow damped down again, the stone returning to dormancy.

I massaged my wrist, more out of reflex than necessity. "Really, you could have just told me."

"But now you know," Lady Arek said. "Which will help you, when you have to trust your life to it."

"What gets through it? When we meet the Inhibitors, they won't be coming at us with knives."

"Nothing in our conventional arsenal. Nothing that we've been able to test using our resources inside this rock. Cutting tools, projectiles, medium-yield laser and boser discharges: nothing breaks the field. Extreme pressure, extreme heat: nothing touches it."

Glass made a scoffing sound. "Call me when you need some real weapons."

"The armouring skein is strong, but not invulnerable," Lady Arek replied. "That we know. If the Grubs were in possession of an infinitely powerful defensive technology, one of their kind would likely not have crashed on Yellowstone. It must have limits. If we breach those limits, we may lose the Gideon stone, or even destroy ourselves. That, we must not risk. Given these dangers, the only testing must be under conditions of fire."

"Do you think this can resist Inhibitor-level weaponry?" I asked.

"We cannot assume so. Perhaps it will offer short-term protection, but that is not what we are depending on. What you just saw—what you just experienced—was a demonstration of the Gideon stone's ability to protect against extreme pressure. A mechanical vice, in this case, but it could just as easily have been the crush of a planetary atmosphere. An object—say, a ship—could endure a great deal of pressure with the assistance of Gideon stones."

"What sort of pressure?"

"Multiple gigapascals," she answered me. "Many hundreds of thousands of atmospheres. That, at least, is what we must be prepared for, depending on factors yet to be decided."

I nearly laughed. "Dear God."

"I do not deny that the task is not without its challenges. But the thing we seek—the thing that the stones will help us find—may well be located at those pressures. We must be prepared."

"But you've only got the one stone. Is that going to be enough?"

Lady Arek shook her head once. "Unfortunately not. The armouring skein has a limited effectiveness, a range of extent. One stone would provide for a small object—say a suit, or a missile, but not a ship."

"Then you'd better have an idea how we get the other stones," Glass said.

Lady Arek looked at Pinky. "Tell them, if you will. The condensed version."

Pinky looked through me rather than at me. Then at Glass. "We had an ally in the city, who helped secure the nine stones. Unfortunately someone in his organisation betrayed him. Before we could get out of Chasm City, we were jumped by the Swine Queen. He was killed, and she has the other eight stones."

"Is she...a pig?" I ventured.

"No." Pinky's stare impaled me. "Not a pig."

"A number of the people you see here, including Probably Rose, were either prisoners of the Swine Queen, or forced to work within the Swine-house. Some had escaped before we arrived, while others got out during the confusion and chaos of the operation. But many remain, and their lives must be considered in any future plans."

I asked: "Will she give up the remaining stones?"

"Not if threatened," Lady Arek said. "In fact, threatening her is the worst thing we could do. From her location, she would only need a few moments to dispose of the stones entirely, scattering them back to the base of the chasm, where we would have no hope of recovering them. That rules out any use of force, including surprise attacks." She directed a forbidding look at Glass. "Even nerve gas. We have run every scenario. Even if we considered the lives of her prisoners to be expendable, no measure works fast enough to guarantee the preservation of the stones."

"There is a way," Pinky said. He finished off what was left of the spirit. "I'm the price she's willing to accept. For me, she'll hand over the eight remaining stones."

"What do you mean to her?" I asked.

"We do not discuss this," Lady Arek said.

"Perhaps it's time we did." Pinky shrugged, the oiled leather patches of his tunic squeaking with the motion. "The Swine Queen got a good look at me before. Knows what I am: the oldest pig alive. That makes me

161

valuable to her. Pig meat's rare, and I'm the rarest kind of all. She wants to cook and eat me."

I shook my head in utter disbelief.

"She can't intend that."

"You bet your life she does, Stinky."

"It's what she does, yes," said Probably Rose. "Keeps pigs. Lots of pigs. Chained up, yes and yes. Fed and fed. Then she cuts them up, a bit a time. And feeds them to the swineherds, yes and verily." She looked down at her hands, as if gripped by sudden shame. "I was…her doctor. The one she kept, to keep them alive. Yes, and yes." She shuddered, but instead of Probably Rose cuffing herself, Omori took her by the shoulders and hugged her until she was still. Even Chersini, the pig with the knife, moved to comfort her.

"It's abominable," I said.

"It's what she does," Pinky answered indifferently. "And I'm the one prize she hasn't got her hands on. Oh, it's not just the way I'll taste, though that'll be part of it. I'm symbolic. A pig with real history, don't you know. I had a reputation in that city, long ago. Makes me totemic. Take me down, and she doesn't just crush the hopes of the pigs left alive, she also sends a message to her rivals. 'Look what I did, everyone! I gobbled up the oldest living pig and robbed Lady Arek of her loyalist deputy.' She'll tape my screams, pipe them on repeat out to the rest of the city—and whenever anyone doubts her steel, or thinks they can make a move on her, I'll get a replay, just for old times' sake."

"A pretty little impasse," Glass said quietly.

"That's all you've got to say? An impasse?" I asked, staggered by her detachment.

She replied coldly: "I merely state the practicalities. Lady Arek will not countenance sending Pinky to his death. Therefore we do not obtain the stones. Forever and ever." She narrowed her eyes in the direction of the other Demi-Conjoiner. "Might I ask: was there ever a plan, or were you just hoping reality would go away?"

"The plan is to wait," Lady Arek answered, with a thunderous calm. "Factional warfare is rife in the ruins of Chasm City. The Swine Queen's position grows tenuous, as Pinky has indicated. Sooner or later she will overreach herself, or be usurped by one of her deputies. Then we shall reopen negotiations."

"Well, that's fine, then," Glass said. "The wolves are at our door, the fires are going out, but we'll just wait." She stiffened, an idea presenting itself. "I brought chequers. Would anyone like a game of chequers? Or we could play rock, paper, scissors, extinction."

162

"Shut up, Glass," I mouthed.

"At last, a useful contribution from Stinky."

I nodded at the pig. "There must be a way to get what we need. If the handover were to proceed, how would it happen?"

"No..." Lady Arek began.

But Pinky was at least willing to entertain my train of thought. "We set up the deal via optical laser, when the weather window allows. Might take weeks. Agree the deal. Then we go down with the shuttle. Verify that the goods are authentic—on both sides—then complete the exchange."

I nodded slowly. "Would she kill you immediately?"

"Not her style. Likes to drag things out, crow over her victories." He fingered the ruin of his ear. "She might want to take another nibble out of me, just for old times' sake. Once you've tasted pig, you don't go back." He smiled at my evident discomfort. "But one thing I'm sure of is that she'd want to make the rest of me last."

I nodded, understanding how close he must have already come to becoming her prize, and what it would mean to go back.

"Are we talking hours, days, longer than that?"

"Pass me a crystal ball and I'll tell you. What are you suggesting?"

I took my time before answering, sensing that I only had one chance to make my point, and that it was likely to be dismissed out of hand.

"If there were a way to go through the motions of the exchange, but still get Pinky back, oughtn't we consider it?" I paused, waiting to be shouted down—or for Glass to encourage me on—but there was only an expectant silence. "We have two ships now, not one. That opens up some possibilities—especially if Glass can operate without detection."

Words were murmured, looks exchanged. Snowdrop seemed to be on the point of saying something, and Pinky seemed equally on the point of silencing her before she began.

"Continue," Lady Arek said.

"You make the exchange and leave with the stones. You get far enough away for there to be no chance of them falling back into the wrong hands. How long would that take?"

"We would only need to be airborne, and out of the immediate range of the Swinehouse's guns. Say, a minute or two after departure." Lady Arek's tone became harder. "Then what?"

"We go in hard with the other ship and extract Pinky. Element of surprise, while the Swine Queen no longer has any hold over the stones."

"No," Lady Arek said, shaking her head. "This is still not feasible. You cannot be blamed for trying, but you do not understand the size of the Swinehouse, the overwhelming disparity in numbers. She has hundreds of armed underlings, and many hundreds more innocent prisoners in chains, waiting to be served. No shock attack, no matter how well mounted, will ever be sufficient. She only needs a moment's warning to kill Pinky, and by the time we go in he could be anywhere inside the Swinehouse."

"Fit him with a tracking implant," I said.

"He will be scanned at the point where we verify the goods. Any concealed weapon or device will be construed as grounds to abort the exchange." She looked disappointed in me, as if she had seen promise, then seen it extinguished. "Do you not think we already considered this, Clavain?"

"There must be a way," I pleaded.

"There might be," Glass said. She paused, enjoying her moment: Lady Arek hanging on her words just as tenaciously as the rest of us.

"Go on," Lady Arek said.

"Inside *Scythe* is an archive of weapons systems, some of them highly specialised. Some of them very old, and barely used. There is . . . a suitable option. A prototype, but well advanced. Synthesised, and used correctly, it could serve as both weapon and tracking facilitator."

"Were you not listening?" Snowdrop asked.

"I was," Glass purred. "The haemoclast is entirely undetectable. Unless your Swine Queen has access to a comparable archive of weapons and countermeasures, she won't be able to find it. This, I guarantee."

Pinky leaned in. "How does it work?"

"The haemoclast is concealed about your person. At an appropriate trigger, it deploys. Anyone near you who has not been marked as an ally or neutral party will die. The effective killing radius is large enough to form a moving bubble, easily sufficient to shield you. You'd merely have to make your way to safety."

"Not much use if I'm tied up and gagged; even less if I'm already turning on a spit."

"The haemoclast can be configured to neutralise restraints."

"It sounds promising," I allowed.

Glass looked pleased with me. "Right answer!"

"No," Snowdrop said firmly, laying her hand over Pinky's. "We're not considering this. We don't know what the hell she's talking about, or how safe it is, or how effective. And meanwhile you'll still be on your own, against hundreds of blood-crazed swineherds."

"We'd agree a rendezvous point," Glass persisted. "Meanwhile, I would go in with *Scythe*'s servitors and a spare suit. The haemoclast will guide me to Pinky. Once I reach him, the suit becomes his armour. We depart."

"No," Snowdrop repeated, but this time with less conviction. It was clear to all of us that every objection she raised would be quietly undermined by Glass.

"If it means a way of obtaining the stones, and not losing Pinky..." I said.

"The choice is simple," Glass said, leaning back. "Act now, secure the objective, be on our way. Or sit and wait for an opportunity that may never come."

"This weapon," I said, Glass turning to me. "If I'm not mistaken, the name you gave it means something like...blood destroyer."

Glass's face creased. "Clever boy."

In the morning Snowdrop came to our rooms and told us to dress warmly and for rough terrain. My room—and I presumed Glass's was the same— had a huge and well-stocked wardrobe, capable of catering to every size and body shape. I put on two pairs of trousers, three underlayers over my upper body, a padded vest and a heavy belted coat with a fur-lined hood, with pockets for gloves and mittens. I found sturdy boots with cleated treads, a good fit over two pairs of socks. Predictably, Glass disdained any clothing beyond the inner suit layer she had been wearing since our arrival.

"You'll catch your death," I said.

"Don't sound so enthusiastic about it."

Snowdrop appraised our arrangements with a disinterested sniff. "Lady Arek wants me to show you the inner core. Your preparations are your own concern: I'm not responsible for any harm you get into in there." Snowdrop was about as well layered as me, with a number of belts, pouches and holsters about her, as well as tools, knives, grapples and a line of rope slung around her shoulder.

"You were the one who said you'd show us around," I said.

"I did," Snowdrop said. "But that was before I got to know you better."

"Then what's the purpose of this, if it isn't a bit of friendly sightseeing?"

Snowdrop glared at me. "You know what, old man? You ask far too many questions."

"There had better be a point to this," Glass said warningly.

"Take it up with your scary half-sister. I'm just doing what she tells me."

"I thought you didn't do orders," I said.

"You're right," she snapped back at me. "I just follow strongly worded suggestions. Good enough for you?"

Knowing when to hold my tongue, at least temporarily, I let Snowdrop lead us through a warren of tunnels and shafts until we were back into the weightless part of the rock, which accounted for most of its volume.

A set of heavy, lock-like doors allowed us to enter the inner core, which was still as gloomy and mist-wreathed as when I had seen it through the observation windows. We were weightless, but not drifting. A series of handholds and guide-lines had been stapled into the face of a crag, and Snowdrop indicated that we should never lose contact with any of these aids. The air was cold and humid, and within a few minutes a clammy chill had worked its way into my clothes. I was glad of the layers I had put on and wondered if Glass was having second thoughts about her insouciance.

We traversed the crag, gradually working around a prominence. There was no real up and down now we were weightless. But the way the rock formations jagged out from the circular walls, grasping towards the middle, made me suspect that the entire core had been designed to be rotated, providing gravity. The Overlook was on an independent axis, though, so it was quite possible that the gravity in the core could be made higher or lower, depending on the wishes of the clients. We could see the Overlook now, looking back towards the way we had come in: a protruding feature on the rim of a slow-grinding wheel, turning against a circular back-plate. The lights were on in the Overlook, a tiny but imperious form regarding us.

"Lady Arek's had time to think about your suggestion, Clavain," Snowdrop said, at last breaking the silence. "She believes there may be some mileage in it, especially when allied to the weapon Glass tells us she can provide."

I shivered. "I don't want to influence any decisions you have to take about the Swine Queen."

"Then why did you suggest the course of action?"

"I thought it was something you might have considered already and wanted to know why it wouldn't be feasible, for my own satisfaction."

"Is he always this bad a liar, Glass?"

"He knows better than to try in my presence. Of course he meant to put that proposal forward. It's the soldier inside him, breaking through to the surface."

"Ready to send another man to his death if it means achieving an objective?"

"He's understood enough to know that we must have the stones."

Snowdrop halted. She was ahead of us, negotiating a crumbling, ledge-like shelf, the mist-cloaked void all around. Despite the absence of gravity my stomach kept turning, convinced that I was on the point of falling. I had not felt this way in the belly of John the Revelator, but that had been an artificial space, made of machinery. The crags and abysses of this tormented landscape snagged ancient parts of my brain, tricking it into thinking that there must be an up and a down.

"Be still," Snowdrop said to us. Slowly she drew a weapon from one of her holsters. The grip was shaped for a pig's hand. She thumbed a safety catch, made lights glimmer in the weapon's dragon-carved muzzle.

Movement caught my eye: something compact, fast and scuttling passing between two shadowed clefts on the next crag over. I tensed, all my expectations undone. I had assumed that the core was abandoned, empty of anything that might harm us.

"I sense it," Glass said. "A machine presence, prickling against my implants."

"It may take a particular interest in you," Snowdrop said, tracking the scuttling form until it disappeared into mist. "We've destroyed most of them, captured others, but there are still a few dozen running loose in here."

"What are they?" I asked.

"Ninecats. Small robot hunter-seeker units, part of the games they used to play in the core."

"Are they dangerous?" I asked.

Snowdrop nodded. "Very much so—don't be fooled by the size. They've also got a very particular lethality where the likes of Glass are concerned. They're drawn to cybernetic systems. The augmented champions who faced them had prosthetics, neural enhancements, built-in weapons, but still the mortality rate was high enough to make for some *very* competitive wagering."

Something flashed into view, much closer. It was on the same formation of rock as us, further along the ledge, and coming closer with a sinuous, scuttling efficiency. It had a featureless, oval, matte-silver body, with fine segmented arms radiating from it, tapering down to needle-like points. It was perhaps a metre across, from arm tip to arm tip. It was impossible to count the arms as they moved, but from the name alone I suspected that there were nine.

Snowdrop let the ninecat come a little closer then blasted it off the crag. I watched it tumble off into the void, legs thrashing. If she had meant to destroy it utterly, she had made a mistake with either her yield or aim. But perhaps destruction had not been her intention.

"Do you still sense them, Glass?" Snowdrop asked.

"Yes. Two in our immediate area, several more at the limits of detection. They have sharp little minds."

"Lady Arek wanted you to see them. After Clavain's suggestion last night, she wonders if they might be useful to the operation." Snowdrop lowered her weapon, but refrained from safing or reholstering it.

"Have you tried to control or reprogram them?"

"With limited success. Lady Arek might have the capability, but—as she would be the first to admit—her experience with military-grade cybernetic systems will never be as thorough as your own. After all, you are one."

Whether this was meant as insult or flattery, Glass was completely unfazed by it. "You say you've captured some?"

"About one hundred and twenty. Some damaged. We keep them locked up very securely, as you can imagine. If they were to break out, they'd very quickly overrun us. We're also reluctant to allow Lady Arek too close to them, in case they hurt her or otherwise find a way into her head."

"I should like to see them."

"Don't overestimate yourself," I warned.

"I tried, but for some reason I keep failing to find my own limits."

"Lady Arek will show you the ninecat cache. If you can override their built-in patterns, they may be useful against the Swinehouse. They can move quickly and slip through very narrow spaces."

"They may be useful. It will depend on the time we have."

"In a day or so Lady Arek will attempt to use the signalling laser to establish dialogue with the Swine Queen. There's no point attempting it until then. The weather is much too impenetrable. There's something else, too."

"Go on," I said.

"We have eyes and ears sprinkled around Yellowstone: sensor motes Lady Arek deployed when she first arrived. Now and then they pick up on wolf activity. Individual cubes are too small to be detected, but when they begin to form into aggregates, our network stands a better chance of seeing them. The ultra-low-frequency alerts have begun to trigger in the last twenty-six hours, and especially since you docked."

"We did nothing," Glass said indignantly.

"Other than create a commotion near that tracking beacon. I'm afraid that may have been all it took. The wolves have been roused to an additional readiness level: cubes are warming up, beginning to aggregate. Some organised movement, precursor flows. Left to itself, and with no other provocation, it will likely die down. That's what always happens. But signalling Yellowstone risks another escalation. Never mind actually going down there, if the Swine Queen agrees to the trade..." Single-handedly, Snowdrop took something from her belt, then offered it to me. "Clip yourself in."

It was a loop of metal with a spring-loaded fastener. Wordlessly I fixed the loop onto my coat, hitching it around the belt. A line ran from the loop, floating loose for the moment. Snowdrop had the other end of it, wrapped around her wrist a few times but otherwise held slackly.

"He's mine," Glass said.

Snowdrop jerked the muzzle at Glass. "Keep out of this."

"What's this about?" I asked.

Snowdrop kicked me away from the crag. I flailed, but within a moment the handholds and wires had already drifted out of reach. I was floating away at about a metre per second, Snowdrop playing out the line as the distance increased.

"I was ready to give you the benefit of the doubt," Snowdrop said, her voice turning hollow and echoing as the space between us increased. "Ready to go along with whatever you brought to the table. But you put that idea in Lady Arek's head. Now she's going to send Pinky down to the Swinehouse, and it's all because of you."

The mist was already clouding my view of Snowdrop and Glass—the latter wisely keeping her distance.

"I wouldn't have proposed it if I didn't think we had a means of making it work. No one's talking about sending Pinky to his death."

"Your conscience is clear, then."

"No! It's not. But this is war. We need those stones."

"They haven't even told you what they need them for."

"They haven't needed to. It's obvious enough to me that we need them to strike back against the wolves. How is for another day."

"That simple?"

"It is, actually. The wolves will find and kill us all eventually. It's just a matter of time. Nowhere's safe, unless we go back to the trees. And maybe even then they won't stop. Without the stones, there's no future. We all die, or our children die, or our grandchildren do."

There was a tug as the line reached its present limit. The mist had closed in almost completely now, offering only furtive glimpses of the crag and the two watchers.

"I could cut you loose now, Clavain. Say it was an accident. Lady Arek can't see a thing from the Overlook, not with this mist. And do you think she'd doubt me over Glass?"

"You'd gain nothing."

"I'd gain you not pushing a stupid, reckless idea that could get Pinky killed. We were doing fine until you showed up."

"Fine doing nothing," Glass murmured, evidently unable to help herself.

"Not helping!" I shouted back at her.

"You see Pinky and all you see is a pig," Snowdrop said. "Maybe you think you see more than that. Maybe you tell yourself that you're not like all those other men and women who see something less than human. *Other* than human, yes. But not *less than*."

"I see a man," I said. "A man with pig genes in him. But still a man. His being a pig isn't the issue here. It's that she has something we want, and she happens to want him in return."

Snowdrop shook her head slowly. "*Sure* it isn't the issue."

"I can attempt an intervention," Glass commented.

"I'd rather you didn't," I called back. Then, to Snowdrop: "Those nine-cats wouldn't take long to find me, would they?"

"When they did, though, you'd have the consolation of it being a relatively quick end. Quicker than being cut up and cooked a piece at a time by some cackling lunatic."

"You wouldn't kill me, not after all the trouble it's taken to get me here."

"I've told you I would." The line went limp, momentarily, and I had a horrible intimation of falling, of being sucked into the mist. But the line retightened and I saw that Snowdrop had released and snatched it again, quite expertly.

"I don't want to die out here, Snowdrop."

"And I don't want Pinky to die down there."

"He won't. I promise you. And I'll..." I hesitated, conscious that there could be no going back once the words were out of my mouth. "I'll guarantee that. I'll guarantee it by going down there with him."

"Anything that he says now is under duress," Glass said. "And therefore void."

"Shut up," I replied.

"Yes, shut up," Snowdrop said.

"We agree on that much, at least," I said, trying to find a scrap of common ground. "A little Glass goes a long way."

"You mean what you just said, about him not being alone?"

"Yes," I said, then with more emphasis. "Yes, you have my word on that. I'll not let him down. I'll not let you down. Pinky comes back with me, and we keep the Gideon stones."

"Understand this."

"I'm listening."

"Pinky can come back on his own. Or the both of you can come back. Either outcome's acceptable to me. But if, for some reason, he doesn't make it out, you'd be doing yourself a great favour if you never saw my face again." The line jerked again as she hauled me in. "Because I'd make you pay. And the things I'd do to you would give the Swine Queen night terrors."

CHAPTER THIRTEEN

I asked Lady Arek to call her associates to the Overlook. Before all the others had taken their seats, I made sure to position myself directly opposite Pinky, so that there was no chance of either of us avoiding the other's gaze. I wanted him to look into my eyes and know that I meant every word of what I was about to say.

But my first question was for Lady Arek.

"How detailed is the Swine Queen's knowledge of your operations here?"

"In what capacity?"

"Does she know the names and faces of everyone involved, the number of people around this table?"

"No," Lady Arek answered carefully, eyeing me with interest, as if she already had a strong sense of where I was going. "Her contact with us was confined to the extraction operation alone. She knows the identities of some of those who escaped back into orbit with us, but nothing of those who were already here."

"Good." I nodded. "Then there shouldn't be any difficulty presenting me as one of your own. When you hand Pinky over to the Swine Queen, you'll make me part of the same exchange."

Some mild interest registered on his face. "You think I need someone to hold my hand, Stink?"

"No," I said evenly, refusing to be baited. "I'm in no doubt at all that you're perfectly capable of doing this on your own, especially if you're sober. But since I initiated the idea, it seems only fair that I accept my share of the risk. We'll go in together. Glass will have to manufacture two samples of the haemoclast, and provide two spare suits instead of one, but it doesn't complicate the operation in any way."

"Unacceptable," Glass said. "I found him. He's my asset. I won't see him risked."

"But you will countenance Pinky being exposed to the same danger?" Lady Arek asked. "Is his life somehow less valuable than Clavain's?"

Glass gave her answer due reflection. "Yes."

"Well, it's good to get your prejudices out in the open," Pinky said.

"Clavain is tactically critical to the second and third phases of this operation. You are...not without your talents. But there is a difference between useful and irreplaceable."

"Thank you for that warm endorsement, Glass," I said. "But I'm going down with Pinky. It's not a question of whether I do or don't, but of how we make it work."

Pinky regarded Snowdrop. "Wonder what made the guy grow a spine overnight?"

"We came to an accommodation," Snowdrop said, eyeing me with something that was not yet approbation, but at least the recognition that I was not totally beneath consideration.

"I had a spine. I just needed reminding." I paused. "I'm not asking for your friendship or respect, Pinky. I know I haven't done nearly enough for that. Just your cooperation. Acting together, I believe we can increase the chances of getting you out of there."

"The terms of the exchange are already settled," Lady Arek said, shaking her head slowly. "Pinky for the stones. The Swine Queen won't understand why I'd offer more than I need to. That will make her suspicious, maybe even expecting a trap. That in turn will jeopardise the stones."

"Which is why we won't do it that way. I'll be a last-minute offering, a scrap of meat thrown to the dogs."

There was silence. I was certain that none of Lady Arek's close associates were comfortable with the idea of Pinky going to the Swinehouse, but each had accepted, in their own way, that there might be no other way of gaining the stones. Snowdrop liked it least of all.

Except for Glass. I do not think she disliked the pig, but she certainly considered him an acceptable exchange for the stones. And if Pinky was willing to submit himself voluntarily, with a chance of surviving, her conscience need not be too troubled.

Now I had complicated things for her.

"Someone else must go with him," she said, looking around for a candidate. "Not I. Nor Lady Arek. Our minds will be...needed."

"And ours won't?" asked Cater.

"It's settled," I said. "I go with Pinky. No one else." Then, to Glass: "I understand that you consider me tactically valuable, although you still haven't had the decency to tell me how I fit in with your plans. But this will only give you more of an incentive to work on those weapons. They must work, now. You can't run the risk of not getting me back alive, and Pinky will benefit from the same advance preparation."

Pinky drew his arms across his barrel chest. "I'll do just fine without riding your slipstream."

"It will help us both," I affirmed, not wishing to be drawn into an argument. "Lady Arek, we've seen the ninecats. I think you're right. If Glass can make them work with us, rather than against us, they'd be a useful infiltration tool."

"Apparently you failed," Glass said.

Lady Arek directed a sharp look at Snowdrop for this indiscretion, but she was much too wise to be goaded into a denial. "Yes, I did, in all senses. Even this Demi-Conjoiner could not get deeply enough into their programming before they began to fight back. But perhaps I lacked your tenacity and insight."

Glass looked sympathetic. "Perhaps you did."

"Be aware of one thing, though, before Snowdrop allows you near our captured samples. From the corpses we found in the core, left there quite deliberately, like architectural flourishes, we know that Conjoiners were sometimes set against the ninecats. They were alone, and likely handicapped, but not even their quick bright minds were enough. The ninecats cut and gored them, and that was not all. Something got inside them, and took them apart from the inside, perhaps not as quickly as one might wish."

Glass flinched; some tiny moment of slippage, her control faltering. But she regained herself just as speedily. "Show me to your toys."

"Can we depend on you with regard to both the ninecats and the haemoclast?" Lady Arek asked, settling her hands before her.

"By all means suggest some other candidates for the work," Glass answered reasonably.

"You know that there aren't any."

"Ah, good—just needed that clarifying, in case there was any doubt." Glass considered. "But I will need some time—some few days, at the very least."

"And when will you be able to give us an idea of your chances of success?" Lady Arek asked.

The question seemed to puzzle Glass. She mock-frowned and cocked her head questioningly, before some dawning realisation broke her spell. "Oh, I see. You think there's some doubt, some likelihood that I won't succeed. Yes—I understand now. How silly of me not to have done so sooner."

"Glass," I said, my patience straining.

"Now. You have my assurance of success now. It will be done, Lady Arek, just as I count on you to facilitate your own small contribution to the operation. The fact that I said I would need days in no way—"

"I think you can start your negotiations immediately," I interjected.

"Good," Lady Arek said, blanking Glass even as she nodded at me. "We shall indeed do so, the instant the weather permits."

"With regard to the haemoclast," I said. "Once it's ready, do we need a period of familiarisation, learning how to use it? You said it would be concealed about our persons. I'm still not sure how that's going to work, if we're examined."

"Did I say 'about'?" Glass asked anxiously. "That was an unforgivable slip, if I did."

"It goes into us, doesn't it?" Pinky said. "Not 'about' our persons, but inside them."

"You could have mentioned that," I said, knowing full well that there had been no mistake.

"The truth is," Glass said, smiling as she gushed false concern, "the less you know about the haemoclast before it's time, the better it will be for you. And from what I can gather about the prototype, there's an additional consideration."

"Which is?" I asked pleasantly.

"There's no record of anyone ever using it twice."

Glass split her time between preparing the haemoclast specimens and taming the captured ninecats. She worked quickly with the latter, and was ready to show off her progress after only three days of study.

A secure, windowless room had been prepared near the Overlook. In its former life, according to Snowdrop, this was where the guests of the gaming complex were required to deposit privately owned weapons and anti-personnel toxins, lest any disputes turn violent. We stood with our backs to the wheel-locked door, Glass facing us with her back to the rear face of the room. She held a pliant ninecat: gripping it by its smooth, matte-silver body with the nine arms draping down like jellyfish stingers.

"Have no concerns," she said, clearly relishing being the centre of attention, even with Lady Arek in attendance. "The unit is now completely subjugated to my authority. It was simple, in hindsight. The ninecats' engineers left a neural back-channel, a means of accessing the deep programming layers. If they wanted to enter the core for maintenance, for instance, or to extract bodies, it allowed them to place all the ninecats into a temporary safe mode."

"Why did none of their Conjoiner victims find it in time?" Lady Arek asked.

"Doubtless they tried. Maybe some did? It was one thing for me to map and probe the ninecat's control architecture at my leisure, when the unit was restrained behind a layer of hyperdiamond. Another for someone to search out those vulnerabilities when the ninecat was closing in on them, in the core, when they were likely already defenceless, weakened and handicapped."

"All the same, I had the same opportunities as you. But I could not breach the fortifications. I felt the ninecat resisting: mounting neural counter-attacks against my own architecture."

"It was why we wouldn't let her carry on, yes and verily," said Probably Rose.

"What can I say?" Glass asked rhetorically. "I persisted. Now, would you like to see what the ninecat can do for us?" She tossed the unit to the floor, bringing the ninecat alive in the same motion. The needle-tipped legs stiffened into arcs, cushioning the impact and elevating the body a few centimetres into the air. The legs' tips skittered against the polished surface, making a nervous pitter-patter.

All of us, even Lady Arek, pressed back a little nearer the door.

"I'll need some reassurance that you really have cracked those security protocols," Lady Arek said.

"I'll let the ninecat demonstrate my control. I am sending it a neural command: asking it to establish a defensive cordon."

The ninecat scuttled from one side of the room to the other, tracing the same line like a neurotic spider. It got faster, the pitter-patter becoming a blur of white noise. Soon it had become a silvery blur, like a low net stretched across the room.

"Traverse it, if you dare," Glass said. "I wouldn't, though; not if you value your extremities."

"How good is it at telling friend from foe?" I asked.

"Sufficient for our needs."

I nodded at her non-answer, wondering what it concealed. "I don't doubt that it's dangerous. Can it actually help us in the Swinehouse?"

"Most certainly. The ninecats have the means to be biometrically locked to individuals, identifying targets, or safe subjects. Again, it's a main-tenance precaution. Before you enter the Swinehouse, the ninecats will be programmed to recognise you as friendly parties. Not only that, but they will zero in on your positions, aided by the haemoclast. Wherever you are in the Swinehouse, no matter how well guarded, the ninecats will find you, and I will follow."

"Quickly, I hope," I said.

"Once the ninecats have found you, they will establish defensive perimeters similar to this. You will be protected for the short interval it takes for the suits to arrive."

"So they'll recognise us," Pinky said. "What about anyone else they meet while getting there?"

"The ninecats will avoid detection at all times. But should it be met, resistance will be neutralised."

"And if these things run into some pissed-off pigs being held in meat racks?"

"They will recognise the phenotype, and mark it at a lower priority for neutralisation."

"All the reassurance I needed, thanks."

"How many will we need?" Snowdrop asked, standing next to Pinky.

"The more I send in, the quicker they can search the Swinehouse. I have tamed one; I can tame a hundred more."

"The question isn't how many you can send in," I said. "It's how many you can keep control of."

"The answer is: as many as I deem necessary."

I turned to Pinky. "I'm not sure I like it. But I like the idea of going in there without the ninecats even less. Are you happy with this part of the plan?"

"Happy's not the first word that springs to mind, Stink." He lifted his snout challengingly, directing the gesture at Glass. "If you can make a few of these things work for you, send 'em in. But you'd better be coming in damn fast afterwards."

"I'll fulfil my part in the exercise," Glass answered. She snapped her fingers at the shimmering fence and the ninecat sprung back at her, lobbing its central body into her palm and curling its legs around her wrist.

She closed her fingers and lowered her hand to her side, the ninecat dangling limply.

"How many would you need?" Lady Arek asked. "I thought you might make do with twenty."

"Twenty would suffice, but the search pattern becomes more efficient if I have another ten, or even twenty. I need hardly remind you that the speed of the search correlates strongly with Clavain and Pinky's survival probabilities."

"No, you need hardly remind me. Thirty, then. But only with the understanding that you remain in complete control."

"May I have ten more, for the purposes of destructive testing?"

Lady Arek's tone was grudging. "If you feel the need. But do not over-exert yourself, Hourglass. You have more than enough to be getting

176

on with in preparing the haemoclast. You are more useful to me function-al than exhausted."

"I know my limits. Fortunately, I can put one or other of my brain hemispheres into a sleeping state while the other remains active. You should try it sometime."

The demonstration complete, Glass's audience filtered out through the open door, back into the warrens of the stronghold. Pinky shouldered past me without a word. I lingered, waiting until I was left alone with Glass.

"That was very well done."

"You were impressed by the ninecat."

"No, not that part. The bit where you hid the injury it just inflicted on you. Open your hand."

"There's no need."

"Then do it anyway. Why not, if you've nothing to hide?" Seizing the moment, I snatched the limp ninecat from her grasp, easily done since her palm was already slick with blood. I prised open her fingers. The blood welled out in pulses from a deep, vivid gash in the meat of her palm. "You fool," I whispered.

"It was an...error, not a loss of control."

"I'm sure in your mind there's a very distinct difference."

"This is nothing, Clavain—just a slip."

"You're lucky you didn't lose your fingers. Those legs must cut like razors and this wound needs treatment. You should go to Probably Rose."

"If Probably Rose speaks to Lady Arek, then Lady Arek will lose confi-dence in the operation, and revert to her original plan of waiting."

"Maybe that's not such a bad idea?"

"Except there are no other options. This must work. It will work." Astonished, I understood that Glass was appealing to me. For the first time in our relationship, I knew something that could be damaging to her, and no amount of coercion was going to help. "It won't happen again. I'm learning the control protocols a little more each time. That's why I want the other ninecats, so I can fully understand their limits."

"I admit there's a part of me that wants to see this through." I passed the blood-lathered ninecat back to Glass, almost as if it were a peace offering. "I won't mention this to Lady Arek. Or any of them. But you should get that wound looked at. If you don't trust Probably Rose, go back to *Scythe* and have the ship fix it."

Glass held the ninecat in her uninjured hand. She stared down at the wound in the other, her face tensing in concentration. It was as if she were trying to puzzle out an equation. The pulse of blood began to slow, then stop altogether.

"I've got it under control."

"You can break," I said, marvelling. "You're not some indestructible mannequin after all. You have limits. And that hurt, didn't it?"

"I chose to allow it to hurt," Glass said defiantly. "Pain is information. Information is..."

"Situational awareness," I said, and then frowned at myself, because the words had come from somewhere within me that I did not care to explore.

"Right answer," Glass said.

I tensed inside my suit, preparing for the shock of entry. The simulations had prepared me for the fact that the loads would come on suddenly, and I was ready for that. Nothing in the mission planners' suite of training methods, though, could ever replicate the real experience of being shackled to a house-sized lump of chondrite rock as it rammed into the iron wall of the Martian atmosphere.

Nor would that necessarily be the worst of what was to come. We were counting on the rock fragmenting a long way off the surface, but the exact timing and severity of that fragmentation was impossible to predict with any accuracy. All that could be said was that the four dropships, and the four suits inside them (and the bodies inside three of those dropships and suits) were capable of absorbing a reasonable spread of predictive stresses. The one mercy was that we would more than likely black out if the conditions were at the extreme end of the range of survivable scenarios. Beyond that range, we would be safely dead, and probably falling to Mars in several molten pieces.

With my dropship still attached to the rock—head first, so that the gee loading would tend to send blood into my brain, rather than away from it—I waited for the first indications of the coming disintegration. There would not be much time between the rock's first encounter with the atmosphere, and the thermal shock that eventually shattered it. But there should be enough of an interval to know when it was starting.

Far from being an iron wall, the atmosphere was, in fact nearly, as tenuous as vacuum. But even a ghost-thin atmosphere presented a formidable obstacle to a lump of rock arriving from deep space at thirty kilometres per second. The majority of these incoming rocks never left any trace of themselves on the surface, shattering high up and leaving only a rain of hot, dusty gravel as a memento of their arrival. Once in a while, a rock stayed intact long enough to leave an impact crater. Mars was large enough that even these impactors were rarely worth the trouble of deflecting.

I felt the first touch of atmosphere. The rock rumbled, like one iceberg grinding against another. I swivelled my view, looking either side, past the other dropships. The horizon—the edge of the rock, only a few metres away—was starting to flicker with purple light. The rumbling sensation intensified. I felt the push of gravity, as the frictional braking slowed the rock down. The purple light brightened to rose, then white. Tongues of flame bannered past, converging behind the rock. The ride was becoming rougher, heavy jolts signifying the rock's imminent destruction. Pieces of it, fist-sized or head-sized, were already splintering. Beyond the curtaining fire, a wide arc of the day-lit Martian surface had come into view. I had trained for visual recognition of landmarks, but nothing looked familiar.

The dropships had drilled acoustic sensors several metres into the rock to detect the exact moment of break-up. The separation needed to be timed too precisely to be left to human control. A fraction of a second too early and we would lose the camouflaging action of the explosion itself. A fraction too late and the fireball would engulf us. I had always known that the moment would come as a surprise, and so it proved. To my eyes the flames were just starting to shine more strongly, veiling Mars, and the jolts becoming more continuous...and then there was whiteness, and I was falling.

The rock had blown up. I had been strapped to a megatonne warhead until the last instant, and now I tumbled away from the expanding edge of the blast, one among hundreds of similar shards of debris surfing that bright billowing edge. It would look convincing...it *had* to look convincing. There were going to be no second chances where the operation was concerned. If luck was on our side, the Conjoiners might just be fooled by our ruse.

Was it worth the risk, knowing we would never be able to pull off the same trick twice?

Of course.

Down there on Mars was the Conjoiner compound. And inside that compound was an extremely high-value prisoner. One of our own. A man like myself: another Knight of Cydonia.

My brother, Nevil.

We knew he was alive. We knew also—through diplomatic back-channels—that he had not undergone the usual fate of those caught by the Conjoined. He had not been converted; not had their machines pumped into his skull, eroding his humanity and turning him into another unit in their massively distributed, conscienceless hive-mind.

They were holding back because of his status as an extremely useful bargaining chip.

For now.

The explosion was a fading, dirt-stained smear far above me. The dropship was falling on exactly the near-parabolic course that would be expected of any piece of fiery debris. It was even sloughing parts of its hull to mimic ablative heating. Somewhere out there were the other three ships, another trio of falling sparks, two of them containing Hope and Charity. But they were long past the point where I stood any hope of visual acquisition. If I could have acquired them—and distinguished them from the real debris—something would have been wrong.

The ground came up hard, like a zoom in on a terrain map. One downside to our plan was that the dropships could not be seen to slow down as they approached the surface. Our mission planners had examined all feasible scenarios for getting three live bodies down onto Mars and concluded that the inhabited dropships could only commence deceleration measures when they were five hundred metres up.

This was going to hurt.

But pain, as I liked to tell my students in military planning, was situational awareness.

One week slipped by, then another. Lady Arek's stronghold swung around Yellowstone, its orbit carrying it to northerly and southerly extremes of latitude, but only occasionally coinciding with the position of Chasm City. As often as not, when it did, the atmosphere was going through one of its periodic fits of intense, colourful storms, smothering any trace of the city's location. Even the thermal hotspot of the Chasm, where gases upwelled from deep in Yellowstone's mantle, was smeared into obscurity. Until the day Lady Arek's laser signal received a pinprick flash of a return pulse, signifying that someone at the other end was listening, and willing to respond.

The transmission window closed before any meaningful dialogue could take place. But conditions remained favourable on the next pass and the Swine Queen joined the communication circuit from inside her lair.

It was voice only, and the window would close in four and a half minutes. There would not be another opportunity for dialogue for three weeks. If the ransom exchange were to happen soon, all negotiations would have to be concluded within this window.

Lady Arek knew it. So did the Swine Queen.

"What've we to say to each other, lovely?" asked the rough-edged voice coming out of the walls of the Overlook. "You haven't called, you haven't asked after me. I thought we was done talking, despite my nice offer."

"Concerning that offer. Would it still be open?"

"Well, if we're talking about the same offer…didn't you say I could shove it down my pork-hole? That you'd never agree to it in a million years? Had a change of heart, have you, lovely?"

"Everyone is entitled to alter their opinion, Your Swineness."

"That they are. But that really don't sound like you. No. Don't sound like you at all."

"You know how much I want the Gideon stones."

"That, I do. I also know how little you want to send your piggy pal down to me. What's changed?"

"That is between me and Pinky. Suffice it to say that I no longer have any objections to the terms of the exchange."

"Oh, but you're going to have to do better than that. You don't just wake up one day and decide to sacrifice your loyalest deputy. You wasn't willing to think about it six years ago, so why now?"

Aware as she was of the clock ticking down, Lady Arek still risked a few seconds of silence. I admired how she held her nerve for the sake of a convincing performance.

"A development has occurred. I thought I could count on that loyalty through thick and thin, but it seems I was wrong. Pinky always agitated for taking more decisive action against you. Immediate, forceful action."

"Whereas you saw the benefits of waiting me out, knowing there's one or two who wouldn't mind sticking a knife in, moment my back's turned."

"Heavy is the head that wears the crown, as a great man once said."

"And you felt the same itch when you had your back to him, did you?"

"I cannot blame him for acting in accordance with his nature." Lady Arek shuddered to say those words in front of Pinky. Doubtless he had heard worse, but they would have a particular sting coming from the mouth of his friend, even as she meant no harm by them. "His kind cannot see the longer game. Waiting is inimical to them. They are creatures of impulse, driven by the need for immediate gratification. In all matters."

The Swine Queen made an appreciative noise. "So the scales've fallen from your eyes after all. Should have listened to me when I told you what him and his sort were about, lovely."

"I admit I saw more in him than was warranted. Until he organised a move against me, and showed his true colours."

"Yet you're still speaking."

"He gathered a small number to his side, but not enough to make a difference. I suppressed his rebellion and came to an arrangement with him. His life, in return for the others being spared."

181

"That's nicer than I'd've been. One turns against me, I gut and skin ten. Nosh on them in front of their pals. Keeps 'em in line."

"Sage advice, your Swineness. Unfortunately, I don't have the benefit of your numbers. Those men and women disappointed me, but they are indispensable. I prefer to make one concrete example and give the others a chance to redeem themselves."

"It's a mistake," the Swine Queen said, with a sort of distant concern, as if they were two business leaders discussing opposing views of managerial strategy. "But it's yours to make, not mine. All the same...I still can't quite believe you've turned against Pinky. Not that I want to talk myself out of some noshing, but you were as thick as thieves."

"I saw a side of him that was hidden before. An animal side, the beast behind the mask. I can't trust him, or be comfortable with his presence now. He is...less than I imagined."

"Can't've been easy. I hate to say this, lovely, but you've nearly got my sympathy."

"And you nearly have my thanks. But I must be honest with you about Pinky. Consider him damaged goods."

"How so?"

"He was hurt quite badly during the failed rebellion. It makes my decision simpler. I know that I am not condemning him to an early death."

"But...just so we're clear...you still know what I mean to do with him?"

"Yes," Lady Arek said earnestly. "And that will be on my conscience, such as it is. But that is part of the arrangement he and I came to. He accepts this price, for the lives of his co-conspirators." Lady Arek drew breath. She looked around at the rest of the gathering, each of us conscious that she had reached the critical point in the negotiation. "May I...presume... your Swineness, that the terms of the ransom are still...applicable?"

"I've still got the stones."

"And I have the pig."

"Then we'll do business. How soon can you get down here, presuming you've still got a ship?"

"We are monitoring heightened wolf activity. A sub-aggregate flow is passing between us and Yellowstone at the moment, but it should disperse in about twenty-six hours. If all is well, we would be able to make a rapid, stealthy insertion at any point thereafter."

"Well, give us a day to dust off the landing stage and put some ammo in our guns. Not that I'm assuming any naughtiness, but..."

"You would only be taking all sensible precautions."

"Glad we're of one mind. You remember how to find us, don't you?"

"I think so."

"Good. We'll roll out the carpet." The signal crackled as the lasers lost their optimum lock. "And don't forget to bring the bacon. We'll have the spits turning, the griddles warmed. The culinary offerings've been a little on the tasteless side lately: this'll perk us up nicely."

A silence fell, once the transmission was finally curtailed. Lady Arek placed a hand over the microphone, as if there was still a measurable risk of her words drifting down to Yellowstone. "I am sorry, friend."

"Don't be," he growled. "You only said what she needed to hear."

"I want you to know that I don't—"

"The only insulting thing would be for you to think I didn't already know how you really feel." He softened his tone minutely. "It's all right. Shit needed to be said."

Lady Arek had not been lying when she mentioned the wolf flow passing between her stronghold and Yellowstone. Snowdrop was monitoring the flow's attenuation, collating whispers of intelligence from the dwindling assortment of sensors sprinkled in orbit around the planet. Some of these devices had been dispersed from the shuttle as it came in from John the Revelator, but others were native to the Rust Belt: beacons, traffic monitors, surveillance nodes and so on, that had been coaxed back into some kind of life and programmed to make stealthy observations in the wavebands and modalities most likely to permit detection of Inhibitor movements. Mostly it was impossible to see individual cubes going about their business, but when larger numbers of the units coalesced into a structural aggregate or an organised flow, there was a chance of detecting mass ripples or the occlusion of background radiation. The second hard part was relaying any of this hard-won data back to the stronghold, in a way that avoided being sniffed out by the wolves themselves. As on Michaelmas, Snowdrop's network relied on ultra-low energy and frequency burst transmissions, disguised as random noise. It meant that the updates arrived sporadically, sometimes with many hours between them.

After thirteen, the flow showed signs of attenuation, breaking up into sub-elements which flocked off in different directions, and by the time a day had passed there was no clear sign of it. Only so much reassurance could be drawn from this, though. The sensor network was patchy, with significant blind spots. What the wolves were doing or planning in the shadows was open to conjecture.

But we would never have any better guarantees.

Scythe was the first ship to leave orbit. Glass took it out alone, exercising extreme caution and running all her stealthing measures. She nosed her way through the ruins of the Rust Belt, and then down into the inter-orbital space between the lowest-flying debris belts and the sickly coloured atmosphere of Yellowstone. Her last signal, tight-beamed back to the stronghold, was confirmation that *Scythe* had not detected any lone wolf elements, nor seen any sign of larger groupings within its limited sensor horizon.

Then *Scythe* dropped into the atmosphere, and we lost contact.

CHAPTER FOURTEEN

Before leaving, Glass had made all the necessary arrangements with Probably Rose. Partially dressed for the mission, but with additional armour and breathing devices still to be fitted, Pinky and I laid ourselves down on adjoining medical couches. Straps were then fastened across our bodies, which did nothing for my confidence. My forearm was left exposed, so that a transfusion catheter could be inserted without difficulty. With Pinky, it was easier to go in through the inner thigh. This part was unpleasant enough, since the catheter had to be large enough to handle a large blood volume. Since there was worse to come, though, it had been agreed that any sort of anaesthetic was pointless.

Then it began. Probably Rose wheeled a trolley into the space between our couches. The trolley had an upright rack, dangling with chilled blood bags, clear and full. Litre by litre our blood was extracted and stored in the waiting bags, ready to be put back in us if we ever made it back from Chasm City. With each litre that was removed, another litre of an oxygen-bearing buffering agent was substituted. This was a medically safe blood substitute, proven for use in field surgery, and would produce no more than mild discomfort and nausea while it was inside us. It was intended to keep a person alive, and no more than that.

The buffering agent was just an intermediate step. Once it was circulating, and we were deemed to have accepted it well, the real process began. Litre by litre—but more slowly this time—the buffering agent itself was replaced by the haemoclast, injected from a pair of upright metal reservoirs.

I had been right about the name. The haemoclast was weaponised blood. It was the right colour and a similar viscosity, and it could keep its recipient alive for an extended period. But there all biological similarities ceased. This blood was a moving fluid made up of quickmatter: tiny machines in a plasma-like suspension medium. Because it was distributed throughout our bodies, and had density and ferromagnetic properties comparable with biological blood, it would pass all but the

185

closest inspection. There would be nothing to show up on an X-ray, resonance, or ultrasound scan. It could manage oxygen transfer, although not as efficiently as normal blood. Inside our bodies, the haemoclast was a functioning, if imperfect, life-support system. Outside of them, it was an adaptive, self-governing killing machine.

But the cost to bear it was torment. It built slowly, litre by litre. To begin with, I thought I might be able to tolerate it quite well, something I could almost push to the back of my mind. By the third litre, I understood how wrong I was. The blood felt like a stream of lava circulating in me, burning me from inside. My heart laboured, sending out sharp protests of its own. My lungs were like two bellows being filled with heavy, molten metal.

Pinky and I tested our restraints. My body writhed and strained, my limbs tensing and untensing so violently that I felt they might rip themselves from their sockets. Within a few seconds, I felt that every already aching muscle had been shredded, every ligament severed. I would have screamed, except that Probably Rose had given me something to bite down on. But even she seemed surprised by the ferocity of the reaction. On the couch next to mine, Pinky tried to swallow back a groan. He had forsworn the biting aid. Now I wondered if he regretted it.

"Glass says this might help," Lady Arek said, as Probably Rose pushed in the last litre of our torment. "The pain is a false signal, your body confused by the new circulatory medium. Merely knowing that may allow you to compartmentalise the discomfort."

"Tell Glass..." Pinky began.

I wrenched open my jaws and allowed the biting aid to loll away from my lips, trailing drool. Probably Rose had finished replacing our blood and was extracting our catheters.

"...to shove it," I finished for Pinky.

By some miracle it did not worsen, and after a few minutes of doing nothing but breathing and thinking, I saw that there might be a point somewhere in my future where the pain could be endured. Just to be able to move and talk and think about something else for one clean second. Could I do that? The answer, when it presented itself, was simplicity itself. I had no choice. I was committed to this operation, and therefore I had to function. Even if there was no room inside me for anything but the pain, I had to lie to myself that it was otherwise, and in the narrow space of that lie, make myself useful.

"It's bad," I said aloud, testing the timbre and steadiness of my voice, and surprising myself by how resolute I sounded. "But I think I can live.

186

Glass is right: it's better when you remember the blood isn't doing as much damage to us as it feels like."

Snowdrop came around, looking down at me. "Does it hurt, Clavain?"

"Yes."

"Keep this pain in mind. It'll be a tenth of what I'll do to you if Pinky doesn't come back."

"Oh, he'll come back," I said, grunting as I twisted around to look at him. "How would I...manage...without his sparkling company?" Then I pushed out a hand. "Help me, Snowdrop. He can look beaten-up: it fits the narrative. But I have to look strong, at least until Lady Arek cuts me loose."

Snowdrop took my hand and yanked me into a sitting position. I breathed. The slight increase in oxygen demand made itself known in my chest, but compared to the fire threading every vein and artery inside me, that was no more than a dull ache.

"Thank you," I huffed.

"I mean what I said."

"I don't doubt it. I'd far sooner have you on my side than against me."

"First intelligent thing you've said since we met," Pinky growled.

"Then we're finding common ground." I braced for pain and swung my legs off the medical couch. "I mean it too, Snowdrop. I saw the job you've done wringing some useful intelligence out of that sensor network. We struggled with the same problems on Michaelmas. The difference was we had hundreds more people and ten times the technical resources you've managed with here. We could have used you."

Snowdrop made a noncommittal sound, not dismissing my words but unwilling to show that she was moved by them. I understood well enough.

"Bring those stones back to us, and maybe some of this won't have been for nothing."

Probably Rose came back with a couple of tablets palmed in her hand.

"Take one of these, yes. Glass said they'll dull the symptoms for a little while, and verily."

The pills looked alike, so I selected one at random and swallowed it whole. It scraped down my throat, dry and tasteless as a pebble. "Why didn't you give us the pills before injecting the blood?"

Probably Rose looked at me as if I had asked a deliberately vacuous question.

"Because you needed to know what it'll be like when they wear off."

"How soon?"

"Two, three hours. Yes, and yes. I'll be in the shuttle, along with Omori, if something goes wrong. Once you're outside, though, you're on your own."

"And if something did go wrong, I don't imagine there'd be much you could do about it? Am I right?"

Probably Rose looked torn between candour and reassurance. Clearly there was little of the latter she could offer.

"And verily."

"Well, luck's been on my side so far. Why would it desert me now?"

"I don't know you very well, Clavain. I think you are a tissue of lies walking around in the shape of a man. I think you may have done many bad deeds."

"Very probably."

"But this is a good thing that you do now. Yes."

"Thank you," I breathed.

Whether it was that crumb of kindness from Probably Rose, or the effect of the pill, I felt an easing in me, a simmering down of the fire. It was still there, nothing that I would call pleasant, but momentarily bearable. I looked at Pinky, who had also taken a pill, and hoped that he was feeling a similar respite. Snowdrop was leaning down to him, whispering some promise in his ear, and I looked away just as they kissed, feeling that I was intruding on their privacy.

I'll bring him back, I vowed to myself. It was as much as I could do.

Chasm City was nowhere beneath us, and then it was everywhere. We had come through the last layer of cloud, above a plain of ruins. It took a few moments for my eyes to adjust to what I was seeing; a few more for my brain to accept the scale of destruction and the toll of murder that it implied. I knew what had happened here; I knew the punishment that had been dealt against us for having the hubris to turn our eyes to the stars. But no intellectual understanding could have prepared me for the visible evidence of our downfall, graven in the ruins of our greatest metropolis. The worst thing was that it was still possible to tell that this had been a city. A blackened carpet of ash, a glass-fused crater, a scoured blank absence, would have been easier to process than the half-incinerated remains beneath us. Ruins told a story.

Kilometre upon kilometre they stretched: the black or ashen remnants of what had once been buildings as big as mountains, now reduced to hunched, crouching, mangled forms like pitiable slouching figures under cowls and cloaks of sackcloth. They were hollow-eyed, hollow-skulled, blown right through. Some of them had fallen over, or taken one or more with them in the same collapse. Pieces of buildings lay among the ruins, jammed upright like jagged tombstones. Draped over everything, yet mostly so diaphanous that we saw right through it, was the collapsed shroudwork of the city's domes. Nowhere was there a trace of movement, nowhere a light or a flash of living matter. I had accepted that there were pockets of survivors down in Chasm City without question, but now it seemed preposterous that any organism, much less any group of people, could have found a way to live there.

The city slid under us, monotonous and terrible, until in the grey haze of distance we could make out the chasm itself, the belching maw at the city's heart. Lady Arek slowed us further as we neared the in-curving lip, the ruined buildings crowding near the edge in tightening spirals, like processions of ships about to tumble into a whirlpool. Turbulence increased. Thick, unhealthy-coloured clouds were still rising from the chasm, hiding anything more than the upper fraction of its depth. The shuttle stopped altogether and began a cautious, queasy descent.

"Are you all right?" Probably Rose asked both of us.

"No worse," I said. "Pinky?"

"No worse," he echoed. And I thought that if we could agree on that much, even in our discomfort, there might yet be hope we'd come through this together.

We lowered beneath the chasm's rim, and I saw how the buildings had spilled over the edge and down into the shaft, pushing ever deeper as the real estate above ground became more congested and expensive. The remains of bridges grasped across the chasm without meeting. Lady Arek navigated us around these buckled, sagging hazards, draped with acres of dome that had come raining down. Slowly the walls were rising past us, the sense of confinement and claustrophobia increasing with each kilometre that we descended. Only a poor sort of daylight made it through Yellowstone's clouds to begin with. There was not much left of it by the time we were five kilometres into the chasm.

Yet as the gloom intensified, and the fluted and striated walls seemed to press in on us like a tightening throat, so I made out the first signs of active habitation. Lights and fires glimmered from a dozen widely spaced points in the wall, like eyes in a night-lit forest. Then a hundred more, as I adjusted to the spectacle. The band of habitation seemed confined within a kilometre or less of the chasm's height.

"They do not use those fires for heat or cooking," Lady Arek said, noticing my interest. "They are territorial markers; lines of division between little dwindling empires. You might as well be looking at a map of planetary systems, slowly being snuffed out by wolves. Already there are fewer signs of life than there were six years ago."

"They're dying off?"

"One by one. Very little else to do, in the long run. There were no sustainable resources left behind when the city fell. The gangs subsist off scraps, stored commodities, what little they can steal or barter from others."

"And if that fails," I said quietly, "there's always a bright future in cannibalism."

"Not the most sustainable lifestyle choice, if history has been any guide."

"You have a gift for understatement, Lady Arek. At times I even think you might have a sense of humour."

"I do. But I've learned from bitter experience that it's best kept to myself." She nodded into the mist, at a structure emerging from the chasm's depths. "There, Clavain. Our destination: the Swinehouse. Study it well. In a few minutes you are likely to be somewhere inside it, suffering terribly."

"Are you a sadist?" I asked.

"No, merely a realist."

"Well, you're right: you really should keep that sense of humour to yourself."

The Swinehouse was built out from the chasm's side like a faceless wall clock, buttressed from beneath by huge splayed and angled supports which rested on natural ledges a hundred or so metres beneath the underside of the lair. That was about as far down as we could see before thicker layers of mist closed in. Augmenting these supports were numerous tensioned cables, radiating out from fixtures in the lair's sides and corners and cleated directly into the wall, through whose narrowing gaps we had to pick our way. It would be exceedingly bad manners to clip one of those lines, even though the loss of any one of them would not be sufficient to send the lair tumbling into the chasm.

"Do you think Glass managed to get all this way without being seen?"

"We must depend on it."

"Not quite the answer I was hoping for."

"She will have achieved her initial objective. *Scythe*'s stealthing systems are far in advance of this shuttle, and besides, we wish to be seen. Hourglass will have come in silently, keeping close to the opposite wall and using the mist and adaptive hull chameleoflage for cover. She will be waiting now, positioned some way beneath the Swinehouse and certainly out of reach of our sensors or any surveillance devices available to the Swine Queen. When we send the signal, she will rise to the base of the structure and commence her infiltration."

"Do you think we can rely on her?"

"We are different in our methods, different in our philosophies. She is the lightning; I am the weather system. But she will not fail in her aspect of the operation."

"And it ain't because she cares about me," Pinky said. "Or pigs in general."

"You may not like me," I said. "Or respect me. And in your shoes, I probably wouldn't either. But I have a feeling you are much more valuable than Glass realises. She would be making an error if she treated your life as worth anything less than my own."

He looked at me sceptically "You done, Stink?"

"Yes."

"Good. I've spent my whole fucking existence being told I matter. Usually about thirty seconds before I become inconvenient to someone."

"Did you matter to Nevil Clavain?"

"He wasn't the same."

"Then nor am I," I said quietly. "If you mattered to *him*, then you matter to me."

The upper part of the lair was too complicated to be called a rooftop. It was a jumble of different levels and lookouts, criss-crossed with ladders and walkways and bristling with spiked defences and slitted, swivel-mounted turrets. The turrets tracked us as we came in. Perhaps there was nothing in them that could do serious harm to the shuttle, but the message was plain enough. We were only one twitch away from a less than cordial welcome. Now would not be the time to get off on the wrong footing with the Swine Queen.

Hemmed in by spikes and turrets, but nevertheless accessible, was a flattened landing surface marked by a crudely daubed cross and lit with flaming beacons. Lady Arek slipped us between the last of the wires, put out the shuttle's landing gear, then set gently down on the pad.

"I think we wait for our hosts before making any moves," she said.

There was time for Pinky and me to fix on the breather masks we would need for the handover. We eyed each other, neither having anything to say. Perhaps a certain taciturn distance was the best way of getting into character for the performance ahead, anyway. Glass's pain-reliever was still doing its work but with every breath I knew that the haemoclast was going to reassert its presence sooner or later, and I needed to be ready for the moment.

Figures came out of a squat building on the edge of the pad. There were six of them, masked and armoured and carrying weapons that resembled long muskets connected by hoses to tanks worn on the figures' backs. Flame-throwers, I guessed. As if any doubt remained, one of the figures elevated the muzzle of their weapon and squeezed out a tongue of blue-edged fire.

"Yes, very good," Lady Arek said aloud. "As if there was the slightest likelihood that your swineherds would come unarmed."

We were ready. Probably Rose, Omori and Lady Arek donned their own breathing equipment. Omori and Probably Rose went through the lock first, taking armaments of their own but evidently not feeling the need to show off their capabilities. Omori and Probably Rose stepped off the shuttle, then walked a short distance across the landing area until they were within speaking distance of the reception party.

Pinky and I watched proceedings through the viewing ports next to the airlock. The reception party all had full-face masks on: old-fashioned, leathery-looking affairs with round portholes for eyes and snout-like protuberances where an air hose went in. I had been staring at them for a few seconds before my perceptions jolted. They were pigs' faces, made into masks.

I started to say something to Pinky, some necessary acknowledgement of this abomination.

"Save it, Stink."

A tense exchange was going on between Probably Rose, Omori and the reception party: clearing haggling over the final terms of the exchange. More than once, members of one or both parties turned away, feigning a breakdown in the agreement. But it was all gamesmanship, all theatre. They were never going to put up an objection to the handover this late in the process, and neither were we. But both parties had an understandable desire to see the goods before the trade.

Something was signalled back to Lady Arek. Outside, two of the reception party went back inside the building. A minute or so later, they reappeared with a trunk hefted between them. A third figure had joined them, one I instantly understood to be the Swine Queen herself.

Around her waist she wore a blood-stiffened leather apron, down which hung an assortment of butchery tools, among other objects whose function was not immediately apparent. She was broader and taller than I had been expecting, her armour more ostentatious, her mask more vis-ibly betraying its origins. It was just a pig's head, mouth and snout, eyes and ears still intact, tilted back so that her masked and goggled face was able to see out between the jaws. If the other masks were made from the faces of hyperpigs, then this was something atavistic, a throwback to the genetic basis of Pinky and his kind. The mask was hideous. Its horror lay not just in the way it was worn, so crudely jammed onto her head, but in the denial it made concrete: that ones such as Pinky or Snowdrop were anything but a small step above the beasts. The Swine Queen had been an abstract antagonist until now, an obstacle we had to work around. Now I saw a madness that needed to be extinguished, a mind gone so far wrong that it was beyond humane salvation.

"Perhaps we should take the stones by force," I said, wanting nothing more than to turn the shuttle's weapons (which I was certain existed, even though I had not been shown them) against her Swineness and her masked retinue.

"And then find out there's nothing in that box except air," Lady Arek said. "No—my nemesis has thought this through, just as thoroughly as we have. I shall inspect the goods. Follow me, but remain by the shuttle until I signal for you to approach." Then, to Pinky: "Whatever happens today, you've shown a bravery beyond words. If there had been no other point to my life, I would consider myself blessed to have shared this little part of space and time with you. You are the best of us, my friend; the reason that we are worth saving. And I promise you this—there will be justice." Then, to me: "Bring him back, Clavain."

Lady Arek went out first, then we followed, waiting as instructed at the shuttle. Slowly and deliberately, Lady Arek drew out a small boser pistol. She held the weapon aloft, cupping it loosely in her semi-opened palm with a finger hooked through the trigger guard. Ready to use in an instant, but not yet aimed at anyone in particular. To be seen to be carrying a weapon was necessary etiquette.

Lady Arek walked to the trunk, now lowered to the ground. The Swine Queen stood behind it, arms folded. At a gesture from the queen, two of the guards flipped open the lid and allowed Lady Arek to look inside.

Lady Arek looked to the queen and mimed dipping her hand into the box. The Swine Queen nodded, her loose-fitting pig mask joggling horribly, and echoed Lady Arek's gesture in an exaggerated, sarcastic manner.

Lady Arek knelt, still with the pistol dangling from her fingers, and scooped out one of the Gideon stones. She turned slightly so that I had a better view of the upraised object. It looked real to me, but then my only point of comparison was the one inside the stronghold. Lady Arek held it close to her eyes, turning the object slowly. She lowered it back into the trunk, gave the queen a peremptory nod, signalling her acceptance that the goods were not counterfeit.

Lady Arek rose to her feet and stepped back. The guards sealed the box again. The Swine Queen made a quick series of gestures. If she spoke, I heard nothing. Lady Arek walked back to about halfway between the two delegations. Two of the guards followed her with the trunk, then set it down again. Unless there was some spectacular sleight of hand going on, the stones must still be inside it.

Lady Arek turned to me only.

"They're good. Bring him, Miguel."

"He can walk on his own."

"I said bring him!" she snarled.

Falling into my role, I seized a buckle around Pinky's back and shoved him in the direction of the Swine Queen. Pinky twisted out of my grip and snarled back at me that he did not need to be encouraged.

The Swine Queen spoke. It was an amplified version of the same rough voice we had heard over the laser-link, but now it emanated from the pig mask.

"Why all the shoving, lovely? I thought you said he'd agreed to come of his own will."

Lady Arek called back: "That was all well and good a day ago. It would seem second thoughts have begun to occur, in the presence of your Swineness."

"Well don't be tenderising him ahead of time. That's my job." The mask fixed itself onto me. "Who's this?"

"Not that it matters, but one of my associates."

"I don't think I know him."

"There's no reason that you should. His name is Miguel de Ruyter. He was one of Pinky's main allies in the move against me."

"Funny that you'd trust him with this, then."

"Who said I do?"

We were nearly at the trunk. This was the moment I had been waiting for, while at the same time mentally blocking as far as possible. Lady Arek did something very quick and deft with the boser pistol, twisting it in her fingers like a party trick and aiming it not at the Swine Queen or any of her party but at me. She fired.

The yield had been dialled down low enough not to be lethal, the beam at its narrowest setting, and her aim had been precise enough to inflict exactly the damage she wished, and no more. The pulse clipped me in the upper thigh, drilling through flesh and muscle.

I yelped and went down, my leg giving way under me.

I let go of Pinky and he staggered away from me as I hit the floor.

Lady Arek's shot had caused the Swine Queen's guards to jab their flame-thrower muzzles in our direction, and one of them let off a quick, sweeping plume, but any further retaliation was curtailed by the queen herself, raising an arm.

"No: don't burn them. That was meant for him, not us." The mask waggled as she nodded some kind of approval. "I take it this man didn't wriggle his way back into your good offices?"

I writhed and groaned. I still had a part to play, though no part of my performance needed to be forced.

"De Ruyter was good, until he wasn't," Lady Arek said, with a distant regret. "After we spoke, I realised I needed to make a firmer statement about my authority. I have you to thank for that, your Swineness."

"In which case, you're welcome."

"Do with de Ruyter as you will. Kill him, if you like, or find some use in him. His loyalty is malleable, as I learned. That may work to your advantage, in the short term."

"Nothing tricky going on here, Lady Muck?"

Lady Arek nodded at my shivering, whimpering form. "Does that look tricky?"

"On balance, maybe it doesn't."

"Have fun with him. I don't know if your taste yet extends to human flesh, but by all means experiment."

"Oh, we will."

"Then, if our business is done…may we consider our exchange concluded?"

The Swine Queen's mask gave a twitch of mild affront.

"In a hurry to be leaving?"

"A hurry to be anywhere but this dying cesspit of a city. No offence."

"None taken…much. But we're not quite done…or were you thinking I'd accept your honesty without question? I might be mad, lovely, but I'm not gullible." The Swine Queen unhooked a thick-rimmed hooplike device from her waist, a sort of metal lasso. The handle ended in a coil of wire which fed back into a box which she held in her other hand.

Four of the guards reached Pinky and me. They took hold of Pinky by the arms, easily lifting him off his feet, and they wrenched me from the ground with no concern for my wound. The Swine Queen walked up and dropped the hoop over my head and down the full length of my body, the guards forcing my arms tight about me so that the hoop could keep descending. Her mask drooped as she studied a flickering grey readout in the box. The device made a musical tone as it worked, rising and falling in pitch. She repeated this procedure for Pinky, evidently satisfying herself that we were not armed.

"Take your stones for now," she said, hooking the hoop and box back onto her waist.

"For now?" Lady Arek asked.

"You've passed the first test. But we'll want to have a closer look at this pair before we let you slip away for good. Hold your ship on the pad, until you get the say-so."

Lady Arek directed Probably Rose and Omori to help with the trunk. "Aren't you the slightest bit curious about what I need them for?"

"Something grandiose, I expect. Something pointless. Something that won't make a difference. You go off and do whatever it is you think will help, lovely. Enjoy yourself. Meanwhile, we'll be down here noshing our faces off on meat and blood until our brains rot or the lights go out, whichever's first."

"That sounds like a very reasonable arrangement," Lady Arek said.

CHAPTER FIFTEEN

They took us into the Swinehouse. Multiple layers of doors closed behind us as we were barged and bullied deeper into the lair. The Swine Queen strode on ahead of the entourage, past jeering and shrieking members of her cult. As they saw her two prisoners, they communicated their enthusiasm through vigorous floor-stomping and the crashing of staffs and weapon stocks against any suitably resonant surface. The only things not being hit or hammered were Pinky and me; even though we passed within easy reach of her swineherds, no one made the mistake of laying a finger on us. There was no encouragement to be taken from that, though. It was just that our flesh was not to be despoiled.

A level beneath the landing stage was a boxy room where we were subjected to further tests, either too complicated or too cumbersome to be done on the surface. Pinky and I both submitted without much resistance: Pinky because he had to give the impression of passively accepting his fate, and me because I was feigning more of an injury than Lady Arek had really given me. True, her aim had been perfect, and it had been suitably painful. But the pulse had gone through soft tissue only, and once the initial shock had passed, some strength and coordination had begun to return to my leg. I masked that by limping and groaning at every opportunity.

The examinations were thorough. We were stripped of our outer armour and then closely inspected for anything concealed. More scanning devices were brought in—some wielded by the Swine Queen, giving us her personal attention, and some operated by various pig-masked acolytes. Everything that was used on us had an improvised look. Fixed and handheld screens were consulted, muffled consultations undertaken. It felt as if we were being given a medical review, rather than being checked for fitness to be detained and eaten. My wound was bandaged up, but it had never bled.

These tests took at least half an hour. The Swine Queen seemed in no rush to conclude them. Perhaps it pleased her to keep Lady Arek sitting

197

anxiously. At last, though, some verdict was reached, the Swine Queen conferring with her lieutenants and, after much nodding of pig masks and muffled exchanges between them, a command of sorts was sent up from the examination room. A level below the landing stage, the only evidence of Lady Arek's departure which reached us was a rumbling vibration as the shuttle's thrusters rattled the Swinehouse. Lady Arek had not been certain how deeply we would be taken inside, though, and had promised us that she would arrange a more reliable signal.

We got it about thirty seconds later: the dull chug of those Gatling turrets, responding to a vindictive shot Lady Arek had lobbed back at the lair. It was the retaliatory blast that counted, since we had a good chance of sensing the activation of those turrets. So too would Glass, waiting far below us.

"I'm surprised she felt the need for that," the Swine Queen said, addressing us both. "Seems to me she got the better side of the deal. I'm the one who ought to feel short-changed."

With our breather masks removed, both of us were now free to speak.

"You don't think we're the equal of those stones, your Swineness?" I asked.

"The stones are in her possession forever, Mister de Ruyter. That *was* your name, wasn't it?"

"It was my name," I agreed.

"You'll see the asymmetry, then. I only get to eat and kill the pig once."

"I like the way you say 'eat and kill,' not 'kill and eat,'" Pinky said. "Any chance of flipping that order, since I'm asking nicely?"

"You're wrong about that asymmetry, your Swineness."

"I am?"

I nodded earnestly. "It's only that way if you choose it. You don't have to eat and kill him." I gave the impression of reconsidering my position. "Well, you can—I'm sure your mind's already made up—but you were never expecting me. I'm the bonus that tips the deal in your favour."

"Because you'll taste as good as the pig? You might not be as nicely aged in alcohol as he is, but we do nosh on men and women sometimes, de Ruyter, just in case you were getting your hopes up."

"But you heard what Lady Arek said about me. I was good until I wasn't. By good, she means *useful*. A valuable adviser."

"Shame there ain't any vacancies open."

"I know about your reach down here," I persisted, playing for time. "This lair is impressive enough—I like what you've done with it—but your control only extends to a tiny part of Chasm City."

"Your ladyship didn't seem to think too highly of the neighbourhood. Why should any of us care?"

"Care or not, I'm the one who can help you consolidate the power you do have, and extend your reach further than before."

"Is he always this weaselly, Pinky?"

"He has his moments. But I wouldn't trust him."

The Swine Queen tilted her mask to look at him. "Hang on. I thought you and he was on the same team, against Lady Muck."

"True," Pinky said. "He was also the first to turn traitor, when it became clear I wasn't going to win."

"That said, I like a man with flexible loyalties."

"Get back to me when he's got a knife to your throat."

"Ah, but you won't be around to see it anyway. Now, I am going to make you last, but no matter how slowly I take you, piece by piece, there'll always be a point where you end."

"I should warn you: I'm already well past my best."

"Aren't we all, Pinky—but we won't hold that against you." The Swine Queen clapped her hands. "To the Carvery! Sound the dinner gong! Supper's ready!"

We were strapped onto upright trolleys so that we could be wheeled deeper into Swinehouse and shown off like the prizes we were. Grilled masks were fixed over our mouths, just in case we got any ideas about biting or spitting.

As we were trundled along, I was sure that Pinky was doing the same mental calculations I was. With a little warning we could release the haemoclast at any time, but its effectiveness lay entirely in conjunction with Glass's infiltration. If we went too soon, the haemoclast would cause a little local havoc but burn itself out before Glass had time to locate us. If we waited too long, we might get killed out of sheer expediency once the Swine Queen knew she was under attack.

Not yet, I told myself.

The Carvery was some way beneath the examination room. We went down ramps, down spiralling corridors, down slow, whining elevators with scissoring doors. At all points there was a gathering throng of hammering, stomping and braying swineherds. Some of them had full-face pig masks on, but as we voyaged deeper into the lair I mapped a hierarchy, with the full-face masks clearly being the relatively elite who were allowed onto the upper floors and permitted into closer contact with the queen. Beneath these trustees—her inner retinue—were several subordinate ranks, where the herds wore partial masks, covering only a portion of their faces. The most numerous had no masks at all. They were all of them damaged in some way: scarred, broken-toothed, cankered, white-eyed. Many of them had a permanent drooling madness, a cackling delight in how low they had come. Some of them shook and gibbered—some bad thing had got into their brains.

The Swine Queen had missed the one weapon I carried about my external form, just as she had missed the equivalent adaptation on Pinky. She could not be blamed for that. Our weapons were tiny and nearly useless. Mine was a slightly barbed nail on my second finger, fixed over my own. I had hidden it by closing my fist. The worst it could have done was puncture an eye or gash an artery: bad news for the one person I reached, but no use at all against massed captors.

I tested it against my palm, unseen in my clenched hand. All I had to do was break the flesh.

But not yet. *Not yet.*

Grand maroon doors, inset with portholes and elaborate chromed pipework, opened at the Swine Queen's approach. We swept into the Carvery. If I had begun to calibrate the numbers of men and women in her cult, now I had to discard my sums and start again. I knew what a thousand faces looked like from the community meetings in Sun Hollow. This was closer to two thousand: two thousand stomping, hammering, whooping lunatics dressed in scraps of pig-flesh, gathered into two steep tiered galleries set either side of a spectacle of pure horror.

The central floor of the Carvery was a rectangular area about twenty metres wide and sixty long. It was made of metal, extensively perforated, and arranged with subtle slopes and numerous interconnecting drainage channels. I understood its function immediately: to gather and contain such blood and fluids as were likely to be spilled during the course of the Swine Queen's ministrations.

Occupying the floor were twelve wheeled plinths. Ten were occupied; the two nearest us conspicuously empty. Pigs lay bound to each of the others, all in different degrees of consumption. They were flat on their backs, strapped to the hard upper surfaces of the plinths, which in turn mirrored some of the floor's design considerations, being as well equipped with drainage runnels. The plinths had something in common with operating tables, or life-support couches. Wheeled alongside each of them was a makeshift arrangement of wheezing, huffing and glugging machines, all pistons, fluid bags, slow-dripping glassware, connected in turn by thick snaking cables which trailed across the floor, off into ducts in the wall. The pigs were all alive, but all of them would have been better off dead. I did not want to look, but when I considered averting my eyes I thought how much worse it had to be for Pinky, and

200

by some force of will I held my gaze, determined to record the crime in its fullness.

The least badly affected of the pigs had had oblongs of flesh removed, but not yet to the point of losing limbs or extremities. What was the most vile was not that these injuries had been done to them, but that there had obviously been time for the wounds to heal over. Probably Rose might have been the agent of some of these repairs, certainly the oldest of them, and I could only begin to guess at the psychological toll such work had taken on her. She would have been doing a healer's duty in the sure and certain knowledge that it was only to facilitate the furtherance of pain. Whoever had been responsible, there had been no lack of skill in their handiwork. There were careful stitch-lines; scar tissue sagging over absences. Now new areas had been marked for excision, delineated by drawn-on boxes in hatched tattoos. The life-support machines would stop the pigs from bleeding out or dying too quickly from shock. I would say that these were the luckiest of the ten, since they might have walked away once the restraints were undone. But another way of looking at it was that these pigs were only at the start of a journey, and the lucky ones were those near its culmination. The ones near the end were the hardest of all to look at. Almost everything had been cut away except a limb or part of a limb, and yet they remained living and, I believed, conscious.

The Swine Queen strode around these tables, banging her own staff against the metal floor, sometimes against the sides of the tables. She jiggled the fluid lines, made the glassware rattle. She bellowed to her audience, raising her arms, waving the staff above her head. The whooping reached its culmination and the Swine Queen called her acolytes to order, or its nearest approximation. They settled down, never becoming entirely still or entirely silent. The anticipation was too great for that.

"Let it never be said that we lack the gift of patience, my flock! We've waited many years for this moment, but never with any lack of faith that it would arrive. We asked for this day, and it was given! The one we sought, the rarest and most precious of them all, has been granted unto us!" The Swine Queen paused, lifting her staff to encourage a whoop of approbation. "Yes, rejoice—all of you! Very soon you'll have your reward! Prize noshing: the flesh of the Old One! I've tasted a little of him, just enough to want more, but now there will be ample meat for sharing! Even the least of you will have your scrap! And as his squeals ring out—as I broadcast them into the city—he'll send a message to others of his kind, and they'll know that I've taken their champion!"

Pinky angled his head to mine. We had been parked upright and near enough to each other to be able to speak.

"You still sure you want to work for this lunatic, de Ruyter? You think that's going to work out for you, in the long run?"

"It's not my time just yet," I said.

"It might be mine."

"No, I think you can hold on a little longer. You heard what she said: you're the one who's outlasted all the others. She'll keep you going as long as she can because she knows you're one of a kind. So now *isn't* your time."

The Swine Queen sidled back around to us. "A little chat between old pals, is it? Passing the time, trading reminiscences?"

"Whatever you mean to do to us," I said, "just get on with it."

"Oh, I shall!" This drew a roaring whoop, but rather than encourage it, the queen gave an angry jab of her staff, bringing down a sudden tense silence. "A little consideration for our guests, please, my flock! They can hardly hear themselves think over your din-dinner-din!"

It was only a silence in so far as the audience had quietened for a moment. The life-support machines were still making their whirring and gurgling noises. I tried to listen out for something coming up below us, shouts or gunfire, some hint that Glass had made her entry and would be with us soon, but there was nothing to be heard. Pinky wanted to start the havoc, and every part of me agreed with him: except for one last rational shred that said we had to wait a little longer.

"He's more use to you alive than dead," I said.

The Swine Queen leaned in. "Friends again, is it?"

"I'm just being pragmatic. You see a pig, your Swineness. I see a survivor. He hasn't made his way through all these years because he's lucky. He's a force of nature. A ruthlessly adaptable tactician and strategist who Lady Arek valued for a reason. He understands pigs, but he understands you and me just as capably. Cut him open, and you'll get to taste his meat. But you'd be wasting something far more valuable."

"I can have my nosh and eat it, you know." The Swine Queen swivelled her attention onto Pinky. "It's all right. I'm not going to cut too many bits off you just now. Just a little appetiser or two. Nothing you'll miss."

Pinky writhed against his upright restraints. He had his fists clenched, so there was no way to tell what was going on with his sharpened nails.

The pain hit me suddenly. The fire in my blood—the fire that was my blood—had begun to rage again. There had been no warning, no transition when the pain-relieving drug wore off. I tensed, crunching my teeth against each other.

The Swine Queen moved to the side of one of the occupied tables, one where the pig was still in the early stages of consumption. An aide took

202

her staff, then she delved among her tools and came out with a little whirring circular saw. She tested its sparking edge against the plinth's side, then began to excise a sliver of tissue from the area of the pig's thigh. The pig was still for a moment, as if drugged beyond any immediate effects of the cutting, but that was only temporary. The pig thrashed against the restraints. The pig squealed and bled, and still the Swine Queen continued. What she was removing was only the finest-possible slice of flesh, yet it was impossible to imagine the pig being afflicted by any higher pain. The Swine Queen finished her work with a sense of unhurried professionalism, refusing to be put off by the thrashing and the squealing. Finally she removed the circular saw, holding it aloft, still whirring, and with her other hand she peeled away a portion of flesh about as large as an eye-patch.

She tossed it into the audience: an offering to the greedy, grateful, masses. They were snared by her, like iron filaments in a magnetic field. Hands strained to grab at the morsel, or to wrestle it from one recipient to another. The Swine Queen watched this commotion for a second or two, pleased or appalled by it, and then returned her attention to the pig. She selected another area of flesh then dug down with the rotary cutter. Then, with her free hand, snapped her fingers at the fully masked men who had come down with us from the examination room. "Get our prizes on the bleeding slabs. A little taster won't ruin the main course, and I'm keen to see if the Old One's meat is as salty as his conversation."

Two of them moved around to the backs of our trolleys and began to fuss with the restraints. The other two remained in front, long-bladed knives drawn and ready. Human eyes moved behind the sagging, ragged-edged holes cut into their pig faces, but there was no humanity left in those eyes to appeal to.

"She's here," I said, not in a whisper, but quietly enough not to be overheard by the Swine Queen, preoccupied with her buzzing saw.

"I don't hear her," Pinky said.

"I don't either. But I trust that she's here and won't be long."

"Are you saying it's time?"

"I'm saying it's time."

"Good. Couldn't come a second sooner. This blood hurts so badly I'm starting to think I'll take the Swine Queen's knives instead."

The guard in front of me had been troubled by this exchange and jabbed the tip of the blade under my chin, cocking his head questioningly. The tip had not touched my skin, but it would only need to jerk up a little more to do me harm.

"What's time?" the pig mask asked.

203

"An abstract concept," I said.

This earned me a jab from the blade, drawing blood beneath my jaw. I flinched but did not cry out. Meanwhile, I continued to work the barbed nail into my palm, gouging open my own flesh. Until the haemoclast began to spill out from me.

There were two points of exit: my hand and my jaw. Neither was a large wound, but that was good. We could only cope with a partial loss of the haemoclast: it might be a weapon, but it still had to do the work of blood. The haemoclastic flow would staunch itself at intervals of about one litre, but it was up to each of us to manage the restarting of that process, until we were too weakened to continue.

I couldn't see the flow from my jaw, except as a spreading redness on my upper chest, but I had a much better view of my hand. The blood was lathering out, behaving in not quite the way blood was supposed to behave. It was a continuous spreading tide, and by the time it engulfed my fingertips, it had begun to self-organise. The lathering became granular rather than smooth, like a sea of red suddenly wind-ruffled into little domains. And those domains then separated from each other, leaving margins of clear, clean, bloodless flesh between them. The haemoclast was forming itself into several hundred sub-elements, each about the size of a small insect.

Small, red, gloss-coated insects.

The guards could see it happening. They understood that it was wrong, they knew this was not what blood was supposed to do, and they all had a long and excellent understanding of blood, its mechanisms of leakage, flow and coagulation. What they were seeing was a violation of those (literally) sacred principles. But as if in some dream paralysis, they were struggling to articulate the wrongness they saw before them, the Swine Queen was still sawing, and the pig still shrieking.

The flow from my palm was abating, but already I felt some small but welcome easing in the fire that the blood had lit within me. The haemoclast spilling from my jaw had formed into a column, joining the primary mass gathered around my hand. For a moment, it was as if I had covered my flesh in honey and dipped my hand into an ants' nest.

Until they lifted off me. It was an eruption, a sudden busy exodus of tiny red forms. They swarmed into the air, dithered for a moment or two—target selecting—and then exploded in about two dozen directions, multiple elements following each vector. They were as fast as darts, and within a second they had reached all their chosen objectives, in every corner of the Carvery.

The havoc came...but before mine struck, Pinky released his own haemoclast too. It was just the one wound in his case, but the effect was comparable. The swarms might not have looked like they were coordinating, but they were in fact acting as a single aggregate weapon, ready to be augmented by the haemoclastic load still within us. The bleeding from my palm had stopped: the weapon detecting that it had expelled about a litre of itself. I jabbed myself again, reopening the gash, and again the red tide surged willingly forth.

Out among the guards and Swine Queen acolytes, the little red forms were inflicting no end of chaos. They searched for orifices, sense organs, wounds and weaknesses. Where none could be identified, they impaled and drilled and corkscrewed in anyway. The masks and partial masks were no impediment. They went in fast and sought out neural tissue. Then they exploded, with a pop of stored energy like a tiny firework. In ones and twos it was enough to knock out specific areas of brain function, incapacitating the host almost instantly. When dozens of haemoclastic units had drilled in at once, the effect was more like a small demolition charge going off behind the eyes. A sort of grey and pink smoke came out of them in a pulse. Mostly, that was not survivable. But the afflicted bodies still jerked and spasmed as they went down.

The Swine Queen was still alive, still upright and able to walk and talk. The haemoclastic units would not have spared her intentionally, but it seemed that she had been lucky or that her mask and armour were offering some additional defence.

She made the circular saw whirr again and pushed the blade up against my forehead, in a top-to-bottom orientation. She let it skim against my skin, but did not depress it any further.

"Make this stop," she said.

She pressed down, beginning to cut into my face. I reached up with my left hand and wrenched the saw from her grip. My arms had been free from the moment her guards released our restraints, but my legs were still bound. Before the Swine Queen could react, I chewed through the remaining bindings with her saw, then tossed it to Pinky. He was nearly free as well. I hoped that, like me, he was starting to feel better as the haemoclast left his body.

The second pulse of units had finished leaving my body from the gash in my hand. Already I felt the giddy, light-headed absence of those two litres. Perhaps a little more was spilling from the wound in my face, but it was hard to tell how deeply she had cut. The first wave was nearing the end of its effectiveness, having taken down as many victims as it could, but leaving many still unharmed. The second wave—combining with units sent out by Pinky—was organising and target-selecting. It was a fuzzy, nervous ball of red, which suddenly dispersed to go after multiple targets.

The Swine Queen dug a long-bladed knife from her personal arsenal. I jerked aside as she swung it, surprising myself with the instinctive speed of my reaction, the ease with which it had by-passed any conscious processing. Pinky, free now, ducked behind the Swine Queen and retrieved something from one of her fallen guards. It was a stubby pistol with an oversized barrel and a short, fussy haft. Pinky's hands were not made for it. He tossed it my way and I caught it deftly, my fingers sliding around the haft and finding the trigger. My hand had been blood-lathered a few seconds ago, but when the haemoclasts detached they left the skin completely unmarred, with no stickiness or slickness. I pointed the barrel at the Swine Queen's mask and aimed between her eyes. The gun coughed and kicked. She dropped, a finger-sized hole bored into her pig-skinned brow. She made to say something, gurgling and thrashing. Haemoclasts swarmed in, finding the wound and piling over themselves to fight their way into her. The Swine Queen screamed as they did their work, and kept on screaming until the detonations which ended her life.

We were free, but in no sense safe. There were still too many swineherds. They were scrambling down from the viewing galleries, almost tumbling over each other in their fear and rage. They might not have understood what had happened, but they had seen enough to realise that it had come from within our bodies. I pressed the barb back into my flesh, hoping I could tolerate the loss of another litre. Pinky and I backed against each other. He had the Swine Queen's knife, and I had the gun. It was enough to hold back the advancing swineherds temporarily, but we would need something more to survive.

It came. There was a new sound rising from the mob now: wild shrieks, somehow more urgent and terrified than anything we had heard so far. Accompanying this sound was a fast metallic lashing. A flicker of silver caught my eye: a dancing, gyring whirlwind working its way through a field of standing and fallen bodies, chopping into them as it proceeded. I watched in numb recognition. It was one of the ninecats. I had already seen something of what it could do when Glass gave her demonstration, but nothing had prepared me for this moving vortex of carnage. The ninecat had become a demonic entity, a whirling quicksilver abomination, moving through our enemies like a razor-edged propeller blade.

There was more than one. A second had found its way into the Carvery, and then a third. There was no defence against these weapons. They went through armour as easily as air, flicked blood and flesh up in their wake, and they gave every impression of never stopping. A storm of body parts rained down on us, and my eyes stung against the blood haze. They would not touch us, I told myself. They had been conditioned to recognise our forensic and biometric traces. I had wanted them to find us. But now that they were here, now that I was seeing their grisly work, my certainties collapsed.

Then I spied a fourth, and a fifth.

The destruction continued. Pinky and I were now incidental to it. The swineherds had stopped trying to kill us; all any of them were interested in was getting out of that room, fleeing to some imagined sanctuary where the whirling horrors might not reach them. Nor were the pigs entirely safe: the ninecats were not attacking them directly, but as the tide of destruction lapped around and past the plinths, some incidental injuries were all but guaranteed. The pigs shrieked as the edges of the blades nicked their already sensitised flesh. The equipment that had been wheeled in to keep some of them alive, or sufficiently buffered from shock, was being toppled and ripped apart without discrimination. Still more of the ninecats were finding their way into the Carvery, springing out of ducts and grilles. Now that the advance forces had located us, the other units were being signalled to converge on this room.

"There are too many," I said, raising my voice above the shrieking and the chaos. "This is more than she was meant to send in."

"If they're here, then so is Glass," Pinky said, grunting as he made a pained lunge with the knife, encouraging one of the masked men to keep his distance.

"She could barely control one of them."

"She doesn't need to—they're doing what they need to do."

"For now. Do you think you can make it to the landing deck? If Glass has commenced her attack then *Scythe* should be moving to the extraction point."

"I can make it. But I'm not the one Lady Arek shot in the leg."

"I'll be all right. She aimed well."

I thought I could find the path back the way we had been brought. Almost lost in the chaos, we moved in the direction of the tall maroon doors. We had only got about halfway there before a fresh wave of swineherds burst through, all of them armed and armoured. They took a moment to appraise the scene before them, then discharged their weapons, partly in the general direction of the ninecats and partly at us. We would have been dead instantly if they'd had a clear line of fire, but the air was still a storm of blood, bone, meat and finely shredded armour. Pinky grabbed my shoulder and drove me into the cover of one of the empty plinths. Bullets clanged against the other side of the plinth. They had projectile weapons, but nothing that could penetrate the plinth's thick metal construction.

The ninecats were still arriving. There had to be a dozen in the room by now, perhaps as many as twenty. One slowed its whirling and sidled up to us, swivelling its blank silver body, its nine needle-tipped limbs varnished with blood.

"It recognises us," I said quietly. "Tell me it recognises us."

Pinky dabbed at his skin and lifted his hand away, crimson-stained. "We're getting a little tainted. Might not be getting so good a biometric fix on us."

The ninecat pushed nearer to me. I pushed back, but there was only so far I could go before I lost the shelter of the plinth. The ninecat lashed out a limb. There was a cold sting against my cheek. The limb withdrew, taking a small sample of me with it.

I shot the ninecat. The pistol blasted it into about three large smoking pieces, dropping to the floor instantly. The disconnected limbs thrashed, but now without purpose. I squeezed away from the ruined machine as best I could.

"Why'd you shoot it?"

I glared at him. "Would you rather I hadn't shot it?"

"I'd rather those other ones weren't suddenly taking an interest in us."

Half a dozen other ninecats had broken off from whatever they were doing and began to whirlwind their way in our direction. I shot, and shot again. With each discharge I feared that the next squeeze of the trigger would produce silence. The pistol was of a type unknown to me and I had no idea of its capacity or recovery time.

A white explosion blinded and deafened me, and I lay numb, shivering. I forced my eyes open, squinting through dust and pain. Three white forms resolved, hovering on the edge of focus. They had blasted their way into the Carvery, and were now dispensing fire from built-in weapons. Two were suits of the same size I knew from *Scythe*; the third was of a similar design but smaller and with different anatomical proportions.

"Our rides are here," Pinky said.

CHAPTER SIXTEEN

Glass and the two slaved suits stomped in through the hole they had blown in the wall, smoke still billowing from the pop-out slug dispensers in their sleeves. Against the remaining numbers of swineherds, the suits were as good as invulnerable. Bosers were doing the main work now, firing from shoulder emplacements on the suits. Their coordination and accuracy was far beyond any human guidance. These in turn were augmented by micro-grenades which the suits extracted from a belt-feed and tossed into the air with unerring accuracy. The swineherds' projectile weapons did more harm to their users than to the suits, ricocheting off the adaptive armour. Their edged and blunt weapons were as useless as kisses. It was almost cruel, seeing this total disparity in preparedness. But I only had to glance at the still-living forms on the plinths to remind myself the swineherds deserved every moment of it.

The suits continued to work their way towards us. Glass was at least showing some restraint: as far as I could tell, none of her direct shots had yet hit any of the pigs. But there was little accounting for the stray fire and ricochets being scattered around.

Then I noticed a development.

The ninecats were reacting to the suits. In ones and twos they were pulling away from whatever they were doing and making lunging, whip-cracking strikes against the suits. Their limbs were not capable of slicing right through the suits' armour, but they were forcing the suits to defend themselves, and direct more and more of their energy into emergency repair. Silver gashes were appearing in the white armour, then melting away...but the ninecats were gathering their numbers, flinging themselves against the suits at a quickening rate.

Glass's plan was going adrift.

The suits began to retaliate. Not just passive defence now, but active measures. The bosers angled down to snap onto the ninecats. Mostly, all it took was one shot. Now and then, a lobbed grenade had the same effect. The fifth or sixth time a ninecat was destroyed, it produced an explosion

209

nearly as powerful as the one that had heralded the suits' arrival. It was enough to tip over two of the plinths, spilling their tormented occupants to the blood-slick floor. Everything was sticky and red: no amount of drainage could cope with the current demand.

"I'm not sure if we'll be safer in those suits or out of them," I confided to Pinky.

"You take your chances either way you like, Stink. Know where I'd sooner be."

The suits had gained a moment's advantage over the ninecats: enough time for Glass to complete her crossing and kneel by us, flanked by the two other suits. Her voice boomed out from the suit's neck. "Are you ready? I'll provide covering fire while you get into the suits. Simply stand and present yourselves to them: they will do the rest."

Bullets were still ringing against the plinth. Glass's weapons began to concentrate on the swineherds who had been targeting us, and the incoming volleys became intermittent as our adversaries were taken out or forced to duck behind cover of their own. They had no hope at all, so long as the suits kept working.

I chose my moment and sprang for the suit. It packaged itself around me with a reassuring brusqueness, indifferent to my suffering a few more bruises in the process. The faceplate was already framed by the familiar pattern of status icons. Glass had also allowed me access to some of the weapons modes that were normally blocked. Next to me, his head only coming up to my shoulder, Pinky had been swallowed by his own suit.

"Now we leave," Glass said. "We'll use minimum necessary force all the way out."

I glanced back at the destruction she had already wrought.

"*That* was minimum necessary force?"

"Difficult as you may find it to accept, Clavain, I used restraint. I don't want to undermine the structure of this place while we're still inside it."

"Fair observation. What do we do about these prisoners?"

"I am already dispensing a painless euthanising gas."

"No, Glass," I said, knowing that to raise my voice would have achieved nothing. "We don't gas them. You have room aboard *Scythe* for hundreds of evacuees."

"Upon my arrival I conducted a rapid situational triage. What has happened here is . . . regrettable."

"I'm so glad you find it regrettable," Pinky said.

"They are beyond any sort of salvation, not helped by being caught in the crossfire of our rescue effort. This is by far the kindest option."

"Take him to the ship," Pinky declared. "He matters, apparently."

I turned to him. "Where are you going?"

"To see what I can do about all the other captives she must have in this place."

"You think you can work that suit well enough to avoid trouble? Those ninecats are starting to turn against us, and only Glass knows how many more she sent into the building."

"How many?" Pinky asked her sharply.

She looked down at him. "More. But the suits will get us to *Scythe*, provided we leave immediately."

"Go," I said. "Get aboard *Scythe* and prepare for departure. Pinky and I will go back and look for her prisoners."

"I wasn't looking for a shadow," the pig said.

"No, but you might benefit from having someone at your side. Glass, do as I say. If you don't, I'll take this helmet off and breathe in some of that gas you just dispensed."

"I wouldn't allow it," she said. "And I'm not allowing this. Your suits will stay slaved to mine. You have comms and weapons authority, but nothing else. And don't think that means you'd be able to shoot me."

"Glass," I said, seething. "Allow us this. If not me, then at least let Pinky search the lower levels."

My visor pulsed with a pink hazard warning: a throbbing triangle bracketing an emerging a ninecat, sawing its way into the Carvery through a solid wall.

"They're here," Glass said. "And we're leaving."

There was no further debate. Glass set off at a fast stride and my suit jerked into immediate pursuit. I had no means of slowing or altering my course: the suit's dominion over me was total. Pinky must have come to the same conclusion because he did not offer a word of protest. I was starting to understand him a little better, to see the calculating intelligence beneath the swagger. Complaint was only effective up to a point, after which it was a waste of energies better kept in reserve. But I wondered what reckoning he planned for Glass, further down the line.

More ninecats were breaking into the Carvery. We made it to the main doors without resistance, and Glass only paused to lob a few grenades and boser pulses back at the emerging ninecats at the far end of the room. Glass shut the doors behind us then used a continuous boser beam to perform a quick fusion-weld down the central seam. Then we were moving again. I felt two cold jabs: one in my thigh, the other in my upper arm.

"I've been hit."

"No, you've been surgically punctured. Your suit is performing a reverse transition to the buffering solution. Or would you rather keep the haemo-clast? Any longer in you, and you'd start to die."

I felt better, at least in a relative sense, as the suit did its work on my blood. I hoped Pinky was feeling the same benefit.

We rose through the levels without difficulty, encountering only light resistance from the remaining dregs of the swineherds. Somewhere inside me was a developing guilt that I was leaving the other pigs behind to their fates. I tried to negate it by reminding myself that I had come to Chasm City not to rid the city of its evils, but to achieve the very specific objective of securing the stones. That had already cost me pain, fear and the very real possibility of losing my life. It was enough to know that we had damaged the lair and decapitated the queen's cult, thereby sowing the likely seeds of its collapse. There were only three of us, and we had risked enough as it was...

But I knew this was going to prickle inside me. It wasn't that I had a choice: I had no doubt whatsoever that Glass could make my suit do anything she wanted it to. But what troubled me was my relief that Glass had taken that choice out of my hands. It was a coward's comfort.

Glass's suit had decided that the most reliable way out of the Swine-house was to retrace our journey down from the landing stage. One of the last places we passed through was therefore the examination room where the Swine Queen had failed to detect the haemoclast. The room thrummed, picking up the vibrations caused by an unusually large spacecraft holding position just overhead, displacing vast quantities of atmosphere as it kept station.

A ninecat blocked our path. It was squatting on its needle-thin legs, fixed to the floor like an inverted candelabra.

Glass shot it: at least they were able to be killed on an individual basis.

"There are more converging. We must move quickly."

"Dear God, Glass: how many of those things did you release?"

"Eighty."

"Eighty! Are you insane? How did you get hold of eighty of them?"

"I...reasoned with Lady Arek. I convinced her that an overwhelming force offered our best chance for success. I brought them inside one of the suits."

"You missed something. Some detail somewhere in their programming. You got arrogant, thinking that there's no system in the universe that the brilliant Glass can't master. Did it occur to you that there might have been a reason those ninecats were left behind? That perhaps they were never to be trusted in the first place?"

We ascended the stairs, Glass's suit taking them two risers at a time, and ours following with the same bounding strides. My visor was clotting over with warning symbols again: detecting the moving, mechanical threats it had already decided were not a good thing. I risked a backward glance, and made out a swift, quicksilver scuttling. Two or three of the ninecats were coming up behind us, advancing slowly but deliberately, as if they too had conducted a threat assessment. We were to be neutralised. Carefully.

Glass blasted open a final set of doors and a howling wind swept in. Murky, yellow-tinged daylight pushed down, interrupted by the clawed shadow of the huge ship hovering just out of sight. Its engines pushed a nerve-shredding scream all the way through my suit.

I could only see part of the landing stage. There were a few bodies lying around, but no living swineherds. The turrets that had covered Lady Arek's ship—those I could see—had been reduced to black-smoking chimneys. In one, I could still make out the remains of a Gatling cannon, reduced to a sagging, drooping sculptural mass, with two goggled and masked skeletons in attendance.

Glass led us out. *Scythe* was about ten metres above the tops of the turrets, hovering horizontally, its long axis more or less parallel with the chasm wall, its belly ramp lowered to skim against the landing stage. A rush of relief surged over me, and for a moment that guilt was gone entirely. I was about to have my own skin saved, and that was enough. We had done it: got the stones, and saved ourselves. A million hard steps might lie ahead of us, but this one was done.

Nearly.

One ninecat emerged from the cover of one of the corpses, then another.

Glass fell back, and suddenly I realised that I had complete control of my suit again.

"Get aboard. You and the pig. I'll provide a covering fire."

I did not argue; it seemed like an excellent plan to me. I might have had weapons authority, but I had nothing to compare with Glass's super-human reflexes. I grabbed at Pinky's shoulder, sensing his hesitation, and as a pair we ran out across the deck, towards the base of the ramp. It was moving, as *Scythe* drifted in response to the winds and turbulence rising in the chasm. Glass took care of the two ninecats that had emerged from the corpses, but others were slithering into view, from apertures and hiding places. Pinky and I dispensed our own weapons with some effectiveness, but since we had to concentrate on running and aiming for the moving platform, our efforts were mixed. Glass was having to take up the slack, and the number of ninecats was taxing her capabilities. She must have depleted her grenades because now her suit was only using its bosers. The ninecats were concentrating their attentions on her, judging Pinky and me to be of less immediate concern.

We reached the base of the ramp just as some gust overwhelmed *Scythe*'s control and sent the ramp bludgeoning into us like a runaway cart. It caught me mid-section and I folded into the impact, my chest and arms overhanging the ramp, my legs dangling beneath it, skimming the ground. Pinky had been knocked over completely: the impact had caught him above his centre of gravity. I hauled myself onto the ramp, grabbed a rail and reached down to scoop Pinky up as we passed over him again. I grunted, and swung him to safety. For an instant our faceplates met, and I saw some reaction in his expression: not gratitude exactly, but at least a twitch in that direction.

"Are you all right?"

"I'd say I'm pretty far from all right." He paused. "But I'm better without that shit inside me. Glass was right."

"How so?"

"I ain't ever doing that again."

Then we were both standing, facing Glass. I ought to prioritise my own survival and hurry up the ramp, but I could not abandon her that easily, not while we had so much unfinished business.

Glass retreated in the direction of the ramp, her back to us. Her boser shots were becoming more sparing now. The ninecats were snipping at her, lashing against her legs and thighs, sometimes flinging themselves against her chest. Silver furrows opened up in the suit, centimetres deep, only to close again as the suit marshalled its repair mechanisms. But the rate at which the ninecats were inflicting damage was exceeding the suit's capacity for healing. The ninecats were getting more brazen. One flung itself at Glass, coiled its legs around her knee joint, and made a sharp savage twist. Glass dropped to a lopsided stagger, then a kneeling posture with her left hand pressed to the floor.

"Move!" I shouted.

Glass hauled herself back to her feet. She covered some ground, limping as her knee refused to bear her weight, testifying to some severe damage in the suit and perhaps to Glass herself. She fell again, this time flat on her front. She was about six metres from the drifting sanctuary of the ramp. I made an instantaneous decision and hopped back onto the deck. A ninecat was already coiling itself around Glass's right leg below the knee, chewing into the armour as it tightened its hold.

I moved into a low, scrambling posture and grabbed Glass's outstretched right hand. Trusting the suit to apply all necessary power augmentation, I yanked her as hard as I could, and nearly fell backwards in the direction

214

of the ramp. I recovered, and the ramp brushed against me: either by luck or intention, the ship had closed the distance. Pinky grabbed me, and I retained my hold on Glass. Pinky pulled harder and by effort and will we managed to get both Glass and myself onto the ramp. Most of Glass was still overhanging, but it was enough. *Scythe* must have detected that its master was now back aboard—in the technical sense—because we began to ascend very rapidly, with the ramp retracting back into the belly. With Pinky still fixed onto me, I adjusted my hold on Glass and pulled more of her onto the ramp, with just her legs overhanging.

I sighted my boser and blasted the ninecat still attached to Glass. The ninecat fell away: a charred, flailing ruin. The pulse had taken a bite out of the suit as well: a blackened, smoking depression in which it was impossible to say where the laminated structures of the suit ended and Glass began.

The ramp continued to seal up into the belly. When it was nearly done, and the chasm walls were racing past us as *Scythe* accelerated, two of the sphere robots dropped out and extracted Glass from our care, spiriting her with immense speed back into the ship. Pinky and I followed, both of us risking a last glance down at the Swinehouse before the ramp closed off our view.

Multiple explosions flowered around the Swinehouse. They hit suddenly and in unison, concentrated around the anchor points where the Swinehouse extended its tethers and wall-braces. The tethers snapped and whiplashed, and the braces and buttresses sagged and ripped under uncontrolled force. The explosions halted. They had done their work, and mechanics and gravity would finish the task. The Swinehouse was detaching from the chasm wall. Instead of dropping like a stone, it seemed to hover for a second or two, unwilling to submit to the inevitable. Then, still moving as one structure, it began a slow, leisurely acceleration. Pinky and I watched in the last seconds before the view was closed to us. The Swinehouse was tumbling forward, facing down, and parts of it were flaking off as the winds of the chasm had their way. Still accelerating, it lost itself in the opacity of the deeper mist layers. It was like watching a dark coffin vanishing beneath roiling white waves. All that remained were the remnants of the buttresses and tethers, the latter still flailing around as if in some terrible agitation.

"It's still a long way down," I said quietly.

"Like I need to be reminded?"

"It might've been the right thing for her to do. If there was no way to save the prisoners inside, then at least they'll be out of their pain very shortly."

"But not yet."

"Not just yet, Scorp."

The ramp sealed up into the belly lock. There were the two of us there: the spheres had already bustled away with Glass. The air exchange proceeded rapidly and our suits peeled away from us as we stepped into the suiting room. Two more robots arrived in prompt fashion and immediately set about attending to our obvious injuries while we remained standing. While that was going on—and our old blood pumped back into us by the same robots—I wondered about Glass, and the price she had paid for our rescue.

"I won't say that went well," I said. "But given how much more badly it could have gone, I think we have to consider ourselves lucky."

I expected some rebuff, but Pinky's answer wrong-footed me. "You think she'll mend, Stink?"

"I think she has a better chance of it than you or I would have in the same situation. The main thing is...for whatever purpose they're going to serve, we have the Gideon stones." I nodded at the floor. Somewhere below us, lost in the mist, I wondered if the Swinehouse was still falling. "Everything else, including your survival or mine, has to be secondary to that."

"I'm not saying this rubs out all my doubts about you."

"I'd be surprised if it did."

"But it's a start. A small one." He paused. "One other thing."

"Yes?" I asked guardedly.

"Why'd you call me Scorp?"

"I didn't."

"Yes, you did. Very distinctly. I didn't mishear. So where'd it come from? What made *that* drop from your lips?"

"Does it mean something?"

"It's my name. A name. One of several. Lady Arek knows it, and she knows that just now I happen to prefer Pinky. But Scorpio is a name I took once, and it didn't fall out of your mouth by accident."

"I can't explain it. Perhaps Lady Arek said it once, and I picked up on it without realising?"

"No, not that. Nor did you hear it from Snowdrop. She doesn't know it. Plenty she does know, but not that. Anyway, you used the form of it *he* always did. I was Scorp to Nevil."

"But I'm not him!" I said, raising my hands in protest. "I might be his brother—maybe I can start to believe that much—but I'm not him." I shook my head, rattled by Pinky's line of questioning, and unable to deny the root of it. I had used that name. For an instant, a piece of the past had swum into my present: a connection between Pinky and me.

As if we already knew each other.

"Glass will know," I said.

Pinky nodded slowly. "You want her to live?"

"More that I don't want her to die before I wring some answers out of her."

"You're deeper than you look, Stink." Pinky went to the door that led out of the suiting room into the rest of *Scythe*. "Let's go see if we can find that cold-hearted ghoul, shall we?"

"That sounds like an excellent plan."

He opened the door.

Glass was not on the other side of it. But a hundred other faces were.

I was the first to speak.

"After everything, she rescued them. Before she came for us, she must have found them and got them aboard *Scythe*."

"We have tongues," said the foremost of the hyperpigs, the one who had been standing immediately in front of the door. "At least, those of us she didn't get around to cutting them out of." The pig, dressed in little more than rags, offered a hand. "I'm Barras."

I took Barras's hand. "I'm . . . something. Call me Warren for now."

"He's working through some issues," Pinky said. Then, to Barras: "I'm Pinky. Maybe you already knew that."

"Word did get round," Barras said, nodding slowly, and with something like admiration. "Especially when you came to the Swinehouse. They were gearing up for the feast of the century."

"So I gathered. Are you going to be all right, Barras? I'm sorry we didn't get to free you personally, but Glass had other ideas."

"I'll be all right, Pinky. We'll all be all right." Barras looked back at the throng pressing up behind him, stretching away along the corridor's length. "This is a good day. This morning we were all going to die, and now we're not. I mean, not just yet, and not in the Carvery. I don't know whether the news you have for us is good or bad in your terms, but I guarantee it'll seem good to us."

"How many of you did she rescue?" I asked.

"We haven't done numbers," Barras said. "But about three-quarters, I'd guess. Some she couldn't get to in time. She said she would save as many as she could, but some would have to stay behind."

"It's gone," Pinky said.

Barras did not need clarification. "It's better. I'm sorry for those we left behind, but . . . this is better."

217

"Do you remember Snowdrop?"

There was a cautious murmur from the gathering. "We do. They say she made it out. Did you have news?"

"Better than that, Barras." Pinky closed his hand around Barras's wrist, squeezing it hard. "You'll see her soon, when we get back to Lady Arek's stronghold. And others. Bruno, Chersini, Maude, Yilin…if those names mean anything to you, they all made it, they're with us, and you'll see them soon."

I felt bad about dragging the conversation back into the immediate reality, but it had to be done. "Did you see Glass after you came aboard?"

"No," Barras said, puzzlement creasing his brow. "Where is she? I thought you'd know."

"Glass was hurt. The ship must be looking after her. But that leaves the question of who's looking after the ship." I braced my hand against the wall, feeling vibrations. The floor was tilted, and my knees were registering an increasing load. "We seem to be climbing, so I think we can assume we're on our way back to space. But I'm not going to sit back and assume the best." I raised my voice. "Ship! *Scythe*! You know me. You knew me well enough to wake me up when Glass was in trouble. Now I'd really like to see her!"

"Can you operate this ship?" Pinky asked.

"Glass assigned me certain controls, but not all of them. And I don't know what the ship will and won't let me do. *Scythe*!"

A door opened before me, in what had previously been the unmarked side of the corridor. Barras and three of the pigs squeezed aside. Floating in the doorway was one of the sphere robots, with its two arms extended in supplication.

"Follow it," Pinky said. "I'll stay with Barras; we have to start discussing plans for these survivors. When you have something, get back to us."

"I will." I hesitated at the point of reaching out to him, wanting to cement whatever new-found respect had begun to form between us, but I worried that it was still too fragile for that, and I might do more harm than good. Instead I contented myself with nodding, meeting his eyes as I did so. "We won't waste the opportunity to help these people, Pinky."

"Damn right we won't," he answered.

I set off after the robot, the door sealing behind me.

The angle of the floor tilted, acceleration rising, and then the floor formed treads into itself and I found myself climbing a steepening stairway. After a turn or two the robot brought me to a room in the ship that I had not seen before, despite my wanderings. It was the medical suite, or infirmary, or whatever Glass called it.

She was in the middle of the bright white room, lit by the angelic glow emanating from its own seamless walls, cordoned by medical machines and enclosed in a large, fluid-filled tank. Glass was restrained by a harness of spiderlike manipulators that were applying gentle contact to various intact parts of her body. She was not wearing any sort of mask or breathing device, so she was either inhaling the pale green support medium or already dead. But if she were dead, or in some way beyond resurrection, I did not think the machines would be showing such obvious devotion.

Whether they were trying to keep her alive, or bring her back to life, I was in no doubt that something was happening. Larger machines moved around outside the tank with speed and purpose. I supposed they were running scans of some sort, or perhaps projecting energies into the tank. Within it, smaller machines swam or undulated through the medium with the busy industry of fish. Now and then one of the machines on the outside made contact with the tank's exterior and seemed to exchange a machine or part of a machine with those on the inside through a matter-permeable region of the container. A constant flicker of blue lights emanated from the machines.

But Glass herself was still, her face a mask of death. It was motionless and her eyes were dark-lidded. If she breathed, I saw no sign of it.

I noticed a familiar-looking device, fixed to a medical console. A tray-sized portable medical scanner, not far removed from the instruments we had in Sun Hollow. I detached the device, thumbed it to power, and swept it across the tank, eyeing the blur of details which played across its display surface. I zeroed in on Glass, and allowed the device to probe into her chest, peeling away layers of anatomy as it scanned and processed.

Now at last I had a clearer view of the implanted mass. Glass was either too preoccupied to override the imagery, or no longer concerned with the keeping of secrets.

It was a fist-sized kernel of dense machinery, lodged deep in her thoracic cavity. An artificial heart or heart-lung machine? When we spoke in Sun Hollow, just before leaving the pressurised part of the tunnel, she had admitted that it was a life-support device.

But I could also see Glass's heart, and her lungs. The heart pulsed, and the lungs inflated and deflated, albeit very slowly. So she was breathing, after all. Was alive.

What did a creature like Glass, already superhumanly strong and resilient, need with a clumsy-looking machine inside her chest?

The scanner freckled over with static.

"Clavain," her voice sounded, ringing from the walls, even as her mouth remained still. "Did no one tell you it's bad manners to pry?"

219

I set aside the scanner.

"I'm sorry that you were hurt."

"Sorry that I was nearly killed, before you had a chance to do it yourself? Or sorry that these injuries have upstaged some of what you might have been thinking of doing to me?"

"I am simply sorry you were hurt."

"That doesn't sound like you. Whatever happened to your pledge?"

I blunted her question with one of my own. "Why in hell didn't you tell us that you'd already saved those pigs?"

"Because I had no reason to justify myself. Because their safety was contingent on the safe departure of *Scythe*, which at that point was by no means assured."

"It was a good thing. A kind thing."

"It was tactically feasible."

"Oh, shut up, Glass. You can drop the act. I see you for what you are. A nearly invulnerable shell wrapped around something that's still a lot warmer and more human than she's ready to admit—a human core that still makes mistakes and still cares."

"It was an error to risk rescuing the pigs. I was already beginning to see indications that the ninecats were reverting to non-compliance."

"Non-compliance. What do you call death? Non-respiration?"

"I call death death. We have a solid understanding." She paused. "But it was an error. I risked compromising the one component of the operation we could ill afford to lose."

"I'm back to being a component now, am I?"

"We're all components."

"Those pigs are people you saved. You can run some cold-blooded calculation after the fact and say you shouldn't have done it, but that doesn't change the fact of their survival. They were going to die; now they get to live."

"We may not have improved their life chances. I received a transmission from Lady Arek as soon as she was clear of Yellowstone. Conditions have deteriorated while we were down below."

"To what extent?"

"The Inhibitor movements we have been monitoring since our arrival have shifted to a more organised level of activity. Lady Arek's stronghold has become the focus of their attentions."

"Then we have to do something."

"Right answer. Go to the control room and ask the ship to put you in contact with Lady Arek. *Scythe* will do what it can to avoid signal interception, but you must refrain from all but essential communication."

"Why are you telling me this?"

"I need time for self-repair. Perhaps several days. The ship will place me in an induced coma, to assist the neural processes."

"This really *isn't* the time."

"There's no choice. I have to skirt death in order to live again. Now go and speak to Lady Arek. She will understand where we have to go next."

"The fabled Charybdis?"

"Not yet. Before Charybdis, we need more information. We will find it on Ararat, in the p Eridani system. Lady Arek will explain."

"Glass," I said softly.

"Yes?"

"Don't die in there."

I placed my hand against the container, half wondering if she might move her hand to press against mine from the other side. But Glass made no movement, and I left her to heal.

Part Four

EVACUATION

CHAPTER SEVENTEEN

To my relief—and no small astonishment—I realised that I was down, alive and mostly unhurt. The dropship was perfectly still. Through my visor, and the curve of the transparent segment of the hull beyond it, I made out a low, rust-coloured ridge which seemed to be a few hundred metres away. Nearer me was an area of sloping ground dotted with small, sharp boulders. The sky was a pale buff, deceptively bright. It did not take many atoms to scatter the sun's radiation in a way that suggested the full, comforting blanket of a breathable atmosphere.

I was on my side, nearly horizontal. None of the other dropships were to be seen, although a few faint smoke trails still lingered in the air. I ran a systems review. If I had a broken limb, or irreparable damage to my suit, my mission was finished. None of us was indispensable, and the others could find workarounds for my absence.

But the suit was intact. A good a thing, too, as I would be totally dependent on it for my entire spell on Mars. The dropship was finished, its outer skin burned to a crisp, but that was to be expected. It had never been meant to do more than get me onto the surface. Its only remaining task was to conceal itself. As for my body, the toll of damage was about as serious as it could be without actually preventing me from continuing. I had neither broken nor dislocated any limbs. I did have a bruised or fractured rib or two, and there was ligament and muscle damage around my hips and knees. I had suffered mild concussion during the landing, and had a small retinal bleed in one eye. I seemed to have bitten my tongue and chipped a tooth.

I could cope with all of that—and would have to, immediately. Before moving, though, I scrolled through the medical diagnostic options and authorised my suit to do whatever was required to make me functional. Micro-syringes pricked my skin around the damaged joints, and pumped a cocktail of steroids, anti-inflammatories and localised painkillers into the affected regions. I soon felt a warm numbness around my hips and knees. As awkward and uncoordinated as it made me feel, it allowed me to begin the work ahead.

Groaning against the pain of my ribs—there was nothing the suit could do for me there—I cracked open the dropship's hull and wriggled out of its close-fitting compartment. Somewhat unsteadily, I stood up and moved around the wreckage. Lying there on the ground, still smoking, the dropship looked far too small to have contained me, let alone to have been my home for the three months it had taken to reach Mars.

Heatproof compartments had been built into its skin for equipment too bulky to be stowed inside along with my suit. I kicked at these scorched hatches until they sprang open, then collected the items stored inside. I fixed them onto the many attachment points on my suit. Survival rations, medical supplies, small arms, ammunition—and one heavy machine gun, which I stowed on a specially engineered rig across my lower back, beneath my rear life-support pack.

I checked the dropship over one final time, making sure I had left nothing, then sent the verbal command that instructed it to self-bury. Parts of its hull moved counter to each other in a complex, spiralling pattern, cutting surfaces digging into the ground and slowly gaining traction. It looked like a dark, squirming maggot. I stood back and watched for the five minutes it took the dropship to fully submerge itself. It would keep going down until it hit bedrock, and then begin an even slower process of auto-catalytic breakdown, denying the Conjoiners any useful components or materials, if they were ever lucky enough to find the burial spot.

I scuffed over the disturbed ground with my heel. The surface disturbance was actually quite minor. Winds were due in a few days and would soon conceal evidence of the burial. In the meantime, it would simply look like the impact point of a piece of debris from the asteroid.

Exactly as planned.

Footprints were more of a problem. Each of us had to cross hundreds of kilometres to the rendezvous point, and still more to the capsule. Fortunately, the mission planners had considered this detail. My suit had thickened bulges around its ankles and sleeves. These were a mission-specific augmentation, containing telescopic stilts. I deployed the ankle stilts a step at a time, teetering on my rising height, until they were at their maximum extension. After a few seconds of unsteadiness my balance came back. We had trained well enough that using the legs was mostly second nature. The sleeve-mounted stilts were reserved for scrambling over difficult terrain, and I would not need them immediately.

The stilts had been carefully engineered to leave the minimum possible ground disturbance, while just supporting my weight. They were also made of a strong thermal insulator, so that we minimised our heat transfer to the terrain—critical as we would need to keep moving in the hours of darkness.

The final adaptation to the suit was a huge, self-deploying camouflage parasol. It popped out of a compartment in the top of my backpack, pushed up on a stalk above my head, then flung out overlapping segments to an adjustable radius of up to three metres. The parasol had a domed profile, so that its edges drooped to within about a metre of the surface. It obstructed my sightline, but the parasol was sewn with arrays of sensors which fed a visual overlay to my visor. In an emergency, I could squat low, blending with the ground under total concealment. The parasol's upper surface was constantly adjusting itself to achieve a seamless match of colour, texture and temperature with the ground underneath it. It was a lot of trouble to go to, given that the Conjoiners had little opportunity for overhead surveillance. But its main purpose was to deceive the neutral Demarchists into believing that the Coalition was still fully compliant with its treaties.

I moved off, making four-metre strides with each swing of my stilts. There was no transition, no easy build-up. I was immediately into my rhythm, moving at the unforgiving pace we had trained for. Through the numbing fog of the drugs, I still felt the protestation of my joints and muscles. If it became unbearable, the suit could increase its anaesthetic dosage. But the one thing I could not do—would not permit myself to do—was to slow or to stop. A pulse on my faceplate showed the direction I needed to go, and the estimated distance to the rendezvous point.

Six hundred kilometres. Under training conditions I had averaged two hundred kilometres a day, if the terrain was not too treacherous.

Three days continual movement, without rest.

Undaunted, emptying my mind of all thoughts except the need to make the next stride, I strode on. Nevil would not thank any of us for delaying his escape, least of all me.

The ship ushered me to the control room without delay. Before I took my seat, the false windows were already giving me a good idea of our position. An ochre haze arced away from the ship to port and starboard, darkening to black overhead. I could see a few stars, and maybe a few dull moving glints from whatever was left of the Rust Belt, but we were not yet in space. There had been ample time, though, given the time I had been with Glass, so *Scythe* must have been delaying its exit for a reason. The only one I could think of was that it was already considered too dangerous for us to lose the relative cover of the atmosphere.

"Ship," I said, buckling myself in. "Glass says that you'll accept my commands, up to a point. Put me in contact with Lady Arek, as securely as you can manage."

Lady Arek's voice emerged from the console a moment later. "Hourglass?"

"No, it's me. Glass is out of action for the time being. How much do you know?"

"Almost nothing: we have our own situation out here and it is not improving. Glass is hurt? What about you and Pinky?"

"We're both all right—both safe on the ship, and clear of Chasm City. The ninecats turned on Glass, but she says the ship can help her recover her from her injuries. Is it safe to remain in communication?"

"You will know the moment it isn't."

I studied the location fix, by which the laser was maintaining its lock on Lady Arek's ship. Her position was a few hundred kilometres higher than my own, well out of the atmosphere, and moving so as to blend in with the flow of debris around the planet, but she was not on any sort of trajectory that would bring her back to the stronghold.

"We have a complication, Lady Arek. I don't know how much Glass or the ship communicated to you, but we're carrying hyperpig evacuees from the Swinehouse."

"How many?"

"I haven't done a head count. Around a hundred, I'd guess, maybe a few more."

"What are your intentions with them?"

"I don't have any: Glass rescued them without telling us. Can the stronghold make room for them, until we come up with something better?" I felt as if I was talking into a void. "Lady Arek?"

Her voice sounded broken, drained of the last drop of hope. "It's finished. The wolves have identified it as a source of organised human activity, and now they're massing. The defences have been activated, but the best they can manage is a delaying action. I've aborted my return. The only safe action now is to dock with *Scythe* and exchange the Gideon stones."

"What about the people still there?"

"I am afraid there is no way out for them. They know this, Clavain. They are as resigned to it as I am."

"We can't just give in!" I protested.

"We're not giving in." There was a fierce rebuttal in her words. "We have the stones. All nine. I brought the single stone with us, in case a comparison was needed. Now all we need is to arrange a rendezvous, for which the destruction of the stronghold will provide a useful distraction." Lady

228

Arek was silent for a moment. "I imagine you think that I take this all a little coldly. You underestimate me. I've thought this through a thousand times, considered every possible response, every possible get-out clause. Nothing works. The only good outcome we can achieve today is not dying. Are you intending to die, Warren Clavain?"

"Of course not."

"Then here are my instructions. Follow them."

I told the ship to instigate my orders in five minutes, which gave me time to get back down to Pinky and the refugees.

"Did you see Glass?"

"Yes—and I think she'll be all right, once she's spent some time in the infirmary. For now we're on our own, though. I've spoken to Lady Arek: our best course of action lies in an immediate rendezvous with her ship."

"Why don't we wait until we're safe inside the stronghold?"

"It's tactically inadvisable."

"Why?"

I nodded out over the heads of the refugees, recognising the most prominent of them and making mental notes of some of the others, and speaking to all of them. "In a few minutes we're going to accelerate hard. If I know the ship, then it will orientate its interior surfaces to minimise the risk of injury, but that doesn't mean it won't be hard. Spread yourself out as best you can and get as low to the floor as possible. If you have clothing or other items that can serve as cushioning, use it. Do what you can for the injured and infirm. The acceleration won't last long, after which we'll be weightless. That carries its own hazards, of course. Do not allow yourselves to drift too far from any surface, in case the ship needs to make a sudden course change." I raised my hands slowly, as if in surrender. "I wish this wasn't the welcome, but for the moment it's all we can offer. In about two hours we make rendezvous with another ship. If that goes well, we can begin to talk about the future. But for now, concentrate on getting through these next two hours."

"Something's not going to plan," said the hyperpig called Barras.

"We're in the woods," I said. "But there's a way out, provided we make the right decisions." I made a lowering gesture with my hands, encouraging them to get down on the floor. In ones and twos they began to comply, until Barras spoke up and made them scramble for a patch of floor. Quickly the pigs rummaged around among their rags, plumping up anything that would offer a degree of cushioning. "You too, Pinky," I said, lowering myself as well. "We'll ride this out down here. The ship knows what it needs to do."

He settled next to me, both of us picking a spot of floor space on the edge of the refugees, but not separated from them.

In a low gruff tone he said: "You didn't answer my question."

I looked down at my folded legs.

"There's a reason for that."

"How bad is it?"

"Bad enough that there are things Lady Arek would rather you heard from her lips."

"Then whatever promise you made to her, you've already half-broken it."

"Actually, I think I may have broken all of it."

"Then you might as well tell me whatever it is she doesn't think I need to know right now."

I felt as if I were sitting next to a bomb, and had just begun to play with a naked flame. I wondered about the rage that might be in him, and the imperfect control he had over that rage. Perhaps Lady Arek had only ever been trying to spare me, as the bringer of bad news. Perhaps she knew what he was capable of doing to me.

"We can't go back."

"Can't or shouldn't?"

"The wolves are already there."

His next question was all the more unsettling for its calm reasonableness. It only made me wonder what was being bottled up, under steadily rising pressure.

"Snowdrop and the others are gone?"

"Lady Arek says they're putting up a defence."

"They know it won't make a difference. Once a wolf agglomeration locks on in force, it's only a matter of time." He settled on his haunches. Squat-trunked and bow-legged as he was, he seemed more comfortable on the floor than I did. "They know it's futile. They could end it in a second by over-loading the stronghold's reactors."

"But they won't," I answered, "because they want to give us a chance. While they can provide a distraction, the wolves won't necessarily pick up on our ships."

"Is Lady Arek in contact with Snowdrop, or inferring this from long-range observations?"

"She didn't say."

"I'd like to know."

I had not been keeping a mental count, but the five minutes must have expired because the acceleration began to rise. It was a gradual shift to begin with and I was relieved to find that my sense of vertical did not begin to wander. The ship was pressing us against the floor, but at least we were not being dashed against the walls, buried in a suffocating, bone-shattering pile. Groans and cries came from the refugees, and I imagined some of them were having old or recent injuries put under unpleasant stress. But if they could get through these next two minutes, I might at least be able to keep them alive for another two hours.

"There's something else we need to discuss," I said quietly.

"Now that we've got that small business of the death of my partner and most of my community out the way, you mean?"

"I don't mean that. Once we're weightless, we'll go forward and see if we can re-establish contact with Lady Arek. But there's a snag with this plan. You and I will be all right: there are acceleration couches in the control room. Glass will be all right as well: she's in some kind of suspension bottle. But everyone else will need to be prepared for ten gees of deceleration."

Pinky lifted his head against the strain of two additional gravities and glanced out at the refugees.

"A snag, you call it."

"There was no other way that made this feasible. The one saving grace is that it won't be for long."

He regarded me for a long moment, then nodded. "You looked at the other options."

"Yes, and they were all significantly worse."

"And when we get the Gideon stones, what then?"

"Glass said something about Ararat: not the first time it's come up, either."

"Have you been to Ararat, Stink?"

"No. Is there a reason I should have?"

He chose his answer carefully. "It's an interesting place."

"You'd know?"

"We were all there. Me, Lady Arek...the old man. Lived there awhile. Bad things happened on Ararat, and then we left. Part of me would be very happy never to have to go back."

"Part of you?"

"Actually, make that all of me."

By the time *Scythe* shrugged itself clear of Yellowstone's atmosphere it was already moving ballistically, with just enough excess speed to intersect Lady Arek's orbit. The pigs took to weightlessness quite well to begin with— even after all they had been through it was a pleasant novelty to experience for the first time—but I knew very well that a host of unpleasant side-effects were likely to come their way shortly, and few, if any, of them would be prepared. The air circulators were going to be dealing with a lot more than just gaseous waste products, so I hoped Glass had insisted on ample redundancy.

Pinky took to the weightlessness with no difficulty. Between us we made quick progress back up to the control room, with me mentally counting down the minutes until we would need a system in place to safeguard the refugees. Pinky and I agreed that we would coordinate our tasks in tandem: he would signal Lady Arek, getting clarification on the situation at the stronghold, and I would try to persuade the ship that it needed to provide protection for the new passengers. If all else failed, I was counting on Glass still being this side of consciousness so that she could instruct the ship directly. But I was starting to worry that she had already withdrawn into herself.

"You can tell Lady Arek we're on our way," I said to Pinky, once I had instructed the ship to open a channel for him. "Our estimated time of arrival will be...one hundred and nine minutes from now. In all like-lihood, she won't see any trace of us until we're right on top of her and slowing down hard, so warn her to stand down any anti-ship weapons she might have armed."

"Worried she'll hurt us?"

"More worried what *Scythe* might do in return."

Pinky and Lady Arek communicated, and although my attention was on the task of making arrangements for the refugees, I still caught most of the exchange. For two old allies—two old friends, as far as I could tell—it was not far off a screaming argument. Lady Arek was furious with me for telling Pinky what was happening to the stronghold. Pinky was furious with Lady Arek for presuming to think that he would not be level-headed enough to process this news like a rational being. Lady Arek in turn was furious at him for having the temerity to presume upon the wisdom of her reticence, and to dare to suggest that it was rooted in anything other than kind concern and a deep-seated understanding of the extremes he might go to in the service of a lost cause.

"You are the bravest of all of us!" she was shouting. "The one who only today offered up his life for the greater cause of our struggle! But then there was a chance, a shred of a hope, just enough reason to believe. With the stronghold we are far past that point. Nothing can be done, nothing at all, and I will not risk the life of my dearest friend twice in one day!"

"How dare you call me brave, and then keep this from me, while telling him—"

"He needed to know that the stronghold was not a viable destination!" she replied, her voice breaking on her fury.

And so it went, while I kept on trying to find some way of alerting the ship that it needed to take care of its own. Perhaps my message had got through, perhaps it had not. There was no way to tell.

Gradually the shouting and screaming gave way to something loosely resembling reasoned dialogue, and after some deliberation Lady Arek was persuaded to share the intelligence she was gathering from the stronghold. We only got a small part of it, since the data had to be compressed to the point where it could share the voice-only laser-link without degrading the signal.

It was enough. From what we were shown it was clear that we had no hope of rescuing Snowdrop and the others. The stronghold was still intact, but it was wreathed in a thickening cloud of black machines, partially or totally obscuring the view of it from the monitoring eyes Lady Arek had sprinkled around the Rust Belt. The wolves were concentrating in shell-like waves, clotting around the little asteroid and then falling inward. Where the view was clearest, we could see that the stronghold was fighting back, with bursts of energy stabbing out from dozens of previously concealed weapons emplacements.

I felt for the burden of decision that must have befallen Snowdrop as she committed to those defences. They were only ever going to be capable of staving off the wolves for a limited time, and in deploying them they removed any doubt that there were humans still around Yellowstone; humans with potent machines and a will to survive. Snowdrop had probably been condemned from the moment the wolves took any sort of exceptional interest in the stronghold. In discharging the defences, she had as good as signed her own death warrant.

But the wolves were not getting their prize for free. Snowdrop's weapons were formidable, and I took some small solace in the way they blasted holes through those curdling shells, annihilating or dispersing wolf elements as if they were no more than buzzing black flies. The shells became ragged, lacy and discontinuous, and then broke apart completely. But there were always more shells forming, like distant breakers marshalling for a charge against the shoreline. Wolf flows were funnelling in from multiple points around the Rust Belt, providing a near-limitless reservoir of reinforcements. As always with the wolves, they would accept surprisingly heavy losses in the early stages of an engagement while they probed and learned and adapted. Sooner or later the units would coordinate a modification to their force-generating mechanisms, either by rapid evolution or by dredging some proven response from their archives of

233

prior encounters. They had workable countermeasures for every weapon we had ever invented, as well as the equivalent efforts of all the other species they had acted against. It was only ever a question of time before they found the right way to overcome Snowdrop, and in the meantime some losses were not only acceptable but perfectly unconcerning to them. These were not soldiers but elements of a single vast war machine, operating on a scale of light-years and a timescale of centuries.

What hope had we of defeating such a thing?

None at all, I thought to myself. To think anything else was species-level hubris.

But there might be other survival strategies. If we could force the wolves to a negotiated stand-off, a point where they recognised that we were too much trouble to annihilate completely, but could be contained, that would count nearly as well as victory. The wolves' greatest strength was their patience, their willingness to sit out an enemy for millions of years. If we put up a sufficiently messy, obstinate struggle, they might move us into a holding category, a problem to be deferred for a galactic rotation or two. To the wolves, that would not count as defeat in any sense: merely a drawing of breath. But we were warm, fleet creatures who operated on timescales utterly beneath their comprehension. A mayfly would regard an extra hour as a welcome stay of execution.

We had to think like mayflies.

"Put me through," Pinky said.

"No," Lady Arek answered. "I can't risk it. I've had no direct contact with Snowdrop for forty minutes. There's too high a chance of wolf interception."

"Do it anyway."

"Dear Scorpio..." Her voice broke on the name that came most naturally to her, the name he no longer wished to carry. "Dear friend."

"Do it," I said, speaking up. "I have a message for Snowdrop as well."

There was a silence, broken only by the occasional static crackle as the weapons discharges burst into our comms circuits. "I've opened the link. Voice only, and no guarantee that it'll hold. Snowdrop and I have already made our farewells."

"Then this is mine," I said. "Snowdrop: I hope you can hear me. I see what you're doing, and it's magnificent. It will fail, as you know it will fail, but your brave actions will have bought us the time and the distraction we need. For that I thank you."

Her voice came through: a thinned, metallic approximation of the real thing. I might not have recognised it had I not already spent time with her.

"Don't feel sorry for me. Every hour that I haven't been trapped in Swinehouse is an hour I never expected to live. The others feel the same way. We have always been ready for this. Make that exchange count. Will you do one thing for me?"

"I'll try."

"Accept your true name. Glass went to a lot of trouble to find you. We were all counting on her to succeed. Now she's brought you to us, you have to accept what you are. Promise me you will do this."

My voice faltered. "I can't promise what I don't believe in."

"But you will, in time. So make that adjustment. No one's asking you to forsake the memories of who you thought you were before Glass arrived. I know you had family, and she ripped them away. I'm sorry about that, Warren. But it was all only scar tissue. Become the man we need you to be. You are Sky Marshall Warren Clavain, a Knight of Cydonia."

I intoned the words she wished me to say: "I am Sky Marshall Warren Clavain."

"Now say it like you mean it."

"I am Sky Marshall Warren Clavain," I said, more forcefully.

"Shout it, soldier. Tell the world who you are."

I raged: "I am Sky Marshall Warren Clavain!"

"And the rest!"

"A Knight of Cydonia!"

"Good…good." Snowdrop became quieter, seemingly satisfied. "That's better. Deep down, you already know. Avenge us, Sky Marshall. You have the Gideon stones. Now slay some wolves."

"Goodbye, Snowdrop," I said.

"Goodbye, Sky Marshall. And now, could I speak to Pinky, please? We've a few things to say to each other, all of them private."

CHAPTER EIGHTEEN

The pigs were in a state of consternation, which had nothing to do with our impending arrival at Lady Arek's ship. They were already being dealt with by *Scythe*: dozens of sphere robots had bustled out of somewhere (I had only ever seen a few of them at a time before) and were now encouraging, or in some cases forcing, the refugees to adopt fixed postures with their backs to the floor. Once they obeyed, the area of floor beneath them puckered in as if it were made of rubber, forming a partial enclosure around the recumbent form. The floor did not close over completely—it left a snug opening so that the occupant could still breathe and communicate. But in all other senses they were totally imprisoned by the floor, unable to move their limbs or in any way free themselves.

I understood instantly: the ship was making provision for the deceleration burst. But to the refugees, it was as if they were being forcibly absorbed into the floor like so many trophies. Some, including Barras, were trying to impose some kind of calm, insisting that this had to be part of some plan for their protection. But for too many of the refugees the whole experience must have brought back sharp memories of imprisonment and torture in the Swinehouse. The worst of the resistors were being pinned in place by the spheres, literally pressed into the yielding floor until the floor swaddled itself around their forms and stopped them thrashing.

Barras was one of the ones not yet interred.

"Tell me this is for our benefit."

"It will be," I said, equally astonished and enraged that the ship had not thought fit to tell me that my concerns had been noted and acted upon. "When this weightless phase is over, which will be in about eighty minutes, *Scythe* will have to brake very hard. If you were left to float around, I don't think many of you would survive the process. This way it will be uncomfortable but survivable."

"Some of us only just made it through the last one."

"I know, and this will be worse. I'm sorry, Barras." I looked out among the confusion of refugees and sphere robots, a storm of rags and scraps

236

littering the air as the unwilling patients resisted their fates. "It will be all right. Can you give them my word that this isn't anything bad, and they'll be let out of the floor once our manoeuvres are complete?"

Barras eyed me quizzically. "You know that for a fact?"

"I don't, but everything I've seen so far suggests to me that this ship wants to protect its occupants, including you."

"They'd feel better if that reassurance came from Pinky."

I wondered how much of the truth to share with him. Then decided that any trust was better consolidated by absolute openness, no matter how unpalatable the news.

"Snowdrop is going to die, Barras. The wolves have hit Lady Arek's stronghold. There are a few folk still inside, and they're using whatever weapons they have to delay the wolf incursion. Ultimately, none of what they have will work. But that delaying action helps us."

Barras absorbed what I had said. I hardly dared wonder about the shared history that existed between this man, Snowdrop and Pinky. It was none of my business and yet I still sensed the edge of something as harrowing and wonderful as any human story of friendship and resilience. They did not have to be human to be people. All had been through far more than I could imagine; far more than I wished to imagine.

"Is he with her now?"

"Some final words," I said softly. "Lady Arek was against establishing a link, but we persuaded her."

Barras met my eyes, a mutual understanding passing between us.

"Some things matter too much. After what Pinky went through in the Swinehouse...this doesn't seem fair."

"Nothing is. Cold as it seems, that's probably the safest philosophy to live by."

"I'll tell them there's nothing to fear," Barras said, looking doubtfully out at the unruly chaos of pigs, shredded clothing and dogged, kindly robots trying to do their best. "And I hope I don't live to regret that promise."

"Thank you."

Before he turned to the others, he had one last question for me. "There is a plan, isn't there? I mean, if we can't go back to the stronghold, then I don't suppose there's any safety to be found in the Rust Belt at all. That means we have to live somewhere else." He paused and repeated himself, this time with a more plaintive note. "There *is* a plan?"

"There will be," I said.

The comms had ceased.

Lady Arek's surveillance assets had gone dark across the Rust Belt.

Flares garlanded Yellowstone as the wolves turned against the largest of the surviving structures. In some cases there was still enough air inside them for fires to burn.

Nothing diverted *Scythe* or caused it to recalculate its approach. It was only quite near the end, in the last minutes of our flight, that we had verification that we were closing in on the right object: a speck of debris that was a little warmer than its neighbours, but not so much that it stood out across thousands of kilometres. Then our darkdrives went into emergency reverse thrust, ten gees of sudden deceleration, and instead of whipping right past our objective we were on it, coming to a bruising but precise standstill only twenty metres from Lady Arek. After that, everything happened very quickly. *Scythe* had already modelled the optimum approach for docking, and we orientated and latched on with indecent, hull-clanging haste. It helped that Glass and Lady Arek had already agreed and coordinated a common lock interface, so there was no need for *Scythe* to go through the troubling business of adapting itself to the other, slower-witted spacecraft.

Just as swiftly, Lady Arek and Probably Rose came aboard with the Gideon stones, as well as several cases of supplies and weapons. We were nearly ready to detach. Almost certainly the wolves had picked up on *something* happening here, for that ten-gee slowdown had forced the darkdrives to operate at a level where their reaction products lingered in this universe a little longer than otherwise.

"We will speak of what you went through later," Lady Arek said, hugging Pinky. "Never think for a second that this debt will be forgotten."

"It's nothing compared to what we owe Snowdrop and the others." He eased himself from her embrace. "You did all right, Rash. So did Stinky."

"You think he might be cut from the old cloth, after all?"

"Jury's still deliberating. But...he didn't let us down."

"I must look at your injuries, Clavain, yes," Probably Rose said, eyeing where I had been shot.

"What am I, pork?" Pinky asked.

"You are made of injuries. If I treated one, I'd have to treat them all, and then where would it end?"

"Fair point," the pig acknowledged.

"Besides," Probably Rose went on. "You are not the one who was shot. Have you recovered from the haemoclast?"

"I'm all right," I admitted. "Lady Arek's aim was true, and the suits flushed the haemoclast out of us while we were still on Yellowstone."

"Was it as bad as they say?"

"No. Much worse. But I'm feeling much better with my own blood back in me, and my wounds have been fixed up well enough. This leg of mine can wait for the time being. Somewhere in here is an exoskeleton Glass provided me for when we were leaving Sun Hollow. If I can find it again, I won't need to put any load on my leg."

"If you find it, see if you can find some others," Lady Arek said. "We may all have need before very long. Probably Rose, can you see what can be done for the evacuees?"

Probably Rose steeled herself for work. "Show me to them. And send medical servitors and supplies, yes."

Lady Arek turned to me. "Is there any word on Hourglass?"

"I found her floating in a bottle, about to be put into a medical coma."

A sharp shake of her head. "Now is not the time for her to abdicate control of this ship."

"I don't think she likes it either, but it's what needs to be done. Glass will come back to us when she can. Until then we're on our own. But the ship will oblige, I think, especially if we can help it understand our requirements." I nodded over her shoulder, into the still-open lock. "Is there anything else inside that shuttle that we need to unload?"

"All essential items have already come aboard."

"Then we'd better close up and we'll be under way," I said, wondering why Omori was taking so long to leave the shuttle.

"There's a difficulty," Lady Arek said, looking back over her shoulder to the airlock where our two ships were still mated. "We took some incoming fire from the Swinehouse, after I sent you that signal. Omori had to fly her out on manual control, and now she won't accept our commands to go away."

"Then we abandon that part of the plan and make a run for it anyway. If the wolves converge on this point in space they'll find a drifting shuttle and assume that was the source of the emissions."

Lady Arek turned back again. "Omori! We shall think of something else!" Then, to me: "I will audit the systems as soon as I can. But in the meantime, you can help me. Does this vehicle still have drone missiles, the ones Hourglass uses for reconnaissance?"

"I think so," I said, unwilling to commit to an answer since the control of those missiles was another question entirely. "I suppose we could attach one of them to the shuttle, boost it that way... as long as it made enough noise and light, it would serve...?"

I trailed off, realising what was happening in the same instant as Lady Arek. Omori had closed the airlock connection from the shuttle's side and was already initiating a forced un-docking, severing our two ships.

Lady Arek hammered on the now sealed lock. "Omori! No! You do not need to do this!"

But Omori was doing it anyway.

The shuttle detached from *Scythe.* We watched it through the false windows either side of the lock, easing away from us on attitude jets until Omori had created enough of a safe margin to engage the engines. The shuttle corkscrewed, then dashed away on an arcing trajectory. I watched it numbly, aware of the sacrifice I had just witnessed, unable to comprehend how it must have felt to Lady Arek. She seemed paralysed, stunned into inaction. I was about to suggest that we would be wasting Omori's sacrifice unless we moved immediately, but I had gravely underestimated her.

"He has made his choice and there is nothing I can do about it," she stated. "Now we had better make it count. There's nowhere safe for us in this system; nothing to delay our departure for Ararat. We'll need to run the darkdrives to the limit of detection, but not one thrust increment beyond that threshold."

"The ship should understand," I said. "The deeper question is whether it can keep all of us alive. I only saw two reefersleep caskets."

"Then it will need to make more. I imagine that will be comfortably within its capabilities."

"Aren't you taking rather a lot on faith?"

She looked at me patiently. "Let me explain something about survival. You do not worry about the third or fourth stepping stone until you have successfully traversed the first and second. Anything beyond them is a diversion of energies away from the immediate moment. And we are in that moment now."

I smiled, accepting my lesson. "Rash?"

"Lady Aura-Rashmika-Els-Khouri," Pinky said. "Arek is much less of a mouthful."

"Show me to the injured," Probably Rose requested.

We fled.

The wolf concentration around Lady Arek's former stronghold was a thick black coating now, the machines pressing in on each other like demented puzzle pieces, locking into some secret configuration. They jostled and surged, settling into denser and denser formations even as more machines arrived from around the Rust Belt, converging along sooty flows that we only saw because they blocked all forms of light. Lady Arek's weapons had either expired or were no longer capable of blasting through any part of that screen. We had to assume the worst: that the inner layer

240

of machines would shortly penetrate the locks and passages that led into the habitable parts of the stronghold, or simply grind their way through rock and rubble until they reached the same objective. No signals were now possible between us, and perhaps that was a mercy. There was nothing we could do for them, and no news they could offer us that would not have been harrowing. It was conceivable, likely even, that Snowdrop and her associates were already dead, and all that remained was the last dogged defiance of a few housekeeping programmes. But the reactors had not blown, to the best of our knowledge.

Nor had wolves yet caught up with Omori. But they were on their way. We could detect sub-flows breaking away from the main movement within the Rust Belt, being assigned to this new target. From four points, spaced around Yellowstone at roughly equal divisions, black wisps were fingering in the direction of the shuttle. They were not wasting energy moving any faster than they needed to. That, I think, was the most terrifying thing of all: that this alien killing system knew that it did not need to be hasty, not against such trifling creatures as ourselves. It would get us in the end.

I was a soldier. I accepted this now. It was in my marrow, no longer to be denied. Every soldierly part of me wanted to take the fight directly to the wolves, to unpick that black scab, to slash at those reaching fingers before they found their objective. But a cooler part of me, borne of experience and survival—the wiser, older warrior—knew that we take our victories where we find them, and accept our defeats with grace and patience.

Stepping stones.

While Probably Rose was down with the evacuees, doing what she could with her own medical supplies, Lady Arek, Pinky and I watched the end of things from the control room. *Scythe* was flying away from the Rust Belt, with its nose pointed towards interstellar space, so the view through the false windows ought to have been one of blackness and stars. But Lady Arek had found a way to have the windows show the view to our stern, of the receding Rust Belt and the planet it orbited.

Our acceleration soon had Yellowstone looking visibly smaller, with a larger and larger fraction of the Rust Belt coming into view, until we could see all of it, from one side of the orbit to the other. Yellowstone's face was lit, so the part of the Rust Belt that bisected the planet was a sooty ribbon, a smear of ash across the brow. No intact structures could be made out within that procession now; it was a flow of ruins, the shards of worlds, dust-wreathed and dream-haunted. It was where humans had tried to be more than themselves, for a few short centuries.

We had seen it on our approach, and it was different now. The wolf flows were dark arteries, curling and spiralling through these broken pieces, throbbing out of the largest remnants, where the machines had gorged and multiplied and waited until their time of release and quickening. Where the Rust Belt lay against a background of space, on either side of the planet, it should have been as invisible as it had been before, its presence betrayed only by the stars it occluded. But now flecks of gold and red burned like lanterns on a slow-flowing river. These were the last human fires, the last gasps of life and oxygen, as tiny warm pockets were at last evacuated to space.

"It's beautiful again," Lady Arek said. "After all this, it gets to be beautiful again. Just for a few hours, on this last day."

"We precipitated this," I said. "Our arrival, Glass and me. If we hadn't come, this wouldn't have happened."

"Maybe not today, but soon enough," she replied. "We were here because the wolves came for us in the first place. And the only reason they did that is because some misguided fish once decided to try breathing oxygen instead of water."

"She does this," Pinky said. "Just when you think you're consequential, she finds a way to bring you down to the level of a fish." He shrugged, shoulders powerful even in three gees. He had buckled on an exoskeleton, helpfully finding one that was adjustable to his frame. He was so short, squat, stocky and muscular that I wondered if he needed its assistance at all. "Still, at least she stopped at something with a nervous system. She's been known to go all the way down to bacteria."

He was distracting himself.

A moment later a pinprick of light stabbed out from one quadrant of the Rust Belt. It was like a little eye, winking open, an eye that disclosed a brighter, purer creation beyond itself. It stared out for a second or two. Then the eye shuttered, the light extinguished.

Pinky was silent. I wanted to say something, to offer some consolation, but any words that came to mind were immediately self-censored, unforgivably trite and demeaning.

"We thank her," Lady Arek said. "Snowdrop and the others. That's all. We thank them, and keep thanking them, while we have breath to do so. There's nothing we can do, except to live, and keep living, and always hold that gratitude in our hearts." She reached out to her friend the hyper-pig, the man I hoped might, in time, become my own friend as well. "And be consequential."

When we were alone—a stoic, brooding Pinky had waddled off in his exoskeleton to see Probably Rose, Barras and the other evacuees—Lady

242

Arek called an image onto one of the screens, drawn from deep in *Scythe*'s archives.

"Hourglass would have shown this to you sooner or later, or you would have found a way to extract it via your own enquiries, but it's as well that you see it now and understand."

I felt as if I were being set a test that I was already in the process of failing.

The image was a square, bisected along a very shallow curve, practically a straight diagonal. The upper left half was black: a backdrop of space, with only a few faint stars speckling into view. The lower right half of the image was a close-up of part of a planet, with the curved limb forming the boundary between the darker and lighter parts of the image. The visible part of the planet was a pale blue in colour, but with bands and swirls of deeper colour, shading to opal and turquoise.

"I don't recognise it."

"I did not expect you to. What does that begin to tell you?"

"I suppose it must be Charybdis, the place Glass has been dropping hints about since we met. She told me that she was the one who applied the name, and that it isn't so far away as to be beyond the reach of a ship like *Scythe*. From that view, I'd say it's an ice giant, something fairly common. We'd need to cross-correlate against the known systems..."

"You are right that ice giants are commonplace. But this planet matches none in any of the systems that have been subjected to any kind of robotic or human exploration. That is our difficulty, Clavain. Tell me: if I asked you to localise this planet, what would you do next?"

"Zoom out, so that more stars fall into view. It should be child's play to back-compute the star patterns and identify which system the planet's in."

"A valid suggestion. Unfortunately, what you are seeing is the extent of the image, and the handful of stars that happened to be recorded offer an insufficient baseline for parallactic triangulation. All other image localisation measures have failed. The brightness of the galactic ridge, the anisotropy of the background radiation—none give us enough leverage. From the spectrum of light falling onto Charybdis we may hazard that its primary is a G-type star, perhaps a G-zero dwarf, but that barely begins to help us. We cannot determine the system in which this planet lies."

"This doesn't make sense, Lady Arek. If you have one snapshot, you should have a billion. Whether someone captured this view through a telescope from light-years away, or from much closer in, it would never be the only thing you have."

"In this instance, regrettably, it is. Let me explain."

"Please do."

"I misled you slightly: this system has been visited. But it was an undocumented visitation, centuries ago, by an early interstellar expedition sent out by the Conjoiners. Specifically, this image was recorded by the *Sandra Voi*, the prototype starship assembled and launched under the aegis of Galiana."

"*The* Galiana?"

"One and the same. In the early decades of the twenty-third century, Galiana and her doughty band of allies pushed deep into interstellar space, looking for sanctuary, and for anything else that pricked their limitless curiosity. They came home, eventually. In time, their discoveries entered the Conjoiner archives. But those archives were very badly corrupted during subsequent troubles.

"Much was lost, or scrambled beyond recognition, including the data logs relating to this system. Only fragments remained legible. Among them was enough information to indicate the significance of Charybdis to the anti-wolf effort, but not enough to help us determine how to find the planet itself. Of course, it is a cold gas giant, and while they are numerous there must be a fixed limit to the number of systems and worlds that the *Sandra Voi* could possibly have reached, allowing for relativistic mechanics. So, if our time and resources were limitless, we could simply send autonomous expeditions to every possible system of interest, out to at least fifty or sixty light-years from Earth. That is a great many systems, Clavain, many thousands, and these are not normal times. Even if we restricted our search space to G-types, the task facing us would still be formidable. The wolves stalk us at every step, as we see. We cannot solve this problem by blunt means." She paused. "Hence, you."

I blinked. "Nevil Clavain was closely involved with Galiana. They were enemies once, I know that much. Then something happened to turn him to her cause. He defected from his own side and threw his lot in with the Conjoiners." When she did not contradict me, I ventured further: "To the extent that he was on that expedition, I suppose?"

"He was. And we know that Nevil Clavain must have died with the knowledge we need. He would have remembered Charybdis as an anomaly, something worthy of further investigation, and he would have known the system in which it lies."

"Then...you're hoping that by some osmosis his dying knowledge will have seeped into my brain as well, just because I'm his long-lost brother?"

"No. We are not fools, Warren. Ararat is the key, because Clavain died there. Normally that would be the end of it, except for one thing: Ararat is an ocean planet. A Pattern Jugglers world. It is...believed by us...that

244

Clavain's memory patterns remain encoded and retrievable, through the Pattern Jugglers."

"I know something of how it works with the Jugglers," I admitted. "If they have preserved his personality—and there's no promise of that—someone else might be able to swim in the same seas and have his patterns imprinted into their own neural matrix. If the Jugglers are willing, and they understand the request. Has one of you already tried it?"

I detected some diffidence in Lady Arek, there and gone in a flash. "Hourglass indeed attempted communion, in the manner you allude to. It was not successful. There would be a much greater likelihood of success if someone with a personal connection to Nevil Clavain were to meet the Jugglers."

"I see." I reflected on her answer, feeling that something larger—and more obvious—lay just out of reach. "I'm guessing her contact attempt wasn't totally unsuccessful. Clearly she reached enough of Nevil to gain some insight into my part in all this."

"Your part?"

"That I existed. That I might be able to stand in for Nevil, to some extent. That I could be found on Sun Hollow."

But a small, doubtful voice whispered to me that my brother could never have known of my intentions to take the *Salmacis* to AU Microscopii. Our paths had diverged after Mars. He might have hated me, in the aftermath of that betrayal, but the years would surely have pushed my memory to the back of his mind, along with all the trappings of his younger days. He had concerned himself with bigger matters than brotherly spite: the fate not just of one ideology but human civilisation itself. There was no reason at all that I should have crossed his thoughts in the last years of his life, and even less reason for me to have mattered to some ghost of him, haunting an alien ocean.

Then again, my brother had never been one to forget a slight.

Lady Arek prompted gently: "Warren?"

"I was just wondering what it would take from me."

"It will not be so onerous. You will swim with them—something millions have done before. There's little risk in that alone. You may be rebuffed before the opening of any window of contact, but if that happens you will survive and we will regroup and make another attempt. Eventually there will be an opportunity for communion. After that, it is just a question of intent and the holding in mind of a clear objective. If you open your mind to the Jugglers, if you submit to them that you are the brother of one who lies within them, there is every chance that they will facilitate the transfer of recorded knowledge. Your mind, and that of Nevil's, will not be so very different. Your neural matrix will accept his: an augmentation of your personality, rather than an erasure. It must and will succeed. You are by far the best receptacle we could hope to find."

"And after this is done, if it's possible, it's your expectation that I'll magically remember everything you need to know about Charybdis?"

"It is not a question of magic, merely one of alien biology. But you see that our hopes must be pinned on the Jugglers. However we calculate the odds, they improve with your involvement."

I tasted salty water; felt the sting of green sunlight on my eyes. A sudden panic of drowning rose in my chest.

"Why am I frightened, Lady Arek? Why do I feel like I've already been to the Pattern Jugglers—already tried this thing you want me to do—and that it didn't end well?"

"You would remember if you had visited them," Lady Arek answered. Then, consolingly: "Don't dwell on it, Warren. It is what lies ahead of us that we must be concerned by—not imagined phantoms. The unknown is always troubling."

"I knew his name," I whispered.

"His name?"

"Scorpio. Or Scorp, as his friends called him. As I think Nevil called him. It slipped out of me without thinking." I looked at her with renewed intensity. "How could I ever know that?"

"I must have used his old name in a moment of indiscretion, and you overheard it without realising."

Sensing an impasse, I returned to my attention to the cryptic image fragment, wondering how it had come into our possession, and how Glass or Lady Arek could be sure that their answers lay there.

"All right. The past be damned. I'll go to your damned Jugglers. But if this does work, what will we find?"

Lady Arek caused the image to disappear and another to spring into its place. It was a machine of some kind: a sort of nightmare fusion of turbine, corkscrew and pine tree, all glittering, intertwining and counter-rotating in ways that made my eyes hurt.

Of course, I had seen it already: if not complete, then in a condition of partial assembly. It was the mechanism I had glimpsed through the little window in the partition, during my first exploration of *Scythe*. The mechanism that Glass had been content to let me see, even if she had not seen fit to explain its presence in anything other than teasing allusion.

"A hypometric precursor device," Lady Arek said.

"Good. I feel enormously enlightened." I paused. "John the Revelator mentioned something about hypometric weapons. Is this the same thing?"

"Let us say that it belongs to the same family of technologies. But it is not in itself a weapon."

"All right," I said slowly. "That fits with what Glass told me when I asked her about the machine I'd seen inside *Scythe*."

"It's helpful that you've seen it," Lady Arek said. "I'm at least spared the tedium of persuading you that such a thing might exist. Permit me to assume a certain degree of ignorance on your part."

"Assume away."

She took a breath. "Years ago, we attempted to gain an advantage over the Inhibitors by the use of hypometric weapons: instruments that performed certain operations on the local structure of spacetime. With the hypometric weapons, we could reach inside the hull of a ship without disturbing a single atom of its structure: tunnelling beneath reality. Or snip a smaller ship or missile entirely out of existence."

"It's possible I heard rumours. The *Salmacis* was picking up all sorts of transmissions as we fled to Michael, and some of them alluded to impossible weapons, or weapons stolen from the future."

"It would have been better if there had never been rumours. The hypometric weapons were a false dawn. They helped us survive a number of engagements, but they were too few in number, and too inexpertly controlled, to offer a decisive advantage. In the end we added them to the roll-call of things that had failed us: dark toys that should have remained in the toy-box."

"You're going to give them a second try?"

"No, that would be as futile as all the other attempts, and besides, the wolves learned from our limited successes and evolved counter-strategies of their own. But we have not exhausted the possibilities of hypometric technology. If our first efforts were atomic bombs, instruments of blunt destruction, what we make next will be an engine of creation. An atomic-force microscope, by analogy."

I thought back to what I remembered from our makeshift laboratories in Sun Hollow, our fumbling efforts to repair or maintain miniature systems. "An atomic-force microscope allows the manipulation of matter at the atomic scale."

"And by extension, a hypometric manipulator—this machine you see in Hourglass's constructor files—will operate on spacetime at an analogous precision. Fed a set of constructional schedules—a blueprint, if you will—it becomes a precursor technology: an intermediate step in the direction of something else, something utterly beyond our comprehension."

"What?"

Lady Arek dropped her voice to a reverential whisper, as if what she meant to utter was too heretical or possibly blasphemous to voice in anything but the most hushed of tones.

"An Incantor."

CHAPTER NINETEEN

My head was swimming by the time I found Pinky conferring quietly with Probably Rose. All three of us were wearing exoskeletons and moving slowly and cautiously even with their protection. An exoskeleton was helpful under *Scythe*'s acceleration, but it was no insurance against carelessness.

Barras and the other evacuees were still pressed down into individual pockets in the floor, like dolls half sunk into quicksand. The sphere robots bustled around them, attending to those who needed more assistance than the others. Most of the refugees were able to cope on their own, but about a tenth needed additional medical support, and the ship was providing it. They had oxygen masks, pressed over their faces like inverted flowers with the stalks emerging from the part of the floor immediately next to their heads. Some had nutrient or anaesthetic lines, provided by similar means, and monitored by the robots. There were broken limbs, fractured ribs and skulls, open wounds and older, badly healed injuries that still gave trouble.

"Have you been able to do much?" I asked Probably Rose.

"A little, yes," she said ruefully. "Until the ship saw what I was doing and decided it could do a much better job, yes and yes."

"I think in general it will always do better than us, provided it understands what we want. It's like a loyal dog: it wants to please, but doesn't always know how. How much Glass is also still pulling strings, I can't say." I paused, eyeing the pig. "Pinky..."

"Nothing to be said, Stink."

"But I might want to say it anyway. I'm sorry. That's all. I wish it had happened differently." I looked beyond him, to Barras and the others. "Have you told them?"

"I thought I'd wait until I knew what the clever people are planning." He planted his hands on his hips. "So what's it to be?"

"We're all in this together, Pinky."

"Sure we are."

"I mean it. And if by clever people you think I'm part of deciding what your fate is, you've got it badly wrong. Glass and Lady Arek had plans for me—plans you were a part of—not the other way around. Have they told you about the machine Glass has been making inside this ship?"

He looked at me warily. "What do you know?"

"Enough to think I should be a little frightened by it all."

He considered my response, nodded curtly. "If you'd seen it in action, you'd understand why."

"Lady Arek says this is something new—something beyond what they've used in the past. They're going to use this technology to make some new order of weapon."

"Helps to have a plan."

He made to turn away but I stopped him with a touch on his shoulder. "The machine needs a blueprint. If we had that blueprint, I imagine Lady Arek would have told me."

"And did she?"

"You know that she didn't. You know that because there's no way she wouldn't have shared every detail of this plan with her loyalist friend. So, tell me."

He met my eyes, and for a moment I felt as if all the rage and grief that had built up inside him had been saved just for me.

"What's to tell?"

"She wants me to meet Nevil Clavain. It's something to do with the location of a planet, and I suppose whatever that planet is hiding has something to do with the weapon Lady Arek wants to make. And I suppose also that the Gideon stones, which have just cost us so much..."

He snarled: "Don't speak to me about cost when you've lost nothing."

"It's hard to have anything to lose when you're a man without a past. A man who keeps being lied to."

"Why would you think you're worth the trouble of lying to?"

"Because something doesn't fit, and you know it." I kept my voice level, trying to reach the core of reasonableness that I still believed lay within him. "I spoke your true name. I called you Scorp."

"Guess you overheard someone else."

"No, I doubt that very much, and so did you when you first picked me up on it. No one around you would be so foolish as to touch a nerve like that."

He grunted something that was not quite disagreement, even if it tortured him to do so.

"So what's your grand theory, Stink?"

250

"My theory is that that knowledge could only have come from Nevil Clavain—this figure I'm yet to make contact with. Yet a little bit of him was already inside me, and I didn't even realise it."

"You were brothers. Supposedly."

"But brothers who last spoke to each other in the crucible of war, half a thousand years ago. Nevil wouldn't have known you then." I shook my head slowly. "It doesn't add up. However that knowledge got into my head from his, it's from much later in his life. But we never met again." I added it more firmly, for the sake of my own sanity. "We never met again." Then, plaintively, "Did we?"

"You think I'd be the one to be told if you had?"

"I think you probably know more than you want to admit to me. Perhaps more than you want to admit to yourself."

"You got the wrong pig," Pinky said.

"Perhaps I did," I answered, moving past him. "Because if you were truly a friend of Nevil Clavain, I think you'd have the decency to tell the truth to his brother."

"You don't..." he began.

Leaving Pinky to fume in his own self-contradictions I knelt next to Barras and explained our predicament and immediate intentions. He was the one I felt the most immediate connection to, and the one I felt could be trusted to keep details in mind. But there was no point in telling only Barras, and he was in no immediate position to spread the word to the others. So once we had spoken, I moved along the rows of embedded bodies, striding the narrow tongues of floor between them, and tried to give as honest an account as I could.

"Lady Arek's stronghold is gone. The only survivors are aboard this ship: Pinky, Probably Rose and Lady Arek herself. Glass, who saved you, is being healed somewhere else in this ship. Snowdrop and the others did us a huge favour, giving us the distraction we needed to make a bolt for interstellar space. Omori is still helping us, providing a distraction with the shuttle. What we're doing now is capitalising on their bravery and selflessness. But I'm afraid it'll mean running the engines very hard for many hours."

"How many hours?" asked one of the pigs, her face staring up from the neat swaddling enclosure of the floor. "We can't move, can't talk to each other..."

"After thirteen hours, we might have some idea how safe we are. Somewhere between half a day and a day, we might have some respite."

"Let us leave," said another. "I can bear this. I can walk around, just like you, and I won't even need that frame."

"I'm sure you could," I answered. "But the ship came up with this arrangement; it decides when it's time to end it."

"Then we're still prisoners," lamented another.

"You're alive," I countered. "And you've got a future. That's more than any of you had in Chasm City."

"You have to agree," Probably Rose called, overhearing our exchange. "He has a point, yes and yes. And we will take care of you, whatever it takes, and verily."

A sharp demand: "Where are we going?"

"A place called Ararat," I answered. "About twenty-two light-years away, or twenty-three years flight time."

"Why'd we want to go there?" demanded another.

"Good fucking question," Pinky interjected, in a surly undertone.

"Lady Arek needs me there. It's a Pattern Juggler planet."

"Pattern what?" a voice queried.

I dredged up the few facts I felt sure of. "They're a form of alien life, distributed throughout a living ocean. An information-storage biomass, intelligent in some respects but not really conscious in any way that we'd recognise. Harmless for the most part, and cooperative on occasions. A sort of living archive, capable of manipulating the deep structure of our minds—rewiring our brains, temporarily or permanently, with new information structures: memories, modes of perception, and so on."

"Water planet?" a voice said.

"Yes," I admitted. "Lots of it. Jugglers are found on several worlds, but they all have similar characteristics."

"Water and pigs don't mix very nicely," the same voice said.

"There'll be some dry land as well, according to Lady Arek. Somewhere we can land and make some kind of camp. We shan't be the first. Pinky has lived there before. He's proof that it isn't some kind of watery hell-hole."

He called out: "Don't go over-selling it, Stink. There are reasons I never wanted to go back."

"There are also reasons why we might not want to rob these people of all hope just right now," I replied, smiling through my teeth.

"First we have to get there, though," Barras said, pleasing me that he at least accepted the fact of our destination without complaint. "And that's not a given, is it?"

"We'll find a way," I answered, with more conviction than was warranted. "This ship will need to keep us alive for the crossing, but it isn't as bad as it sounds. Time will slow down for us once *Scythe* gets close to the speed of light, which will take less than three months of steady acceleration. About ten years will pass: a long time, but quite a bit less

252

than twenty-three years. My hope is that the ship can put us all into hibernation. But to do that it'll need to provide more than a hundred caskets."

"I heard that pigs don't do too well in those caskets," commented a woman, perhaps one who had a little more knowledge than the others.

"I won't pretend otherwise," I said, nodding slowly. "It's not right, but it's the way things are. The minds who spent centuries perfecting reefer-sleep technology weren't really thinking about hyperpigs. But we know it can be done. Pinky is the proof of that, and Lady Arek says they've learned some useful measures—measures that ought to work on any of you."

"These caskets...are aboard, somewhere?"

It was a question I had been hoping to skirt, for now. "If they aren't, we'll make them. The ship can do that. And if for some reason it can't, or doesn't understand our needs, then we go through those ten years the hard way."

Pinky grumbled: "You'd better mean that, Stink."

"Oh, I do," I said, fierceness breaking through my reserve. "Trust me."

"I think he does," Probably Rose confided to her friend, but loudly enough for me to hear. "Yes, and verily. And you should start taking him at his word, too."

Yellowstone was small enough to cover with my fist. It was still showing its dayside, and the Rust Belt still bisected it, but it would not be long before the planet, its belt, its moon, and the furthest of its habitats could be encompassed in my grasp. It meant nothing, almost no distance at all on an interplanetary scale (let alone interstellar) but I allowed myself some slow-growing encouragement that we might yet make our escape unhindered. The brightest of the fires had begun to ebb, that dark garland returning to a procession of unlit ashes. But Omori was still trackable, still managing to keep apace of the flows.

"He'll exhaust his fuel any time now," Lady Arek said. "After that, it'll be a matter of time until they close in on him. Those flows are almost over-kill for what he represents: one small ship, unlikely to be carrying more than a few of us, and which can't ever leave this system. They understand us well enough to know all that."

"They've been missing their sport," Pinky said, from the seat next to hers.

Lady Arek shook her head in bitter regret. "Omori did not have to do this."

"But he did, and nothing you could have done would have stopped him. Now at least we still have one point of distraction." I nodded at the displays grouped around Lady Arek's control seat: they were in a markedly different configuration compared to when I had left. "You seem to have made progress with the ship. Do you think you can get it to accept direct commands, or is it still going to be a case of telling it what we want and letting it choose how to interpret our wishes?"

"I've made some small progress. For now, I am grateful that it's taking us anywhere at all."

"So am I. But Barras and the others can't stay in those acceleration pits for the rest of our crossing."

"What do you propose?"

"As soon as it's safe to do so, we reduce our acceleration. Even if it's only for a day, it'll give Probably Rose time to assess the condition of the refugees and make them feel that they're more than inconvenient cargo we just happen to have been saddled with."

Lady Arek looked at me sharply. "Is that what they believe?"

"I think they may have cause to, if this goes on."

"We have to survive, Clavain." A hardness entered her voice, too obviously forced to convince me that it was part of her character. "I am sorry that it is hard on them, but if we let the wolves catch us, a few bone fractures will be the least of their problems."

"Stink has a point, though. Glass brought 'em aboard. The moment she did it, they became our responsibility."

"I do not deny that, but...a moment, please, Pinky."

"What is it?" I asked.

"I cannot be sure. I know only what I do not wish it to be."

Pinky purred: "A little less cryptic, your ladyship?"

Lady Arek made an enlargement of Yellowstone, swelling back up as if we were still within its gravitational clutches. "I have been monitoring a possible development, and it troubles me. There has been a drop in albedo in this area of the face."

I understood her words, but not their significance to our plight. "A drop in albedo means less reflected light?"

"Or less light reaching us. There's something getting in the way of our view of Yellowstone. If it were a single solid object, we would see it. But at this distance there's nothing to resolve, just a drop in the reflected light across a circular region about a third of the diameter of the planet, like a faint grey thumbprint on a picture."

Lady Arek made some adjustments to the display parameters and the face of Yellowstone gained a new disfigurement beyond the bisection of the Rust Belt. The two were interlinked, but not the same phenomenon.

"Wolf flow," I said.

"But aimed directly at us, so we stare down the column, rather than seeing it from the side as we have the others. It's been growing over several minutes, spreading in its extent and deepening the albedo drop."

"Then they've locked onto us after all. The distractions helped, but not enough to give us time to slip free." I was hearing my own words, marvelling at their cold detachment. "Do you have a distance estimate, an interception solution?"

Lady Arek gave a shrug of precise helplessness. "They could be ten thousand kilometres astern of us, or a hundred thousand. If we change course, we should see the albedo locus shift relative to the planet, and that will give us an idea of their distance and spread. But it won't help us run any faster, and our turn will only confirm that we are a viable target."

"Looks like they've already made their minds up about that to me," Pinky said.

"I do not think this flow is as concerted as the other," Lady Arek demurred. "It's exploratory: a relatively small commitment compared to the total aggregate around Yellowstone. That suggests to me that the wolves do not believe we are worth throwing all their resources at."

"Then we hold our nerve," I said. "Keep running, but with no change in our course or acceleration. And hope that the flow loses interest in us."

Lady Arek looked at the display, then back to me. "I see little point in informing Barras and the others about this. There's nothing they can do, so why add to their concerns?"

I disagreed. "We have to build trust, here. I think the safest way to do it is to be as open and transparent with Barras and the others as we are with ourselves."

"They won't thank you," Lady Arek said.

"They won't," Pinky said. "But he's right, too. If we only share the good news, they'll never know when to believe us."

Lady Arek was neither right, nor entirely wrong. The refugees took the news of our predicament with the full range of responses, from fury that I had burdened them with worry about a situation totally out of their control, to a grumbling but mostly stoic acceptance, to a cheerful resignation, to heartfelt gratitude that I had spared them nothing of the truth. Mostly it was somewhere in the middle, but verging on the opinion that it was better to be informed than to remain in ignorance.

"I won't deny that we're in trouble," I told them, walking along the aisles between the pits, each footfall a fresh lesson in pain despite the exoskeleton. "But if any ship has a chance of escaping the wolves, this is it. We think it likely they picked up something, enough to tease their interest: maybe some interaction of ours with the debris around Yellowstone, or a perturbation of the magnetosphere. But they aren't sure we're any-thing but a ghost signal. That's why they've only sent a relatively small number of elements after us. It's a fishing expedition, not a committed action. In the meantime, our friend Omori is giving them something real to chase..."

My timing could have been better.

Lady Arek called down, interrupting my sermon to inform me—and my audience—that the shuttle had blown up. Omori had used munitions, or the shuttle's last drops of fuel, to deny the wolves a fresh source of material for their transformations.

"Pinky and I risked our lives to obtain the Gideon stones, but both of us had hoped to make it back alive. Omori knew exactly what he was doing when he took that shuttle. There was no way back for him, no hope of survival. But he wanted to give us a tiny advantage, and he did."

"A good man, yes and yes," Probably Rose affirmed.

Someone asked if it was too late to go back to the Swinehouse.

"The Swinehouse is a pile of rubble at the bottom of the chasm," I said. "But you're welcome to lodge a complaint. Perhaps when we next make port you'll be lucky or stupid enough to find a ship going back in the other direction."

The question had not been meant seriously, but in that moment I was feeling an acute awareness of the sacrifices made for us by the others. "We're not finished, not by a long margin. Ahead of us will be fresh problems and worries. But if I'm to treat you with the respect you all deserve, then you need to know the worst of it, as well as the best."

"It was the right thing to tell them," Barras murmured to me as I passed his station. "And they'll come to understand that. In the meantime... did you know this man, Omori?"

I thought about another lie, one that would make the sting of his death seem more personal to me, and therefore more noble.

"I'd like to say I did. But until a few weeks ago, we'd never met."

"Whatever he did, whether he saved us or not, I think we can agree that he gave us time."

"I think we can."

"To live is better than not to live. Even for a few hours, in the company of friends."

Yellowstone was a dulling coin, nearly eclipsed. I stared at the image for long seconds, processing my own thoughts, not wanting to arrive at the inevitable conclusion.

"It's thickened," I said. "They've been pumping more units into the flow."

"There's no doubt," Lady Arek said. "I think we might be looking at around a million elements, at a conservative estimate."

"*Scythe* was able to deal with them in small numbers. Glass even brought a single unit inside the ship, so I could watch her destroy it in person."

"But a million will be a little more than we can fight off. By a factor of about ten thousand, is my guess."

"This change in the flow happened after Omori's death?"

"No, it started before," Pinky said. "But now they can afford to fling more of themselves at us."

I closed my eyes, breathed in. My leg had been bothering me all the way back from the refugees, but now it had reduced to an itch, barely any trouble at all.

"It seems they've decided we're more than just a sensor ghost."

"It's possible. Or else, they're taking no chances now that the other two distractions have been neutralised."

"This ship can accelerate harder."

"But at the expense of stealth," Lady Arek countered. "Pushed much harder, the darkdrives will begin to emit detectable by-products and the cryo-arithmetic modules will struggle to keep up with heat dissipation. We will light ourselves up."

"But if we're already lit..."

"We don't know that we are."

"It doesn't matter how hard we run," Pinky said. "We saw how futile it was when we swung past this system on our way to Hela. Ships tried to run. Sometimes the wolves let 'em get a little bit ahead. But it only ever ends the same way."

"I'll countenance a small increase in our engine output," Lady Arek declared. "There are...measures, which can mitigate the reaction over-spill, for a short while. And if we bias the cryo-arithmetic cooling to our stern and let our bows run hot, we can still keep a cold face to the wolves."

"And if there are wolves ahead of us?" I asked.

"Then have some very short, snappy prayers in hand," Pinky said.

Lady Arek's manner became businesslike. "Your assessment, Clavain: could the pigs withstand an increased gee-load, for a few more hours?"

"Only if it's a question of our survival. Probably Rose says some of them are barely hanging on, with the injuries they came aboard with. This may be more than they can tolerate, until we begin treating them properly.

"I must consider the overall outcome."

"Split the difference, then," Pinky said. "Give us one more gee, and I'll inform them that it's a temporary increase."

"You'll go to them?" I asked.

He was already moving. "Can't have them thinking that the only one with tact and sensitivity on this ship is a human, can we."

The measures Lady Arek would need to instigate within the darkdrives and cryo-arithmetic systems could not have been implemented instantly even if she had complete command of the ship. She first had to formulate her desires within the narrow control protocols that the ship seemed willing to listen to, and then she had to proceed a step at a time, verifying each alteration before moving to the next. This was delicate, unorthodox work: to tinker with the reaction balances inside a Conjoiner drive, especially a darkdrive, was to risk invoking immediate catastrophe. But—as I had to understand—Lady Arek carried the secret knowledge of Conjoiners within herself, and her gifts (as I was now learning) were prodigious.

"We'll initiate in ten minutes," she announced, when she had done all that she could. "That should give Pinky time to get back from the evacuees."

"I'm sorry for what both of you have had to go through today."

"But you've a feeling it will be hitting him the hardest."

"Am I wrong?"

"Pinky is a shot fired into the future. Tumbling, fragmenting. He ought to have slowed down by now...ought to have stopped. But he just keeps moving, gaining scar tissue. Sometimes I think the pain is what stops him dying. Snowdrop's death and the loss of the stronghold will not end him, Clavain. He will be hurt by it, and it will increase the pressure behind those eyes, and add to the scars...but it will not be more than he can take."

"How can you know?"

"Because I know a tenth of what Pinky has already been through. And that is enough."

"I'm daring to hope..." I shook my head, smiling at my own conceitedness. "No, never mind."

"What?"

"That at some point he might not consider me the most contemptible thing he's ever seen. That maybe, just maybe, I might earn about one per cent of his respect."

"Perhaps you're nearer than you realise. But give yourself time, as well. His friendship is not easily won. Once made, though, no force in the universe can undo it. Clavain, would you..." But she trailed off, her attention snagged back to the displays of Yellowstone.

"What?"

"Something may be happening. The locus is showing an elongation."

I frowned, unable to perform the necessary three-dimensional contortions to make sense of the changing data. "A pincer movement?"

"Too soon to rule out a bifurcation in the flow, which would be a precursor to a pincering..." Lady Arek became immobile, her attention so laser-focused that I was reminded of some ambush predator, poised in perfect stillness before springing for its prey. "No. Not that. At least, I do not believe so. The elongation is due to an angular deflection in the column. It's no longer aligned exactly with our vector, so we are starting to see down the length of it..." She snapped her eyes from the readouts, looking at me with a strange pleading intensity. "I want to believe it, Clavain, but I am not sure that I dare. They were hard on us, and now they deflect?"

"Wolves don't just give up, do they?"

"Not in my experience. Unless this an attack mode I haven't seen before, something new..."

Without warning, Glass's voice cut across the control room: "It's not something new."

"You're back," I said, surprised and relieved.

"Careful, Clavain: you nearly sound pleased to hear me."

"Are you back?"

"Only temporarily, dear friends. *Scythe* has raised me above a minimum consciousness threshold for one reason alone: to offer analysis and guidance in an extreme situation, one far beyond the ship's library of past scenarios."

"Your assessment, Hourglass?"

"The flow is indeed deflecting, Lady Arek. The wolves have abandoned this target and selected another."

Lady Arek shuffled through *Scythe*'s readouts, adjusting thresholds and filters accordingly.

"I see it now," she said. "Hourglass is right. There's something else drawing the flow. More fool me not to have spotted it sooner."

"Spotted what sooner?"

"A radio-frequency emission, Clavain. Very strong, omnidirectional. A broadcast, unmistakably a hallmark of human intelligence...a lure." She smiled deliciously. "Wolf bait. We like wolf bait, don't we, Hourglass?"

"We do indeed, Lady Arek—especially when we are not the bait."

"*Scythe* is in receipt of a simple transmission. Audio only. Shall I play it?"

"I think you should," Glass said. "I very much think you should."

Voices sang:

Tell me who's that writing? John the Revelator.
Tell me who's that writing? John the Revelator.
John the Revelator wrote the book of the seven seals.

"He anticipated that there would be difficulties," Glass said. "Anticipated them, and decided that you would most definitely benefit from a larger distraction."

Lady Arek directed my attention to one of the displays. "Darkdrive emissions, hotter and noisier than our own. Easily detectable across several light-minutes. There's only one other ship in this system that could be putting out that much energy, in addition to the radio signals."

"He's come in, from the edge of the system," I said, awed and astonished in the same instant. "He can't have waited for us to run into trouble: he must have made this decision days ago, perhaps as soon as we left him behind."

"He's positioning himself at the trailing Lagrange point behind Marco's Eye, where ships used to gather during trade stopovers," Lady Arek said. "Wolf activity will already have been intense there. They'll have picked apart any wrecks that survived the first part of the cull. This is a taunt, a deliberate provocation."

"One that, judging by the actions of the flow, is working," Glass remarked.

Lady Arek returned to the images of the Yellowstone. "It's abandoning us. I can't say that every element in the flow's given up on the chase, but if any are left it's a small percentage of the total."

"Will John the Revelator be able to escape?" I asked.

"No," Lady Arek said, with a weary finality. "No. No hope of that at all. You've seen that ship, Clavain. It's forty times bigger than *Scythe*, and it was old and broken when it reached this system. John the Revelator knows that just as well as we do. This is only going to end one way."

"He's becoming visible," Glass said. "He's pushing those darkdrives far outside their safe regime. They're glowing like stars."

"He doesn't want to give the wolves any reason to turn around," I commented, keeping my voice to a near-whisper. "And he must know that we're aware of his actions, and using them to our advantage. Which we must."

I called down to Pinky and Probably Rose.

"This is Clavain. We have an opportunity to shake the wolves loose and make a clean break for interstellar space. But only if we push as hard as we can. We'll be throwing everything into the fire, and it will be hard on the weakest of the evacuees. Once we open up the engines, you'll be unable to move around or offer any sort of assistance to the injured."

"Is there going to be any debate about this?" Pinky asked.

"None. I just thought you should be ready."

There was a silence before he answered.

"Spoken like the old man."

So we pushed harder, all the way up to four gees. Under that load, almost any movement was impractical and even speaking and concentrating became less easy. With each breath, I felt as if my ribs were heaving against a pile of books on my chest. The best we could do was remain still and observe.

John the Revelator was now the brightest energy source anywhere in the system, with the exception of Epsilon Eridani itself. His drive emissions were two close-set beacons, two miniature suns flaring and flickering with incipient instability. But an ashen veil of wolf machines was beginning to cloud our view of them. It was not just the flow that had been assigned to us that was converging on that other ship. Ten times as many elements were oozing in from different points around Yellowstone. It was as if all the destruction that we had witnessed today was but a prelude to this greatest of conquests.

Perhaps, in the long run, his efforts made no difference to our chances. But I wanted to believe that across those light-minutes (not so very far) some part of John the Revelator was able to detect our movements, picking up on a whisper of exotic radiation from our faint but unavoidably heightened darkdrive emissions, or seeing the heat spiking from the parts of the hull no longer blanketed by the cryo-arithmetic engines. His angle of view was different to that of the wolf flow that had been behind us, and he might have seen some trace of us and known that we were responding. We had to trust that the other flows did not have a better angle on us, or at least that they were otherwise so fixated on this new prize as to fail to notice us.

Supposition, never to be proven or disproven. But it suited me to believe that one more noble act went knowingly recorded, that against the long ledger of questionable deeds that made up his strange, distended life, perhaps the longest, strangest life ever lived, John the Revelator, writer of the book of the seventh seal, felt absolved, if only in those last sweet moments of his existence.

"If I know him," Lady Arek said, "something will happen just before he succumbs. He will try to take as many of them with him as he can."

We had warning, but only a little. The two close-set stars diverged. John had cut them away from himself, like two old-style chemical boosters detaching from the main core of a rocket. At a certain separation—Lady Arek said it could not have been more than a handful of kilometres—the engines detonated. We needed no magnification or image enhancement to see the consequences of that: if *Scythe* had possessed real windows, we would have seen the flash with our own eyes, and probably had to squint away to avoid temporary blindness. The explosion had been instantaneous and singular: so huge that it seemed to emanate from the volume between the engines, swallowing them instantly. And, in the same silent deflagration, taking every atom of the ship with it, and perhaps some useful number of wolf elements.

The chorus had been continuing, until the moment it ceased:

Tell me who's that writing? John the Revelator.
Tell me who's that writing? John the Revelator.
John the Revelator wrote the book...

He was gone.

And still we fled.

CHAPTER TWENTY

We held at four gees for an hour, then reduced to three, and after six hours agreed to drop the acceleration to one gravity for as long as it took to tend to the refugees and address the worst of their ailments. Pinky, Probably Rose and I went down to them while Lady Arek kept an eye on the ship and its surroundings, all of our nerves still on edge.

We dared to hope that we had given the wolves the slip, and perhaps we had, but it would be many days or weeks before we had any certainty. The feelings that rose in me were bitterly familiar from our time in the *Salmacis*. I had learned then, and was relearning now, that there was only so much worry a human being could tolerate. Never mind the next days or weeks: they were as irrelevant as the next million years. What mattered was that for the next hour I did not have to think about dying.

When we arrived at the holding area, the refugees were still snug in their pits. There was no screaming, and the moans and grumbles of discomfort were strangely lulling to me.

Barras looked up from his Barras-shaped enclosure.

"Talk to us," he said.

I looked at Pinky, thinking he ought to be the one to address the pigs, but his nod gave me permission. He was waddling off along the aisles, joining Probably Rose in seeking out those most in need of attention.

"We think the wolves have lost interest in us."

"You think?"

I smiled. "There's rarely any certainty. But the indications are that the flow broke away from us, seeking another target."

"When will we know if we're safe?"

"Maybe never. But it probably won't be the wolves that kill us today."

"Is that what counts as a morale-raising speech?" But Barras met my eyes and nodded. "You got us out of Swinehouse, Clavain. Whatever else happens when we get to this waterworld, you have my gratitude for that."

Pinky called over to me. He was leaning over one of the refugees, knees bent, hands propped against them for support. "Something's happening, Stink. The floor's pushing her back out again."

"Who are you?" I asked.

The pig looked at me. "Mira."

Pinky and I reached down, trying to help her as the floor oozed back towards the level, filling in the pit.

"Are you hurt, Mira?" I noticed at a badly swollen wrist and wondered if the bones were broken beneath it.

"There's those hurt worse than me. But it doesn't sting so much as it did before we went into these pits. Now it just tingles, mostly."

"It'll still need treating."

Four of the sphere robots came into the chamber. Pinky and I watched them guardedly, conscious that we had no direct control over these machines. They were operating at the whim of the ship, beyond any authority we might possess.

The robots swooped over to Mira. They extended their arms, reaching to lift her out of the in-filling pit. I stepped back, sensing that it would be futile to obstruct their actions. Pinky was a fraction slower—or more stubborn—and got a less-than-gentle shove in the belly, sending him stumbling backwards, arms flailing until I reached out and grabbed him by the elbow.

"Doctor knows best, I think," I said.

Pinky grunted something back: not quite a thanks, but close enough to pass as one.

Mira resisted the robots, as might anyone in the same circumstances. But they had more limbs than she could kick or thrash against, and they were able to restrain her with what seemed like reasonable gentleness. They hauled her into the air, distributing their pressure points evenly.

"They're going to help you," I said.

Mira quietened, becoming limp. The transition was so sudden that I could only guess that one of the robots had jabbed some sedative into her. With her body suspended between them, the robots left the chamber.

Pinky whispered: "You don't really know what they are going to do to her."

"The ship's taken care of everyone until now. Unless it's psychotic, I think we can assume it means to continue as it began. It'll be taking her away to the medical suite, just as it did with Glass."

In time, more robots came. It appeared that pigs were emerging from the floor in the order of those most in need of treatment, the ship performing some inscrutable calculus of triage behind the scenes. Evidently it lacked the capacity to deal with them all at once, so the pigs were being spirited away in ones and twos only. By then it was clear that just being in the pits had provided some anaesthetic effect on the worst injuries, with most of the wounded reporting a numbing or reduction of pain. But the mechanisms in the floor could only do so much, and so further treatment had to be conducted somewhere else.

"This ship isn't mad," I said quietly, for Pinky's ears alone. "If anything, it's saner than Glass."

"As comparisons go, Stink..."

I smiled. "It could use some work. I know."

At Lady Arek's persuasion, the ship allowed us back to the medical suite where I had last seen Glass. That meeting felt much longer ago than a day, consigned to some more innocent part of my life. Snowdrop, Omori, and John the Revelator had all been alive when I was last in here. Now their deaths seemed to mark some dividing line between the man I had felt myself to be and the one I knew, deep down, I truly was.

We gathered around the room's focal point: the container in which I had last seen Glass. She might still have been in there for all we could tell, but now there was no way to see into it. The support medium had become a murky yellow-green, hiding its secrets, and the surgical machines had pulled away from whatever activity they had been engaged in before.

"Are you in there, Glass?" Lady Arek asked, touching a palm to the enclosing shell.

"She'd better be," I said.

"Not helpful," Lady Arek snapped.

"She can't be anywhere else, can she? I saw her in this bottle. The machines were fussing over her."

"Damn those ninecats. I never liked them." Lady Arek removed her palm from the container. It left a cold imprint, blushing away after a few seconds. "We need her. Not just because there will always be aspects of this ship that she understands better than me, but the rest of it, too. Her tactical and strategic expertise dovetails with my own." Her eyes flashed onto me. "And yours—when you relearn it."

"Glass!" I called. "If there's a part of you still alive enough to hear this, you find a way to come back to us!"

"Giving her orders now?" Lady Arek asked mildly.

Pinky made a low cough. "Was that there when we arrived?"

Another door had opened on the opposite side of the medical suite, beckoning us to investigate. Stepping into the chamber beyond, I took an involuntary breath, taken aback that such a large space could have been in the ship all along, hidden from my exploration. It was twenty times larger than the medical suite, big enough to contain another spacecraft entirely. All it was, though, was a larger annex of the medical suite, filled with multiply duplicated samples of the same equipment.

We moved from bottle to bottle, quickly confirming that each contained the faint but unmistakable form of a pig. Judging by the quick whirring processes going on in and around the bottles, various forms of surgery and healing were taking place.

"Thank you, *Scythe*," I said, not caring what the others made of my talking to the ship. "You're trying to help them, and we understand. Please continue doing what you're doing."

"Healing them is only half the battle," Lady Arek said. "None of this will help if they cannot be kept alive afterwards. That either means reefersleep or life-support, or..."

"I think we can trust that the ship has things in hand," I said. "Or that it will do, very shortly."

The far wall was not fixed. It was moving back very slowly, like the barrel of a piston. As it retreated, it was leaving a structure behind it. It had a soft, improperly formed look to it, like a casting that had been removed from the mould when it was still molten. But it was sharpening as we looked, gaining form and function. It was a reefersleep casket, all but identical to the ones Glass and I had used.

The retreating wall finished forming the casket. Then a new one began to bud out of the same moving surface.

"Something got the message," Pinky said.

Our friends and allies—even such a doubtful and mercurial ally as John the Revelator—had turned the wolves from our scent. But it was only when we were a month out of Yellowstone that we allowed ourselves to believe it. Lady Arek used every passive sensor at her disposal and finally decreed that there was no trace of the enemy ahead or behind us—at least not out to a range of several light-minutes. Of course there could be no certainty in that, but since no better reassurance could be hoped for, we all accepted it gratefully. Under pressure, as I had learned in Sun Hollow, the human mind will settle for a lot less than certainty.

Day by day the ship had continued healing pigs and manufacturing reefersleep caskets. Neither process could be accelerated, but once we had a sense of the schedule we could begin to plan around it. There was food, water and life-support in abundance. We never saw where our sustenance was coming from, and perhaps that was for the best. All that mattered was that the tireless robots came and went without cessation, and if food of one kind was rejected (the pigs could be fussy, due to their hypertrophied sense of smell and taste) then an alternative was quickly offered. Over the early days of that month the machines—and by implication *Scythe*—came to an understanding of its guests, and gradually tailored its offerings and amenities until all were satisfied. Washing and toilet facilities were created, as well as furniture and concessions to privacy including personal sleeping spaces. Garments were offered, the rags taken away, and the pigs rummaged through hoppers of clean colourful fabric, trying on pieces for size and style. With the ship holding at one gee for the time being, it was as close to a normal life as most of the pigs had ever known.

One by one the healed ones came back to us. I was glad of that, preferring to have the proof of their recovery than having them sent straight into the new caskets. The other pigs saw that their friends had been made well and began to believe that this frightening, unpredictable and automated environment might be trying to help them. By then, most understood that it was our hope to have them all go into reefersleep. But that brought its own concerns, too. The pigs were either alarmed at the general prospect of being frozen, or more specifically aware of the particular risks associated with hibernation and pigs. On this matter, we could only offer so much reassurance.

All the same, the ship clearly meant for us to sleep. When we all went into the caskets, the acceleration could be ramped up as steeply as *Scythe* desired. It would be a lot less complicated if none of us needed to breathe or walk around in that interval.

Barras turned out to be key. He was wise enough not to be completely persuaded that any part of this was going to be safe. By submitting to reefersleep, the pigs were accepting a reasonable chance of death. But it was a risk that came from considerations of physics and biology, not the mad whims of the Swine Queen or the cold predation of the wolves. They could deal with that, in their fashion. Not all the pigs would see it that way, but a small number of dissenters could be press-ganged into the caskets if it came to open resistance. Barras, though, was confident that a majority of the pigs would come to an understanding that this was still the best hope for them collectively, and the doubters would eventually fall in with the rest, grudgingly but peacefully.

We left them to it. If we were to instil trust in the pigs then we had to let them manage their own affairs, with a de facto leader and something approaching an ad hoc democracy. I reiterated my earlier pledge: if for some reason reefersleep was not an option for the pigs, then I would remain awake and see out the long watch with them. But at the same time I made it clear that I expected to be able to offer very little assistance.

In the end there was unanimity among the pigs. How they got there was no concern of mine: all that mattered was that Barras had persuaded them to go into the caskets. By then, nearly all the cabinets had been created, stretching in a long, ordered row down the length of that huge chamber. The robots played no further part in the process, leaving us to coordinate how the units were occupied, configured and their revival clocks set.

Lady Arek ran various simulations of *Scythe*'s crossing under different thrust patterns. The worldtime for our journey hardly varied with one parameter or another, but the competing scenarios did make a significant variation in elapsed shiptime, amounting to nearly a year's difference in our on-board clocks. That would be a long time to wake up early, if the revival points were set too early. The trouble, as Lady Arek made clear, was that *Scythe* could only begin detailed intelligence gathering when it was already within a few light-months of Ararat. If it found wolves, or some other threat, it might need to adjust its deceleration and final approach profile. The exact details of our flight's end stages were therefore impossible to predict in advance, giving us no way to be sure when to set the revival clocks.

"The pigs can wait until we're sure that there's a planet we can land on," Pinky said. "The rest of us can come out earlier."

"By how much?" Lady Arek asked, when it was just the four of us left warm, standing by our waiting caskets: the two that Glass and I had already used, one of which would suit Lady Arek just as well, and the two new units that had been forged for Pinky and Probably Rose.

"A month. Six months. Maybe even a year. Sniff out the system, see how it lies, then refine our plans."

"If those plans demand high acceleration," I said, "staying awake for the rest of the voyage might not be an option."

Pinky glanced at his casket. Outwardly, it looked the same as the other two. But its interior space was smaller, configured to provide a snug fit around a pig. "So we go back in."

"And each time, we roll the dice on whether we come out again," I said.

"That'd be for me to fret about, not you."

But Lady Arek sided with me. "Clavain is old as well, Pinky—older than either of us. The things Hourglass did to him have reset some of his morbidity markers, but reefersleep still presents a non-negligible risk. None of us must take any part of this lightly."

He lifted his snout. "Do I look like I'm taking it lightly?"

"If I might offer an opinion?"

We all stopped and turned to face the voice. Glass was standing in the doorway: she had appeared silently, without warning. She looked just as she had before she went to the Swinehouse: steady on her feet, lacking any visible injury, and entirely in command of herself.

"I was only ever caretaking," Lady Arek said decorously, extending a hand by way of welcome, even though they were standing far apart. "It is good to see you, Hourglass. We were becoming concerned, after your absence."

"So concerned that you were ready to jump into my reefersleep casket?" Glass asked.

"You can't blame us for making arrangements," I said. "For all we knew you'd be in that bottle for months. Besides, the ship has shown that it can make reefersleep caskets at will."

"You're quite correct, Clavain." She walked over to us, her gait steady. Perhaps she had grown marginally thinner or paler since I had last seen her clearly, but it was hard to be sure. "In any case, there are no hard feelings. It is right that you should take to the caskets, now that I am restored. In fact, I will be here to supervise all four of you as you go into reefersleep."

"What of you?" Lady Arek asked suspiciously.

"I will enter in good time," Glass answered. "There are a number of technical matters I'd like to attend to while *Scythe* is in transit. First of all, I will overview the final measures necessary for the completion of the hypometric precursor device, the nature of which you were good enough to explain to Clavain. "Our layover on Ararat will provide the ideal environment to perform a number of low-energy system tests, safe from wolf interference."

"And between now and then?" Lady Arek asked.

"I was about to come to the other matter: the testing and integration of the Gideon stones. This will be delicate work, and it would do well not to be rushed. I shall remain awake for a period—anything up to several months, depending on my progress—and I shall wake earlier, as well, to complete whatever loose ends remain."

"I could assist," Lady Arek said.

"And you most certainly shall, if for any reason I find myself unable to complete the work in a timely fashion."

"When you begin poking about with those stones...is there a danger of destroying the ship?" I asked.

Glass nodded enthusiastically. "Very much so."

"Then for the sake of my nerves, I think I'd rather be dead while you're doing it."

Pinky had made his own mind up. He was already clambering into the casket. I met his eyes, nodded some wordless encouragement, and made similar arrangements of my own.

Part Five

PHOTOSPHERE

CHAPTER TWENTY-ONE

The sun was still ten degrees above the horizon when I reached the Muskie ruin. Not much was left of it now, with dust already smothering its lines, but the feature had been well documented and easily mapped from orbit, and it was a prime candidate among our possible rendezvous points. I was glad that the impactor and dropships had not veered too far from their predicted landing zone because none of the other shelters were as handy as this one, nor as close to the initial objective.

It had been a quintet of pressure domes, with one main dome in the middle and four smaller units around it, linked by semicircular tunnels. The domes had long ago ruptured or caved in, so that all that was left was their foundations and a metre and a half or so of crumbling, curving walls. Anything useful, such as solar collectors, airlocks or life-support systems, had been plundered long ago. These abandoned, crumbling homesteads—there were hundreds more, all over Mars—were already fading into invisibility. They had been here only a century or more, but I easily imagined myself crouching among the vine-ridden walls of some jungle temple from a thousand years earlier.

Mars already had a long and bewildering history of ambition, conquest and abject, harrowing failure. The Muskies, with their cultish, over-reaching aspirations, were just one small chapter in that narrative.

While the others converged on this position, I set about preparing our temporary camp. I retracted my stilts and set equipment pods on the darkening ground. I unwrapped a four-metre-wide thermal mat and secured it to the ground with burrowing pitons. Kneeling on the mat, I laid out more tools, weapons and supplies. Using the walls as cover, I deployed a camouflaged awning, resembling a bigger version of my suit's adaptive parasol. Now even the neutral, vigilant Demarchists would have trouble spotting us from space.

The sun had gone down by the time I was done. Without image amplification it was totally dark under the awning; totally dark beyond it. There was no airglow, no moonlight. A thin, cold wind whipped and chivvied the adaptive fabric. I heard it, faintly, through my suit's acoustic sensors. Conserving energy, I sat very still with my knees tucked up to my chest.

Hope was the first to arrive. My suit alerted me to his approaching footfalls, picking up even the minor seismic signal of the stilts. There was almost nothing to see until he was climbing in through a gap in the wall, crouching into the space under the awning. I studied him through the image-amplification overlay, alert for signs of injury or damage. My visor painted a pale purple outline around his form.

Our suits established an ultra-short-range comms handshake.

"Status?" I asked.

"Bruised and battered, but otherwise functional. How was it for you?"

"Nominal."

"Always one for the small-talk, Faith."

"Small-talk won't get us off Mars with the mission objective."

"No, but it might make the time pass a little more easily. You know, by the time they extracted me from my last surface mission, I was talking to anything that looked like it had a face."

"By all means talk to yourself. Unless it compromises our operational effectiveness, I don't have a problem with it." I gestured at the items on the ground. "I've commenced the parts inventory."

Hope unpacked his own equipment pods and began laying the contents next to the things I had already set out. Weapons, ammunition, suit components, medical instruments and supplies. Some of the bigger weapons and tools had been split between us; now their parts could be organised and assembled.

"The drop was rougher than the simulations," Hope commented, clicking together the two main sections of an armour-piercing rifle.

"Everything's rougher than simulations. We made it down. If they saw us, or suspected anything, there'll be some activity by day-break." I sighted down the bore of a magnetic pistol, then snapped it back into its housing.

"Any sign of Charity?" Hope asked.

"Not yet."

"The fourth suit?"

"Not yet."

I carried on organising our equipment.

Charity arrived an hour later, exhausted but relieved to have found the rendezvous. She unpacked her gear, and after a quick inspection we confirmed that it had all arrived undamaged.

Which was good: each of us had our role to play, but Charity's was the first, and arguably most critical, part of the mission. If it failed, then the operation as a whole was shot.

"Rest while you can," I advised her. "We're still waiting on the other suit, but even if it arrives soon we'll need storm cover before we set out."

"About the other suit, sir."

"Yes?"

"I think I saw it go down, sir. Something came in very hard about twenty klicks north of my drop-point. I don't think it was an ordinary impactor shard. It looked small and sleek, like a dropship. But I didn't see any sign of a slowdown. The horizon line was near, though, so I suppose it might have flared when it was out of sight..."

The storm came, and the storm persisted. There was night, and there was night's close cousin: daylight smothered to a grey, shadowless twilight by the rushing dust clouds. At its fiercest, the storm felt as it might already blanket all of Mars and never surrender its hold. But we knew better. At this season, and this latitude, it might only last a day. That would still be enough for us.

I was the only one receiving updates from orbit. They were highly encrypted, low-energy transmissions that were being beamed out in all directions, not just down to the surface. If the Conjoiners detected these signals, it would not necessarily alert them that an operation was in progress. The content itself was extremely terse: just enough to give us guidance as to whether it was safe to proceed, and what sort of time margin was in force.

"Twelve hours until we lose storm cover," I reported. "No other storm of comparable extent predicted for the next seven days."

Hope made a diffident sucking sound. "Couldn't be nearer the knuckle."

"It's sufficient. Five hours to the objective, one on site, five back. Maybe less than one on site, if all goes well. We'll be back under shelter with at least an hour's margin—but only if we leave now."

"Or sit it out until a longer storm."

"The longer we delay, the more chance we'll give the spiders to reach the capsule ahead of us. We've planned for this." I turned to Charity. "Five hours will be tough on all of us, and there'll be no chance to stop. It all hangs on you when we get to the Defection Capsule. I know we're all tired after the drop, but this is probably our only opportunity."

"I'm ready," Charity affirmed.

"Good—we're depending on you." Almost as an afterthought I added: "By the way, control confirms your observation, Charity. The fourth dropship malfunctioned at the last moment."

"So no fourth suit," Charity said.

I nodded, examining the spare visor that had come with our supplies. "A complication. But we'll find a workaround."

Hope, next to me, said nothing.

We stowed our inventoried equipment, selected what we would need for this part of the operation, and left the rest in the shelter where the walls would keep off the worst of the dust. The force of the storm was actually very slight. There was no chance of anything being blown over, or blown away—but the invasive, scouring dust was a constant problem. It always had been. Always would be on Mars. Now we depended on it, for no surveillance capability accessible to the Conjoiners should be able to track our movements under the storm's screen.

We deployed our stilts and moved out in close formation, guided by the transponder signal from the Defection Capsule.

Two human faces were there as I emerged from reefersleep.

Lady Arek had not changed to any noticeable degree. But Glass was a different version of herself. She had become thinner and steelier, the bones around her dark-margined eyes more sharply defined, her skin drawn tighter onto the armature beneath it. I thought of war drums and bowstrings.

"Clavain, talk to us."

"Give him time, Glass. You forget how hard this is, for those without our gifts."

I tried to speak. My tongue felt like some dry, swollen maggot cramming my mouth.

"Lady...Arek. Glass."

I blinked some of the gumminess out of my eyes. The lids were stiff canvas, rough against my eyeballs. Everything in me was glued to every other part, as if I had been part mummified in some hard-setting resin.

"He remembers names, at least," Lady Arek commented to Glass.

"More than names. Where are we?"

Glass reached in and bundled me out of the casket with as much consideration as if I were a sack of meat with a few old bones tossed in. "What do you remember about our destination?"

"Mars," I coughed, as she rough-handled me. "We were going to Mars."

She flung me onto some kind of couch she must have brought alongside the casket. "Not Mars, you bloody fool. Definitely not Mars."

"He is confused," Lady Arek said, with a faint pitying smile.

Glass slapped my cheek. "Concentrate, Clavain! John the Revelator died.

You remember John the Revelator. For pity's sake tell me you remember John the Revelator..."

"Something about..." I had to wait while my brain shuttled impulses around its warming loom and dredged up fragments of memory. It was like a cold engine trying to run up to speed. "Gideon stones. And on our way to..." I grunted, trying to force it out of me. "Albertine. Amduman."

"Ararat," Lady Arek said.

I nodded fiercely. "Ararat. Where the Pattern...the Pattern..."

"Jugglers," she helped.

"Pattern Jugglers," I echoed. "To swim with them. To learn something." Like a lifting fog, some sort of clarity began to form. "Did we make it to Ararat? Glass was going to wake up before the rest of us..."

"I did," Glass said. "We're nearly there."

I pressed a finger to my brow, massaging away a knot. "How nearly is nearly?"

"In-system, about to complete our slowdown phase. We just need to trim a little more speed, then we can make a ballistic crossing to Ararat."

"Tell him the rest," Lady Arek said.

I swung my legs off the couch, forcing mobility into my limbs. "There's a problem. If there wasn't, you wouldn't be waking me with this urgency. You said you'd bring us out well in advance of our arrival. An hour or a day here or there shouldn't matter if we're still weeks from Ararat. So what is it?"

"A problem arose with the integration of the Gideon stones," Glass said.

"Try rephrasing that in something other than the passive voice, there's a good Glass," said Lady Arek.

Glass shot a glare at her. "I attempted to embed three of the Gideon stones. If they're to be useful to us, they must work in conjunction with the cryo-arithmetic engines. Unfortunately, there was a conflict."

Lady Arek chided: "And instead of waiting for my counsel, how did you react to this conflict?"

"I pressed on, because only I have the necessary understanding of this ship's systems."

"An understanding that proved lamentably insufficient when put to the test."

Their bickering was worse than the reefersleep revival. "Enough," I said, raising a hand. "What happened? Clearly the ship is all right, or we wouldn't be here. Are the stones damaged? The cryo-arithmetic engines?"

"There has been no lasting damage," Glass said.

"Good."

"But there is a complication," Lady Arek said. "A significant one. We

277

have…not been able to arrive at a joint position concerning the best course of action ahead of us."

"What about Pinky?"

"Pinky has declared his opinion," Glass said.

"Fine. I'll declare mine, as soon as I know what the hell it is I'm supposed to be declaring one on."

"Can you walk, Clavain?" Lady Arek asked.

"Give me a moment. Or several."

She jammed an arm under my left armpit and heaved me off the couch. Glass grunted and took my other side. Between them they dragged me out of the room while I tried to get my legs to make slippery contact with the floor. They felt like two flimsy tentacles scraping beneath me.

"You are right about the ship," Glass said. "All systems are now nominal. As you will have noticed, we are in a deceleration configuration."

"Barras, Probably Rose and the others?"

Lady Arek seemed pleased by my concern. "They are well. But still asleep, for now. It is probably for the best that they remain that way, until we have resolved the complication ahead of us. We shall wake them once we are on Ararat. If all is well, that will be as far as they ever need to travel."

"Are there wolves around Ararat?"

"If there are, they are concealed for now," Glass answered.

"The problem is that their presence must be assumed, even in the absence of evidence," Lady Arek said.

I nodded. "This ship can run silently, if it needs to."

"So it would have done," she said. "Unfortunately, Glass's experiments have made that impossible. Tell him. He will hear all of it before long, from your lips or mine."

"The systems conflict…" Glass, for once, was tongue-tied. "The conflict I created."

Lady Arek urged: "Continue."

"I pressed on when I should have backed away. My tests led to a cascade of failures and the ship went into a coma, save for life-support power. The darkdrives defaulted to a failsafe condition."

"In other words," Lady Arek said, "they stopped."

"When we should have been slowing down, we were not," Glass went on. "It took time to bring the ship back to normality. As a consequence, we're now coming in too fast."

"Too fast for what?" I asked.

"To avoid being seen," Lady Arek said. "If we operate the engines at the necessary level to complete our approach to Ararat, we will emit detectable drive products. If there are wolves in the vicinity, they will undoubtedly track us."

We had come to the control room. Pinky was already there, occupying one of the command seats, spooning something into his mouth and reviewing a set of scrolling simulations. The ship had configured its manual controls to suit his fingers. We nodded at each other, two acquaintances who had only lately spoken, and whose last exchange was separated only by a single sleep. That the sleep had taken a decade, and might well have been our last was, for the moment, immaterial.

"How much've they told you, Stink?"

"That we have to slow down a little more, and it's hard to see how we can do it without making ourselves known to the wolves. How are you?"

"Doing well for a pig."

"Then I'm glad."

"Outline the proposition, Pinky, if you would be so good."

"My very great pleasure, your ladyship." He rubbed at his snout, thoughtfully. "Okay. You settled, Stink? Buckled in? You'll need to be."

"Tell me."

"We need cover. That's the essence of it, Stink. Some nice moon or planet we can screen ourselves behind while we kill this extra speed Glass has so kindly given us."

"I see."

"But the kicker is, there isn't any moon or planet that works for us. Not with our approach vector the way it is, and not with any reasonable guess as to where wolves might be hiding, if they're here at all."

"Wouldn't it be nice if they weren't."

"It certainly would, Stink. Still, there is an option on the table. A concealment method. Works very well under almost any set of assumptions. We use P Eridani A: the star we used to call Bright Sun."

"Good...?" I said provisionally, certain there was an aspect to this that I was not yet seeing. "There's a vector that lets us hide behind the star while we complete our slowdown?"

"Not quite," Glass said. "We won't be employing Bright Sun as a mask. We'll be using the star itself. *Scythe* has projected a course that allows us to skim close to the star, dip beneath the photosphere and execute our final slowdown while we're within it."

I laughed. It was the only sane response. "I must have some post-revival confusion. I could have sworn you said *inside* the star."

"It isn't as bad as it sounds."

"No," Pinky said. "It's much, much worse."

279

I regarded Glass. "You're not stupid, and I'm reasonably sure you're not suicidal. Explain how this helps us."

"Good, Clavain—at least you're open-minded. The fact is, we're only considering a brief dip into the photosphere of the star: barely different to skimming the atmosphere of a planet."

"Except it's a star."

"Don't get too hung up on that. The photosphere is merely a transitional zone where the mean free paths for photon collisions undergo a large change. From *Scythe*'s point of view, it will be no different to moving from one plasma environment to a somewhat denser, more excited environment containing the same plasma."

"Except it's a star," I repeated.

"Inside the photosphere," Glass continued, undaunted, "the ambient energy background will screen our emissions very effectively. We can complete our slowdown and emerge at the correct speed to make a safe crossing to Ararat. Some thermal transfer will have taken place during the passage, but simulations indicate that it will be within the dissipative capacity of the cryo-arithmetic engines."

"'Simulations' and 'indicate.' Two words to inspire confidence, if ever there were any."

"He's as thrilled about it as I was," Pinky said.

I turned to Lady Arek. "You're at least as smart as Glass. Is any part of this even remotely feasible?"

"It is...not without its challenges. But I have reviewed the same projections as Glass. I believe the proposal to be fundamentally sound."

"Now tell him the fun part," Pinky said.

"The manoeuvre isn't feasible without a contribution from the Gideon stones," Glass said. "The dynamic loads on *Scythe*, both from the ambient forces, and the deceleration pattern, result in terminal hull collapse under all simulations, absent the Gideon stones."

"Absent these almost entirely untested Gideon stones," I said. "Exactly how many did you get to work, Glass, before it all went wrong?"

"Three. Two, if you wish to split hairs."

"And how many will it take to work?"

"All nine."

I shrugged. "Well, that's no problem at all."

"With my assistance in coordinating the integration," Lady Arek said, "it may not be so difficult as the first time. There is, also, a secondary consideration. The stones must be made to work eventually. If they fail us now, at least we will know that the rest of our plan is hopeless."

"All right," I said, sighing my acceptance. "That's the extreme option. I don't like it, but I'm prepared to believe that it might work, if Glass and Lady Arek both work at it. What's the back-up plan?"

"We abandon our approach," Glass said. "Slip through the system at our current speed, hope that we're not detected, return to interstellar space, wait until we've gained enough distance, then reverse our course."

"Which will add time to our rendezvous."

Glass nodded. "About two years, with an unavoidable margin of uncertainty—and at the end of it we'll still have to make the Gideon stones work en masse."

"I think I like being late better than I like being burned to a crisp inside a star. But it's not that simple a comparison, is it?"

"Any moving object runs a chance of detection, especially passing through the dusty, magnetic environment of a solar system," Lady Arek said. "The more times we do it, the greater likelihood of being seen."

I looked back at the scrolling simulations. "Give me your honest answer, both of you. If the systems work as they should, is this really something we can survive?"

I watched Glass for the slightest trace of hesitation or equivocation. But her answer was immediate and firm.

"Yes."

"Lady Arek?"

"It is within our capabilities."

I turned to Pinky. "They tell me you've already weighed in."

"I have, Stink."

"And your position?"

"I think it would be better if you answered first," Lady Arek said. "Pinky and I are split on how best to proceed, so your vote will settle things. You may reflect on it for a little while. Our course needs to be modified one way or the other, and the earlier we do it the smaller the possibility of detection. A decision within the hour would be exceedingly helpful...not least because there will be work to be done if we go with the sun-skimming manoeuvre."

"I could spend ten hours weighing those alternatives and it wouldn't help."

"There is that," Lady Arek agreed.

"If we don't get to Ararat, I don't get to meet my brother. Without the information you expect to learn from him, no other part of our plan has a hope. And without our plan, the wolves will ultimately destroy us." I breathed in. "In essence, you're telling me to make a decision which could save or condemn whatever's left of humanity."

"No pressure, Stink."

"Then I go with my intuition. It's all or nothing: we try to reach Ararat on this pass."

Lady Arek nodded solemnly. "Is that your final decision?"

"It is." Then, to Pinky: "I hope you won't resent me for that."

Rolls of frown corrugated his forehead. "Why would I? You just sided with me."

"I assumed you'd have regarded this as complete madness."

"Because pigs are said to be risk-averse?"

"Because pigs are sane."

"The dissenting opinion was mine," Lady Arek said. "I was moved to reject Glass's plan. I still am. But now the majority has spoken, and I abide by it. You and Pinky have decided our course."

She closed her eyes.

With the engines damped, Pinky and I suited up and went outside. We floated out of the weightless ship and allowed our momentum to drift us a couple of hundred metres away from the hull before slowing down with suit thrusters. Then we turned around to inspect the transformations that had already been wrought on *Scythe*.

We could just about see the ship. It was a black form against blackness, but faint lustres of highlight played across the form, defining its shape.

P Eridani was a double star, made up of two similar K-type dwarves. Ararat only orbited one of these stars, P Eridani A, the so-called Bright Sun, with the B component always being more distant. Bright Sun was obvious to us now, much more luminous than the seemingly smaller and fainter counterpart. But although it was the most obvious thing in the sky, even at our present distance Bright Sun only emitted a dim golden pall. Most of the light available to us was coming from the floodlights built into our suits. The ship could have made itself darker still, soaking up all the photons we fired at it, but we were still far enough out to be able to dispense with such precautions.

Pinky and I carried the remaining seven stones, three with him and four with me. The two that had successfully integrated were tiny in comparison to the ship, but they stood out like warts on an otherwise smooth face.

I had handled a single stone before, and been shown something of its capabilities. Their real usefulness only came out when they were employed in numbers, though, according to functional principles Lady Arek and Glass had done their best to explain to me.

Each stone had been placed in contact with the skin and allowed to undergo a process of limpet-like attachment, pushing roots deep into the existing hull armour. The stones did this on their own: if I had kept hold of one long enough, it would have tried to anchor itself into me as well. Once so anchored, the stones co-opted some of the ship's local fabric to grow meandering interconnections, linking themselves up and also searching for a native technology with which to bind and establish a control protocol.

Once we were done appraising the hull from a distance, Pinky and I told our suits to take us to separate worksites about a hundred metres apart and well out of sight of each other. I clamped on with my boots and dug into a pouch fixed to my chest. I took out one of the remaining stones; Pinky confirmed that he had done likewise.

A ruby glow slipped between my fingers.

"Glass, Lady Arek: I'm ready."

Lady Arek called back: "Pinky, are you in position?"

"Just getting there." I heard him grunt as he settled onto the hull. "I've got the magic pebble. Just say the word."

"Integration seems to go more smoothly when the stones are introduced synchronously," Lady Arek said. "You will lay the three remaining pairs at the designated positions, then the ninth and final stone. Hourglass? Tell them how to proceed."

"Offer the stone up to the hull. You need not press too firmly. In fact, it would be advisable to remove your fingers from the attachment site as soon as contact is established."

"Why's that?" Pinky asked.

"Because you may find your fingers useful in later life."

"Thank you, Glass. Is there a reason Stink and I drew the short straws on this one?"

Lady Arek said: "If you feel you have the neural workflow to manage two conflicting system integration tasks with an optimum intervention lag on the order of zero point three seconds, by all means come on in."

"The thing I like about her," Pinky said, "is that she's never in a rush to protect my feelings."

"I think we're outflanked, Pinky," I said confidingly. "Are you ready?"

"Ready as you are, Stink."

"Deploy," Glass and Lady Arek said in unison.

I held the stone in both hands, cradling it between my fingers, then almost flung it at the hull. I pulled back, fingertips tingling as if some part of the Gideon stone's energy had already begun to penetrate them. The stone seemed to have jumped out of my grip, slamming into the hull with some sudden magnetic attraction. It was already anchoring itself, partially submerged into what, only a moment ago, had been almost impermeable armour.

"In," I reported.

"In," Pinky confirmed.

"Good," Lady Arek said. "Now proceed to your second installation points. Hourglass and I will commence initial integration of these stones as soon as the tendrils marry with *Scythe*'s avionics."

"Take your time," I said quietly.

Pinky and I worked efficiently but carefully, and within an hour we had laid in the last of the four pairs of stones. That left me with the odd one to finish the job.

"Do not delay your return to the lock," Lady Arek said, as I knelt with the stone in my grip. "Something happens with an unpaired stone. It seems to be the factor that encourages the others to begin skein initialisation."

"Nice to know. Shouldn't Pinky go inside ahead of me?"

"We started this together, Stink," came his voice. "May as well see it through."

I pushed the ninth stone nearer the hull until I felt it trying to wriggle out of my fingers. I let it go, the stone speeding out of my grip as if on a sling. It rammed into the hull, and I began my retreat.

Pinky and I arrived back at the lock within a second of each other. Once we were within the lock, even with the outer door still open, I assumed we were safe. But our mistresses urged us to cycle through and complete the sealing off of the outer hull. "The skein is surface-conformal," Lady Arek explained. "It will tend to suck itself into any cavity. You would be ill-advised to be inside that cavity when it does."

"I like this more by the hour," Pinky said.

We came through the lock, back into *Scythe*.

The engines were already coming back on: Glass and Lady Arek not wanting to waste a second in which we might be decelerating ahead of our encounter with Bright Sun. We slipped out of our suits, stowed them, and made our way back to the control room.

Glass and Lady Arek barely acknowledged us as we came in. They were already knee-deep in the mental task of initialising the seven new stones. Their backs were arched, their necks rigid, their mouths open, their eyelids fluttering: ill-matched cousins caught in the same rapturous fit. I was seeing what it meant to be a Demi-Conjoiner now: how each of them was able to tap into the mental resources of their progenitors, to coordinate and share mental tasks between themselves, yet without dissolving into the absolute hive consciousness of the Conjoiners.

They had left a schematic of *Scythe* active, showing the meshlike connections between the Gideon stones—worming yellow lines readapting, thickening and consolidating by the second, like eldritch lightning playing over and around the hull.

"Ladies weren't kidding," Pinky said in a low voice. "It's happening quickly."

"How much did they tell you about all this?"

"Oh, plenty." He cocked his head, reflecting on his answer. "How much I understood, different question."

The ship juddered. Various alarms sounded. On the schematic, the yellow lines had stabilised. But now a secondary influence was asserting itself. A colourless, frosted, scale-patterned membrane was spreading out from each of the stones, clinging to the hull and merging at the contact points between the stones.

"The skein?" I asked.

"Trying to form, I think."

I thought of the pearly, faceted membrane that had bled out of the stone when I was shown it in the stronghold, oozing over my hand—gloving it against the impact of a blade. "It spills out from the nodes, becomes a kind of armour sticking close to us. I don't think we need to know *what* it is, Pinky, just that there are a whole range of things that won't be able to get through it."

"That's the level of understanding that's worked for me for most of my life."

"It's a sensible philosophy."

"It'd better be. It's the only one I've got."

The ship juddered again, but less violently than before, with the alarms becoming more muted. I had the sense that these were merely protestations of irritation as the alien and human technologies came to a grumbling, bad-tempered accord.

Lady Arek jerked and coughed. She was coming out of her trance. On the display, the pearly bloom was thinning and curdling, breaking back down into distinct regions, then sucking back into the Gideon stones.

"We have stable coordination across nine," Lady Arek said.

"Will nine do?" I asked.

Glass echoed Lady Arek's emergence. For a second her eyes were still rolled back in their sockets, as if they had stuck there. She shook her head as it to rattle them loose.

"Nine will have to." Glass nodded at the woman beside her. "You did well. We did well."

"It was...taxing," Lady Arek answered. Her chest heaved, as if she had just come up from under water. "But not unenjoyable."

"Between us, we should be able to manage the stones as we pass through the photosphere," Glass said. "It won't be easy; the magnetohydrodynamic loads will require constant adjustment. But it will be..."

"Fun," Lady Arek said, tilting her head slightly, as if the word was new to her.

CHAPTER TWENTY-TWO

Bright Sun grew larger and brighter by the day. *Scythe*'s windows were able to simulate a perfectly realistic view, and already the star's disc was becoming uncomfortable to stare at for any length of time. Holding my squinting eye to the curdled, storm-ridden boundary where its glare met the black of space, I marvelled at our brilliant madness. We were going into that: dipping ourselves willingly into those molten shallows. And here was the real madness: hoping it wouldn't kill us.

Although we were committed to the manoeuvre, there were still many variables that needed to be considered. Everything was a brutal trade-off. The harder the ship decelerated, the less time it would need to spend in the photosphere, minimising the load on the Gideon stones and the cryo-arithmetic devices. Above a certain threshold, though, no guarantees could be made for the safety of any of us, including our sleeping passengers. The further we cut into the photospheric layer—which formed a thin, bright rind around the star of about one hundred kilometres in depth—the better hope we had of concealment when we performed the slowdown. But then everything *else* got harder. I was glad that Glass and Lady Arek had taken it upon themselves to weigh these factors and offer what they considered the least-bad option.

Neither Pinky nor I quibbled with it.

From the moment we dipped into the photosphere, until the moment we emerged from it, about an hour would pass. When we touched the photosphere, we would be travelling at about eight hundred and fifty kilometres per second relative to Bright Sun. By the time we emerged, our speed would have been reduced to a still-fast four hundred and ninety kilometres per second. That was manageable: we could shed that excess with slow, stealthy deceleration measures between the star and Ararat. But to gain that advantage we needed to decelerate continuously at ten gees while inside the photosphere.

There was a complication.

We couldn't just arrow straight through the star, taking the path of

287

least distance. That would have bored us deep into the convection layer, beyond any hope of survival. Our trajectory had to follow a precise curve, keeping within the incredibly narrow boundary of the photosphere: a margin no thicker than a planet's atmosphere. But since our speed would be so high when we came in, we would be travelling *faster* than the motion of any object that just happened to be in orbit around the star at the same altitude. The effect of that would be an outward force far greater than our deceleration burn: around one hundred and four gees at the start of the manoeuvre. That was made slightly more bearable by the star's own gravitational field, acting in the opposite direction, but it was by no means neutralised. Bright Sun was less massive than the sun, but also more compact. The result was a surface gravitational acceleration of thirty-four gees, meaning our net outward force would be a mere seventy gees.

Against that, our ten gees of deceleration was barely consequential. We would feel it only as a slight deflection in the local vertical. But then we wouldn't be *feeling* anything: those levels were far beyond any point where consciousness was feasible, even with artificial measures. Even Conjoiners were incapable of thinking at seventy-plus gees.

But things would get better as we slowed down and the radial component of our acceleration diminished. Eighteen minutes into our manoeuvre, when we passed the midpoint of our journey through the photosphere, the outward gee-load would have reduced to just forty-five gees, which (according to Glass and Lady Arek) was approaching the point where Glass could begin to resume normal cognitive operations, and therefore have both knowledge and influence over the ship. Lady Arek would follow some while after. But it would be a lonely wait before Pinky and I were able to approach the same functionality. By the time the outward force was reduced to ten gees, the same magnitude as our deceleration, another half-hour would have passed. Even then we would feel fourteen gees, because by then the deceleration vector was no longer negligible.

The acceleration couches were designed for sustained loads of three gees, and transient loads of between ten and twenty. Beyond that, we all needed specialised protection and life-support measures, including Glass and Lady Arek.

For those of us who were still awake, these turned out to be our suits, already engineered to cushion their hosts against a range of stresses. The suits were normally full of air, but each was capable of immersing their subjects in a dense but breathable fluid. No part of that would be enjoyable, but it would be survivable. As for the evacuees, their reefersleep caskets could be auto-modified to provide an equivalent degree of protection. *Scythe* knew what it was being called upon to do and had taken it upon itself to make the necessary arrangements. The caskets had gained additional footings, rooting them more solidly to the floor. Within them, a dark-tinted gel seemed to have been introduced to fill the space around the bodies, and perhaps provide some support from within. Elsewhere, similar signs of preparation were evident. The ship was steeling itself, reinforcing weaknesses, eliminating superfluous design features, consolidating its maze of rooms and corridors. It was becoming an iron needle, with the sole purpose of slipping through the winking eye of the photosphere. It was a living castle that had begun to gird and buttress itself for war, shedding the fineries of peace.

As Bright Sun kept growing, so Glass and Lady Arek kept refining the simulations, calculating to the second when they were likely to be able to issue their last useful commands. One might last a little longer than the other, but by the time they had both succumbed, the ship would need to be a master of its own fate. They had given it some leeway to deflect its course up and down, steering around any developing storms in the photosphere—or perhaps exploiting them for maximum cover.

By the same token, we knew exactly how late we could delay our entry into the suits. Too late, and the cushioning medium would not have time to build up to the necessary support pressure before the seventy gees came in.

The last two hours saw Bright Sun swelling to a third of the sky, then half of it: a blinding orange-yellow furnace, as if the end of the universe were a blazing wall. Like nearly any star, it only looked calm and unchanging from a distance. This close, its surface had become a storm-tossed sea of prominences and rifts, with vast convection cells welling up from beneath.

Scythe went into free-fall for its final approach, and at thirty minutes before contact, Pinky and I took refuge in the suits, with Glass and Lady Arek monitoring.

The immersion fluid lapped into my mouth, into my throat and nasal passages. No part of my body was yet ready to give in to drowning, and the gag reflex was beyond any conscious control. I convulsed several times before succumbing to the inevitable.

Glass came through: "Can you hear me, Clavain?"

"Yes."

"Good. You'll start feeling drowsy very shortly. The suit will use mechanical and electrical intervention to keep you alive, so don't be surprised when you wake up with a few cracked ribs and a headache the size of a solar system. Since you don't have to do anything except survive, unconsciousness need not concern you."

"In other words, I'm baggage."

"Valuable baggage," Glass said, as if that were meant to make me feel better.

On the long fall in from the last million kilometres, the stresses on *Scythe* continued to mount. The bulk of it was thermal. To begin with, the conventional materials and cooling systems of the ship were easily able to re-radiate the heat, but not without cost. Within a vacuum a re-radiant object could only stay cool by glowing, and to glow was to make oneself known. The background temperature of space was a little under three kelvin above absolute zero: a ship only had to stand out against that by one or two kelvin to make itself a very tempting target.

So, long before we needed them, the cryo-arithmetic engines had already spun up to algorithmic speed, performing acts of occult calculation. By moving symbols around, playing chequers with the basic informational granularity of local spacetime, the engines were able to swindle the incorruptible bookkeeping of classical and quantum thermodynamics. The individual cheats were subtle and bought almost no gain, but the cryo-arithmetic engines ran them over and over again, thrashing through the same cycles until the effects became first measurable and then macroscopic.

It worked. But the nearer we got to Bright Sun, the more furiously the engines had to compute, and the closer they came to a feared instability—a cliff-edge beyond which their algorithmic cycles became self-reinforcing, self-accelerating. It was said that a ship succumbing to this condition opened a mouth inside itself to the winds of hell, a mouth that might never close. It was down to Lady Arek and Glass to push the cryo-arithmetics all the way to that brink, but never once over it.

No cryo-arithmetic engines had ever had to work so hard as those of *Scythe*. Normally all they were asked to do was cool areas of a ship by a few hundred kelvin. Now the demand was for thousands of degrees, and the cooling gradient was inversed. It no longer mattered how hot the outside of the ship got: there was no chance of detecting it now, within the gathering howl of the photosphere. But the inside had to remain cool enough not to overload the hundreds of life-support devices, each of which contained a warm, salty bag of water and cells with a mind and memories.

As *Scythe* dipped into the photosphere, it was hitting an atmosphere of entirely ionised particles. Ships encountered plasmas all the time, and mostly sailed through them without consequence. Indeed, we had already descended through a coronal plasma that was hundreds of thousands of times hotter than the photosphere. But while the temperature of the particles in that plasma might have been high, meaning that each had an enormous kinetic energy, there were not nearly enough of them in a given volume to begin overwhelming our systems. It was not like that down in the photosphere. There, the temperature was a modest five thousand kelvin—but the heat capacity of a given volume was far greater. We were flying through a medium with a particle density comparable to a breathable atmosphere at sea level, except that it was as hot as a furnace and we were passing through it at hundreds of kilometres per second.

I saw us. In my mind's eye I looked down from above the photosphere, into a blinding sea. A black, needle-sharp form arrowed through that sea, parting it like a hypodermic. Mach cones swept back from its tip and tail, barbs of savage shock. They made me think of feathered plumes, diamond-patterned. A curdled wake, tens of thousands of kilometres long, followed our passage. At its boundary it became fractal, consumed in diminishing recursive iterations. But the sea was ever-seething and soon swallowed any trace of us.

The cryo-arithmetic engines were safeguarding *Scythe* from the heat of the star, but it took the Gideon stones to armour the ship against the pressure and shock of moving through the photosphere. The problem was that these two forms of defence tended to squabble...and it took a pair of human minds, or at least a pair of augmented minds, to resolve each knot of discord before it engulfed the ship. When the stones and the engines tussled, one or both had to be adjusted, backed off, or sometimes strengthened. If an error were made, an instability allowed to propagate, the ship would have all the durability of a moth's wing touching fire.

And all the while this was happening, every other system of the ship had to operate at its limit, including the Conjoiner drives, pushed as hard into the red as was ever the case. But the engines only gave us ten gees of deceleration along our line of flight: they were insufficient to provide the seventy gees of downforce needed to maintain that curving path. That component came from the magnetohydrodynamic interaction of *Scythe*'s hull with the plasma, with the ship using its engine spars as control surfaces. Without the Gideon stones, Glass had assured me, the spars would have buckled and torn away under the load, taking the engines with them.

Then our difficulties would have been of an entirely different complexion, but at least they would have been mercifully brief.

*

I dreamed of a beach.

A flat black beach, stretching limitlessly, and a lone figure buckled nearly to the horizontal as they stooped against the wind—a wind as luminous and scalding as molten metal, searing the eye until the figure melted away into the whiteness, diminishing to a little star-shaped speck, and then flaking away into scouring white oblivion.

"Clavain. Stop mumbling."

Hands were easing me out of the suit. I let them. I had no power to either resist or assist them. I was a sack of body parts, a gristly mess held together by pain and stubbornness and the distant, nagging sense that I still had unfinished business.

"Where," I said, too weary to frame my word as a question.

"We're out, on our emergence trajectory. *Scythe* is weightless now, but we have more than enough speed to escape the gravity well. Once the ship has run a self-repair cycle on itself, fixing damage from the stresses we accrued in the photosphere, I will begin our gradual slowdown for Ararat. Our atmospheric entry interface will be in approximately... fifty-three hours."

"I'm all right, thank you."

"I didn't ask. You are conscious, therefore the suit did its job. Do your ribs hurt?"

"There's no part of me that doesn't hurt. How's Pinky?"

"Unconscious for the time being. We'll keep him that way for now. He's going to need to be strong when we get to Ararat, for your sake, because there'll be a limit to my effectiveness. Now, we need to talk about Lady Arek..."

Through everything, I still managed to frown.

A little warm spark flaked away from Bright Sun. This was not unusual. Tongues of plasma were lifting from the surface all the time, snagged in pincers of magnetic flux. Sometimes they fell back; on other occasions they broke off into phlegmatic fragments, coughed all the way into space. For a little while, as it rose, that warm spark gave no indication that it was anything other than one of these spitballs of stellar material, destined to thin out and cool and eventually lash its way across the magnetic fields of the planets orbiting Bright Sun. Nothing about it was odd or distinctive enough to warrant further interest.

The blob cooled, but it did not disperse. It was our ship, rapidly chilling itself back down to two point seven kelvin above absolute zero. By the time it broke free of the star's chromosphere, it had become undetectably dark and cold, and even as its propulsion systems cycled back to readiness, they did so stealthily, emitting nothing that could be detected by human or wolf faculties.

Inside that ship, still weightless, Glass and I floated in seated positions facing each other, while my friend Scorpio remained in his suit.

"Something happened as we were completing our slowdown," Glass said. "An instability developed in the interplay between the stones and the cryo-arithmetic engines. More than we could neutralise. A flutter, on the outside of the ship, magnifying instead of diminishing. The stresses increased. The conflicting influences put a torsional load on the hull... and a stone began to detach, peeling away from its anchorage. It was the ninth, the one we placed last of all."

"You said nine stones would suffice. I'm sure, with your talents, you could have found a way to make do with eight."

"And now we must, because eight is all we have left." Glass composed herself. She was more rattled, more distraught, than I had ever known her. "It was not just the fear of losing one stone. Unless there was an intervention, there was a danger of the loose stone ripping the others away as it detached. We could not allow that. Would not allow it. One of us had to go outside, Clavain. Out onto the hull, during the photospheric passage. One of us had to resecure the stone, or cut it away sacrificially, before it took the rest... and Lady Arek went."

"No one could have survived going outside, Glass. We were *inside* a star."

"It was survivable, provided Lady Arek moved quickly. It was survivable." She repeated it, as if to assert the fact of it against her own crumbling judgement. "It *was* survivable. If the suit remained in contact with the hull, the armouring skein would have conformed to its surface, protecting Lady Arek against the plasma shock. The cooling demands on the suit would have been extreme, but so long as it maintained thermal contact with the ship, the cryo-arithmetic engines would have taken over most of the refrigeration burden..."

"Glass, don't tell me you sent another human being outside while we were inside a *star*. Don't tell me you ever thought this was sane."

"One of us had to go."

"Why the hell couldn't you have sent a suit, or a drone?"

"Autonomy was needed. The plasma would have blocked any control signals. Sometimes you just have to send meat in a tin."

"She's not meat!"

"We're all meat. One of us had to remain, to coordinate the stones as they readjusted to the intervention. We...debated, Clavain. Traded scenarios. Formed a duelling adversarial network. Each tried to convince the other we were right." Glass shook her head in wonder. "But she triumphed over me. She was best suited to going outside, and I was best suited to controlling the ship. No ambiguity, no doubt, no hard feelings. This wasn't about courage or sacrifice or nobility, it was about functional usefulness."

"We're here," I said slowly. "And you said we're on our way to Ararat. So whatever happened out there...we didn't die." My voice broke on rising anger. "So what the hell happened? How is it we are here and Lady Arek isn't?"

"We were in contact. Neural exchange. But the packets were fragmenting, the further she got from the lock. She was struggling against the plasma front, moving towards the instability...we were inside each other's heads, Clavain. In those last few seconds she opened up more of herself to me than I ever saw before. As if she trusted me, finally. As if she knew."

"That she wasn't going to make it?"

"She must have reached the ninth stone in time to cut it loose. That's all I know. *Scythe* detected..."

"What?"

"*Scythe* detected something falling away from it, very quickly. Falling away into the plasma." Glass reached around her back and retrieved something that she must have had clipped to her waist. It was a boser pistol.

She pressed it into my fingers. I closed them around its cold, weightless heft.

"There's a point to this?"

"I've set the yield to an appropriate setting. It won't do any damage to the ship, just to me. I've disabled any intervention protocols."

"I'm not going to kill you."

"Why not. Isn't that what you want?" Before I could react—for all her infirmity, Glass was still fast—she had grabbed my wrist and twisted my arm so that the gun was aimed directly at her forehead. "Do it. Kill me. Kill me again."

"I won't."

"Do it."

"No!"

"I let Lady Arek die. My mistake, in the first place. My errors."

"You weren't to know."

"I knew what I was doing to you! I destroyed everything you cared for. I stole your life away. The moment you had happiness, I crushed it. I ripped you away from the people you loved, and who loved you. And you

294

promised to kill me for it." Her voice became a snarl. "So do it!"

I tried to deflect the pistol, but Glass was stronger. "I'm not going to kill you. Not now."

"You made a vow."

"No. *I* didn't." I breathed in hard, every part of me shaking except my hand and wrist, which remained in her grasp. "*I didn't.* A dead man made that vow. He's gone now." I paused, shuddering from within. "I was never him." I started weeping, fiercely and uncontrollably. "Whatever I am, it's not the good man who made that vow." I swallowed, used my other hand to scrape the tears from my eyes. "What is it you want from me, Glass? What did I ever do to you? What the hell did you mean by kill me again?"

"You murdered me once. Left me for dead. But it turns out, not quite dead enough. Now, all I'm asking is that you do the job properly." She nodded, her eyes meeting mine encouragingly. "Go ahead, Clavain. Finish it off."

"No."

There was a finality in my answer that must have persuaded her. Glass moved my hand aside, took the boser pistol back. "You won't do it now. Not ever?"

"No."

"I needed to know. I thought that this was the simplest way." Glass reached out again, but instead of pinning my hand she drew me into her, hugging me close, showing no consideration for my bruised or fractured ribs. I wrapped my arms around Glass, and between us we stilled the tremors running through our bodies.

"What are we?" I asked.

"Two ragged soldiers," Glass said. "A long way from the war that made us."

"You're not as angry with me as I thought you'd be," I said to Pinky, after I had helped him out of reefersleep and explained the bare facts of our situation.

"Why would I hold you responsible for this, Stink?" he asked, looking at me oddly.

"It's all because of me. Us being here. It's on me, in the end. I didn't ask for it, but that doesn't mean I'm absolved of responsibility."

"Some of it's on you," he admitted thoughtfully. "But not all of it. This was Glass's screw-up, all along. If she hadn't messed around with those stones, we'd never have needed to do any dumb shit like trying to fly through a star."

"Lady Arek always thought it was unwise."

295

"It was."

"It's not right that she's the one who ended up paying for it."

"There we're on the same page, Stink. But I've got some news for you. Universe doesn't give a damn about what's fair and right. And Lady Arek knew that better than any of us." He paused, shook his head. "No, it's not all on you, not this time. And you know why you can be sure of that?"

"No."

He looked down at his wrists. "Because I've got two good hands, and you're still breathing."

Part Six

ARARAT

CHAPTER TWENTY-THREE

We saw nothing of the Defection Capsule until the last possible moment, when it loomed out of the scudding dust, angled onto its side and partially buried.

I slowed my stilt-walk, struck by the way that the capsule seemed larger, darker, and more ominous than the orbital scans had led me to expect. From space it had seemed a clear tactical objective: a fallen metal object with useful things inside it. That did not mean that we had been blasé about our chances. There had been numerous things to be concerned about, from the possibility of our activities being detected, to the occupants being dead, to Charity's takeover protocol not working in the way it was intended. All I knew was that my team had been as prepared as it could be, and if some aspect of the mission failed, it would not be due to any negligence on our part. For all that, though, I had not been ready for the physical presence of the capsule, its brooding inertness, the sense that it was waiting for us, inviting trespass.

I went a little closer while Hope and Charity circled around the back. There were no bad surprises so far. If the capsule had come down in such a way that its door was buried, we were in trouble. We would have to dig it out, in the middle of the storm, and then put things back in a way that looked completely natural, while making sure no dust got anywhere inside the lock itself. The scans had offered some confidence about the orientation, but there had still been room for doubt. Until now.

I played wrist and helmet torchlight across the hull, and after a moment the others turned on their lights as well. It felt reckless, but we had planned to use the torches. While the storm continued—blacking out the noonday sky as if it were midnight—there was no chance of detection.

Considering the violence of its approach, re-entry and landing, the Defection Capsule was in excellent condition. A beacon blinked on and off near the narrower end of the roughly cone-shaped vehicle. The transponder signal was still sounding its two-tone lullaby. The airlock door was entirely exposed, but not tilted so far off the ground that we would have trouble climbing up to it.

Really, it could not have been more helpfully orientated.

"Charity?" I asked.

"Proceed."

"Hope?"

"Proceed."

"Concurrence." I reached up and attached the magnetic limpet that contained the override and control mechanism for this type of lock. We had tested it on captured Conjoiner assets and had no reason to expect it not to work...but still there was a moment of unbearable tension before the limpet's status lights pulsed red to green and the lock ground open against the rush of the storm.

Leaving the limpet in place, we climbed into the lock, only retracting our stilts at the last moment. It was a squeeze, but we had trained for it and expected that the lock would accommodate all three of us.

The lock was of rugged but dependable design. The outer door closed, and an automatic sequence flooded the chamber with air from the capsule's pressure tanks. After two minutes, our suits detected one standard atmosphere and the inner door opened to a dim, red-lit interior.

I went first and swept my torch around the cramped confines of the capsule. There was just one compartment, with six Conjoiner recruits strapped into hammock-like webs around the in-curving walls. Between the hammocks were windows and some rudimentary controls and life-support devices.

My light fell on the faces of the recruits. They were either unconscious or dead. None wore spacesuits, but each had a transparent plastic mask over their nose and mouth. Their eyes were closed. In repose, they looked saintlike and calm.

"Your show, Charity."

She unpacked her medical diagnostic devices and went to work. There were paste-on trans-cranial neural scanners and clip-on blood-sampling cuffs. She fixed them on without fuss. The devices performed their rapid scans, analyses and cogitations, and a series of summaries scrolled across Charity's wrist and faceplate readouts.

"All viable."

"Why aren't they awake?" I asked.

She indicated drug catheters in the recruits. "Deep, medically induced comas to conserve shipboard resources. They'd have known there was a high likelihood of a long wait on the surface, so they came prepared to

300

go into comas. It's not as efficient as hibernation, but much simpler to instigate."

"Are they all spider?" Hope asked.

"Confirmed."

Not all recruits to the Conjoiner cause had been touched by the Transenlightenment. Some were just misguided pilgrims, convinced that there was a better life for them on the Martian surface. But in this case, according to Charity's devices, all six were already primed and ready to join Galiana's army. Their neural hardware had been infected and transformed. Each would have already experienced some foretaste of life among the Conjoined.

"Interneural traffic?" I enquired.

"Minimal protocols only," Charity answered. "If they were to crank up their brains to normal Conjoiner clock-speed, they'd soon burn through whatever's left in this life-support system."

"Choose your best candidate," I said. "And one for the short straw."

There was not really much of a choice to be made. The six were all of similar vigour, similar age. But one had to be the host, and one had to be the stooge, to conceal our use of the lock.

Charity made her choices, and offered them to Hope and me.

"Proceed," I said.

Charity took out more equipment. The injection device was a skeletal crown, which she fitted and adjusted around the skull of the middle-aged woman she had selected. Studded at intervals around the crown were the yellow nubs of nano-injectors which would wage shock warfare on the Conjoiner hardware. They had been tested and tested, and left only microscopic blemishes after the injection process. But the process was still fraught.

"Weapons at readiness," Hope said.

Faith and I took out small, semi-automatic pistols, ready to shoot and kill any of the five other Conjoiners should they respond to the injection process being performed on the sixth. The paste-on devices were designed to block or spoof short-range neural traffic, but until now they had never been tested in field conditions.

"We're ready," Charity said.

"Continue," I said.

She issued a command via her wrist interface and the injection crown plunged its yellow fangs into the subject's skull. Instantly there was a reaction: a jerk from the subject, a shocked surfacing to consciousness, eyes wide and fearful. The Conjoiner systems were detecting the onset of the attack and raising their host's cortical alert level.

301

Sweat beaded on the woman's high, imperious forehead.

We had expected nothing less. While it pushed the nanotherapeutic devices into the skull, the crown would be blocking neuromotor control with a multitude of electrical and chemical blockades. The subject went palsy-stiff, eyes wide, pupils dilated, restraints taut.

"She's trying to alert the other five," Charity said coolly. "But the signals are being blocked and spoofed. They're only seeing the normal house-keeping background."

"Status," I said.

"We're in. Level one barricades overwhelmed. Level two beginning to lose resilience."

"She's choking," Hope observed, as the woman's eyes bulged and steam misted her mask.

"Switching autonomic dominance to our control pathways," Charity answered. "She'll hold."

"Status on level two defences?" I asked.

"We're through. Commencing level three assimilation."

"The tricky stage," Hope remarked.

I smiled behind my visor. "Not for us."

"She's ours," Charity said.

We still had our semi-automatic weapons drawn and ready. My hand tightened on the grip as Charity removed the crown. She examined the woman's skin and scalp, unable to detect the puncture points with her own eyes.

"It looks good," I observed.

The woman was drowsy again, losing her stiffness. The drugs still in her system would ensure that she retained no recollection of this episode, even if she returned to full consciousness. Their work done, the drugs would undergo a chemical breakdown, leaving only normal metabolic products. By the time the Conjoiners were likely to be taking an interest in this woman's biochemistry, though, it would be far too late for them to stop the takeover protocol. As soon as she came into contact with another Conjoiner, or any of their neurally linked systems, the contagion would spread.

The paste-on monitors were only picking up routine traffic now, so it was safe to remove them. Charity did this with all but one of the six, leaving the monitor in place on the man she had selected to go out the lock. The monitor would keep him from broadcasting any distress signals while he was euthanised.

"I don't like this detail," she said.

"None of us do," Hope answered. "But the mission planners looked at

302

every aspect of the operation, and this was the only practical workaround."

I clapped a hand to her shoulder. "You've done your part."

Charity euthanised the subject with a drug that would closely simulate death by vacuum asphyxiation. She waited until the drugs had taken effect, then packed away her medical equipment.

"Leave nothing," I reminded her.

Charity performed a rigorous visual sweep of the cabin.

"Clear, sir."

We were done. It was time to go, while we still had storm cover.

Charity went out first, taking the man into the lock. Hope and I followed as soon as the lock had cycled. We put out our stilts and dragged him about ten paces from the capsule, then left him face down in the soil. Charity removed the monitor.

The dead man served one purpose only: to conceal our use of the airlock. Simulations had shown that there was no way to prevent dust ingress to the lock while the outer door was open. If the Conjoiners found any such dust traces, they would realise that the lock had been operated from the outside, most likely during the visual blackout of the storm, and be more cautious about integrating their new recruits. The only solution was to contrive a scenario where it looked as if the lock had been operated from within, with one of the occupants making a confused attempt to leave the capsule without a suit. Such incidents were not unknown, according to our analysts. Early-term recruits sometimes exhibited disorientation or a sort of delirious risk-denying euphoria.

It was all we could do. I removed the magnetic limpet, allowing the lock to close itself and, with one last glance at the fallen man, the three of us retreated into the curtaining storm.

We came in from above the ecliptic, the world's face turning below us with the northern pole tilted into our line of sight. It was a ball of blue-green, a humid waterworld for the most part, but with enough of an axial tilt to produce seasonal variations in climate and weather. Small, brittle-edged icecaps covered the northern and southern poles, glinting back with fierce reflectivity, as if they were little shards of mirror pressed in the planet's flesh. These only accounted for about five per cent of the globe's surface, with another five given over to a sprinkling of islands, mostly gathered into chainlike archipelagos, and concentrated more in the northern latitudes than the southern. The islands were produced by bouts of volcanic activity around weaknesses in the underlying crust, pushed up over relatively short intervals and then doomed to a gradual process of erosion and retreat back into the ocean. Few of them were older than ten million years, and most of them had been only sparsely colonised by living organisms. As far as we knew, these arid outcroppings were the only places that humans had ever found shelter on Ararat, albeit for a very short interval. But as we closed in, our sensors picked up none of the technological signatures that would have suggested a continuing human presence

"It's a beautiful planet," I remarked.

"I'm glad you think so. Is there anything else that strikes you about it? Such as a certain familiarity?"

She had touched an itch I had only just become aware of. "I must have seen similar waterworlds. Images, experientials. I suppose it's even possible that I may have visited some world like this one, long ago. But I don't remember any specifics. If there were memories, they've been polished away as thoroughly as my time on Mars."

"But you'd remember if you'd come to Ararat, specifically?"

"I think I would."

"You were here," Glass stated bluntly. "As was I. It's our second time, for both of us."

"You as good as told me I couldn't have been here before."

Ararat grew larger, almost perceptibly so with each passing minute. *Scythe* made deft adjustments to its course, finessing the final approach.

"It wouldn't have helped you to know the truth. If you'd come to a full appraisal of what happened here, you would have been reluctant to return."

"And why would that be?" I asked angrily. "The truth now, Glass: not your idea of which version of the truth happens to suit me right now. Start with the obvious question: why the hell would I have tried to make contact with a brother I didn't even know about?"

"Because you *did* know, back then. Consciously or otherwise, you knew that this was the place to find some peace with Nevil. Doubtless you were already on a journey of self-forgetting by that point, trying to put as much distance between yourself and what made you, the crimes and glory of a war on Mars. But if you still have doubts, ask yourself this question, Clavain: how did I trace you to Sun Hollow? The answer's simple—before I attempted to reach Nevil, you had already *been* here. You met the Jugglers and swam with them, hoping they'd provide a conduit to your brother. In doing so, you left a fading, echoing trace of yourself. I failed to reach Nevil, but your echo was still here. It told me enough of your intentions to guide me to Michaelmas and Sun Hollow."

"I worry that this is just another of your lies."

"Why would I do that?" Glass looked at me with a thin sympathy.

"I expect it's coming through on some level. Those bright skies and grey-green seas. The brine in your eyes. The salty smell of all that seaweed. The sea trying to dissolve any human machine, any human tool. Surrendering yourself to the biomass, going naked into that alien sea."

I felt a pressure on my chest, a sharp rising terror.

A drowning terror.

"Stop."

"Your memories of Mars are one thing: you blocked them deliberately. I've been able to undo those blockades, just as deliberately, a piece at a time. But what happened on Ararat would have been a different order of experience. Your time here may have been so traumatic that you laid down almost no lasting impression of it. The sea remembers more of your visit than you did."

In a broken voice I said: "I did something terrible to my brother, didn't I? Something so bad that when I last tried to reach him, I nearly died."

"Let's hope that time's a healer," Glass said.

No wolves harried us on our final approach to Ararat. They were around us, almost certainly, sprinkled through the system and most likely gathered in the fragmented remains of the moon, just as they had haunted the Rust Belt, but we were as dark and cold and silent as ever we could be, and we kissed Ararat's atmosphere as delicately as if it were the face of a new lover, still unexplored—producing no ripples, shockwaves or thermal blooms—and we descended to the waters with the same grace and stealth.

We skimmed the sea at an altitude of one kilometre, the hull's surface employing chameleoflage to make itself nearly invisible to any distant watcher. Sky-coloured underneath, sea-coloured above, a rippling, hazy indeterminacy between, the ship a silent skimming chip of blue-grey-green jade or turquoise. We maintained our subsonic flight path above the patches of ocean where the Juggler concentration was at its slightest, never becoming more than an inky darkening on the horizon. We were playing the polite guests, doing nothing that might offend or aggravate our alien hosts. The Jugglers did not pose any sort of threat to us inside *Scythe*, but if we got on the wrong side of them we might forestall any possibility of contact for years to come.

Gradually a landmass loomed: the western extent of one of the island chains. A low tongue of rock, a partial bay, a sprinkling of random pale structures of various sizes and spiriform shapes, standing at jumbled angles like seashells jammed into mud. Some of them were hundreds of metres tall, nearly reaching our altitude. Behind, far to the east, rose mountainous purple-browed thunderheads.

"Conch structures," Glass identified confidently. "Nestbuilder ruins. Alien technology. The remains of their ships and weapons, fallen to Ararat during some engagement that must have happened thousands of years ago. Now they are inert and largely harmless. The settlers found them and repurposed them for their larger shelters and administrative offices."

Pinky looked on intently, saying nothing.

We circled the remains of First Camp. From a distance it was possible to believe that it had been abandoned, but left relatively intact. Once we were near, though, all such illusions evaporated.

Great waves and winds must have torn loose anything not firmly bedded to the ground. Scant traces remained of any human presence between the conch structures, mostly just scoured ground, barren except for a green fringing within a narrow band close to the sea, and a few dyke-like mounds where a mass of shanty-like structures had been swept up and rammed against the unyielding side of a conch structure. Some of the conch structures had themselves been uprooted or had toppled into each other. Larger shattered parts had come to rest in the relative shallows, a few hundred metres into the water.

It was pitiful.

"I am sorry," Glass whispered, and Pinky nodded.

"What happened?" I asked.

"We left a settlement here, after John the Revelator departed Ararat for Hela. There was a battle in orbit... a big one. Human and wolf weapons." Pinky sniffed, holding something back. "We could never be sure what sort of collateral damage affected Ararat. Even a moon got blown apart. Even if none of those weapons had touched the planet directly, the debris from the battle..."

"There would have been a bombardment episode," Glass said. "Major impact events and subsequent oceanic upheaval. Enhanced volcanism and tsunami-like episodes."

"Perhaps someone made it," I said.

Pinky said nothing.

We came lower and lower, watchful for traps. It would have been unusual for the wolves to establish a presence in the biosphere of a Juggler planet, but we dared not trust to that. Tentatively, now that it had the blanket of an atmosphere above it, *Scythe* risked active scanning measures. They came back negative for all indications of wolf presence. Our nerves were too shredded to take much relief from that, but it was better than the alternative.

"We'll have to find a way to cross the sea," Glass said. "We can't make a direct approach by ship. The Jugglers will not permit contact unless we come in quietly."

"I thought you'd have made arrangements."

"I did. When I was last here I had *Scythe* construct me a skimmer. A high-speed, minimum-contact catamaran, mostly ceramic and capable of enduring prolonged contact with the sea without being dissolved. I anchored it to these rocks, knowing I'd be back eventually. But it's gone. The sea must have overwhelmed the island and digested my skimmer."

"Inconvenient."

"*Scythe* will still have the builder templates. It should be able to spit out a new one in a few days."

Glass sent out her drones, snooping into openings in the conch structures. There were no survivors, no warm machines, but her mechanical spies did find evidence of prior human usage, their wreckage gathered into ungainly, rotting piles at the backs of the structures. Biological breakdown was obviously quite advanced: this close to the shore, even the atmosphere was laden with Juggler micro-organisms. But along with the dykes, some of the materials inside those debris mounds might be useful, if they could be salvaged.

Glass identified an area of gently sloping terrain on the seaward side of the green margin, within walking distance of the main collection of conch structures. She hovered *Scythe* over this submerged ramp and brought the ship down very slowly, sinking into a floating carpet of seaweed, churning and boiling the waters with *Scythe*'s landing thrusters, until the ship was about three-fifths concealed. Once we were down, and the disturbance in the water had subdued, the seaweed closed in again, forming a green girdle that helped add to the ship's disguise. The dissolving processes of the seaweed and other marine organisms would already be at work, Glass said, but at least in the shallows they were slow enough to be rebuffed with only mild interventions from the ship's defences.

Glass's experience, and all records pertaining to Ararat, showed that the air could be breathed with relatively few complications. She opened a dorsal hatch and Glass, Pinky and I climbed out onto the back of *Scythe*, standing on a little railinged platform like bold submariners surveying a new continent.

"Breathe," Glass encouraged, when it was obvious to all that I was having difficulty drawing a full-lunged breath.

"I'd forgotten the taste of this place," Pinky said, before sneezing explosively. A prodigious quantity of bright green material splatted onto his sleeve. "Better out than in, I s'pose." He knelt, rubbing the verdant mass against *Scythe*. "Here, ship, have some practice. If you can't deal with a little healthy pig-snot, we're in more trouble than we think."

"Does it take you back?" I asked cautiously.

Pinky nodded. "We're mammals, Stink. Smell and taste matter to pigs even more than humans." He sniffed, wrinkling his snout, as if staunching another sneeze. "Good and bad happened here. Mostly bad. But now that I'm smelling it again, I remember the good, too. Antoinette. Xavier. Old friends." He shook his head, as if ashamed where his thoughts were taking him. "They don't feel like they're long gone. More like we just missed them, and if we stick around a little they'll be back." His voice turned quiet. "I'd like to see my friends again."

Glass extended a hand, causing the railings to drop away and a flattened walkway to form along the spine of the ship, running all the way back to the swollen bulge of the tail, which I now understood to contain the hypometric device. We walked the length of it, which took us in the direction of dry land, with the tail meeting the rising slope as it emerged from the water. Ladder-like handholds puckered the side of the hull, allowing us to scramble down the last ten metres onto the solid ground of First Camp. Our boots squelched onto slippery, slime-covered rock.

Each of us took a faltering step, waiting for our soles to find traction. We had come with very little equipment, and only a modest addition to the clothes we wore inside the ship. It was hard to say whether we needed more or less protection. The air was sticky and humid one minute, chilly and biting the next. If we decided we needed more, we would have to go back for it, or have the servitors bring it out.

I kept looking up at the sky, drawn to its hypnotic shimmering vastness. I knew that the atmosphere was not going to fall away into space. But it was unsettling to realise that my life depended on that thin skin of air, trapped in place by nothing more than its own heaviness. Those thunderheads had neared while we made our landing, teetering over us like curious stooping ogres, and a few drops of rain stung my cheek. Pinky sneezed again, and I watched Glass stumble, only just concealing one of her shuddering episodes.

"What's up with her?" Pinky asked.

"Something she's been trying to hide since we came out of reefersleep."

"We need the two of you, Stink. Even more so without Lady Arek."

I nodded. "I know."

We picked our way through the green skirting, until we reached drier ground, overshadowed by the conch forms. They were cloud-coloured and only slightly translucent. Here and there, human-proportioned windows and doors had been cut into them by some arduous means, probably involving a great deal of energy and time. I could tell it was difficult because they had only done a few of them. The usefulness of this alien material lay in its invulnerability, but that also made it awkward to work with. I could imagine how grateful these settlers had been for anything that helped them weather the seasons of Ararat.

We examined the mounds built up on the outside of the conches. Boxy buildings and tents had been crushed like paper toys, reduced to a collapsed, soggy mass. Perhaps there were things in there that we could use, but it would take a kind of diligent mining to extract them. Glass found the remains of a hovercraft, which would have suited us very well for travelling over water, but it was crushed and buckled beyond any sensible repair. It would have been quicker to have *Scythe* fabricate a new one.

Ground-level entrances led into the conch forms. Some of them were natural arches: clefts or fractures that had already been there when the settlers arrived. Others had been cut by human tools, some door-sized and others tall and wide enough to allow heavy equipment or cargo to be brought under cover. Once or twice we found faded but still-legible symbols or writing above the doors, such as Central Amenities or Security. It was a reminder that this had been much more than just a temporary outpost. There had been a functional self-governing community, on this island and others, a place not so far removed from Sun Hollow, but where the skies were made of air rather than rock. I wondered how well I would have adapted.

We picked our way through the interiors of the larger conch forms, confining our explorations to the lowest levels. A milky light suffused the conch walls, enabling us to move around without using torches. The structures were not hollow, for the most part, but subdivided into smaller chambers and with multiple levels. Most of these partitions, floors and ceilings had been put in by the settlers, and they had all suffered some degree of damage and deterioration. There had been staircases and ladders leading to the upper floors, but nearly all of them had been damaged during the upheavals. To reach the higher levels, we would need to come back with more equipment.

That could wait. There was more than enough to keep us occupied down below, searching for clues and anything we might use—especially to cross the sea. The piles of debris reached two or three times as high as a person, but they were loosely organised and shallowly pitched, so it was not too difficult to scramble up and into their lower flanks and begin to survey the contents. It was in the third building that we found the hull of a boat, wedged upside down and at an angle, but still seemingly intact, and light enough that between the three of us (and mainly Pinky) we were able to wrestle it loose and jump out the way before it came free and tumbled onto us.

It was a small boat, tin-coloured and traditionally shaped. Its function, if not its means of manufacture, would have been instantly familiar to any human who had lived within a hundred kilometres of the sea at any point in the last three thousand years. It was open, lacking any sort of enclosed cabin. A handful of cross-planks sufficed for seating. Six people would have been its limit, and no more than four could be accommodated in any sort of comfort.

Near the back was a fixture where a motor might have been attached.

Glass squatted, examining the absent component. "I can adapt an existing propulsion solution." She stood up, rubbing her palms. "It's a good find. We'll keep looking in case there's something better, but if not, this hull should suffice for our crossing."

I eyed the metallic grey hull, doubtful as to its suitability. We were on dry land now, so it looked more capacious than it would when immersed.

"Let's hope the sea stays nice and calm. And that whoever made this boat understood the part about the Jugglers digesting anything we put into the water."

Glass shot a hard, frowning stare at the boat. "I've tagged it. The hull is metalloceramic so should resist the ocean for as long as we have need of it. I'll have the servitors come and drag it out into the open air. If we choose our weather window wisely, a boat of this size should meet our needs."

"We've come all this way in an invisible spaceship with force-fields, and now we're doing the rest by a dissolving boat?" Pinky asked.

"You were here," Glass replied sternly. "You know how it works. The Jugglers respond to certain subtlety of approach. My skimmer was at the limit of the technologies they tolerate. And since we can't swim all the way..."

"I can't even swim my own body length," Pinky said.

"I'm assuming you had other priorities besides learning to swim," I said.

"The boat will suffice, unless we turn up something better."

We did not. We found broken helicopters, mangled hovercraft, some land vehicles, several things that were unrecognisable, and a couple of boats four times the size of the first. But bigger was not necessarily better, Glass said. They would be harder to move into water, and the larger craft would likely be slower and clumsier, without any gains in safety.

"We'll keep looking," I said. "There's no telling what might be in these

310

debris piles: even a weapon or a medical kit could benefit us down the line."

"There's something I'm not looking forward to," Pinky said.

"What?" Glass asked absently.

"Finding dead people in these ruins. But you were here more recently, Glass. You'd know."

"I would. Except I never found any bodies. There was a memorial site, not too far from here, while I was testing the skimmer. But it must have predated the final catastrophe."

Eventually, exhausted and dispirited by what we had found, we gathered back outside on the sloping ground just above the green margin. A shelf of cloud lay over us like a blackened boot heel, ready to stomp down. The rain arrived in greasy, fitful spalls. Sometimes it smelled of the sea, at other times of electrical burning. Glass was shivering and shuddering, and at one point she bent over and vomited something dry onto the ground.

Pinky caught her before she lost her footing.

"Time for some truth. What's wrong with you?"

"Nothing."

"She's lying," I said. "And she's not our only concern, either. Somehow or other, we have to make a home here for the refugees. Shelter's taken care of—or it will be, once we have enough hands to clean the worst of the debris out of these buildings, bodies or not. Then we can adapt what's inside, or have *Scythe* make us new walls and floors that we can fit together into rooms. Shouldn't be asking too much of a spacecraft that can remodel itself at the drop of a hat."

"*Scythe* has already reallocated internal mass resources to create the hypometric precursor device."

"I'm sure it has. I'm also sure that it wouldn't miss a thousand tonnes or so, and that'd be more than enough to make a self-sufficient community, given that we already have a head start with the conch structures."

Glass seethed and fizzed. "I suppose a small mass allowance would be within *Scythe*'s capabilities."

"See, that wasn't too hard, was it? But we need to start now, and we also need to send a clear sign to Barras and the others that they're more than just some inconvenient cargo we happen to have saddled ourselves with."

"What do you propose?" Pinky asked.

"Let's revive Probably Rose, Barras and a dozen or so of the fittest pigs. We bring these few out and show them what they've got to work with. Your voice will be useful, Pinky. You've lived here; you know what's possible—and just as importantly what isn't." Then, to Glass: "If we're to mean what we say, you should assign Barras authorisation to command

Scythe. I don't mean all the functions, but enough that he can tell the ship what it needs to make, tools and materials, and have your servitors help with moving things around and assembling them into bigger units."

Some battle of wills seethed within Glass. "All right. It's not an unreasonable proposal. They won't be able to come with us when we use the boat, so at least they will be usefully occupied while we're at sea. Pinky?"

"You remember my name? She remembers my name, Stink. I've gone up in the world."

"Chose the fittest of them to be revived first. You can oversee their orientation while Clavain and I prepare the boat."

"That wasn't an order," I said. "Was it, Glass?"

"A suggestion," she clarified, through half-gritted teeth.

"And not a bad one," I said. I nodded back at the ship which, wreathed as it was in seaweed, resembled some hump-backed behemoth breaching water. "I suppose the ship can keep everyone fed and clothed for the time being, even if they're outside. But by the time we leave, we'll need to have established a self-sufficient settlement. Do you think that's feasible in . . . what, a matter of days, weeks at best, depending on the weather and the Jugglers?"

"We made it work once." Pinky was looking out to the west. I wondered what his eyes saw, or perhaps what they now failed to see. "It helps if you can develop a taste for seaweed tea. And seaweed soup. And seaweed everything else."

"How long did it take you?"

He looked at me with surprise. "I said it helps if you *can*, not that you ever do."

Glass was showing an interest in the conch forms, wandering around their bases. I watched her from a distance, wondering what it was that she sought or thought she saw.

Glass stopped at one of the conches, where a smooth surface rose up from the ground, rooted into it like a standing stone. She smeared a green film away from the Nestbuilder's construct, exposing the off-white translucence of its surface. She studied this cleared patch for a few moments, hands on hips, head slightly cocked, as if trying to make sense of a piece of abstract art. Then she tilted forward, pressing out an arm to lean against the conch, as if she were suddenly exhausted. The arm moved, Glass's hand stiff and curled, so that it was the heel of her palm in contact with the conch rather than her fingers. Where some of the green still lingered, her palm etched a narrow, curving trace. Glass stepped back and deliberated. She used her other palm to etch a curve that cut across the first at a diagonal, making a loose shape like a pair of crossed cutlasses. Glass studied her handiwork again, hands dropping to her sides, a quiver of animation running from her shoulders to her hips. Glass began again. She leaned in and made parallel marks with both hands at the same time. Her gestures become faster: rapid scrubbing strokes, as if she were trying to erase some error or blasphemy that was lost to my senses. The shaking intensified, overcoming her whole body. Now her hands criss-crossed in a fury of negation, scuffing the conch far too quickly for me to visualise the individual traces. Glass dropped to her knees, flinging her arms above her head, palms whisking against the conch. Her head wrenched itself from one extreme to the next, as if it were trying to tear itself off her neck.

Something showed itself in the conch: a faint darkening, a sort of shadow moving behind the material. Where Glass was still scrubbing, the conch seemed to my eyes to become momentarily rough, catching the light in a way that hinted at a leathery texture. But it was there and gone in a second. Glass's shaking consumed her, and her arms flailed away from the conch. She lolled onto her side, her head thudding against the ground.

I dashed to her, as perhaps I should have done the instant I saw her being taken by the fit. She was still writhing when I slid down next to her, ramming my knees into the rock. I cupped my hands under her head. It was like trying to stop the movement of a machine, something bigger and more powerful than me. I slumped back and dragged all of Glass with me, hugging her shuddering form close to mine. By gradual increments her fitting began to reduce. A white froth bubbled from her lips.

I looked up at the area of the conch where she had conjured something into being.

"Glass," I said quietly, not even sure that she could hear me. "We need to talk."

When there was a moment, I made her sit down next to me, our haunches on the slippery rock, the darkening sea beyond us, a margin of salmon-coloured light breaking between striated cloud layers close to the horizon.

"Tell me what's wrong."

"Nothing is wrong."

"Stop lying about there being nothing wrong. If I hadn't got to you by the conch, you'd have dashed your brains out in about five minutes. And what was all that about, anyway?"

Glass brooded. Her eyes searched the west. "I was attempting to verify a set of Nestbuilder gestural commands. They didn't work."

"Something nearly worked."

"I wasn't even close. And the conch is damaged: shorn from its proper place and therefore unable to function properly."

"You said these things used to be part of a ship."

"Or many ships, or a structure that could break apart and reorganise itself however it wished. I need to be sure that when we meet one of these ships, we understand enough of it not to get ourselves killed."

I looked around at the ruins. "And why would we be likely to run into one of these ships? Unless you already had a good idea where to look for one."

"When the *Sandra Voi* made an examination of Charybdis, it detected something inside the ice giant's atmosphere. A large, solid mass. Unfortunately, neither Clavain nor Galiana had the background knowledge to interpret their finding correctly, nor the means to do more than send in a few high-atmosphere sounding probes. But with the benefit of centuries, I know exactly what it was: an intact, or near-intact, Nestbuilder vehicle."

"How can you know?"

"I know." She gathered herself. "And we'll locate it, once we reach Charybdis. The floater will still be there. You mustn't make the error of thinking on human timescales when it concerns the Nestbuilders. But it would help if I had confidence in these command protocols, ahead of time."

"You over-reached yourself."

"I assigned too many mental resources to the conch. I left myself unguarded."

"Unguarded against what?"

She sighed. It was an oceanic sigh: an immense and painful admission of imperfection. "The ninecats."

"The ninecats? We left them on Yellowstone."

"They did more harm to me than I admitted. They contained an engineered weapon, something specifically designed to hurt Conjoiners, or those like me who have Conjoiner proprietary neural architecture."

"Snowdrop and Lady Arek told us that was a risk. Why didn't you listen?"

"I thought I had the better of the ninecats." She grimaced, shaking her head. "Even when I was hurt and taken into *Scythe* to be treated, I didn't realise the extent of the trouble I was in. But the diagnostics showed that parts of the ninecats' limbs had broken off inside my wounds: little slivers of them. Microscopic, autonomous splinters, independent weapons in their own right. They've been in me ever since, working their way into my head. *Scythe* tried to . . . flush them out. Then to cut them out, or hunt

314

them down with nanophages of its own. But the slivers were adaptable and easily able to devise counter-strategies of their own. They had already seen and defeated many Conjoiner countermeasures."

"But you, Glass. You? You broke every system in Sun Hollow; rewrote our records and turned our own guns against us. How the hell did this catch you out?"

"I hate to disappoint you, but defeating Sun Hollow was never more than child's play. I told you I liked games." She smiled at my innocence. "This, though...this is an adult game. It's far less forgiving."

"You can't lose."

"Can't I?"

"No. Now that we've lost Lady Arek, who else has the tactical knowledge to see this through? Not me, not Pinky. This was your fight, Glass. I may have been the weapon you needed, but you were the mastermind guiding it. So you don't get to die on us."

"The work on the Gideon stones needed to be completed. If I had permitted *Scythe* to treat me properly, we would never have had time to achieve the full integration of the stones." She breathed in, tightening her arms around her upraised knees. "I...made a calculation, Clavain. I traded my health against the stones, and that saved us."

"It was the wrong calculation, then!"

"Do you recall what Lady Arek said about stepping stones? I was listening in, whether you realised it or not. And she was right. This was the step that needed to be taken."

"And now you die, is that it?"

"No—at least, I hope not. But since the ship's remedies have failed me, and the slivers are knocking on my last defences—as you have noticed—there is only one other treatment option open to me. I'm afraid it's a radical one."

The evening chill was working its way into my bones. "Go on."

"I'll come with you to the Pattern Jugglers. We'll both swim, but for different reasons. You, to make contact with your brother. Me, to be restored to an earlier biological template: a back-up condition in which I don't contain the slivers."

"Can it be done?"

"I entered the sea once before and attempted partial communion with the Jugglers."

"And failed."

"Not entirely. I detected your intentions, which means there was at least a partial breakdown and reintegration of my own memories. That means the Jugglers have known me once, and perhaps retained an echo of that encounter. I am only asking to be restored to that echo."

"Drastic," I agreed.

"Right answer."

"What about the memories you've acquired since you were last on Ararat? What happens to them?"

"In all likelihood they'd be lost—or at least surrendered to the sea. But I could reconstruct them, over time. The ship knows what I did. So do you. You have stood witness."

"This is madness, Glass."

"It is. Glorious madness. Glorious necessary madness. Will you help me? I may be weaker than you expect, by the time we get to them. I can't do this on my own."

"I can't do it on my own either."

Glass shook her head in wonder. "What a pair of broken monsters we make, Clavain. Do you think the sea will put us back together again?"

I looked out to the dulling horizon, to the despair and promise that it held for the both of us.

"I think it'll either mend us, or be the death of us," I answered.

CHAPTER TWENTY-FOUR

Night came: our first on Ararat. The clouds that had been gathering solidified into a storm, pouring continuous sheets of rain onto the island. Lightning shattered the sky, sometimes striking near enough to light the remains of First Camp in a spasm of counterfeit day. The sea swelled in slow, dark, green-crested waves like the breathing rhythms of some world-wrapping monster, something enormous, black, tentacular and foul-tempered, that we were in abject danger of rousing.

We returned to the warmth and security of *Scythe*, where nothing of the storm touched us. Although all three of us had visited Ararat before (even if I remembered almost no part of my time here) Glass was still insistent that we should be subjected to thorough examinations in case something had changed in the biological environment of the planet. But if anything harmful had got into us, it was too subtle to be picked up by Glass's methods. Beyond runny noses and mildly irritated eyes, neither of which were expected to last, we were experiencing no ill-effects directly attributable to Ararat.

Before we rested, Pinky and I went to the hibernation bay and made a revised inventory of the sleepers according to physical fitness and age. Barras and Probably Rose had already been agreed upon, but it took some further deliberation to settle on the other ten to rouse first. We needed pigs who were old enough to work and take decisions independently, but not so infirm that any manual labour was too much for them. If we were too slow in establishing a settlement, the survivors were going to have to travel with us regardless of any risk that lay ahead.

Having made our choices, we set the caskets to a slow revival cycle, knowing it would be at least thirteen hours before any of them reached any awareness. We needed sleep ourselves, but before we spoke to the twelve, we also needed the ghost of a plan so that Barras and the rest did not feel they were being thrown to the fates.

"Glass is getting worse," I said, while Pinky folded shut the last of the manual override panels on the twelve caskets.

317

"And Glass probably has ears in every part of this ship."

"Then she won't be surprised by any part of this conversation. She's pinning her hopes on the Jugglers being able to fix whatever went wrong with her in the Swinehouse, winding her back to the version of Glass that visited here the last time."

"What do you think?"

"I think we might be asking a lot of something that no one understands." I dropped my voice in deference to his earlier comment. "But she is getting sicker, and I'm certain we're only seeing the tip of it. You saw how she nearly collapsed out there. If you hadn't caught her, she'd have probably dashed her head on those rocks."

"I'd be more worried about the rocks."

"I'm concerned that we may not have much time, now that we're here. As soon as that boat is ready, and this storm dies down to the point where it isn't suicide to go out into the water...I think we ought to be leaving."

"And you want me with you."

"If Glass is right, things didn't go so well the last time I was here. It may be that I never reached my brother. But it's also possible that I reached him—whatever remains of him in this ocean—and he fought back. I need an advocate: someone who my brother will recognise as a friend and an ally."

"Then maybe go with someone other than the person who killed him."

"Whatever happened between you and Nevil, I know this much just from the time I've spent with you: whatever you did, you did it with love in your heart."

He began to scoff, but I carried on regardless.

"The universe gave you no choice. It held your hand in an iron glove and made you do its bidding. And if your hand was on that knife, so was my brother's, at every step."

"Maybe it was." He held a fragile calm for a moment, before exploding. "But I still killed him! His mind understood why it had to happen. But that was his *living* mind. Whatever's left of him out there, the two aren't necessarily the same. What if all that's left of Nevil Clavain is hate and rage and regret, and a faint memory of someone who cut him open while he was still screaming?"

"Then we may need to be each other's advocates."

"Is that the best reassurance you've got?"

"For now."

"Well, if it does take madness to go out in that boat...I'd say you've got that part covered." Pinky gave a dog-like shiver that I took to be equal parts fury and exasperation. "You're fuckers, all of you. Clavains. Why

318

does my life keep getting tied up in your problems? Why am I always the salvation? Why can't you find some other pig?"

"Look on it this way: we have excellent taste in allies."

In the morning the twelve were revived. Glass, Pinky and I were waiting for them as they came to life, ready to dab lips and eyes and offer succour to dry throats. Scorpio and I bore the brunt of the work, since Glass was having trouble controlling her trembling.

They had the obvious questions. Had we made it to Ararat? Where was Lady Arek? Why were the others still sleeping? What was going to happen next?

We answered them patiently, imagining ourselves in the same states of ignorance, and were not at all annoyed when our account of skimming Bright Sun was either dismissed outright or accepted without dispute. Our twelve fell into two camps, it seemed: either knowledgeable enough to think our exploit an outrageous falsehood until we stressed that it had really happened, or sufficiently ignorant of stars and their properties not to consider it in any way remarkable.

They were soon disabused of that notion. We explained that the ship had come close to catastrophe, and only Lady Arek's bravery had held it together. But that bravery had taken her from us.

The pigs could not mourn her as Pinky and Probably Rose did—not even as much as Glass, who had lost a collaborator, if not a friend—but they understand that her absence cost us very dearly.

"It's nearly the worst thing that could have happened," I told them. "But the very worst would have been all of us dying, and we have Lady Arek to thank that that's not the case. She's given us a chance to carry on, a chance to regroup and continue our fight. Which we will, in her name, and those who gave themselves so that we could escape from the wolves around Epsilon Eridani." I drew myself up, looking each of them in the eye. "Now we need to work without her guidance. And we do have work ahead of us."

When Barras, Probably Rose and the other ten were fit enough to walk around and leave *Scythe*, we ventured back onto land. The worst of the storm had played out overnight, with rain only falling in spurts, and never as heavily as it had at its fiercest. That did not mean that the weather was treating us kindly. The sea was still wind-ruffled and restless, and more clouds were marshalling to the north-east. It was not exactly how I might have wished to present this new world to the refugees. But I supposed it was better they were acquainted with its moods now, than be disheartened later on.

Yet the twelve seemed unconcerned. It was a wonder to them just to be able to breathe outside or walk more than a few strides without running into cage bars or a wall. They tripped, stumbled, fell face down on the slippery rocks, and got up laughing again. There would be many bruises and gashes by the time the day was done, many stinging eyes and runny noses, perhaps an aching bone or two, but all seemed to consider the price of survival a fair one. Even Probably Rose, who had never been incarcerated, was glad to be somewhere not bounded by artificial surfaces, and where her life did not depend on the immediate and continual functioning of machines.

"We can live here," she said to me, gesturing at the conch structures. "If they did, we can, yes and yes. I know they didn't have it easy, but we've been through worse."

"I don't doubt it. And we're not necessarily talking about a place that no one ever leaves, just a world where we have to live for a few decades." I smiled at myself: how easily I spoke of decades as if they were mere inconsequential episodes in a lifetime, soon forgotten. I knew better, but the old habits lingered.

"We as in yes, 'you,'" Probably Rose said.

"*Scythe* will return." A rash promise, but if I did not bank on success I might as well have ended myself now. "And we may not be the only ship. I'm sure there are others out there, somewhere. If we succeed, then eventually there won't be any need for us to hide. Those of you who've adapted to Ararat can remain, but it doesn't have to be a life sentence."

"But first, and verily, we have to build."

The twelve had already been briefed on the burden placed on them. Pinky was there to assist, but it was up to them how they went about the division of labour and responsibility. First it was agreed that they would explore the conches and decide which were the most suitable for early occupation. After that, the work would be at least twofold: one group would spend time learning how to collaborate with *Scythe*, persuading it to manufacture what they needed. The other group would be preparing the ground—clearing out debris and drawing up blueprints for partitions, floors and ceilings, interlocking with what was already present, building on the ruins.

"Nothing needs to be perfect," I stressed. "It just has to work well enough for now. The ship will remain here while three of us go off in the boat, so there's always that fallback. You can come and go as you please, and depend on the ship for your basic needs. But we always need to be thinking ahead to the day when the ship has to depart, and that may not be too far in the future."

320

"Months?"

"Sooner, unless things go badly wrong with the Pattern Jugglers."

I watched all the hope drain out of Probably Rose between one breath and the next.

"I take back what I said just now." The strain of the moment brought on one of her twitching fits, and she cuffed her forehead violently. "It's yes, yes, and yes, impossible!"

"No, just difficult. Every part of this has been done before, and Pinky knows all of it. You'll never starve. Pinky tells me that provided you take certain precautions, you can eat almost anything that washes up against the island. I won't say you won't get bored of it, but it'll keep you alive. And you won't suffocate, or die of anything contagious. Nor will you die of hypothermia. Clothes, blankets and heaters will be easy to provide. This isn't the end: it's the start of something. Ararat is about as compatible a planet as we could ever land on."

"It killed the others."

"No," I stressed. "Not Ararat, and not the Pattern Jugglers. They were both tolerant hosts. It was the war that happened in space that spelled their end, and it won't come again."

"You're very sure of yourself."

"There'll be a war," I clarified. "But not the kind we fought before. The next one will be different."

She measured me with a gently cocked head. "You've changed from the man who came to us, the man I stuck my needles into on that first night in the stronghold. Yes and yes. I knew it was you from the genetic samples, but I still didn't believe it, not quite. Now I do. There's another man looking out at me from behind your face. Colder. Harder, yes and yes. More sure of himself. More willing to think the unthinkable."

"I didn't ask for this. But now that it's here, it feels like it was always waiting to come back." I stomped my foot onto rock. "We make a stand here. We build something. We build to say that humanity's not done. That we've been pushed back, cornered, forced to cower and hide, but we're not finished. We've been into the darkness, all of us. This is the cusp, the point where we turn to the light again. It starts on Ararat, and it starts with you."

She considered my words, nodded slowly. "So, build."

"So build," I echoed.

"Go and tend your boat, old man," Probably Rose told me. "Some of us have real work to be getting on with, yes, and yes."

*

Part of me would have been very glad to depart that morning: not because I was in any way looking forward to meeting the Jugglers, but because there could be no room in my thoughts for much else. I had felt the same way on Sun Hollow, when I knew I had to have a tooth taken out. I just wanted it over; to be on the other side of all the pain and uncertainty.

But we would not be leaving for a day or two. Glass expected to be ready with the adaptations to the boat by the evening, and the provisioning could be done an hour or two before we were ready to depart. But the weather had other plans for us. The overnight storm might have broken temporarily, but those clouds on the horizon had continued to swell and mass their ranks, and now they looked like dark-bellied galleons, hulls prickling with cannon fire. The sea roared and spat. A bigger craft with an enclosed cabin could have set out, but our open-topped boat would have been tossed to the waves within minutes of setting sail. It was laughable that it had come to this: that all our travelling, all our boldness, had brought us back to the Stone Age, watching the skies and setting our eyes to the wind. We had no forecasts and no idea of the weather conditions beyond the horizon. Glass had been unwilling to leave monitoring eyes in orbit, and now that we were safely down she was adamant that it was too much of a risk to send any drones or servitors out on scouting trips beyond First Camp, in case they registered with the wolves. It would be dangerous enough setting off in a boat, but that was the one part of our expedition that could not be avoided.

So we had to wait. While it tested my nerves, the delay did at least allow time for Barras and the others to get into their stride, and for Pinky and me to lend our wits and muscles where we could. *Scythe* and its servitors had been busy, spitting out stacks of simple modular forms which could be locked together to make chairs and tables, as well as providing the tools and bonding agents to allow these forms to be adapted into more complicated designs. Already the Administrative conch contained a long, ramshackle galley where legs could be rested and food and drink served, and a number of basic partitions had already been established to provide toilets and washrooms, furnished using basic but reliable templates from *Scythe*'s libraries. It was all haphazard to start with, and both the food and waste products had to come and go from the ship. But over time, as Pinky's experience told us, there was nothing to stop the settlement becoming dependent solely on the sea. Knowing that a thing could be made to work was a very powerful incentive to short-term problem solving, and his assurance and swagger soon communicated itself to the twelve. Pinky was also wise enough to step back when he saw a solution,

322

but knew that it would help the twelve to discover it for themselves. I watched him with a powerful sense of pride, as if I had ownership of his accomplishments, and then rebuked myself for that fallacy.

By the end of the second full day, when the worst of the eye and nasal irritation had begun to wear off, there was talk of bringing out more of the sleepers to accelerate the preparations. But Barras and Probably Rose had established the outlines of a democratic process and the matter was voted on, and narrowly rejected. The twelve would continue building at their own pace, and only revive another portion of the refugees when they had something to show them besides acres of slimy rock, draughty conches, and sad moraines of human debris.

The twelve worked in shifts, alternating between the physical labour of clearing out the conches, and the mental tasks of learning how to communicate with *Scythe*. Glass had arranged control interfaces for the ship's manufactory, enabling the pigs to work with natural language, written code, or abstract symbol manipulation. The interfaces were custom-manufactured weatherproof compads, sturdy enough to be dropped on rock or into shallow water, and with their tactile controls suitable for pig digits.

None of this was straightforward for the pigs, since few of them had ever had to submit instructions to a machine. But on the other hand, they had almost nothing to unlearn and therefore came to the problem without pre-established ideas. I was pleased to see how quickly they overcame their initial hesitancy and persuaded the ship into creating fully finished objects and machines that already met a need, rather than just raw materials. The process of furnishing the conches was already gaining pace, and the pigs were coming up with ever more inventive and efficient solutions to help in turning these damp, wind-haunted shells into something liveable. It was as if all the years and decades of free will that had been denied them in Yellowstone was now finding expression in a matter of days.

Still no bodies had turned up. Glass had found none on her earlier visit, but she had admitted that her search had not been thorough. And I had no sense that I had found bodies either, although in that respect all I could go on was the emotional tenor of my still-buried memories. There was drowning in there, and fear, but nothing like the horror of coming across unburied dead. Perhaps I too had spent only the minimum time in and around First Camp, with all my significant experiences confined to the open waters.

I told Glass that I should like to visit the memorial ground she had mentioned before we set off for the Jugglers. It felt necessary; a paying of respects. But Glass demurred. What had been an hour's travel in her skimmer would be far more arduous in our boat, and she was against anything that counted as an unnecessary journey.

"This isn't tourism, Clavain. We didn't come here to sightsee."

"I feel like we're already treading on their bones."

Glass's rejection was final. "The moment the weather cooperates, we leave. But not for the memorial ground." Her eyes searched me "What are you hoping to find? Some fond message from your brother, some absolution from beyond the grave?"

"If I was here, then perhaps I left a message for myself."

"You didn't," she said flatly. "I'd have found it."

The next day the weather was as bad as the first storm, and there was no easing in it for another fifty-two hours. It made any sort of work difficult, so even the pigs had to slow their labours. They had put down meandering high-friction walkways around and between the conches (another of the things they had asked *Scythe* to manufacture) but between the rain, the wind, and the eye-stinging foam flecking in from the sea, it was impossible for any sort of productive labour to go on. The pigs rested, either back on the ship, or in the conch where the work was already most advanced. It was a time for wounds to be addressed, sprains and strains to be eased, bellies replenished, stories told and boasts exaggerated. They had heating and as much hot water as they needed by then, and the ship had no trouble providing food and drink in the desired quantities and varieties. Pinky, in a spirit of solidarity, had even shown the pigs how best to collect, prepare and consume the seaweed; which varieties to look for, which to avoid, and how best to make it semi-palatable. It seemed like the basis for a crushingly monotonous diet, and perhaps it was. But I thought of the similar lessons we had endured on Sun Hollow (though they had happened to some man who was not quite me) and how our palates had gradually found a way to detect surprising nuance and variety in the few basic foodstuffs we had been able to grow in those caverns, and how that discriminatory faculty had only been amplified with each successive generation.

The weather did break, in the end, although we dared not jump at the first easing of it in case there was worse to come just over the horizon. But after another day the rains and winds had passed, the skies had cleared to the limit of vision, and the sea had settled into a blue-green torpor barely marred by a wave. The air became warmer and drier, and by evening the stars overhead were as bright and unwavering as if they were lanterns, lowered by watchful gods. We all observed them with the same thought:

somewhere in the darkness between those lit motes lay our enemy, and perhaps closer to hand than we might wish. But for now, we were power-less against the wolves, and we all pushed them to the backs of our minds as well as we could.

Glass's boat was ready. The hull was much as we had found it. To power the boat, *Scythe* had provided an outboard propulsion system based around three of the shipboard servitors. Their spheres were joined in a row, with a framework around them. They ingested air and accelerated it within themselves, the second and third spheres boosting the output of the one before them, before blasting it out as a cold, high-velocity jet. The thrust was enough to move the boat across water at about forty kilometres per hour, less if there was wind resistance or rough seas. It was barely faster than one of the electric carts we had in Sun Hollow, but it would suit our purposes. The line of spheres was attached to the rear of the boat by a swivelling mounting, and a manual tiller could be worked by someone seated on the last cross-plank. Glass had neural control of the power output, but there were manual inputs built into the tiller for lesser mortals. Nothing in Ararat could be guaranteed against erosion by the sea's biochemical and molecular agents, but at least our motor was not immersed in water, which ought to extend its lifetime long enough to get us to the Pattern Jugglers and back.

At the time of our landing, Glass had determined the nearest large Jug-gler mass as lying two hundred and twenty kilometres from First Camp. If it had not moved, and the sea conditions remained in our favour, we could be there in under six hours. Contact with the Jugglers did not happen on any sort of predictable schedule, but if we were rebuffed it was likely to be over with fairly quickly. At this latitude and time of year, Bright Sun was above the horizon for around eighteen hours. There was at least the chance of making a first bid and returning to base before nightfall, and while travelling at night would be riskier, Glass ought to be able to handle the navigation.

We agreed to set off just before first light. Although we expected to be back before nightfall, we still made preparations for a longer expedition. We took three days' worth of food and water, medical supplies, additional clothing, buoyancy aids, and a sun screen which could be strung over the boat should we end up becalmed under warm skies. We also took two pairs of oars, found in the debris and stowed under the cross-planks until we needed them. We brought knives and one gas-powered harpoon, but no other weapons. A radio-frequency communicator allowed us to remain in touch with Probably Rose, although we would limit its use to the minimum. According to Glass, any sort of energy emission was likely to deter the Jugglers. We could not avoid using an engine, but the less of our technological culture we brought with us, the better our chances.

Glass and I were already in the boat, settling in and rearranging the stores, when Pinky, Barras and Probably Rose came alongside.

"He says you need him for this," Barras said.

"I do."

"Bring him back," Probably Rose said, underlining this imperative with a cyclopean glare. "He doesn't think we need his help, but we do, yes. Yes yes." She flicked the back of her hand against her forehead. "Bring him back, yes yes."

"We're all coming back," I said, and then wished that I had not, because it sounded like empty bravado. "But we'll take particularly good care of Scorp. He doesn't need to be here. I've asked him along because I need a friend, and I think his presence will improve our chances, but he knows he could walk away and I wouldn't force him to join us."

"I might," Glass muttered.

Barras helped Pinky with the difficult stride into the boat, while I assisted from the other side. "You've decided you can't live without my sparkling company, Glass?" Pinky asked, grunting as he planted his feet on one of the few open spaces between the cross-planks.

"I've decided Clavain might be right about your usefulness." She lifted her face to the two figures still on dry land. "We're not likely to be back before at least thirteen hours have passed. Don't become too concerned if we're a lot later than that."

"Signal us if you, yes, yes. Signal if you...yes. Signal if you run into yes, difficulties, yes yes."

"Do you think you'd be able to help us, with no boat, and no other means of crossing open water?"

"We'd still want to yes, still want to know, yes yes, and verily."

"You think you would," Glass answered.

Pinky tucked himself low on the middle cross-plank. Glass was at the back, with the motor and tiller; I was at the front. Without a word from Glass we began to move, sluggishly at first, because seaweed had already begun to cloy itself around the hull, but then with gathering speed as the boat knifed out of the seaweed and forged into the relatively open and calm waters beyond the rocks. The motor made a thin, keening whistle, and the turbulence from its jet ruffled the water about ten metres behind us.

Glass increased our speed to what I took to be the boat's maximum. Wind and spray lashed my face, and I soon averted my gaze from the direction of travel, leaving Glass to worry about navigating.

We were heading west, with Bright Sun at our backs. For the first half-hour there were reference points to measure our progress, as First Camp gradually fell away and the conch structures became smaller and smaller, until the land they were on dipped beneath the sun-hazed horizon and finally the tips of the structures vanished as well. After that, and with no other islands near enough to be visible, we were just a small moving point in the ocean, and progress became harder to gauge. The storm was gone, but the sea was choppier than it had looked when we set out, and the criss-crossing patterns of the waves confused my sense of motion. The boat had settled into a semi-regular bumping rhythm, the prow pitching up since most of the weight was near the back. Sometimes the waves grew large enough for the boat to steepen against their swell; at other times we cut through them in a slap of stinging spray.

We had said nothing since departure. Glass was steady enough now, and focused on the job of guiding the boat, but I wondered at the reserves she was drawing on to hold herself together. Pinky was stoic, snout held to the wind, eyes pink-slitted and fixed on the south-westerly horizon. The fine white hairs on his brow were flattened against his skin.

"All right?" I asked after the first hour, when I had begun to swallow down the first hints of motion sickness.

"This isn't my first boat trip."

"This might be mine. I suppose I must have crossed water to reach the Jugglers before, but I don't remember any part of the journey. The last time you were in a boat...was it here?"

"Not much call for boats on Hela." He squinted at me. "Got any other topics, especially ones that don't involve boats and Ararat?"

I smiled once. "I'm sorry. I know how hard this must be for you."

"You don't know half of it."

"You remember what happened on this planet, and you don't want to revisit it. I don't remember what happened to me, except that it left me with an aftertaste of fear and drowning. But I have to revisit it. Perhaps this will help us both."

Glass watched us silently. It was hard to tell how much she was listening, or indeed if she cared.

"And if it doesn't help us, let's hope it doesn't leave us even more fucked-up than we already are. You'd better be ready for that, because I've discovered this weird thing where life doesn't always grant us our fondest wishes."

"I'm ready. Frightened, but ready. I also know that the worst thing this ocean will do to me will be a kindness compared to extinction by the wolves."

"For once, a valid observation," Glass commented.

"So you were listening."

"I always listen. Whether I process is a different matter. Sometimes the noise inside my head is preferable to any human babble."

"Congratulations," Pinky said, eyeing me. "You made it through her threshold. You're less annoying than white noise." But he paused, still regarding me. "I know what happened here, and what my part in it was. Nothing can change that. I've made my peace with what I did. Get back to me when you've killed your only true friend in the universe, and then maybe we'll talk."

"You killed my brother," I said softly. "I think that gives me a stake."

Pinky said nothing. Glass kept her hand on the tiller, and the engine's keening note drilled into my soul.

CHAPTER TWENTY-FIVE

The sea was all that there was, with all reference points long behind us. We were more than two hours out from First Camp and the rhythm and sounds of the boat had become lulling enough that my thoughts strayed into the logic-less margins of sleep. I kept blinking to keep myself awake.

Then I jolted to alertness. About one hundred metres off to our port side, I thought I had seen something break the water, surfacing briefly above the waves. Glass was preoccupied with the motor, but Pinky must have caught my twitch as I snapped to life and tried to track the fleeting form.

"What?"

It was the first word he had spoken to me since our exchange about my brother's death.

"Nothing," I answered, for the waves had reclaimed whatever it was I might or might not have seen. Then, unwisely: "I just thought..."

"You saw something in the water." He was silent for a second or two. "Yeah. Me too. Not that time, but a couple of minutes ago, and maybe once before that."

Glass was paying attention to us now. "You should have spoken."

He swivelled to face her. "Did you see it?"

"No."

"Then you wouldn't have taken me seriously."

"A pig's visual acuity is lacking compared to..."

"Whatever he saw, I saw," I said, levelling my gaze at Glass. "There's something else out here, besides sea and micro-organisms."

"Ararat contains no macro-scale ocean forms. The Jugglers are the only large, organised life form besides the seaweed rafts."

"I don't care what your database says this ocean does or doesn't contain," I said, reaching down into the base of the boat to unship the gas-powered harpoon. "Something's following us, maybe more than one something. Could the Jugglers have some part of themselves swimming out here alone, detached from the main node?"

329

"What I saw looked like an animal," Pinky said. "Just a glimpse of it, but enough to tell. Big, dark and powerful."

"As big as this boat?"

"I don't know. Maybe not."

I nodded slowly. "I couldn't tell either. I'm not even sure if I saw a head or a fin. But it was real, and solid, and moving nearly as quickly as us. This wasn't some mass of micro-organisms bobbing along the water. What I saw looked like whale skin." I inspected the harpoon gun, having paid it little enough attention when we loaded the boat. It had a barbed projectile loaded into the barrel, with two spares tucked into a slot in the stock. I armed it, drew it close to my body, sighting along the barrel, and realised how comfortable and familiar the weapon felt. Another dark form caught my eye, this time to starboard, and I tracked onto it with a smooth confidence that surprised me. My finger tightened on the trigger. But I did not fire. This one, at least, was a trick of the light and waves, melting back into green surf.

"If the things you saw were real..." Glass began.

"No if about it," I snapped back.

"Then they don't fit any established template for Juggler manifestations. The ocean *could* support other life forms, clearly—it's just that the records say that it doesn't."

"Didn't when were you here?" I asked. "Before you chased me to Michaelmas. And that was a long time ago now. I don't even know what the date is any more. Or that it matters. But there's been time for things to happen here."

"Whatever it was, we don't know that it's dangerous," Pinky said.

"You want to take that chance, after all we've been through?" But I lowered the harpoon gun slowly.

Glass was the first to see the Pattern Jugglers. Still guiding the boat, she used her right hand to draw my gaze to a spot on the western horizon. "There," she said, her voice flat and matter-of-fact. "The leading edge of the node."

We had been under way for nearly seven hours: longer than expected and proof that the mass had moved or reorganised itself in the days since our approach from space. The swimming forms, whatever they had been, had not returned since our earlier sightings, and I think Glass was still doubtful that they had been real in the first place. Some of that scepticism had lodged inside me as well. Had I really seen something? And if Pinky had been so sure of his sighting, why had he not mentioned it sooner?

One thing was certain: the node was real. After five minutes I could see

330

it clearly for myself, without any direction from Glass. It was a low, fixed smudge, like the first hint of a landmass emerging around the world's curvature. It was altering the weather in that direction: conjuring a train of clouds above it, condensing moisture where the air was slightly cooler than out over the open water. I stared at it as we continued our approach, and within a few minutes Pinky confirmed that he was seeing it as well. The smudge widened, more and more of the mass emerging over the horizon. It was as low as a reef, at least on its margins, but hugely extended to the north and south: thousands of square kilometres of it, still mostly out of sight.

"Look," I said excitedly, my eye catching movement to the south of us. "A flying fish, or a bird."

"No flying fish or birds on Ararat," Glass responded. But she was also watching the fast-fleeting thing as it skimmed the waves. "It's a messenger sprite, flying between two nodes. Packaged with information at its point of origin, sent off to be received and digested by the recipient node. They send information by other means, including biochemical signals in the water and living transmission cables floating just beneath the surface and extending for hundreds or even thousands of kilometres. But these sprites are what they use when a large packet of information needs to be conveyed very rapidly."

"Does it mean we've been noticed?"

"Let's not get above ourselves, Clavain. They've noticed us, most certainly. There's nothing they don't notice. But these information exchanges go on all the time. Think of the nodes as a vast collective bureaucracy, constantly auditing itself."

Pinky asked: "What about the other things we saw?"

Glass looked at him patiently. "Irrelevant to our present concerns."

Glass reduced our speed as we crossed the last few kilometres between open water and the boundary of the node. The transitions had looked sharp from space, but that had been deceptive. The node spread into the surrounding sea, thinning out, but pushing its influence far beyond the point where it resembled a distinct, raft-like mass. The sea was becoming more grey-green, more opaque and more sluggish, carrying a denser cargo of micro-organisms. The boat's motion became more ponderous, the motor having to do more work to keep us pushing forward through the thickening resistance. The green mass slipped past our hull on either side. It had a slurry-like texture, but with increasing hints of structure and organisation. There were meshlike patterns and ropelike tubes embedded within it, and as the biomass moved on the remaining swell it gave the uneasy impression of countering the action of the waves, rather than going along with them. I had been feeling the edges of seasickness before; now the full force of it rose in my throat and I had to work very hard not to vomit.

Our speed reduced to about half our progress in open water. I peeked over the sides, noticing that the green slurry was adhering to the hull, not just in random splotches but in a deliberate, connected manner, like the crystalline patterns formed by frost on glass. Pinky and I dragged out a pair of oars and used them to flick away the larger concentrations before they took hold.

"We'll bog down before we ever reach the main part," I said.

"There's an open channel a little to the south," Glass said, turning the tiller. "If we can't make it directly, we'll back out and circle around."

The boat could not have been making more than a fast walking pace by the time our speed had dropped to its lowest, but at least we were still moving, and by concentrating our efforts with the oars, we kept the visible part of the hull relatively clean. Now we were heading more or less due south, travelling parallel to the node's edge and hoping to pick up the inlet Glass had seen. I had to trust that she was right. I had no doubt that such channels existed, for I had seen the signs of them from space, cutting back into the node in glinting filigrees of reflected sunlight.

The boat pitched forward, sharply enough that I had to grab onto the sides to stop myself tumbling into the bows. We came to a sudden halt, just as surely as if we had run aground. Glass increased the motor, but it made no difference, merely churning the green-scummed water behind us.

"I think we've tangled with something," I said, creeping forward to where the nose of the boat was jammed down at an angle, half buried in a ropy green mass which emerged from the sea on either side of us. "It must be one of those cables you mentioned, Glass, or a bundle of them. It didn't show above the surface until we ran into it. Can you back us out?"

"Get down," she said. "If you don't, the thrust will blow you out of the boat."

Pinky and I crouched low on the cross-planks. Glass put the motor into reverse thrust and brought it up through stages of power. The boat surged, trying to free itself, but whatever we were tangled with was refusing to yield.

"It has us," Glass said, resignedly. She eased the engine down. "There's no choice. We'll have to cut it loose. Use the knives."

I opened the stores box which contained the knives, thinking how much easier things would be if we had brought a boser pistol or excimer rifle. I passed a knife to Pinky and we leaned over the boat on either side of the bow. I was ready to hack away, but caution stilled my hand. "Glass. If we do this, aren't we harming the organism? I thought the whole point was not to antagonise it?"

"These connections must form and re-form all the time," Glass said. "The biomass has to be able to tolerate a certain level of damage due to environmental factors, without necessarily considering itself under attack."

"I hope you're right, and I also hope we ran into these tentacles accidentally, not because the node is warning us off." I nodded at Pinky, indicating that we should coordinate our cutting. "Ready?"

"Ready."

"Glass? Wait until I give the signal, then gun the engine. We'll cut what we can, and hope to jerk clean of whatever's left underneath the water."

We began to cut. The knives were sharp, and went through the fibrous green strands with very little resistance. At least to begin with. There were dozens of strands, knotted around each other in complicated fashion, and it almost seemed as if they were becoming hardier the more we worked at them. After a minute, my hand and wrist slathered in green, I paused to inspect the blade's edge. It had already gained a shimmering, olive discoloration. "It's fighting back. Try the engine, Glass."

The boat surged back a good metre, straining the remaining tangles, but failed to free itself. The hull had been smooth, with nothing on it that could snag an underwater obstruction, but the fibres were still clinging on tenaciously. Perhaps they were already forming sticky bonds with the craft, striving to begin the slow but inevitable process of chemical breakdown and digestion.

"We'll have to work faster," I said, as Glass eased the motor. "We don't have too much time before these knives give out."

"Should've kept Nevil's knife," Pinky said. "That'd go through anything."

I doubted that we had hacked our way through more than half of the entanglement. What remained was harder to reach, even at a full stretch, and there might be far more of it underwater than I imagined. When we seemed to have made more progress I made a motion to Glass and she gave the engine all it could take. The blast warmed my neck and we struggled back and then jerked free, at least temporarily, while still dragging a mass of the entanglement with us. Our speed increased, still in reverse.

I saw it then, about twenty metres north of our moving position. A form had broken the green-scummed water: a rounded hairless head blending into muscular shoulders. Breaching the green carpet next to the gleaming form was a spiked implement, a shaft festooned with green ribbons which

333

trailed back into the water. Instinctively I looked to the south, sweeping the green slurry until I picked out the counterpart to the other form. They were about forty metres apart, swimming humanoids each holding a similar spiked implement, with a netlike trap stretched between them.

I tossed the blunted knife back into the bottom of the boat and took up the harpoon gun again. I levelled it what I judged to be the easier of the two targets, the one to the north, and fired. The gun coughed, expelling the harpoon with a single explosive gas discharge. I watched the projectile arc over the water, deploying further barbs, and extending its range with a secondary gas thruster of its own. My aim had been true, and the harpoon swift. But the swimmer pulled beneath the water in the instant before impact, and there was no way to judge whether I had hit it.

I began to retract the harpoon, using the manual winching handle built into the side the gun. I had only turned it a few times when the line went slack, and I knew instantly it had been severed. Rather than reel in the useless filament, I ejected the entire spool and loaded one of the two remaining barbs from the stock.

Glass kept us powering in reverse. Pinky was still hacking away at the remaining green threads adhering to the bow. At last the bulk of them seemed to slough away, and Glass reversed the boat's thrust and took us on a looping course further to the south. For now, both swimming forms had disappeared.

"Well, Glass," I said.

Pinky scraped his knife against the hull. "Well indeed."

"Would you like to offer an opinion on what the hell those things are?"

"I have nothing to offer."

"Have you seen anything like those creatures before?"

"No," she answered with uncharacteristic hesitancy. "Not here, not anywhere. Clearly they are derived from human genestock."

"Clearly," I echoed.

"You...did well, Clavain. I took their intentions to be hostile."

"Laying a net is not generally the best way to open friendly negotiations." I set down the harpoon gun. "I don't think I killed it. I also don't think I want to run into any more of those until we've completed our business here. Maybe they're just defending their territory, but I'm not much in the mood for politics."

"Everything is politics in the end," Glass said.

With a surge, the boat pushed through into clearer, less obstructed water. Glass turned hard to starboard, and we advanced along a passage where the green growth was hardly more than a surface dusting, offering minimal resistance. Banks of thicker green marked the channel's boundaries, hemming us in and guiding our course. As we progressed, so these banks became more steeply sided and higher. First fifty centimetres, then a metre, and then high enough that we could not see over the top either to the south or north. My motion sickness was easing now, as the channel was waveless, but replacing it was a growing sense of claustrophobic encroachment. As the banks rose higher, and the channel narrowed, meandering its way into ever-rising green, I felt the age-old apprehension of the wanderer straying into the darkening forest, unsure of the secrets and terrors it held.

I looked back, wondering if any of the swimming forms were likely to follow us.

Glass reduced our speed to about twenty kilometres per hour, then further still. The boat's wake was slapping off the green walls, and the turbulence from the motor was stirring patterns into them.

"Should we think about rowing?" I asked. "I know we'll be slower, but this is starting to feel...impolite."

"We're nowhere near enough to the core," Glass said. "Caution is a good thing, Clavain. But too much of it will kill you."

"Too much of anything will kill you. That's the definition of 'too much.'"

"Caution or otherwise," Pinky said. "I'm not liking the look of that."

I followed the line of his gaze.

The channel split into two even narrower forks. By now the rising walls on either side of us were house-high in places and leaning inwardly. The two forks went off in divergent directions, but neither was more or less inviting than the other. They were thickening, narrowing corridors of green, with sagging, ropelike connections strung between their walls.

"This one," Glass said, taking us into the left fork. "It should be the most direct route to the core, if things haven't changed too much. Don't be alarmed by these cross-connections: they're just to enable the node to communicate with itself. Think of us as a cell moving through the commissural gap between brain hemispheres."

"I'm not sure that helps," Pinky said.

We continued down the channel, which stayed relatively constant in width for about a kilometre. I knew what Glass was hoping to find: a lagoon-like enclosure of open water within the node, one of several that had been apparent from space. These lagoons, deliberately maintained by the biomass, were often the best prospect for any swimmers hoping to make contact. They were a sign that the node was at least receptive, even if there could never be any guarantees of success.

Glass's likening of the node to the structure of a brain stayed with me.

There was still no definite opinion on the matter of whether the Pattern Juggler nodes were themselves conscious. But the nodes were certainly rich in biological methods of information storage, manipulation and dissemination. The Jugglers stored many different informational forms, from nuggets of pure, discorporeal knowledge to species-specific templates for particular modes of cognition. A person could swim in the Juggler waters and have the node's micro-organisms rebuild their mind to permit the acquisition of some new gift, such as heightened mathematical insight or the grasping of some long-dead alien language. Such Juggler-derived talents tended to be temporary, though: after an interval—sometimes only a matter of hours—the imprinted structures would wither away. Very rarely, the change was enduring enough for the swimmer to accomplish some one-off challenge. Repeat visits to the Jugglers were uncommon, and rarely successful. It was also said that in the rare instances where the changes were permanent, there was wisdom in being careful what you wished for.

What had happened to my brother was not like that. If any part of him still existed, it was because his body had been absorbed into the Pattern Jugglers. Others had been taken by the Pattern Jugglers, but it usually only happened after an extended sequence of contact episodes, with ample warning along the way. Those individuals usually understood the risk that they were taking and made a calculation that the potential rewards were worth it. By the time they were taken, the seas' organisms would already have insinuated themselves into their bodies to a high degree, marking them as likely candidates for absorption. My brother, according to those who had known him, had never swum. He had been too fearful of what he would find—or rather, what he would *not* find.

The sea had already taken something precious from him. Felka was a child of the Conjoiners, and for Nevil she was the nearest thing to a daughter. Her mother, in a sense that only Conjoiners could understand, had been Galiana, founder of the entire Conjoined movement. The Inhibitors had killed Galiana—in all likelihood she had been the first human being to encounter them—but long before her demise she had visited Ararat, and perhaps left a trace of herself in the ocean. If any human mind could be said to be of interest to the Jugglers, it would be the strange and beautiful brain that belonged to Galiana. Felka had been trying to make contact with her mother when the sea swallowed her whole. Nevil's grief had been so all-consuming that even hope was a torment. Felka might have transmitted herself into the sea, and through his beloved Felka he might find a conduit to Galiana. Was it possible that both Felka and Galiana might have left conscious shadows of themselves, even as the

336

medium in which they were stored was itself perhaps less than conscious?

But though he shut himself away from his affairs, and lived alone by the sea, Nevil could never bring himself to take the step into the waters that might have answered all his questions. It had taken death—death administered by the hand of his oldest and dearest friend—to finally bring him to the sea.

To these three lost souls might now be added a fourth. But I had no desire to be taken; just to make contact.

The boat scraped deeper into the node. Now the channel was a cloying green corridor with furry walls and a ceiling made of cross-fretted tendrils, through which Bright Sun, quite near its zenith, flickered hypnotically with our motion. It was humid and much warmer than it had been out at sea. My nose prickled with a green haze of airborne organisms.

Glass brought the engine to a halt.

"The motor is creating too much disturbance. We'll row from here on in."

"Excellent idea," I said, fixing my oar onto its mount. "Wish I'd thought of it myself."

Pinky and I did the rowing, since I wanted Glass to conserve her energies. Rowing was not really the word for what we did, though. It was more a case of levering the tips of the oars against the resistance of the walls, which were soggy on the surface and then firmer and firmer the more we pushed in. We were doing well to move at a slow walking pace, and I was soon prickling with sweat. But there was something lulling about the mechanical activity of rowing that helped settle my nerves.

Something whirred past my cheek. Startled, I nearly dropped the oar. There was just time to see one of the messenger sprites, streaking ahead of us down the green tunnel. Now that the shadows were deeper, it was possible to see that the sprite glowed with bioluminescence. Another came streaking back a few moments later. Then, over our heads, we watched with a dreadful fascination as a pair of green horns extended out from either side, meeting in the middle like the halves of a cantilever bridge. The green tube thickened in throbbing pulses, and I caught a glimmer of colour and movement within it.

"Heightened organisational activity," Glass said, as another pair of sprites fluttered by us. "All this takes energy. There's no doubt that the node is reacting to us, aware of our presence."

"Did this happen to you before?"

I caught her hesitation. I think she meant to lie, then decided better of it. "No, not to this degree. But I wasn't known to the ocean prior to my visit. That is no longer the case for either of us."

"It recognises us?" I asked.

"Something in it may recognise us."

"Again, not helpful," Pinky said.

A sprite sped down the tunnel, then looped around our boat three times. Now that it was near to us, I had the first opportunity to study it in any sort of detail. It had a bird-sized body, speckled with glowing dots, but no recognisable head or sensory appendages. The only limbs were the whirring wings, fine-veined and translucent. I wondered how it could draw in any information on its surroundings.

The sprite broke off from its inspection and zipped away.

We kept rowing, moving with the punting rhythm of the oars. The walls were no longer just an organised green slurry with designs on digesting our boat. Now there was a breathing, undulating quality to them, as if we were moving along the digestive tract of some great monster. When the oars sunk into the slurry, ripples spread away from the point of contact. The ripples rebounded off each other and generated second-order patterns through their interference. Colours glimmered beyond the green. Were we moving at all? It was hard to be sure. We had no reference points whatsoever, and I doubted that anything in Glass's head was able to track our movement relative to *Scythe* or First Camp. I had a horrible vision of us trapped forever between these oozing walls, thinking we were rowing but actually motionless.

"I see faces," Pinky said.

Under any other circumstances I felt sure that Glass would have been swift to contradict him, telling him that his brain was playing tricks on his conscious mind. Instead she nodded. "Yes. I see them as well. Momentary coherent forms, emerging and disappearing. Do you see them, Clavain?"

"Yes," I answered, stopping punting for a moment, as Pinky had done. "It's only started in the last few moments, hasn't it? Something's been roused."

"The faces mean nothing to me," Glass said. "But Pinky might recognise them, if they relate to the citizens of First Camp."

"We aren't always good with human faces. You know how it is. Something about your lack of a decent pair of ears and a snout." But after a silence he added: "I don't see anyone I remember. But they come and go so quickly, it's hard to be sure. It's like seeing phantoms in a fire."

"It's possible that these faces are drawn from the memories of those who swam here, or who were absorbed, not necessarily people who ever visited Ararat." Glass nodded peremptorily. "Keep rowing. This is encouraging."

"I've never felt so encouraged." But Pinky sighed and resumed his half of the rowing, and so did I.

"Only human forms so far," I commented.

"That we recognise," Glass said. "If there were alien faces in those patterns, our visual systems might have missed them completely. Assuming aliens even *have* faces. But I think it likely the biomass is drawing on information patterns that it understands to be pertinent to us, as humans, rather than the vast collective memory of other visitors who were here thousands or even millions of years ago. Again, I am inclined to see it as an encouraging overture."

I forced a smile, hoping it would lift my spirits. "I'd hate to see your idea of discouraging."

We continued down the channel, which had now become a squeezing corridor of faces, constantly forming and dissipating in the slurry. They were there and gone in much less than a second; just long enough for the eye to snag the proportions and know that it was detecting something meaningful. The faces were green masks, blank-eyed forms with a strange constancy of expression, like vaguely amused theatregoers roused from distracted trains of thought by our passage. Ripples rippling into ripples, become faces, dissolving back into randomness, over and over again. I recognised none of them, and saw nothing that looked like my own face.

Glass lunged for the gas-harpoon. She grabbed it double-handed and swung it back to aim at the disturbed water we had already passed through. Her hands were shaking, jerking the barbed barrel.

I reached out and steadied the harpoon.

"What?"

"One of those things. I saw it for a second, behind us in the channel. Just its head, but a clearer view. It's humanoid. Human-derived, I should say."

"It's not there now."

"It was," Glass said.

We kept rowing, but slowly, with nearly all our focus directed back along the green-shadowed channel. The torrent of faces had eased, seemingly detecting our nervousness. Glass's hands were still shaking. It was not apprehension, in her case, but a neuromuscular consequence of whatever was happening in her brain.

Gently I took the harpoon gun from her while Pinky managed both oars, dipping them languidly into the water rather than levering them against the banks.

"Somewhere in the gaps in our records," I said quietly, "someone must have come here and adapted to the ocean. Or been forced to adapt. Whatever the case, we're the newcomers now. Those swimmers would be dead unless they'd found some equilibrium with the sea and the Jugglers: some way of life that allows them to coexist with the nodes." I smiled. "Out of all this chaos and darkness, something new. Speciation, adaptation, biogenesis. Life always finds a way."

"Until it doesn't, and there's nothing left to mourn it but decaying cell cultures. Adaptation's all well and good. But unless you've got something to fight the wolves with, you've just found a slower, quieter way of becoming extinct."

"You said they don't touch Juggler worlds. Perhaps that's our solution: merge with the oceans and wait until the wolves have gone."

"And while we're at it," Glass said, sounding like Lady Arek for a moment, "we can de-evolve spines and central nervous systems as well."

"Maybe we should wait until we've met these people before we pass judgement on their choices."

"Now might be your chance," Pinky commented.

The swimmer was emerging from the water again, perhaps fifteen metres behind us. A head rose above the green, then a widening neck, then the shoulders and sternum of a muscular, broad-chested torso. I couldn't tell if the swimmer was treading water, or standing on some extension of the biomass beneath the surface, only that it seemed confident of its posture.

Glass had been right when she spoke of human genestocks; of that I had no doubt. Compared to some of the wilder strains of people that had existed in the Rust Belt or out among the Skyjacks or Ultras, its adaptations were almost unremarkable. It had a flattened, seal-like face with slitted nasal openings and wide, forward-facing eyes that were clearly well evolved for light-gathering underwater. Whiskers fanned out around the nose and mouth: a useful sensory augmentation in dark or confined spaces. The creature had external ears, but they were vestigial affairs and folded tightly to the skull, which was covered in a dark, glistening integument that I imagined must have very efficient thermal properties. The creature had a mane of green-stained hair fanning down over the shoulders, and what I first took to be oddments of scrap contamination caught in the hair were in fact ornaments or trinkets, deliberately braided in. The skin glimmered here and there with paler, almost luminous patches of gold and green. Only the upper third of the creature was so far visible but I could see nothing of clothing.

All this I took in within a second of Pinky's words, adding these observations to the impressions already gained with our earlier encounters. We had already seen that the creatures possessed tools, and the desire to trap us, so my assumption was that this swimmer also had hostile intent.

"Go back!" I shouted, jabbing the barrel of the harpoon gun in what I hoped was a sufficiently unambiguous fashion, regardless of which spoken languages the creature did or did not comprehend.

A moan came from the swimmer.

"NOoo...!" it bellowed, on a long, deep, falling note. "NOooo...! NOoo...GOoooo...! NO GO! NO GO!"

Unless my brain was filling in meaning where none existed, I felt that the utterance had been quite clear enough. Our tongue might not have been the one preferred by the creature, but it knew it well enough to issue a directive.

"Not your decision to make, I'm afraid." I made another lunge with the harpoon gun. "Leave us alone, friend, and we'll leave you alone. Our business is not your business."

"Shoot it," Glass said.

Two barbs remained in the gun, one ready to be fired and the other still stowed in the stock. I considered a warning shot, firing above the creature, but if that did not have the desired effect and the creature made a lunge I would not have time to load the third barb.

"Go!" I shouted. "You understand 'go'! Go or I'll hurt you! Don't make me do this!"

"NO GO! Not swim! Bad time!"

Glass turned on the motor, aiming its blast at the creature. It howled as the hot air lashed its face, then drew its left arm from the water, using a large webbed hand to shield its eyes. The boat accelerated away from the swimmer, sluggishly at first, then with gathering momentum. The swimmer's other arm came out of the water, and it had something in it. It was a sort of clawed grapnel on a line, and the creature swung it in widening, quickening arcs, letting out the line a little at a time, all in the fingers of one hand.

I fired, but I still could not bring myself to aim directly for the creature. I knew it to be intelligent and on some level I understood that its injunction had been as much warning as threat, and perhaps a warning that we would have been wise to heed. But we had come too far, and overcome too much, to be deterred now.

The shot was aimed at the swinging grapnel, not the creature's hand, but the effect was not very different. The barb collected the grapnel and its line, tangling with them, and in so doing ripped the line from the creature's grip, taking some portion of flesh with it. The creature bellowed, the tips of its fingers bloodied, and the webbing between those fingers lacerated and flapping loose. I released the barb's line. The creature was still looking at us, holding its wounded hand by the wrist even as it sank back into the water. Slowly the curving corridor of green sealed it from sight, almost like a curtain closing, and we were alone again.

CHAPTER TWENTY-SIX

When it seemed unlikely the creature would find us again, Glass quietened the motor and we resumed our progress with the oars. I had reloaded the harpoon gun with the one remaining barb, but after that encounter had seen nothing that merited raising the weapon.

Which was not to say that we were relieved, or in any way confident. Although very little was said of the matter—what *was* there to say, since we had all seen the same thing—each of us in our private fashion must have been mulling the creature's motives and wondering if its intentions were as belligerent as they had seemed at the time. If we had surprised these creatures with our presence on Ararat, then perhaps they had been forced into actions which only looked to be hostile because barriers of language precluded any reasoned persuasion. Maybe they had tried to net the boat not because they meant harm to us or our craft but because by the time they knew of us we were moving too quickly to be dissuaded by other means. When that had failed, one had followed us into the node... and if the creature had meant to hurt us, then by the time he surprised us we were in easy range of spears, arrows, poison darts, or any throwing weapon I cared to name. But the creature had asked us to stop, and when we had refused it had only demonstrated an intention to grapple our boat. Perhaps others would have arrived soon after, to augment the effort.

Or perhaps I was being charitable where no such assumption was merited. Perhaps, if I had not fired that barb, one of us would have lost an eye or a hand to that grapple. Who was I to decide what was a weapon, and what was a tool?

"Ahead," Glass called, snapping me from my thoughts. "The lagoon. We've reached it."

The channel widened, disclosing an area of relatively open water about two hundred metres across. Walls of green surrounded the lagoon, at least as tall as any part of the channel, and beyond these walls rose ever higher terraces of dense green, climbing in ziggurat-like steps until they were at least fifty or sixty metres above the level of the sea. Some immense architecture of living matter must have supported these prominences, scaffolding them like the interlocking limbs of a forest canopy, but all complexities were hidden beneath the green mantle.

The air was still, humid and heavy. The only way in or out of the lagoon was the channel that had brought us and now that we had passed it that aperture looked narrower, less navigable. The weather system that we had glimpsed over the node from a distance was now a dark, squatting mass directly above us. The clouds were moving in a restless, slithering, cross-hatched formation, like a nest of eels. No rain yet fell on us, but my skin prickled as if there was an ocean of water suspended over us by the thinnest of threads. Thunder rumbled some way off. A tick-like creature nipped my neck and I swatted it away.

The boat had reached the middle of the lagoon. I arrested its drift with the oar, which I then set down in the bottom.

"So," I said, addressing Glass. "We've arrived. This is the lagoon, or a lagoon. Do you have a script for the next part?"

"We commune," Glass said. "The node has permitted us passage, and the presence of this lagoon indicates a tacit invitation to proceed. We shall swim: you with the intention of contacting your brother, me to be restored to my earlier template."

"Nothing big, then."

"The Jugglers rarely do anything in small ways." Glass began to disrobe. "Take off your clothes, Clavain. They'd only be consumed by the water, so if you want them afterwards you'd better leave them on the boat."

"Naked humans," Pinky said, with a faint disgusted shudder. "You've no idea how much you look like pigs, under all those layers. It's unsettling."

"Be glad you're not expected to swim," I said, beginning to strip off.

"I would if my life depended on it. Which it would have to, because any other time swimming's almost certainly going to get me killed. You sure you don't want to slow down a bit, you know, take in the scenery?"

I nodded. "Every sane part of me, Scorp. But Glass is right. We're here now. No amount of delay is going to make any difference, and since I very, very badly want to be on the other side of this..."

"Then I'll just sit here and think happy thoughts."

"No," I said firmly. "You're still my advocate, remember? You don't have to swim. But if the node's aware of us, it's aware of you. Start telling it that I'm not here to do any harm, and that it would be very good to meet my brother. Remind him who you are—and that you're here to vouch for me."

"At least there's nothing awkward about any of that."

"Do what you can. But above all else, no matter what happens here, you protect yourself. And if Glass and I don't return...you turn that boat around and return to First Camp."

"You know that ain't happening. But nice sentiment."

"You'll give us six hours from the point where you lose contact with us," Glass said firmly. "No longer. Your bravado doesn't concern me. But I'd like knowledge of our failure to make it back to Probably Rose."

"How will that help?" I asked.

"They'll know what not to do. They'll have to try, nonetheless. If we don't succeed, they must—even though the odds decrease with each degree of separation from your brother. This is all we have, Clavain: we either reach the knowledge held by Nevil, or we fail, eternally."

I finished undressing. Although the air was sticky, and a storm felt as if it were building pressure, straining to burst through some incredibly thin membrane, I still shivered. I felt weak and cadaverous. Glass regarded me with clinical disinterest, and I nodded back at her, ready and not ready, full of wonder and terror and the deep apprehension that preceded any long-delayed family reunion.

"Into the water?"

"Into the water." Glass slid off the boat, making a splashless entry into the lagoon. She submerged her whole body then came back up with just her head and shoulders above the green surface. But now she was lathered in a fine marbling of green and instead of wiping it from her eyes she stared back with an unblinking ferocity of spirit. "My advice is not to resist the organisms. Let them into you willingly, no matter how uncomfortable the process. Whatever will happen will happen anyway, but resisting the contamination only delays the inevitable."

I eased myself onto the edge of the boat, Pinky counter-balancing it, then slipped into the lagoon, a couple of metres from Glass. I dipped my head under, closing my eyes by reflex, then pushed my face back into the air. My skin itched and I had a strong sense of a gummy mass wanting to ooze its way into my nostrils.

Glass paddled backwards from the boat, still keeping her head elevated from the water, with only her black-nailed fingers and toes breaking the surface.

"Follow me. We should put some distance between us and the boat. The node must recognise that our entry is deliberate, and that we are not seeking to return to the boat's sanctuary."

"When will we know if something's happening?"

"I doubt there will be much ambiguity. Your only clear memory of your last visit here was a sense of drowning. That should indicate the level of experience typical of Juggler communion."

I still had my face to the boat as I kicked alongside Glass. Pinky was standing up, astride the boat's middle now that he no longer had to balance my weight. He puffed his chest, worked his shoulders, and cupped two hands around his snout.

"Hey, Nevil. Wondering if you can hear me. It's Scorp. You remember me, I guess. Hard not to, given how it went down the last time you and I were together. Part of me never thought I'd ever come back to this place. Part of me never wanted to. But here I am. Ain't life a surprise, sometimes?" He paused, shuddered, and seemed on the point of sitting down, overcome by the ridiculousness of the role I had placed on him. I would not have blamed him in the slightest. I had spoken truthfully when I said I wanted him to accompany me to the Pattern Jugglers, but only a small part of that had anything to do with his advocacy. I had come to regard him as a protector, a talisman whose mere presence was enough to keep harm at bay. He had been at my brother's side until the end, and it was not through any failings of Pinky that Nevil had perished.

Yet after that deliberation he regathered his purpose. "You know I was never good at this stuff. After you were gone, they made me run this place. I guess I didn't do the worst job, all things told. Quite a lot of us made it, even if it wasn't exactly happy ever after once we got off Ararat. But the speech-making part of it? Never my finest hour." He tapped his forehead. "They say there are things in here that aren't so well developed: little circuits that help with reflection, strategic planning, delayed gratification, that kind of thing. And I suppose if those aren't working too well, then speaking out loud, being all persuasive and rhetorical, ain't likely to be my strongest suit, either. But this little piggy is the last straw in the pack, so I guess we have to work with what we're given, and that's me. And I remember you, my friend. There hasn't been a day when I haven't brought you to mind. We were either together too long, or not nearly enough, ain't worked that one out just yet, and maybe I never will. But here's what I have to tell you." Pinky angled his head in my direction, giving me—what? Forewarning? That my name and identity was about to be invoked, and once uttered, there could be no undoing it? "I've brought someone to meet you. Maybe you already know who he is. I like to think you do, because then it takes the burden off me to do the introducing... but seeing as I was asked, and I don't like to let my friends down... this is your brother. His name is Warren and I know there's some... not so great stuff between you. Shit that went down, hundreds of years ago. Shit you never told me about, probably because the wounds were still raw, even after all that time. Now, it ain't my job to say that none of that mattered, now or then. But I do have a duty to state my feelings. Warren doesn't measure up to you, Nevil. He hasn't seen or done half the things and I doubt he's known half the heartache you went through. But in the time I've known him—which I admit is just a scratch against a life. Against a human life, leastwise—I've seen enough to make me say a good word for him. And if a word of this reaches you, and if any of it has any chance of you moving to accept him, even to speak to him in the way he wants, and open up about the things you still know—the things you might not even know matter to us—then I beg you to remember our friendship, and consider that any friend of mine must be a friend of yours, no matter how strange the course that brought us together."

Pinky fell silent and buckled back down onto his haunches, worn out and perhaps aware that he had offered all that could reasonably be presented in my defence, and any further words were not likely to make any difference. By the time he finished, Glass and I had paddled most of the way across the lagoon, and with the green biomass forcing its way into me with each breath, stifling my breathing, it was all I could do to nod a grateful thanks for his intercession. It might not help, but it was all I could have hoped for, and I was very glad indeed that he had accompanied us.

"Are you frightened, Glass?"

"Would it help if I am?"

"I'm frightened. But I think my fear's of a different kind than yours. This is either going to kill me or not. If it doesn't kill me, then I think I may come away with something of Nevil, something that can help us. If I die, then nothing ever matters again. But you're expecting to lose part of yourself: every new experience since you were last on Ararat. The Jugglers might preserve something of your memories since then, but there's no guarantee of that."

"It's an acceptable sacrifice. And there's no guarantee that they will reset me to my earlier condition. There are informational structures in my brain that they may find enticing, sufficient to grant a favour. But a request does not have to be honoured."

"Then you're between two hard places: dying in pieces, here, or dying for good, a little while from now. I don't envy you, Glass. But if you won't admit that this is a little terrifying, I'll do it for you. I don't want to lose the part of you that's known me. You've been a witness, and a catalyst, to my changes. Whatever's become of me, whatever man I've now become, you were the instrument that made it happen. I won't say I'm grateful...although perhaps I should be. The truth is always better than the lie."

"You do not need me to tell you what you are."

"But I need you to hold these threads together. You're the only one

346

who saw what I was, and what I've become. You're half my story. If you crumble away, I don't know what will happen to the rest of me."

"You were a survivor. You'll stay a survivor."

"Here's my promise to you, Glass. If either of us comes out of this, and you've been reset, I'll help you recover the things you've lost. We'll be each other's crutches, two broken souls that can't exist without each other. I'll help you remember, and in remembering, you'll help me find myself."

Glass considered my words, then said: "Can I tell you something, Clavain? You talk too much."

The sky over us crackled.

Around the lagoon, the green walls and terraces shimmered with faces, a constant dance of them. Now the faces were larger than before: house-sized visages leering at us, forming and collapsing back into the green substrate almost quicker than the eye could follow. It was more than just faces, too. Less familiar forms were appearing in the endless, overlapping confusion of solid images. Now alien bodies and body parts interposed themselves between the faces, interlocking like clever wall-paper designs: claws, tentacles, compound eyes and scissoring wings among them. The waves of change hastened. The forms were blurring into a continuum, an infinite, disarticulated carnival of all the creatures that had ever touched this sea, and perhaps all the monsters and phantasms they ferried with them in their deepest nightmares and phobias.

The waves of change, now a furious, flickering tumult, had begun to agitate the water of the lagoon. Disturbances sloshed from side to side, lifting us on one swell, crashing us down on the next. The rising and sinking waves brought the boat in and out of view. For a moment I thought that Pinky had been knocked overboard, but on the next glimpse I was relieved to see him pressed to the cross-planks, presenting as low a centre of gravity as possible. I feared for him, but as long as the boat stayed upright I thought he had a chance.

Glass was still close to me, but the force of the water's movement was starting to push us apart. Even as I gave all of myself to the act of swimming, holding my head above the surging green swell, I tried to reach out to her. My fingers closed on something, but not firmly enough. I paddled, snorted green muck from my nose, and struck out again. But Glass was out of reach, and now the airborne haze was blurring my vision. All was turning green.

"Glass!" I called out, with one good breath. "Glass!"

But Glass was gone.

I fought it for a little while, even as I knew that the wisest course was

347

to submit; to allow the green into my lungs, to drown so that I might be reborn. But half a billion years of land-based evolution had wired my brain with a powerful aversion to the notion of drowning. It was not the same as getting into one of the acceleration tanks on *Scythe*, surrounded by all the reassurances of modern civilisation. I was alone now, devoid of tools or protection, naked to the core, just a small, frightened mammal about to drown, and all my higher faculties turned and fled in the face of that most primal of fears.

So I fought, and fought, but always with ebbing strength, until at last I had nothing more to give, and the green tide flooded into me with eager enthusiasm, citadel gates at last flung wide to the besieging army. The organisms stormed my throat, my windpipe, my lungs. They fissured through me like a green lava flow, finding every crevice and channel to every other part of me. They followed nerves and blood vessels, infiltrating my brain, establishing lines of communication out of my body and into the wider node, and from there to every other node on Ararat. There was a point of maximum terror, then submission, then a dawning acceptance. Then the green bliss of dissolution. Even as my sense of self evaporated, I lost sight of why it had ever mattered in the first place. The sea was old and warm and welcoming. I was just another set of patterns to be folded into the whole.

I remembered Glass and Pinky, and that I had come here for a reason. The urgency of my mission had not deserted me, but now it was just one imperative fighting for attention against a welter of new impulses and sensations. Because I knew that it mattered, I held onto it with what felt like a superhuman effort of will. My brother. I had to sift through the impressions battering my mind and identify his distinct presence. Then reach out to it, with all the humility and submission I could muster.

Memories stroked my consciousness, bursting against its limits. They were not mine. They were not, for the most part, anything that I would have called human. I saw alien skies, alien suns, birthing nebulae, the scattered ashes of worlds and stars, vistas of great magnificence and equally great desolation. Time dizzied me. I had thought I understood time, but now my ignorance left me reeling. Time was vaster and colder and lonelier than anything I had ever imagined. There had already been so much of it: heavy oceanic layers of time, plunging into deep, still blackness, and my consciousness was just a feeble thing drifting in the highest sunlit layer. A galaxy's worth of history had already passed into this ocean and been memorialised. All our human adventuring was no more than a scuff on the final page; unwarranted, barely noticed.

I retained some sense of my physical embodiment. I had been blurred at the edges, but not destroyed. Something resembling a man was still immersed in the lagoon, although now I was no longer swimming, no longer breathing air. I was a man-shaped density gradient in the green slurry. A concentration of living matter that could be dispersed or reconsolidated with equal disregard.

I formed a thought: *Help Glass*. And another: *Don't hurt Scorp*.

The lagoon's movement had become a bottled storm. I was in it somewhere, tethered to the node like a billion-stringed puppet. I rose and fell on the surges. By some means I remained aware of my surroundings, even as I no longer had a clear sense of my own point of view. Encircling the lagoon, the play of forms had become a frenzy of transformation. Lights lit the flickering, ever-shifting mass. Sprites cross-knit the air. Purple clouds bellied down. Lightning arced between the node and the sky, over and over, some monstrous circuitry completing itself.

A form began to bud from the lagoon's side, maintaining integrity against the changing background. It was a rounded protrusion, a green stump gradually extending itself, as if it meant to form an arcing connection from one side of the lagoon to the other.

The stump ceased its projection. It began to reshape itself, the green slurry flowing and reorganising in deliberate waves. The stump was becoming five-budded. The buds were becoming distinct in form and size. Four were fingers. One was a thumb.

The green hand reached down from the sky and plucked me from the lagoon. It pinched me between its fingers and I saw myself as it did: a straggly, fibrous starfish, dripping tendrils.

The hand lifted me higher. Now the point where it emerged from the lagoon's wall was gaining definition and stability, becoming a lumpy, towering torso. Another arm began to bud from the torso. Then a boulder-like head. Two trunk-like columns differentiated themselves and lifted the torso and head ever higher.

The hand elevated me until I was level with the head. It was crudely carved, lopsided. There had been a face there once, but now it was time-eroded, ruined, blasted by eternity. All that remained were suggestive creases and folds. Two eye-holes, the crease of a mouth, the line of a beard.

And still I knew it.

I formed his name.

Nevil.

Nevil.

Nevil.

And the face spoke into me: *How dare you call me that. How dare you use my name.*

I felt the hand's embrace around my soggy, sagging body. The hand and I were made of the same matter, intertangling and inter-penetrating.

You know mine. I'm Warren, your brother.

The fingers squeezed tighter. *You shouldn't have come back. Didn't you remember what I promised? Didn't I make it clear what I'd do to you if you returned?*

The face was gaining depth and symmetry, becoming a mirror to my own. Ageless eyes of blank green formed beneath the overhang of massive brows.

I need your help, Nevil. We all need your help.

The face formed a sneer. *Isn't it enough that I already died for you once?*

Your friends are here. They know they can't ask more of you. But there's something you know, a piece of information you've carried with you, that will help us. Help us all, Nevil. Help humanity, all that's left of it.

The lips defined a mirthless smile. *And for this . . . they send you?*

If there were a part of me still breathing, a ribcage, lungs and heart within that green concentration, I forced myself to take two slow measured breaths.

No. I sent myself.

Then you forget our last meeting. The one where I nearly killed you and left you with that as a warning never to trouble these seas again. The head cocked, quizzically. *I thought I was clear. What part of that wasn't clear?*

You left a part of you within me, last time. I came with a hyperpig called Pinky . . . only I called him Scorp once, and the only way I could have known that name is because you left it with me, the last time I was here. Scorp spoke for me. If anything that he said reached you, then you'll know that I am not here to cause you hurt, or to seek forgiveness. He knows me better than I know myself. And he knew you.

The hand tightened.

You've tricked my old friend.

No. I haven't tricked him. I tricked myself. I blocked my memories and made a new life for myself to escape the truth of what I am, and what I did to you. I deny none of that, and I'm ready to pay whatever price you deem necessary for returning here. But before you punish me, we must have the information. You owe that: to Scorp, to Ana Khouri, to all the dead of Ararat. To the memories of Felka and Galiana.

It was a risk to invoke those who had been dear to him, and I was willing to take it. With that invocation I knew that I would either breach his defences or turn him fully against me. There could be no middle ground.

The hand squeezed tighter, and tighter still. I felt myself oozing out between his fingers, a loosening slurry that had once been a man called Warren Clavain.

And still the hand kept squeezing.

CHAPTER TWENTY-SEVEN

Our suits guided our return to the Muskie shelter, backtracking via inertial compasses. The storm was abating as we moved into the cover of the camouflaging awning.

"If they take the bait," I said, when we were unpacking the equipment again, and enjoying sips through our nutrient straws, "it will be sooner rather than later."

"Is there a chance they'll just let them die?" Charity asked. "Isn't that the most likely outcome, given what we know of their group-mind psychology? There've been numerous cases of individuals or groups being sacrificed to offset a risk to the main nests."

"It's true." I nodded. "But these are raw recruits, who ran the gauntlet to get to Mars. The other Conjoiners won't want to do anything that might deter similar ventures. The mother nests need fresh bodies to replace those we kill. Even if it is only a question of not handing us a propaganda coup, they'll be strongly disinclined to abandon these fresh young puppies."

"I don't understand how they think," Charity said. "After all my time in Psychosurgical Ops, I understand what goes on inside their heads, probably better than anyone. But I still don't have a sense of how it would feel to be a Conjoiner."

"Be glad," Hope said.

"It feels marvellous," I said, removing the cartridge from my semi-automatic and slipping in a replacement. "It must feel marvellous, or they'd try to undo it. That, or it's a trick of memory. It might feel terrible in absolute terms, but if the subject's tricked into believing that it's still better than what they had before, they'll accept the transformation unquestioningly. Accept it and not want it taken away from them."

"Your brother's given this a lot of thought," Hope said.

I caught Charity's frown. Whose brother, she must be thinking. She had no brother. Was the statement meant for me? But none of us were supposed to know about our respective backgrounds. Not even so much as our real names, let alone familial relationships.

Something about the casual way Hope had made the observation had undoubtedly left Charity discomfited, feeling on the outside of something.

I empathised. It was a familiar, skin-prickling sensation.

"I doubt anyone's given it more thought," I said, clicking the magazine back into the handle of the semi-automatic. "My brother might even get to see what the process feels like for himself."

"Your brother?" Charity asked.

"The prisoner—our extraction objective. The man we've come to Mars to steal away from the spiders."

"I didn't know."

"You weren't meant to know," I answered, not without some kindness. "Anyway, it's not tactically relevant. All that matters is that he's a high-value asset that we'd like back for ourselves, and now we're a step closer to getting him home."

"Are you...Sky Marshall Clavain, sir?"

I wondered if she detected some distant, merciless amusement in my answer.

"Would you think it likely, Charity?"

"I don't know." She swallowed hard. "I thought that the Sky Marshall... one of the Marshalls, I mean...was on a diplomatic mission to Europa."

I answered her patiently. "Sky Marshall Nevil Clavain has been on Mars for three and a half months, Charity. That whole story about Europa was a smokescreen to explain his absence. It's embarrassing to us that he's been taken—even more embarrassing that we haven't yet got him back. But we're close now—thanks to you."

"Then you must be...Sky Marshall Warren Clavain, sir."

"I must."

"I am...honoured to be part of this operation, sir. I always took it seriously, but now that I know the prisoner's identity, and that you're with us..."

"Let me turn this around, Charity," I said, interrupting her gently. She would still keep thinking of me as Faith, until I gave her permission to use my actual name and rank. "Things have gone well so far. Almost exactly according to plan. Apart from one detail."

A salty wind snapped against my cheeks. I was sitting on my haunches, knees drawn up, arms wrapped around grazed shins, pale grass tickling my calves, shivering.

Another boy sat next to me. Beyond us was a sloping shoreline of grass, hemming a thin strand of colourless mud, and beyond it a seething grey sea, rows of whitecaps stretching unbroken to a horizon the colour of digital static.

"Did you really think this was a good idea?" the other boy said, rolling a smooth grey pebble between his fingers. "I mean, after everything?"

"I had no choice. If our roles had been reversed, you'd have come back to Ararat just as I did." The wind flicked my hair against my eyes. I brushed it away, squinting irritatedly. "This isn't about what I did to you, or what you said you'd do to me."

"Isn't it?"

"I know that I wronged you. Set you up to die for the sake of a political stunt...because I desired the continuation of the war, rather than the peace you knew was possible. That was wrong, I know. But it wasn't because I loved war itself. It was because I believed in our cause, and I thought war was the only way for it to prevail."

"So you wronged me, but it was all right because you believed in a higher cause."

I ground my teeth. "Not what I'm saying."

"Let's be clear about the nature of your betrayal, shall we? You didn't just set up my peace initiative to fail. You arranged for me to stumble into a lethal trap. You plotted my murder."

"You didn't die."

"Which must have been a weight off your conscience."

"You gave as good as you got," I said, casting my eyes to the slate-coloured indeterminacy of the horizon. "When you turned your loyalties over to Galiana, and fled the solar system...what was the last message you sent back to the world? One of high-minded forgiveness, befitting one who has finally risen above the pettiness of war?" I sniffed, shaking my head slowly. "No, you reserved all your energies to announce a brotherly vendetta. You said that you'd kill me if you ever got the chance, and that you'd never revoke that promise. That no deed on my part could ever atone for my one crime against you. That I shouldn't even attempt to live a better life, because it was mathematically impossible to ever earn your forgiveness."

"And yet, you live."

"For now."

"Did it occur to you that I might not want to be found on Ararat?"

After a silence I said: "I was here before. I tried and failed, but for some reason you left me alive."

"You remembered?"

"I remembered the terror of drowning. I remembered that I didn't want to return to this place, even if I didn't quite know why."

"You should have listened to your fears. Perhaps, in a moment of weakness, I pitied you enough not to kill you there and then. But those fears should have made it very clear that I was serious about what would happen the next time."

"And yet, here we are."

I reached down, uprooting a clump of grass with a nub of muddy soil at the end of it. "I haven't come back to test the seriousness of your threat. I'm not here to seek atonement or persuade you that I deserve another chance. I'm not even here as a brother. I'm here to speak to you as one soldier to another, about a war that makes the one that divided us seem ludicrous and tiny. I'm talking about extinction. Something which makes our lives look about as significant as this piece of dirt, compared to that ocean."

He reflected on an answer, then said testily: "It's not an ocean. It's the North Sea."

"You saw something," I persisted. "In your explorations, when you and Galiana took the *Sandra Voi* off into interstellar space, forging beyond any of the systems that had already been mapped and explored. Skimming close to a gas giant, your instruments picked up the signature of something that didn't belong: a physical anomaly deep within the planet's atmosphere. It was far too deep for your ship to reach, and your sturdiest probes only got close enough to glimpse its presence. You could get no nearer, so you did the only sensible thing: filed the anomaly away for future reference, a puzzle to be explored when Conjoiner science had advanced by a couple more centuries." I tossed aside the clump of grass. "But that advancement never came. History got in the way. The anomaly remained a footnote, too far away and too speculative to be worth the investment of a return expedition. Perhaps it was a mirage after all, a data ghost, or the result of some clever little trick of natural science, like a Brocken spectre. Interesting in its own right, but not likely to win a war." I paused. "But you were thinking about the wrong war."

"Wars used to occupy me," Nevil said, sighing. "Now they don't. Being here...being what I am, in the green becoming...you'd be surprised how my perspectives have changed. I was weary of it all near the end. Now I'm so far past the point of weariness you wouldn't even recognise my state of mind."

"I'm weary too," I admitted. "We've both been through it."

He gave a small chuckle. "Through the wars. Literally."

"But this is different. Those old wars were the result of human failings. We made them happen because we were too lazy to think our way to something better. We could have walked away at any point. But not this one."

He turned to me with a wry amusement crinkling the corners of his eyes: the lines of a man rather than a boy.

"You think such a distinction matters to me now?"

"It had better. The sanctuary that you've found here may not be as permanent as you imagine."

"The wolves won't touch these waters."

"I wondered if you remembered what brought you here."

"Hard to forget."

"Then put your faith in the wolves if you wish. Maybe there's an instruction in their deep programming to avoid harming Juggler planets. Maybe that's held in the past. But do you have absolute confidence that it still holds true, across all space and time? The wolves are still dangerous— we've seen ample evidence of that. But the fact that we got as far into space as we did, and for as long, shows that they're not as efficient as they used to be. Things have been going wrong inside them for millions of years—slow failings. Entropic breakdown. All systems succumb in the end, even ruthless machine ones. With that breakdown, all manner of programmed boundaries might become blurred."

"That's supposition."

"Perhaps. But you can't deny that damage has already been done to Ararat. The shattering of the moon, the infall of the debris, the enhanced volcanism and tectonic activity following that cataclysm. The seas have risen, islands been swallowed up."

"The sea will heal. You underestimate its resilience."

"But I don't underestimate your instinct for caution. There's a seed of doubt there, Nevil. Don't deny it."

He was silent for at least a minute. The waves crashed, the grasses swayed. The sky was the same grey as the sea, the wind relentless.

"You say you came with Scorp."

"I did."

"I didn't sense his presence."

"He's here. Or there. In the lagoon. We came with Glass...are you aware of Glass?"

"There was another. This wasn't her first time."

I nodded eagerly. "She came here looking for you, just as I did. I was rebuffed, and so was Glass. Do you remember something of her?"

"I looked inside her head."

"Now, or then?"

"The first time. She wasn't aware." He chuckled, amused by himself.

"I picked her apart like a fruit, studied what little was interesting, re-assembled her. Do you know who she is, Warren? Have you worked it out yet?"

"Glass isn't the puzzle I came to solve."

"Well, we don't always get to choose. She was with you on Mars. That's how far back her memories go. She was there, part of the extraction team. You remember, don't you? You came to rescue me."

"No."

"You don't remember?"

"No, I *do* remember. But Glass couldn't have been part of that. It's not possible. We left her for dead."

"You mean, after you killed her."

My next question left Charity at something of a loss.

"What planet would you say we're on?"

But for her nervousness, I think she might almost have laughed at the absurdity of my enquiry. I was being deliberately cruel. I was not normally cruel—ruthless, single-minded, yes—but now that the opportunity was here I found that I felt comfortable with cruelty; comfortable and more than a little regretful that I had not tried it sooner. It was like a garment that turned out to suit me more than I had expected it could; a surprise and a delight.

"This is...Mars, sir. We're on Mars."

"Can you be sure that this is Mars, and not a simulation?"

I caught her hesitation. "It's not a simulation, sir. I've been through the training simulations, all of us in Psychosurgical Ops have, and they're good...very good...but I'm certain that this is a real operation, happening in real-time, and that we're really on Mars."

"Well, you're right about that."

"Thank you, sir."

"Next question: is there air on Mars?"

"No, sir. I mean, almost none. There's barely any atmosphere and what there is isn't breathable. I know there's thicker, warmer air inside the Great Wall, but it's building up slowly, and what there is..." Charity faltered. "What there is...isn't really breathable yet. No one can survive anywhere on Mars, outside the pressurised compounds or capsules, unless they're in a suit."

"Well, there's the nub of it."

Hope made a quiet chuckling sound. "There it is."

"Suits are the problem, you see. If the extraction goes as planned—and thanks to your excellent work, Charity, there's no reason it won't—we've still got to get our prisoner, my brother, out of that camp and off the surface of Mars."

Hope put in: "What would come in handy, do you think?"

"A suit, sir. Sirs."

"It most certainly will," I said. "When we were younger, and used to go swimming in the loch near our home, my brother and I would sometimes play a game to see who could hold their breath underwater the longest." I dropped my voice to a confiding register. "I have to tell you that Nevil always won. He had far better lungs than me—or far better willpower; I'm not sure which. But even Nevil couldn't hold his breath long enough to get off Mars."

"Perhaps the Conjoiners will have been kind enough to leave one nearby," Hope said. "Pre-tanked and ready for just such an escape attempt. What do you think, Charity?"

"I...don't think they'd be likely to do that, sir."

"Nor do I," I agreed. "We could try and take one of their own suits off them, of course, but that won't be much good if we're in a hurry. Those suits aren't like anything we use."

"Neurally linked to the occupants," Hope said, nodding in agreement with me. "No conventional controls at all. If we had a day or so, we could patch in our own control harness—but the one thing we won't have is time. We have to get in and out very quickly—but you know that."

"I...do," Charity said. "It's why a fourth suit came with us. The one that didn't make it down. You said there'd be a workaround, sir."

"You're the workaround," I answered.

Charity became emboldened. "My mission deliverable lies in the administering of the neural protocols. I am an expert in that field. I was trained to deliver that element of the operation...and I did. I did what I was meant to do. The rest is...not my responsibility."

"And rest assured that we will always be indebted to you," I said.

Quickly, smoothly, I aimed the pistol and shot her through her visor.

Air geysered out through the hole in the glass, until Hope jammed his finger into the hole, giving me time to turn off the life-support valves and prevent further loss of closed-cycle pressure. The flow was reversed and the remaining air sucked back into the reservoir, allowing the suit to be dismantled and removed from Charity and then reassembled as an empty unit. Hope confirmed that the damage to the back of the helmet was minimal: the bullet had not broken through. The old visor was swapped for the new one: a simple field procedure that we had rehearsed until our fingers could do it blind.

It was good that we had brought spares.

"I hope she was right about those protocols being self-adaptive," Hope commented, as we peeled back the mat and dug out a shallow grave.

"I don't doubt for a minute that she did everything asked of her," I answered. "I meant what I told her: we're indebted. When all this is behind us, she'll get her due recognition. She deserves nothing less."

While we worked to bury the rapidly freezing corpse, I reflected on what had been required of me. If and when the operation was declassified, there would be no lie about what had happened here. The facts would be presented exactly as they were: I had shot one of our own, for the sake of the mission. It would not be passed off as an accident or the result of enemy fire. It was cold-blooded—on some level quite indefensible—murder, but there was, in my view, no moral distinction between my killing Charity and a military planner sending a group of soldiers into battle knowing that a third of them were bound to die.

It was just what had to be done.

"I wonder why she didn't say something when I put that visor down," Hope said.

"She was task-orientated. She lacked overview." Inside my helmet I smiled once. "There's no shame in that. We'll need both mindsets to win this war."

"I hope I've got the right one."

"I hope both of us have."

We completed the burial. After that, it was only a question of waiting. The storm had passed and the skies over the shelter were clear and cloudless. Hope and I had no knowledge of the weather conditions outside of our immediate locality, nor could any information be communicated to us, but it seemed likely that the clear conditions extended all the way to the Defection Capsule, now exposed again after the storm.

The storm had been our ally in two aspects: providing cover for our approach and retreat, but also blasting the ground after us, scouring away any traces we left. Still, there would only need to be one lingering hand or stilt print to alert the Conjoiners that someone had been at the capsule, and I was in no doubt at all that they would be looking for signs of interference.

Equally, I was sure the prize would be too tempting for them to ignore.

I shook my head.

"No. We would never have done that."

"Of course we would, brother. It was war." He stared out to sea, lost in the past. "The Coalition for Neural Purity: doesn't that suggest a certain...self-righteous certainty of purpose? And you and I...what part of that were we? The Knights of Cydonia? Masters of war, masters of Mars? We did whatever was needed. Murdering one of our own, even a brilliant, loyal and courageous volunteer, because she needed to die for me to survive? Not a moment's hesitation."

"If I killed Charity..." And this time I stopped short of absolute denial, remembering Glass's insistence that I had already murdered her once.

"No if. Would you like to see it, brother? Would you like to remember, properly, what it was you did?"

"No—" I began to reply.

"The trouble is, I think you're quite a way past the point of getting to have that choice." He added helpfully: "Let me reach into you a little further. Let me strip away the last of those mental blockades, so that you can finally know yourself."

"Nevil, please..."

He laughed aside my pleading. I felt him delving into my soul, flicking aside my feeble screens and blinds. Shredding and discarding them like the thin, disposable phantasms of self-denial they had been. Until Charity came back to me, her face behind the visor, the snapping trapdoor logic of that moment, the cold, clear realisation of what I was about to do to her.

The merest distress in her eyes. The tiniest bend to her mouth, as she began to frame a counter-argument, a new plan for our consideration. The squeeze of my finger on the trigger. The release, the recoil. The bullet's gyring trajectory: barrel to thin vacuum, thin vacuum to visor glass. The visor puncturing as the bullet spun through it. The shards of glass.

The bullet's continuation. Into air, moist and warm, even as it sucked itself out into the pitiful atmosphere of Mars. Its progress into the first part of her face. Into skin, into the flesh beneath her skin, into muscle and bone and frontal cortex.

Her mouth still struggling to form a word, because nerve signals were still reaching her larynx.

He looped the memory. Made it play back over and again, slower and more horribly each time, until he had eroded me to a sobbing core. A moral remnant that finally understood what it had done to another human being.

Finally understood. Finally knew.

"How did she come back?"

He answered matter-of-factly: "The Conjoiners found her, eventually. Brought her corpse into the nest and took it upon themselves to see what could be salvaged of her. A kind of pet project: an internally run Conjoiner experiment in radical neural reconstruction. Think of the benefits. If they could bring her back to life, after days of exposure, after no end of damage to her brain, then the same principles of memory and personality reconstruction could be applied to their own wounded."

"It doesn't sound all that different to what they did to those of ours they took prisoner. Dragged them to the recruitment theatres, opened up their skulls, stuffed Conjoiner machinery into their heads. Instant conversion to the cause." I paused. "But Glass isn't one of them. She has all the gifts of the Conjoined, but she acts alone."

"That was another aspect of the experiment. Being Conjoined gave them strength in numbers. Gave us, I should say."

I nodded, reminded of my brother's ultimate defection to Galiana's movement.

"But like you, Glass was not quite one of them."

"In my case, I made a deliberate decision not to commit to full Transenlightenment. I thought I could be more useful, more agile, if I retained a degree of neural autonomy. So it proved, I think. That same autonomy was imposed on Glass by design, from the outset. And made more extreme. It would be an exaggeration to say that she was given engineered sociopathy...but also not entirely divorced from the facts."

"What were they hoping to achieve?"

"Insurance, I suppose. One loyal to their cause—our cause—but who could act independently, far from the mental support of other Conjoiners. A lone agent, sent out into the world. Doubtless there were others. But perhaps only Glass has come to us across the centuries."

I reflected on his words, picking up sand and allowing it to trickle through my fingers. I wondered if the grains were sufficient to count the years that Glass had been travelling.

"When she found me on Michaelmas, I thought her only interest in me was as a means of defeating the wolves. But that was only half of it. The rest of it was punishment. She knew what I had done, and she required me to remember it too."

"You think of this as punishment? Isn't the truth supposed to set us free?"

I looked down, my eyes stung by the wind. "I was a good man on Michaelmas."

"You were a lie. Now you have to live with what you are, not with some comforting fiction." Nevil shifted, as if he was getting cramp from sitting in the same position. "I'll tell you what. Are you really serious about wanting the name of that world?"

"We need the location, the identity of the ice giant Glass called

Charybdis. *Scythe*—the ship we came in—has the means to reach whatever you saw inside that atmosphere."

"To what purpose?"

"Glass believes you saw a Nestbuilder vehicle. We know they exist; you
saw their relics littering this planet."

"Relics don't bode well."

"Glass's intelligence suggests that the Nestbuilders are the only species
within this sector of the galaxy to have attained any sort of technological
parity with the Inhibitors."

"Then why haven't they wiped them out already?"

"It seems they prefer a strategy of managed containment. They have
a stick that can poke the wolves, but if they use it too many times the
wolves will evolve a countermeasure. So for the Nestbuilders the best
approach is to survive by stealth and only use their weaponry as a last
resort, even if that means accepting the occasional defeat. Think of the
weapon as a supremely powerful antibiotic, to be used only in direst need,
lest the bacteria develop resistance."

"And the name of this weapon?"

"An Incantor. That's Glass's translation: the nearest approximation in
human terms."

"And your aim is…what? To extract the Incantor from this wreck."

"Better than that: to harvest the information that lets us make our own
Incantor, using hypometric technology as an intermediary step. Once
we've made one, we can make others."

"Ambitious."

"There is no other course."

"Doesn't it concern you that the Nestbuilders won't take kindly to this
misuse of their technology?"

"They shouldn't have been careless with their secrets in the first place.
We won't use it indiscriminately. But if it's a choice between extinction
tomorrow, and incurring the wrath of the Nestbuilders, I'll take the wrath.
If all we do is push the wolves back out from this corner of space, we'll still
have bought time. Besides, Glass told me something else."

Nevil looked at me with the first real interest since the start of our
meeting.

"Oh?"

"There's something that helps us—some leverage. Something she knows
that could work to our advantage when it comes to securing the Incantor."

"A bargaining ploy?"

I shifted, uncomfortable with my ignorance. "Something like that."

"Glass knows a lot about these Nestbuilders. A strange amount, considering how sparse our own knowledge base was at the time of my demise. Almost everything...apart from that location."

"Glass only tells me what she needs to, and then only under duress. Will you help us?"

Nevil deliberated. I wondered how much of that was real, and how much was for no other reason than to torment me. This had never occurred to me: that I might reach him, but not make a persuasive enough case.

"How did you take to Scorp?"

I sifted through the possible answers I might offer, finally settling on the truth. "Not well, to begin with."

"An aversion to pigs?"

"An aversion to his having an aversion to me. He didn't believe any part of the story he was presented with. Certainly didn't believe I could ever be half the man you'd been. He made no secret of the fact he considered me unworthy of his friendship."

"Yet by some means, you've turned him around."

"I put my life on the line. He was ready to put himself forward for a slow, painful death. I wouldn't let him face that alone, or without an escape plan. We made it out and obtained the technology that *Scythe* needed to reach the Nestbuilder vessel."

"You think that made him your friend?"

I shook my head. "No, I wouldn't be so callow as to imagine his opinion could be altered by a single deed. But it was the start of something. I know I'll never be your equal, in his eyes. But I think he's accepted that I'm not an impostor."

"I should have liked to have spoken to Scorp again. To have thanked him for being there, at the end. To have wished him well, and listened to his voice again. He was a better man than any of us."

"Let me be the one to pass on that message."

"Do you think you'd be up to it?"

"I wronged you very badly, in ways that can't ever be undone. But I can start to become the better human being I always believed I was on Michaelmas. Let me carry your friendship back to Pinky."

"There's a small problem with that." He began to rise, pushing himself up by his knees. "I made you a promise, Warren. I said that if you ever came back here, I'd kill you. Now, if a man breaks his word..."

I rose as well, the cold seeping into my spine. I had allowed myself to believe I was getting somewhere with him, that there might be a way to convince him. "Nevil. Put aside what's happened between us. Humanity matters more than a couple of feuding brothers. Give me the information. Once we have the Incantor, I'll return here. You can do as you will with me. But allow me this stay of execution. And if that isn't acceptable to you, find a way to pass the information directly to Glass."

"I still don't know that you really came with Scorp. Why should I trust your word? The Inhibitors got into others. They could have got into you, or Glass, or anyone. You might want that information so you can finally destroy any chance of the Incantor falling into human hands."

"It's not that!" I pleaded.

"Then prove it! The last thing I said. Out of those that survived that day, only Scorp was there. Only he knew. He'd remember. And if he meant me to trust you, he'd have told you that word."

A quiet anger rose in me. I was wearying of these brotherly games. "You may have become the better man, Nevil, but you were always a monster to me. Nothing's changed."

"So you don't know."

I shook my head, sneering. "These sands? That sea? That grey, dreary sky? I always knew where we were, you stupid fool. This is Scotland. Where we were born, where we grew up. The word is Scotland."

Two figures appeared from the mist behind us. They were indistinct; grey silhouettes. But I thought that one was an older woman and one a younger, and the two of them gestured for Nevil Clavain to turn from the iron sea.

"Scotland," I repeated, more softly.

Nevil nodded. Without seeming to change—some trick of perception being worked on the deep architecture of my brain—the boy became a man, and the man became very old. His eyes were infinitely cold, infinitely patient and infinitely sorrowful. He had seen and endured more than any soul should.

"You'll remember what needs to be remembered," he said, and turned to rejoin Galiana and Felka.

I came up for air and gasped the first sweet, life-giving breath into my lungs. I was alive; I had been spared. And although I could not momentarily bring it to mind, I knew that there was a piece of knowledge inside me which had not been there before, and which I would soon be able to express.

I wiped green scum from my eyes and trod water, breathing heavily, pleased not to be dead but not sure that I had the strength to keep myself from drowning. I looked around through stinging, watery eyes, squinting into the trembling light. The lagoon's green walls had passed away. I could see nothing of the node, and nothing of the weather system. With no other reference points, it was impossible to say which of us had moved. I could not allow myself to die out here, but my limbs felt heavy and my muscles nearly empty of strength. How absurd it would be to have succeeded in my mission with Nevil, then to perish before ever communicating the information to my allies. But that was exactly the kind of sick joke the universe had no qualms about playing on its inhabitants.

No, I vowed. Not here, not now. I was going to live. While I had the energy to hold a conscious thought, I had the energy to swim. Or at least keep myself afloat.

Something glinted at the edge of my vision. It came and went, bobbing on the waves, snatched in and out of view. The boat. If I could see it at all it had to be near, but in that moment nothing had ever seemed so distant. A wave slapped me and I took in a mouthful of water. I coughed it out, spluttering, but not quickly enough to stop some of going down my windpipe. A velvety darkness lapped at the edge of my thoughts. The boat was gone and I wondered if I had imagined it. Then it was back again. I fixed its position against a pattern of clouds, hoping neither the boat nor the clouds would move against each other too swiftly, and struck out in that direction. My swimming was so feeble that any current would have negated it completely, but the boat did not seem to be moving, so I hoped that any movement of the waters would act us on equally.

It had been a smudge of tin-coloured metal, identifiable as the boat only because no other artificial thing could be anywhere near me. Now at last I could discern more of its details. I was hoping to see Pinky, perhaps not yet aware of me, but waiting.

The boat was on its back. No wonder it had been so hard to see, as it moved up and down on the swell. I stared at it in shock, unable to accept what I was seeing. Not after all this. Not *this*.

"Scorp..." I mouthed, before spitting out water.

In that moment I hated everything about this world. I hated the sea, the Jugglers, the minds within them. The capricious and unforgiving tyrant that was my brother, and the uncaring will that had allowed this to happen. But since the boat was still my only point of sanctuary, and I retained enough of my own will not to want to drown, I kept swimming. Perhaps, as a mirage within a mirage, the boat would invert itself as I got nearer, and I would see my friend the pig beckoning me to close the distance.

I swam, and swam. The boat became more constant in its presence, but nothing about it changed. Like some demonstration of Zeno's paradox, my energy halved with each halving of the distance yet to swim. I was going to have to shatter some infinities to make it to that doubtful objective.

How long it took me, I have no idea. In all likelihood the entire interval between my coming up for air and touching the boat was no more than minutes in extent. But there was room in my struggle and despair for endless days.

I stayed in the water for a long while, holding onto the boat but without the strength to do more than that. Intuition told me that I had no hope of turning the hull around again, but when I regained some tiny measure of strength in my limbs I still tried it. The hull was much too heavy for a lone swimmer to tip over. Then I gathered a deep breath and poked my head under the water and up into the inverted hull, where there was still a pocket of air. I had very little hope of finding Pinky there, and he was absent. So was all of our equipment. No matter how carefully we thought it had been stowed, it had not survived the capsizing.

The water was starting to feel cold. I could not survive immersion for very much longer. With one last exertion I ducked out again, heaved myself up onto the boat's belly, hooking an ankle around the keel and stretching as far as I could until my fingers found one of the mounts for the oars. I dragged myself onto that baking metal, sprawled face down against it, content that if I had to die then at least I would not give myself to the ocean. Then I lay in a fog of half consciousness, broken and exhausted, and with too many impressions storming the edges of my thoughts for any one of them to gain precedence over the others. Somewhere in them was the realisation that when my fingers scratched against the boat's side they had been tipped with black.

But there was not enough left of me to think deeply about that.

There was sun and light, cold and sea spray. Straddling the boat, face down on the bobbing swell, living by the merest thread, I grew weaker rather than stronger. By the time they came I had nothing to offer by way of resistance. They emerged from the waters, pressing webbed hands to the boat's flanks, studying me with those inscrutable proud-whiskered faces that were half human, half seal. I think I screamed, or at least mouthed some failing protestation. But one of them pressed a finger to my lips as if silencing a child against the night's terrors, and by some strange persuasion I was moved to submission.

Then they swept me into the darkening waters.

CHAPTER TWENTY-EIGHT

I had feverish dreams of stars.

Victorine was standing on the kitchen chair, precariously balanced, paintbox in one hand, brush in the other. She was dabbing stars onto the ceiling: speckly smears of blue or gold or red, like little painted flowers. They glowed where she left them, as if in her meagre assortment of improvised materials were marvellous luminous pigments that she had never discovered until now. Or perhaps never deemed worthy of use until she came to make this starscape.

The stars floated in a dizzying trickery of depth. Rather than being fixed to the ceiling's plane, each had its own distance, its own implied luminosity. It was as if the ceiling had soared away to an infinite elevation, with the stars suspended by threads. Looking up at her patient work, my head swam with vertigo. My feet loosened from the floor, as if I were about to fall into that aching vastness.

"I made you some stars," Victorine said, looking down from her perch. "They'll help you get to where you need to go."

"I made you a machine," I answered, as if that were the only possible response.

Later I would learn that three full days passed between my entering the lagoon and my return to proper, lasting consciousness. I had no reason to doubt the accuracy of that, but if I had been told it had been three hours, or three eternities, I do not think I would have quibbled. I had been stripped down to the components of sentience by the Pattern Jugglers, dismantled and remade like a broken toy, and somewhere in that process all continuities of time had been severed.

Beyond the immediate fact of not being dead, or in the process of drowning, or being slowly mummified on the back of the boat, I arrived at some qualified observations. I was in a room or chamber of some kind. There were walls around me and a ceiling above and the air was cool but not so cold as to be uncomfortable. Something of the room's pale textures and curving contours (revealed by a high-placed window, elaborately and pleasingly fretted, and set with chips of coloured glass) brought to mind the conch structures we had surveyed, and begun to prepare for our own use, at First Camp. But I did not think I was in any part of First Camp. There had been nothing like this room, and none of its furnishings bore the stamp of the modular components and materials I had authorised *Scythe* to manufacture. There was a bed, on which I rested, and near the bed two long, sinuous, chair-like forms made up of vertebrae, pelvic girdles, ribs and flukes. There was a thing like a low table, crouched on a quartet of mottled crab's legs, and a sort of dresser or cabinet pressed into the wall's concavity, and seemingly made of a whale's baleen screens. Adhering to the wall at random intervals were lacy accretions of bone or coral, forming winding, branching chains.

The room rocked gently. The light coming through the windows, stained by the coloured facets, wandered up and down the walls and floors on a lulling rhythm.

I had come through something daunting and my reserves of endurance had been tested to their limits. I also knew that I had rested long enough and was ready to move back into the world. I got out of the bed, limbs aching only slightly from the suddenness of my exertions. Keeping a sheet wrapped around myself—there was still a dampness to the air—I shuffled to the wall, until I was just under the lowest part of the window. I stretched to level my eyes with the lowest facet, and through its green tinting I saw waves, clouds, and the edge of another conch-like form, but which did not seem firmly anchored to the one I was inside. Although they had been used and modified in different ways, these were clearly the same kinds of alien structure that had been used in the land-borne settlement.

In the wall behind me, a baleen-fretted door swung open.

Pinky came in. He was dressed as I remembered, and seemed no worse for wear. He appraised me guardedly, then made a gesture back in the direction of the bed.

"They want you rested. It's good that you're up and about, but they have a good idea how long it takes to recover from a Juggler encounter."

"They?" My voice sounded off, so I touched a hand to my throat, as if there were something there that needed to be cleared. "You're alive, Pinky. I can't tell you how glad I am. When I saw that upturned boat..."

"And knowing my capabilities as a swimmer." He nodded, still giving off a wariness. "Please humour them, Glass. We don't want to start coming over as bad guests, not this early in negotiations. They've been kinder than we had any right to expect, especially after those little

368

misunderstandings out at sea, but we don't want to push our luck."

"I'm not..." I stopped, already questioning myself.

"You're not what?"

"I was going to say that I'm not Glass. But that would be silly. I am Glass." Moving back to the bed, my gaze settled on my fingertips again. "I *am* her. I am Glass."

"I'm glad you're in no doubt."

"I also think something odd may have happened." Suddenly unsteady on my feet—it was either the room's movements or the undermining of my own certainties—I lowered back onto the bed. It was only a partial respite, since the bed moved with the room. I felt seasick, unmoored from myself. "What happened to Warren?"

"Stink never came back."

"Are you sure?"

"The storm got worse. All hell broke loose in that lagoon. I cowered down and tried to ride it out, but eventually I got separated from the boat. I thrashed around a bit, tried to keep from drowning. I don't remember too much of what happened after that, except that when I came around two of the mariners were keeping me afloat. I don't know how I got to them or what had happened to the node. They spoke, a little. Just enough to stop me thrashing. They weren't the ones we'd run into earlier. Probably for the best, given what we did to them." Pinky lowered himself into the strangely shaped chair. It was no more suited to his frame than mine, and his legs and feet dangled awkwardly to either side of it. "They were only ever trying to keep us out of trouble. Turns out they've established a rapport with the Jugglers, a sort of diplomatic channel. They know when it's a good time to swim, and when it's not such a good time. Guess we ought to have taken a little more notice when we had the chance."

"You think we lost Warren?"

"Only two people came out of that storm alive, Glass. You and I. They were looking for you when you reached the boat. By then, they'd already found his body."

"He didn't die, Pinky. He's part of me."

His snout puckered. He cocked his head, eyeing me as if he might be the victim of a particularly tasteless prank. "I'm just a pig, and I don't really know what can and can't happen when you dance with the Jugglers. But you have to admit that's going to take a little persuasion."

"I met Nevil. I was with him, and I told him the word only you could have known. Could...Glass...have known any part of that?"

"There's no telling what Glass did or didn't know." He pinched at his brow. "Wait. Who's talking now? Who do you think you are?"

"I think I'm both Glass and Warren," I answered carefully, feeling I owed him that much consideration. "I have clear memories of swimming in that lagoon, Glass next to me. Then I lost sight of her, and you. But I also remember being Glass before any of this began. I remember floating in space, waiting for him to find me. I remember being trapped by John the Revelator, and thinking I'd die alone in that room, with only a mad captain and his reanimated corpses for company. Hearing that song he sang over and over again, about opening the seventh seal…" I shuddered, as if those threads of memory were clinging around me, dragging me back into that horror. "That was me. That was also me. There's no easy answer to what I've become, Scorp, nothing simple and binary."

He nodded slowly. I think he understood, or at least believed me. There was no earthly reason for me to lie, and no reasonable case in which my dual identity could be put down to post-traumatic confusion.

"There you go, calling me Scorp again. Dragging me back into a past I'd sooner forget about."

"I didn't even think about it. I've known you a long time—long enough for names not to matter."

"I'll be the judge of that. All right. Accepting this, just for now, next question. Excuse me if I'm blunt, even for a pig. Why the fuck has this happened?"

I laughed. "Excuse me if I'm equally blunt. I have no fucking idea, my friend. Except that Nevil made a vow to kill Warren if he ever came back to Ararat. Perhaps this is his way of honouring that promise, in word if not in spirit."

"Did Glass get a say?"

"I remember nothing of what happened to Glass after we separated in the lagoon. But we do know that Glass was already badly damaged. Perhaps this was the best possible outcome for both of us: stitching Warren into Glass to make a whole personality again."

Pinky shook his head. "Just when I thought the universe was done throwing weird shit at me."

I met his observation with a half smile. "It gets stranger. I think there's a little bit of Nevil in with us. Not his personality, but a few shards of what made him. Enough to help us with what needs to be done next."

"Got to say, the old man really did a number on you."

"But we got what we came for. I know where to find Charybdis. It's an ice giant planet in the Zeta Tucanae system, about six and half light-years from Ararat—say a little under eight years of flight time. As soon as *Scythe* is ready, and the refugees are established…why are you looking at me like that?"

"We need to talk about the refugees. And our hosts."

"That was going to be my next question. Are they as friendly as you make them seem?"

"Allowing for the odd slip-up in communications, I think they're on our side."

"I suppose that's better than the alternative. Who are they, and how did they get here?"

"It's complicated, and I think you still need to rest awhile. We agreed not to wear you out in one go. Whatever you are, whatever's in you, you need to be strong."

"Who is 'we'?"

"Probably Rose and Barras are with me. We call ourselves the Temporary Floating Embassy. The mariners call this place Marl—it's not their only floating settlement, but I think it's one of the biggest. The others are still at First Camp. When the mariners saw our boat, and realised what was happening, they sent another party back to the island to make contact."

"Why did they wait?"

"Until we set out in the boat, they didn't have a clue we'd even landed on the planet. We didn't see them, they didn't see us." He shrugged. "What's done is done. Our hosts have tried to make us comfortable. Me, I've been seasick nearly the whole time. Have you any idea how much puke comes out of a pig? Even I'm a little appalled by it."

"They say it helps if you widen your stance."

Pinky pushed himself up from the chair. "I'll have some food sent to you. I hope you like the colour green, because that's all you'll be eating and drinking for a few days. Most of what comes out of you'll be green as well."

"I can't wait. And concerning the refugees?"

"Eat, rest, and then we'll talk." He was about to leave the room when he turned back. "I don't know what you are, exactly. But I'm working on the assumption we're better off with you than without you."

"So am I." I paused, remembering something. "Pinky?"

"Yes?"

"Nevil said he wanted to thank you. He said he misses you, and was glad it was you with him at the end. He said you were the best of us."

He was right: I needed more rest than I realised. I both knew and did not know the limits of my own body. There could be nothing more familiar than my own flesh, and at the same time nothing more alien. When the oddness tripped me up, it was Warren behind my eyes. When Warren stopped dwelling on himself, accepting what was absent and what was

371

new, it was Glass gaining dominance. We flickered between each other like a spinning mirror. Somewhere in that dazzle was the person we might be merging into, perhaps with whatever figment of himself Nevil had lodged within this shimmering union. It was a peculiar condition to find myself in, and not one I would have chosen. But it was preferable to non-existence.

Food was brought to me at intervals, and I ate and rested. I was given the means to wash myself, and when the need arose I made use of the toilet that I found within the dresser, which turned out to be a sort of disposal chute, funnelling my waste into the sea beneath us. I squatted over it awkwardly at first, easily losing my balance, but after those initial trials I came to accept its essential utility. Let what came from the sea return to the sea.

Pinky brought in the food most of the time, and if it was not him than it was Barras or Probably Rose. The mariners had brought them here (wherever we were) aboard a boat or raft that used the wind for propulsion and which, with the right handling and sea conditions, was hardly any slower than the powered boat that had carried us from First Crossing. But when I tried to get more out of them concerning their journey, and what exactly had been discussed before my revival, they answered only in the tersest of terms.

I did not blame them. Pinky had been to this world before and knew something of the Pattern Jugglers and the unpredictability of their gifts. He could believe what the others found harder to accept, with so little proof. Barras and Probably Rose had no trouble accepting that I was Glass, because I looked like her. But when I addressed them as Warren, the same voice still came out of my mouth. It was no help pleading that I had the memories of a dead man, a man whose body had been fished from the sea. They had seen some of Glass's capabilities (mine) and had no trouble believing that she (I) could have accessed and internalised my (his) memories, and that what seemed to be Warren (me) was merely an adept piece of mimicry. Not that they voiced those thoughts to me, but I could read it in their eyes. Would I have believed myself? I wondered. Almost certainly not. And could I have offered anything by way of corroboration? Not a hope.

My only advocate remained Pinky, because he had known Warren a little, and known Nevil very well, and by his testimony the doubters might be won around. In the meantime, all I could do was tolerate their guardedness with good humour and understanding, and do nothing that might undermine their slowly changing opinion of me.

It was clear that I was being isolated from our hosts for the time being, and clear also (from the questions I asked, and the evasive answers I almost always received) that some difficult business remained to be resolved where the matter of First Camp was concerned. Wisely, I stopped pressing against an unmoving wall. I concentrated on regaining my energies and satisfying myself that my broken body had indeed been remade and the battles within me put to rest.

This seemed clear. I remembered being very ill indeed. I remembered fighting to conceal the severity of it from Warren and the others, lest they lose all confidence in me as an ally. The hostile entities which had broken through my defences on Yellowstone had been close to killing me. But they had been purged by the Jugglers, and I felt clear and clean.

Nearly. There was still something inside me, wasn't there? Something lodged deep. But I had put that there, and like house cleaners the Jugglers had understood to leave that one precious thing intact. They had dusted around the priceless heirloom, but never touched it.

I stopped. It was as if a clock gear within me had snagged on a broken tooth.

Oh, I'm sorry, Warren. You didn't know about that? I must have omitted to mention it.

Or omitted to remember it yourself. We each had our secrets, Glass. Mine was the lie I chose to live, the bed of false memories I made for myself. Yours was the thing lodged inside you. You might have put it there. But it became such a part of you that you eventually forgot what you'd done. What you'd allowed into yourself.

I didn't forget...

One of us gave a wry chuckle.

But you didn't exactly remember, *either.*

Pinky gave off a controlled nervous energy as he took me along the winding, conch-walled passages of Marl which led to the others. Evidently such negotiations as had been proceeding were still at a delicate stage and an indiscretion from me might undo days of good work. But I was in no mind to ruin the efforts of the Temporary Floating Embassy. All I wanted was to leave Ararat before the knowledge I held melted away.

"They have language and writing all of their own," he was saying. "And you can see where there are little bits of Canasian and Russish and Norte jammed into the pudding. But it's not really comprehensible to any of us."

"So they're derived from human stock. A ship must have come here, with genetically augmented colonists, pre-engineered to survive in the ocean. Something went wrong: the ship must have crashed, or abandoned them, and they slipped back into the Dark Ages. Only now are they rebuilding some kind of aquatic culture."

"Wow," he said, looking at me with amazement. "That's so far from what happened it's almost beautiful. These aren't colonists, Glass." He paused in his stride. "Glass? Do I call you Glass, or Warren? We're going to have to help me sort that one out. I'm just a pig: I'm not wired to deal with this shit."

"Nevil called him War, when they were boys. Now War and Glass are in the same body." I thought on that for a moment. "So call me Warglass. I like that. It makes me think of something fused at high temperatures, a substance that wouldn't otherwise exist."

"All right," he said doubtfully, going along with me for the sake of argument. "Warglass it is. Who is speaking now?"

"I'm not sure it matters."

"Is it one person inside your head, or two?"

"Two becoming one."

"That's a great help."

"It's the best I can do. I feel as if we're two fluids poured into the same container. We each have access to each other's memories, and the more that sharing happens, the less it matters that we were ever two different people. The fluids are mixing. Our voices are becoming one. That's why it makes sense for us to have a single name."

He walked on, clearly unsatisfied by my answer. "Well, Warglass. News for you: these aren't colonists who arrived on Ararat after the fall of First Camp. These are the survivors. Or rather, the descendants. These are the people we left behind."

"It's not possible," I stated flatly. "I was there, Pinky. I remember."

"Ah, so now it's Stink stepping up?"

"No, it's me, Warglass, but with access to two sets of memories. The people who stayed behind on Ararat were human, not merfolk. They had no technology that could have let them reshape their bodies, and no time to do it even if they had."

"You're right on that score. They didn't do it to themselves. The sea did."

"By which you mean the Pattern Jugglers?"

"Probably, but don't go looking for hard evidence. You won't find it. It's been a hundred and eighty-odd years since we left them behind. To us, it's recent history. But these people have lived through it the slow way, generation after generation. We're six or seven of them beyond any direct memory of what happened here. What they have is oral testimony, songs, stories, pictures." He stiffened in his stride. "Don't judge them for that.

374

They could have thrown me back into the sea, but they didn't."

I patted his shoulder. "They know an ally when they see one. As did I. Did *we*. I never did thank you for smoothing the way with the Jugglers, but consider a debt owed to you."

"Pigs don't hold anyone in debt."

"Why not?"

"Bitter experience. We tend to die before anyone has a chance to pay us back."

"And yet, I have a distinct feeling you'll outlive all of us."

During my confinement I had formed a tentative view as to the nature of this place. Pinky had said that it was like a boat that never went anywhere, by which he meant a floating structure that was tethered to the seabed, or at least anchored against drift by some means. In fact, it was a whole flotilla of such objects. The main part of each was a large conch, watertight enough to bob up and down on the waves, and of which some larger or smaller portion remained permanently submerged. Some of these conches were fused together, so that they moved as a whole, even while trapping areas of open water between them. We stepped between these fixed conches by archways or precariously narrow hump-backed footbridges, with balustrades that were too low for my liking. At times it was a thirty- or forty-metre drop down to the sea. Evidently the mariners had no fear of falling, since they could survive almost any plunge into water.

I saw glimpses of them below, swimming in the enclosed waters, tending rafts, fixing nets, scrambling high up the sides of the conches on trellises. I heard their barked instructions, their laughter, and their shanties.

The other conches, especially the outlying ones—the community was about the size of one chamber in Sun Hollow—were only loosely tethered, and moved on independent swells, one rising where another might be falling. They were lashed together by larger, stronger versions of the material that had been strung up to trap our boat. Ropes and nets of this stuff were used in abundance, lending the conches the look of white shells which had been lathered in masses of sticky, cloying seaweed.

Nowhere did I see anything that depended on power to function. There were complicated devices—drawbridges, locks, winches and cranes—but they all used muscle power or some clever arrangement of waterwheels and water reservoirs. They were fashioned of something like wood or bamboo, stiff and green-veined, but which I presumed was some marine organism that could be harvested and worked in a similar manner, and nothing like anything growing on the fringes of First Camp. Where I saw metal, or some artificial material which must have been scavenged from the abandoned colony, it was used with deliberation and care: they knew it to be precious and irreplaceable. Elsewhere there was much use of bone, or the baleen-like material, and a kind of coral-like cement which I presumed to have been built up in laborious layers, by hand, to form the bridges and other structural flourishes which were not part of the original conches. Once in place, it must have set rock-hard and appeared perfectly strong enough for the uses it was put to. They had fire and light, dispensed by candles and lanterns, which seemed to burn strongly and enduringly, and emitted a sweet smell as they combusted, but I could only guess at the materials and methods behind them. Was the glass in the windows and lanterns really glass, or just some translucent, tinted natural substance, like a kind of keratin?

There were a hundred things about which I could only speculate. What was clear to me was these were not a primitive people. They were clever and resourceful, with an innate understanding of many subtle principles of engineering and geometry. All the same, I could have been looking at civic amenities from any point in the last four thousand years. It was an impressive and defiant act of survival, a means of living that kept the mariners beneath the threshold of interest of the Inhibitors. By the same token, though, they had surrendered their lives to the moods of a world, to the capricious governance of weather and climate and geological catastrophe. They could persist here, I thought, and in some comfort, but that was all. They could never make their world safer, or avert destruction from the skies, or escape to some better sanctuary. But it was community, and life, and since I had lost one and nearly lost the other, I was moved by their resilience and adaptability.

At length, we emerged into a large, high-ceilinged chamber lit by grander versions of the coloured windows in my stateroom. The space was ornately decorated, with relief work formed from the same rocky cement I had seen earlier, only this time employed purely for ornamentation. Between pediments and curlicues of layered-on cement were friezes, marked on the walls in blue, gold and turquoise pigments, and depicting marine men and women engaged in acts of drama and antiquity, as if I looked upon a history that was millennia deep, rather than a scattering of decades. There was writing, too: chains of winding, antennae-like symbols garlanding the drawings, some of which snagged my eye with the illusion of meaning. Somewhere in the lineage of this writing were language forms known to me, ghostly traces that my brain detected, but which had been shattered and recombined so many times that I could read no part of them. Yet I knew that human minds were behind this work.

Barras and Probably Rose were waiting, along with about twenty mariners, including a pair of enthroned eminences who I took to be their leaders. Their chairs were mounted on a raised dais of conch material, with the other mariners flanking them at different levels in some kind of ceremonial hierarchy. Other than the seated pair, all were standing. I had only seen them in the water before, or from far above, and had not really formed any definite opinion as to whether they were capable of walking upright. But out of the water's protection they were not so far from baseline humanity as I might have imagined. Their skins were dark, but mottled with flecks of grey, green and gold. Their fingers and toes had been adapted for swimming, and their chests and shoulders were wide; each of them had a thick, muscular neck that supported their head like a plinth. They had large dark eyes, slitted noses, whiskery faces, a sort of mane, often green-stained, but beyond those generalities each was an individual, and I soon made tentative guesses as to age and gender. Their clothes, such as they were, consisted at the minimum of a skirt or loin cloth of some green woven material. To this might be added augmentations of woven plates, almost like armour, but which surely had only a decorative function, as well as diagonally worn belts and various sheaths and pouches containing weapons and tools, including two of the spearlike stanchions that had been used in the attempted trapping of our boat.

"The ones on the thrones are the king and queen," Pinky told me in a whisper. "Least, that's the nearest we've got to their titles. The man is Rindi, the woman Ivril. They seem to run things equally between them. As far as we can tell there's a ruling lineage going back about seventy or eighty years, when there was some sort of upheaval. That's not even half their history, but they talk as if it were somewhere back in the Bronze Age." He gave me a gentle shove. "Introduce yourself. Speak slowly, and their interpreters will pick up enough to be going on with. And if you want my advice, go easy on the two fluids in one head bit. We're trying to build some bridges here, not send our allies running for the hills."

"I'm that unnerving?"

"You were unnerving before any of this. Both of you were."

I stepped a little closer to the raised thrones. The king and queen nodded at my approach, but said nothing.

"I am Glass," I said, touching a hand to my chest. "At least, that's the name I used to be known by." I directed an apologetic shrug at Pinky, for I was about to do exactly what he had cautioned against. "But I am also Warren Clavain, brother to Nevil. I think you must know Nevil. He's been a part of your ocean for longer than you've swum in these seas."

The queen—Ivril—leaned forward in her throne. One of the other

377

mariners approached her and whispered into her ear. She nodded at intervals: that gesture, at least, had transmitted itself through all the changes wrought on these people. Ivril regarded me as she listened, then spoke back to the interpreter. She kept her voice low, but the fragments that reached me were nothing I understood.

The interpreter turned to face me. He spoke slowly, in a high, querulous, thick-accented tone that still required great concentration on my part to decipher.

"You are...two...in one?"

"Yes, and it's as strange for me as it must be for you. If it makes things any easier, I'll be taking a single name from now on. You may call me Warglass, if you wish. The first part of my name is the form that Nevil Clavain knew his brother by, when they were small. His name was Warren: War for short. Glass is the short form of Hourglass, who was the woman who used to inhabit this body."

I waited for this to be translated. It was slow process, with much back-and-forth conferring between the aides.

Queen Ivril's answer came: "You...are...blood...to...Green Man?"

I nodded sombrely. "Yes. I am—or was—blood to Nevil Clavain. His brother. And I saw him, in the Juggler node."

A further exchange took place between Ivril and her interpreter.

"We warned you. Green Man is angry. Angry and...powerful. This season not good season."

"We could not wait for a better season. But I am sorry that we misunderstood your good intentions." I paused, wondering how far I could go before I strained the abilities of the interpreters. They had a frowning, scholarly, faintly pedantic look to them. I supposed that they were mariners who had made a point of tracking the shifts in their language from its origins, and who retained enough knowledge of the old forms to be able to piece together my meaning and offer faltering translations of their own. "But you are right," I continued. "My brother was angry, and he was not happy to see me. That is my fault, or rather the fault of the part of me that was once Warren. Warren wronged Nevil and was warned not to visit him again. I came here once before, you see. Perhaps you were already here, swimming in these seas, but I did not see you and I do not think you saw me. If you had, you would have tried to stop me then."

"Many have come. Many have failed."

"I did not fail," I replied. "Not this time. There was something Warren wanted of his brother, and now I have it."

"We found you with nothing."

"He told me of a place, a world, that my friends and I must travel to. About eight years of flight from here, around another star, one called Zeta Tucanae." I nodded in the direction the play of light through the windows told me the sun lay.

"We know of stars." This was delivered to me in a mildly chiding tone, as if I were in danger of assuming my hosts to be ignorant of their place in the wider cosmos. "We know of ships and worlds. We know what we were, and where we came from."

"I do not doubt that," I said.

"You will take ship? All will leave?"

Barras met my gaze and although I would never read pigs as well as I read humans, I saw the concern and warning in his expression. I was entering troubled waters.

"With your permission, some would remain."

"Why?"

"Our ship is not designed to carry many people. Where we are going will be very dangerous. Some of us have entered this fight willingly, but that isn't true of everyone. The ones we have left behind at First Camp... do you know of First Camp?" I shook my head, amused at my own stupidity. "Of course. You were the ones who took my skimmer, weren't you? And I wouldn't be surprised if you tended those graves."

"No one can live in First Camp," said Rindi, speaking through his own favoured interlocutor.

"Not as it stood," I said. "But we have already begun making it habitable again. The settlers there won't trouble you unless you desire contact, and they'll only take as much from the sea as they need."

"No one can live in First Camp," Rindi repeated. Then, after a clarifying exchange: "No one *shall* live. It is forbidden."

I bridled. "They won't be in competition with you. If you avoid those islands you need never know they're there."

"It is not yours to decide."

"I'm afraid it is. These refugees have come from a more terrible place than you can imagine. This is no paradise, but being able to live on Ararat— to live freely, without fear—is the least that they deserve. You'll allow it, Rindi. And you, Ivril. I'm afraid there's no other alternative."

"You will be stopped."

I shook my head, more in sorrow than in anger. "No. I'm afraid not. We won't hurt you, but if you force us we'll set up a defensive cordon around First Camp and the surrounding islands. Machines that prevent you ever reaching the settlers."

"Machines will fail," Ivril stated, drawing a nod of weary agreement from her companion. "Do you not see? We have no machines. They failed. Yours will fail. All shall fail."

"You do not know the machines my ship could make. Machines to make more machines. Machines to repair any damage the sea does to them." Realising that my diplomacy was running hard onto the rocks, I attempted to steer back into more clement waters. "I see that you are a kind and noble people, and very resourceful. You have done well to make a life here, and these chambers of yours are beautiful. But you would be unwise to resist our settlement, and you should not attempt it."

"It would not be us," Rindi answered.

"*Green Man* would not allow," Ivril put in. "Green Man would grow angry. Angry-er. Angrier grow!" She made a sharp sweeping motion with her hand, webbed fingers spread wide. "Green Man take."

Barras spoke gently: "We've been over this with them. They seem to be serious. It's not a threat. It's a warning. Green Man...whoever or whatever Green Man is...won't allow settlement of First Camp."

"It's...yes," Probably Rose said. "Yes, yes. Your brother, yes. He's the one. The one with the say, yes. He won't let it happen. He knows it's too yes, risky, yes yes. To be seen. Yes, from space, and verily. By the wolves. Won't let it. Because of them, because of these, yes, yes. Because he loves them."

Pinky picked up the same train of thought. "He's protecting 'em. Them and whatever else got sucked into this ocean, over millions of years. The sea shelters the mariners, and they keep a low enough profile not to attract the interest of the wolves. And the Jugglers preserve the memory of everything else."

"Warren's brother is just one mind in that mix."

"But a new and dominant one. A soldier. The Butcher of Tharsis! A Knight of Cydonia! I knew the man: he had his light moments but mainly he was a heavy customer. Perhaps there's a sort of spirit, a custodial force, that he's become part of. If so, I wouldn't mind betting he's dominating the room. But it doesn't matter whether it's him alone, or an ocean's worth of other minds. The king and queen have laid it out for us. If we leave a settlement behind on First Camp, it'll be swept into the sea before *Scythe* reaches interstellar space. And no boasting about weapons and machines is going to change that."

"I wasn't..." I began. But I trailed off. He was perfectly right. As soon as the mariners put an objection in my way, I had responded with an aggressive overture.

"I'm sorry," I said, beginning anew. "There'll be no more talk of force. This is your world, and I accept your wisdom concerning First Camp."

I glanced at the others, desperately hoping I was not overstepping the mark. "We'll...make no further plans for settlement. What we have done, we will reverse. Once our ship has left, there'll be no evidence that we were ever here."

"The ones you speak of, who were to live in First Camp?" Ivril enquired.

"We'll take them with us. They survived the crossing to Ararat, so they can survive another. It won't be comfortable, or safe, but they'll be alive, at least for a while, and perhaps we'll find another world where they can make a home."

"They can stay," Rindi said. "But they must change."

I wondered if I understood him. Before I could seek clarification, Ivril was speaking through her interpreter. "The sea will take them and change them. To become more like us. If they wish."

"And if they do not?"

"The sea will still take. But they will not live."

I needed to sit down. It was almost too much to take in, much less to think through rationally. Dizzied, I turned to Barras. "They must have put this to you already. Are they seriously suggesting that the refugees can become mariners, like our hosts? That all you have to do is swim, to be adapted similarly?"

"I don't think they'd bring it up if it wasn't possible. But that doesn't mean it'll be easy, or that there's any guarantee of success." He was keeping his voice low, as if he worried about offending the mariners by speaking so bluntly. "It's not something they control. But it seems that if we accept this fate, they'll petition the sea, or the Jugglers, and make it more likely that we'll be altered the way they were. But if the Jugglers aren't receptive, or the Green Man's in a bad mood, or it's just the wrong season..." He shrugged. "This is as far as we got."

"Perhaps it's all the assurance we can expect. Would they go for it, Barras, to live on Ararat?"

He tugged at a long hair springing from his chin. "Some would. They haven't put down roots here, but they can see it's better to live on a world than be squeezed into a tiny little ship and forced to sleep most of the time. And given where they came from, and what the Swine Queen meant to do with us, it's not such a bad thing to think of throwing our luck in with the Pattern Jugglers. These...people...aren't so bad." He hesitated. "But I don't think they'd all go for it. It'd be different if none of us were ever planning to leave Ararat, but if some get the choice of leaving and some don't..."

"Everyone will have that choice," I affirmed. "*Scythe* will take as many as

381

needed. But anyone who comes with us must understand that it's going to be hazardous."

"Worse than committing ourselves to the sea?"

"I can't say. Everyone will need to weigh that for themselves."

"We told Ivril and Rindi that we'd talk it over with you. They asked us if you were our queen, and I told them that you weren't, but you did have a ship."

"And now you have my answer." I gave him a sympathetic smile. "Which I imagine has only made things harder."

"Yes, it would have been so much easier if you'd been a tyrant and decreed we weren't getting a ride off Ararat. What happened to the old Glass?"

"She got fractured into lots of pieces, like one of those windows. When they got put back together, some were missing, and some had never been part of her before." I returned my gaze to the king and queen of the mariners. "I hope I am not speaking out of turn before my friends. We thank you for the honest words you have spoken. We accept that there can be no life for us at First Camp. But what has been put to us will need more than a day or two to settle. With your permission, we would like to return to First Camp and speak of this matter with the refugees. They have already met mariners, when you sent for the Temporary Floating Embassy, but it would be good if a delegation came with us." Seeing that my words had caused puzzlement, I added: "Mariners should come with us. Old, wise, strong mariners, who can speak well."

"This will be done," Ivril said, nodding sagely. "In a day, the winds will turn, and you shall make the voyage."

"Thank you."

"Before then," Rindi said deliberately, "there is the other matter."

"The other matter?" I asked.

"The funeral for the one who did not come back alive. It is strange, what has happened to you. But it does not avoid the fact that there is a body needing a funeral. If you have customs of your own, let them be said. But ours is to return his body to the sea."

CHAPTER TWENTY-NINE

Pinky pleaded with me not to take any part in the ceremony. Perhaps he was wise in that. But there was another wisdom guiding me, an instinct that said I needed to accept what had become of War and Glass, to embrace the fact of our union, and that witnessing the mariners' funeral would aid that consummation. I needed to know that part of me was dead.

"You mean well, friend," I told him. "But I have to see this through. I think it will help, too, if the mariners see we are all willing to respect their traditions. Whatever happens at First Camp, I think some of the refugees will see their future in the sea. They will need friends in the mariners, and the sooner we show our openness the better." Then I pressed his shoulder. "If one of us were to be spared this, Scorp, it should be you. You've buried my brother at sea already. No one would blame you for not wanting to repeat the exercise."

"It would be harder if I didn't see another Clavain behind those eyes of yours."

"Not all the time, I hope," I said gently. "Glass has to have her time in the light as well." Then, emboldening myself: "It's just a body. It served me well enough for a few centuries, but I think this one is better suited to the times. Glass was a warrior. And we still have a war to win."

"I'll say one thing. You smell better than you used to."

"Trust a pig to notice that." I smiled. "Come on—we should be going down to the dock. It would be bad form to keep the mariners waiting."

The dock was one of the embarkation stages where I had seen mariners fussing with their rafts and rigging. It faced an apron of enclosed water, mostly calm, but with a tall, arched outlet giving access to open seas, and where the more distant conches could be seen rising and dipping like children on see-saws. The sea was dark, the sky star-strewn: by mariner custom funerals were always midnight affairs.

The boat that would carry us back to First Camp was being readied for the crossing, stocked with provisions and trimmed for sail, but we would not be leaving until the following morning. It was a bigger version of the mariners' rafts, with a base formed from eight treelike spars, and a mast from a ninth. It looked fragile, but it was the same sort of craft that had brought Barras and Probably Rose to Marl, and I promised myself not to have the bad grace to doubt either its seaworthiness or the skill of its masters.

The funeral raft lay moored to another platform, at right angles to the boat. Torchlit mariners were crowded around it in solemn preparation, some in the water and some clambering gingerly around on their webbed hands and feet. By some sign the workers attending to the boat stopped conversing, broke off from their duties, and moved around to the funeral raft. I could still see very little of it through the press of glistening bodies, but at my approach the mariners opened up like a curtain.

The raft was about as simple as any floating thing could be. It had no sail or means of steering. It was just going to be released to drift and find its own path. It would not need to do so for long.

A catafalque had been raised up on the raft, an openwork box made of interlaced struts of baleen. It was wreathed in green vines, forming a lacy connection between every part of the raft and its contents. Four lanterns were arranged on struts at the corners of this catafalque. Stretched out on top of it, facing the sky, and also partially wreathed, was my body.

It was an exceedingly odd thing to be looking at the dead form that one used to inhabit. For a few long moments—perhaps a minute—I thought that I was going to be able to maintain a cold objectivity, as if I had been called to a mortuary and asked to identity the corpse of a person known to me, but not intimately. The version of Warren Clavain laid out before me was both familiar and unfamiliar. I had grown used to the toll time had enacted on my body, especially in the last few years of life in Sun Hollow. Glass had undone some of that attrition, though, and I was taken aback at the vigour of the person on the catafalque. It was not youthfulness, for this was still an old man's frame, but I looked so much younger and stronger than my mental image of myself. I had never become fat, but where muscles had begun to wither away there was tone and definition, even in death. I had been readied for something, an ordeal that never came. Or perhaps this had been the ordeal: the challenge of the sea, the defiance of my brother's vow.

I looked peaceful. My eyes were closed, my posture restful: just a strong old man snoozing on his back. However I had died, by drowning, or some deeper intervention, there was no visible injury. My limbs were intact, unbroken, unbruised. A blanket of woven green covered me from shin to sternum, an extension of the wreaths, but I doubted very much that it was concealing any visible trauma.

Something inside me slipped. The objectivity crumbled in an instant, and I sagged, the strength going from my legs. Pinky seized me. It was no mere body on the catafalque; no mere empty receptacle, it was me. It was the last tangible thread connecting me to the life I had lived when I considered myself a better man, when I had known the love and security of family, the bonds of a small but decent community to which I had given my last strong years. Lives had touched this life. Good lives and good people, a web of love and friendship, gratitude and trust, service and dignity, responsibility and humility. I saw it, shimmering out from the catafalque. Endless quivering strands of silver light, linking Miguel de Ruyter to the rest of his tribe, and via finer extensions of that same silver web, the rest of humanity. No life was worthless, not even a life built on lies. He had made something that was better than the materials given him.

You were a good man, and you were loved.

I was crying; weeping not for myself but for this dead man who had been mourned. By the twist that had united our selves within one body, I knew that I was both victim and accessory to that crime, and I could condemn and console myself in the same thought.

"This . . . was a mistake," Pinky whispered. "And next time you'll listen."

I found the will to say: "No, not a mistake. I needed to be here, I needed to feel it."

"I never doubted you were you."

"I know."

"But if I had kept a little doubt back . . . this would've settled it." He turned his snout to the catafalque. "You have to let go now. We both have to let go."

"He gave you a thread back to Nevil. Now it's been broken."

"I never depended on it." His grip on me intensified. "But we're depending on you. Say goodbye, Warglass."

Ivril and Rindi had arrived at the funeral raft, flanked by courtiers. Their garb was more elaborate than before, both of them wearing spined head-dresses and with their bodies daubed in glowing inks. They met my gaze, then set about the formal part of the ceremony, intoning words for the dead, solemn recitations which were interspersed with sung passages and slow, bellowing moans, some of which were accompanied by those gathered, and some of which were the prerogative only of the king and queen. I stood back, allowing the waves of sound to wash over me, devoid of surface meaning but transparent in their emotional intensity. It was not necessary to know the mariners' tongue to understand words of farewell. They did not know this man; had no inkling of his life, carried

385

no catalogue of his deeds or misdeeds. But he had come to their sea and died by it, and if it was a mark against him that he had not heeded their warnings, the mariners were ready to forgive such transgressions.

A silence fell.

I gathered some composure and eased myself out of Pinky's supportive embrace.

I spoke, in a voice still broken by tears: "Please tell Ivril and Rindi that this man would be thankful for these words. I do not know what has been said, but I feel the kindness communicated. It is more than we expected, and more than he deserved." I touched my throat. "I know because a small part of him is still within me, and he would have wanted this to be said. You have honoured him."

Through her translators Ivril answered: "We would not anger Green Man by disrespecting his brother, even a brother that was shunned."

I nodded, not wanting to contradict her, but feeling that she was justifying an act of remembrance that would have been extended to any soul lost at sea, almost as if her charity embarrassed her.

"However it is meant, it is good."

"Then you shall finish it," Rindi said.

They were cutting the ties to the raft, ready to cast it loose. Mariners were gathered in the water with long staves, ready to encourage the raft out through the arched opening. But something remained to be done before it was out of reach. The courtiers brought forward a burning torch, and it was passed first to Rindi and Ivril, then offered to me.

I took it, and was ready to lean out from the dock and ignite the raft. But I hesitated, and turned to the one who had been at my side since we left First Camp.

"This is Pinky," I announced, addressing all who were gathered. "You know him a little by now. Trust me when I say that you could spend another life with him and not know a tenth of what he has seen and done. He was a friend to my brother in his last days, a true and loyal friend, and when my brother called on him to perform a task that should never be asked of any friend, Pinky was willing. Had he not been, then our history—and yours—would have been very different. He has carried the mark of that day ever since. But when I touched my brother's mind— when Green Man spoke to me—the only message he wished me to communicate to Pinky was one of gratitude and fondness. I wronged my brother, and there are some wrongs that are beyond forgiveness. But if there is one thing that united us, it is our common friend Pinky." I nodded to my body. "He knew this man. Perhaps for not as long as either of them might have hoped, but for long enough. And he should be the one who accepts this torch." I passed it to him, nervous about his reaction, and gladdened when he did not immediately thrust it back.

"I'm a pig," he said, diffidently. Then, indicating me: "She's...something else. You fishy lot are some other things. Barras, Probably Rose... there isn't one of us that doesn't have a story about how we got here, and what made us. Same as the one you call Green Man. You want my advice? Fear the old guy's moods a little less. Throw your weight around a little. His bite was never as bad as his bark, and this is your world just as much as it is his." He gave a shudder of sudden self-awareness. "Well, all I'm saying is, we're a weird bunch. Pigs, mer-people, hemi-demi-Conjoiners...but somehow we're here, and we're not dead. That's got to mean something, hasn't it? We keep not dying. We're hanging in. We're a jumble of different ideas and different ways of living, and we squabble, and some of us smell a little funny...actually, some of us smell *really* funny, but the main thing is this: we're not a bunch of identical black cubes with only one idea in the universe. We're messy and broken and we make stupid mistakes but we aren't stupid, mindless machines that are too dumb to realise their programming no longer makes any sense. We're people. Fish people, pig people, people-people, creepy-zombie-spider-people...no offence, Warglass..."

"I've heard worse."

"And yet we...stick around. Maybe like a bad stain, but so what? Many stains make a universe. And we aren't done yet." The torch was still burning, but it was wavering and blackening at the edge of its flame, and I could see the slightly concerned looks of the courtiers, that it might gutter out before the big moment. Presumably none of their previous funeral ceremonies had had to contend with an overly loquacious pig, and they had no contingency in place.

"We soon will be, if you don't light that thing," I murmured.

"Always there with an encouraging word." He leaned in and touched the torch to the base of the catafalque. The raft did not erupt into flames instantly, but began to consume itself unhurriedly, a river of sparks racing along the paths formed by the wreaths. They must have been soaked in the same slow-burning preparation used in the torch and the candles. A mariner extended a hand to Pinky and took the torch, daubing it at other points around the raft's extremities, encouraging the fire to burn symmetrically. Then the torch was passed back to Pinky, and from him to me. It was ebbing out, flame turning sooty.

The raft burned brighter: latticed in fire. The mariners nudged it on its course, employing their staffs deftly. The flames crept up the side of the catafalque and curdled around the reposed form on top of it. I watched for as long as I could, but when the skin on my face began to crisp and blacken it was more than I could endure, and I risked the tolerance of our hosts by averting my gaze so that I was viewing proceedings through narrowed eyes and peripheral vision.

By then, the raft was nearly at the gate. The flames swooped up, formed a pair of swan's wings, enclosing the body, and underlighting the arch as it slipped through. A dozen or more mariners swam after it at a respectful distance, occasionally offering it an encouraging prod, but mostly content that it was following whatever strange currents flowed through Marl. Flames daubed the swelling sea, and sparks challenged the stars.

"He didn't do too badly in the end," I said to Pinky in a low voice.

"He acquitted himself."

"And would the old man have agreed with you?"

"I think he would."

"Right answer," I murmured.

I gave my old body one last squinting farewell before the walls of the arch snatched it from view, and then I tossed the spent torch into the waters. I did not know whether that accorded with mariner custom, but I felt that the right to do it was mine.

Then I turned from the sea. In the course of the funeral, I felt that some chemical marriage had been completed. The fluids had intermixed, become inseparable. Glass was dead, and so was Warren.

I was one.

I was Warglass.

We returned to First Camp. The crossing was easier than I had anticipated, for the winds were blowing well and sea conditions were mostly favourable. I thought of the seconds that it would have taken *Scythe* to traverse the same stretch of water, seconds that might make a difference in some future calculation. But even if it had been ready for flight, my ship could not have been summoned; it was not until we were much nearer to First Camp that I felt the whisperings of its thoughts. More than that, though, I thought of how curious an omission it had been to have lived two long lives and never once been swept across water by wind and sail before.

Barras, Pinky and Probably Rose were the first ashore, and they had some delicate groundwork to lay. The mariner delegation followed next, and then I ventured onto land, conscious of the many eyes on me. It was no good asking them to accept what I was without question, so I decided my best course was to keep out of their way and say as little as possible, leaving the refugees to the more difficult business of deciding whether their best hopes lay with me or the sea.

Nothing would be settled in a day, but certain steps could already be taken. There was no point carrying on with any of the preparations for the resettlement of First Camp, so they were abandoned. This was difficult for those who had put their backs into the early work, feeling that their labours had been for nothing. Barras and Pinky reported that some of the revived pigs were extremely disinclined to stop, but in this matter at least I was perfectly happy to assert my authority. I had seen what my brother's rage could do, and I had no doubt that we would not be permitted to remain on these rocks. After returning to *Scythe*, I had the robots begin reclaiming the materials I had provided, even if that meant tearing apart tables and chairs. I left just enough amenities to keep the revived cases comfortable for another five days, which was all the time I was giving them to decide their fate. The others, still sleeping, would need to be woken and polled as well. But if the twelve came to some kind of agreement among themselves, even if wasn't quite unanimous, that might guide the others to a speedier decision.

I had vowed to offer no opinion of my own. Since I was not going to remain on Ararat, it would have been hypocritical of me to take a stance. And I envied them neither course. Coming with us back into space would be hard on our passengers, and with no guarantee of survival. But who would submit to a kind of drowning and rebirth, emerging into an alien body, without very reasonable qualms? Even the mariners could offer only a shrugging assurance that the sea would welcome the pigs and reshape them for their new lives on Ararat. It was starting to anger me that they had offered this option without the additional clause that it was likely to succeed. Things had been simpler before.

So I was content to have enough distractions to keep me within *Scythe*, fussing it back to life. The ship had done well while I was away. My first fear was that it might not recognise my command authority at all, seeing in me an impostor who only looked and spoke like Glass. My second was that it might only recognise the limited subset of commands I had assigned to Warren Clavain. But the ship welcomed me back with all the unquestioning loyalty of a puppy. It was keen to show me the repair schedules it had completed, the deferred upgrades it had worked on itself now that it had the opportunity. It was nearly ready to fly. In fact, quite a lot of the repair stages still to be done could be conducted while it was already under way.

"Good ship," I murmured.

I went to the infirmary and submitted myself to a full-body examination, including a deep neural trawl. The Jugglers had changed no part of me on the outside, but it was harder to know what had gone on beneath my skin. Large areas of my idiosyncratic brain structure had been remodelled to accept the memories and personality traits of Warren Clavain. There was going to be no easy way to tell which of Glass's memories had been deleted or degraded to make room for the new ones, not until I stumbled on some odd absence within myself. I had expected to come back from the Jugglers with less of me than before, so I could not feel too hard done by if this or that had been sacrificed. Memory was indeed holographic, distributed across multiple embedded encoding structures, not at all like some clean digital ledger. But the Jugglers took apart and reassembled minds at a holographic level as well. Human science could never chase out a memory completely, without leaving fuzzy traces, but Juggler methods could.

Once the scans and trawls were finished, I returned to the command deck and reviewed the results. I zoomed and scrolled through images of myself, peelings and sections, flowering eruptions of cortical structure. My neural augmentations were still in place: the silvery shimmer of implants and cross-connections which marked my brain as at least partly the work of Conjoiner neuromedicine.

Were they indeed intact, or was it only my imperfect memory deceiving me? I checked against earlier trawls in *Scythe*'s database. Although my organic tissue had undergone some changes, areas of brain enlarging and shrinking like districts of a city, jostling against each other and negotiating new boundaries, the implants were unaltered. Warglass was still like Glass, in that respect. Every gift that those augmentations had given me was still mine.

What of the rest of me? What of the real question?

Was it still within me?

I intensified the scan's depth and resolution, peeling back layers of myself, until a hard metallic form emerged from a fog of tissue and bone.

It was still there, still whole.

Good.

We'll have need of you soon; need of you in Charybdis.

Something snapped me out of myself, back to the immediate moment. It was *Scythe*, snagging my attention with the faint repeating tone of a sensor contact.

CHAPTER THIRTY

I called a meeting. Pinky, Barras, Probably Rose, the mariner delegation.

They sat in a loose semicircle near the shore while I knelt and tried to work out the best way to convey the news I needed to share: the complicated, joyous, troubling fact of it, and how much of a mess it was going to make of our already fractured plans.

"Wolves," Pinky said, searching my face.

"Not wolves," I said. "At least, I have no evidence of any near enough to cause us trouble."

"What then?" Probably Rose asked.

"I don't want any of us to have false hopes. At this point, I know only as much as the ship can tell me, from a very faint reading. But I couldn't not bring it to your attention. If we decide that it's real, we have no choice but to act on it immediately."

Pinky scratched at the stub of his ear. "This isn't helping."

"I'm glad you said it," Barras agreed.

I worked my jaw. Then I spoke. "Lady Arek may still be alive. *Scythe* has picked up a weak moving signal, consistent with a localisation pulse of the kind emitted by my suits."

There was silence, as I had anticipated. I could see Pinky straining to be the first to comment on my observation, yet holding himself back by sheer force of will, not wanting to expose himself to ridicule or contempt by showing too much haste to believe.

"You told us she was lost in the star," Barras said.

"She was," I affirmed. "In the photosphere of Bright Sun, when we were completing our slowdown. But here's the thing. We were moving very quickly when it happened; faster than the star's escape velocity. Lady Arek would still have had that velocity when she fell away from us. If she had the luck to make it out of the photosphere, out of the stellar envelope and into clear space...she'd have kept moving, far faster than *Scythe*. She'd have passed Ararat long before we did." And I nodded out to the horizon, to a patch of pearl-coloured sky above it. "The trajectory fits, within a margin of error. The signal is moving at the right speed, and in the right direction."

"If it all fits, yes," Probably Rose said, "if it all fits...why did we not go looking for her already?"

"Because by all that's sane, she shouldn't be alive. I knew the capabilities of my suits. It was dangerous enough for Lady Arek to go out on the hull when she did, but at least she had the armouring skein to protect her, and some benefit from the cryo-arithmetic engines, sucking heat through her soles. But when she broke away..." I shook my head, disappointed in myself. "I neglected one possibility: Lady Arek went outside because we had a problem with the ninth stone. When it was missing, I assumed that it had broken away at the same time, going off on its own trajectory."

"But Lady Arek was a survivor," Pinky said.

I nodded. "Yes, she was."

Probably Rose said: "So she took the stone, yes, and yes?"

"It's the only way she could have survived long enough to escape Bright Sun. In her stronghold, the first time she showed us a stone, she said it wasn't enough to protect a ship. But she did say it would have sufficed to protect a single spacesuit. That's what she must have done. She didn't choose to break away from us, but in the moment when she knew it was inevitable, she must have managed to take the stone along with her. The conformal skein wrapped her like a second skin. The forces on her would still have been hellish, but because she was moving quickly they'd have fallen away quickly as well."

"But without any protection from the cryo-arithmetics," Pinky said.

"There's that. But Lady Arek said the Gideon stones have some thermal shielding properties as well. Combined with the emergency life-support measures of her suit, the acceleration buffering she was already experiencing...I believe it's possible that she lived. Is alive."

"But she's been silent until now," Barras said.

"There are two possibilities, I think. Either she was aware of wolf activity, and was withholding her transmissions, or the suit has only just brought her back to consciousness. I don't think it's very likely to be the former."

Pinky looked at me with all the intensity of which he was capable. "This had better not be a mirage, Warglass."

"I sincerely hope it isn't."

"I need more than 'hope.'"

"So do we all. Which is why I advocate an immediate departure. There's no telling how close that suit is to the end of its life-support capability, or what condition Lady Arek is in. The pulses are very faint, even allowing for the suit's distance."

Pinky looked uneasily at Barras. "When you say immediately..."

"Within the next twenty-six hours," I answered. "Sooner still, if I had my way. And I'm afraid it can't be a question of going out there, finding Lady Arek, and returning to Ararat. Every time we move through this system, or come and go from this planet, we endanger ourselves and everyone here. When we leave, we leave for good. And anyone not aboard *Scythe* will have to learn to live here, with all that that entails."

"Some hard choices just got harder," Pinky said.

Barras shook his head slowly. "I'm not sure that they did. I think this may even help us. We could spend weeks talking about living here or leaving here, and never get any closer to a decision. But if there's a life to be saved, and if that life also happens to be Lady Arek's..." He made to stand up from the loose circle. "We'll put it to the others. But as far as I'm concerned, my mind's settled. You've given us a world to live on, somewhere a lot better than the last place, and I trust that these people will help us make it work."

The mariners had been content to listen until then, passing no judgement or observation.

One said: "The road to the sea is not an easy one. But many have walked it."

"We will be there to guide, and to welcome," said another.

Probably Rose stood up next to Barras. "They should vote, as Barras says. But the less time it takes you to leave, the better."

"There's a place on *Scythe* for anyone who wishes to come with us," I said, noting that Probably Rose had already cast her lot with the remainers. "If we leave in twenty-six hours, or thirteen, that promise still holds."

"We know," Barras said. "And I'll make sure the message gets around. But I know the pigs, and I've already seen the way the mood is turning. They're ready to join the mariners."

"Not all," I said.

"The doubters'll see the light. Lady Arek's name always carried a lot of weight in the Swinehouse. They'll want to do what they can for her now. And delaying even a few hours won't help her at all."

"No one should be cajoled," I said.

Barras made a dismissive gesture in my direction. "Go and do what you need to do to get that ship ready to leave, Warglass. And, Pinky? You know you'll be keeping her company, so do what you need to do as well."

Pinky scratched a heel against the green-slicked rock beneath him. "Just when this place was starting to grow on me."

*

In the end, thirteen hours was all it took. Barras had been right about his promise of unanimity, however it was achieved. I was already on the back of the ship, looking down as Pinky hugged Probably Rose, whispering something to the human woman before turning away and scrambling up laddered recesses onto the hull. Then it was a brief wave to Barras and the others: doubtful promises made and fond hopes offered.

It was all happening too quickly and I felt pangs of guilty abandonment. I believed in the good intentions of the mariners; that they would do all in their power to shepherd their new flock into the sea. But we were still leaving these people to a desperately uncertain fate. The only shred of forgiveness I could offer myself was that our own future was no more settled. Perhaps less so. But whatever hopes we had, they would be improved by the presence of Lady Arek. Therefore, we were compelled to leave, and every hour that we delayed was another hour in which she was at the failing mercy of her suit.

"I'm sorry that it's ended up this way," I said to Probably Rose. "Sorry that we've been forced to make this choice. But I'm not sorry to put this burden on you. I think you can take it. I think you're at least as strong as any of us."

She glanced away, as if my praise stung her. "Find Lady Arek for us, and verily."

I nodded heartfelt affirmation. "We will. And when we've gone out there and found whatever it is we need in Charybdis, we'll come back to Ararat."

"It won't be the same, yes and yes."

"No, I doubt that it will be. But I do know that it will be better for your being here. I'm sorry about Snowdrop, Omori and the others; they were your friends, just as surely as they were Pinky's. But we'll make sure that their sacrifices weren't in vain."

"You never did ask me about my name, Warglass."

"Were you expecting me to?"

"Most do, yes and verily. They think it's..." She made the self-cuffing gesture, gently smacking the side of her forehead as if a gear had stuck. "They think it's strange."

"It is. But strangeness isn't bad. Look at me."

"Yes," she admitted. "Look at you, Warglass." Then, as if continuing the same thread: "There was a pig, in the Swinehouse. After what I'd done to her, she couldn't live. But she never blamed me for any of that. She forgave me, yes. Yes and yes."

Gently I asked: "Was her name Rose?"

"Probably. They weren't sure. No one was. She didn't have a tongue by then."

Something in me tightened like an overwound mainspring. "Did they make you take her tongue?"

"And verily."

"I'm sorry for what they made you do."

"Later, when I had my chance to escape, she was the one who helped me get out. She knew she wouldn't leave herself. And she knew what the Swine Queen would do to her." Something terrible played behind her one remaining eye. "Yes, yes and yes. So I said I'd take her name. I couldn't take her, but I could take her name. I said I'd always be Probably Rose, and I'd never be anything else." She looked out at the sea. "Do you think I'll remember, when it changes me?"

"I think you'll remember everything that matters," I said. "And Rose... Probably Rose? Thank you for everything."

"You should go now, Warglass," she said with a certain sternness. "Go and save Lady Arek. Yes."

"Yes," I answered.

"And verily."

Farewells completed, Pinky and I went inside and sealed up. We were silent together for a few minutes, preoccupied with our thoughts. There was so much to say that neither of us knew where to start. The act of departure was just too big, too monumental, to begin to talk about. I felt simultaneously as if we were fleeing one responsibility and throwing ourselves headlong into another. That we were turning our backs on friends because of the pull of another friend who needed us.

It was good to have the technical business of the ship to focus on. Rather than taking off directly, I opened ingestion ports in *Scythe*'s flanks, sucking in seawater, running it through hyperdiamond compressors and using it for thrust. Gradually the seaweed loosened its hold on the hull and we drifted away from First Camp, moving gently into deepening waters. I waited until we were a kilometre clear of land, and the gathered onlookers, before lifting from the sea, still using the jet compressors. We executed a farewell circuit of First Camp, then arrowed for space, making a quiet departure from the atmosphere, ruffling it to the minimum extent, darkdrives and cryo-arithmetic engines working to cloak us from the notice of wolves.

"They'll be all right," Pinky said at last.

"They will," I agreed.

But almost immediately Pinky dashed my already fragile confidence by adding: "I hope."

Lady Arek had travelled five hundred million kilometres since breaking away inside Bright Sun. Her course had been nearly straight, with just the smallest deflection due to the gravitational influence of the star, its nearest worlds, and the distant influence of its twin. We would have caught up with her whichever way she was moving, but it happened that her vector was aligned with the same quadrant of sky in which Charybdis lay. That was luck, and nothing else, but it saved us time and minimised the velocity changes that we needed to make while still within the stellar environment of Bright Sun.

Scythe could have passed Lady Arek's position within a couple of days of leaving Ararat, but the need to match her speed made the rendezvous more time-consuming, and it took more than a week to close in on her pulse. In the last two days of our approach, the pulses became weaker still, with the gaps between them elongating. By then, though, it hardly mattered whether the pulses kept coming. Pinky and I had narrowed down her expected position to a moving volume about ten kilometres across. When we got there, we could use passive sensor methods to locate the suit.

Pinky was anxious about those diminishing pulses. I felt for him, but there was nothing I could offer by way of reassurance. He had been through the loss of her once, then offered the promise of her still being alive, and now his fortitude was being tested a second time, by the thought of finding her dead and drifting.

"The universe won't do this to us," I whispered to myself. "It's indifferent, but it isn't actually cruel."

Perhaps I believed myself, for a moment or two.

Fifty-two hours out from contact, Lady Arek went completely silent. Most of the next two days was spent with Pinky and I saying as little to each other as we could get away with. It was not that we had fallen out, but that our nerves were equally strained, and our mutual capacity for patience and tolerance nearly exhausted.

Scythe's first glimpse of Lady Arek was a moving speck of warmth, about the size of a person. Warm enough to be alive? I dared not speculate. She had been inside a star not too long ago. Perhaps all we were seeing was the slow fading out of a cinder, a dying spark falling into interstellar darkness.

I brought *Scythe* nearer, until we were about a kilometre out. At that range, even though we were far beyond Ararat's orbit, there was still enough light from Bright Sun to illuminate the suit. Pinky and I watched the slow-spinning form from within the control room, neither of us offering comment. In my mind's eye I had imagined her speeding into

396

space with her visor to the stars, but the reality was less dignified. At some point in her crossing, she had begun to tumble end over end. Other than that continuing movement, there was no trace of mobility. *Scythe* could read some systems activity from the suit, picking up thermal and electromagnetic signals, but to my own neural senses it was mute. Diagnostic queries went unanswered. Nor could I detect any aspect of Lady Arek's mind within it. But there was one thing to which we could pin our hopes, however feebly. Lady Arek was bent nearly double, pressing something to her belly. She must still have the ninth stone, even though we could see no sign of its skein.

Without a word of preamble Pinky said: "I'll go."

I offered no debate, merely a nod of understanding. He knew how to use the suits and airlock systems well enough by now. A couple of minutes later I watched him depart, using cold-gas thrusters to speed over to the tumbling form. His suit was smaller than hers, of course, and to begin with her momentum overwhelmed his own. But by gradual taps of gas Pinky was able to stabilise the two of them, and then haul the unresponsive suit back into the ship. I was rather glad when he did, for this was the last bit of business we needed to attend to before committing for deep space. I felt nervous and exposed until the lock sealed over.

Trusting *Scythe* to manage itself for a while—and preferring not to leave anything to the robots—I went down to the lock and met Pinky as he emerged back into pressure. He hauled the other suit behind him, an awkward job even in temporary weightlessness.

"It's in a bad way," I said, appraising the suit's visible damage. The outer layer of it was mostly black and blistered, with a bronzy sheen over the least-damaged parts. The visor was fogged, and no status indications shone from any parts of the suit. I breathed slowly, reminding myself that Lady Arek would have had no cause to adjust her system preferences to make those indications visible.

"I can see it's in a bad way." He was out of his own suit by then, barely giving it a glance as it shuffled itself back into storage. "Tell me something I can't see with my own two eyes, Warglass."

The suit was not disclosing its contents automatically. Gently I dug around Lady Arek's hands and extracted the Gideon stone from her grasp. I felt it in my own bare fingers, reacquainting myself with the familiar roughness of its texture, its density and coldness. The scarlet light still throbbed within, but weakly.

"It's dormant," I said quietly. "But I don't think it's dead. I think likely that the stone gave up a lot of itself getting her clear of Bright Sun, and now it's in a recuperative phase."

"Would she have needed it, once she was clear?"

I had no good answer to that question. "She was travelling quite quickly, and with only the armour of her suit for protection. The skein would have been useful, if she ran into any micro-meteorites. But she can't have run into anything big."

"Or she wouldn't be here."

"The skein would have barriered her, but there wouldn't have been much it could do about a sudden deceleration, beyond anything the suit could have protected her from." I sketched my hand over the charred form. "This damage looks bad, and it's clear the suit lacked the energy or material reserves to heal itself externally. But that doesn't tell us anything about what's inside."

He looked at me, or rather at the space just above my eyes, behind my forehead. "You still not getting anything?"

"Not yet."

"The suit should open on its own, shouldn't it?"

"Not if it doesn't know where it is, or what's happened. If its sensors are really badly damaged, it won't even know it isn't in vacuum." I frowned, trying various command-and-control protocols, attempting to override the suit's perfectly reasonably instincts towards host preservation. But my signals were bouncing off it, charms that had lost their potency.

I sighed.

"What?"

"We'll have to cut our way in. There's nothing else for it. The suit's stone-dead, except for some very low-level functionality which could mean anything and nothing."

"You're a bundle of reassurance, Warglass."

He needed his mind taken off the matter at hand. "Go to the weapons archive, Pinky. Bring blades and short-range cutters. Even a boser pistol."

"Is that an order?"

"A friend asking nicely."

He pondered that for a second.

"All right."

He was gone, and that was all that I wanted. Of course, I needed no extra equipment to break into her suit: everything I could have wanted was available in the suits already. I summoned a suit, stepped in, and cycled through the minimum functionality tests. I detached the self-merging helmet and set it aside. It was only the suit's tools and weapons that were of use to me now, and I thought it would be easier on Pinky to see my face if he came back before I was done.

I straddled Lady Arek, then commanded my right glove to form a precision cutting function. My forefinger elongated, the tip flattening and sharpening to a scalpel-like shape. I touched the blade to the crown of Lady Arek's helmet and dug in slowly and carefully, alert to the materials-diagnostic telemetry issuing from the cutter. My glove vibrated faintly as the blade engaged its microscopic cutting mechanisms. The blade was both tool and laboratory, and would deactivate itself the instant it strayed into anything that resembled living tissue. But I dared not place undue confidence in its infallibility.

The blade cut through the suit's layers with only moderate resistance. It helped that these were compatible technologies, products of a common engineering philosophy. According to the diagnostics, the charring was confined to the last few millimetres of the suit's integument, with progressively less damage the further in I went. That was encouraging. The innermost parts, just before I burst through into the body cavity, were showing normal consistency. Lady Arek's suit was not fighting back against this intrusion, though.

I worked my way down. I cut a narrow groove down the visor, through the neck joint, into the upper chest. The damaged layers of the suit gave off a powerful, acidic stench, and I had to keep blinking away tears of irritation. All along I was waiting for something horrible to hit me from further in: the choke of cooked or corrupted flesh.

I worked my down Lady Arek's belly, stopping just above her hip. The groove was still only a black line, the edges nearly touching. I deactivated the tool, returning my glove to its default condition. Glancing back at the entrance to the suiting area, half expecting to see Pinky returning, I pressed my fingers into the groove, just above her ribcage. It took effort to force my way in, more than my muscles alone could have managed. But with a gasp and a creak, the suit relented. It split open along a widening fissure, and as the smell hit me from within I nearly fell back in distaste. It was a very bad smell, and I batted it away from my nostrils, gagging on a cough. But it was not the smell of a body that had been cooked or allowed to rot. It was just the human consequence of being bottled inside a suit for too many days, with the usual filtering and waste-recycling measures running at a reduced efficiency.

Just the natural result of being alive.

I pulled Lady Arek out of the suit. She came out in a slithering, greasy mass, like something that had just been born. She was unconscious, and unresponsive, but she was not dead.

"Oh, you..."

I turned to Pinky. "Not a word, Scorp. Not a fucking word."

"You tricked me, you bastard."

"And now you don't have to be the one who opened this suit." I brushed Lady Arek's hair away from her forehead. "I didn't know what we'd find. If it was as bad as I feared, I didn't want you to be the one who saw her. You've seen enough. You've been through enough."

Some of his anger bled away. But his chest was still heaving up and down, his hands still tight on the excellent assortment of cutting implements he had come back with.

"I could use these on you."

"You could try." I paused, and pressed my forehead against Lady Arek's, hugging her into me as if she were the last fixed thing in the universe, the last and final point of reference. "There's something. Neural housekeeping, just enough to read. She's in there." My eyes were closed, her skin sticking to mine. It was the cushioning gel that had been inside the suit when she went outside *Scythe*, broken down into a viscous, lumpy grease. "She's there."

"I want her back," Pinky said. And he let go of the blades, allowing them to float from his fingers.

Three days later Lady Arek came back to us.

Pinky and I were waiting, keeping vigil at her bedside. We had been observing her for hours, saying very little. *Scythe* had been accelerating steadily since retrieving the suit, and I anticipated no further difficulties before we reached Charybdis.

"Pinky," she said, her eyes settling on him. "Dear Pinky. You found me, in the end. Either that, or some undocumented part of my brain is giving me a very agreeable fantasy."

Pinky pinched himself. "I think I'm real."

"I think you are real as well. How long has it been?"

"You were out there for twenty-six days," he told her. "Falling through the system at few hundred kilometres per second. We picked you up three days ago, but it's taken until now for you to come around. You were a long way under."

"Did I still have the stone?"

"Yes, and we'll add it back to the collection."

"That is good. Our plight will be marginal with nine; with eight we would have very little hope at all."

"I see you haven't lost your talent for morale-building, your ladyship."

"Nor you your talent for reminding me of my limits, Pinky." She smiled. "For which I remain grateful."

She turned to me next.

"I felt you, Hourglass. You were trying to pull me back into the light.

400

Thank you. You gave me something to struggle towards."

"You were a long way in," I said.

"You must have seen the condition of my suit. Almost the last thing it was capable of doing was keeping me alive, and even that became a struggle in the end."

I said: "Your pulses were fading out."

"My decision, to conserve energy. I took a gamble, which was to count on you detecting and acting on my pulses when they were at their strongest. I presumed that you had launched the ship and were closing in on my position. If I was right in that presumption, it was safe to reduce the pulse intensity, because you should be close enough to detect and localise them."

"It was quite a gamble."

"I would think it the sort of thing you admired, Hourglass. All or nothing. Every iron in the fire." But she tilted her head finally. "It *is* you, Hourglass. But something is different." Then some redawning clarity of mind had her looking beyond our faces. "Clavain. If you are here, I would have expected him to be here as well."

"Something happened on Ararat," Pinky said.

"Did you obtain the intelligence?"

"Yes," I said, bristling a little at her directness. "The information is secure. We know our destination. It's locked in as we speak. As soon as the ship declares you strong enough, we'll go into reefersleep."

"Clavain swam?"

I nodded. "Clavain swam."

"And he met his brother?"

"I did, Lady Arek."

She frowned at me, puzzlement giving way to doubt and then a brittle comprehension. "Oh, Hourglass."

"Oh indeed."

"What have you become?"

"Something that didn't exist before. Something new in the universe."

"What strange times we find ourselves in."

"Said the woman spat out by a star," Pinky said.

Part Seven

NESTBUILDER

CHAPTER THIRTY-ONE

Charybdis was nothing much to look at, just another ice giant with some mildly interesting weather and common-as-muck hydrogen-helium chemistry. It was a fifty-thousand-kilometre-wide pale blue ball accompanied by a garland of wiry, thinned-out rings and a litter of runtish moons, mostly dirty iceballs of one kind or another. Nothing about the world or its satellites was noteworthy. The galaxy made worlds like Charybdis as easily as beaches made pebbles, grinding them out with monotonous regularity. But it was exactly that unexceptional nature that had made the ice giant such a suitable place to hide. If you had a choice of trees to use for concealment, you would never pick the one that stood out.

Had Nevil and Galiana come to it later, after they had already catalogued a dozen similar giants, they might not have been inclined to give it as thorough an examination as they had. It was our luck that they had, because without that close-up inspection, the *Sandra Voi*'s sensors would never have detected the signature of something anomalous lodged deep beneath the outermost cloud layers, and seemingly floating.

Ice giants had no definite surfaces, unless one counted their cores. They were atmosphere nearly all the way down, gas transitioning to a liquid-like state, and then to a mantle of icy slush, wrapped around an Earth-sized nugget of iron where the pressures nudged into the thousands of gigapascals.

We knew from the fragmentary records that the *Sandra Voi* had dropped atmospheric sounding probes into Charybdis. These devices had gathered radar-returns and sonar traces, enough to tantalise. But the gathering pressure and temperature of the deeper cloud layers had crushed the probes long before they got any sort of detailed view of the floater. Beyond that, there was nothing more the *Sandra Voi* could do. The anomaly was intriguing, but it was far from the only mystery collected in their travels, and it had to wait its turn for a follow-up expedition. Some while later, it was expected, Conjoiner science would have advanced to the point where probes could penetrate further into Charybdis, deep enough to at

405

least determine the nature of the anomaly, even if reaching it was still a goal too far.

The science might well have improved, but by the time it did there were more pressing concerns besides pure exploration, such as surviving an interstellar war. Almost without anyone realising it, Charybdis was all but forgotten: its significance reduced to a few puzzling data fragments and one cryptic image.

No human, Conjoined or otherwise, could have synthesised those fragments and appreciated their true significance.

But Glass had. That former part of me knew what was there, what it contained, and that the Gideon stones would be required to reach it. The only thing she did not know was how to get to Charybdis.

Now we were here, though, our task had only become more daunting. It was one thing to find a world: it had taken decades of travel, numerous sacrifices, my own little death, to bring us to our destination. Until now, I had allowed myself to think of the world as a point of light, a thing unto itself which would immediately disclose all its secrets. But now we were orbiting this vast, cool crypt of a planet, its treasures (if any remained) screened behind millions of square kilometres of mute blue cloud, lost in plunging, fathomless depths, I realised we had barely begun.

Lady Arek put one matter to rest: it *was* the right planet. Using her system privileges, she had again called up the image fragment, and now she was able to cross-compare it with the real view of Charybdis turning beneath us as we orbited.

Nothing matched precisely, but after centuries that was to be expected. The earlier bands and storms had shifted, evaporated and re-formed elsewhere. But what was below us was consistent in its colour, brightness, and implied chemistry. Better still, using our present vantage, Lady Arek was able to obtain high likelihood identifications for the stars that had appeared in the fragment. No amount of brute computation could have matched them previously, not with any reliability, but now we were here the problem was much more tractable, and once I saw the correlations I put aside any doubts that we might have followed a false lead. Better still, a dark patch on the image turned out to be exactly where one of the moons' shadows was expected to fall.

Scythe orbited and scanned. It was using minimally invasive measures to peer into the atmosphere, but these were at least as effective as anything available to the *Sandra Voi*. They had seen something worth the trouble of getting in closer, worth the loss of the probes.

It ought to have been easier for us.

Ten orbits, then twenty, looping around the planet for maximum coverage. Twenty, then fifty. By the hundredth orbit we knew a great deal about the conditions in the outermost cloud layers: chemistry, physical parameters, wind shear. It was almost certainly the most detailed picture of Charybdis ever assembled, at least by human minds. But nothing in that portrait hinted at anything anomalous.

"It's been a while," Pinky said, voicing the fears that Lady Arek and I were doing our best to keep to ourselves. "I know Glass had her reasons to think there'd still be something waiting for us...but who knows? Maybe whatever it was, it moved on."

"It's still there," I said.

"Faith won't make it so," Lady Arek.

"It's not faith," I answered doggedly. "The floater won't have left. It didn't have the means, not in the condition it was in. If we don't see it now, then it can only be because it's gone deeper since Nevil and Galiana last saw it."

"You know this, or you just want it to be the case?"

"I know."

Pinky scratched at an eye, digging deep into an inflamed duct. He had been looking tired since we came out of reefersleep and I wondered at the particular toll it had taken on him.

"The old man wouldn't have led us on a goose chase."

"Who is to say Nevil was any better informed than Glass?" Lady Arek asked.

"Nobody. But between the time he went into the ocean, and the time he appeared to Stink, who's to say what else didn't get into his head? He certainly had time to reflect on things. Time for other bits of information to soak into him. Maybe, by the time Stink showed up, Nevil had figured that there was something worth looking into after all. And maybe he knew enough to guess that the floater would still be present."

I nodded, liking this argument even if I had no reason to accept it as fact. "Nestbuilders were present on Ararat—or at least their remains were. Only a tiny part of their technical lore might have reached the Jugglers, but that would have been enough to convince Nevil that returning to Charybdis wasn't futile. It's been centuries, which feels like an awfully long span to us. But we're human. To a Nestbuilder, that might be a long afternoon."

"But the floater's missing," Lady Arek said.

We were in the control room, surrounded by ever-changing images and graphs of the orbital scans. It had been exciting, at first, to see these datasets assemble. But over those hundred orbits our feelings had shifted to prickling doubt and then a growing despondency.

"So, we're not looking closely enough," I said. "That's all. We go lower and use the active measures we've avoided until now. We drop missiles and use them as advance probes. We keep trying, however long it takes, until we get a return. If we take *Scythe* all the way to its crush depth, and then all the way down to the crush depth of the Gideon stones, and still see nothing, we still don't give in. There's nothing to be gained by turning away now. Either our salvation's here, or salvation's lost, for the rest of time." I stiffened in my acceleration couch, facing my two doubting allies. "Warren and Glass played a game, after she stole him from Sun Hollow. Actually, a series of games. Glass promised him that if he won, she would let him have his family back. In truth, the odds were always against him, even when Glass dropped her cognition level just to even things out a little. But Warren knew that, and it didn't stop him. He never gave in, not when there was still a move to be made. Glass knew he was the person we needed, then. And I won't accept anything less from us now."

"And if he'd won, even by a fluke?" Pinky asked.

"Glass would have honoured her promise."

"Not if I know how much this victory meant to her," Lady Arek said, shaking her head.

"Glass accessed the medical records of Sun Hollow: the register of births and deaths. By the time she got to them, the average life expectancy for his wife was about twenty years. Victorine would have lived a little longer, but not by very much: childhood diseases were in the ascendant, and their medicine was crumbling by the hour. So Glass would have waited long enough for him to bury his family, and then continued with her mission. We'd be here, exactly as we are now, if just a little later in the life of the universe." I nodded to the scans. "And the floater—wherever it is—would still be here."

Pinky folded his arms tendentiously. Between the shared experiences of Warren and Glass, I had become quite adept at reading the pig. I knew when he was settling in for an argument: it was a sort of itch that needed periodic scratching. "If you had a way to keep War alive, presumably the same kindness could have been extended to the rest of them?"

"He lost the game," I said brightly. "Nothing else mattered."

The pig huffed and shook his head, but my candour had blunted any possible response.

"I always knew we'd benefit from a sharp, sterile blade," Lady Arek said. "I knew that's what you were, from the moment I made you whimper before me. But sometimes it frightens me how *very* surgical you became."

"I am glad that Glass proved not to have been a disappointment," I answered. "But do not mistake her for me. Now, shall we discuss plans for a closer look at Charybdis?"

Scythe dropped lower: inside the orbit of the rings and all the major moons, barring a few stray shards that had been knocked loose by some relatively recent gravitational encounter, and which would be destined to burn up in the atmosphere in a few short centuries. I turned up the energy and spectral-response of all the electromagnetic scanning modes. Now we would be starting to illuminate Charybdis in frequencies and intensities that were not part of its usual emission pattern, and our reflected radiation might alert anything nearby—even as far out as hundreds or even thousands of light hours—that something odd was going on. Like a foolhardy civilisation, pumping a planet's worth of radio waves into space, *Scythe* was easily capable of generating the necessary energy output to betray its own presence.

But this was a gamble I was willing to make. So, after reflection, were Lady Arek and Pinky. It was an endgame gambit. All or nothing. If we brought all hell down upon us, so be it.

Still nothing showed. *Scythe* increased the diversity of its scanning modes, moving into exotic radiation forms that could not be generated by any natural means, and were therefore a clear marker for technological intelligence. These reached a thousand kilometres or so into Charybdis, but still not far enough to find something. Given time, and an asteroid's worth of resources, we could have set up a sphere of emitters and detectors, girdling the planet completely, and allowing for a much more efficient search process. But other than its missiles, which had some limited capability to act as receivers, *Scythe* had to rely solely on itself, and the hope that some signal would be bounced back into the detection cross-section of its sensor batteries.

Failure did not daunt me. If the floater had descended, then I would not be at all surprised if it had gone down a long way, perhaps beyond the range of all but the most extreme scanning modes. So we dipped further, until *Scythe* was partially within the upper layers of the atmosphere, and the missiles were sent streaking off on hunter-seeker search patterns that would involve successively deeper passes into the cloud deck. The missiles had nothing like the energy budget of *Scythe*, and by comparison with the ship, they were slow and vulnerable. But I had enough to use them wisely. By sprinkling missiles around the planet at a range of latitudes, longitudes and cloud depths, as far down as the point where the pressure reached a hundred atmospheres—their effective operating limit—I managed to establish an improvised acoustic monitoring network. It was only going to be useful as long as the missiles had fuel, or avoided being crushed, so I needed to work quickly. Selectively, the warheads in some of the missiles were triggered. We were over the nightside of Charybdis when this happened, and there was a certain desolate beauty in watching these pale flowers bloom from beneath the clouds, lighting them up in dizzying stacks. But seeing these pinprick flashes against the face of the planet was also a reminder as to how pitiful even our major weapons were against the effortless scale of nature.

It was not the brightness of the yields that counted, though, so much as the amount of energy they injected into the atmosphere at each detonation point. These energy bursts created waves in the gas, propagating away from each explosion, with the lowest frequency waves travelling the furthest. The remaining missiles only had to listen for the reports of the distant events and report their findings back to *Scythe*. The ship had already modelled the pattern of sounds it expected if there were no reflecting surfaces suspended somewhere in the atmosphere, with the sound waves reverberating unimpeded around the transition zone between the lowest gas layer and the onset of the liquid mantle beneath it. Any localised deviation between model and observations—allowing for the noisy reality of weather systems—would be a strong hint that we were zeroing in on our objective.

If we had taken risks by scanning at higher energies, then letting off warheads in the clouds of Charybdis was another level of provocation still. But that could not be helped, and in any case the acoustic search would be necessarily brief in duration. I only had so many missiles to spare, and the more I detonated the less I had available to act as listening posts.

"There *is* something," Lady Arek said, after thirteen hours of steadily refining our models and watching a faint but suggestive signal begin to rise from the noise background.

"I thought so, but I didn't want to pre-empt your judgement."

The localisation trace was hardly a bullseye: all it did was point to a density anomaly at a certain latitude, longitude and depth, with an error margin still taking up about six per cent of Charybdis's surface area. But I had kept some missiles in reserve so that the acoustic net could be tightened.

Was it real, or just a phantom of atmospheric physics? We would find out soon enough, once the missiles had repositioned. But if it was not the thing we sought then our remaining search options were rather limited. Faith won't make it so, Lady Arek had said. But faith was starting to look like the last thing left in our arsenal.

While we waited for the acoustic search to recommence, we busied ourselves with the final checks on the hypometric device.

"How does it look to your eye?"

"Perfectly hideous and terrifying, Warglass. It is perfectly wrong, by all that is sane. Perfectly perverse. Which is as it should be."

"Remind me to find another two travelling companions, if I ever get the chance," Pinky said.

We were floating in vacuum suits, drifting through the narrow space between the outermost parts of the device and the bulb-shaped cavity that the ship had opened within itself. The device filled nearly the entire volume, fifteen metres across and twenty from end to end. No part of it looked like anything it was wise to be nearby, even before it had started to function. It was inert now, but as the light of our suits played across its numerous blade-like elements it was impossible to escape a sense of slow, slithering motion, as of a great coiled monster rousing from dormancy. Glass had made this device, or at least given permission for it to be birthed within her ship, but I was its inheritor and I was not so sure that I liked it.

"Hypometric technology doesn't belong to us," Lady Arek said. "It's a fire that we stole—a fire that we haven't earned, a fire that may yet scald us."

"Maybe have a word with the one who gave it to us," Pinky said.

Lady Arek pressed on. "It served us temporarily, but we were never its master. I do not regret the means by which it came into our possession, nor that I was a conduit for that knowledge. Perhaps, without the advantages it gave us, we would not have reached the point where we have the means to go beyond it. But I hardly dare speculate what that stranger fire will do. I ask myself: are we right to do this, after all?"

"Let me mull it over," Pinky said. "Extinction, or...not extinction? You know, call me rash, but I'm going with the *not extinction* option. And after all the shit we've been through, I think you should as well."

"My doubts were silent until this moment. But now that we have reached the cusp, now that the final step is upon us...I feel as if we are about to commit some grave, irrevocable act of harm against the universe itself. An act that may leave us wondering if extinction were not the better path after all. There may be stigmas we can never erase: a psychic stain on the conscience of a civilisation."

Pinky swept his arms magnanimously. "Then let it be all on me. My conscience is grubby enough as it is; a few more blemishes won't show."

"My concerns are more pragmatic," I said. "Will it work? Will it accept the construction schedules for the Incantor, or spit them back at us?

We've done the best we can, but is that enough? We're off the map now. Frankly, we're off *all* maps. The tests have only proved so much. We won't know if it even functions as a hypometric device until we turn it on, and that still won't be any guarantee that it'll behave once we start asking it to work for us."

"I suspect," Lady Arek said, "that if something were to go wrong, we would make quite a pretty spectacle. My only regret would be not being around to witness the consequences our own magnificent folly. But at least we would have tried."

"It's not going to get any less scary the more we look at it," Pinky said. "Start the damned thing rolling, I say."

"The readiness checks are all complete," Lady Arek said. "The order to commence spin-up may be issued at any time, by any one of us. Our command pathways are neurally addressed, Pinky, but I reserved a voice-only channel for you, just in case."

"What's the word?"

"Two words. Among equals."

Pinky drifted for a few seconds. "You've said them, but nothing's begun."

"The words are for you alone. If you would rather some other ones, they may be arranged. But I thought they might be fitting. We would not have reached this point without you, but I do not always think you grasp how much we have depended on you. A tripod is a very stable structure, but if one leg is weaker than the others, it collapses."

"The words'll do," Pinky said grudgingly, as bad at taking praise as he was at accepting criticism. "But I don't suppose we want to be inside this room when baby wakes up."

"Spin-up will not be a rapid process. Besides, would it not be a shame to deny ourselves a little harmless spectacle, this late in the game?"

"Fun," I said.

"Indeed, Warglass. If of a very specific kind."

"You two are weird," Pinky said.

"Yet you travel with us," Lady Arek said amusedly.

Pinky was silent for a moment or two. Then he spoke firmly: "Among equals."

Nothing happened for a second or two. Nor was there any sound when the hypometric device did indeed begin to activate. But through vacuum and our suits we nonetheless felt some imagined protestation, some deep grinding groan as the vast components of our machine began, at last, to move against each other. Every part of the device mobilised with respect to every part: blades rotating and counter-rotating, blades interleaving, seeming to touch but never quite doing so, a sort of lethal, silent clockwork made of threshing metal. Only the shallows of hypometric physics were comprehensible to me, but I understood that these near-misses, blade surfaces kissing close but not quite contacting, was in service to the generation of microscopic slivers of Casimir potential, and that by the repeated conjuration and negation of these effects, a series of resonances built, a sort of harmonic song that the deeper mysteries of the engine would use to sing apart spacetime, unravelling it at Planck scales, as idle fingers messed with the broken weave of a carpet's edge, and eventually teased it to ruination.

The device quickened. It was a slow but steady acceleration, the machine self-checking its function at every stage. The blades whisked and danced. As they moved faster, the eye began to pick up secondary waves of motion, sinuous and corkscrewing, implying patterns of movement that seemed completely at odds with the static form of the device. As it spun ever faster, it was unshackling itself from the rational rules of geometry and mechanics. From the scanty technical documents Lady Arek had furnished Glass with, I knew that there would soon be a point where human recording systems were unable to obtain coherent snapshots of the whirling form. No matter how fine-grained our analysis, the device would always seem to have moved between two contradictory states, becoming—as Lady Arek described it—"weakly acausal."

Physics was turning uncanny in the vicinity of the device. It was starting not to recognise itself. It was starting to wonder whether it had other things to be doing.

It was therefore time to be out of the chamber.

The machinery was awake.

By the time we returned to the command room, my missiles had converged on the refined search area and repeated the echolocation procedure. Their grid was tighter now, and concentrated at a lower level in the atmosphere. From orbit, the flashes were dimmer. They had a lot of overlaying gas to pass through before reaching us, and their energies looked paltry: meagre flickers limping up from the dark.

But something was down there, beyond any doubt.

"*Scythe's* best guess is that our objective lies about three thousand kilometres beneath the outer cloud layer," I announced, primarily for Pinky's benefit, since Lady Arek was more than capable of accessing and analysing the same data returns. "That is quite a bit deeper than the reach of any instruments on *Sandra Voi*, which is both good and bad news. Which would you like first?"

"I've spent a lifetime wondering why people bother to ask that question," Pinky said.

Lady Arek looked at him tolerantly. "The good news first, I think."

"Our objective must be extraordinarily robust for it to have survived at all, and for this long. That bodes well for it still containing the information we seek. I would be a lot more concerned if the acoustic net had picked up multiple returns, because then we would be looking at dispersed wreckage. But the floater must still be intact."

"We shall see. The bad news is self-evident: such a depth is at the very limits of our capabilities. *Scythe*'s existing cryo-arithmetic systems will help with the thermal load, but the pressures are far beyond anything the ship can tolerate. Or would be, if we did not have the Gideon stones."

"Good job we didn't nearly lose one of them inside a star?" Pinky said.

"With nine, there'll still be absolutely no margin of failure. But if one or other defence fails, then at least our deaths will be nearly instantaneous."

"You know, I was on board with that until the 'nearly.'" He gave a shrug. "Still, they got us through Bright Sun. I guess we weren't planning on that test, but it's nice to have it behind us. It can't be any worse inside a planet, can it?"

"It can indeed," Lady Arek said, with the sort of sadistic enthusiasm she could only have reserved for a friend. "The dynamic forces will be much less severe, that is true—we are not hitting a plasma at multiple Mach numbers, and the effect of gravity will never exceed one gee. But pressure and temperature will rise sharply: approaching three hundred thousand atmospheres, and three thousand kelvin respectively."

"You were blown off the hull inside the photosphere," Pinky said. "You lived."

"Indeed I did. But the thermal strain was much less problematic. I was inside a hot plasma, but it was also tenuous. Temperature depends on the kinetic energy of particle collisions—a room may be defined as hot if it only has a single atom in it. Heat capacity is a bulk property, and where we are going will be extremely hot and extremely dense. The cryo-arithmetic engines will cope, but of necessity we will be running close to some dangerous thresholds."

Pinky nodded. "I was wondering when the dangerous part was coming up, because it was all sounding safe until then."

"In addition," Lady Arek said patiently, "the armouring skein may be relied upon to have a thermal insulation effect, as a secondary property of its defensive membrane. But I am not minded to depend on it too thoroughly."

"Well, if I had multiple fingers I'd be crossing them." He looked at us both in turn. "We're doing this, right? All of that was...just to make sure Pinky doesn't get any unrealistic ideas about life expectancy?"

"To make sure none of us do," I said. Then, with a decisive sweep to the controls: "The remaining missiles can keep refining the position while we commence our approach. There's no logic in delaying now. If this return isn't the floater, we'll never find it. Buckle in; I'm preparing to take us into Charybdis."

Lady Arek was monitoring the hypometric device as it continued powering up. While she assured me that any accelerational forces we cared to impose on it were of no consequence to its safe functioning, I still kept *Scythe* from darting out of orbit too violently, and I made sure we met the ice giant's upper atmosphere in as gentle a manner as possible, with a vertical descent rate of only one kilometre per second. *Scythe* was handling oddly, to begin with, and I had to continually remap the control parameters. The device in the bud of its tail was acting like an infernal gyroscope; one with only a disdainful regard for the conservation of angular momentum.

Charybdis's blue horizon flattened from an arc to a straight line. The ice giant's face swallowed more and more of the sky, horizontal perspective foreshortening until the hazy stratification of water and methane-ice cloud layers became apparent. As useful as it might have seemed to time our expedition to coincide with day, the light now reaching Charybdis was destined to travel only a few hundred kilometres closer to the core. At the level of the floater, where those photons never reached, it would be as perpetually dark as the deepest marine trench.

The ship syringed into the upper atmosphere without fuss. Gravity was close to a standard gee, for although Charybdis contained about seventeen Earth masses, it was also four times larger. This was the one aspect of our mission where I had over-compensated, working on the assumption that we might have to operate in a high-gee environment. Even if Warren's old body had made it this far, he would not have found it troublesome, especially after the rejuvenation measures. But it was Glass's body that carried us now, and one gee was beneath contempt.

As we descended, maintaining the same sink-rate of one kilometre per second, the pressure climbed towards one atmosphere: about what *Scythe* had experienced before landing on Ararat. But it was still much colder, and the air around us was nothing that could have sustained life. Although we did not yet have need of them, I initialised the cryo-arithmetic engines and Gideon stones, warning them that they would soon be called upon and to verify their integration. Our experience in the photosphere was that the two systems needed to be meshed in harmony, or else one would exert a destabilising dominance over the other.

Pressure and temperature rose with each kilometre of descent. At ten atmospheres we were already under a thick, ashen pall of overlying cloud, turning daylight into dusk.

Beneath us, light billowed from the last of the acoustic probes. The localisation was complete now, and as accurate as it was going to get until *Scythe* was close enough to use its own sensors. The floater had been tracked down to a cubic volume about one hundred kilometres along a side, and the echo analysis pointed to a single solid form with a complicated asymmetric geometry, somewhere between ten and twenty kilometres in extent, orientated with its longest axis pointing down, like a dagger.

By twenty atmospheres the last traces of daylight had surrendered their struggles to reach any deeper. It was as black as a crypt out there, with even *Scythe*'s false windows offering no hint as to what was up and what was down. The darkdrives were inefficient now, compared to cold gas thrusting, so gill-like ingestion intakes opened up along *Scythe*'s flanks and began to suck in atmosphere, before compressing and expelling it without combustion. Attitude control vanes sprung out of the hull, and my flight controls morphed into something more befitting a submarine.

"This is a very capable ship," Lady Arek said, at one hundred atmospheres. "I think I might like one of my own, just like it."

"Save your praise: nothing has begun to test it so far. We might as well still be in vacuum, compared to what's below."

"Does it help our chances, to constantly mention how terrible it is out there?" Pinky asked. "Or could we, you know, take that as read?"

I took my eyes off the controls for a second. "Would that make you happier, Pinky?"

"Right now, you could drop an electrical probe into my pleasure centre and it wouldn't cheer me up."

As the atmosphere warmed and thickened, it began to behave more like a warm fluid than a mixture of gases. Five hundred atmospheres came, then a thousand. *Scythe* was untroubled, but as the hull tightened and consolidated itself, dull clangs and groans sounded throughout the ship. I decided that calm reassurance was the last thing Pinky needed to hear from me, so I held my tongue.

At ten thousand atmospheres, stress indices lit up in hues of mild concern. Now the medium being sucked through *Scythe* was more like a hot, sluggish lava than anything resembling air. It was time to turn to our augmentations, stabilising their influence before we really needed it. I advanced the cryo-arithmetic cooling cycles in logarithmic steps, pausing at each interval to allow the Gideon stones to reach a temporary equilibrium. The armouring skein spread out from the nine nodes, merging and congealing into a sticky, closely adhering film, like the slippery slime covering a hagfish. *Scythe*'s sensors fogged over, then adjusted. They could still see through the skein, and by applying rapid selective dampening and re-establishment measures, the skein could be made to flicker on and off around certain critical parts of the ship, keeping the propulsion and steering functions operable. Provided this was done smartly, the atmosphere never had a chance to break through these weak zones.

Long minutes of descent ensued. Since the blackness outside never changed, and there were no visual cues to indicate the increasing pressure and temperature, it was easy to imagine that we were inert, floating at a fixed level. But while our rate of descent had slowed—*Scythe* was now having to resist its buoyancy, fighting to get deeper—we were still moving at hundreds of metres per second. The hull's pressure and temperature gauges were no longer reliable due to the influence of the skein, and all we could rely on were theoretical predictions based on our assumed motion. At fifty thousand atmospheres, any probe that *Scythe* attempted to extend beyond itself, pushing out through the skein like a snail's antenna, was instantly consumed.

The floater was still thousands of kilometres beneath us. A cold awe touched me. Not because I was impressed that an alien machine could withstand these conditions, but because the wreckage we had seen on Ararat attested to the fact that even *that* level of invulnerability was ultimately insufficient against the wolves and their weapons. Why were we so imbecilic as to think there might be something in the floater that could best the wolves, given the evidence that had already been presented to us?

Because the Incantor is no ordinary weapon, and even the Nestbuilders shirked from using it, except as an absolute last resort.

And I knew that...how, precisely?

Again: because.

Because. Because. Because.

"You are mumbling to yourself, Warglass," Lady Arek said. "It is rarely a good habit, and especially not now."

"Is the hypometric device behaving itself?"

"Indeed it is. Spin-up confirmed. It is...pensive, you might almost say. It knows that it is a maker, rather than a weapon. Now it has an almost insatiable need to know what to make. It grows fidgety. We should not deny it fulfilment for too long, or else—" Lady Arek stopped, frowning slightly, the first distant intimation of concern beginning to cloud her features.

"I know that look," Pinky said. "It bothers me."

"It's the monitors that we left around Charybdis, on our approach. They have signalled. Warglass would have noticed, if she were not preoccupied with *Scythe*."

I had noticed, and only a second or two after Lady Arek. But I felt chastened: a second or two was a lazy afternoon, by the standards of Conjoiners. "That does not augur well."

"It most certainly does not."

Pinky growled: "There's a third person on this ship, in case you'd forgotten."

"If we had forgotten you, Pinky, we would have taken our conversation entirely off-line. The monitors have detected wolf activity."

"Fine, my day needed livening up."

The ship could handle itself for a few moments, I decided. Quickly Lady Arek and I assessed the intelligence fragments beaming into Charybdis from the monitors, squirted through the black ceiling above us via neutrino.

The wolf elements were stirring from hiding places around the rings and moons, as well as drifting in from further out. The numbers were large enough to be troubling, without approaching the concentrations we had seen around Yellowstone. What we were seeing—if the monitors' initial summaries were accurate—was a relatively small aggregation, the sort that the wolves could be expected to seed around any system that might at some point be of interest to humans. The only thing that had spared us such attention around Sun Hollow was the evident madness of trying to live there in the first place. Even the wolves knew better than to spread their eyes and ears too thinly.

"While I would not describe this development as welcome—" Lady Arek began.

"You can stop there," Pinky said. "Because I can just feel one of your 'nonetheless' coming along."

"Lady Arek would be right," I said. "From a practical standpoint, the emergence doesn't change anything, except to throw the consequences of failure into sharper focus. Now failure won't be some distant extinction fifty years or a hundred from now: death will be ours to face as soon as we leave Charybdis. I don't know if they'll attempt to follow us into the atmosphere, but I know this: we have to have made the Incantor before we leave."

"I am glad that they are here," Lady Arek said. "The sooner we show how far we are prepared to go to, the sooner the message will spread among them."

"I don't know how they saw us. We were so quiet coming in, and our search was risky, but didn't trigger their interest."

"We were cautious, Warglass," she agreed consolingly, as if I carried some guilt about me. "It is inescapable that their emergence coincides with the activation of the hypometric device. I think it likely that the wolves may have become sensitised to the signatures given off by such technology: the local metric perturbation, the daughter events of causal breakdown."

"Then whenever one of our allies receives the construction templates for an Incantor, they'll need to act on it very quickly. The instant they start to make the precursor device, any wolves nearby will sniff it out and move in to pounce."

"A certain boldness will be necessary," Lady Arek agreed. "The blade, once tempered, must be used without compunction. Without mercy and without hesitation. As I know it shall."

Pinky scratched his snout. "Is there a place to get a drink on this ship?"

CHAPTER THIRTY-TWO

Not long after that the monitors went silent. It was perhaps for the best. Knowing what the wolves were up to, and how much interest they were taking in us, would not assist in any way. There was only one objective, and only one way of getting to it, and however much time we needed when we got there was entirely out of our control. If the breath of wolves was already on our necks, no good came from glancing behind.

One hundred thousand atmospheres came, and then two hundred thousand. The black stillness descended with us. For the most part the cryo-arithmetic engines and Gideon stones were meshing agreeably. Now and then a flutter of instability would need to be damped before it got out of hand, by altering one or more control parameters. But if all those systems did was bicker and tussle with each other, I was content.

It was as hot as the surface of a star outside now—admittedly a rather cool star—but a star nonetheless. All this energy had been trapped in the ice giant since its formation, bleeding slowly out into space across billions of years. I tried not to take it personally, that we had to suffer for our share of it. The universe was not trying to be cruel or difficult; it was just massively, magnificently indifferent.

"The gravitometer is reading something," Lady Arek said.

It was. The gravitometer was a passive detector, emitting nothing, so safe to use. But until now it had been confused by the strange emissions boiling out of the hypometric device, unable to identify a signal above an elevated background noise. Now, it seemed, we were near enough to the floater to begin to feel its effect.

Floater, I decided, was not quite the right word. If the object was in equilibrium with the fluid-like atmosphere it would be displacing exactly the same mass of hydrogen-helium as itself, and would therefore be invisible to the gravitometer. But it was much heavier than the volume of gas that it had pushed aside. It ought to be sinking: ought, indeed, to have sunk long ago, until perhaps it ended up bobbing along somewhere within the transition zone between atmosphere and the truly liquid mantle, still far below.

The gravitometer sketched a form in red vector graphics overlaid with green technical summaries: a sharpening of the impression already gleaned from the acoustic probes.

The floater was fifteen and a half kilometres from top to bottom, and widest near the top. It tapered down with increasing depth, but not with any regularity. It had a lopsided, crudely chiselled form, as if parts of it had already broken away. Down near the bottom there was not one point of culmination, but several: jagged fingers grasping for the core of Charybdis.

A many-spired castle, inverted.

The going was now very sluggish and the fluid-intake drives were reaching their operable limit. I had no choice but to re-engage the dark-drives. They produced thrust, but no detectable emissions. The downside was the increased thermal load they placed on the ship, necessitating a higher toll on the cryo-arithmetics. This pushed them closer to the brink of runaway algorithmic cycles, and also generated more conflict with the Gideon stones. I imagined myself a hunter with two fine but unruly hounds, slathering and yelping at each other. They were loyal to me, but perfectly ready to rip each other's throats out.

This was going to be delicate.

"If *Scythe* can take it," Lady Arek said, "we should loop around and under, conducting a thorough examination. There may be an obvious point of entry that we won't see from this approach angle."

"If you're expecting a front door with a doorbell, you might need to downgrade your expectations," Pinky said.

"We won't be ringing any doorbells," I replied.

The hull creaked and groaned as we descended the last few tens of kilometres to the uppermost level of the floater. These complaints were no indication of the actual forces assaulting the ship: they were merely the distant echoes of the tiny residual stresses that were not quite fully neutralised by the armouring skein. The skein was generated by the stones attached to *Scythe*'s hull, but under normal operation it formed its own cagelike tensile field, absorbing the crush forces but not transmitting them. But at a third of a million atmospheres, even the skein was approaching its limits.

"I forgot to mention that I never did find that drink," Pinky said.

I smiled: he had not even gone looking.

We sank slowly, at a few metres per second. Nothing was out there except a curtain of absolute black. *Scythe*'s floodlights were at maximum illumination, blasting through the pearly filter of the skein, but since there was nothing larger than an ice-grain for them to scatter against, they might as well have been switched off. Until the moment when *something* rose from the depths. My hands stiffened on the attitude controls. I had been ready for this moment of contact, but it still surprised me.

"Large," Lady Arek said drily.

If the Nestbuilder spacecraft had some preferred orientation, a front and a back, a top or a bottom, it was beyond our means to judge. We had only ever seen the wreckage of their endeavours. All we could say about the floater was that the thick end, the roots or foundations of that many-spired palace, was the highest and widest point. The floodlights only picked out the nearest few hundred metres of it: the rest was still swallowed in the dark crush of Charybdis.

From what we could see it was clear that the structure was not a continuous form, but a fluted, piped, densely packed assemblage of many conch-like sub-elements, arranged at every conceivable angle. The forms had either grown together, been fused, or were conceivably only the remnants of some mountainous solid mass that had been sculpted nearly hollow. By extrapolation from the small part that we could see, the entire vessel must have been made up of tens of thousands of conches, fixed into a vast barnacled and sea-shelled mass like some mad architect's dream of a cathedral. There were passages between the conches: deep black fissures leading hundreds or even thousands of metres into the interior. Lady Arek had been sensible to suggest that we looked for a door, but even a cursory mapping of the outside form would take many hours. To map the innards would be the work of weeks or months.

Instantly a panic of confinement rose within me. To be lost in that maze, in a slowly overheating, buckling ship, fighting to find a way out of one darkness into the vaster one beyond if...

"My missiles won't survive at these depths," I said, in case there was any doubt. "And even if we could use them to scout for us, I'd like to keep some behind for later."

"I should insist on it, Warglass," Lady Arek said, resting a hand on mine, where it still gripped the attitude tiller. "You have done well to bring us here. We have done well, merely to have made it this far. Nevil Clavain would be astonished, I think."

I felt a prickle of negation inside me. "Astonished that it took us so long."

"The old man could have saved us all a great deal of trouble by mentioning this place to someone before he died," Pinky said. "He wouldn't thank me for saying that, but it's still true."

"He could not have grasped its ultimate significance," Lady Arek said. "None of us could. Even now, it has taken leaps of imagination. Were it not for Glass, none of us would have guessed to look here for an Incantor. Or even considered that an Incantor might exist."

She was valorising Glass, not Warglass, so I made no comment. If I was not to be bound by her misdeeds, then equally I could take no praise for her insights.

Scythe tracked slowly down the tapering form of the floater, keeping within a few tens of metres of its side. Conches, pressed into steps, terraces, spires, turrets, ascended past us. Some jagged out like bowsprits; others were attached to angled arms like down-pointing candelabra. Now and then our lights excavated a rugged-outlined cleft in the ship, as if some large part of it had been blasted away. It was a reminder, if any were needed, that the Nestbuilders had never overcome their enemies: they had merely evolved strategies that minimised the likelihood of an interaction.

Fifteen kilometres of additional depth was a scratch compared to the distance we had already travelled into Charybdis, but all our systems were now being pressed to their limits. The cryo-arithmetic engines were fighting heat flowing in from outside and heat emanating from the dark-drives, a war on two fronts. The Gideon stones were picking up on the elevated algorithmic cycling of the engines, crimping and buckling the skein around these vortexes of anti-entropic activity, as if they considered them a form of threat, needing to be contained or even neutralised. We could go deep enough to survey the floater, but anything deeper than that would be taking *Scythe* into treacherous waters, beyond the comfort of anything we had already experienced or simulated.

It was a relief when the lowest parts of the floater, the spirelike tips of its down-pointing conches, passed above us.

We swept slowly back up to the level of the base, spiralling around the floater to achieve the most efficient mapping. We had seen no door, no docking port: at least none that was recognisable to us.

We would just have to make one of our own.

Consulting with Lady Arek and Pinky, I selected an area of the ship about halfway down the taper: a wartlike outgrowth of twenty or so interlinked conches, at least two kilometres beneath any obvious sign of damage. I did not want to go into one of the damaged zones. The architecture of these ships was cellular, divided into independent volumes by bulkheads of conch matter. Even if part of the ship had ruptured, allowing Charybdis's atmosphere to flood in, an adjoining part might still be at the normal pressure tolerated by Nestbuilders.

I orientated *Scythe* vertically, then brought it in slowly until the dorsal airlock was about a metre away from the convex surface of one of the conch outgrowths. *Scythe* laser-mapped the contour of this area very precisely, then adjusted the form of the airlock to provide an exact counterpart, a pair of opposing surfaces that would kiss together with barely an atom's worth of disagreement. I then completed the closure, narrowing the distance until the skein dimpled inwards against contact with the floater. Initially it resisted any further movement, until I increased the pressure from the thrusters and forced the skein to snap onto the floater, becoming surface-conformal. Now the skein had the topological form of a bag with an out-puckering mouth, enclosing *Scythe* but pressing its lips against the convex skin of the conch. It was stable and provided a form of anchorage, enabling me to reduce the output of the darkdrives. Now the floater was doing most of the work of holding us at depth.

"Very good, Warglass."

I took my hands off the attitude controls. They were slippery with sweat.

"Thank you, Lady Arek."

Scythe took a few minutes to reorganise its internal layout to provide a convenient route to the suiting room and the dorsal lock. It was useful, to have those minutes. We all needed time to compose our thoughts and compartmentalise accordingly. One step at a time.

We got into our suits, nervously and silently, as if we were dressing for an execution. For now, the tools, weapons and sensor instruments of the suits would be all we took with us.

Scythe's airlock was pressed hard against the opposing surface. It detected no pressure on the other side, nor any toxicity or radiation that we needed to be concerned about.

We cycled the airlock down to vacuum. Without a word I opened the outer door. It irised back to disclose the off-white, faintly translucent sheen of conch material. We had all seen and touched it before, but never in its intended application as part of a ship that had still had some functionality. The shards and hulks of conch that we found on Ararat were, by definition, damaged specimens. Even then, it had been astonishingly difficult to work with the conch material.

"Where shall we begin?" Lady Arek said. "Lasers, bosers, pressure cutters?"

I dabbed my hands against the surface. I made a series of precise gestural strokes, using the heels of my palms to imitate the narrow but elongated contact area of a Nestbuilder secondary appendage. I worked quickly, since I had to emulate the effect of four limbs with only two of my own. Lady Arek and Pinky looked on, wisely saying nothing. The surface blistered and darkened in definite geometric patches, indicating a query as to my credentials and intentions. It was no small thing to demand admittance to a Nestbuilder ship, even in the language of their kind. I composed replies in the same speedy fashion, asserting my authority with politeness and confidence.

The surface formed an opening. It began as black dot and swelled wide, becoming a circular aperture about a metre and a half across, stopping before it reached the border defined by our own airlock. Beyond was a dark space of indeterminate size. The wall of the conch, where it had peeled back, was no thicker than a fingernail. I shivered at the thought of what that material was resisting, beyond the immediate boundary of the lock and the portion of the skein that had attached to the ship.

"We can go through now," I said.

"There might not be another human who has thought as long and hard about the Nestbuilders as I have done," Lady Arek said. "Nor one who has gathered and assimilated so many scraps of lore about them. Apart from you, Warglass. But even you cannot have learned their language. No records or traces were ever found..."

"Then I must have been spectacularly lucky," I said, showing the lead by clambering through the opening. "Please, let's not delay. The door recognises my authority, but it might close as soon as I'm inside."

"Just checking that it's too late to go back for that drink?"

"Too late for most things, Pinky." But I needed to assuage his nerves. "About two hundred years ago Glass came across a codex for a subset of Nestbuilder gestural commands. Until now, it was largely untested. Glass didn't want to raise our hopes beforehand. If it hadn't worked, we would have resorted to mass-energy, or even a limited use of the hypometric device in its weapons-instantiation."

"Just me, or is she getting more disturbing by the minute?"

"Yet, indisputably, she *has* opened the door. Go through, Pinky. I am right behind."

I stopped on the other side of the opening, reaching out a hand to help Pinky and Lady Arek. Besides the glow from *Scythe*'s lock, the only light was that provided by our suits. My suit radar-pulsed the space we were in and came back with a smooth-surfaced volume about sixty metres across. I turned up my suit's helmet light until a faint milky reflection bounced back from the continuous curving wall enclosing us. There was a floor beneath my feet, but it was really only a sill projecting a few metres inward from the opening. Beyond it, the level dropped away sharply.

"We're in something like a lock," I said. "It's in vacuum now, just as ours would be. That must be a universal design feature, regardless of the species. I know we picked an almost random point of entry, but I imagine the ship's skin will be honeycombed with these cells, so that the Nestbuilders could come and go as they pleased. They weren't required to use a fixed set of locks as we are: they could create a functioning lock anywhere it suited them, just by making the right gestures. Lady Arek: are you through?"

"Both clear, Warglass—and the door seems to be sealing behind us, just as you said it might."

"I'm encouraged. It means the cell is still functioning as it should. If I'm right, there should be a pressure equalisation very shortly."

"Since you seem to be well informed, what can we expect of their atmosphere?"

"Oxygen dominated, but much too warm, corrosive and dense to be breathable. All the same, a fragrant breeze compared to Charybdis. We may also notice—"

Sharply, Lady Arek said: "Gravity is decreasing."

I noted the readout on my faceplate, as well as the neural correlate of the same reading spooling inside my head.

"Yes. For Nestbuilders, a gee is far too heavy to move around in without augmentation. Most of the ship must be creating its own microgravity environment. The lock handles both transitions: pressure and gravity."

"As long as it goes down, rather than up, we should not be inconvenienced. I am still reading *Scythe*, Warglass, is that the case for you?"

"Yes—I'm still in contact, and the door doesn't seem to be blocking the link to any significant degree. Test commands are still being received and acted on, too."

"It would be good to know the moment that stops being the case."

"Or even sooner," Pinky said. "You two are in neural contact as well, aren't you?"

"Interneural handshake protocols remain established," I answered. "That means we can communicate via Conjoiner channels, as soon as it becomes expeditious to do so. But for your sake, I think it would be a little rude if we did too much of it."

"If it's a question of saving my neck, ladies, don't spare my feelings."

"We shall not," Lady Arek said. "But there is a secondary consideration, which Warglass has not mentioned. Verbal communication, via our suits, may be safer than mind-to-mind binding. We do not yet know how the ship regards us, or what measures it may use against us, especially if it finds a vulnerability in the neural channels. Remember, we are dealing with an extraordinarily long-lived and resourceful survivor-species. They have not endured this long by being careless or overly trusting of outsiders, especially not galactic Johnny-come-latelies such as ourselves. They may not regard us as automatically hostile, but they may not welcome us either."

"If this is the welcome, it needs work," Pinky said. He stepped off the lip, arms wide, and began a slowly accelerating drift down to the bottom of the chamber.

"Rash," I remarked.

By the readings on our suits, gravity had decreased to one-hundredth of a gee: about the force we would have felt on a small moon or large asteroid. It would still have been very easy for Pinky to hurt himself, or at least put his suit into a position where it needed to take drastic action to preserve its occupant. But the thickening atmosphere meant that his terminal velocity was also much lower than it would have been under terrestrial conditions of pressure and gravity. Pinky's lights gleamed across an expanse of gently upcurving floor, sheened like ice, and he landed about as daintily as any pig could. Lady Arek and I followed our friend, and we landed neatly either side of him. The sill—and the area where the doorway had been—with *Scythe* on the other side—was now about ten metres above us, with a smooth, slippery cliff of conch material underlying the sill. As we had landed gently, though, with some coordination it ought to be possible to jump back up onto the sill. Failing that, the suits' thrusters would be able to overcome the gravity. But I was not too concerned either way: I had created a lock once; if so obliged, I could create another elsewhere. If I remained in neural linkage with *Scythe*, I could reposition the ship as needed.

I looked more closely at the floor. Beneath a thin translucency was an impression of fast, fleeting movement along circuit-like flows. I thought of shoals of impossibly organised silver fish, darting with the efficiency of nerve signals. Through my boots I felt the throb of distant processes, constant as a city's waterworks. The floater might be dormant, but it was anything but dead. Perhaps, in its way, it was rousing through layers of slumber, stirred by our presence.

I tore my gaze from the floor. We moved in bounding leaps, until we came to a sheer wall directly opposite the point of entry. An opening was already forming as we approached, needing no intervention from me. A pale blue light shone out of the inner doorway, washing over our suits. There had been no change in the air currents, so we must now be experiencing the normal atmosphere of the ship's habitable portions.

The doorway was a semicircle, with its flat edge along the floor. The three of us passed through it at the same time without difficulty. Before I had assessed the new space beyond the doorway, I turned back to watch it close over.

"Still in contact, Warglass?"

"A little attenuation, but nothing I can't compensate for."

I turned back to survey the blue-lit chamber in which we had arrived. It was an enormous bright vault, circular in plan with a domed ceiling, and according to my suit, just under eight hundred metres across. The surfaces were smooth and unadorned, gleaming back at us with the usual slippery lustre of conch material. Beneath or beyond them was the same shivering, eel-like rush of movement that had underpinned the floor. Blue light emerged from all the surfaces, obliterating shadows and making estimates of distance and perspective tricky. There were no Nestbuilders here, nor any objects that—allowing for human preconceptions—I perceived as distinct machines or larger modular components of the ship. I decided that this was not a control room in any recognisable sense, but rather something like an atrium or hallway. I could see no obvious points of exit or entry in the lower parts of the walls or the higher curvature dome.

But there was a way to progress. The floor had a spiralling path cut into it, a tightening helix which vanished down into the middle of the chamber at an ever-steepening angle.

"The ship is obviously functional," I said. "Likely its crew will be in the Nestbuilder equivalent of hibernation, a sort of desiccation, while they wait out whatever hazard compelled them to hide here. A thousand years, ten thousand, is nothing to Nestbuilders. All we need to do is find a means of accessing the ship's native data architecture, from which we'll be able to extract the Incantor construction schedules."

"All we need to do," Pinky repeated.

"Will we recognise the means to access this data architecture, when we find it?" Lady Arek asked.

"I will," I said, and tipped my head to the ceiling. "The propulsion and defensive componentry is above: cubic kilometres of dangerous machinery that rarely needed any attention from the crew." Then I nodded to the spiralling path. "Beneath us lie the command and control cores, the nursery banks, the shell cribs and desiccation vaults. Those are our best places to look for a direct portal into the data architecture. I don't think we will need to go too far down to find what we are looking for."

"Anyone would think you'd been here before," Pinky said.

"I haven't."

"Speaking for Warglass, Glass, or the Old Man?"

"Not one of us."

"But you have acquired knowledge hitherto undisclosed to us," Lady

Arek said. "Including, I imagine, that repertoire of gestural commands. Was there ever really a codex, Warglass?"

"I may have simplified one or two things."

"Simplified as in totally lied about?" Pinky asked. His question was to the point, but his tone was matter-of-fact, almost agreeable, as if now that he was in this situation he might as well make the best of it.

I could see why Nevil had liked him; why Nevil had been glad to have him at his side.

His side. Our side. My side.

"The essentials haven't changed. We've come for the Incantor. We're going to get the Incantor—the schedules that need to be fed back to *Scythe*—and we're going to leave." I set off for the spiral path. "I suggest we make use of this walkway, rather than waste suit propellant. On some level, the ship must be aware of our presence, and we won't want to be rude guests."

Lady Arek and Pinky were following. "And hacking the data architecture won't be considered bad manners?" Pinky asked.

"We'll reserve that act of rudeness until the last possible moment," I replied. "Because I expect there will be repercussions."

Pinky paused, bent forward with his hands on his hips. "Well, just as long as we don't leave ourselves too long a stroll back to the ship...we really *are* going down this scary plughole thing, aren't we?"

"We really are," I said cheerily. "Enjoy it, Pinky. This is a glorious day. You're getting to do something novel. Nothing with a spine has ever been inside one of these ships."

He straightened up. "And it'll be an even better day if something with a spine gets to leave."

We walked single file, following the winding path as it spiralled in on itself and descended, with the blue radiance becoming harder and brighter as the surfaces closed in. Beneath the path, the shimmering patterns chased and teased us, writhing in logical knots around the pressure points under our feet.

"What do we know about Nestbuilders, Lady Arek?"

"Very little, Warglass. Scraps of intelligence, little glimmers of fact: impressions and half-memories reported by the more lucid Juggler contactees, some of which correlate with each other, others of which do not. Added to that, my own fragmentary impressions gleaned from my time in the Hades matrix, when I was not even properly alive."

"But from those disparate traces..."

"They are a long-lived galactic species; one of the very few that has managed to avoid total extinction. They are organic, rather than machine. Their native form is analogous to a terrestrial arthropod: a sort of large, intelligent crab or lobster. The name derives from the vast, free-floating space structures known to have been made by their kind—enormous nest-like agglomerations of conch-like elements, hundreds and thousands of times larger than this ship. But since the Inhibitor purge, the Nestbuilders have largely abandoned these objects and become migratory."

"All of that is correct," I stated. "All of that is also wrong."

CHAPTER THIRTY-THREE

The path had become constant in pitch and radius now, corkscrewing down beneath the floor, with a plunging well running through the middle. There were no barriers to the path, and in the microgravity it would not have been difficult to step off the floor and descend directly, using suit thrust to slow us down when needed. But I had been serious in my determination not to provoke the ship unduly.

"How is it wrong, Warglass?"

"The Nestbuilders did not survive. They are dead."

Pinky hummed to himself. We carried on down.

"I do not grasp the point of that assertion. This ship is functional. You say that it is crewed, even if they are in hibernation. How can the Nestbuilders be dead?"

"Because what we are seeing here is not really the work of Nestbuilders. Let me explain."

"Please do," Pinky urged.

"Quite a long time ago—the timescales no longer matter, but we are talking about much less than a million years ago—another species encountered the Nestbuilders. They too were in flight from the Inhibitors. The distinction was that this second species recognised no ethical bounds on its own behaviour. Observing that the Nestbuilders had devised a viable survival strategy, with a robust and well-developed spacefaring and life-support capacity, this second species decided to parasite itself upon them."

"In what manner?" Lady Arek said.

"They took over their bodies. They completely co-opted the Nestbuilder starfaring civilisation: using them, in effect, as vehicles. The Nestbuilders' minds were degraded to a purely housekeeping function, while the new hosts did all the thinking. They have a name for themselves, but it would break our sanity to utter it. Call them *Slugs*. The Slugs are the new masters: the custodians of what we see around us. They haunt the bodies of the Nestbuilders, running a zombie civilisation that only looks like the Nestbuilders from outside."

"That's—"

"Darwinian, Lady Arek. No more, no less. The wolves push us all to extremes. In extremes, one finds expressions of both beauty and cruelty. But we should not judge the Slugs too harshly. Earth's biosphere has thrown up equal horrors of usurpation and genocidal self-interest. If you doubt me, ask a Neanderthal."

"This is of some theoretical interest," Lady Arek admitted. "But we come for their weapons, not their consciences."

"That is wise, because they have none."

"You have arrived at knowledge that surprises me, Warglass. I do not doubt that it is reliable: presumably springing from the same source that showed you how to break into this ship and understand its organisational structure. You have always known more than we understood to be possible. The mere fact of the Incantor...please, reassure me that we were not wrong about that, as well?"

"No, the Incantor is very real."

"And now that we are here—you are confident that we can take it?"

"The Nestbuilders would not have willingly relinquished such a thing, and neither will the Slugs. To each, the Incantor was a weapon of absolute last resort. They believed, probably with cause, that any lesser species would not be able to resist using it indiscriminately."

"Will we be any better than that?"

"That's a question for a thousand years from now. Today, we do whatever we must to survive. But in answer to your first question: I am confident that we can take it."

"And that confidence is predicated upon...?"

"We have an ally, Lady Arek. An insider. I made a generalisation just now: it would not be entirely true to say that all Slugs lack an awareness of their crime. One did. One does."

"You've met one," Lady Arek said marvellingly, as if she had just found the solution to a puzzle that had been greatly troubling her: a solution that was as charming as it was inevitable. "That is the only answer. In your travels, before you fell into my orbit, you encountered one of their kind. There was knowledge transfer. That is how you recognised the significance of the floater: how you knew that it would contain an Incantor. And how you have brought us this far. Is that true?"

"True enough for our purposes."

"Kind of a big deal not to have mentioned that," Pinky observed.

"Glass never concealed any part of it. You just didn't ask the right questions of her." I slowed my drifting pace, indicating a blur of large, immobile forms beyond the blue walls that enclosed the spiral. "The desiccation

432

vaults. We're passing through them. Do you see the Nestbuilders?"

Beyond the blue walls—beyond the thin shimmer of the logical flows—were ranks of spiralling alcoves, each containing the cancroid form of one of the host aliens. They were faint, watery shapes pinned behind that restless blue translucence. Contrary to what Lady Arek might have thought, I had never seen a Nestbuilder before, in any state of animation. The hardshelled organisms were all of a very similar size and state of development, indicating a cohort that had come up through the shell cribs at the same time, discarding exoskeletons in lockstep. Their main body was a metre across, an ornately folded shell with numerous crimped and puckered outlets for limbs and sensors. The main legs and manipulators were tucked in close, lending the form a shrivelled-up look.

"Never was one for crab," Pinky remarked. "Even less so now."

The desiccation vaults went on and on—many turns of the spiral, a good hundred metres of vertical descent. But this would only be one of the hundreds of vaults dispersed through the ship, arranged so that there was always numerical redundancy in the event of an accident or attack. Eventually, the spiral widened again, and we emerged into the upper part of a chamber just as large as the first, with the path cutting a helical groove around the inner surface of a domed ceiling. Beneath us, bleached in the same directionless blue light, was a much more promising prospect. It was a geometric division of the floor, almost like a formal garden, but with frond-like functional components of the ship rising from the ground at the intersections and borders.

"I feel I should mention something," Lady Arek said. "There is large, organised movement below."

"Yes," I agreed. Fifty metres beneath us, pale scuttling forms were leaping and scrabbling along the floor's pathways, spilling out of holes in the floor and lowest parts of the walls and coming in along different radial lines and organising into larger ranks. In microgravity they moved with astonishing speed, like liquid pouring into runnels.

"They were meant to be hibernating," Pinky said.

"Let us see what they want with us," I said. "They don't seem to be carrying weapons or armour."

Pinky twisted his suit to look at me. "They're giant armoured crabs. What part of them isn't weapons or armour?"

The Nestbuilders were flowing onto the helix, gathering into single file. These spiral walkways seemed like an inefficient means of connecting different parts of the ship, until one saw how speedily and effortlessly the aliens moved along them.

"Press back," I said, leading by example. I pushed myself hard against the outer wall of the spiral—the wall of the dome, now—and bid Pinky and Lady Arek to follow. "They aren't responding to us. If they'd detected our presence, and considered us a threat to their ship, we'd have been stopped or killed by now. This is something else."

"They'll notice us when they pass!" Lady Arek said.

"I don't think they will. But the best way of testing that is by not squeezing in against the wall."

"I'll put off the testing part for now," Pinky said, grunting as he encouraged his suit to flatten itself even more firmly against the wall.

The Nestbuilders completed each loop of the helix a little faster than the last the nearer they got to us. I tried to count them. Perhaps sixty, in all, identical in size and form to my eye, but doubtless varying in ways both minor and significant were I to study them carefully. I had a theory, but there was no point voicing it aloud until the aliens had swept past us.

They came around the last loop beneath us. Although we were not breathing the atmosphere outside, our suits were still using it for auditory pickup. The advance of the Nestbuilders was a roaring, continuous whisking, like a thousand swords being drawn and drawn again. There was no other sound: no cries, no language, no breathing, no hint of coordination between the advancing elements.

They came past us in the same frenzy of scuttling and leaping: as oblivious to our presence as I had hoped. Ten, twenty: carrying on up the tightening coil, in the direction of the desiccation vaults and the parts of the ship above us. Thirty, forty. They were low enough, even as they leapt, that their ridged, crenulated backs never came above hip-height. Only near the end did one come closer to the wall than the others, catching the toe of Lady Arek, losing its footing momentarily, even with all those legs, and in the moment of chaos that followed not only tumbling over the edge of the path, but taking two more with it. They fell slowly, their limbs stilled, and when they crunched gently against the floor—seemingly undamaged—they gathered themselves and resumed their climb.

"These are functionaries," I said, as the last of the fallers passed by again, hurrying after the others. "There are no Slugs inside them. Or if there are, they are Slugs that have been mentally downgraded, either by accident or punishment, to a kind of lobotomised docility. These functionaries are kept animate when the rest of the crew are still in the desiccation vaults. They retain just enough of their original Nestbuilder nervous system to be used as biological robots, tending to the ship. They were never interested in us, nor even properly aware of us, even as they passed. They saw us, but we didn't concern them. They had been tasked to go to some other

434

part of the ship, for some other reason, that had nothing to do with us." I qualified myself. "Or nothing directly."

"The wolves," Lady Arek said.

"I think it likely that the ship has detected their presence around Charybdis, and is now moving to a different readiness condition. The functionaries are part of that preparation."

"Battle stations?" Pinky asked.

"I don't think so. They've survived until now by avoiding engagement. It will take a lot to change that."

There was no second surge of Nestbuilders as we completed our descent to the floor. Again, I reminded myself that whatever we saw in any given area of the ship would only be a small part of the overall activity. Hundreds, even thousands, of functionaries might be moving through it as we walked. Meanwhile, some small percentage of the sleeping crew might be in the process of being roused—undesiccated—so that their higher states of sentience could be queried.

We moved across the floor, eyeing the entry points and wary of another eruption of Nestbuilders. If they came, I was as certain as I could be that their interest in us would be negligible, but they might still become a nuisance. And very soon, too. I expected to provoke the ship in ways that would be much harder for either it or its functionaries to ignore.

The floor's frond-like extrusions were numerous and varied. Each was a pulpy, translucent bag rising to about chest-height, sheathed in a pink or purple membrane and with moving, glowing forms within. The floor's patterns crowded and brightened around these extrusions: logical pathways thickening like fat-sheathed axons. The fronds all had different shapes, sizes and configurations of pseudopods, some of which were jelly-like nubs and others of which were so finely differentiated as to glimmer with glories of refracted colour. In human terms, these fronds were control terminals, status boards, data-entry ports, and perhaps a dozen other things including medical diagnostic devices or even punishment or euthanisation stations. I reached for the patterns of knowledge and recognition I expected to come naturally—the same reserves that had shown my hands how to work the gestural commands—and nothing came. I understood what I was looking at, the class of objects; I understood something of what they might be, but not the detailed particulars of any one item.

"Is this the place?" Pinky asked.

"It will be as good as any other. But I'll need to do some trial and error on these interfaces, until I find the right path into the ship, the one that will lead us to the Incantor schedules."

"Well, who doesn't like a bit of trial and error, when you're inside an alien spaceship, floating at three hundred thousand atmospheres, in a sea hot enough to singe a star."

"Let her do what she must," Lady Arek cautioned.

"Believe me, I wasn't about to stop her."

Since I had to start somewhere, I began at one of the fronds with a crown of long, finger-sized pseudopods. While Lady Arek and Pinky watched, I reached into the mass of pseudopods and allowed them to probe my glove and sleeve, gently testing its properties. The fronds were stimulating my suit with chemical and electrical signals and expecting the suit to respond in kind, just as if it were a Nestbuilder's sensory appendage. Cautiously, following a set of pre-programmed decision steps, my suit reciprocated the contact. It was generating localised electrical and chemical emissions at the points where the fronds touched it: attempting a kind of deeper, more intimate form of the gestural grammar.

In a manner the frond terminal was talking to me, or at least attempting to talk. The impulses picked up by the suit were packaged and translated into forms compatible with my neural systems. But that did not mean that I understood them. It was a discussion going on at a level beyond my own direct comprehension: alien machinery negotiating with Conjoiner machinery, and me only listening in.

The voice within me said to disconnect.

I wrenched my glove and sleeve away from the fronds. They stretched, sticking in place, then relinquished sharply, curling in with a curious brooding resentment.

Lady Arek took my hand and arm, examining it for injury or signs that the suit had been breached.

"What happened, Warglass?"

"I'm all right. I got a little way with this terminal, but it's only a local node, not strongly connected to the rest of the ship. Let me try the next."

"What is happening when you make contact with those things?"

"There's a flow of information between the frond, my suit, and then my hardware. I don't understand all of it. But I'm primed to recognise when we're getting warm, and we're not there yet."

"First the gestural commands, and now the means to process Nestbuilder data patterns. You really are a wonder." Her remark was sardonic, rather than complimentary. "When might you care to tell me how this is possible, Warglass? You said Glass met one of their kind. I can only conclude that the transfer of intelligence was considerably more than a few clues about how to break into one of their ships."

I was at the next frond, one with the larger nubs. Steeling myself for whatever was to come, I dipped my hand in. They closed around it, probing me with the soft, exploratory curiosity of nursing fish. The nubs had padded mouthlike extremities, sucking and tasting.

"Glass found a Slug, Lady Arek. Or the Slug found Glass. It was the one exception to the rule I mentioned earlier."

"A Slug with a conscience?"

"Or at least one with a grievance against its kind. It had been wronged, and it wished to see justice. The Slug had been told a lie, you see. A great, all-encompassing lie, one that cut to the very core of its being. It had been told that the Nestbuilders were devoid of intelligence before the Slugs found them. That the only crime of the Slugs was to inhabit and repurpose the mindless bodies and technologies of a post-sentient civilisation. An act of cosmic indecency, perhaps, cosmic grave-robbery, and an act of gruesome ventriloquism, but not actual xenocide."

"None of them knew?"

"All civilisations move to an accommodation of their past atrocities. Some do it by acceptance, some by forgetting. The Slugs chose to erase the fact of their crime, to pretend to themselves that the Nestbuilders were never more than empty hosts. To pretend and pretend until the pretence became fact. But Glass's Slug discovered counterfactual data. Nestbuilder relics, pointing to a retention of sentience very late in the day: entirely at odds with their species-level narrative. For that, her Slug was punished in ways that would seem mostly unfathomable to us and, after a thousand strange cruelties, they were divested of a host body: torn out of a Nestbuilder. *That* we recognise. Being left to die, like a snail without a shell. But they lived. Hatred is a very strong survival imperative."

"It's worked for me," Pinky said.

Something flowered inside my skull: a bright intrusion, like a neon fireworks display flickering across the underside of my brain-pan.

"I have..."

"I feel it too," Lady Arek said urgently. "It's *Scythe*: emergency signal."

She was right: the flowering was nothing to do with the Nestbuilders.

"Wolves?" Pinky asked.

"No," I answered, forcing myself to focus on the emergency status pulse, unpicking its threads. "Not wolves. *Scythe* is reporting inertial movement. It's still attached where we docked it, but it's being dragged further down into Charybdis. We're moving, this whole ship. We don't feel it because of this microgravity field, but it's real enough. That's how they're responding to the Inhibitors: not by going to a battle condition, but sinking deeper into Charybdis."

"They wouldn't do it if the floater couldn't take it," Pinky said, plaintively. "Would they?"

"There must be a higher level of risk, or they'd have gone as deep as they could right from the start. But it's not the Nestbuilder ship that is the problem."

He nodded behind his visor. "*Scythe* won't be able to take it."

"How much deeper can it go?" Lady Arek asked.

"With our understanding of the Gideon stones? It's impossible to predict. Another ten thousand atmospheres, another hundred thousand. Or it could be that we're almost at crush depth as it is."

"Then we abandon the extraction. Do you still have a command linkage with *Scythe*? Summon it as close as you can, then create another exit point. If you cannot do that, then we begin to retrace our steps."

"We came for the Incantor," I said stubbornly.

"And we accept failure, this time, but we fight another day. Issue the commands, Warglass. This was a noble effort, but the three of us dying here won't help anyone."

"You forget the wolves outside. We were lucky around Yellowstone, but that was because we had friends to act as distraction. Here we have nothing. We'll need the Incantor to break through them."

"We can still evade them if we leave now and leave quickly."

"Do it, Warglass. You said it yourself: we may already be close to crush depth."

I gave up on the second frond. This failure was of a different kind: not because it was too local a node, but because it seemed formatted to only understand and reciprocate a limited subset of queries, like a simplified terminal made for the use of children. Perhaps that was indeed what it was—an educator for underdeveloped Nestbuilders who had only passed through a small number of shell cribs.

I moved to the third: the kind with the fine, whiskery fronds, bursting with refraction patterns.

"I'll summon *Scythe*."

"Good."

"Lady Arek, do you trust me? I am going to ask something very demanding of you, something difficult for any Conjoined, even a Demi-Conjoiner. I should know. I'd find it just as difficult if our places were reversed."

I heard her sigh, made up in equal parts of resignation and sorrow. "You wish me to disable all my mental barricades. To give you absolute, unfettered access to my mind."

"How do you know?"

"Because I can already feel you breathing at my windows."

438

"I'm sorry, I didn't realise it was that obvious."

"Never mind." There was no rancour in her voice, just a fearful understanding. "What is it, Warglass? What are you going to do?"

The fine fronds wrapped me like vines. Their hold was firm, and as soon as they made contact the electrical and chemical information flow was going to be richer than before, demanding more of me in return.

"Three things," I said. "The first is to assign you complete control of *Scythe*, along with all associated neural command routines. You said you'd like one just like it. Well, now you have the ship itself. *Scythe* will be yours, as soon as you allow it. You will have total access to its systems and archives, forever."

I caught a swallow before her answer. "Go on."

"The second is to give you the gestural syntax, in its entirety. You will only need a small part of it: just enough to form a lock, and pass through it. I'll isolate and highlight that particular set of gestures. I think the ship will oblige—we have not been too impolite until now."

"And the third?"

"You will establish a data flow between my mind, your mind, *Scythe*, and the hypometric device. As soon as I have the Incantor schedules, they will be transmitted directly to the precursor: provided that flow remains open."

"You could do all this yourself," Pinky said, addressing me.

"She could," Lady Arek said, understanding what I intended. "But not if she remains with the Nestbuilder ship as it descends. That is your intention, isn't it, Warglass? To remain here, while Pinky and I depart?"

"There's no other way. We must get the schedules now, but I'll need more time than we have and we cannot risk *Scythe*. But if you detach, and move *Scythe* to a safer altitude, we should still be able to remain in contact. We'll only need long enough to transmit the schedules. That won't take as long as you think: they're arcane, but not complex."

"Once you go deeper, *Scythe* won't be able to return."

"I know."

"And this ship could be down here for...years, centuries."

"I know also."

"Eventually your suit will exceed its life-support endurance."

"I know."

"And you will die."

"I think it highly likely, Lady Arek, that my suit will not be the limiting factor."

"I think it also, Warglass." She regarded me silently, immense processes of deliberation going on behind the locked seals of her mind. But already

439

those seals were loosening. "We don't need a duelling adversarial network to settle this matter, the way we did inside Bright Sun. We can do it as friends and allies. I am...readily persuaded that there is no better course. If I had the means to speak to this ship, to know its secrets as you do, I might insist on our trading places. But I lack your capabilities."

"Did you feel that?"

"Feel what?"

"The universe moving on its axis. You just admitted to a deficiency."

I heard the smile in her voice. "I hope it was worth it."

"Nearly."

"I am lowering all neural barricades: do with me as you must. I suppose you will be able to verify that the conduit back to *Scythe* is working as it should?"

"I'm sending you the gestural syntax, scripting it directly into procedural memory. The conduit is established, but the flow won't begin until I have the schedules. Until then, I'll send a continuous stream of test packets, to confirm that the link remains viable. You'll feel a little like a high-pressure pipeline between me and *Scythe*, but you'll get over it."

"Doubtless I will, Warglass." Lady Arek looked down at her hand, watching as her fingers curled and uncurled, seemingly without volition. "That must be the syntax. It wants to be expressed, like an itch that needs scratching! How curious to feel as if I've always known something that was only injected into my head a few seconds ago."

"Sorry for the short-cut, but it will be easier that way." I shifted my attention for a moment. "*Scythe* is detaching now. I've instructed it to descend until it's level with our present position, just a few hundred metres below the original docking point."

"Yes, I feel it move. Your command authority is already transferring to me. May I ask something?"

"Provided it doesn't need too lengthy an answer."

"This decision of yours...I admire it, and accept it. Pinky and I will play our part. But I must know...has it been formed unanimously?"

"There has only ever been unanimity, Lady Arek. Glass was a soldier. Clavain was a soldier. We have had our minor differences, most certainly. But in the prosecution of war, there has never been any dissension. Warglass speaks with one voice."

"You say that as if this were the easiest thing in the world."

"It is."

"Old man," Pinky said. "If there's a part of you still in there, then know this. You did all right in the end. And I hope I did too. You put a lot on

440

me, back on Ararat, but I don't think I screwed up too badly. For a pig, at least." He paused. "And, Stink?"

"Yes?"

"Guess you made the grade, in the end."

"Thank you for advocating for Warren," I replied. "I think it made all the difference. And if I may speak for Warren, I can speak for Nevil as well. You never let anyone down, not once in your life. I know the Clavains have not always made things easy for you... but they chose their friends as carefully as they chose their enemies."

Pinky swallowed back something.

"Glass?"

"What is it you would say to her?"

"We'll make this count. I'll be at the ladyship's side, making sure of that."

"I do not doubt it." I smiled tightly: the eternal awkwardness of the drawn-out farewell. It was a human trait we had carried with us from prehistory, from hunting parties leaving the safety of cave mouths to the iron crush of Charybdis, it was a thing no amount of practice ever helped us get right. "And now you need to go and get aboard *Scythe*, and I need the presence of mind to make this terminal deliver me the Incantor. Go, now. The gestures will come naturally, and your intuition will guide you to the right spot in the wall. Work quickly and detach as soon as you are inside. Ascend cautiously: a sudden reduction in pressure could be just as dangerous as going any deeper."

"We shall be cautious." Lady Arek raised her hand, fingers now stilled after the in-laying of the gestural syntax. "Farewell, Warglass."

"Goodbye," Pinky said. "It's been... something."

"It has indeed," I said.

I turned my back on them then, not because I was careless of my friends, or did not wish to see them to safety, but because I needed all of my concentration, and I knew they had the wherewithal to leave without any further guidance or encouragement.

I continued with the terminal, fully engaging with the electrical and chemical interaction, assigning larger and larger areas of my mind to the task. The Nestbuilder ship was a brutal mistress: the more I gave of myself, the more it demanded. But the seriousness of its dialogue, the complexity and depth of its interrogations, assured me that I was getting close. It was disclosing layers of itself, whispering precious secrets. It thought I was someone to be trusted.

A little while later, something pricked at the edges of my attention. It was *Scythe*, informing me that it had detached from the ship and was now retracing its steps back to the relative shallows of three hundred thousand atmospheres. But the Nestbuilder ship was still on its way down. We were now five hundred kilometres deeper than when we had first docked.

I worked. Veils of formidable security and cunning misdirection vanished beneath my gaze. I glimpsed the holy citadel: the kernel in which the schedules lay treasured. It was nearly mine. I batted aside the ship's last nagging questions, the final checks before it surrendered the prize. The citadel flung itself open, and the spell for casting an Incantor flowed into my mind, and out of it—all the way back to Lady Arek, and from her mind into the waiting registers of *Scythe*, where the precursor machine waited for something to feed upon.

"Glass?"

"Yes, Clavain."

"I think our rudeness may finally have crossed some threshold. There are more Nestbuilders coming into this chamber."

It was not by conscious choice that we had disassociated again, breaking down into our component personalities. But I think it served the higher purpose of survival, to have two foci for our attention: Glass attending to the problem of the Incantor—the sort of informational-intelligence work that had always been her metier—and Clavain maintaining situational awareness, cold eyes levelled to the horizon. I was still Warglass, but within me were two assets I would be foolish to neglect.

These new Nestbuilders, emerging into the chamber, arrived in far fewer numbers than the first group. I counted no more than twelve. But by their independence of movement, their caution and curiosity, I recognised that these were not the robotic functionaries we had seen before. These were the sort that had fully intelligent Slugs within them, perhaps more than one, driving these armoured bodies as if they were expendable mechanical exoskeletons. Undoubtedly these were members of the crew who had been summoned from desiccation, initially because of the detection of the wolf concentration. But now, having been revivified, they had been alerted to investigate anomalous activity in this chamber. What they were in the process of discovering was a human, in a spacesuit of human manufacture (they knew of us, albeit distantly, and with only a dry disregard) and engaged in stealing technical secrets from their data vaults. Perhaps, already, some systems audit had confirmed that the data flow related to the Incantor.

I—or rather Clavain—did not hesitate. The suit began to repel the Nestbuilders. It did so non-lethally, for our interest lay in stealing from the aliens, not adding them to our toll of enemies. By blasting small puncture wounds into their shells, the tissue beneath could be locally superheated to the point where it produced steam, sending Nestbuilders skittering across the floor in microgravity. If that did not work, or was insufficient deterrent, the suit was authorised to snip away at the peripheral limbs. It could do that without causing harm to the Slugs.

But we would kill them if we had to, and meanwhile Glass left an indelible message at every point in the ship's data architecture that I was able to access. The message was in the language of Slugs, a matter of personal business. In terms that we might comprehend it said: *Allow the humans to leave with the Incantor, allow them to duplicate it, and use it as they see fit, and I will hold my silence concerning the act that was perpetrated against the Nestbuilders. Impede the humans, act against them at any point in the future, and the truth that was told to me will propagate and poison every one of our kind, until the stars choke and die. Do not doubt that I have the means.*

The degree to which it had any effect was difficult to say. No more Nestbuilders were coming…but perhaps this was as many as the ship could muster at short notice and with it already under the strain of sinking deeper into the ice giant.

But those that were here were not being easily deterred. Even with parts of their shells and limbs missing, they were returning to the fray. Steadfastly I refused to escalate to more lethal modes of persuasion. This was not mere prudence, but a sober reflection on our predicament. If I started using high-energy weapons, there was no gauging the incidental damage that might be done to the ship, nor how vulnerable it might have become since descending further.

"How far along are we?"

"About twenty per cent of the schedule is now with *Scythe*."

"Can you make it go faster?"

"I don't know, Clavain, what do you think?"

"Just a question."

"Not a particularly helpful one. I'm doing all that I can, but this is a very slow sensory modality. The suit is the bottleneck, not the connection between my mind and Lady Arek."

"Then I might make a suggestion."

There was a long wait for elaboration. "Which is?"

"We are going to die, Glass. Neither of us is any doubt about that. We are never leaving Charybdis. And even if I thought there was a chance of *Scythe* returning to these depths to rescue us, I wouldn't countenance putting Pinky and Lady Arek at risk."

After brooding on an answer: "Nor would I. We've asked enough of them. This is our grave, whatever happens."

"So the question becomes…not *do* we die…"

"But what useful thing can we do in dying."

After an interval of consideration: "How long do you think we could survive without the suit, Glass?"

"A very short, unpleasant while."

"Quantify it."

"A few minutes. Four or five at the most."

"But there would be no bottleneck. Especially if..."

"Especially if we were not inside the suit. If we can establish a direct physical link between the Nestbuilder ship and our mind...with no suit in the way, slowing things down..."

"It must be done, Glass. The sooner the better."

New fronds were emerging from strategic points in the floor. The Nestbuilders that were still capable of movement—those that had not been too badly incapacitated—were gathering at these fronds, plucking fruit-like nubs from their fleshy crowns. They were assembling these nubs into larger forms.

"You are aware, Clavain, that there will be no going back. When the alien air hits us, I will do my best to make it bearable. There are pain blockades that should make those last few minutes tolerable. But tolerable will not be the same as pleasant."

"However we end, Glass, I think we will have had a better deal than many. What about the one inside us..."

Amusedly: "I wondered how long you had known."

"Longer than you think. But not as soon as I should have. I'll give you this much: you never once lied. I asked you if it was a life-support device and you answered truthfully. The error was all mine: assuming the means of life-support applied to you."

"Would you have trusted me sooner, knowing I carried an alien—a Slug—inside my chest?"

"I think, in time, I would have come to an understanding of it."

"Liar."

"All right. You've got me there. But I tried."

The Nestbuilders were massing around us with their new tools. Once joined, the nubs had morphed and merged into larger items. They were veined and glistening, throbbing with internal circulation. The Nestbuilders attacked our suit in several different ways. Some of the nubs spat a blue fire, a sort of liquid flame which, once in contact with the suit, moved with a vague, amoeba-like intelligence. Where it had passed, the suit showed a blistered wound which defeated its self-repair routines. Other nubs seemed to secrete an acid, etching deep furrows into the armour. While all this was going on, the Nestbuilders were using their other limbs to snip and wrestle with us. We thrashed them away. The suit's weapons were still functioning, and permitted to exceed the earlier thresholds, albeit narrowly.

For a moment, with bodies and limbs scattered around us, the nubs turned to withered black husks, there was an interlude. The remaining Nestbuilders were circling, lurching and limping, contemplating their next move. Very soon they would elect to destroy or damage the terminal itself, if that was within their means. That they had not already done so spoke to the possibility of inflicting injury on their ship, but it would not be long before that became an acceptable outcome.

It was time.

"Open the suit."

"Are we sure?"

"Yes. We're sure. Do it now, while we still can."

The command was given. The suit naturally needed superhuman persuasion before it was convinced to expose its occupant to an atmosphere it knew to be incompatible with the preservation of life. But between us we had become very good at superhuman persuasion. The disassociation was gone again, now: our differences erased. In this moment, as we had promised Lady Arek, there was only unanimity.

I was Warglass again.

Inside my chest, something broke free of the layers of willing confinement it had wrapped around itself. When the last seal broke, there was only a little curtain of muscle, bone, and skin to be flung aside before the blue light flooded in. Mere disposable human tissue, nothing of consequence. There was, as I had expected, some discomfort as the Slug ripped its way out of my chest, on its way to a closer union with the Nestbuilder ship. But all things told it was not, in the end, quite as bad as it could have been.

A voice that might have been mine sent one last query: "Do you have it, Lady Arek?"

"Yes. It's complete. The check sums are validated. I am feeding the schedule to the precursor immediately. If we are wrong, if there has been an error, I imagine we shall know very, very shortly."

"I imagine we shall too. But there won't be an error." I smiled, allowing myself one last boast. "I don't do errors. Happy hunting, Lady Arek, and please, take *very* good care of your ship."

It was timely. The link back to *Scythe* was losing coherence. Somewhere above us those vast, dark megatonnes of compressed atmosphere were closing the door on the rest of creation. It was just us now, in a dying body, in a dying ship, falling into Charybdis, hoping that the work we had done was sufficient. Whatever happened out there, whatever became of Lady Arek, whatever became of Pinky, whatever became of the Incantor or of the wolves—their fates entwined—it would not be ours to know.

But that was all right. We had done what we had come to do. The precursor machinery had its schedule, the knowledge to forge an Incantor. And what had been done once could be done again, in other systems. With these dark, dangerous gifts, humanity could begin to push back. To emerge from its hiding places, out of the shadows and into the light. To draw a line against the wolves and begin to retaliate. And if these little victories only gained us a few centuries, then in those times granted us we would think of something else. Yes, it was indeed all right, here at the end. We had known and seen enough.

I said goodbye to Clavain.

I said goodbye to Glass.

I thought we were done with each other. We had been cruel to each other, each in our fashion, and there were crimes that could not be forgiven. But there had been kindness, too, and consolation, and a kind of atonement.

But Glass had one last gift to give.

CHAPTER THIRTY-FOUR

At last I felt some relaxation in the tension between the Gideon stones and the cryo-arithmetic engines. *Scythe* had climbed two thousand kilometres nearer to the outermost cloud layer, and while I believed that we were still deep enough to be safe from wolves, the pressures and temperatures now confronting the ship were entirely manageable.

"What?" Pinky asked, after regarding me for long minutes.

"What, what?"

"That look. The one that says that you know something the rest of us don't."

"By some criteria that would be the look I have carried my entire life. But you are right, my friend: there has been a development." While the hypometric device threshed and whirled at a higher rate than before, kneading and stretching spacetime like dough, bringing the Incantor into existence, I smiled fondly, more grateful than ever to have my loyalest ally at my side. "While Warglass was trying to find her way to the Incantor, she told me she was sending test packets, to make sure we had a stable connection. That was true enough. The packets served that purpose very well."

"And beyond that?"

"Warglass embedded non-essential data into those packets. I recognised that there was deeper structure in the packets, but I set it aside until I was sure that the schedules had come through cleanly. Only now have I taken the time to unpack the embedded data."

"What is it?"

"I think you can already guess, Pinky. Shards of a life. Shards of two lives, more accurately. Pieces of Glass are within me now, and the pieces of Clavain that came with her from Ararat."

"The question a pig might ask is... which Clavain?"

"I think we will both need some time to work that one out. Certainly there are traces of Warren in these fragments: specific memories and emotional affectations that can only be derived from his life before Glass,

447

as real or unreal as that was. But if a part of his life thereafter involved contact with the Jugglers, and through them some communion with whatever remained of his brother? I dare not say. All I can assert, with any certainty, is that I am now the custodian of these shards."

"But they aren't alive within you. This isn't the way it was with Warglass, two minds in the same skull?"

"No," I said, not without some regret. "Not like that. Their voices are silent, for now. Perhaps they will speak again, but not today. Yet while I have these shards, while I carry them within myself, I do not think it would be correct to say that Glass and Clavain are truly dead."

"They'd better budge up, then. It must be getting crowded in that head."

"My mind is a mansion with many rooms. There is always space."

He shook his head wonderingly.

"Did I ever tell you how scary you can be?"

"Perhaps I am no more than what is required. These are indeed scary times, after all."

Pinky nodded to the control room console. "Do any of those readouts help me understand how our new toy's doing? I feel like a dog being shown hieroglyphics."

"Something is busy being born. Something slouches its way towards us. I think, in a few minutes, we shall have some idea of what it is, and what we may do with it."

"And when that time comes...are you the one to know?"

"The Incantor's functioning is beyond our comprehension—beyond even mine. But the set of commands by which it may be used is not complicated at all." Knowing that nothing I did or said could hasten the processes now instigated, I forced my attention onto the more immediate matter of our departure from Charybdis. With the utmost insouciance, I used every active and passive sensor to scan the thinning layers of atmosphere above our position, and the near-orbital space just beyond it. I no longer cared that by doing so I removed any possible ambiguity about our presence.

"There's a thing that troubles me," Pinky said.

"Just the one?"

"The Nestbuilders had this weapon. But something held them back from using it."

"They used it. But sparingly."

"And the reason for that restraint?"

"I expect we shall find out, in time. But that is the crux of it. In time. We saw the lights go out, you and I. We have seen the ships stop flying and the worlds fall into silence. One by one we have watched the beacons

448

of civilisation gutter into darkness. We have stood vigil in the twilight. There is no future for us now except a few squalid centuries, and only then if we are very lucky. But the Incantor buys us possibility. It hinges our history onto another track. It may be better, it may even be worse, but the one thing we can be sure of is that it will be different. And if after a few centuries we begin to understand that there have been consequences to our use of the Incantor, we shall meet them. We shall pay for our actions. But we shall have lived, and that is better than the alternative."

After a moment, the pig nodded; understanding, if not yet fully persuaded. "The old man would have seen it similarly."

"And you?"

"I suppose the human thing is to buy time."

"Always and forever."

"But one of these will only do so much good, won't it?"

"Then it's as well that there will be more," I answered. "Glass laid the preparations. Wherever she went, she had *Scythe* bud off parts of itself: self-assembling seeds, which used ambient matter to grow themselves into manufactory units like the one in which we made the hypometric device. Hela, Sun Hollow, Yellowstone, wherever there might be allies to make use of them, Glass left these seeds. All these manufactories needed to do was wait for the arrival of the Incantor schedules. And now all we have to do is transmit them."

"Someone will have to know what to do when they arrive."

"They will," I said. "Glass made sure of that, as well."

Within the hypometric device, a process neared fruition. The threshing machinery was slowing, the blades opening, the entire bizarre structure loosening apart like a time-lapsed recording of an exploding bomb. While *Scythe* loitered inside the cover of the atmosphere the wolves, undoubtedly as aware of us as we were of them, but not yet persuaded that it was worth the trouble of closing in on us while we were still inside Charybdis— for where else could a little human ship go but back into space?—I left Pinky in the control room, put a suit back on and passed back into the bulb-shaped assembly volume. It was cavalier of me, I suppose, but I wanted to see the evidence of our work with my own eyes, in the first moments of its existence.

The hypometric machinery had stilled. It had disconnected and disassembled itself and retreated to the outer walls of the bulb, becoming a glittering, many-edged plaque.

Where the main mass of the hypometric device had been, in the bulb's core, there now floated an Incantor.

It was beyond my powers of description. I could say with some confidence that it occupied a volume of space of a certain size and shape: approximately a cylinder, about three metres across and twenty long. It was smaller than I had anticipated. But on some level I understood that matters of size and form became slippery in the context of an Incantor. This was an artefact anchored to a layer of reality that was not quite congruent with ours. What I saw—what I thought I saw—was some partial shadow or projection of the true entity. I was not capable of apprehending the true form of it. I might go to the Jugglers and have my perceptual limits remodelled, so that the nature of the weapon became comprehensible to me. But if I did that I would never be able to explain or describe it to anyone else, even via the mind-to-mind channels of the Conjoined.

What could I say, truthfully? There was a light. It bled out of the Incantor. It was something close to purple, being made up of red and blue photons. Where they had come from, and what dark bargains had been struck to keep the universe's bookkeeping square, I could not say. I found it hard not to stare into the light's depths, into the seductive, shifting, layered mysteries of the Incantor. There were details within it, glories of structure and componentry, some teasing promise of rational organisation. But I could not hold any part of it clearly long enough to relate it to another. My head swam, my thoughts twisted back around themselves like Möbius loops. Cross-eyed and fuzzy-headed, I realised that I had forgotten to breathe.

I drew life into my lungs and turned from the Incantor. It was ready, and I knew what to do with it. But it was not mine to understand or admire.

"Are we ready?" Pinky asked, when I returned to him.

"We are."

We shrugged off the last of the atmosphere. Beneath us, an energy pulse flared once within Charybdis, and we guessed that the Nestbuilders had gone too deep after all.

Then we swung to face the wolves, and I made ready.

Nicola drew back the kitchen chair and invited me to sit. She was older than I remembered, but not so aged that I failed to recognise her. The years had been gentle to her in some ways, less so in others, but the patience and tolerance I had so often called upon was still present, breaking through the lines and blemishes.

"I never forgot you," I said.

"Nor we you," said Victorine, who was already seated.

She was a woman now, about as old as Nicola had been when we first met, back in the first year of Sun Hollow. Though I could still see the child in her, it was like glimpsing something through many nested shells of experience, each a hard, bitterly won layer. She wore these layers as *Scythe* wore its armouring skein: clinging close to her, surface-conformal. There had been grief, sadness, anger, despair, hope, sorrow, disillusionment. And again hope, again despair, a dozen times over, grinding away at her human core as if she were some foreign thing that the universe very much wished to annihilate. But she had endured.

"You came through," I said, scraping my seat forward, as Nicola lowered into hers, facing me next to her daughter. Two grown women now, similar in so many regards, even to the common threads of grey hair and the particular way time had grooved their faces, as if working from the same diagram.

"Things nearly fell apart," Nicola said. "Not just because she took you from us. You were important, but not that important. But then, I don't need to tell you that. You had many sins, Miguel. But pride was never one of them."

"How bad was it?"

"Very bad," Victorine said. Her voice was deeper than her mother's, her delivery somehow more measured and judicial, as if each utterance were a verdict in stone, incapable of being overturned. I sensed that she would never be someone who spoke unnecessarily, and that many would listen when she did. "A third died in the five years after your departure. But things got a little better after that. Glass had left instructions in Sanctum's archives: better ways of making do with what we had. It took a little while to learn how to use them, but once we did, it was never as bad again. And the manufactories she had left us began to spit out things that helped our medicine, agronomy and life-support. We have something better than torpor boxes now, as well. That's useful, because there's good reason for some of us to sleep out the years and decades, from time to time."

"And the defences?"

Nicola answered: "She made them better as well. Improved our surveillance and our weapons. Eventually, in the seventeenth year after you left, a small number of wolves arrived in our system. We thought it was the end of us, but Glass's weapons dispersed them quite effectively. Of course, we knew they would come back one day, and that there would be more, and that we would need something better than those weapons. But we survived."

"Did other ships ever come?"

"No," they answered in unison, with something between regret and relief. "No other ships."

"Then no one else needed to die. That's good, I think. Though I would have liked to have known that there were others still out there."

"Are there?" Victorine asked.

"I think so. I think I may have met some. There were some people in the sea, a king and a queen. But it's a little hard to remember." I worked my fingers together restlessly. "I'm not even sure what it means to be having this conversation. I think I might be dead, or dying. I think I might still be inside a planet. Is this real? Are we really talking?"

"Did you want to see us again?" Nicola asked, deflecting my question.

"Yes," I answered forcefully.

"Even though we were from a part of your life that was never quite true."

"It was all true. It doesn't matter what name I had, or where I thought I'd come from. I cared for you."

The two women glanced at each other: some delicate crux had arrived. "Glass left us other things," Victorine said. "One was the means to have this conversation. We're not speaking to you directly. That would be impossible, with so much time and distance between us. But Glass said that if we spoke of you often enough, and talked between us about what you had been, and what we might want to say to you, her machine would gather these impressions and put them into a transmission. When it was safe to do so, it would be sent out into space, to be picked up wherever you were. We could send it at any time, but in the instructions she left us, Glass said that it was important to wait until we were ready to make the Incantor."

"You have one?"

"Not yet," Nicola said, smiling gently at my confusion. "But the hypometric machine is ready and primed to activate, as soon as the schedules arrive. They'll come, one day. It might be a year from now or several decades, but they'll arrive, and we'll be ready."

"Have you tested it?"

"No: Glass warned that the activation alone might function as a wolf lure, so we should never be tempted to activate the device until we are quite sure that the schedule is with us."

"And so we wait," Victorine said, squeezing her mother's hand. "For the day we know will come. We sleep, through the quiet years. Sun Hollow grants us this. It knows that it will have need of us in the future." A touching awkwardness came about her. "We thought that it would be good for you to know this, wherever you are."

"Tell him," Nicola said.

Some additional diffidence—humility or shyness—creased Victorine's lips. "I am the one it's chosen. Or rather, Glass chose me. The hypometric device will answer only to me, and when the Incantor forms, I will be its guardian. I did not choose this; it was chosen for me."

I shook my head, awed by the wonderful and frightening being that she had become.

"Victorine the Wolf-Slayer. It seems...fitting."

"I will be wise," she said, as if I had begun to voice a suspicion to the contrary. "I do not need to know what the Incantor will do, to know that it cannot be borne lightly."

"There will be others," I said. "It will be a difficult burden, I'm sure, but you'll have the knowledge that you're not alone. Other systems, other Incantors, other wolf-slayers. I just wish I could be there to help."

"You would be dead by now," Nicola said.

Her bluntness amused me. As tempting as it was to blame it on an infelicity of Glass's machine, it was entirely true to character. I had loved her for it once, and some part of me still did.

"Yes, that's probably true. Glass made me younger again, on her ship, but only because she needed me that way. In the end, I'm not sure it made much difference. But until we got to...this place...she couldn't know what would be needed of either of us."

"Where are you?" Victorine asked.

I had to fight both to summon the name and force my mind onto the true nature of my predicament, and its inescapability. "A planet called Charybdis."

With her mother's unsparing directness she asked: "And will you die there?"

"I think I may have already died. Or be dying. But I know this: Glass must have received this transmission from you, or it wouldn't be possible to know any of this. It must have reached *Scythe* many years ago, though: anything else would be a ridiculous coincidence. But Glass didn't want me to know about it until now."

"Cruelty?" Nicola asked.

"No, I think it was actually a strange sort of kindness."

"Then why now?"

"Because we've succeeded. The Incantor schedules are inside *Scythe*. And very shortly those same schedules will be on their way to you. They'll be spreading out across space, ready to be received and acted upon by all the hypometric devices Glass left in her wake. It will take time: many decades. But it doesn't matter if the wolves intercept those signals: they'll never get ahead of them. And by the time they arrive, wherever they follow the signals, they'll meet an Incantor."

"You won't see it," Victorine said.

"No. But I've had this moment. This knowledge. It's enough. It's more than I deserved."

"You call that kindness?" Nicola asked.

"I do," I said.

Some prickling sense told me that I might be in danger of overstaying my welcome. I made to push back my chair, and leave Nicola and Victorine in peace. But Nicola laid a hand on mine. "Stay awhile, Miguel de Ruyter. Remember what I said to you, at the end. You were a good man."

Victorine met her mother's words with a nod, and the three of us linked hands. I sat down again, knowing this time I could stay, while the white light of love filled our hearts and seemed to swell out into the room itself, cleansing everything with its radiance.

ACKNOWLEDGEMENTS

A number of friends were kind enough to read and offer comment on this book. I would like to thank, in no particular order: Bernt Handl, Kotska Wallace, Tim Kaufmann, Frank Perrin, Merryn Jongkees, Sam Miller, Roy Miller, Paul McAuley, Louise Kleba, Bob Pell, William Donelson, Kate and Carol Sherrod, Malcolm Galloway, Ulla-Maija Borg, and my wife Josette Sanchez. Such flaws as remain in the book, of course, are entirely my responsibility. I would also like to thank my editors, Gillian Redfearn, Abigail Nathan and Brit Hvide for their continued insight and encouragement, and I would also like to express my appreciation to the rest of the teams at Orion and Orbit. Thanks also to Robert and Yasmin at United Agents. Finally, although she did not live to see this novel finished, I remain grateful to my mother Diane for the kindness and encouragement she showed me throughout my writing career, back to the very earliest days when I was thinking up places like Chasm City and Yellowstone.

END NOTES

Here are some additional notes on the Revelation Space universe, including a timeline, key characters (as they relate to the current book) and a brief glossary. I've also appended some notes on the internal consistency of the timeline, which I hope will be of interest.

Condensed timeline for Revelation Space universe and Inhibitor Phase

2190—	Coalition-Conjoiner War on Mars
2205—	Nevil Clavain defects to Galiana's side
Circa 2300–2500—	A "Belle Epoque" period of expansion, colonisation and great prosperity. Perfection of relativistic starflight. Mind-uploading. Numerous extrasolar planets settled. Speciation of humanity into many distinct factions. Realisation that most alien civilisations appear to be extinct
2510—	Melding Plague afflicts human space
2567—	Human activity in Resurgam system triggers Inhibitor Phase
2675—	Nevil Clavain dies on Ararat
2750—	Glass leaves Hela en route to Sun Hollow
2791—	Glass's arrival at Sun Hollow
2828—	Glass and Miguel rendezvous with Lady Arek
2850—	Bright Sun manoeuvre and return to Ararat
2858—	Events in Charybdis
2882—	Victorine receives Incantor schedule
Circa 2900–3300—	Human reprisal against wolf incursion, second Belle Epoque before Greenfly emergence forces human diaspora

KEY CHARACTERS IN THE TIMELINE

Aura: daughter of **Ana Khouri,** one of the crew aboard the *Nostalgia for Infinity*. Due to the odd circumstances of her conception, Aura was born with advanced tactical knowledge relating to the Inhibitors. Her brain incorporated some elements of Conjoiner neurocybernetic architecture, making her a Demi-Conjoiner.

Brannigan, John: a very long-lived human who eventually ended up cybernetically fused with the starship *Nostalgia for Infinity*.

Clavain, Nevil: a soldier, born in the mid twenty-second century, who became a significant figure in the first war against the Conjoiners, a sect of rogue neuroscientists led by **Galiana** who established an experimental compound on Mars.

Els, Rashmika: a pseudonym adopted by **Aura.**

Galiana: figurehead of the Conjoiner movement, and an ally of **Nevil Clavain** following his defection to her cause.

Gideon: an alien, a survivor of the "grub" species, kept alive and exploited via cruel means by criminal factions in Chasm City.

Khouri, Ana: a former soldier, assassin and weapons specialist aboard *Nostalgia for Infinity.*

Pink, Mister: a pseudonym adopted by **Scorpio**.

Scorpio: a hyperpig and close friend and ally of **Nevil Clavain**.

Skade: a ruthless Conjoiner whose methods were fiercely opposed by **Nevil Clavain.**

Veda, Irravel: a starship captain who made one of the longest relativistic voyages in history, taking her across many centuries and far out into galactic space.

Voi, Sandra: a political figure in the Demarchist movement, who adopted a moderate, conciliatory stance in the war against the Conjoiners. An early Conjoiner starship was named in her honour.

Volyova, Ilya: senior crewmember on *Nostalgia for Infinity*: mentor and eventual friend to Ana Khouri.

SELECTED GLOSSARY

Ararat: a Pattern Juggler-dominated water world around p Eridani.

Boser: directed energy system employing coherent (Bose-Einstein condensate) matter, usually with a laser or particle-beam precursor.

Canasian: a language incorporating elements of Cantonese and Quebecois French. The main language of **Demarchists**.

Chasm City: the largest conurbation in human space, constructed around a gas-belching void on the otherwise inhospitable **Yellowstone**. Closely aligned economically with the **Glitter Band**.

Coalition for Neural Purity: an amalgamation of conservative states opposed to mind augmentation technologies.

Conjoiners: a human faction employing extensive mind-to-mind linkage. Emerging from Mars, Conjoiner technology made human starflight practicable.

Conjoiner drive or C-drive: propulsion system manufactured by **Conjoiners** and sold to various clients including **Demarchists**.

Cryo-arithmetic engine: quantum-computational cooling system, employing local thermodynamic violation. **Conjoiner** invention.

Darkdrive: a modified **Conjoiner drive** with no detectable emission products.

Demarchists: a human faction using implants to achieve real-time participatory democracy.

Glitter Band: in pre-plague years, the ring of 10,000 habitats orbiting **Yellowstone**.

Great Wall of Mars: a 200-kilometre-tall ringlike "atmospheric dam" built on Mars. Designed by Europan Demarchists under Sandra Voi, the wall employed advanced, actively strengthened materials science. Dismantled by **Coalition** forces on the eve of the second **Conjoiner** war.

Haven: a colony world orbiting Gliese 687.

Hela: an icy moon in the 107 Piscium system, orbiting the gas giant Haldora.

461

Hyperpig: pig-human chimera of human-level intelligence.

Hypometric: a class of technologies involving manipulation of space-time at the Planck or sub-Planck level.

Inhibitors: self-replication robots of alien origin, utilising cube-like modular sub-elements of variable size. Also known as **wolves**.

Lighthugger: any large space vehicle with a relativistic cruise ceiling.

Medichine: subcellular nanotechnology, usually of a biomedical rather than military/cybernetic nature.

Melding Plague: nanotechnological virus of probable alien origin, responsible for collapse of the **Demarchist** golden age in 2510.

Nestbuilders: symbiotic intelligences who have retained starfaring capability despite the emergence of the **Inhibitors**.

Norte: a language incorporating elements of English and Spanish.

Pattern Jugglers: amorphous, aquatic alien organisms forming a single information processing entity. Jugglers have been encountered on several isolated worlds, implying some earlier seeding programme. Jugglers record and update the neural patterns of sentient organisms entering their seas.

Reefersleep: the cryogenic freezing technology adopted by **Demarchists**, **Conjoiners** and **Ultras**.

Russish: a language derived from Russian and English elements.

Rust Belt: in post-plague years, the band of mainly ruined habitats still orbiting **Yellowstone**.

Torpor: a less advanced form of hibernation technology compared to **reefersleep**, suitable only for short intervals.

Ultras: a loose, anarchic affliliation of starship crews (derived from a variety of factions) who spend their entire lives on ships, often at relativistic speed.

Wolves: informal term for the Inhibitors.

Yellowstone: the major settled world in the Epsilon Eridani system, home to **Chasm City**.

A NOTE ON CHRONOLOGY

When I began writing this novel I had a story in mind, one that I hoped would fit into the existing chronology of events laid out by other books and stories set in the Revelation Space universe. Things are rarely that simple.

The principal events that happen in the foreground of this novel are indeed broadly compatible with the existing canon, since they mostly take place after *Absolution Gap*, chronologically the last novel in the sequence before now. The only exception is the framing passages in AG, which are set further in the future again—around about the year 3300.

Where we run into difficulties is in the latter stages of the novel, and how those events mesh with the timeline of *Galactic North*.

Irravel's narrative in that story has her communing with a representative of the Nestbuilders around a star in the Hyades, in the year 2931. It's clear from Irravel's discussion that humans have already deployed Nestbuilder weaponry against the Inhibitors, just as they are setting out to do in 2858, at the conclusion of *Inhibitor Phase*. While these dates might not seem to contradict each other, on closer inspection they introduce a difficulty.

Although it might be 2931 by Irravel's reckoning, the latest news she could hope to receive from back home would be from about 2780, a century and a half earlier. That's because the Hyades star cluster is very much further out than any of the locations we've visited in this or the other novels.

The first and least problematic get-out is to assume that the entry in Irravel's narrative must be considered erroneous. Her next entry isn't for another four hundred years, so there's plenty of room to adjust the chronology without throwing her timeline out of joint.

The second approach is to assume that, since Irravel is clearly heading further and further from Earth, she has decided that she no longer needs to synchronise her clocks to any local reference frame. By that reckoning, although she calls it 2931, the real date when the signals reach her would be nearer to 3080, from the point of view of someone on Earth. The later dates in her narrative can be reconciled with Irravel making stopovers, following a circuitous route, or just changing her mind.

As for the framing events in *Absolution Gap*, these remain consistent within the timeline regardless of either assumption above.

extras

orbit

meet the author

Photo Credit: Barbara Bella

ALASTAIR REYNOLDS was born in Barry, South Wales, in 1966. He studied at Newcastle and St. Andrews universities and has a PhD in astronomy. He stopped working as an astrophysicist for the European Space Agency to become a full-time writer. *Revelation Space* and *Pushing Ice* were shortlisted for the Arthur C. Clarke Award; *Revelation Space*, *Absolution Gap*, *Diamond Dogs*, *Turquoise Days*, and *Century Rain* were shortlisted for the British Science Fiction Award, and *Chasm City* won the British Science Fiction Award.

Find out more about Alastair Reynolds and other Orbit authors by registering for the free monthly newsletter at orbitbooks.net.

if you enjoyed
INHIBITOR PHASE

look out for

TERMINAL WORLD

by

Alastair Reynolds

In a far-distant future, Spearpoint, the last human city, is a vast, atmosphere-piercing spire. Clinging to its skin are the zones: semiautonomous city-states, each of which enjoys a different—and rigidly enforced—level of technology.

Following a botched infiltration mission, enforcement agent Quillon has been living incognito, working as a pathologist in a morgue. But when a near-dead angel drops onto his dissection table, his world is wrenched apart.

For the angel is a winged posthuman from Spearpoint's Celestial Levels. And with the dying body comes bad news: Quillon must leave his home and travel into the cold and hostile lands beyond Spearpoint's base. But he can neither imagine how far the journey will take him, nor comprehend how much is at stake....

CHAPTER ONE

The call came in to the Department of Hygiene and Public Works just before five in the afternoon. Something messy down on the ledge, maybe a faller from one of the overhanging buildings up in Fourth, maybe all the way from Circuit City. The dispatcher turned to the wall map, surveyed the pin lights and found a clean-up van close enough to take the call. It was one of the older crews, men he knew. He lifted the black handset of his telephone and spun the dial, taking a drag on his cigarette while the switchboard clunked and whirred.

"Three oh seven."

"Got a smear for you, Cultel. Something out on the ledge, just west of the waterworks. Not much else out there so you should spot it easy enough. Take the service duct on Seventh and Electric and walk the rest of the way. Keys on the blue hook should get you through any municipal locks."

"We're loaded here. And we're about a minute from coming off shift. Can't you pull in someone else?"

"Not at rush hour I can't. We wait for another van, smear's going to start attracting a crowd and smelling bad. Seagulls are already taking an interest. Sorry, Cultel, but you're going to have to suck it up and earn some overtime."

"Fine. But I was serious about being loaded. You'd better get another van to meet us, case we have to move some stiffs around."

"I'll see what I can do. Call in when you've peeled it off the concrete; we'll start the paperwork at this end."

"Copy," Cultel said.

"And watch your step out there, boys. It's a long way down, and I don't want to have to call Steamville and tell them they need to deal with a couple of smears of their own."

470

In the clean-up van, Cultel clicked off his handset and hung it back under the dashboard. He turned to his partner, Gerber, who was digging through a paper bag for the last doughnut. "You get all that?"

"Enough."

"Another fucking ledge job. They know how much I love ledge jobs."

"Like the man said, suck it up and earn some overtime." Gerber bit into the doughnut and wiped the grease off his lip. "Sounds good to me."

"That's because you've got a sweet tooth and expensive girlfriends."

"It's called having a life outside of scraping pancakes off pavement, Cultel. You should try it sometime."

Cultel, who always did the driving, grunted something derogatory, engaged the flywheel and powered the van back onto the pick-up slot. Traffic was indeed already thickening into rush hour, cars, taxis, buses and trucks moving sluggishly in one direction, almost nose to tail in the other. Being municipal, they could go off-slot when they needed to, but it still required expert knowledge of the streets and traffic flow not to get snarled up. Cultel always reckoned he could make more money driving taxis than a clean-up wagon, but the advantage of ferrying corpses around was that he mostly didn't need to make conversation. Gerber, who generally had his nose into a bag of doughnuts, didn't really count.

It took them twenty minutes to make it to Seventh and Electric. The service duct was accessed by a sloping ramp between two buildings, the ramp facing out from Spearpoint, an arched grill-work door at the bottom of it. Cultel disengaged the pick-up shoe and flywheeled down the slope, hoping he'd still have enough spin to get back up it when they had the smear loaded. No sign of the other van yet. He snatched the keyset from the blue tag, grabbed the equipment from behind his seat and left the corrugated-sided van, Gerber carrying a camera and a heavy police-style torch.

When Cultel was new in Hygiene and Works, the cops were always first on the scene at a faller, with the clean-up crew just there to go through the menial business of peel-off and hose-down. But the cops couldn't keep up lately, and so they were perfectly willing for Hygiene and Works to handle the smears, provided everything was documented and signed off properly. Anything that looked like foul play, the cops could always get involved down the line. Mostly, though, the fallers were just accident victims. Cultel had no reason to expect anything different this time.

They passed through the municipal gate and walked down the concrete-lined service duct, which was dark and dank, with bits of cladding peeling off every few spans. Rainwater run-off seeped through the cracks and formed into a slow-moving stream deep enough to soak through Cultel's shoes. It smelled a little bit of sewer. Beyond, at the far end of the service duct, was a half-circle of indigo sky. Cultel could already feel the cool evening wind picking up. Back from the ledge, with buildings all around, you didn't feel it much. But it was always colder towards the edges. Quieter, too: it didn't take much to absorb the hum of traffic, the rattle of commuter trains, the moaning of cop car sirens as they wound their way up and down the city's lazy spiral.

Beyond the duct, the concrete flooring gave way to Spearpoint's underlying fabric. No one had ever bothered giving the black stuff a name because it was as ubiquitous as air. The ledge began level and then took on a gradually steepening slope. Cultel watched his footing. The stuff was treacherous, everyone knew that. Felt firm as rock one second, slippery as ice the next.

Gerber waved the torch downslope. "There's our baby."

"I see it."

They edged closer, walking sideways as the angle of slope increased, taking increasingly cautious footsteps. The faller had come down about thirty spans from the very edge. In the evening gloom Cultel made out a head, two arms, two legs, all where they ought to have been. And something crumpled beneath the pale form, like a flimsy, translucent gown. You could never be too sure with fallers but it didn't look as though this one had come down very far. Dismemberment was commonplace: limbs, heads tended to pop off easily, either with the impact or from glancing collisions on the way down, as the faller bumped against the sides of buildings or the rising wall to the next ledge. But this jigsaw came with all the pieces.

Cultel looked up, over his shoulder, and lifted the rim of his hat to get a better view. No buildings or overhangs near enough for the faller to have come off. And even if they'd stepped off the next highest ledge, with the way the winds were working they'd have ended up at the base, back behind the rising tide of buildings. Should have been a lot more damage, too.

"Something's screwed up here," Cultel said.

"Just starting to feel that way myself." Gerber raised the camera to his eye singlehandedly and flashed off two exposures. They crept forwards some more, planting each footstep gently, hardly daring to breathe. Gerber directed the torch a bit more steadily. It was then that Cultel knew what they were dealing with.

Crushed beneath the form: that wasn't any gown. It was wings.

"It's—" Gerber started saying.

"Yeah."

What they had was an angel. Cultel looked up again, higher this time. Not just to the nearest line of buildings, but all the way up. Up past the pastel flicker of Neon Heights, up past the hologram shimmer of Circuit City. Up past the pink plasma aura of the cybertowns. He could just see them circling around up there, leagues overhead, wheeling and gyring around Spearpoint's tapering needle like flies around an insect zapper.

And he thought to himself: How the fuck did one of them get down here? And why did it have to happen on my watch?

"Let's bag and tag," Gerber said. "Thing's creeping me out already."

"You ever dealt with one of these?"

"First time. You?"

"Once when I was new on the job. Fell onto the third rail of the Green Line elevated. Fucking thing was toast by the time we pulled it off. Then again three, maybe four years back. That one was a lot more mashed up than this. Not a whole lot you could recognise at first glance."

Gerber fired off another shot with the camera. In the after-flash Cultel had the weird feeling that the corpse had twitched, shifting almost subliminally from one position to another. He crept up beside the fallen creature and knelt down with his equipment next to him. Overhead the seagulls really were taking an interest, mewling and squabbling in the evening air. Cultel examined the creature, taking in its nearly naked form, the wings the only visibly broken part of it. It had come to rest with its head lolling to one side, looking at him with huge midnight-blue eyes. It could have been alive, except there was nothing happening behind those eyes.

"Damn thing must have been alive almost all the way down," he said. "This was a controlled landing, not a crash."

"What a way to go," Gerber said. "You think it was suicide, or did it just, you know, lose its way?"

"Maybe there was a fault with its pack," Cultel said, fingering the hard, alien alloy of the angel's propulsion harness. "Hell, who knows? Cover all the angles, then we'll get it zipped up and into the van. Sooner this is off our hands the better."

They got the angel bagged and tagged, taking care not to worsen the damage to the wings or break any of the creature's stick-thin limbs. Lifting the bag, Cultel could easily manage it on his own. It was like carrying a sack of bones and not much else. They didn't even need to hose down the ground. The angel hadn't shed a drop of whatever passed for blood in its veins.

The other van hadn't arrived when they called back to the dispatcher.

"Sorry, Cultel. Had to send them over to the boundary with Steam—had a report that the zone was shifting around again."

"Well, you might want to rethink that. We got the smear." He glanced at Gerber, grinning in the moment. "You ready for this? It's an angel."

"No reports of anything falling down from the Levels, three oh seven."

"This one didn't fall. It must have flown almost all the way. Then died."

"As they do." He could hear the practised scepticism in the dispatcher's voice. Didn't much blame him, either. It wouldn't be the first time an angel corpse had been faked up for someone's twisted amusement. Might even be the kind of sick joke someone in Hygiene and Works would play on another clean-up crew, to see how gullible they were.

But Cultel knew this was a real one.

"You want us to squeeze the angel in, we will. Might get a little crumpled in there, but we'll manage. Just so you understand, I'm not taking responsibility for any breakages. I take it you'd like us to ship this thing over to Third?"

"If you think it's the real deal."

"I'll take the fall if it isn't."

"Fine; stop by at Third. But remove anything technical. Bag them separately, and we'll box them over to Imports."

Cultel hung up.

"Why Third? We never deal with Third," Gerber said.

They secured the angel, closed up the van and flywheeled back up the access ramp. It was another twenty-minute drive to the Third District Morgue, dodging through short cuts and back alleys, winding their way a little further up the spiralling ledge. The building was an ash-grey slab with a flat roof and a frontage of small square windows, lower than any of the office and apartment blocks crowding in around it. They drove to the rear and backed the van up to the dock, where a white-coated receiving clerk was waiting for them.

"Dispatch phoned through," the clerk said as Cultel unlocked the van's rear doors. "Said you had something juicy for Quillon." He scratched a pen against his nose. "Been a while, you know. I think he was starting to wonder if you'd forgotten about the arrangement."

"Like we'd forget," Cultel said, countersigning the delivery form.

"What's this all about?" Gerber asked.

"Quillon likes to get first dibs on anything freaky," the clerk explained. "Kind of a hobby of his, I guess."

Gerber shrugged. "Each to their own."

"Suits everyone," the clerk said. "Quillon gets his kicks. The other morgues don't have to wade through a ton of paperwork—and there's always a lot of triplicate when one of these things comes in." He peered at the bagged form as Cultel and Gerber eased it onto a wheeled stretcher. "Mind if I take a look?"

"Hey, be my guest," Cultel said.

The clerk zipped the bag down half a span. Wrinkled his nose at the dead, pale, broken thing inside.

"They look so beautiful flying around up there, wings all lit up and glowing."

"Cut him some slack." Cultel zipped the bag tight. "He's not been having the best of days."

"You sure it's a he?"

"Now that you mention it—"

"Wheel it through to Quillon if you want," the clerk said. "Take the freight elevator to the third. He'll be up there someplace. Gotta wait down here to see in another delivery."

"Busy night?"

"Busy week. They say the boundary's getting itchy feet again."

"What I heard," Cultel said. "Guess we'd better batten down the hatches and get our watches wound."

They pushed the wheeled stretcher into the building. It was all green walls, stark white tiles and the chlorine reek of industrial cleaning solution. The lights in the ceiling were turned down almost to brown. Most of the staff had gone home for the day, leaving the morgue to the night shift and the ghosts of former clients. Cultel hated the place, as he hated all morgues. How could anyone work in a building where all they did was cut open bodies? At least being on the clean-up crew got him out into fresh air.

They took the freight elevator to the third floor, heaved open the heavy trelliswork door and rolled the stretcher out into the corridor. Quillon was waiting at the far end, flicking the butt of a cigarette into a wall-mounted ashtray. It had been three or four years but Cultel recognised him straight away. Which wasn't to say that Quillon hadn't changed in all that time.

"When I heard there was a delivery coming in, I was hoping it was the new medicines," Quillon said, in his slow, measured, slightly too-deep voice. "Cupboards were any barer, we'd have to start turning away dead people."

"We brought you a present," Cultel said. "Be nice."

"How's work?"

"Ups and downs, Quillon, ups and downs. But while there's a city and corpses, I guess you and I don't have to worry about gainful employment."

Quillon had always been thin, always been gaunt, but now he looked as if he'd just opened his eyes and climbed off one of the dissection tables. A white surgical coat draped off his thin-ridged shoulders as if it was still on the hanger and a white cap covered his hairless skull. He wore glasses, tinted slightly even though the lights in the morgue were hardly on the bright side. Green surgical gloves that still made his fingers look too long and skeletal for comfort. There were deep shadows under his cheekbones and his skin looked colourless and waxy and not quite alive.

No getting away from it, Cultel thought. The guy had picked the ideal place of employment.

"So what have you got for me?"

"Got you an angel, my friend. Came down on the ledge."

Quillon's reaction was hard to judge behind the glasses. The rest of his face didn't move much, even when he spoke. "All the way down from the Celestial Levels?"

"What we figured. Funny thing is, though, there's not much sign that this one was going fast when it hit."

"That's interesting." Quillon said this in the uninflected tones of someone who'd be hard pushed to think of anything less interesting. But Cultel wasn't sure.

"Had some gadgetry on it, we removed all that. What you've got is essentially just a naked corpse with wings."

"That's what we deal with."

"You…um…cut many of these things open, Quillon?" Gerber asked.

"The odd one or two. Can't say they drop in with great regularity. Have we met?"

"I don't think so. What is it about them you like so much?"

"I wouldn't say 'like' comes into it. It's just a speciality, that's all. We're set up for it here. Got the positive-pressure room, in case anything toxic boils out of them. Got the blast-proof doors. And once you've done one, the paperwork's fairly routine."

"Takes the pressure off the other morgues," Cultel said.

Quillon flexed his scrawny neck in a nod. "Everyone's a winner."

There was an awkward moment. The two of them by the trolley, Quillon still standing there with his green-gloved hands at his sides.

"Well, I guess we're done here," Cultel said. "Docket tells you everything you need to know. Usual deal: when you're through with the bag, send it back to Hygiene and Works. Preferably hosed down."

"I'll see to it."

"Well, until next time," Cultel said, backing into the still-open freight elevator.

"Until next time," Quillon said, raising a forearm by way of farewell.

"It's been great meeting you," Gerber said.

Cultel closed the elevator doors. The elevator descended, the motor whining at the head of the shaft.

Quillon stood still at the end of the corridor until the panel over the door told him that the elevator had reached the ground floor. Then he walked slowly up to the stretcher, examined the docket and placed one gloved hand on the black zip-up bag containing the angel.

Then he wheeled it into the examination room, donned a surgical mask, transferred the bag onto the dissection plinth and carefully removed the angel from the bag.

extras

It seemed to Quillon to be beautiful even in death. He had placed the angel on its back, its eyes closed, the ruined wings hanging down on either side so that their tips brushed the tiled floor, the floor's sloping runnels designed to channel away bodily fluids. Under the hard lights of the dissection plinth, it was as ghost-pale, naked and hairless as a rat foetus.

Not expecting to be disturbed, he took off his glasses.

He pushed a squeaking-wheeled trolley next to the table, pulling aside the green sheet to expose an assortment of medical tools. There were scalpels, forceps, bone-cutting devices, gleaming sterile scoops and spatulas, and an array of glass and stainless-steel receptacles to receive the dissected tissue samples. These tools had once struck him as laughably crude, but now they fell to hand with an easy, reassuring familiarity. A microphone dangled from the ceiling; Quillon tugged it closer to his face and threw a heavy rocker switch in its side. Somewhere beyond the room, tape reels started whirring through recording heads. He cleared his throat and enunciated clearly, to make himself heard through the distorting mask.

"Doctor Quillon speaking. Continuation of previous record." He glanced up at the row of clocks on the far wall. "Time is now... six-fifteen p.m. Beginning autopsy of a corpse, docket number five-eight-three-three-four, recently delivered to the Third District Morgue by the Department of Hygiene and Public Works." He paused and cast his eyes over the corpse, the appropriate observations springing to mind with a minimum of conscious effort. "Initial indications are that the corpse is an angel, probably an adult male. Angel appears uninjured, save for impact damage to the wings. There are some longitudinal bruises and scars on the limbs, together with marked subepidermal swelling—recent enough to suggest they might be contributory factors in the angel's death—but the limbs appear otherwise uninjured, with no sign of major breaks or dislocations. Indications are that the angel's descent was controlled until the last moment, at which point it fell with enough force to damage the wings but not to inflict any other visible injuries. Reason for the descent is unknown, but the likely cause of death would appear to be massive maladaptive trauma due to sudden exposure to our zone, rather than impact onto the ledge." He paused again, letting the tape continue recording while he reached for a syringe. He punched the needle into a small rubber-capped bottle—one of the last dozen such bottles in the morgue's inventory—and loaded the tube, taking care not to draw more than was strictly necessary.

"In accordance with protocol," he continued, "I am now administering a lethal dose of Morphax-55, to ensure final morbidity." He tapped the glass until there were no more bubbles, then leaned over to push the needle into the bare skin of the angel's chest.

In the six years that he had been working as a pathologist, Quillon had cut open many hundreds of human bodies—victims of accident, homicide, medical negligence—but only eleven angels. That was still more than most pathologists saw in their careers.

He pressed the tip of the syringe against skin.

"Commencing injection of—" he started.

The angel's left arm whipped over to seize his hand.

"Stop," it said.

Quillon halted, but it was more out of reflex than a considered response to the angel's actions. He was so startled that he almost dropped the syringe.

"The angel is still alive," he said into the microphone. "It has exhibited comprehension, visual awareness and fine motor control. I will now attempt to alleviate the subject's suffering by..." He hesitated and looked into the dying creature's eyes, which were now fully alert, fully and terrifyingly focused on his own. The angel still had his hand on Quillon's wrist, the syringe hovering dagger-like above the angel's sternum.

"Let me do this," he said. "It'll take away the pain."

"You mean kill me," the angel said, speaking slowly and with effort, as if barely enough air remained in his lungs to make the sounds. His eyes were large and blue, characteristically lacking visible structures. His head rolled slightly on the dissection table, as the angel took in his surroundings.

"You're going to die anyway," Quillon said.

"Break it to me nicely, why don't you."

"There's nothing nice to break. You've fallen out of the Celestial Levels into Neon Heights. You don't belong down here and your cells can't take it. Even if we could get you back home, too much damage has already been done."

"You think I don't know that?" The angel's piping, childlike voice was just deep enough to confirm him as male. "I'm fully aware of what's going to happen. But I don't want your medicine. Not just yet." The angel let go of his hand, allowing Quillon to place the syringe back on the trolley. "I need to ask you something."

"Of course."

The angel was looking at him, the blue eyes windows into an alien soul. His head was only a little smaller than an adult human's, but almost entirely hairless, beautiful and unworldly, as if it were made of porcelain and stained glass rather than living matter and machines. "You must answer me truthfully."

"I will."

"Are you Quillon?"

He was silent for a few seconds. He had often wondered how it would happen, when his pursuers finally caught up with him. Strangely, he had never envisaged the encounter taking place in the morgue. He had always assumed that the time would come in some dark alley, a packed commuter train, or even his own apartment as he clicked on the light after returning home. A shadow moving into view, a glint of metal. There would be no reason to ask his adopted name. If they had managed to track him down that efficiently, his real identity would have been beyond question.

The only reason for asking, in other words, would be to taunt him with the sure and certain knowledge that he had failed.

"Of course," he said, with as much dignity and calm as he could muster.

"That's good. They said I'd be brought to you."

The unease had begun deep in his belly and was now climbing slowly up his spine.

"Who said that?"

"The people who sent me here, of course. You don't think any of this happened by accident, do you?"

Quillon thought about killing the angel there and then. He still had the Morphax-55 to hand, ready to inject. But the angel knew he was capable of doing that and was still talking. His mind raced. Perhaps trying to kill the angel would be the very trigger that caused him to kill Quillon.

He kept his composure. "Then why did you fall?"

"Because I chose to. This was the quickest—if not the least risky—way." The angel swallowed hard, his whole body flexing from the table. "I was under no illusions. I knew this was a suicide mission; that I would not be returning to the Celestial Levels. But still I did it. I fell, and stayed alive long enough to be brought to you. They said when an angel falls into Neon Heights, it almost always gets taken to Quillon to be cut open. Is that true?"

"Most of the time."

"I can see why that would work for you."

The tape reels were still running, recording every detail of the conversation. Quillon reached up and clicked off the microphone, for all the good that would do.

"Can you?"

"You were once one of us. Then something happened and... now you live here, down amongst the prehumans, with their stinking factories, buzzing cars and dull electric lights."

"Do I look like an angel?"

"I know what happened to you. You were remade to look prehuman, your wings removed, your body reshaped, your blood cleansed of machines. You were sent to live among the prehumans, to learn their ways, to prove that it could be done. There were others." The angel drew an exhausted, rasping breath. "Then something went wrong and now there's just you, and you can't ever go back. You work here because you need to be on guard, in case the Celestial Levels send agents down to find you. Ordinary angels can't reach you, so you know that whatever they send will have to be unusual, or prepared to die very soon after finding you."

"There's just you and me in this room," Quillon said slowly. "Why haven't you killed me yet?"

Follow us:

/orbitbooksUS

/orbitbooks

/orbitbooks

Join our mailing list
to receive alerts on our
latest releases and deals.

orbitbooks.net

Enter our monthly
giveaway for the chance
to win some epic prizes.

orbitloot.com